DANIELLE STEEL

DANIELLE STEEL

THE RING

CHANGES

FULL CIRCLE

CHANCELLOR PRESS

The Ring first published in Great Britain in 1980
by Hodder and Stoughton Limited

Changes first published in Great Britain in 1984
by Sphere Books Limited

Full Circle first published in Great Britain in 1984
by Hodder and Stoughton Limited

This collected volume first published in Great Britain in 1992
by Chancellor Press
an imprint of
Reed International Books Limited
Michelin House
81 Fulham Road
London SW3 6RB

by arrangement with Hodder and Stoughton Limited.

ISBN 1 85152 243 3

Printed in Great Britain by The Bath Press, Avon

CONTENTS

THE RING

To Omi

Love
d.s.

BOOK ONE
KASSANDRA

Chapter I

Kassandra von Gotthard sat peacefully at the edge of the lake in the Charlottenburger park, watching the water ripple slowly away from the pebble she had just thrown. The long, graceful fingers held another small smooth stone, poised for a moment, and then threw it aimlessly into the water once again. It was a hot, sunny day at the end of the summer and her golden strawberry hair fell in one long, smooth wave to her shoulders, pushed away from her face on one side with a single ivory comb. The line of the comb in the smooth golden hair was as perfect and graceful as everything else about her face. Her eyes were enormous and almond shaped, of the same rich blue as the bank of flowers behind her in the park. They were eyes that promised laughter, and yet they whispered something tender at the same time; eyes that would caress and tease, and then grow pensive, as though lost in some distant dream as far removed from the present as the Charlottenburger Schloss just across the lake was distant from the bustling city. The old castle sat timelessly, watching her, as though she belonged to its era rather than her own.

Lying on the grass at the edge of the lake, Kassandra looked like a woman in a painting or a dream, her delicate hands sifting gently through the grass, looking for another small pebble to throw. Nearby, the ducks were waddling into the water as two small children clapped their hands with glee. Kassandra watched them, seeming to search their faces for a long moment, as they laughed and ran away.

'What were you thinking just then?' The voice at her side pulled her from her reverie, and she turned towards it with a slow smile.

'Nothing.' Her smile broadened and she held out a hand towards him, her intricate, diamond-encrusted signet ring gleaming in the sun. But he didn't notice it. The jewels she wore mattered nothing to him. It was Kassandra who intrigued him, who seemed to hold the mystery of life and beauty for him. She was a question to which he would never know an answer, a gift he would never quite possess.

They had met the previous winter, at a party to celebrate his second book, *Der Kuss*. In his outspoken fashion, he had shocked all of Germany for a time, but the book had nonetheless won him still more acclaim than his first. The story had been deeply sensitive and erotic and his seat at the pinnacle of Germany's contemporary literary movement seemed assured. He was controversial, he was modern, he was at times outrageous, and he was also very,

very talented. At thirty-three, Dolff Sterne had made it to the top. And then he had met his dream.

Her beauty had left him breathless the night they met. He had heard of her; everyone in Berlin knew who she was. She seemed untouchable, unreachable, and she looked frighteningly fragile. Dolff had felt something akin to a shaft of pain when he first saw her, wearing a silky, clinging dress of woven gold, her shimmering hair barely covered by a tiny golden cap, a sable coat draped over one arm. But it wasn't the gold or the sable that had stunned him, it was her presence, her separateness and silence in the clamour of the room, and finally her eyes. When she turned and smiled at him, for an instant he felt as though he might die.

'Congratulations.'

'On what?' He had stared at her for an instant, struck almost dumb, feeling his thirty-three years shrink to ten, until he noticed she was nervous, too. She wasn't at all what he had expected. She was elegant, but not aloof. He suspected that she was frightened of the staring eyes, the milling crowd. She had left early, disappearing like Cinderella as he greeted still more guests. He had wanted to run after her, to find her, to see her again, if only for an instant, to look again into the lavender eyes.

Two weeks later they had met again. In the park, here at Charlottenburg. He had watched her looking up at the castle, and then smiling at the ducks.

'Do you come here often?' They had stood side by side for a quiet moment, his tall, dark good looks in striking contrast to her delicate beauty. His hair was the colour of her sable, his eyes brilliant onyx looking into hers. She nodded and then looked up at him with that mysteriously childlike smile.

'I used to come here when I was a little girl.'

'You're from Berlin?' It had seemed a stupid question, but he hadn't been sure what to say.

She laughed at him, but not unkindly. 'Yes. And you?' 'München.' She nodded again, and they stood in silence for a long time. He wondered how old she was. Twenty-two? Twenty-four? It was difficult to tell. And then suddenly he heard a peal of crystal laughter as she watched three children, cavorting with their dog, elude their nurse and wind up knee deep in the water, the recalcitrant bulldog refusing to join them on the shore again.

'I did that once. My nurse wouldn't let me come back here for a month.' He smiled at her. He could have imagined the scene. She seemed young enough still to hike into the water, yet the sable and the diamonds she wore made it seem unlikely that she had ever been unfettered enough to chase into the water after a dog. He could almost see it though, with a governess in starched uniform and cap berating her from the shore. And when would that have been? 1920? 1915? It seemed light-years away from his own pursuits at that time. In those years he had been struggling to manage school and work at the same time, helping his parents at the bakery every morning before school and for long hours every afternoon. How far removed that had seemed from this golden woman.

He had haunted the park at Charlottenburg after that, telling himself that he needed air and exercise after he wrote all day, but secretly he knew better. He was looking for that face, those eyes, the golden hair ... and at last he found her, again at the lake. She had seemed happy to see him when they met again. And then it became a kind of silent understanding. He would take walks when he finished writing, and if he timed it right, she would be there.

They became spiritual guardians of the castle, surrogate parents of the children playing near the lake. They took a kind of possessive joy in their surroundings, telling each other stories of their childhood, and each listening to the other tell about his dreams. She had wanted to be in the theatre, much to her father's horror, but it had always been her private dream. She understood perfectly that it would never happen, but now and then she dreamed that in her later years she would write a play. She was always fascinated when he spoke of his writing, how he had started, what it felt like when his first book became a success. The fame still didn't seem quite real to him, and perhaps it never would. It had been five years since his first successful novel, seven years since he had left Munich and come to Berlin, three years since he'd brought the Bugatti, two since the beautiful old house in Charlottenburg had become his ... and still none of it was quite real. Not quite believing it all kept him youthful, and kept the look of delight and astonishment in his eyes. Dolff Stern was not blasé yet, not about life, or writing, and least of all about her.

She was enchanted as she listened. Listening to him talk about his books, she felt the stories come alive, the characters become real; and being with him, she felt herself come alive again, too. And week after week as they met, he saw the fear in her eyes grow dimmer. There was something different about her now when he met her at the lake. Something funny and young and delicious.

'Do you have any idea how much I like you Kassandra?' He had said it to her playfully as they walked slowly around the lake one day, enjoying the balmy spring breeze.

'Are you going to write a book about me, then?'

'Should I?'

But she lowered the lavender eyes for a moment and then, looking back up at him, shook her head. 'Hardly. There wouldn't be anything to say. No victories, no successes, no accomplishments. Nothing at all.'

His eyes held hers for a long moment, the lavender and the black saying words that could not yet be said. 'Is that what you think?'

'It's what is true. I was born into my life and I will die out of my life. And in between I will wear a great many lovely dresses, go to a thousand proper dinners, listen to countless well-sung operas ... and that, my friend, is all.' At twenty-nine, she already sounded as though she had lost hope ... hope of life ever being any different.

'And your play?'

She shrugged. They both knew the answer. She was a prisoner in a diamond cage. And then, smiling up at him, she laughed again. 'So, my only hope for fame and glory is for you to make something up for me, put me in a novel, and turn me into some exotic character in your head.' That much he had already done, but he didn't quite dare tell her. Not yet. Instead he played the game with her, tucking her hand into his arm.

'All right. In that case, let's at least do it to your liking. What would you like to be? What seems to you suitably exotic? A spy? A woman surgeon? The mistress of a very famous man?'

She made a face and laughed at him. 'How dreadful. Really, Dolff, how dull. No, let's see ...' They had stopped to sit on the grass as she flung off her wide-brimmed straw hat and shook loose the golden hair. 'An actress, I think ... You could make me a star of the London stage ... and then ...' She tilted her head to one side, winding her hair around the long, graceful fingers as her rings shone in the sun. 'Then ... I could go to America and be a star there.'

'America, eh? Where?'

'New York.'

'Have you ever been?'

She nodded. 'With my father when I turned eighteen. It was fabulous. We were –' And then she stopped. She had been about to tell him that they'd been the guests of the Astors in New York and then of the President in Washington, DC, but somehow it didn't seem quite right. She didn't want to impress him. She wanted to be his friend. She liked him too much to play those games with him. And it didn't matter how successful he had become, the truth was that he would never be part of that world. They both knew it. It was something they never discussed.

'You were what?' He had been watching her, his lean, handsome face close to hers.

'We were in love with New York. At least I was.' She sighed and looked wistfully at their lake.

'Is it anything like Berlin?'

She shook her head, squinting, as though to make the Charlottenburger Schloss disappear. 'No, it's wonderful. It's new and modern, and busy and exciting.'

'And of course Berlin is so dull.' Sometimes he couldn't help laughing at her. To him, Berlin was still all of those things she had said about New York.

'You're teasing me.' There was reproach in her voice, but not in her eyes. She enjoyed being with him. She loved the ritual of their afternoon walks. More and more now, she escaped the fetters and restrictions of her daily obligations and came to meet him in the park.

His eyes were kind when he answered her. 'I am teasing you, Kassandra. Do you mind very much?'

She shook her head slowly. 'No, I don't.' And then, after a pause, 'I feel as though I've come to know you better than anyone else I know.' It was disturbing, but he felt the same way. Yet she was still his dream, his illusion, and she eluded him constantly, except here in the park; 'Do you know what I mean?' He nodded, not sure what to say. He still didn't want to frighten her. He didn't want her to stop meeting him for their walks.

'Yes, I understand.' Far more than she knew. And then, seized by a moment of madness, he took her hand, long and frail, in his own, yet encumbered by the large rings she wore. 'Would you like to come to my place for tea?'

'Now?' Her heart had fluttered strangely at the question. She wanted to, but she wasn't sure ... she didn't think ...

'Yes, now. Do you have something else you should do?'

She shook her head slowly. 'No, I don't.' She could have told him that she was busy, that she had an appointment, that she was expected somewhere for tea. But she didn't. She looked up at him with those huge lavender eyes. 'I'd like that.'

They walked side by side, laughing and talking, secretly nervous, leaving the protection of Eden for the first time. He told her funny stories, and she laughed as she hurried beside him, swinging her hat. There was a sudden urgency to their mission. As though this was what they had been building up to with their months of walks in the park.

The heavily carved door swung open slowly and they stepped into a large marble hall. There was a huge, handsome painting hanging over a Biedermeier desk. Their footsteps echoed emptily as she followed him inside.

'So this is where the famous author lives.'

He smiled at her nervously as he dropped his hat on the desk. 'The house is a good deal more famous than I. It belonged to some seventeenth-century baron and has been in far more illustrious hands than mine ever since.' He looked around him proudly and then beamed at her as she stared up at the carved rococo ceiling and then back at him.

'It's beautiful, Dolff.' She seemed very quiet, and he held out a hand.

'Come, I'll show you the rest.'

The rest of the house fulfilled the promise of the entrance, with tall, beautifully carved ceilings, wonderfully inlaid floors, small crystal chandeliers, and long, elegant windows looking out on a garden filled with bright flowers. On the main floor were a large living room and a smaller one that he used as a den. On the next floor were the kitchen and dining room and a small maid's room where he kept a bicycle and three pairs of skis. And above that were two huge, beautiful bedrooms, with views of the schloss and their park. There were handsome balconies perched outside each bedroom, and in the larger of the bedrooms was a narrow winding staircase tucked into a corner of the room.

'What's up there?' She had been intrigued. The house really was a beauty. Dolff had good reason to be proud.

He smiled at her. He enjoyed the admiration and approval he could see in her eyes. 'My ivory tower. That's where I work.'

'I thought you worked downstairs in the den.'

'No, that's just to entertain friends in. The living room still intimidates me a little bit. But this' – he pointed skyward from the foot of the narrow stairs 'is it.'

'May I see?'

'Of course, if you can wade through the papers around my desk.'

But there were no papers around the well-ordered desk. It was a small, beautifully proportioned room with a three-hundred-sixty-degree view. There was a cosy fireplace, and in every imaginable corner there were books. It was a room one could virtually live in, and Kassandra settled happily into a large red leather chair with a sigh.

'What a wonderful, wonderful place.' She was looking dreamily out at their schloss.

'I think this is why I bought the house. My ivory tower, and the view.'

'I don't blame you, even though the rest is lovely, too.' She had curled one leg under her as she sat down, and she smiled up at him with a look of peace that he had never quite seen on her face before. 'Do you know what, Dolff? This feels like I'm home at last. I feel like I've been waiting all my life just to come here.' Her eyes never wavered from his.

'Perhaps –' his voice was whisper soft in the room –an 'the house has been waiting for you all these years ... just as I have.' He felt a wave of shock ripple through him. He hadn't meant to tell her that. But her eyes showed no anger. 'I'm sorry, I didn't mean to.'

'It's all right, Dolff.' She held out a hand to him, her diamond signet ring catching the sun. He took her hand gently, and without stopping to think, he pulled her ever so slowly into his arms. He held her there for what seemed like an eternity, as they kissed beneath the bright blue spring sky, and they held tightly to each other in his ivory tower. She kissed him with a hunger and passion that only fanned his flame, and it seemed hours before he had the presence of mind to pull away.

'Kassandra ...' There was both pleasure and torment in his eyes, but she stood up and turned her back to him, looking down at the park.

'Don't.' Her voice was a whisper. 'Don't tell me you're sorry. I don't want to hear it ... I can't ...' And then she turned to him, her eyes blazing with a pain akin to his own. 'I've wanted you for so long.'

'But ...' He hated himself for his hesitations, but he had to say it, if only for her.

She put up a hand to silence him. 'I understand. Kassandra von Gotthard doesn't say things like this, is that it?' Her eyes hardened. 'You're quite right. I don't. But I wanted to. Oh, God, how I wanted to. I didn't even know how much I wanted to until just now. I never have before. I've lived my life until now just as I was meant to. And do you know what I have, Dolff? Nothing. Do you know who I am? No one. I am empty.' And then, with tears misting her eyes, 'And I was looking to you to fill my soul.' She turned away again. 'I'm sorry.'

He came up softly behind her and put his arms around her waist. 'Don't. Don't ever think that you are no one. You are everything to me. All these months, all I wanted was to know you better, to be with you, to give you something of what I am, and to share some part of you. I just don't want to hurt you, Kassandra. I don't want to pull you into my world at the risk of making you unable to live in your own. I have no right to do that. I have no right to take you away to a place where you couldn't be happy.'

'What? Here?' She turned to look at him with disbelief. 'Do you think I could be unhappy here with you? Even for an hour?'

'But that's just it. For how long, Kassandra? For an hour? Two? An afternoon?' He looked anguished as he faced her.

'That's enough. Even a moment of this in my lifetime would be enough.' And then, the delicate lips trembling, she lowered her head. 'I love you, Dolff ... I love you ... I ...'

He silenced her lips with his own, and slowly they walked down the narrow staircase again. But they went no further. Taking her hand gently, he led her to his bed and peeled away the fine grey silk of her dress and creamy beige satin of her slip, until he reached the exquisite lace that lay beneath, and the velvet of her flesh. They lay there together for hours, their lips and their hands and their bodies and their hearts blending into one.

It had been four months since that day, and the love affair had changed them both. Kassandra's eyes sparkled and danced; she teased and she played with him, and sat crosslegged in his big, beautiful carved bed, telling him funny stories of what she had done the day before. As for Dolff, his work had taken on a new texture, a new depth, and there was a new strength about him that seemed to come from his very core. Together they shared something that they felt sure no one had ever shared before. They were a meshing of the best of two worlds: his hard-won, hard-earned, determined struggle to excel, and her fragile fluttering to break free of her golden bonds.

They still walked in the park sometimes, but less often, and when they were together out of his house now, he often found her sad. They were too many other people, too many children and nannies and other couples strolling in the park. She wanted to be alone with him in their own private world. She didn't want to be reminded of a world outside his walls that they did not share.

'Do you want to go back?' He had been watching her quietly for a time. She was stretched gracefully on the grass, a pale mauve voile dress draped over her legs, the sun catching the gold in her hair. A mauve silk hat lay cast aside on the grass, and her stockings were the same ivory colour as her kid pumps. There was a heavy rope of pearls around her neck, and behind her on the grass were her kid gloves and the mauve silk bag with the ivory clasp that had been made to match her dress.

'Yes, I want to go back.' She stood up quickly, with a happy smile. 'What were you looking at just then?' He had been staring at her so intently.

'You'

'Why?'

'Because you're so incredibly beautiful. Do you know if I wrote about you I'd be totally at a loss for words.'

'Then just say that I'm ugly and stupid and fat.' She grinned at him and they both laughed.

'Would that please you?'

'Immensely.' She was teasing and mischievous again.

'Well, at least no one would recognise you if I wrote about you like that.'

'Are you really going to write about me?'

He was thoughtful for a long moment as they walked towards the house they both loved. 'One day I will. But not yet.'

'Why?'

'Because I'm still too overwhelmed by you to write anything coherent. In fact –' he smiled down at her from his considerable height – 'I may never be very coherent again'.

Their afternoons together were sacred, and they were often torn about whether to spend them in bed or sit comfortably in his ivory tower talking about his work. Kassandra was the woman he had waited half a lifetime for.

And with Dolff, Kassandra had found what she had always so desperately needed, someone who understood the odd meanderings of her soul, the longings, the fragmented pieces, the rebelliousness against the lonely restrictions of her world. They had come to an understanding. And they both knew that, for the moment, they had no choice.

'Do you want some tea, darling?' She tossed her hat and gloves on the desk in the entrance hall and went to her bag for her comb. It was onyx and ivory, inlaid and beautiful, and expensive, like everything else that she owned. She put it back in her bag and turned to Dolff with a smile. 'Stop grinning at me, silly...tea?'

'Hmmm ... what? Yes. I mean, no. Never mind that, Kassandra.' And then he firmly took her hand in his. 'Come upstairs. Planning to show me a new chapter, are you?' She smiled her incomparable smile as her eyes danced.

'Of course. I have a whole new book I want to discuss with you at length.'

An hour later as he slept peacefully next to her, she looked down at him with tears in her eyes. She slipped carefully from the bed. She always hated to leave him. But it was almost six o'clock. After softly closing the door to the large white marble bathroom, she emerged again ten minutes later, fully dressed, with a look of great longing and sadness about her face. She paused for a moment next to the bed, and as though sensing her standing next to him, he opened his eyes.

'You're going?'

She nodded, and for an instant they shared a look of pain. 'I love you.'

He understood. 'So do I.' He sat up in bed and held out his arms to her. 'I'll see you tomorrow, my darling.' She smiled, kissed him again, and then blew him another kiss from the doorway before she hurried down the stairs.

Chapter 2

The drive from Charlottenburg to Grunewald, only slightly further from the centre of the city, took Kassandra less than half an hour. She could make it in exactly fifteen minutes if she kept her foot on the floor in the little navy blue Ford coupe; she had long since established the quickest route home. Her heart pounded slightly as she glanced at her watch.

She was later than usual today, but she still had time to change. It annoyed her that she should be so nervous. It seemed absurd to still feel like a fifteen-year-old girl late for curfew.

The narrow, curved streets of Grunewald came rapidly into view, as the

Grunewaldsee lay flat and mirrorlike to her right. There wasn't a ripple on the water, and all she could hear was the birds. The large homes that lined the road sat solidly behind their brick walls and iron gates, concealed by trees and shrouded in their conservative silence, as in bedrooms upstairs maids assisted their ladies to dress. But she still had time, she wasn't too late.

She pulled the car to a quick halt at the entrance to their driveway and hopped rapidly out of the car, fitting her key into the heavy brass lock in the gate. She swung both sides open and drove the car through. She could have someone come back to close the gate later. She didn't have time now. The gravel crunched noisily beneath the wheels of her car as with a practised eye she surveyed the house. It had been built in something of a French manner and stretched out endlessly on either side of the main door. There were three sober-looking storeys of discreet grey stone, topped by yet another floor with lower ceilings nestled beneath the handsomely designed mansard roof. The upper floor housed the servants. Beneath that was a floor that she noticed now was lit by lights in almost every room. Then there were her own rooms, as well as several guest rooms, and two pretty libraries, one looking out over the garden, the other over the lake. On the floor where her own rooms were shone only one light, and beneath that, on the main floor, everything was ablaze. The dining room, the main salon, the large library, the small smoking room panelled in dark wood and lined with rare books. She wondered for a moment why every single light on the lower floor appeared to be on that night, and then she remembered, and her hand flew to her mouth.

'Oh, my God ... oh, no!' Her heart pounding harder, she abandoned her car outside the house. The huge, perfectly manicured lawn was deserted, and even the abundantly stocked flowerbeds seemed to reproach her as she ran up the short flight of steps. How could she have forgotten? What would he say? Clutching her hat and gloves in one hand, her handbag jammed unceremoniously under her arm, she fought the front door with her key. But as she did so, the door opened and she stood staring into the intransigent face of Berthold, their butler, his bald head gleaming in the bright light of the twin chandeliers in the main hall, his white tie and tails impeccable as always, his eyes too cold even to register disapproval. They simply gazed expressionlessly into her own. Behind him a maid in a black uniform and white lace apron and cap hurried across the main hall.

'Good evening, Berthold.'

'Madam.' The door closed resolutely behind her, almost at the same moment as Berthold clicked his heels.

Nervously Kassandra glanced into the main salon. Thank God everything was ready. The dinner party for sixteen had been the last thing on her mind. Fortunately she had gone over it in detail with her housekeeper the morning before. Frau Klemmer had everything under control, as always. Nodding to the servants as she went, Kassandra rushed upstairs, wishing she could take the stairs two at a time as she did at Dolff's when they were running up to bed ... to bed ... a glimmer of a smile floated to her eyes as she thought of it, but she had to force him from her mind.

She paused on the landing, looking down the long grey carpeted hall.

Everything around her was pearl grey, the silk on the walls, the thick carpets, the velvet drapes. There were two handsome Louis XV chests, magnificently inlaid and topped with marble, and every few feet along the walls were antique sconces with pretty flame-shaped lights. And set between them were small Rembrandt etchings, which had been in the family for years. Doors stretched to her right and left, and a glimmer of light shone beneath only one. She stopped for a moment and then ran on, down the hall towards her own room. She had just reached it when she heard a door behind her open, and the dimly lit hallway was suddenly flooded with light.

'Kassandra?' The voice behind her was forbidding, but when she turned to face him, the eyes were not. Tall, lithe, still handsome at fifty-eight, his eyes were an icier blue than hers, his hair a mixture of sand and snow. It was a beautiful face, the kind of face one saw in early Teutonic portraits, and the shoulders were square and broad.

'I'm so sorry ... I couldn't help it ... I got terribly delayed ...' For an instant they stood there, their eyes holding. There was much left unsaid.

'I understand.' And he did. So much more than she knew. 'You'll be able to manage? It would be awkward if you were late.'

'I won't be. I promise.' She eyed him sorrowfully. But her sadness was not for the dinner party she had forgotten, but for the joy they no longer shared.

He smiled at her from across the vast expanse of distance that seemed to separate their two lives. 'Hurry. And ... Kassandra ...' He paused, and she knew what was coming, as waves of guilt surged upward towards her throat. 'Have you been upstairs?'

She shook her head. 'No, not yet. I'll do that before I come down.'

Walmar von Gotthard nodded and softly closed his door. Behind that door lay his private apartment, a large, stark bedroom furnished in German and English antiques in dark woods; a Persian carpet in deep wines and sea blues blanketed the rich wood floors. The walls of his bedroom were wood panelled, as were those of the study that was his private sanctum just beyond. There was also a large dressing room and his own bathroom. Kassandra's apartment was larger still. And now, flying through her bedroom door, she tossed her hat on to the pink satin comforter on her bed. Her rooms were as much like her as Walmar's were like him. Everything was soft and smooth, ivory and pink, satin and silk, draped and gentle, and hidden from the world. The curtains were so lavish that they obscured her view of the garden, the room so draped and enclosed that, like her life with Walmar, it hid her from the world beyond. Her dressing room was nearly as large as her bedroom, a solid bank of closets filled with exquisite clothes, an entire wall of custom-made shoes faced by endless rows of pink satin boxes filled with hats. Behind a small French Impressionist painting hid the safe that held her jewels. And beyond the dressing room, a small sitting room with a view of the lake. There was a chaise longue that had been her mother's, and a tiny French lady's desk. There were books she no longer read now, a sketch pad she hadn't touched since March. It was as though she no longer lived here. She only came to life in the arms of Dolff.

Kicking off the ivory kid pumps and hastily unbuttoning the lavender dress, she pulled open the doors of two closets, mentally reviewing what hung inside. But as she stared into the closets' contents, she had to stop, barely able to catch her breath. What was she doing? What had she done? What kind of mad existence had she let herself in for? What hope did she have of ever having a real life with Dolff? She was Walmar's wife forever. She knew it, always had known it, since she had married him at nineteen. He had been forty-eight then, and the marriage had seemed so right. A close associate of her father's, head of her father's sister bank, it had been a merger as much as a marriage. For people like Kassandra and Walmar, that's what made the most sense. They shared a life-style, they knew all the same people. Their families had intermarried once or twice before. Everything about the marriage should have worked. It didn't matter if he was so much older, and it wasn't as if he were elderly or half dead. Walmar had always been a dazzling man, and ten years after their marriage he still was. What's more, he understood her. He understood the frail otherworldliness about her, he knew how carefully she had been cloistered and nurtured during her early life. He would protect her from life's coarser moments.

So Kassandra had her life cut out for her, from a pattern well worn by tradition and cut by hands more skilled than her own. All she had to do was what was expected of her and Walmar would cherish and protect her, guard and guide her, and continue to maintain the cocoon that had been spun for her at birth. Kassandra von Gotthard had nothing to fear from Walmar; in fact, she had nothing to fear at all, except perhaps herself. And she knew that now, better than she had ever known it before.

Having torn one tiny hole in the cocoon that protected her, she had fled now, if not in body, then in soul. Yet she still had to come home at night, to play the role, to be who she was meant to be, to be Walmar von Gotthard's wife.

'Frau von Gotthard?'

Kassandra wheeled nervously as she heard the voice behind her in her dressing room. 'Oh, Anna ... thank you. I don't need any help.'

'Fräulein Hedwig asked me to tell you –' Oh, God, it was coming; Kassandra turned away from her, feeling guilt pierce her once again to the core – 'the children would like to see you before they go to bed.'

'I'll come upstairs as soon as I'm dressed. Thank you.' The tone of her voice told the young woman in the black lace uniform to go. Kassandra knew all the tones to use to perfection, the right intonations and right words were part of her blood. Never rude, never angry, seldom brusque, she was a lady. This was her world. But as the door closed softly behind the maid, Kassandra sank to a chair in her dressing room with tears brimming in her eyes. She felt helpless, broken, pulled. This was the world of her duties, the existence she had been bred to. And it was precisely what she ran away from each day when she went to meet Dolff.

Walmar was her family now. Walmar and the children. She had no one to turn to. Her father was dead now. And her mother, gone two years after her father, had she been this lonely too? There was no one to ask, and no one she knew who would have told her the truth.

From the start she and Walmar had maintained a respectful distance. Walmar had suggested separate bedrooms. There were little evenings in her boudoir, champagne chilled in silver coolers, which eventually led them to bed, though very seldom since the birth of their last child, when Kassandra had been twenty-four. The child had been born by Cesarean section and she had almost died. Walmar was concerned about what another pregnancy could do to her, as was she. The champagne had cooled less and less often after that. And since March there had been no evenings in her boudoir at all. Walmar asked no questions. It had taken little to make herself understood, the mention of several trips to the doctor, a mention of an ache, a pain, a headache; she retired early to her bedroom every night. It was all right, Walmar understood it. But in truth, when Kassandra came back to this house, to his house, to her bedroom, she knew that it wasn't all right at all. What would she do now? Was this what life had promised? Was she to go on just like this, indefinitely? Probably. Until Dolff tired of the game. Because he would, he'd have to. Kassandra knew it already, even if Dolff did not. And then what? Another? And another? Or no one at all? As she stood staring bleakly into her mirror, she wasn't sure any more. The woman who had been certain in the house in Charlottenburg that afternoon was no longer quite as poised. She knew only that she was a woman who had betrayed her husband and her way of life.

Taking a deep breath, she stood up and went back to her closet. It didn't matter what she felt now, she had to dress. The least she could do for him was look decent at his dinner. The guests were all fellow bankers and their wives. She was always the youngest at any gathering, but she carried herself well.

For an instant Kassandra wanted to slam the door to her closet and run upstairs, to be with the children – the miracles hidden from her on the third floor. The children playing at the lake at Charlottenburg always reminded her of them, and it always pained her to realise that she knew her own children as little as she knew those tiny laughing strangers at the lake. Fräulein Hedwig was their mother now. She always had been and always would be. Kassandra felt like a stranger with the little boy and girl, who both looked so much like Walmar and so little like her ... 'Don't be absurd, Kassandra. You can't take care of her yourself.'

'But I want to.' She had looked at Walmar sadly the day after Ariana was born. 'She's mine.'

'She's not yours, she's ours.' He had smiled at her gently as tears filled her eyes. 'What do you want to do, stay up all night and change diapers? You'd be exhausted in two days. It's unheard of, it's ... nonsense.' For a moment he had looked annoyed. But it wasn't nonsense. It was what she wanted, and she knew also that it was what she would never be allowed to do.

The nurse had arrived on the day they left the hospital and whisked the baby Ariana to the third floor. That night, when Kassandra had walked upstairs to see her, she had been admonished by Fräulein for disturbing the baby. The infant was to be brought to her, Walmar insisted; there was no reason for Kassandra to go upstairs. But her little girl was brought to her only once in the morning, and when Kassandra appeared in the nursery later, she was always told it was too early or too late, the baby was sleeping, fussing, cranky, unhappy. And Kassandra would be sent away to languish in her room. 'Wait until the child is older,' Walmar told her, 'then you can play with her anytime you want.' But by then it was too late. Kassandra and the child were strangers. The nurse had won. And when the second child came three years later, Kassandra was too sick to put up a fight. Four weeks in the hospital, and another four weeks in bed at home. Four more months of an overwhelming sense of depression. And when it was over, she knew it was a battle she would never win. Her assistance wasn't needed, her help, or her love, or her time. She was a pretty lady who would come to visit, wearing pretty clothes and smelling of wonderful French perfume. She would sneak them cakes and candy, spend fortunes on exotic toys, but what they needed from her she was not allowed to give them, and what she wanted from them in return they had long since bestowed upon the nurse.

The tears having subsided, Kassandra pulled herself together, took her dress from her closet, and crossed the room to find a pair of black suede shoes. She had nine pairs of them for evening but she chose the ones she had acquired most recently, with pear-shaped openings over the toes, leaving her brightly polished nails visible. Her silk stockings made a whispering sound as she took them from their satin box and changed from the ivory-coloured stockings she had worn earlier. She was grateful suddenly that she'd taken the time to bathe at Dolff's. Now as she stood there, sliding carefully into the black dress, it seemed incredible that she existed in Dolff's world at all. The house in Charlottenburg seemed like a distant dream. This was her reality. The world of Walmar von Gotthard. She was irretrievably and undeniably his wife.

She zipped herself into the dress, which was a long, narrow sheath of black wool crepe with long arms and high neck, stopping just short of the black suede shoes. It was striking and sombre, and only when she turned around was its full beauty and her own revealed. A large oval opening, like a giant teardrop, revealed her back from neck to waist; her ivory skin glimmering in the opening, like moonlight reflected on a black ocean on a summer night.

Putting a short silk cape over her shoulders to protect the dress, she carefully combed her hair and swept it off her neck, piercing the neat twist she created with long black coral pins. Satisfied with the effect she had created, she wiped the mascara from beneath each eye and redid her face, took one last look in the mirror, and fastened a large pear-shaped diamond to each ear. On her hands were the large emerald she often wore in the evening and the diamond signet ring she always wore on her right hand. The ring had graced the hands of women in her family for four generations. It bore the initials of her great-grandmother in diamonds and glimmered as it caught the light.

With a last glance over her shoulder she knew that she looked as always, striking, lovely, tranquil. No one would have dreamed that underneath there was torment. No one would have guessed that she had spent the afternoon in the arms of Dolff.

In the long, quiet grey hallway, she paused for only an instant at the foot of the stairs leading up to the third floor. A clock in the corner sombrely chimed the hour. She was actually on time. It was seven o'clock, and the guests were expected at seven-thirty. She had half an hour to spend with Ariana and

Gerhard before they went to bed. Thirty minutes of motherhood. She wondered, as she climbed the stairs to see them, how much that would add up to in
their lifetimes. How many thirty minutes multiplied by how many days? But
had she seen her own mother more often? She knew, as she reached the last step
on the stairway, that she had not. And that what she had that was most vivid
and tangible was the signet ring, which had always been on her mother's hand.

At the door to their large playroom she paused for a moment and knocked.
There was no answer, but she could hear squeals and laughter beyond. They
would have eaten hours before, and by now they would have had their baths.
Fräulein Hedwig would have made them put their toys away, and the nursery
maid would have assisted them in this monumental task. But at least they were
back now – for most of the summer they had been in the country, and
Kassandra hadn't seen them at all. This year, for the first time, Kassandra had
not wanted to leave Berlin, because of Dolff. A convenient charity had provided her with the desperately sought excuse.

She knocked again, and this time they heard her, Fräulein Hedwig bid her
come in. As she entered, there was sudden silence, the children startled from
their playing with a look of awe. Of all of it, it was that that Kassandra most
hated. The look they gave her, always as though they had never seen her there
before.

'Hello, everybody.' Kassandra smiled and held out her arms. For an instant
no one moved, and then, at Fräulein Hedwig's prodding, Gerhard came first.
He only needed a moment's urging, and then would fly unharnessed to her
arms. But Fräulein Hedwig's voice was quick to stop him.

'Gerhard, don't touch! Your mother is dressed for the party.'

'That's all right.' Her open arms never wavered, but the child backed off to
just beyond her grasp.

'Hello, Mummy.' His eyes were wide and blue like hers, but the face was
Walmar's. He had lovely perfect features, a happy smile, blond hair, and still
the chubby body of a baby, despite his now almost five years. 'I hurt my arm
today.' He showed her, still not having arrived in hers. She reached out to him
gently.

'Let me see it.' And then, 'Oh, that looks awful. Did it hurt a lot?' It was a
small scrape and a smaller bruise, but to him it was important, as he looked
from the injured arm to the woman in the black dress.

'Yes.' He nodded. 'But I didn't cry.'

'That was very brave of you.'

'I know.' He looked pleased with himself and then bounded away from her
to collect a toy he had forgotten in another room, which left Kassandra alone
with Ariana, who was still smiling shyly at her from Fräulein Hedwig's side.

'Don't I get a kiss today, Ariana?' The child nodded and then approached,
hesitant, elflike, with delicate looks that promised to outshine even her
mother's. 'How are you?'

'Fine, thank you, Mummy.'

'No bruises, no cuts, nothing for me to kiss?' She shook her head and they
exchanged a smile. Gerhard made them both laugh sometimes. He was so
much a little boy. But Ariana had always been different. Pensive, quiet, much

shier than her brother, Kassandra often wondered if it would have been different if there had never been a nurse. 'What did you do today?'

'I read, and I drew a picture.'

'May I see it?'

'It isn't finished yet.' It never was.

'That doesn't matter. I'd like to see it anyway'. But Ariana blushed furiously and shook her head. Kassandra felt more than ever an intruder and wished, as she always did, that Hedwig and the nursery maid would disappear into another room at least, so that they could be alone. It was only on rare occasions that she was alone with the children. Hedwig stayed near to keep them from getting out of hand.

'Look what I have!' Gerhard had returned to them, bouncing along in his pyjamas, with a large stuffed dog.

'Where did you get that?'

'From Baroness von Vorlach. She brought it to me this afternoon'.

'She did?' Kassandra looked blank.

'She said you were going to have tea with her, but you forgot.' Kassandra closed her eyes and shook her head.

'How awful. I did. I'll have to call her. But that's a very handsome dog. Does he have a name yet?'

'Bruno. And Ariana got a big white cat.'

'Did you?' Ariana had steadfastly kept the news to herself. When would they ever share things? When the girl was grown, perhaps they would be friends. But now it was too late, and yet too soon.

Downstairs the clock chimed again, and Kassandra looked at them, feeling anguish clutch her. And Gerhard looked at her, crestfallen, tiny, chubby, 'Do you have to go?'

Kassandra nodded. 'I'm sorry. Papa is having a dinner.'

'Aren't you having one, too?' Gerhard looked at her curiously and she smiled.

'Yes, me, too. But it's for people from his bank, and some other banks.'

'It sounds very boring.'

'Gerhard!' Hedwig was quick to reprimand him, but Kassandra laughed.

She lowered her voice conspiratorially as she spoke to this delicious child. 'It will be ... but don't tell anyone ... that's our secret.'

'You look very pretty anyway.' He looked her over with approval, and she kissed the chubby little hand.

'Thank you.' She pulled him into her arms then and kissed him softly on the top of his blond head. 'Good night, little one. Are you taking your new dog to bed?'

He shook his head firmly. 'Hedwig says I can't do that.'

Kassandra stood and smiled pleasantly at the heavyset older woman. 'I think he can.'

'Very well, madam.'

Gerhard beamed up at his mother and they exchanged another conspiratorial smile, and then her gaze turned to Ariana. 'Will you take your new cat to bed with you, too?'

'I think so.' She glanced first at Hedwig and then her mother, as Kassandra felt something deep inside her die again.

'You'll have to show him to me tomorrow.'

'Yes, ma'am.' The words cut to the quick, but her pain didn't show as Kassandra gently kissed her daughter, waved at both children, and softly closed the door.

As quickly as the narrow black dress would allow, Kassandra made her way downstairs, arriving at the foot of the stairs in time to see Walmar greeting their first guests.

'Ah, there you are, darling.' He turned to smile at her, appreciative, as always, of how she looked. He made the introductions as heels clicked and hands were kissed. It was a couple Kassandra had met often at functions for the bank, but who had not yet visited their home. She greeted them warmly and took Walmar's arm as they entered the main salon.

It was an evening of civilised exchanges, lavish food, and the very best French wines. The guests spoke mostly of banking, travel. Children and talk of politics were strangely absent from the conversation, although it was 1934, although President von Hindenburg's death that year had removed the final threat to Hitler's power. It was a subject not really worth discussing. Since Hitler had become Chancellor the year before, the bankers of the nation had maintained their position. They were important to the Reich, they had their work to do, and Hitler had his. However little some of them might have thought of him, he was not going to stir up problems in their lair. Live and let live. And there were those, of course, who were pleased with Hitler's Reich.

Walmer was not among them, but it was a view he shared with few. He had been astonished at the gathering power of the Nazis, and he had warned his friends several times privately that it would lead to war. But there was no reason to discuss it on that evening. The crêpes flambées, served with champagne, seemed of far more interest than the Third Reich.

The last guest did not leave until one-thirty, when Walmar turned tiredly to Kassandra with a yawn. 'I think it was a very successful dinner, darling. I liked the duckling better than the fish.'

'Did you?' She made a mental note to tell the cook the next morning. They served gargantuan dinners, with an appetiser, soup, fish course, meat course, salad, cheese, dessert, and at last fruit. It was expected, so it was what they did.

'Did you have a pleasant evening?' He looked down at her gently as they walked slowly upstairs.

'Of course I did, Walmar.' She was touched that he would ask. 'Didn't you?'

'Useful. That Belgian deal we've been discussing will probably go through. It was important that Hoffmann came tonight. I'm glad he did.'

'Good. Then so am I.' As she followed him sleepily, she wondered if that was her purpose, then, to encourage him with his Belgian deal, and Dolff with his new book. Was that it, then? She was to help both of them achieve whatever it was that they were going to do? But if them, why not her children? And then it came to her, and why not herself? 'I thought his wife was very pretty.'

Walmar shrugged, and then as they stood on the landing, he smiled at her, but there was a ghost of sorrow in his eyes. 'I didn't. I'm afraid you've spoiled me for everyone else.'

She smiled back into his eyes. 'Thank you.'

There was a moment of awkwardness as they both stood there on the stairs. It was the moment of parting. It seemed easier on the evenings when they had nothing to do. He would retreat to his study, she would go upstairs alone to read a book. But climbing the stairs together left them with a fork in the road that never grew less poignant and left them both feeling so much alone. Before, they had always known they might meet in her bedroom later, but now it was no secret between them that they would not. And there was an aura of adieu each time they reached that landing. It always seemed so much more than just good night.

'You're looking better lately, darling. I don't mean in terms of your looks.' He smiled gently. 'I mean your health.'

She returned his smile. 'I'm feeling better, I suppose.' But there was something gone from her eyes as she said it, and she quickly dropped her eyes away from his. There was an instant of silence as the clock softly chimed the quarter hour.

'It's late, you'd best get to bed.' He kissed the top of her head and walked resolutely to the door of his room. She saw only his back as she whispered softly. 'Good night, and then walked quickly down the hall to her own.

Chapter 3

The wind whisked briskly around their legs as Dolff and Kassandra walked along the lake at the Charlottenburger Schloss. This afternoon they were alone in the park. The children were back in school, and the lovers and old people who came out to feed the birds were too sensible to go out on such a cold day. But Dolff and Kassandra were happy with their solitude as they walked along.

'Warm enough?' He looked down at her smilingly and she laughed.

'In this? I'd be embarrassed to admit it if I wasn't.'

'You should be.' He glanced admiringly at the new sable coat, which danced only a few inches above the ground. She wore a matching hat tilted to one side of her head, and the sleek golden hair was tied in a knot at the nape of her neck. Her cheeks were pink from the cold, and her eyes looked more startlingly violet than ever. He had an arm around her shoulders and he looked down at her with pride. It was November and she had been his now for more than eight months.

'How do you feel now that you've finished the book?'

'Like I'm out of a job.'

'Do you miss the characters very much?'

'I miss them terribly at first.' And then he kissed the top of her head. 'But less so when I'm with you. Are you ready to go back now?' She nodded and they turned back towards his house, hurrying the few blocks until they reached his door. He pushed it open for Kassandra as they stepped into the front hall. She felt more and more at home here. The week before they had even ventured into some antique stores together and bought two new chairs and another small desk.

'Tea?' She smiled up at him warmly and he nodded comfortably in answer, following her into the kitchen. She put on the kettle and pulled out one of the well-worn kitchen chairs.

'Do you have any idea how lovely it is to have you here, madam?'

'Do you have any idea how lovely it is to be here?' She was coming to terms with the guilt now. This was simply her way of life, and she had been greatly comforted to learn inadvertently several months before that one of her father's sisters had had the same lover for thirty-two years. Perhaps that was her destiny, too. To grow old with both Dolff and Walmar, useful to them both, the fabric of her life irrevocably meshed with that of Dolff's and bordered by Walmar's protecting arms. Was it so terrible after all? Was anyone really suffering? She seldom felt the pangs anymore. Only when she was with the children did she still feel any kind of pain, but she had felt that long before Dolf came along.

'You're looking serious again. What were you just thinking?'

'Oh, about us ...' She grew pensive again as she poured his tea. How different it was here in the comfortable kitchen, unlike the elaborate ceremony that took place in the house in Grunewald when she invited friends in to tea, with Berthold the butler staring gloomily down at them.

'Does thinking about us make you look so serious?'

She turned to face him as she handed him his cup. 'Sometimes I take this very seriously, you know.'

He looked at her gravely. 'I know. So do I.' And then suddenly he wanted to say something to her that he had never said before. 'If things were ... different ... I want you to know that ... I would want you for always.'

Her eyes bore into his. 'And now?'

His voice was a caress in the warm room. 'I still want you for always.' And then with a small sigh, 'But I can't do anything about it.'

'I don't expect you to.' She sat down across from him with a gentle smile. 'I'm happy like this.' And then she told him something she had never said before. 'This is the most important part of my life, Dolff.' It meant everything to him to have her be part of his life. So much had altered in his life over the past year. The rest of the world was changing around them, but he was far more aware of it than she. She touched his hand softly, pulling him back from his own thoughts. 'Now tell me about the book. What does your publisher say?'

But as she said the words, an odd expression came into his eyes. 'Nothing much.'

'He doesn't like it?' She looked shocked. The book was marvellous, She had read it herself, tucked into his bed, on the cold winter afternoons. 'What did he say?'

'Nothing.' She saw his eyes go hard. 'They're not entirely sure they can publish it.' So that was the shadow she had seen in his eyes when she'd arrived right after lunch. Why hadn't he told her sooner? But it was like him to hide his problems from her at first. He always wanted to hear about her.

'Are they crazy? What about the success of your last book?'

'That has nothing to do with it.' He turned away from her and stood up to put his cup in the sink.

'Dolff, I don't understand.'

'Neither do I, but I think we will. Our beloved leader will show us soon enough.'

'What are you talking about?' She stared at his back and then at the anger she saw in his eyes when he turned around.

'Kassandra, do you have any idea what's happening to our country?'

'You mean Hitler?' He nodded. 'It'll pass. People will get bored with him and he'll fall out of favour.'

'Oh, really? Is that what you think?' And then bitterly, 'Is that what your husband thinks?' She was startled at the mention of Walmar.

'I don't know. He doesn't talk about it a greal deal. At least not with me. Nobody reasonable likes Hitler, obviously, but I don't think he's as danger-ous as some people think.'

'Then you're a fool, Kassandra.' He had never talked to her in that tone of voice before. But suddenly she saw anger and bitterness that he had never unveiled to her before. 'Do you know why my publisher is sitting on the fence? Not because my last book didn't sell, not because he doesn't like the new manuscript. He was stupid enough to let me know how much he liked it before he cooled off. But because of the Party ...' He looked at her with an anguish that tore at her heart. 'Because I'm Jewish, Kassandra ... because I'm a Jew.' His voice was a barely audible whisper at the last. 'A Jew isn't supposed to be successful, isn't supposed to win national awards. There will be no room at all for Jews in the New Germany, if Hitler has his way.'

'But that's crazy.' Her face said that she didn't believe him. It was some-thing that they had never discussed. He had told her about his parents, his past, his childhood, the bakery, but he had never talked to her at any length about being Jewish, about what it did and did not mean to him. She had simply assumed that he was and forgotten about it after that. And on the rare occasions when she did think about it, it pleased her, it seemed different and exotic in a very pleasant way. But it was something that simply never entered their discussions, and seldom her mind. But the fact of that difference never left him. And the truth of what it could mean to him was coming slowly clear.

Kassandra thought over the implications of what he had just said. 'You can't mean it. It couldn't be that.'

'Couldn't it? It's starting to happen to some of the others. I'm not the only one. And it's only happening to the Jews. They won't take on our new books, they don't want to publish our articles, they don't answer our calls. Believe me, Kassandra, I know.'

'Then go to another publisher.'

'Where? In England? In France? I'm a German, I want to publish my work here.'

'Then do it. They can't all be fools.'

'They're not fools. They're much wiser than we think they are. They see what's coming, and they're afraid.'

Kassandra stared at him, shocked at what she was hearing. It couldn't be as bad as he thought it was. He was just upset over the rejection. She let out a long sigh and reached for his hand. 'Even if it is true, it won't be forever. They may relax once they see that Hitler isn't going to cause as much trouble as they think.'

'What makes you think he won't?'

'He can't. How can he? The power is still in the right hands. The backbone of this country is the banks, the businesses, the old families – they're not going to fall for all that garbage he spouts. The lower classes might, but who are they, after all?'

Dolff looked grim as he answered. '"The old families," as you put it, may not fall for it, but if they don't speak out, against it, we're doomed. And you're wrong about something else. They aren't the power in this country anymore. The power is the little man, armies and armies and armies of little men, men who are individually powerless, but strong as a group, people who are tired of the "backbone" you're talking about, tired of the upper classes and the "old families" and the banks. Those people believe every word that Hitler is preaching; they think they've found themselves a new god. And if they all get together, that will be the real power in this country. And if that happens, we'll all be in trouble, not just the Jews, but people like you, too.' It terrified her to hear what he was saying, lf he was right ... But he couldn't be ... he couldn't.

She smiled at him and stood up to run her hands slowly over his chest. 'Hopefully nothing is as dire as you predict.' He kissed her gently then and led her slowly upstairs with an arm around her waist. She wanted to ask him what he was going to do about the new book, but she hated to press it, she didn't want to revive more of his fears. And for an author of his magnitude, it seemed unlikely that Hitler's prejudice against Jews and Jewish authors could be of any major importance. After all, he was Dolff Sterne.

That evening Kassandra was pensive as she drove back to Grunewald, mulling over again what Dolff had said. The look in Dolff's eyes was plaguing her when she let herself into the house. She had an hour to herself before dinner, and tonight, instead of going to see the children, she sought refuge in her room. What if he were right? What could it mean? What would it mean to them? But as she sank slowly into a tub of warm water, she decided that the whole thing was probably nonsense. The book would be published. He would win another award. Artists were sometimes a little crazy. She smiled as she remembered other moments of the afternoon. She was still smiling to herself when she heard the knock on the door of her bedroom and she called out absently for the maid to come in.

'Kassandra?' But it wasn't Anna. It was the voice of her husband in the other room.

'Walmar? I'm in the bath.' She had left the doors open and wondered if he would come in, but when his voice reached her again, it wasn't approaching, and she continued to talk to him through the open door.

'Will you please come and see me when you're dressed?' He sounded serious, and for an instant she felt fear stir in her heart. Was he going to confront her? She closed her eyes and held her breath.

'Do you want to come in?'

'No, just knock on my door before dinner.'

He sounded more worried than angry.

'I'll be there in a few minutes.'

'Fine.'

She heard the door close again softly and hurried through the rest of her bath. It took her only a few minutes to put on her makeup and run a comb through her hair. She put on a simple dove grey suit for dinner, with a white silk shirt that tied in a loose cravat at the neck. Her shoes were grey suede, her stockings the same subdued hue, and she quickly slipped on the double rope of black pearls that had been her mother's favourite, along with the earrings that matched. She looked subdued and serious as she glanced at herself before walking down the hall. The only touch of colour was her hair, and the deep Wedgwood blue of her eyes. When she reached his door, she knocked softly, and a moment later she heard his voice beyond.

'Come in.' She stepped across the threshold, feeling the silk skirt of the suit rustle against her legs. Walmar was sitting in one of the comfortable brown leather chairs in his study, and he was quick to put down the report he had been reading when she came in. 'You look lovely, Kassandra.'

'Thank you.' She searched his eyes and saw the truth, the pain. She wanted to reach out to him, to ask him, to offer him comfort. But as she watched him, she found that she couldn't approach him. She suddenly found herself staring at him from across an abyss. It was Walmar who had stepped back.

'Please sit down.' She did and he watched her. 'Sherry?' She shook her head. In his eyes she could see that he knew. She turned her face away from him, pretending to enjoy the fire. There was nothing she could say to him. She would just have to live through the accusation and come to some solution in the end. What could she possibly do? Which man would she abandon? She needed and loved them both. 'Kassandra ...' She kept her eyes on the fire, and then at last turned them to his.

'Yes.' It was a painful rasp.

'There is something I must say to you. It is ...' He seemed agonised, but they both knew that now there was no turning back. '... it is extremely painful for me to discuss this with you, and I'm sure it's quite as distasteful to you.' Her heart pounded so horribly in her ears that she could barely hear him. Her life was over. The end had begun. 'But I must speak to you. For your sake. For your safety. And perhaps ours.

'My safety?' It was only a whisper, but she stared at him, confused.

'Just listen to me.' And then, as though it were too much for him, he sat back in his chair and sighed. When she looked at him, she also saw the bright light of unshed tears in his eyes. 'I know ... I've been aware that ... for the past several months ... you have been engaged in a somewhat ... difficult situation.' Kassandra closed her eyes and listened to the sound of his voice drone in her ears. 'I want you to know that I'm ... I do understand ... I'm not unsympathetic.' The huge sad eyes opened again.

'Oh, Walmar ...' Slowly the tears began to roll down her cheeks. 'I don't want to ... I can't.'

'Stop it. Listen to me.' For a moment he sounded like her father, and after another sigh he went on. 'What I'm going to say to you is terribly important. I also want you to know, since this situation is somewhat out in the open now, that I love you. I don't want to lose you, whatever you may think of me now.'

Kassandra shook her head and, taking a lace handkerchief from her pocket, blew her nose through her tears. 'I have nothing but respect for you, Walmar. And I love you, too.' It was true. She did love him and she died a little over his pain.

'Then listen to what I have to say. You're going to have to stop seeing ... your friend.' Kassandra stared at him in silent horror. 'And not for the reasons that you think. I am twenty-nine years older than you are, my darling, and I am not a fool. These things sometimes happen, and they may hurt a great deal for the people involved, but if they're handled properly, one can survive the ordeal. But that's not what I'm telling you now. I'm telling you something very different. I'm saying that for reasons entirely other than me, our marriage, you must stop seeing ... Dolff.' It seemed to cause him anguish to say the other man's name. 'In fact, even if you were not married just now, if you had never been, it is a relationship in which you could not afford to indulge.'

'What do you mean?' She jumped to her feet angrily, her gratitude for his benevolence instantly gone. 'Why? Because he's a writer? Do you think he's some kind of Bohemian? For God's sake, Walmar, he's a very decent, wonderful man.' The absurdity of her defending her lover to her husband had not yet occurred to Kassandra as she looked into Walmar's eyes.

He sat back in his chair with another sigh. 'I hope you don't think me sufficiently small-minded to eliminate writers and artists and their kind from the roster of those I choose to befriend. I have never been guilty of such narrow opinions, Kassandra. It would do you credit to remember that. What I'm speaking of here is entirely different. I'm telling you' – he leaned forward in his chair and spoke to her with sudden vehemence – 'that you can't afford to know the man, to be with the man, to be seen at his home, not because he's a writer ... but because he's a Jew. And it makes me sick to tell you that, because I think that what is starting to happen in this country is disgusting, but the fact is that it *is happening* and you are my wife and the mother of my children and I won't have you murdered or put in jail! Do you understand that, dammit? Do you understand how important this is?'

Kassandra stared at him disbelievingly. It was like continuing the nightmare of what Dolff had said to her that afternoon. 'Are you telling me that you think they might kill him?'

'I don't know what they'll do, and the truth is that I don't know what I think anymore. But as long as we lead a quiet life and stay out of what's happening, we're safe, you're safe, Ariana and Gerhard are safe. But that man isn't safe. Kassandra, please ...' He reached out and grabbed her hand. 'If anything happens to him, I don't want you to be a part of it. If things were different, if these were other times, I would be pained at what you are doing, but I would close my eyes, but I can't do that now. I must stop you. You must stop yourself.'

'But what about him?' She was too frightened to cry now. The magnitude of what he had said to her had cleared her head.

Walmar shook his head. 'We can't do anything to help him. If he's smart and if things go on like this, he'd be wise to leave Germany.' Walmar looked at Kassandra. 'Tell him that.' Kassandra sat staring into the fire, not sure what to say. The only thing she was sure of was that she wouldn't give him up. Not now, not later, not ever.

Her eyes found his in a moment, and despite the anger, there was something very tender there for him as well. She went to him and kissed him gently on the cheek. 'Thank you for being so fair.' He hadn't berated her for being unfaithful. He was only worried about her safety, and perhaps even that of her friend. What an extraordinary man he was. For a moment her love for him fanned as it hadn't in years. She looked down at him with her hand on his shoulder. 'Is it as bad as that, then?'

He nodded. 'I think perhaps it's worse. We just don't know it yet.' And then after a moment, 'But we will.'

'I find it difficult to believe that things could ever get so out of hand.'

He looked at her with urgency as she stood up to leave the room. 'Will you do what I asked you, Kassandra?' She wanted to promise him, to assure him that she would, but something had changed subtly between them. He knew the truth, and it was better that way. She didn't have to lie to him any more.

'I don't know.'

'You have no choice.' His voice was angry then. 'Kassandra, I forbid you –' But she had quietly slipped out of the room.

Chapter 4

Six weeks later one of Dolff's writer friends disappeared. He was far less well-known than Dolff, but he, too, had had trouble publishing his most recent work. His girlfriend called Dolff in hysterics at two o'clock in the morning. She had driven home from visiting her mother in Munich that night, and the apartment had been broken into, Helmut was gone, and there was blood on the floor. The manuscript he'd been working on was scattered around the room. The neighbours had heard shouting and then screaming but that was all she knew. Dolff had met her near Helmut's apartment and then driven her back to his place. The next day she sought refuge with her sister.

When Kassandra arrived later that morning, she found him in the depths of depression, and insane with grief over Helmut's disappearance.

'I don't understand it, Kassandra. Little by little, the whole country's going mad. It's like a slow-moving poison travelling in this country's veins. Eventually it will reach our heart and kill us. Not that I'll have to worry about that.' He stared at her gloomily and she frowned.

'What's that supposed to mean?'

'What do you think it means? How long do you think it will be before they come for me? A month? Six months? A year?'

'Don't be crazy. Helmut wasn't a novelist. He was a highly political non-fiction writer who has openly criticised Hitler since he came to power. Don't you see the difference? What do you think they'd be angry about in your case? A novel like *Der Kuss?*'

'You know, I'm not sure I do see the difference, Kassandra.' He glanced around the room with displeasure. He didn't even feel secure in his house anymore, it was as though he expected them to come for him any day.

'Dolff ... darling, please ... be reasonable. It was an awful thing to have happened, but it can't happen to you. Everyone knows you. They're not simply going to make you disappear overnight.'

'Why not? Who's going to stop them? Will you? Will anyone? Of course not. What did I do for Helmut last night? Nothing. Absolutely goddamn nothing.'

'All right, then leave for God's sake. Go to Switzerland now. You can publish there. And you'll be safe.'

But he only looked at her bleakly. 'Kassandra, I'm a German. This is my country, too. I have as much right to be here as anyone else does. Why the hell should I go?'

'Then what are you telling me, dammit?' It was the first fight they had had in years.

'I'm telling you that my country is destroying itself and its people and it's making me sick.'

'But you can't stop that. If that's what you believe, then get out before it destroys you.'

'And what about you, Kassandra? You stay here pretending none of it will ever touch you? You think it won't?'

'I don't know ... I don't know ... I don't know anything any more. I don't understand any of it.' The golden woman had been looking tired for weeks. She was getting it from both of them now, and she felt helpless in the face of their fears. She looked to them for reassurance, for the confirmation that everything she believed in would never change, and they were both telling her that everything was changing; yet all Walmar wanted to do about it was for her to stop seeing Dolff, and all Dolff wanted to do was rail, at something that none of them had the power to change. He went on talking in disjointed circles for another half hour, and suddenly she jumped to her feet in a rage. 'What the hell do you want from me? What can I do?'

'Nothing dammit ... nothing ...' And then as tears streamed down his cheeks for his lost friend, he pulled her tightly into his arms as he sobbed. 'Oh, God ... Kassandra ... oh, God ...'

She held him that way for an hour, holding him close, as she would have her son. 'It's all right ... it's all right, darling ... I love you ...' That was really all that was left to say, but the finger of fear that she had been avoiding began to crawl up her spine now, too. What if it were Dolff who were dragged screaming into the night? What if it had been she in the shoes of Helmut's hysterical girlfriend? But that couldn't happen to her ... or to him ... those things didn't happen ... and it wouldn't happen to them.

When she got home late that afternoon, Walmar was waiting for her, not in his study, but in the main salon. He motioned her to join him and quietly closed the double French doors.

'Kassandra, this is becoming impossible.'

'I don't want to discuss it.' She turned her back to him, staring into the roaring fire beneath the portrait of his grandfather, whose eyes always seemed to follow everyone in the room. 'This isn't the right time.'

'There will never be a right time.' And then, 'If you don't do as I ask you, I will send you away.'

'I won't go. I can't leave him now.' It was madness to be discussing this with Walmar, but she had no choice. It had been out in the open for almost two months now, and whatever it cost her, she was going to stand her ground. She had given up too many things in her life already. Her dreams of the theatre, her children – she would not give up Dolff.

She turned to face him. 'Walmar, I don't know what to do. It's very hard to believe what I'm hearing these days. What's happening to us? To Germany? Is it all because of that silly little man?'

'It would seem to be. Or perhaps he has aroused some incipient insanity we had somewhere in our soul all along. Perhaps all of these people who have welcomed him have simply been waiting for someone to lead them on.'

'Can't somebody stop him before it's too late?'

'It may already be too late. He excites the people. He promises them progress and riches and success. For those who've never tasted that, it's hypnotic. They can't resist.'

'And what about the rest of us?'

'We wait and see. But not your friend, Kassandra. If things go on as they are, he won't have the luxury of waiting. Oh, God, please listen to me, you must. Go and stay with my mother, for a few days. Think it over. It'll give you time away from us both.' But she didn't want time away from them. And she knew she didn't want to leave Dolff.

'I'll think about it.' But he knew from the tone of her voice that she would not. There was nothing more he could do. For the first time in the almost sixty years of his lifetime, Walmar von Gotthard felt like a beaten man. She watched him stand up and walk to the doorway, and then quietly stretched out a hand. 'Walmar ... don't look like that ... I'm ... I'm sorry ...' But he only turned to look at her from the door.

'You're sorry, Kassandra. And so am I. And so will the children be before this is over. What you are doing will destroy you, and perhaps in the long run destroy all of us.'

But Kassandra von Gotthard didn't believe that.

Chapter 5

It was in February that Walmar and Kassandra attended the Spring Ball. The weather was still icy, but it was cheering to celebrate the prospect of spring. She wore her full-length ermine over a starkly simple white velvet gown.

The top was cut halter fashion, and the skirt fell in total perfection from her waist to her white satin-clad feet. Her hair was an upswept mass of delicate tendrils, and she looked lovelier than ever and as though she had not a care in the world. The fact that Dolff had been testy all day again over the unpublished manuscript and that Walmar and she were barely speaking as their battle raged on didn't show. Trained from the cradle to show nothing but graciousness beyond the sanctum of her own bedroom, she smiled benevolently at every introduction and danced willingly with all of Walmar's friends. As always their entrance had caused a small sensation, as much for the clothes that she wore as for the face with its striking beauty, which outshone even her clothes.

'You look ravishing, Frau Gotthard. Like a snow princess.' The compliment came from the man she had just met, some banker or other. Walmar had greeted him with a curt, friendly nod and quick assent when he had asked his permission to escort Kassandra to the floor. They were waltzing slowly as Kassandra watched Walmar chat with some friends.

'Thank you. I take it you know my husband?'

'Only slightly. We have had the pleasure of doing business once or twice. But my ... activities have been a little less commercial in nature during the past year.'

'Ah? Enjoying a sabbatical?' Kassandra smiled pleasantly as they waltzed.

'Not at all. My efforts have been engaged in assisting our leader in establishing the finances of the Third Reich.' He said it with such force that Kassandra was startled and looked into his eyes.

'I see. That must keep you busy.'

'Decidedly so. And you?'

'My children and my husband keep me busy most of the time.'

'And the rest of the time?'

'I beg your pardon?' Kassandra felt herself growing uncomfortable in this bold stranger's arms.

'I understand that you're something of a patron of the arts.'

'Really?' Kassandra found herself praying for the dance to end.

'Indeed.' He smiled pleasantly at her, but there was a glint of something chilling lurking in his eyes. 'I wouldn't waste a great deal of my time on that, though. You see, our concept of the arts is going to change greatly with the assistance of the Third Reich.'

'Is it?' For a moment she felt faint. Was this man warning her about Dolff? Or was she growing as crazy as he was, fearing threats at every turn.

'Yes, it is. You see, we've had such ... such inadequate artists, such sick minds holding the pen.' Then it was Dolff he meant. 'All of that will have to change.'

But suddenly she was angry. 'Perhaps it already has. They don't seem to be publishing the same people any more, do they?' Oh, God, what was she doing? What would Walmar say if he could hear? But the dance was coming to an end. She was about to be free of this evil stranger. But now she wanted to say more.

'Don't worry about all of this nonsense, Frau Gotthard.'

'I wasn't planning to.'

'That's encouraging to hear.' What was? What did he mean? But he was leading her back to Walmar now. It was all over. And she didn't see the man again that night. On the way home she wanted to tell Walmar, but she was afraid of making him angry – or worse, afraid. And the next day Dolff was back in such good spirits that she didn't tell him what had happened either. And after all, what did it mean? Some moron banker who was in love with Hitler and the Third Reich? So what?

Dolff had come to a decision. He was going to write whether they published him or not. And he was going to go on trying to publish. But if he starved to death, he was going to stay. No one was going to drive him out of his homeland. He had a right to be there, and to prosper, even if he was a Jew.

'Can I interest you in a walk near the castle?' She smiled at him. It would be the first time they had gone out for a walk in two weeks.

'I'd love that.'

They walked for almost two hours, near the schloss and next to the lake, watching the few children who had come to play there, and smiling at other strollers passing by. It felt at long last like their first winter, when they had met by chance there time and time again, anxiously seeking each other, yet afraid of what might lie ahead.

'Do you know what I used to think when I looked for you here?' He was smiling down at her, his hand tightly clasping hers as they walked.

'What?'

'I used to think that you were the most elusive, mysterious woman I had ever known, and if I could only spend one day with you, I'd be happy for the rest of my life.'

'And now? Are you happy?' She drew closer to him, her short fur jacket a ball of fluff over a long tweed skirt and dark brown suede shoes.

'I've never been happier. And you? Has the last year been too hard on you?' He still worried about that much of the time. She was the one with the pressures, with Walmar and the children, especially now that Walmar knew. She had told him of Walmar's warning.

'It hasn't been hard. It's been lovely.' She looked up at him with the fullness of their loving in her eyes. 'It's all I ever wanted – and always thought I couldn't have.' And she still couldn't have it. Not really. Not all the time. But even this was enough. Just these precious afternoons that she shared with Dolff.

'You'll always have me, Kassandra. Always. Even long after I'm dead and gone.'

But she looked up at him unhappily. 'Don't say things like that.'

'I meant when I was eighty, silly lady. I'm not going anywhere without you.' She smiled then, and they found themselves running hand in hand along the lake. Without explaining or asking, they made their way home and wandered happily upstairs after making tea. But they drank it quickly, they had other things on their minds, and their lovemaking was passionate and urgent, as though each of them needed the other desperately and more than anything on earth. At the end of the afternoon they lay sleeping, Kassandra curled tightly in her lover's arms.

It was Dolff who stirred first, aware of someone pounding on his door on the floor below them, and then there was the sudden battering of feet on the steps leading up from the main floor. He lay listening for an instant and then came fully awake and sat straight up in bed. Feeling the motion of his body, Kassandra stirred, and then, as though sensing danger, her eyes went wide. Without saying anything at all to her, he flung the covers over her and sprang from the bed, standing naked in the centre of the large bedroom just as they pressed through the door. At first glance it looked like an army of brown uniforms and red armbands, but there were only four.

Pulling his robe around him. Dolff stood firm. 'What is this?' But they only laughed. One of them grabbed him roughly and spat in his face.

'Listen to the Jew!' He was suddenly pulled taut between two of them, as a third delivered a ferocious punch to his belly, and Dolff grunted with the pain and bent double towards the floor. This time the third man kicked him, and instantly blood gushed from a gash near his mouth while calmly the fourth surveyed the room.

'What have we here under the covers? A Jew bitch keeping our illustrious writer warm?' With a sudden motion he pulled back the covers, exposing every inch of Kassandra to their interested gaze. 'And a pretty one. Get up.' Immobile for a moment, she did, sitting upright, and then gracefully slipping her legs on to the floor, her lithe, supple body trembling slightly, her eyes wide in terror as she stared silently at Dolff. The four men watched her, the three around Dolff questioningly gazing at the fourth to see what he would do. He surveyed her carefully, his eyes scouring her flesh, but she could only watch Dolff, still gasping, standing hunched and bleeding between the two uniformed men. And then the fourth turned to them with a sneer. 'Get him out of here.' And then in amusement as he touched his belt. 'Unless he'd like to watch.'

Suddenly Dolff came to his senses, his eyes frantically reaching for Kassandra and then turning furiously to the man in charge. 'No! Don't touch her!'

'Why not, Mister Famous Author? Has she got the clap?' The four men laughed in unison as Kassandra gasped. The full realisation of what was about to happen filled her with a terror she had never known. At a signal from their sergeant, they shoved Dolff from the room, and an instant later a resounding crash told her that Dolff had just been pushed down the stairs. There was an exchange of angry voices and Kassandra heard Dolff's above them all. He was calling her name and attempting to fight his captors, but a series of scuffling noises silenced him quickly, and then there was a dragging sound at the bottom of the stairs, and Dolff's voice did not rise to her ears again as, horrified, she turned her eyes to the man who was about to unzip his pants.

'You'll kill him ... oh, my God, you'll kill him!' She shrank back from him, her eyes wide, her heart pounding wildly. She could barely think of herself now, only of Dolff, who may even already have been dead.

'And if we do?' Her assailant looked amused. 'It's no great loss to our society. Perhaps even not so great a loss to you. He's only a little Jew boy. And you my sweet? His pretty Jewish princess?' But now Kassandra's eyes flashed; there was anger mixed with terror in those wild lavender-blue eyes.

'How dare you! *How dare you!*' It was an anguished scream as she ran from the wall towards him, clawing at his face. But with one deft sweep of his arm he slapped her, backhanded, across the face.

When he spoke to her, his voice was quiet, but his face was tense. 'That's enough. You've lost your boyfriend, little Jewess, but now you will find out what it is to be had by a better race. I am going to teach you a little lesson, dear one.' And with that, the belt whipped swiftly from its loops and cracked her mightily across the breasts. Stung by biting wings of pain, she clutched her bosom and bowed her head.

'Oh, God ...' And then, knowing she must do it, she looked up at him with anger mixed with shame. He would kill her. He would rape her and then kill her. She had to tell him. Had to ... she had no choice. She was not as brave as Dolff was. She looked in fury at the man who had just whipped her, still holding tightly to her bleeding breasts. 'I am not a Jew.'

'Oh, no?' He approached her now, the belt waiting to bite her yet again. As she stared at him, she saw the undeniable erection clawing at the front of his trousers. The calm he had sported only moments earlier was giving way to a frothing frenzy that Kassandra feared was already beyond control.

'My papers are in my handbag. I am –' she winced at the agony of what she was doing, but she had no choice. 'Kassandra von Gotthard. My husband is the president of the Tilden Bank.'

For an instant the man paused, eyeing her with anger and suspicion, not quite sure what to do. And then his eyes narrowed. 'And your husband doesn't know you're here?'

Kassandra trembled. To tell him that Walmar knew was to doom Walmar into the bargain. To tell him that Walmar did not was to doom herself. 'My housekeeper knows precisely where I am.'

'Very clever.' The belt slipped slowly back into the loops on his trousers. 'Your papers?'

She pointed. 'Over there.' In two strides he had reached the brown alligator handbag with the gold clip. He almost tore it open, fumbled for a moment, and found the wallet concealed inside. Roughly, he pulled out her driver's licence and identity cards and threw them to the floor. He almost snarled as he did it, and then menacingly he walked back towards her. It hadn't worked. He didn't give a damn who she was. Kassandra stood bracing herself for what would come next.

He stood looking down at her for an endless moment and then slapped her hard again across the face. 'Whore! Filthy whore! If I were your husband, I would kill you. And one day, for something like this, you will die, like that bastard Jew. You are filth. Filth. You're a disgrace to your race, your country. Filthy bitch!' And then, without another word, he turned and left her, his boots clattering down the stairs as he went, until at last she heard the front door slam. It was over ... over ... With every inch of her body trembling, she fell to her knees on the floor, a double trickle of blood still running from her breasts, her face bruised, her eyes filled with tears, as she lay down on the floor and sobbed.

It seemed hours that she lay there sobbing, keening for the last instant when she had seen Dolff, and terrified of what would come next. And then suddenly it occurred to her what might happen. They might come back, to destroy his house. Frantically then, glancing hurriedly around her, she pulled on her clothes. Standing for a last moment in the bedroom where she and Dolff had given birth to their dreams, she gazed, sobbing, at the spot where she had last seen him, and then without thinking she reached out a hand to the clothes he had worn only a few hours before. Discarded on the floor before their hungry lovemaking, still smelling of the special spice and lemon scent he wore, she felt them for a moment and ran them through her fingers, pressing his shirt to her face with a sob. And then she ran from the room and down the stairs. It was at the bottom landing that she saw it, the pool of blood where he had lain, and the trail it made where they must have dragged him, unconscious, from his own house. She fled the building and ran frantically towards her car, parked only slightly further down the street.

She was never quite sure how she had got back to Grunewald, but she had driven home, still sobbing, clutching the wheel. She had crawled out of the car, unlocked the gate, driven on to their doorway, and let herself in with her key. Silently, and with tears still streaming from her eyes, she had run up the stairs to her bedroom, slammed the door, and looked around her. She was back, she was home ... it was the pink bedroom she had seen so often ... the pink ... the pink ... it was all she could see as it spun around her and she sank at last, unconscious, to the floor.

Chapter 6

When Kassandra came to, she was lying on her bed, a cold compress pressed across her head. The room was dark and there was a strange buzzing. She realised in a moment that the sound she heard was in her own head. Somewhere in the distance there was Walmar, staring down at her and applying something damp and heavy to her face. In time she felt her blouse stripped off; and she was aware of a terrible stinging, and then of something warm draped across her naked breasts. It seemed a long time before she could see him clearly, and then at last the buzzing stopped and he sat down quietly in a chair beside her bed. He said nothing, he only sat there as she lay staring at the ceiling, unwilling and unable to speak. He asked her nothing. He only changed the compresses from time to time. The room stayed dark for hours, and when now and then there came a knock at the door, it was Walmar who sent them away. She looked at him gratefully and then drifted off to sleep. It was midnight when she woke again; a dim light burned in the distance in her boudoir, and keeping his silent vigil, he was still there.

At last he couldn't hold back any longer, and he could see from her eyes that she was conscious and no longer in shock, and he had to know what had happened, for her sake and his own. 'Kassandra, you have to talk now. You have to tell me. What happened?'

'I disgraced you.' Her voice was the merest whisper, and he shook his head and took her hand.

'Don't be silly.' And then after another moment, 'Darling tell me. You must tell me. I have to know.' Anna had come to him screaming that something terrible had happened to Frau von Gotthard and she was lying near death on her bedroom floor. In terror, he had run to find her, not near death, but beaten and in shock. And then he had known. 'Kassandra?'

'He was ... going to kill me ... to rape me ... I told him ... who I was.'
Walmar felt a chill of fear run through him.

'Who was it?'

'Them ... they took him ...' And then she whispered horribly. 'They took
Dolff ... they beat him ... they ... he was ... bleeding ... and then they ...
dragged him ... down ... the stairs ...' She sat up in bed and retched, emptily,
on to the bed, as Walmar sat by helplessly, holding out a monogrammed pink
towel. When it was over, she stared blankly at her husband. 'And one of them
stayed behind ... for me ... I told him ... I told him ...' She looked at
Walmar pathetically. 'They thought I was a Jew.'

'You were right to tell them who you are. You'd be dead by now if you
hadn't. They may not kill him, but they would probably have killed you.' He
knew that more likely the reverse was true, but he had to lie, for her sake.

'What will they do to him?'

He took her in his arms then and she sobbed for almost an hour. When it was
over, she lay there, spent and broken, and he laid her back quietly on her
pillows and turned off the light. 'You must sleep now. I'll be here with you all
night.' And he was, but when she woke up in the morning, he had at long last
gone to rest. For him it had been a night of anguish, watching the pale face
writhe and contort in her nightmares beneath the ugly bruises that had darkened it. Whoever the man was who had slapped her, he had spared not an
ounce of his strength when he did. And as he watched her, hour by hour,
Walmar came to hate them in a way he never had before. This was the Third
Reich. Was this what they had to look forward to in the coming years? Was
one meant to count one's blessings that one was not a Jew? Walmar would be
damned if he'd see his beloved country turn into a nation of thugs and
marauders, beating women, raping the innocent, censuring artists for their
heritage. What had happened to their world that this was the price his beloved
Kassandra had to pay? He was outraged, and in his own way he also mourned
for Dolff.

When he left her to bathe and have a cup of coffee, he glanced at the
newspaper with dread. He knew just how they would do it, and he fully
expected to find a notice that some 'accident' had befallen Dolff. That's how
they had done things like that before. But this time there was no small, 'unimportant' news item. Or rather, it was so small that he didn't notice it on a back
page.

When Walmar returned to Kassandra's bedside two hours later, she lay silent
and awake, her gaze empty as she stared at the ceiling. She had heard Walmar
come into her bedroom, but she didn't turn her eyes to him.

'Are you feeling any better?' But she only stared at the ceiling in answer, and
now and then she closed her eyes. 'Can I get you anything?' This time she
shook her head. 'It might make you feel a little better to take a nice warm bath.'
But for a long time she just lay there, staring at the ceiling and then finally the
wall, and then as though the effort was almost too much for her, she dragged
her eyes to his.

'What if they come to kill you and the children?' It was all she had thought of
since she woke up.

'Don't be ridiculous, they won't.' But now she knew differently. They were capable of anything. They dragged people trom their beds and killed them, or at the very least took them away. 'Kassandra ... darling ... we are all safe.' But even Walmar knew he was lying. No one was safe anymore. One day it wouldn't be just the Jews.

'It's not true, they'll kill you. Because I told them who I was. They'll come here ... they'll ...'

'They won't.' He forced her to look at him again. 'They won't. Be reasonable. I'm a banker. They need me. They're not going to hurt me, or my family. Didn't they let you go yesterday when you told them who you were?' She nodded mutely, but they both knew that she would never feel safe again.

'I disgraced you.' It was her only refrain.

'Stop it! Now it's over. It was a nightmare. An ugly, horrible nightmare, but it's over. Now you must wake up!' But to what?' Dolff gone? The same nightmare all over again? There would only be emptiness, and added to that, pain, and a horror that she knew she would never forget. All she wanted to do was sleep. Forever. A deep black sleep from which she would never have to wake. 'I have to go to the office for two hours, for that Belgian meeting, and then I'll be back and I'll stay with you all day. Will you be all right?' She nodded. He bent low next to her and kissed the long, delicate fingers of her left hand. 'I love you, Kassandra. And everything will be all right again.' He left orders with Anna to bring her a light breakfast, leave it on a tray next to her bed, and then go. And whatever she saw was not to be discussed with the other servants.

Anna nodded sagely and delivered the breakfast half an hour later to Kassandra's side. It was the breakfast tray Kassandra used every morning, of white wicker, covered with a white lace cloth. A single bud vase held a long red rose, and the breakfast service had been her grandmother's favourite Limoges. But Kassandra said nothing when the tray appeared. It was only after Anna left the room that Kassandra took an interest, seeing the morning paper tucked into the side basket of the tray. She had to see it, had to – maybe some small item would appear. Some few words that would tell her something of Dolff's fate. Painfully, she struggled up to one elbow and unfurled the paper on the bed. She read every line, every page, every story, and unlike Walmar, her eyes found the story on the back page. It said only that Dolff Sterne, novelist, had had an accident in his Bugatti and was dead. As she read it, she cried out, and then suddenly the room was filled with silence.

She lay there very still for almost an hour, and then resolutely she sat up on the edge of the bed. She was still shaky and very dizzy, but she made it to the bathroom and ran the tub. She stared into the mirror and saw the eyes that Dolff had loved, the eyes that had watched him dragged from the room, from his home, from his life and hers.

The bathtub filled very quickly, and she quietly closed the door. It was Walmar who found her there an hour later, her wrists slashed, her life gone, the bathtub filled with her blood.

Chapter 7

The dark brown Hispano-Suiza carrying Walmar von Gotthard; his children, Ariana and Gerhard; and Fräulein Hedwig rolled solemnly behind the black hearse. It was a grey February morning, and on and on since daybreak there had been mists and rain. The day was as bleak as Walmar and the children, sitting rigid, holding tightly to the hands of their beloved nurse. They had lost their pretty lady. The woman of golden hair and lavender-blue eyes was gone.

Only Walmar fully understood what had happened. Only he knew how deeply and for how long she had been cleft. Not just between two men, but between two minds, two lives, two lifestyles. She had never quite been able to adjust to the rigid rules of the life to which she had been born. Perhaps it had been a mistake to force her into the mould. Maybe he should have been wise enough to leave her to a younger man. But she had been so young, so free, so lovely, and so warm, so entirely what he had always dreamed of having in a wife. And other thoughts nagged at him. Maybe he had been wrong to keep her from the children.

As they rode mercilessly onwards, Walmar cast an eye at the nurse to whom his children now belonged. A rugged, sturdy face, kind eyes, strong hands. She had been the governess to his niece and nephew before this. Fräulein Hedwig was a good woman. But Walmar knew that, in part because of her, his wife was gone. She had been a woman without a cause or a reason to live after the tragedy of the day before. The loss of Dolff had been too shocking, the fear of what she had perhaps brought down on Walmar too great to bear. It was perhaps an act of cowardice, or madness, yet Walmar knew full well that it was more. The note she had left beside the bathtub had been written in a trembling hand. Only 'Goodbye . . . I'm sorry . . . K.' His eyes filled with tears again as he remembered . . . *auf Wiedersehen*, my darling . . . goodbye . . .

The brown Hispano-Suiza halted finally outside the gates of the Grunewald cemetery, its gentle mounds of green bordered by bright flowers, its handsome stones staring solemnly at them beyond the rain that had begun again.

'We're leaving Mama here?' Gerhard looked shocked, and Ariana only stared. Fräulein Hedwig nodded. The gates opened and Walmar signalled the chauffeur to drive on.

The service had been brief and private in the Lutheran church in Grunewald, with only the children and his mother present. That evening mention of Kassandra's passing would be printed in the press, attributed to sudden illness, an inexplicable bout of a lethal flu. She had always looked so fragile that it would not be difficult to believe. And the officials who knew would be too intimidated by Walmar to reveal the truth.

The minister from the Lutheran church had followed them to the cemetery in his own bedraggled car. They had been unable to hold the funeral in the Catholic church they normally attended. Her suicide had ruled out that possibility, but the Lutheran minister had been kind. Now he stepped quietly from his automobile, followed by Walmar's mother, the Baroness von Gotthard, emerging from her chauffeured Rolls. The two liveried Von Gotthard chauffeurs stood discreetly by as the casket was lowered from the hearse to the ground. A man from the cemetery was already waiting, his face sombre, his umbrella unfurled, as the minister reached into his pocket, taking from it a small Bible that he had marked.

Gerhard was crying softly, clutching tightly to Fräulein Hedwig's and his sister's hands, and Ariana looked around her. So many markers, so many names. Such big stones, such large statues, so many hills, and such eerie-looking trees. In spring it would be green and pretty, but now, except for the patches of lawn over the coffins, it all looked so awful and so bleak. She knew as she watched them that she would never forget this day. The night before, she had cried for her mother. She had always been a little frightened by the dazzling beauty, those huge, sad eyes, and the shining hair. Fräulein Hedwig had always said not to touch her or they'd put a spot on her dress. It seemed so odd to leave her here now, in that box, out in the rain. It made Ariana sad to think of her, all alone, under one of the smooth green mounds.

Kassandra was to be buried in the Von Gotthard family plot. It was already populated by Walmar's father, his older brother, his grandparents, and three aunts. And now he would leave her with the others, his sparkling bride, the fragile wife of the elusive laughter and the wondrous eyes. His gaze shifted from the headstones to his children; Ariana looked only faintly like her mother, and Gerhard not at all. Ariana, with her long colt legs stood beside him, wearing a white dress, white stockings, and the dark blue velvet coat with the ermine collar, trimmed with the remains of her mother's splendid coat. Beside her stood tiny Gerhard, a portrait much like his sister, in short white trousers, white stockings, and the same dark blue. They were all Walmar had now, these two small children standing at his side. He vowed silently to protect them from the evil that had so brutally destroyed his wife. No matter what happened to his country, no matter how badly their values were betrayed, he would let nothing happen to the children. He would keep them safe from the venom of the Nazis until Germany was free again from Hitler and his kind. It couldn't take for ever, and when the storm had passed, they would still be safe at home.

'... to keep Your child, Father, in the eternal peace she has found now at Your Side. May she rest in peace. Amen.'

The five onlookers silently made the sign of the cross and stood quietly for a moment staring at the dark wood box. Walmar's and the minister's umbrellas stood high above them as the sky opened up its heart and cried, too. But none of them seemed to notice the rain as they stood there, as it fell around them in driving sheets. At last Walmar nodded and touched the children's shoulders gently.

'Come now, children, we must go.' But Gerhard wouldn't leave her; he only shook his head and stared. In the end Fräulein Hedwig simply led him back into the car and lifted him inside. Ariana was quick to follow, with one last glance over her shoulder to where the box lay and where her father stood alone, now that Grandmother had also gone. The minister hurried back to his own car, and only Walmar stood there, looking down at the coffin covered with a single wreath of large white flowers. There were orchids and roses, and lilies of the valley, all the flowers that she loved.

For an instant he wanted to take her with him, never to leave her in this place with the others who had been so unlike her. His aunts and his father and the older brother who had died at war. She had been so childlike, and she was still so young. Kassandra von Gotthard, dead at thirty. Walmar stood there, unable to believe she was no more.

It was Ariana who finally came to find him. He felt the small fingers lace into his own and looked down to see her standing there, her blue coat with the ermine collar drenched with rain.

'We have to go now, Papa. We will take you home.' She looked so old and wise and loving, her huge blue eyes a distant shadow of those others he had known. She cared nothing about the rain as she stood there. She only looked up at him, holding tightly to his hand. And then, silently, he nodded, his face wet with tears and winter rain. His Homburg was dripping water on to his shoulders, and the tiny hand was held fast within his own.

He didn't look back over his shoulder, and neither did the child. Hand in hand, they climbed silently into the Hispano-Suiza, and the chauffeur closed the door. The men of Grunewald cemetery then slowly began to cover Kassandra von Gotthard's coffin until it, too, would become a green mound, to rest with all the others who had come before her and whom she had never known.

BOOK TWO
ARIANA
BERLIN

Chapter 8

'Ariana?' He stood at the bottom of the stairs, waiting. If she didn't hurry, they would be late. 'Ariana!' The nursery floor lay above him, transformed now into the rooms more suitable for teenagers. Now and then he had thought of moving the children downstairs to be near him, but they had grown accustomed to their own floor, and he had never been able to bring himself to reopen his wife's room. The doors to Kassandra's empty apartment had stood closed for seven years.

The clock chimed the half hour, and then, as though on cue, light flooded the upper hall. As he looked up, she stood there, a vision in layers of white, organdy, with a spray of tiny white roses woven into her golden hair. Her long neck was like ivory rising above the snowy dress, her features a perfectly curved cameo, and as she looked at him, her bright blue eyes danced. Slowly, she came down the stairs to him, as Gerhard grinned from above her, peeking from what had once been their playroom door. He broke the spell of the moment, calling down to his father, who waited, stunned, at the bottom of the stairs, 'She looks good, doesn't she? For a girl.' Both Ariana and her father smiled then. Walmar nodded and cast his son a tired smile.

'I'd say she looks extraordinary, for a girl!' Walmar had just turned sixty-five that spring. And times weren't easy, not for a man of his years, for anyone these days. The country had been at war for almost three years now. Not that it changed how they lived. Berlin was still vivid with beauty and excitement, almost to the point of frenzy, with constant parties, theatre, opera, and endless novel forms of entertainment that he found tiring for a man of his age. In addition there was the constant strain of maintaining order for his family, running his bank, keeping clear of trouble, and sequestering his children from the poison that now ran freely in the country's blood. No, it had not been easy. But so far he had managed every turn. The Tilden Bank was still solid, his relations with the Reich were good, his lifestyle was still secure, and because of his importance as a banker, as long as he continued to be useful to the Party, no one would disturb his children, or him.

When Ariana and Gerhard had reached the age when participation in a youth group was expected, it was quietly explained that Gerhard was having trouble with his studies, had a touch of asthma, and was agonisingly shy around children his own age. Ever since the death of his mother ... of course you understand ... and Ariana ... we're not at all sure she will ever recover from the shock. A noble widower of aristocratic background, his two young

children, and a bank. One needed nothing more to survive in Germany, except
the patience to endure, the wisdom to be quiet, the willingness to be blind and
mute.

He still remembered Ariana's horror when she had gone to see her mother's
furrier one day three years after her mother's death. When she was a little girl,
Rothmann, the furrier, had always given her hot chocolate and cookies, and
now and then some small mink tails. But when she had gone to find him, she
had found instead a dozen men with armbands standing guard outside the
store. It was dark and empty, the marquee torn, the windows smashed, the
huge, luxurious emporium empty, and on the windows one single word –
Juden.

Ariana had run to her father's bank crying, and he had shut the door and
been firm. 'You must tell no one, Ariana! No one! You must not discuss it or
ask questions. Tell no one what you saw!'

She had stared at him in confusion. 'But other people saw it, too. The
soldiers, they were all standing outside with guns, and the window ... and,
Papa ... I know it – I saw blood!'

'You saw nothing, Ariana. You were never there.'

'But—'

'Silence! You had lunch today with me, in the Tiergarten, and then we came
back to the bank. We sat in here for a while, you drank a cup of hot chocolate,
and then the chauffeur drove you home. Is that quite clear?' She had never seen
him like that, and she didn't understand. Was it possible that her father was
frightened? They couldn't touch him. He was an important banker. And
besides, Papa wasn't Jewish. But where had they taken Rothmann? And what
would happen to his store? 'Do you understand me, Ariana?' Her father's
voice had been raised harshly, almost angrily, yet she had sensed that he was
not angry at her.

'I understand.' And then in a little voice that pierced their silence, 'But why?'

Walmar von Gotthard sighed and sank back into his chair. It was a large,
impressive office, an enormous desk, and across from him, despite the fact that
she was twelve, Ariana looked so small. What could he tell her? How could he
explain?

A year after that incident the worst had happened. In September war had
come. Since then he had steered his own course with caution, but he knew that
it had paid off. The children were safe and protected. Gerhard was twelve and a
half now, and Ariana just sixteen. Very little had changed for them, and
although the children always suspected that he hated Hitler, it was a suspicion
they never discussed, not even with each other. It was dangerous to admit that
one hated Hitler. Everyone knew that.

They still lived in the house in Grunewald, went to the same schools,
attended the same church, but they seldom visited other people's homes.
Walmar kept a tight rein on them for their own sake, he explained carefully,
and it made sense to them. After all, the country was at war. Everywhere were
uniforms, laughing soldiers, pretty girls, and at night they sometimes heard
music when their neighbours gave large parties for officers and friends. In some
ways, all over Berlin it was a time of gaiety beyond measure. In other ways the

children knew that it was sad, too. Many of their friends' fathers were off fighting. Some of them had already lost fathers and brothers to the war. But for Ariana and Gerhard, despite other children's teasing, it was a relief to know that their father was too old. They had already lost their mother, they couldn't have borne to lose him, too.

'But you're not too old for parties,' Ariana had told Walmar with a waiflike smile. This was the spring of her sixteenth birthday, and she desperately wanted to attend her first ball. She was old enough to remember that while her mother was alive her parents had been very social. But in the seven years since her passing, Walmar had spent almost every waking moment either at his bank or at home in his rooms or with them playing cards. The life of balls and parties had ended when Kassandra took her own life. But the children knew very little of their mother. The facts of how and why their mother died were painful truths that Walmar had never shared. 'Well, Papa? Can we? Please?' She had looked at him so pleadingly, and Walmar had smiled.

'A ball? Now? During the war?'

'Oh, Papa, everyone else goes to parties. Even here in Grunewald they stay up all night.' It was true – even in their staid residential district, the carousing went on regularly into the wee hours.

'Aren't you a little young for that?'

'Hardly.' She had stared down her nose at him, looking oddly like his mother rather than her own. 'I'm sixteen.'

At last, with the assistance of her brother, Ariana had prevailed, and now she stood there, like a princess in a fairy tale, wearing the white organdy dress Fräulein Hedwig's expert fingers had made.

'You look so lovely, darling.'

She smiled, childlike, at him, admiring the white tie and tails. 'So do you.'

But Gerhard was still watching, and they heard him giggle from the top of the stairs. 'I think you both look silly.' But he looked proud of them, too.

'Go to bed, you monster.' She shouted it gaily over her shoulder as she tripped lightly down the last flight of stairs.

The Hispano-Suiza had been replaced just before the war had come with a black and grey Rolls, and now it waited for them in the driveway, the elderly chauffeur standing beside the door. Ariana had a light wrap around her shoulders, and the white dress swirled around her as she swept into the car. The party was being held at the Opera House, and all the lights were blazing as the Von Gotthards approached. The broad boulevard looked as beautiful as ever, Unter den Linden had not been changed by the onset of war.

Walmar looked proudly at his daughter, sitting like a fairy princess at his side in the Rolls. 'Excited?'

She nodded happily. 'Very.' She was enchanted by the prospect of her first ball.

And it was even better than she had expected. The stairs leading into the Opera House had been carpeted in red, the main hall with its wondrous ceiling was ablaze with light. And everywhere around them were women in evening gowns and diamonds, while the men all wore uniforms and decorations or white tie and tails. For Walmar the one damper on the evening was the large red flag that hung before them with the black and white emblem of the Reich.

The music whispered at them softly, coming from the main hall, and around them swirled and eddied countless bodies bedecked, bemused, bejewelled. Ariana's eyes looked like two huge aquamarines in the delicate ivory face, her mouth a delicately carved ruby.

She shared the first dance with her father, and afterwards he was quick to move her into the safe confines of a group of his friends. There were several familiar bankers clustered at a table near the floor where couples waltzed.

She had been chatting happily with them for some twenty minutes when Walmar became aware of a tall young man standing near them. He was watching Ariana with a look of interest and conversing quietly with a friend. Walmar turned his gaze away from the soldier and invited his daughter to dance with him again. It wasn't quite fair to do that, but he felt he had to postpone the inevitable for as long as he could. He had known when he had brought her that she would dance with other men. Yet the uniforms ... the uniforms ... it was unavoidable ... he could only pray that they would all think her far too young to have any great appeal.

But as Walmar and Ariana slowly circled the floor together, he knew that she would catch the eye of any man. She looked young and fresh and lovely, but more than that, there was a lure to Ariana, a quiet power that pulled at anyone who looked into those deep blue eyes. It was as though she had the answers to a secret. He had seen the reaction in his own friends. It was a quality that hypnotised most men. It was the quiet face, the gentle eyes, and then the sudden smile, like summer sunshine on a lake. There was a quality to Ariana that drew one, a magic and a spirit of which one wanted to know more, despite her youth. She was far smaller than her brother and still more delicately boned. The top of her head barely reached her father's shoulder, and her feet seemed to fly as they waltzed.

It was when he returned her to their table that the young officer finally approached. Silently, Walmar tightened. Why couldn't it have been one of the others? Someone not in a uniform – a man and not a Reich. That's all they were to him, those uniforms, they weren't people, they were simply one band of gluttonous, self-indulgent evildoers, and in unison, with what they stood for and they threatened, they had killed his wife.

'Herr von Gotthard?' Walmar gave a curt nod and the young man's right arm immediately shot out in the familiar signal. 'Heil Hitler.' Walmar nodded again, this time with a frozen smile. 'I believe this is your daughter?'

Walmar wanted to slap him but, glancing at Ariana and then back at the intruder, he gave a curt answer instead. 'Yes. She's a bit too young to be here tonight, but I gave my consent as long as she remains with me.' Ariana looked shocked at his pronouncement, but she did not protest. And the young man nodded understandingly and then gazed at the fairy princess with a dazzling smile. He had a long row of perfect snowy white teeth, enhanced still further by the curve of his lips and the beauty of his smile. The blue of his eyes was not unlike the colour of Ariana's, but where her hair was palest blonde, his was raven dark. He was tall and graceful and with broad shoulders, small hips, and long legs accentuated by his uniform and gleaming boots.

This time the young officer bowed to Ariana's father, in the fashion of a time before right arms had shot into the air; he clicked his heels and then stood erect again. 'Werner von Klaub, Herr von Gotthard.' The gleaming smile shot towards Ariana again. 'And I can see that Miss Gotthard is indeed a very young lady, but I would be honoured if you would entrust her to me for just one dance.' Walmar hesitated. He knew the boy's family, he realised now, and to refuse would be a slight, both to his name and to the uniform he wore. And Ariana looked so hopeful and so pretty. How could he refuse? He couldn't fight the uniforms when that was what had taken over their whole world.

'I suppose I can't object to that, can I?' He glanced gently down at his daughter, his voice filled with tenderness and regret.

'May I, Papa?' The eyes so large, so hopeful, and so blue and bright.

'You may.'

Von Klaub bowed again, but this time to Ariana, and then led her away. Slowly they danced, like Prince Charming and Cinderella, as though they had been perfectly made for each other's arms. It was a pleasure to watch them, the man at Walmar's elbow said. Perhaps it was, but not for Walmar. He realised as he did so that a new threat had just come into his life. And more importantly, into Ariana's. As she grew older, she grew more lovely, and he could not keep her eternally a prisoner in his house. Eventually he would lose her, and perhaps to one of them. How strange, he thought to himself as he watched them. In another life, another era, Von Klaub would have been welcome in his home and in his daughter's life, but now ... that uniform had changed everything for Walmar. The uniform and what it stood for. It was more than he could bear.

When the dance ended, Ariana glanced at her father, an open question in her eyes, and he was about to shake his head, denying his permission, but again he found he could not do that to her. So again he nodded. And after that, once more. And then, wisely, the young German officer led her back to her father, bowed again, and bid Ariana good night. But something in the way he smiled at her told her father that they had not yet seen the last of Werner von Klaub.

'How old is he, Ariana? Did he say?'

'Twenty-four.' She looked directly at her father with a small smile. 'He's very nice, you know. Did you like him?'

'The question is, did you?'

She shrugged noncommittally and for the first time all evening her father laughed. 'So it begins, does it? My darling, you are going to break a thousand hearts.' He only hoped that among them, she would not break his. He had kept her so carefully from that poison that it would kill him now if she countered his beliefs.

But she showed no sign of betraying him, or his principles, as the next few years wore on. Werner von Klaub had indeed come to visit them, but only once or twice. He had found her as ravishing as he had that first evening, yet he also found her very young and more than a little shy. She wasn't nearly as amusing as the women who had fallen prey to his uniform in the past three years. Ariana wasn't ready, and Werner von Klaub wasn't interested enough to wait.

Her father was relieved when the visits ended and she didn't seem particularly saddened by the loss. She was happy with her life at home with her father and her brother, and she had lots of friends her own age at school. Walmar's determined battle to protect her had left her, in some ways, young for her years. Yet countered by that innocence was the wisdom she had gained from loss and pain. The loss of her mother, however remote Kassandra may have been, however well veiled the realities of that loss, had marked Ariana, and the absence of a mother she could turn to had left a sadness lurking somewhere in the tiny beauty's eyes. But it was a private kind of sorrow, a window to something amiss within it was not due to any exposure to the price of war. Despite the considerable increase in the bombings of Berlin since 1943 and the amount of time she spent in their cellar with Gerhard, her father, and the servants during the air raids, Ariana had no real contact with the pain of war until she was eighteen, in the spring of 1944.

All that spring the Allies had increased their efforts, and Hitler had recently issued new decrees confirming his commitment to total war.

Ariana had come home from school to find her father closeted in the main salon with a friend, according to Berthold, who was now quite elderly and also very deaf.

'Did he say who?' Ariana smiled at him. Berthold was one of her earliest memories. He had always been there.

'Yes, miss.' He smiled benignly, the stonelike face cracking into warm creases just for her. He nodded as though he had understood her, but she knew immediately that he had not.

Familiar with his foibles, she spoke louder, unlike her brother, who often teased him openly about being deaf. But from Master Gerhard, Berthold would take anything. Gerhard was his pet. 'I said, did my father say who was visiting?

'Ah . . . no, miss. He did not. Frau Klemmer let them in. I was downstairs for a moment assisting Master Gerhard with his chemistry equipment.'

'Oh, God, not that.'

'Yes?'

'Never mind, Berthold, thank you.' Easily, Ariana swung through the hallway. The house and its vast crew of servants had also been a constant in her life. She couldn't imagine living elsewhere.

She passed Frau Klemmer in the upper hallway on the way into her room. She and Frau Klemmer had been discussing a secret that morning, about reopening her mother's room. It had been nine years now, and Ariana was about to turn eighteen. It annoyed her to share the upper floor with Gerhard, who was noisy and constantly blowing up his chemistry concoctions, trying to make small bombs. And she and her father had already decided that she would put off going to university until after the war. So when she finished school in two months, she would be busier around the house. There was volunteer work that she had planned for herself. She already worked in a hospital two days a week. But somehow it seemed to her more suitable that after she graduated from gymnasium, she should at the same time advance her status in the house. The prospect of occupying her mother's quarters pleased her greatly ... if only she could get her father to agree.

'Have you asked him yet?' Frau Klemmer asked it in a conspiratorial whisper and Ariana shook her head.

'Not yet. Tonight. If I can get rid of Gerhard after dinner.' She sighed and rolled her eyes. 'He's such a pest.' He had just turned fifteen.

'I think if you give your father time to think it over, he'll probably agree. He'll like having you that much nearer. Climbing all those stairs up to the third floor to see you wears him out.' It was a sensible reason, but Ariana wasn't sure that it was the one that would win him over. At sixty-eight, her father did not enjoy being reminded of his age.

'I'll think of something. I wanted to talk to him now, but there's someone with him. Do you know who it is? Berthold said you let someone in.'

'I did.' She looked briefly puzzled. 'It is Herr Thomas. And he doesn't look well at all.' But who did look well these days? Even Ariana's father looked exhausted now when he came home from the bank. The Reich was putting more and more pressure on all of the country's bankers to come up with funds they didn't have.

As Frau Klemmer left, Ariana mused for a moment about whether or not to go back down and join her father. She had wanted to slip into her mother's rooms again, to admire the handsome bedroom and to see if the boudoir was large enough to accommodate her desk. But she could do that later. She would prefer to visit for a moment with her father's friend.

Herr Thomas was some thirty years younger than her father, but despite the gap of years between them, her father had a great fondness for the soft-spoken man. He had spent four years working for her father and had then decided to go into law. During law school he had married a fellow student, and they had had three children in four years. The youngest child was three now, but Herr Thomas hadn't seen him since four months after his birth. His wife was Jewish, and she and the children had been taken from him. For the first two years of the war, Max had been able to stave off the Nazis. But in the end there was no putting off the inevitable. Sarah and the children had to go. In 1941, three years before, they were taken away. The shock of losing them had almost destroyed him, and now when he visited Ariana's father, he looked fifteen years older than his thirty-seven years. He had fought desperately to find them, and in the past year Ariana knew he had all but given up hope.

Gently she rapped on the double doors, but all she heard was the soft hum of conversation within. She was about to turn away and leave them when at last she heard her father call out.

She opened the door slowly and peeked inside with her soft smile. 'Papa? May I come in?' But what she saw startled her and she didn't know whether to close the door and go, or stay. Maximilian Thomas was sitting with his back to her, his shoulders shaking gently, his face dropped into his hands. Ariana stared at her father, expecting to be sent away again, but to her surprise, he motioned her to stay. He was at a loss now. There was so little to be said. Perhaps his daughter could offer Max some comfort beyond what he had been able to give. It was Walmar's first act of recognition that Ariana was no longer a child. Had it been Gerhard in the doorway, he would have sent him back upstairs again with an urgent wave of his hand. But Ariana was not just a girl now, she also had the gentleness of a woman. He motioned her towards him, and as she approached, Max dropped his hands.

What she saw when she approached him was a look of total despair. 'Max ... what happened?' She dropped to her knees beside him and without thinking held out her arms. And just as naturally he went to her and sobbed softly as they embraced. He said nothing for long minutes, and then at last he wiped his eyes and pulled slowly away.

'Thank you. I'm sorry to ...'

'We understand.' Walmar went to the long antique table where a large silver salver bore several bottles of cognac and the remains of his stock of English Scotch. Without asking Max his preference, he poured him a glass of brandy and silently held out the drink. Max took it from him, sipping slowly and wiping once more his still streaming eyes.

'Is it Sarah?' Ariana had to ask. Had he had news? He had sought information unsuccessfully from the Nazis for so long.

His eyes sought hers in answer, and the pain of what he had learned that day was there, etched in all its horror, his worst fears confirmed. 'They're all ...' He couldn't bring himself to say the word. '... dead.' He took a deep, ragged breath and put down the brandy. 'All four of them ... Sarah ... and the boys ...'

'My God.' Ariana stared at him in anguish and wanted to ask him why. But they all knew why. Because they were Jewish ... *Juden* ... Jews. 'Are you sure?'

He nodded. 'They told me that I should be grateful. That now I can start fresh with a woman of my own kind. Oh, God ... oh, God ... my babies ... Ariana ...' He reached out to her again without thinking, and once again she held him tight, this time with tears running down her cheeks as well.

Walmar knew he must get Max to think about leaving at once. He could no longer stay in Berlin. 'Max, listen. You have to think now. What are you going to do?'

'What do you mean?'

'Can you stay here? Now? Now that you know.'

'I don't know ... I don't know ... I wanted to leave years ago. In thirty-eight, I told Sarah then ... but she didn't want to ... her sisters, her mother ...' It was a familiar refrain to them both. 'And after that I stayed because I had to find her. I thought that if I knew where she was, I could bargain with them, I could ... Oh, God, I should have known ...'

'That wouldn't have changed anything, would it?' Walmar looked down at his friend, sharing his pain. 'But now you know the truth. And if you stay, they will torment you. They will watch what you do, where you go, who you do what with and where. You have been suspect for years, because of Sarah, and now you really must leave.'

Max Thomas shook his head. Walmar knew only too well what he was saying. Twice Thomas's law offices had been destroyed with 'Jew Lover' carved in every piece of furniture and painted on the walls. But he had stayed. He had to. To find his wife. 'I guess I don't understand yet that it's over, that ... that she ... that there's no one to look for any more.' He sat back in his chair, his eyes full of terrible understanding. 'But where would I go?

'Anywhere. Switzerland, if you can get there. Afterwards maybe to the United States. But get out of Germany, Max, she will destroy you if you stay here.' ... *just as she destroyed Kassandra ... and before her, Dolff* ... The memory of that was fresh again as he looked into the young man's face.

Max shook his head. 'I can't go.'

'Why not?' Walmar was suddenly angry. 'Because you're so patriotic? Because you love the country that has been so kind? Good God, man, what is there to stay for? Get the hell out.'

Ariana watched them, frightened; she had never seen her father look like that before. 'Max ... maybe Daddy is right. Maybe later you could come back.'

But Walmar stood there glowering. 'If you're smart, you won't want to do that. Start a fresh life somewhere. Anywhere, Max, anywhere, but get out of here before it all comes down around your ears.'

Max Thomas looked at Walmar bleakly. 'It already has.'

Walmar sighed deeply and sat down in his own chair again, never taking his eyes from his friend. 'Yes, I know, I understand that. But, Max, you still have your life. You have already lost Sarah and the children.' His voice was gentle, but Max shed fresh tears. 'You owe it to them and to yourself to survive now. Why add yet another tragedy, one more loss?' If only he could have said that to Kassandra. If only she could have understood that, too.

'How would I go?' Max stared at him, thinking, yet not really understanding what it meant to leave his house, his heritage, the country that had once given birth to his sons and his dreams.

'I don't know. We could think it over. I suppose with all the chaos these days, you could just simply disappear. In fact' – Walmar seemed to be thinking – 'if you did it now, immediately, they might well think that you went mad from the news. You could have run off, killed yourself, done anything. They won't be suspicious right away. Later they might.'

'And what does that mean? That I leave your house tonight and start walking towards the border? With what? My briefcase and my overcoat and my grandfather's gold watch?' The watch he spoke of rested, as it always did, in the pocket of his vest.

But Walmar was still thinking. He nodded quietly. 'Perhaps.'

'Are you serious?'

Ariana watched them, shocked at all she was hearing. Was this what was happening, then? They were killing women and children, leaving others to flee on foot to the border in the middle of the night? It filled her with a kind of fear she had not yet known, and the tiny ivory face seemed paler than it ever had before.

Walmar looked at Max then. He had a plan. 'Yes, I'm very serious. I think you should go now.'

'Tonight?'

'Perhaps you shouldn't leave tonight, but as soon as possible, as soon as

papers can be arranged. I think that you should disappear tonight though.'
And then after another sip of cognac, 'What do you think?'

Max had been listening carefully to Walmar's words, and he knew that what
the older man was saying made a great deal of sense. What reason did he have to
cling to a country that had already destroyed everything that he held dear?

Silently he nodded. And then after another moment, 'You're right. I'll go. I
don't know where – or how.' His eyes never left Walmar's, but now the elder
man looked at his daughter. This was a turning point in all three lives.

'Ariana, would you like to leave now?'

For an instant none of the three stirred in the room, and then she looked
questioningly at her father. 'Do you wish me to, Papa?' But she didn't want to.
She wanted to stay here with him and Max.

'You may stay if you like. If you understand the importance of keeping all
this quiet. You must discuss it with no one. Not Gerhard, not the servants. No
one. Not even with me. What will happen, will happen in silence. And when it
is over, it never happened at all. Is that clear?' She nodded and for an instant he
questioned the insanity of involving his daughter, but they were all involved.
Soon it could be happening to them. It was time she knew. He had thought that
for some time. She had to understand how desperate the situation was. 'Do
you understand me, Ariana?'

'Perfectly, Papa.'

'Very well.'

He closed his eyes for a moment, and then he turned to Max. 'You will leave
here this evening, by the front door, looking even more troubled than you did
when you came in, and you will very simply disappear. Walk towards the lake.
And then later you will come back. I will let you in myself after the house is
dark. You will stay here for a day or two. And then you go. Quietly. To the
border. Into Switzerland. And then, my friend, you are gone for good. To a
new life.'

'And how am I supposed to finance all this? Can you get my money out of
the bank?' Max looked worried and Walmar shook his head.

'Never mind that. All you have to worry about is getting back here tonight.
And then getting to the border after that. Let me take care of the money and
the papers.'

Max was impressed, if somewhat surprised, by his respectable old friend.
'Do you know anyone who can do that sort of thing?'

'Yes, I do. I researched it about six months ago, in case ... the need ever
arose.' Ariana was astonished but she kept quiet. She had no idea that her
father had ever considered such a thing. 'Are we clear, then?' Max nodded. 'Do
you want to stay for dinner? You could leave rather obviously after that.'

'All right. But where will you hide me?'

Walmar sat silent for a moment – he had been wondering the same thing.
This time it was Ariana who had the answer. 'Mother's rooms.' Walmar
looked at her in quick displeasure, and Max watched the exchange that passed
silently between their eyes. 'Papa, it's the only place no one goes near.' Except
that she and Frau Klemmer had been there only that day. It was what had
brought the rooms in question so quickly to her mind. Ordinarily the family

and the household almost pretended that Kassandra's room were no longer a part of the Von Gotthard house. 'Papa. It's true. He would be safe there. And I could tidy up again after he's gone. No one would ever know.'

Walmar paused for what seemed an endless moment. The last time he had been in that apartment, his wife had been lying dead in a bathtub filled with blood. He had never entered her rooms again. He couldn't bear the pain of those last memories, that bruised face and those desperate eyes, the breasts shattered from the belt buckle of the Nazi who had almost raped her. 'I suppose there is no choice.' He said it with an agony that only Max understood. They both knew what the Nazis were capable of.

'I'm sorry to be a problem for you, Walmar.'

'Don't be ridiculous. We want to help you.' And then, with a small wintry smile, 'Perhaps one day you will help us.'

There was a long silence in the room then and at last Max spoke. 'Walmar, do you really think of going?'

The older man looked pensive. 'I'm not sure I could. I'm more visible than you are. They watch me. They know me. They need me more than they need you. I am a source of funds to them. The Tilden Bank is important to the Reich. It is the albatross around my neck, but it is also my salvation. One day it may prove to be the gun held to my head. But if I have to, I would do the same as you are doing.' Ariana was shocked to hear him say it. She had never suspected that her father thought one day to flee. And then, as though by exact prearrangement, Berthold knocked and announced dinner, and the three of them left the room in silence.

Chapter 9

Walmar von Gotthard tiptoed silently through his own house and waited in the front hall. He had warned Max Thomas to come barefoot through the garden. It would make less noise than walking on the gravel in his shoes. And he had given him his own key to the front gate. Max had left them around eleven and now it was a few minutes before three. The moon was round and full and it was easy to see him, running quickly across the expanse of lawn. The two men exchanged no greeting, only curt nods as Max Thomas carefully wiped off his feet with his socks. The dirt from the flower beds would have left tracks on the white marble floor. Walmar was pleased with Max's clear thinking. He was a different man now than the one who had sat sobbing and broken in his study only ten hours before. Now that Max Thomas was fleeing, his very survival would depend on his quick wits and his cool head.

The two men walked rapidly up the main staircase and in a brief moment reached the door at the end of the long hall. For an instant Walmar paused there, waiting, as though not sure whether he should go in. But Ariana had been waiting for them and now, sensing their presence, she opened the door a crack to peek. Seeing Max's intent face in the doorway, she opened the door wider to let them in, but Walmar only shook his head as he stood there, as though he could not yet force himself to go in. Max quickly entered. Perhaps it was time for Walmar to open the doors again; perhaps, like Max, it was time for him to forge ahead.

He closed the door soundlessly behind him and followed as Ariana beckoned them into the small room that had been her mother's study, now faded into a still softer pink. The chaise longue still stood in the corner, and Ariana had put warm blankets on it so Max could sleep there.

She put a finger to her lips and whispered softly. 'I thought if he slept there he'd be safer. Should anyone look in, they won't see him from the bedroom.' Her father nodded and Max looked at him gratefully, but there were lines of fatigue crowding round his eyes. Walmar looked at him one last time, nodded, and then left the room with Ariana following quickly behind. Walmar had promised that he would get the papers as quickly as possible. He hoped for Max's sake to have them by the next night.

Ariana and her father left each other in the hallway with their own thoughts and no words. She returned to her room then, thinking of Max and the lonely journey he was about to undertake. She still remembered little Sarah, a tiny woman with dark, laughing eyes. She had been so full of funny stories, and she had been kind to Ariana whenever they met. It all seemed so long ago now. Ariana had often thought of her over the past three years, wondering where she was and what they had done to her ... and the boys ... Now they knew.

They were the same thoughts Max was thinking as he lay quietly on the pink satin-covered chaise longue in the room of the woman he had seen only once when he first met Walmar. She had been a dazzling woman with golden, almost copper-coloured hair. He had thought her the most striking vision of his lifetime. And shortly after, he had learned that she was dead. Of flu, they had told him. But as he lay there, he sensed that there had been some other reason for her death. Some odd feeling had communicated itself from Walmar, as though he knew, as though he, too, had suffered at the Nazis' hands. It didn't seem possible, but one never knew.

In his own room Walmar stood looking out at the lake in the moonlight, but it was not the lake he saw there, it was his wife. Golden, shining, beautiful Kassandra ... the woman he had loved so desperately so long ago ... the dreams they had shared in the room. And now it was empty, solemn, draped, forgotten. It had torn a part of him away that night, crossing that doorway with the man they were hiding, and Ariana with those same bottomless lavender-blue eyes. He turned away from the moonlight in sorrow, and at last he undressed and went to bed.

'Did you ask him?' Frau Klemmer asked her after breakfast when they met in the hall.

'About what?' Ariana had other things on her mind.

'The room. Your mother's apartment.' What a strange girl she was, so distant, so withdrawn at times – had she already forgotten? Frau Klemmer often wondered what mysteries lay behind the deep blue eyes.

'Oh, that ... yes ... I mean no. He said no.'

'Was he angry?'

'No. Just very definite. I guess I'll just stay where I am.'

'Why don't you push him a little? Maybe he'll think about it some more and give in.'

But Ariana shook her head with determination. 'He has enough on his mind.'

The housekeeper shrugged and moved on. Sometimes it was hard to understand the girl, but then again, her mother had been strange, too.

When Ariana left for school that morning, Walmar had already left the house in his Rolls. She had wanted to spend the day at home – in case, because of Max – but her father had insisted that she go on with her life as always, and to be sure of Max's protection, Walmar had himself relocked Kassandra's door.

It seemed hours before she could get back there, but at last it was time to go home. She had sat in school all day, distracted, thinking of Max and wondering how he was. Poor man, how strange it must feel to him, to be a captive in someone's house. With a calm step, Ariana walked down the main hallway, greeted Berthold, and went upstairs. She declined Anna's offer of tea and went into her bathroom to comb her hair. It was another fifteen minutes before she dared walk back downstairs to the next floor. She paused for a moment at the door of her father's bedroom and then glided past it with the key she had borrowed from Frau Klemmer only two days before.

The door opened easily as she turned the key and then the handle, and she slipped quietly inside and disappeared. On silent feet she ran through the bedroom, soundless, breathless, and then she stood there, in the doorway, a smiling vision in front of the tired, unshaven Max.

'Hello.' It was barely a whisper.

He smiled and invited her to sit down. 'Have you eaten?' He shook his head. 'I thought so. Here.' She had brought him a sandwich hidden in the deep pocket of her skirt. 'I'll bring you some milk later.' That morning she had left him a pitcher of water. They had told him not to run the taps. The pipes would be too rusty after so many years, and they might squeak horribly, alerting the servants that there was someone in these rooms. 'You're all right though?'

'I'm fine.' He gobbled the sandwich quickly. 'You didn't have to do this.' And then he grinned at her. 'But I'm glad you did.' He looked younger somehow, as though years of care had been dropped from his face. He looked worn, and different now that he was unshaven, but still, he didn't have the gaunt, pained look he had worn yesterday. 'How was school today?''

'Awful. I worried about you.'

'You shouldn't have. I'm fine here.' It was odd, he had only hidden there for a few hours, but already he felt cut off from the world. He missed the buses, the noise, his office, the telephone, even the sound of boots goose-stepping down the street. It all seemed so remote here. As though he had drifted into another world. A faded, forgotten world of pink satin, in the boudoir of a woman long since gone. Together they stared around the small study and their eyes met at the same time. 'What was she like ... your mother?'

Ariana looked around her strangely. 'I'm not sure. I never really knew her. She died when I was nine.' For an instant she remembered Gerhard at the cemetery and then standing in the rain beside her father, holding tightly to his hand. 'She was very beautiful. I'm not sure I know much more than that.'

'I saw her once. She was incredible. I thought she was the most exquisite woman I'd ever seen.' Ariana nodded.

'She used to come upstairs to see us, in evening clothes and smelling of perfume. Her dresses made wonderful sounds as she crossed the room, the swishing noises of silk and taffeta and satin. She always seemed terribly mysterious to me. I suppose she always will.'

Ariana looked at him with her big sad eyes. 'Have you thought about where you're going?' Speaking to him in the whisper they had to use to converse, she seemed like a child asking him a secret, and he smiled.

'More or less. I think your father's right. Switzerland first. Then maybe when the war is over, I'll see if I can get to the States. My father had a cousin there. I'm not even sure if he's still alive. But it's a start.'

'Won't you come back here?' She looked shocked for a moment as he shook his head. 'Never, Max?'

'Never.' And then he sighed softly. 'I never want to see this place again.' It seemed strange to Ariana that he should cut himself off forever from what had been his whole life. But then, perhaps he was right to shut the door so firmly. She wondered if it was like her father's never re-entering her mother's bedroom until the night before. There were places one simply never returned to. One couldn't bear the pain. When she looked up at him again, he was smiling gently. 'Will you and your father come and see me in America after the war?'

She laughed softly. 'That seems a long way off.'

'I hope not.' And then, without thinking, he reached out and took her hand. He held it for a long moment, and then she bent slowly towards him and kissed him softly on the top of his head. There were no more words needed between them; he only held her, and she gently stroked his hair. Soon he made her leave, telling her it was dangerous for her to be there. But the truth was, he was thinking the unthinkable while hiding out in his old friend's house.

Later that evening Walmar came to see him, and he looked far more tired and subdued than Max. He already had the travel papers and a German passport in the name of Ernst Josef Frei. They had used the picture from Max's passport, and the official seal they'd stamped on it looked real.

'Quite a job isn't it?' Max stared at it with fascination and then glanced back at Walmar sitting uncomfortably in a pink chair. 'What now?'

'A map, some money. I also got you a travel permit. You can make it close to the border on the train. After that, my friend, you're on your own. But you should be able to make it –' he paused for a moment – 'with this.' He handed him an envelope filled with money, enough to keep him handsomely for several weeks. 'I didn't dare take out more than that, or someone might have wondered why.'

'Is there anything you didn't think of, Walmar?' Max stared at him in admiration. What a remarkable old man Von Gotthard was.

'I hope not. I'm afraid I'm a little new at this. But I think it might be good practice.'

'You really think of leaving?' Walmar looked pensive. 'Why you?'

'A number of reasons. Who knows what will happen, at what point they'll lose control. And I have Gerhard to think of now, too. In the fall he'll be sixteen. If the war doesn't end soon, they may draft him. At that point we go.' Max nodded quietly. He understood. If he still had a son to protect from the Nazis, he would do the same thing.

But it wasn't only Gerhard that worried Walmar, it was Ariana too. The flood of uniforms in the city worried him almost all the time. She was so delicately pretty, so enticing in her quiet, distant way. What if they were to harm her, to grab her, or worse, if some high-ranking officer were to take a fancy to his only female child? It frightened him increasingly now that she was older, and in a few months she would no longer be in school. Knowing that she was doing volunteer work at Martin Luther Hospital terrified him most of all. He sat there thinking while Max looked at his new passport again.

'Walmar, what can I do to thank you?'

'Be safe. Start a new life. That's thanks enough.

'It seems nothing at all. Can I let you know where I am?' 'Discreetly. Just an address. No name. I'll know.' Max nodded. 'The train leaves from the station at midnight.' Walmar fished in his pocket and handed him the keys to a car. 'In the garage behind the house you'll find a blue Ford coupe, an old one. It was Kassandra's. But I checked it myself this morning. Miraculously, it still works. I think the servants still drive it around from time to time to keep it running. Take it, drive it to the station, and leave it there. I'll report it stolen in the morning. You'll be long gone. We'll go to bed early tonight, so there shouldn't be any problem. Hopefully by the time you leave at eleven thirty everyone will be asleep. And that, my friend, takes care of everything – except one thing.'

Max couldn't imagine anything more. But Walmar had thought of one thing further. He walked quietly into Kassandra's bedroom and lifted two paintings from the wall. With his pocket knife he prised them from the frames that held them, and then sliced them carefully from the wood stretchers that had held them taut for twenty years. One was a small Renoir that had been his mother's, the other a Corot he had bought his wife in Paris on their honeymoon twenty years before. Without saying anything to the man who watched them, he rolled both canvases tightly and then handed them to his friend. 'Take them. Do whatever you have to. Sell them, eat them, barter them. They're both worth a great deal of money. Enough to start you on your new life.'

'Walmar, no! Even what I'm leaving in the bank here would never cover those.' He had spent much of his money trying to find Sarah and the boys.

'You have to. And they do no one any good hanging here. You need them
... and I could never bear to look at them again ... not after they were here.
They're yours now, Max. Take them. From a friend.'

Just then Ariana slipped quietly into the room. She was puzzled when she
saw the tears in Max's eyes and then, when she saw the empty frames beside her
mother's headboard, she quickly understood.

'Are you going now, Max?' Her eyes grew wide.

'In a few hours. Your father has just ... I don't know what to say, Walmar.'

'*Wiedersehen*, Maximilian. Good luck.' They shook hands firmly as Max
fought back tears. A moment later Walmar left them, and Ariana stayed for
only a few minutes. But before she left him to go to dinner, Max reached out
for her and they kissed.

Dinner passed with the utmost propriety, except for Gerhard, who shot
small breadballs at Berthold's retreating back. Reprimanded by his father, he
grinned and shot one a moment later at his sister's back.

'We're going to have to send you back to Fräulein Hedwig for your dinners
if you continue to do that.'

'Sorry, Father.' But despite his friendly chatter, he was unable to rouse either
his father or his sister to a great deal of conversation, and eventually he, too,
fell silent as he ate.

After dinner Walmar retired to his study, Ariana to her bedroom, and
Gerhard to his pranks. She wanted to return once more to Maximilian, but she
was afraid to. Her father had insisted that they must take no more chances of
drawing the servants' notice. Max's escape depended on no one's knowing
where he was, and their safety on no one's knowing where he had been. So she
sat in her room for hours, and dutifully, at ten thirty, as per her father's orders,
she turned off her lights. But silently she waited, thinking, praying, until at last
she could bear it no longer, and at twenty minutes after eleven, she tiptoed
softly down the stairs until she reached her mother's door.

She let herself in without a sound and found him waiting, as though he knew
that she would come. He kissed her long and hard this time, holding her tightly
until she could barely breathe. They kissed for one last long moment, and then
buttoning his coat around him, he pulled away. 'I have to go now, Ariana.' He
smiled softly. 'Take good care, my darling, until we meet again.'

'I love you.' It was the merest whisper, as much spoken with her eyes as with
her words. 'God be with you.'

He nodded, the briefcase with the priceless paintings hidden in newspapers
at the bottom clutched in his right hand. 'We'll meet again after it's over.' He
smiled as though she were going to the office. 'Maybe in New York.'

She giggled softly then. 'You're crazy.'

'Maybe.' And then his eyes grew serious. 'But I love you, too.' And it was
true. She had touched him, come to him in a moment when he needed a gentle
friend.

And then, saying nothing further, he tiptoed softly past her to the door. She
held it open, locked it behind them, and waved one last time as he tiptoed
softly down the stairs. She quickly took refuge in her bedroom, and then at last
she heard the sound of her mother's car driving swiftly through the gate.

'*Auf Wiedersehen*, my darling.' She watched from her window and stood there for almost half an hour, thinking of the first man she had ever kissed and wondering if they would ever meet again.

Chapter 10

There was nothing evident in her father's manner the next morning that would have led anyone to suspect that something was amiss, nor in Ariana's when they shared breakfast. And that afternoon when the chauffeur reported solemnly that Frau von Gotthard's old Ford had been stolen, Walmar immediately called the police. The car was found later that evening, abandoned near the train station and unharmed. And it was slyly but amusingly suggested that Gerhard had been the culprit and had gone for a little ride. The police attempted to conceal their amusement, and Gerhard behaved with appropriate outrage when he was called. But the matter was left to the family to handle, the police were thanked, and the car was put back in the garage.

'But I didn't take it, Father!' He blushed hotly, standing facing Walmar.

'Didn't you? Well, in that case, then I suppose everything is all right.'

'But you think I did!'

'It doesn't matter. The car is back in the garage. Please see to it, however, that neither you nor your friends attempt to ... er ... borrow ... your mother's car again.' It was an attitude he detested taking, but there was no choice. Ariana understood it clearly, and she attempted to console Gerhard as she ushered him from the room.

'But it's so unfair! I didn't!' And then he stared at her. 'Did you?'

'Of course not. Don't be silly. I don't know how to drive.'

'I'll bet you did!'

'Gerhard, don't be silly!' But suddenly they were both laughing, and they walked arm in arm up the stairs to their rooms, Gerhard convinced she'd done it.

But despite her jovial manner with her brother, Walmar saw that there was something much amiss. She was more quiet than usual in the mornings, and when she returned from school or her volunteer work in the evenings, she disappeared immediately into her room. She was difficult to draw into conversation, and at last, a week after Max had left them, she sought her father alone in his study, and her eyes were washed with tears.

'Have you heard anything, Father?' He knew instantly. It was just as he had feared.

'No, nothing. But we'll hear. It may be some time before he's settled enough to let us know.'

'You don't know that.' She sank into a chair beside the fire. 'He could be dead.'

'Perhaps.' His voice was sad and soft as he watched her. 'And perhaps not. But, Ariana, he is gone now. Gone from us. To his own life, wherever that will lead him. You can't hang on to him. We are only part of the old life he has left.' But it frightened him to see her, and the next words escaped him before he could make them stop. 'Are you taken with him, Ariana?'

She turned towards him, shocked at the question. She had never known her father to ask something like that. 'I don't know I ...' She closed her eyes tightly. 'It's just that I was worried. He could have ...' She blushed faintly and stared into the fire, unwilling to tell him the truth.

'I see. I hope you aren't. It's difficult to dictate these things, but ...' How could he tell her? What could he say? 'In times like these it is best to save our loving for a brighter day. In wartime, in difficult circumstances, there is a sense of romance that is often unreal and may not endure. You may see him again years from now and find him quite different. Not at all the man you remember from last week.'

'I understand that.' It was why she so carefully avoided any involvement with the wounded men at the hospital where she worked. 'I do know that, Father.'

'I'm glad.' He sighed deeply as he watched her. It was another turning point for him. Yet another fork in their ever more treacherous road. 'It could also be dangerous to love a man in Max's position. Now he is fleeing, someday soon he could be hunted by the Nazis. And if you attach yourself to him, they could hunt you, too. Even if no harm comes to you, the pain of it could destroy you, as in some ways the pain of losing Sarah almost destroyed him.'

'How can they punish people because of whom they love?' She looked angry. 'How can one know beforehand which is the right side and which is the wrong?'

Her childish question, so naïve, yet so right, brought the memories of Kassandra floding back ... he had warned her ... she knew ...

'Father?' Ariana watched him search himself. He seemed a million miles away.

'You have to forget him. It could be dangerous for you.' He looked at her sternly and her eyes never wavered from her father's.

'It was dangerous for you to help him, Father.'

'That's different. Even though, in a sense, you're right. But I'm not tied to him with that same bond, the bond of loving.' And then he looked at her more closely. 'And I hope neither are you.'

She didn't answer, and at last he walked to his window looking out over the lake. He could almost see the Grunewald cemetery from his windows. But in his mind's eye, he saw her face. As she had looked when he had warned her. As she had looked the night before she took her life.

'Ariana, I'm going to tell you something that I never wanted to tell you. About the price of loving. About the Nazis ... about your mother.'

His voice was a gentle, distant sound. Ariana waited, baffled staring at her father's back. 'It is not a judgement I make of her, or a criticism. I am not angry.

I am not telling you any of this to make you feel ashamed. We loved each other deeply. But we married when she was very young. I loved her, but I didn't always understand her. In some ways she was different from the women of her times. She had a kind of quiet fire in her soul.' He turned to face her then. 'Do you know that when you were born she wanted to take care of you herself, not to have a nurse? It was unheard of. And I thought it was silly. So I hired Fräulein Hedwig, and I think something happened to your mother. After that she always seemed a little lost.' He turned away again, silent for a moment, and then he went on. 'When we had been married for ten years, she met someone, a younger man than I. He was a very famous writer, he was handsome and intelligent, and she fell in love. I knew about it almost from the beginning. Perhaps even before it began. People told me they had seen them. And I saw something different in her eyes. Something excited and happy and alive again, something marvellous.' His voice grew softer. 'And I think, in a way, it made me love her more.

'The tragedy of Kassandra was not that she was in love with a man other than her husband, but that her country had fallen into the hands of the Nazis, and the man she loved so desperately was a Jew. I warned her, for her own sake and for his, but she wouldn't leave him. She wouldn't leave either one of us, in fact. In her own way she was loyal to us both. I can't say I ever really suffered from her attachment to this man. She was as devoted as she had been before, perhaps more so. But she was equally devoted to him. Even when they stopped publishing his work, even when they shunned him, and at the last ...' His voice cracked and he could barely go on. 'Even when they killed him.

'She was with him the day they took him. They dragged him from his house, they beat him, and when they found your mother, they ... beat her ... they might even have killed her except that she thought to tell them who she was so they left her alone. She made her way home. And when I got here, all she could talk about was that she had disgraced me and how afraid she was that they would hurt us. She felt she had to offer her life to secure ours ... and she couldn't live with what they had done to him. I went to a meeting for two hours, and when I came home, she was dead. In the bathroom of her rooms down the hall.' He waved vaguely towards the rooms Max had occupied only a week before.

'That, Ariana, is the story of your mother, who loved a man the Nazis wanted dead. She couldn't bear the pain of the reality they had shown her ... she couldn't live with the ugliness and the brutality and the fear ... So -' he turned to face his daughter - 'in a sense they killed her. Just as, in a sense, they may dare to kill you, if you choose to take the risk of loving Max. Don't do it ... oh, God, please, Ariana ... don't ...' His face sank into his hands and for the first time in her life Ariana heard her father cry. She went to him, trembling and silent, and held him tightly in her arms, her own tears falling on to his jacket as his mingled with the gold dust of her hair.

'I'm so sorry ... Oh, Papa, I'm so sorry.' She said it to him again and again, horrified at what he had told her, and yet for the first time in her life, her mother had become real. 'Papa, don't ... please ... I'm sorry ... I don't know what happened ... I'm so confused. It was so strange, having him here in that bedroom ... in our house, hidden, frightened. I wanted to help him. I felt so sorry for him.'

'So did I.' Her father raised his head at last. 'But you must let him go. There will be a man for you one day. A good man, and I hope the right man, in better times.' She nodded silently as she dried a fresh cascade of tears.

'Do you suppose we'll ever see him again?'

'Perhaps one day.' His arms went around his daughter. 'I hope we will.' She nodded and they stood there, the man who had lost Kassandra and the little girl she had left him with instead. 'Please, my darling, be careful now, while we're at war.'

'I will. I promise.' Her eyes turned up towards his then as she bestowed on him a tiny smile. 'Besides, I never want to leave you.'

But at that he laughed softly. 'And that, my darling, will change, too.'

Two weeks later Walmar got a letter at the office. It had no return address and contained a single sheet of paper with a hastily scrawled address. Max was in Lucerne. It was the last that Walmar von Gotthard ever heard of him.

Chapter 11

The summer passed uneventfully. Walmar was busy at the bank, and Ariana was busy at the hospital three mornings a week. With school no longer an obstacle, she had more time for her volunteer work and more time to run the house. She and Gerhard and her father went on a week's holiday to the mountains, and when they returned, Gerhard turned sixteen. His father announced with amusement on the morning of his birthday that now his son was a man. That was apparently also the opinion of Hitler's army, because in the desperate last puch of the fall of 1944, they were drafting every man and boy within reason. Gerhard received notice that he was being drafted four days after the birthday that he and his father and sister had celebrated with such glee. He had three days to report.

'I don't believe it.' He stared at the notice over his breakfast. He was already late for school. 'But they can't do that ... can they, Father?' His father looked at him gloomily.

'I'm not sure. We'll see.'

Later that morning Walmar visited an old friend of his, a colonel, and learned that nothing could be done.

'We need him, Walmar. We need them all.'

'It's that bad, then?'

'It's worse.'

'I see.'

They had discussed the war, the colonel's wife and Walmar's bank for a few moments, and then resolutely Walmar had gone back to his office. As he sat in the back of the Rolls-Royce driven by his chauffeur, he pondered what he had to do. He would not lose his son. He had lost enough.

When Walmar got back to his office, he made two calls. He returned to the house at lunchtime, extracted some papers from the wall safe in his study, and returned to work. He didn't get home that evening until after six, and when he did, he found his children upstairs on the third floor, in Gerhard's bedroom. Ariana had been crying and Gerhard's face was filled with fear and despair.

'They can't take him, can they, Father?' Ariana believed her father was able to move mountains. But her eyes held little hope. And neither did Walmar's when he answered softly.

'Yes, they can.'

Gerhard said nothing; he sat there, stunned at what had befallen him. The notice still lay cast open on his desk. He had read it a hundred times since that morning. Two other boys in his class had also received their notices. But he had said nothing of his own. His father had told him to remain silent, lest there be something that he could do. 'So that means I'm going.' He said it in a dull, flat voice and his sister gave way to fresh tears.

'Yes, it does mean that, Gerhard.' Despite the stern voice he eyed his children gently. 'Be proud to serve your country.'

'Are you crazy?' He and Ariana stared at their father in shocked horror.

'Be still.' On his last words he closed Gerhard's bedroom door. With a finger to his lips, he urged them closer and then whispered softly. 'You don't have to go.'

'I don't?' It was a jubilant stage whisper from Gerhard. 'You fixed it?'

'No.' Walmar shook his head seriously. 'I couldn't. We're leaving.'

'What?' Gerhard looked shocked once more, but his father and sister exchanged a knowing glance. It was like Max's flight only a few months before. 'How will we go?'

'I'll take you into Switzerland tomorrow. We can say that you're sick here at home. You don't have to report until Thursday that's not for another three days. I'll take you over the border and leave you with friends of mine in Lausanne, or in Zurich if I have to. Then I'll come back for your sister.' He glanced gently at his daughter and touched her hand. Perhaps she would see Max again after all.

'Why doesn't she come with us?' Gerhard looked puzzled, but his father shook his head.

'I can't get everything ready that quickly, and if she stays here, they won't suspect that we're pulling out for good. I'll be back here in a day anyway, and then I'll leave with her for good and all. But you're all going to have to be absolutely, totally quiet about this. Our lives depend on it. Do you understand?' They both nodded.

'Gerhard, I've ordered you a different passport. We can use it at the border if you have to. But whatever you do in the meantime, I want you to look resigned to going into the army. I even want you to seem pleased. That also means in this house.'

'Don't you trust the servants?' With all his sixteen years Gerhard was still naïve. He overlooked Berthold's preoccupation with the Party, and Fräulein Hedwig's blind faith in Adolf Hitler.

'Not with your lives.'

Gerhard shrugged. 'All right.'

'Don't pack anything. We'll buy everything we need there.'

'Are we taking money?'

'I have money there already.' Walmar had been prepared for years. 'I'm only sorry that we waited this long. We should have never come back from vacation.' He sighed deeply, but Ariana tried to console him.

'You couldn't know. When will you be back from Switzerland, Papa?'

'Today is Monday. We leave in the morning ... Wednesday night. And you and I will leave on Thursday night after I go to the bank that day. We can say we're going out to dinner, and then we will never come back. It will take a little manoeuvring to get the servants to think Gerhard reported to the army without saying goodbye. As long as you keep Anna and Hedwig out of Gerhard's rooms tomorrow and Wednesday, we can just say he left too early Thursday morning to see anyone at all. If you and I are here, no one will suspect anything. I'm going to try and be back in time for dinner.'

'What have you told them at the bank?'

'Nothing. I won't have to explain my absence. There are enough secret meetings going on these days that I can easily cover myself there. All right, both of you? Is everything clear now?

'The war is almost over, children, and when it ends, the Nazis will pull everything down with them when they go. I don't want either of you here for that. It's time for us to go. We can pick up the pieces later. Gerhard, meet me in the café around the corner from my office at eleven in the morning. We'll go to the train station together from there. Is that clear now?'

'Yes.' The boy looked suddenly grave.

'Ariana? You'll stay up here tomorrow and look after Gerhard, won't you?'

'Absolutely, Father. But how will he leave the house in the morning without being seen?'

'He'll leave at five before anyone gets up. Right, Gerhard?'

'Right, Father.'

'Wear warm clothes for the trip. We'll have to walk the last part.'

'You, too, Father?' Ariana was worried as she searched her father's eyes.

'Me too. And I'm quite capable of doing it, thank you. Probably a great deal more so than this boy.' He stood up then, rumpled his son's hair, and prepared to leave the room. He smiled at them, but there were no answering smiles from his children. 'Don't worry. It will go safely. And one day we'll be back.' But as he closed the door behind him, Ariana wondered if they would.

Chapter 12

'Frau Gebsen.' Walmar von Gotthard looked down imperiously at his secretary, his Homburg in his hand. 'I will be gone for the rest of the day, in meetings. You understand ... where I'm going.'

'Of course, Herr von Gotthard.'

'Very well.' He marched quickly from the room. She had no idea where he was going. But she thought she did. To the Reichstag of course, to see the Minister of Finance again. And if he didn't appear on the morrow, she would understand that the meetings had resumed again. She understood about those things.

Walmar knew that he had timed his exit perfectly. The Minister of Finance was spending a week in France, consulting over the situation of the Reich's finances in Paris and taking inventory of the vast store of paintings they were sending back to Berlin. Quite a windfall for the Reich.

He had told his driver not to wait for him that morning, and he walked quickly around the corner to the workers' café. Gerhard had left the house on schedule at five that morning, with a kiss from his sister and a last look over his shoulder at the home he had grown up in, before he walked the twelve miles to the centre of Berlin.

As Walmar entered the café, he saw his son there but offered no sign of recognition. He merely walked towards the men's rest room, his face obscured by his Homburg, his briefcase in his hand. Once behind the locked door of the rest room, he quickly stepped out of his suit, putting on a pair of old work pants he had taken from the garage. Over his shirt he pulled a sweater, on his head a nondescript old cap, then an old warm jacket, and back into the briefcase went his suit. The Homburg he shoved brutally to the bottom of the trash. A moment later he joined Gerhard and with a vague nod and a coarse greeting signalled for him to go.

They took a cab to the station and were quickly lost in the milling throng. Twenty minutes later they were on the train bound for the border, their travel papers in order, their identification secure, their faces masks. Walmar was increasingly proud of Gerhard, who had played his part to perfection. He was overnight a fugitive, but learning quickly how to be a successful one.

'Fräulein Ariana? ... Fräulein Ariana?' There came a sharp knocking at the door. It was Fräulein Hedwig, her face peering into the girl's as Ariana gingerly opened the door. But Ariana was quick to press a finger to her lips to silence Hedwig, and she rapidly joined the older woman in the hall.

'What's going on here?'

'Sshh ... you'll wake him. Gerhard isn't feeling well at all.'

'Does he have a fever?'

'I don't think so. I think mostly just a dreadful cold.'

'Let me see him.'

'I can't do that. I promised him that we'd let him sleep all day. He's terrified he'll be too sick to go to the army on Thursday. He just wants to sleep it off.'

'Of course. I understand. You don't think we should call the doctor?'

Ariana shook her head. 'Not unless he gets much worse.'

Fräulein Hedwig nodded, pleased that her young charge should be so anxious to serve his country. 'He's a good boy.'

Ariana smiled benevolently in answer and kissed the old woman on the cheek as they stood in the hall. 'Thanks to you.'

Hedwig blushed at Ariana's compliment. 'Should I bring him tea?'

'No, it's all right. I'll make him some later. Right now he's asleep.'

'Well, let me know if he needs me.'

'I will, I promise. Thank you.'

'Bitte schön.' And a moment later Fräulein Hedwig went on her way.

Twice that afternoon and once that evening she pressed her services on Ariana again, but each time Ariana insisted that her brother had awakened earlier, eaten something, and then gone back to sleep. It was by then late Tuesday evening, and she only had to play the game until her father returned on Wednesday night. After that they were home free. Her father could claim that he had taken Gerhard to the army himself at the crack of dawn. All they had to do was make it through Wednesday. It was only a matter of another twenty-four hours. She could do that. And on Thursday evening she and her father would be gone, too.

Her body felt tired and achy when she went downstairs late Tuesday night. It had been a strain, listening all day for Hedwig or Anna, keeping up the ruse, and standing guard near Gerhard's room. She needed to escape the third floor, if only for a few minutes. So she let herself into her father's study and sat staring at the ashes in the grate. Had he only been in the room that morning? Had this been where he had said his quick goodbye? It seemed like a different room now without him, the papers carefully ordered on the desk, the books so neatly put away in the bookcase. She stood up, looking out at the lake, remembering his words when he had said goodbye ... 'Don't worry, I'll be back day after tomorrow. And Gerhard will be fine.'

'It isn't Gerhard I'm worrying about. It's you.'

'Don't be silly. Don't you trust your old father?'

'More than anyone alive.'

'Good. Because that is precisely how much I trust you. And that is why, my darling Ariana, I am going to show you some things now, which one day may come in very handy. I think they're things you need to know.' He had shown her the secret safe in his bedroom, another in the main library, and the last one in her mother's bedroom, where he still kept all her jewels. 'One day these will be yours.'

'Why now?' Tears had sprung to her eyes. She didn't want him showing her all this now. Not the day he was leaving to spirit Gerhard away.

'Because I love you, and I want you to know how to take care of yourself you must. If something happens, you must tell them that you knew nothing about it. Tell them you thought Gerhard was sick upstairs and you had no idea he was gone. Tell them anything you have to. Lie. But protect yourself, with your fine mind and with this.' He showed her a small pistol and a dozen stacks of freshly minted bills. 'If Germany falls, these will be worth nothing, but your mother's jewellery will always take care of your needs.' He then showed her the false volume of Shakespeare, in which were the large emerald, which had been her engagement ring, and the diamond signet ring she had worn on her right hand. As Ariana saw it, she unthinkingly reached out to touch it. Its glimmer was familiar. She could remember seeing it on her mother's hand so many years before. 'She always wore that.' Her father's voice had been dreamlike as together they looked at the diamond signet ring.

'I remember.'

'Do you?' He seemed surprised. 'Remember it is here if you need it. Use it well, my darling, and her memory will be well served.'

As she thought back on the morning, she realised that standing in her father's study wouldn't bring him back to her any faster than if she went to bed upstairs. And she had to be up early in the morning to resume her vigil, lest Fräulein Hedwig grow zealous and insist on seeing Gerhard for herself.

Silently, Ariana turned off the lights in her father's study, closed the door, and went back upstairs.

At the Müllheim station Walmar gently nudged Gerhard, sleeping peacefully in his seat. They had been on the train for almost twelve hours, and the boy had been asleep for four. He looked so young and innocent as he lay there, his head tucked away in the corner, pressed against the wall of the coach. Soldiers had come aboard at several stations, and their papers had been checked twice. Walmar had only referred to Gerhard as his young friend; the papers appeared in order, and when he spoke to the officers, his tone had been deferential and his accent coarse. Gerhard had said little, only widening his eyes in awe of the soldiers, and one of them had ruffled his hair and teasingly promised him a commission soon. Gerhard had smiled winningly, and the two men in uniform had moved on.

At Müllheim no one boarded and the stop was brief, but Walmar wanted him awake before they reached Lörrach, their last stop. He would come awake quickly then in any case, in the cool night air. They had a nine-mile walk then, and their greatest challenge – to cross the border and reach Basel as early as they could. From there they would take a train to Zurich. Walmar had decided to leave him there – he would be safe in Switzerland. He would return two days later with Ariana, and they could go on together to Lausanne after that.

He was anxious to return to Ariana as soon as he could. She would not be able to keep up the charade forever, and the main thing was to get Gerhard safely to Zurich. But first, Lörrach, and their long walk. It was eighteen miles from Müllheim to Lörrach, and half an hour after Gerhard had stirred sleepily in his seat and gazed absently around him, the train came to a full halt. It was the end of the line for them.

At one thirty in the morning, with a handful of others, they stepped down, and for an instant Walmar felt his legs tremble beneath him at the unfamiliar sensation of solid ground. But he said nothing to Gerhard, he simply pulled his cap down, pulled up his collar, gestured towards the station, and they moved on. An old man and a boy going home. In their rough clothes they did not look strange in Lörrach: only Walmar's carefully manicured hands and well-barbered hair would have given them away, but he had worn the cap during the entire journey and had seen to it that he got his hands good and dirty in the dusty station before they left Berlin.

'Hungry?' He glanced at Gerhard, who yawned and shrugged.

'I'm all right. You?'

His father smiled at him. 'Here.' He handed him an apple he had pocketed from the lunch they'd bought on the train. Gerhard munched it as they walked along the road. There was no one in sight.

It took them five hours to cover the nine miles. Gerhard would have done it faster, but Walmar couldn't walk quite as quickly as he had as a young man. Still, for a man of almost seventy, he had done remarkably well. And then they knew that they had reached the border. Miles of fence and barbed wire. In the distance they could hear border patrols rumbling past them. Two hours earlier they had left the road. But in the dark before the first light of daybreak, they looked like two farmers getting an early start. No bags to attract suspicion, only Walmar's briefcase, which he would have thrown into the bushes had he heard someone approach. From his pocket he quickly pulled wire cutters as Gerhard watched, and as he snipped, the boy held back the wires. In a few minutes there was a hole big enough to crawl through.

Walmar felt his heart pounding ... If they caught them, they would be shot ... He didn't care for himself now, but the boy ... Quickly, quickly, they climbed through and he could hear his jacket tearing, but a moment later they both stood in Switzerland, near a clump of trees in a field. Silently Walmar gestured, and they both began to run, darting through the trees for what seemed like hours until at last they stopped. But no one had followed, no one had heard. Walmar knew that a year or two earlier it would have been much harder to get across, but in the past months, the army had been in such desperate need of soldiers, there were ever fewer on the Swiss border patrols.

They walked for another half hour, reaching Basel by the first bright light of day. There was a splendid sunrise on the mountains, and for an instant Walmar put an arm around Gerhard's shoulders and stopped to watch the mauves and pinks streak across the sunlit sky. He thought in that brief moment that he had never felt so free. It would be a good life for them there until the war was over, and perhaps for even longer than that.

With aching feet they reached the train station and were just in time to catch the first train. Walmar bought two tickets to Zurich and settled back in his seat to rest. He closed his eyes and felt sleep begin to pull him deeper. It seemed only moments later when Gerhard was tugging at his arm. For the four-and-a-half-hour journey, glancing at the pleasant views of the Frick Valley, Gerhard had not wanted to wake him.

'Papa ... I think we're here.'

Walmar looked sleepily around him, glancing out at the familiar Bahnhof Platz and the Grossmünster cathedral in the distance, and further away he could just glimpse the mountains of the Uetliberg. For that moment it felt like home. 'We are.' As they stepped down safely from the train in Zurich, despite his tired back and aching legs, Walmar wanted to take his son's arm and dance. Instead a long, slow grin lit his face and he put an arm around his son's shoulders. They had done it. They were free. Gerhard's life was assured now. He would never serve in Hitler's army. They would never kill his son.

They walked quickly to a small pension that Walmar remembered vaguely. He had had lunch there once while waiting for a train. And it was still where he remembered, small, unimportant, quiet, friendly. It was a place where he felt comfortable leaving Gerhard while he went back for his last hours in Berlin.

They ate a mammoth breakfast and then Walmar took him up to his room. He looked around, satisfied, and then turned to face the boy who had grown to manhood in so few days. It was a precious moment between father and son. It was Gerhard who spoke first, looking with damp-eyed admiration at the father who had led him to safety, cut the wires, walked across the border, and brought him here. 'Thank you, Papa ... thank you.' He flung his arms around his father's neck. This was the father his friends had sometimes teasingly called 'old'. But this wasn't an old man who held him, it was a man who would have walked barefoot and bleeding across the mountains to save his son. For a long moment Walmar held him, and then slowly he pulled away.

'It's all right. You're safe now. You'll be all right here.' He walked swiftly to the simple desk then, pulled out a piece of paper and his carefully concealed gold pen. 'I'm going to give you the address and number of Herr Müller ... in case Ariana and I get delayed.' The boy's face clouded over, but Walmar ignored his fears. 'Just a precaution.' He never thought to give him Max's number. It was too dangerous. The other man was a banker whom Walmar knew well. 'And I'm going to leave you my briefcase, there are papers, some money. I don't think you'll need much of that in the next two days.' All he was taking back with him was a slim purse filled with money, cash, nothing with which he could have been identified should they stop him this time on the road. 'This time it would be harder. It would be broad daylight, but he didn't want to take a chance delaying his return to Ariana. He wanted to get back to her by that night. He turned then to face Gerhard and saw that the boy was crying. They embraced again and said goodbye. 'Don't look so worried. Get some sleep now. When you wake up, have a good dinner, walk around, and see the sights. This is a free country, Gerhard, no Nazis, no armbands. Enjoy it. And Ariana and I should be back here by tomorrow night.'

'Do you think Ariana can make that walk from Lörrach?' Even for them it had been rough.

'She'll manage. I'll tell her not to wear her fancy highheeled shoes.'

Gerhard smiled through his tears then and held tightly to his father for one last time. 'Can I see you to the station?'

'No, young man, what you can do now is go to bed.'

'What about you?' He looked exhausted, but Walmar only shook his head.

'I'll sleep on the way back to Basel, and probably all the way back to Berlin.'

They looked at each other long and hard then. There was nothing left to be said.

'*Wiedersehen*, Papa.' He said it softly as his father waved at him and hurried down the stairs to the pension's main hall. He had ten minutes to catch the train back to Basel, and he ran the few blocks to the station, just in time to buy his ticket and board the train. At the pension, Gerhard was stretched out on the bed and already fast asleep

Chapter 13

'Well, how is he?' Fräulein Hedwig looked worriedly at Ariana as she stepped out into the hall to pick up their trays for breakfast. With an air of reassurance, Ariana smiled at their old nurse.

'He's much better, but he's still coughing a little. I think after another day in bed he'll be just fine.'

'That and a visit from the doctor, Fräulein Ariana. We don't want him reporting to the army with pneumonia. That would be a fine thing for the Reich.'

'Hardly pneumonia, Fräulein Hedwig.' Ariana looked at her kindly but with hauteur. 'And if his bad humour is any sign that he's improving, then he ought to be in fine shape for the Reich.' She made to re-enter their apartment with her brother's tray. She would come back in a moment for her own tray, but Fraulein Hedwig had already picked it up. 'That's all right, fräulein, I'll get it in a minute.'

'Don't be so independent, Ariana. If you've been taking care of that boy since yesterday, trust me, you need help.' She clucked and muttered, and in their little sitting room set down Ariana's tray.

'Thank you, fräulein.' She stood expectantly, clearly waiting for the old nurse to leave.

'*Bitte*.' And then she reached out for the tray Ariana was still holding. 'I'll take him his.'

'He won't like that. Really, you'd better not.' Her grip was firm. 'You know how he hates being treated like a baby.'

'Not a baby, Fräulein Ariana, a soldier. It's the least I can do.' Sternly, she was reaching for the tray.

'No, thank you, Fräulein Hedwig. I have my orders. He made me promise that I wouldn't let anyone else in.'

'I am hardly "anyone", fräulein.' She drew herself up to her full height. On any other occasion Ariana would have been intimidated. In this case she had no intention of being out-maneouvred by their old nurse.

'Of course you're not "anyone," but you know how he is.'

'Even more difficult than he used to be apparently. I think the army will do him good.'

'I'll be sure to tell him you said so.' She smiled gaily, whisked the tray into Gerhard's room, and closed the door. She set the tray down instantly, leaning her full weight against the door lest Fräulein Hedwig persist, but a moment later Ariana heard the door to the sitting room close firmly and she let out a long sigh of relief. She hoped her father returned on schedule that night. It would be impossible to keep Hedwig at bay for much longer.

She sat nervously in the sitting room that morning and eventually put out both trays, with evidence that there had been damage done to both. She thanked Anna for a stack of fresh towels, and thanked God that Hedwig did not come up again until that afternoon.

'How is he?'

'A lot better. I think he'll be all ready for the army by tomorrow. He may even blow up his room before he goes. He's saying something about dragging out his chemistry equipment for one last try.'

'That's all we need.' She glared at Ariana disapprovingly. She did not like the high-handed way the girl had been behaving at all. At nineteen, she may have been a grown woman, but not as far as Fräulein Hedwig was concerned. 'Tell him he owes me an explanation for hiding like this, like a spoiled schoolboy, in his room.'

'I'll tell him, Fräulein Hedwig.'

'See that you do.' She stalked off again, this time ascending to her own room on the fourth floor. And twenty minutes later Ariana heard another determined knock on the sitting room door. Expecting to see Hedwig, she opened the door with a strained smile. But this time it was Berthold, still panting from his long climb up two flights of stairs.

'It's a phone call from your father's office. Apparently it's urgent. Will you come down?' For an instant Ariana hesitated – should she leave her guard post? But after all, Hedwig had already been staved off. For a few minutes it would be safe. She hurried after Berthold and took the call in the alcove in the main hall.

'Yes?'

'Fräulein von Gotthard?' It was Frau Gebsen, her father's secretary at the bank.

'Yes. Is something wrong?' Perhaps she had some word of her father? Had there been some change of plans?

'I don't know ... I'm sorry ... I don't mean to worry you, but your father ... I assumed ... He mentioned something when he left yesterday morning. I rather thought that he was with the Minister of Finance, but I realise now that he was not.'

'Are you quite sure? Perhaps he had some other meeting. Does it matter?'

'I'm not quite sure. We had an urgent call from Munich, and I had to reach him, but he wasn't there. The minister is in Paris, and he has been all week.'

'Then maybe you misunderstood him. Where is he now?' Her heart was pounding.

'That's why I called. He didn't come in this morning, and if he wasn't with the Minister of Finance, then where is he? Do you know?'

'Of course not. He's probably at some other meeting. I'm sure he'll call you later.'

'But he hasn't called all day, fräulein. And –' she sounded vaguely embarrassed, after all Ariana was still young – 'Berthold said he didn't come home last night.'

'Frau Gebsen, may I take leave to remind you that my father's nocturnal whereabouts are none of your concern, or Berthold's, or my own.' Proper outrage shook her voice, or so it seemed; in point of fact it was raw fear.

'Of course, fräulein. I must apologise, but the call from Munich ... and I was concerned, I thought perhaps he'd met with an accident. It's unusual for your father not to call.'

'Unless he's in a secret meeting, Frau Gebsen. The Minister of Finance can't be the only man of importance with whom my father disappears. I really don't understand why this is so important. Simply tell them in Munich that momentarily he can't be reached, and as soon as he gets home, I'll have him call you. I'm sure it won't be long.'

'I do hope you're right.'

'I'm quite certain of it.'

'Very well, then please ask him to call.'

'I shall.'

Ariana hung up gingerly, hoping that her terror didn't show as she marched with proper outrage back up the stairs. But she paused on the first landing to catch her breath before continuing upstairs. And when she reached the second landing, she saw the door to the sitting room ajar. Hurriedly, she pushed it open, only to find Berthold and Hedwig in grim conference in front of her brother's open door.

'What are you doing here?' She almost shouted it.

'Where is he?' Hedwig's voice was an accusation, her eyes cold as ice.

'How do I know? He's probably hiding somewhere downstairs. But as I recall, I distinctly asked you –'

'And where is your father?' Now it was Berthold's turn.

'I beg your pardon. My father's whereabouts are none of my business, Berthold, nor yours.' But as she faced them, her face went deathly pale. She prayed that her voice wouldn't tremble and give her away to Hedwig, who knew her so well. 'And as for Gerhard, he's probably gone off somewhere. He was here the last time I looked.'

'And when was that?' Hedwig's eyes filled with suspicion. 'That boy has never made his bed in his life.'

'I made it for him. And now, if you would both be good enough to excuse me, I would like to take a nap.'

'Certainly, fräulein.' Berthold bowed with precision and he signalled Hedwig to follow him from the room. When they had left her, Ariana sat pale and trembling in Gerhard's favourite chair. Oh, God, what would happen now? With her hands pressed to her mouth and her eyes closed, a thousand terrifying images ran helter-skelter through her head. But none of them as terrifying as what happened half an hour later when there came a firm knock on her door.

'Not now, I'm resting.'

'Are you really, fräulein? Then you must excuse this intrusion into your private rooms.' The man who spoke to her was not a servant, but a full lieutenant of the Reich.

'I beg your pardon.' She stood up in astonishment as he strolled in. Had they come for Gerhard? What was he doing here? And not just the lieutenant – she saw as he wandered confidently into the room that there were three more soldiers walking up and down her third-floor hall.

'I'm afraid I must beg your pardon, fräulein.'

'Not at all, Lieutenant.' She stood up with a decided presence, smoothing her soft blonde hair into the tidy figure-eight chignon she wore. She dropped a dark blue cashmere sweater around her shoulders and attempted to walk unhurriedly towards the door. 'Would you care to talk downstairs?'

'Certainly.' He nodded pleasantly. 'You can pick your coat up on the way.'

'My coat?' Her heart was pounding.

'Yes. The captain thought we might get down to business more quickly if you came to see him at his office, rather than playing tea party with you here.' His eyes glittered unpleasantly and she found herself hating his steely grey eyes. This man was to his very core a Nazi, from the lapels of his uniform to the depths of his soul.

'Is something wrong, Lieutenant?'

'Perhaps. We will let you explain that to us.' Had they caught Gerhard and her father, then? But no, it couldn't be. She wouldn't allow herself to believe that as she followed him, seemingly calm, to the second floor, and then she understood. They had come to question her, but they knew nothing. Not yet. And she mustn't tell them. No matter what.

Chapter 14

'And you thought your father was in a secret meeting, Fräulein von Gotthard? Really? How interesting. With whom?' Captain Dietrich von Rheinhardt looked her over with interest. She was a very pretty piece. Hildebrand had told him as much before he escorted her into the room. And a cool one, for a girl so young. She looked totally unruffled, a lady from the top of her shining blonde head to the tips of her black-alligator-clad feet. 'With whom did you say you thought your father was meeting?' This had gone on for almost two hours, ever since they escorted her from the big black Mercedes on to the Königsplatz, over which rose the forbidding six-columned splendour of the Reichstag, and then hastily into the building and this impressive-looking room. It was the office of the commanding officer, and it had chilled many before her, to the very bone. But she showed no terror, no anger, no exasperation. She merely answered their questions, politely, calmly, and with that unshakably ladylike manner, again, and again, and again.

'I have no idea whom my father was meeting with, Captain. He doesn't share his professional secrets with me.'

'And do you think he has secrets?'

'Only in terms of the work he does for the Reich.'

'How charmingly said.' And then as he sat back and lit a cigarette, 'Would you care for some tea?' For a moment she wanted to snap at him that they had said they didn't want to play tea party, which was why they had brought her here, but she simply shook her head politely.

'No, thank you, Captain.'

'Some sherry perhaps?'

The amenities were wasted on Ariana. She could not be put at ease here, with a life-size portrait of Hitler staring her in the face.

'No, thank you, Captain.'

'And these secret meetings of your father's? ... Tell me about those.'

'I didn't say he had secret meetings. I just know that on some evenings he comes home rather late.' She was growing tired, and in spite of herself, the strain was slowly beginning to show.

'A lady perhaps, fräulein?'

'I'm sorry, Captain, I don't know.'

'Of course not. How rude of me to suggest it.' Something ugly and angry and wicked jumped at her from his eyes. 'And your brother, fräulein? He goes to secret meetings, too?'

'Of course not, he's just barely sixteen.'

'But he doesn't attend youth meetings either, does he? Does he, fräulein? Is it possible, then, that your family is not as sympathetic to the Reich as we had previously thought?'

'That's not true, Captain. My brother had a great deal of trouble with his studies, as well as asthma, and of course ... since the death of my mother ...' She trailed off, hoping to discourage further questions, but that was beyond hope.

'And when was it that your mother died?'

'Ten years ago, Captain.' *Thanks to people like you.*

'I see. How touching that the boy even remembers his mother. He must be a very sensitive young man.' She nodded, not sure what to answer, and let her eyes stray from his face. 'Too sensitive for the army, fräulein? Could it be that he and your father have deserted their homeland in its final hour of need?'

'Hardly. If they had done that, why would they leave me here?'

'You tell me, fräulein. And while you're about it, perhaps you could tell me something about a friend named Max. Maximilian Thomas? A young man who used to visit your father on occasion, or was it that he visited you?'

'He was an old friend of my father's.'

'Who only five months ago fled Berlin. Interestingly, he disappeared on precisely the same night that one of your father's cars was stolen, and then found again, of course, safe and sound, outside the train station in Berlin. A happy coincidence, of course.' Oh, God, did they know about Max, then? And had they tied her father to that after all?

'I don't think the car being stolen had anything to do with Max.'

He took a long drag on his cigarette. 'Now let's talk about your brother again for a moment, fräulein. Where do you suppose he could be?' He spoke to her in a singsong voice of someone speaking to the mentally retarded or a very young child. 'I understand that you've been nursing him through a very bad cold for the past two days.' She nodded. 'And then, miraculously, when you went downstairs to answer a phone call, the boy disappeared. Annoying of him, of course. What I'm rather wondering, though, is if he didn't disappear several days earlier. Like yesterday morning perhaps, around the time your father was last seen at his office? What kind of coincidence do you suppose that might be?'

'A very unlikely one, I'd say. He was in the house all day yesterday, last night, and this morning, in his room.'

'And how lucky he is to have a devoted sister like you. I understand that you guarded him with the zeal of a young lioness guarding her cubs.' And he said the words, a chill ran down her spine. There was only one way he could have known that. From Hedwig or Berthold. A wave of nausea seized her as she understood the truth. For the first time Ariana felt the full force of the facts. And then suddenly she felt raw fury run through her for their betrayal. But she couldn't let him see it. She had to play the game, at any price.

The captain pressed relentlessly on. You know, fräulein, what I find intriguing is that they seem to have run off and left you here, your father and your brother together, perhaps to save the boy from joining the army, or perhaps for even more malicious purposes than that. But whatever the reason, they seem to have abandoned you, my dear. And yet you protect them. Is it that you know your father is coming back? I assume that's what it must be. Otherwise I'm afraid I don't understand your unwillingness to talk.'

For the first time she snapped at him in irritation; the strain of the interrogation was finally fraying her nerves. 'We have been talking to each other here for almost two hours, but I simply don't have the answers to the questions you ask. Your accusations are inaccurate, and your presumption that my brother and father have run off and left me is ridiculous. Why would they do that?'

'In truth, my dear lady, I don't think they would. And that is precisely why we're going to wait and see. And when your father returns, he and I will talk over some business.'

'What kind of business?' Ariana eyed Von Rheinhardt with suspicion across his desk.

'A little trade, shall we say? His charming daughter for ... well, let's not discuss the details. I'll be happy to arrange it with your father when he gets back. And now, fräulein, if you'll excuse me, I will have Lieutenant Hildebrand escort you to your room.'

'My room? I'm not going home, then?' She had to fight to keep the tears from springing to her eyes. But the captain was shaking his head firmly while still wearing his unbearable false smile.

'No, fräulein, I'm afraid we'd prefer to show you our hospitality here, at least until your father returns. We'll make you quite comfortable in your ... er ... room here with us.'

'I see.'

'Yes.' He looked at her sombrely for a moment. 'I suppose that by now you do. I must offer your father my compliments when I see him, if I see him, that is. He has a most impressive daughter, charming, intelligent, and extra-ordinarily well bred. You haven't cried, begged, or pleaded. In fact, I've thoroughly enjoyed our little afternoon.' Their 'little afternoon' had consisted of hours of gruelling interrogation, and she wanted to slap his face when she heard the words.

He rang a buzzer at the side of his desk then and expected Lieutenant Hildebrand to appear. They waited for a long moment and the captain buzzed again. 'The good lieutenant appears to be busy; apparently I'll have to find someone else to escort you to your room.' He spoke of it as of a suite at the Danieli in Venice, but Ariana knew full well that what awaited her was not a hotel room, but a cell. With his boots gleaming in the lamplight, the captain, obviously irritated, strode to the door. He pulled it open by its large brass doorknob and glared angrily outside. It was almost seven o'clock in the even-ing and Lieutenant Hildebrand had apparently gone in pursuit of his dinner. The only officer visible outside the office was a tall man with a stern face and a long narrow scar that ran down one cheek. 'Von Tripp, where the hell are all the others?'

'I believe they've all gone to eat. It's –' he glanced at the clock and then at his captain – 'it was getting late.'

'Pigs. All they think of is filling their stomachs. All right, never mind. You'll do just as well. And why aren't you with them, by the way?' He glared in annoyance at the chief lieutenant, who returned his superior's look of annoyance with a small, frigid smile.

'I'm on duty this evening, sir.'

He waved back in the direction of his office at the woman who was partially concealed by the door. 'Take her downstairs, then. I'm through with her.'

'Yes, sir.' He stood up, saluted smartly, clicked his heels, and walked rapidly into the room.

'Stand up.' He issued a brisk order and Ariana jumped in her chair.

'I beg your pardon?'

Captain von Rheinhardt's eyes glinted malevolently as he returned to the room. 'The lieutenant has ordered you to stand up, fräulein. Be so kind as to do what he says. Otherwise, I'm afraid ... well, you know, it would be awkward ...' he touched the riding crop at his waist.

Ariana instantly rose to her feet, trying to stem the thoughts running through her mind. What were they going to do to her? The tall blond officer who had ordered her to stand up so brusquely looked terrifying, and she was not encouraged by the small, nasty scar on his cheek. He looked cold-blooded and machinelike and he stood by like an automaton as she walked out of the room.

'Have a good evening, fräulein,' Von Rheinhardt smirked at her back.

Ariana did not answer the captain, and in the outer office the lieutenant grabbed her firmly by the arm. 'You will follow me and do exactly as I tell you. I do not enjoy quarrelling with prisoners, and most particularly women. Be good enough to make this easy for yourself, as well as for me.' It was a stern warning, and despite his long strides, she walked along quickly beside him. He had made himself clear. She was a prisoner now. Nothing more than that. And suddenly she couldn't help wondering if even her father would be able to get her out of this.

The tall blond lieutenant led her down two long corridors and then down a long flight of stairs into the bowels of the building, where it was suddenly both damp and cold. They waited for a heavy iron door to be opened after a guard had peeked through a window and nodded his head at the man at her side. The door closed horrifyingly behind them, was bolted, then locked, and she found herself travelling down another flight of stairs. It was like being led to a dungeon, and when she saw the cell where her journey ended, she realised that it was just that.

The lieutenant said absolutely nothing as a woman sergeant was called and Ariana was frisked and searched. She was then shoved into the cell and the lieutenant stood by as the woman locked the doors. In cells around them women were calling and crying, and once she thought she heard the wails of a child. But she couldn't see any faces, the doors were solid slabs of metal with barred windows only a few inches square. It was the most terrifying place Ariana could imagine, and once inside the dark cell, she had to fight every moment so as not to scream and totally lose control. In the tiny shaft of light that came through the minute window, she could see what she thought was a toilet, and discovered moments later was only a large white metal bowl. She truly was a prisoner – somehow that made it real.

In the stench of the cell she began to cry softly, until at last she sank into a corner, dropped her head on her arms, and was wracked by sobs.

Chapter 15

When Walmar von Gotthard left the station in Basel that morning, he looked around him carefully before beginning his long walk back to Lörrach, to catch the train back to Berlin. Every muscle in his body ached, and he looked finally as dirty and ragged as he had pretended to be the morning before. He looked very little like the banker who ran the Tilden, sat in meetings with Minister of Finance and was in effect the most eminent banker in Berlin. He looked like a tired old man who had had a long journey, and no one would have suspected him of having the vast amount of cash that he secretly carried.

He reached the border by noon without problem, and now the long haul was about to begin: the nine-mile walk back to Lörrach, which he had finished with such victory at the Swiss border only six hours before. Then came the most difficult part of the journey, the road back to Berlin. And then he had to undertake once again the same terrors with Ariana. And once both his children were safely on the Swiss side of the border, he didn't care if he dropped dead in his tracks. In fact, as he crawled through the wires he had cut that morning, he thought that he would be very lucky if he didn't drop dead long before. For a man of his years it had been quite an adventure, but if he could save both Ariana and Gerhard, nothing mattered. He would have done anything in his power, and beyond that, for them.

Once again he stopped, looked around, and listened. Once again he hurried towards the cover of the trees. But this time he was not as lucky as he had been that morning, and he heard footsteps in the brush only a few feet away. He tried to run deeper into the bushes, but the two soldiers were instantly on his heels.

'Hi there, grandpa, where you going? To join the army in Berlin?'

He tried to grin stupidly at them, but one of the two men on the border patrol nonetheless cocked his gun and took aim at his heart.

'Where you going?'

He decided to tell them, in a thick country accent. 'To Lörrach.'

'How come?'

'My sister lives there.' He felt his heart dancing in his chest.

'Does she? How nice.' He waved his gun again in the direction of Walmar's breastbone and signalled to the other to commence a search. They tore open his jacket, patted his pockets, and then felt his shirt.

'I have my papers in order.

'Oh, yeah? Let's see.'

He began to reach for them, but before his fingers got there the soldier who had been searching felt something long and smooth concealed under Walmar's right arm.

'What's this, grandpa? Hiding something from us?' He laughed coarsely and winked at his friend. The old ones were funny. They all thought they were so smart. The soldiers tore open the shirt that was now wilted and dirty, never noticing the fine fabric they tore. They had no reason to suspect him. He was just an old country man. But what they found in the secret wallet impressed them, for there was a fortune in large bills and small ones, and their eyes grew round with amazement as they counted what they had found. 'You were taking this to the Führer?' They laughed at their own joke and grinned happily at the old man.

He kept his eyes cast down lest they see the anger there and hoped they'd be content just to take his money. But the two soldiers were wise in the ways of war by now. Exchanging a quick glance, they then did what had to be done. The first man stood back while the second one fired. Walmar von Gotthard fell lifelessly into the tall grass around him.

They dragged him firmly by the heels into the deep brush, stripped him of his papers, pocketed the money, and went back to their hut, where they sat down to count the money in earnest and threw into their open fire the papers of the old man. They never bothered to read them. It didn't matter who he had been. Except to Gerhard, waiting in a hotel room in Zurich. And to Ariana, sitting terrified in her cell in Berlin.

Chapter 16

Lieutenant von Tripp signalled to the soldier with the large key ring to open Ariana's cell. The door creaked slowly open, and both men attempted not to react to the stench that always emanated from inside. All the cells were like that because of the dampness, and of course because no one ever cleaned them out.

Freed from her darkness, Ariana was instantly blinded unable to see in the bright light. She didn't know for how long she'd been there. She only knew that she had been crying for most of the time. But when she heard them coming, she had quickly dried her eyes and attempted to wash the mascara she knew had run down her face with a corner of her lace slip. She smoothed her hair down quickly, and she waited as she heard them unlock her door. Perhaps there was news of her father and Gerhard? She waited and she prayed, longing to hear familiar voices, but there was only the metallic sound of their keys. At last she could see dimly, and she saw the outline of the tall blond lieutenant who had led her there only the day before.

'Walk out of your cell, please, and come with me.' She stood up shakily, steadying herself against the wall of her cell, and for an instant he wanted to reach out and help her as she stumbled. She looked so incredibly small and so frail. But the eyes that looked into his a moment later were not those of a fragile beauty begging for help; they were the eyes of a determined young woman desperate for survival and trying to maintain an air of dignity against impossible odds. Her hair had come loose from the sleek figure-eight she had worn the previous evening. It hung down her back now, like a loose shaft of wheat. Her skirt was wrinkled, but expensive, and despite the appalling stench in which she had lain for almost twenty-four hours, a faint hint of her perfume still lingered about her hair.

'This way, please, fräulein.' He stepped carefully to one side and walked just behind her, so he could be sure that she didn't escape him, and as he watched her, he felt even sorrier for her than before. She straightened the narrow shoulders and held her head high as they walked, her heels clicked determinedly down the corridors, and again as they walked up the stairs. Only once did she falter, for an instant, bowing her head as though she were too dizzy to go on. He said nothing as he waited, and in a moment she continued up the stairs, grateful that he hadn't pushed her or shouted at her for not moving on.

But Manfred von Tripp was not like the others. Only Ariana did not know that. He was a gentleman, as she was a lady, and not for an instant would he have pushed her, or shouted, or prodded, or whipped. And there were those who didn't like him for that. Von Rheinhardt himself didn't particularly like Von Tripp. But it didn't matter too much because Von Rheinhardt was the captain and he could make Von Tripp dance if he so chose.

As they reached the top of the last flight of stairs, Lieutenant von Tripp once again took a firm grip on her arm and led her back down the familiar hallway, where once again, the captain was waiting, grinning and leisurely smoking a cigarette, as he had been the day before. The lieutenant rapidly saluted, clicked his heels, and disappeared.

'Good afternoon, fräulein. Did you spend a pleasant evening? I hope you were not too ... er ... uncomfortable in your ... ah ... room.' Ariana didn't answer. 'Sit down. Sit down. Please.' She took a seat without speaking and stared at him from her seat. 'I do regret to tell you we have not heard from your father. And I rather fear that some of my conjectures may have been all too true. Your brother has also not surfaced, which makes him, as of today, a deserter. All of which leaves you, dear fräulein, for the moment, rather high and dry. And somewhat at our mercy, I might add. Perhaps today you'd like to share with us a little more of what you know?'

'I know nothing more than what I told you yesterday Captain.'

'How unfortunate for you. In that case, fräulein, I will not waste your time or mine interrogating you further. I will simply leave you to your own devices, sitting in your cell while we wait for news.' *Oh, God, for how long?* She wanted to scream as he said it, but nothing showed on her face.

He stood up and pressed the buzzer, and a moment later Von Tripp appeared again. 'Where the hell is Hildebrand? Every time I call for him, he's off somewhere.'

'I'm sorry, sir. I believe he's out to lunch.' In fact Manfred had absolutely no idea where he was, nor did care. Hildebrand was always wandering, leaving everyone else stuck with his damn errand-boy job.

'Escort the prisoner back to her cell, then. And tell Hildebrand I want to see him when he comes back.'

'Very well, sir.' The lieutenant shepherded Ariana from the room. She was familiar with the routine now, the long halls, the endless walk. At least she was not confined in her cell and for these moments she could breathe and move and touch and see. She wouldn't have cared if they had walked her down those halls for hours. Anything except the horrors of the tiny, filthy cell.

It was on the second stairway that they ran into Hildebrand, smiling happily and singing a snatch of a tune. He looked up at Von Tripp, startled, and then with interest his eyes combed Ariana, as they had done the morning before when he had walked into her room in her father's house.

'Good afternoon, fräulein. Enjoying your stay?' She didn't answer, but the look she gave him would have burned holes in rocks. He glanced back at her with irritation and then smiled at Manfred. 'Taking her back?' Manfred nodded with disinterest. He had better things to do than talk to Hildebrand. He couldn't bear the man, or most of the officers he worked with, but ever since he'd been wounded at the front, he'd had to put up with jobs like this.

'The captain wants to see you. I told him you were out to lunch.'

'I was, dear Manfred. In fact, I was.' He grinned again then, saluted briefly, and moved on up the stairs as they continued down. He cast a last glance over his shoulder at Ariana as Manfred moved her through the last door, back down the halls, and into the bowels of the building and at last to the door of her cell. Somewhere nearby there was a woman screaming. Ariana shut her ears to the sound and found herself relieved at last to collapse on the floor of her cell.

After three days she walked the corridor again to see the captain; again he told her that her father and brother had not returned. But now she could not understand it, and she knew that either they were lying – that they had found her father and Gerhard – or something had gone desperately wrong. If they were in fact telling her the truth, then there seemed to be no news of either her father or her brother, and after a few brief moments in his office, Von Rheinhardt sent her away.

This time it was Hildebrand who led her down the corridors, his fingers pressing her flesh to the very bone, yet at the same time, his hand was placed high enough on her arm so that with the back of his hand he could touch her breast. He spoke to her in odd familiar bits and pieces, as though she were some animal to be urged on, with kicks and shoves if necessary, and as he never failed to mention, there was always his whip.

This time when they reached the door to her private dungeon he did not wait for the woman to conduct the search. He slipped his hands slowly over her body, down her stomach, up her buttocks, and across her breasts. With every inch of her body, Ariana shrank from him, looking with hatred into his face as he laughed and the woman firmly shut the door between them. 'Good night, fräulein.' And with that she heard him walk away then, but the footsteps stopped only a few feet away. She heard him bark curtly at the matron.

'This one. I haven't tried this one before.' Listening intently with her eyes closed, Ariana heard the keys rattle, the door open, and then his footsteps disappeared. Moments later she could hear screams and pleading, the sound of his crop whizzing through the air and into flesh, and then silence, no more screaming, only a long series of horrific grunts. But she could no longer hear the woman, and in her worst fantasies, she couldn't quite imagine what he'd done. Had he beaten the woman into unconsciousness? Had he whipped her till she died? But at last she heard quiet sobbing, and she knew the woman was alive.

Standing pressed against the wall in her tiny cell, she waited, listening for the footsteps, fearing that they would approach her door again, but instead they turned down the long corridor and rhythmically disappeared. Sighing softly with relief, she sank back to her seat on the floor.

It went on for days and weeks, and regular visits to the captain, who informed her that they had heard nothing of her father and he had not returned. By the end of the third week, she was exhausted, filthy, starving, and she couldn't understand what had happened, why they hadn't come back for her. Or was Von Rheinhardt lying? Perhaps Gerhard and her father had been captured and were prisoners, too. The only answer she couldn't let herself accept was the worst one. They had been killed.

It was after her last visit to the captain, after three weeks of those visits, that Hildebrand escorted her back to her cell. Up until then it had often been the other lieutenant, and now and then it had been someone else.

But today it was he who held her arm as they made their way into the depths of the prison. She was exhausted and three or four times she stumbled. Her hair hung in a tangled mass down her back and around her face. She swept it back often with long, delicate fingers, but the nails were broken now, and there was no longer any trace of perfume in her hair. The cashmere sweater she had first worn so jauntily around her shoulders, she clutched tightly around her for warmth, and her skirt and blouse were torn and dirty – her stockings she had thrown away after the first few days. He took it all in with a look of interest, like a man investing in a herd of cattle or buying sheep, and on the last stairway in the prison they ran into Lieutenant Manfred von Tripp. He greeted Hildebrand curtly, and his eyes avoided Ariana's gaze. He always looked just above her, as though he had no particular interest in her face.

'Good afternoon, Manfred.' Hildebrand was oddly casual as they passed, but Von Tripp saluted and murmured only, 'Afternoon.' And then as though to watch them, he turned briefly and stared. Ariana was too tired to notice, but Hildebrand cast him a knowing look and grinned. Von Tripp turned away then and went upstairs, back to his desk. But as he sat there, his anger burned. Hildebrand was taking much too long to come back to work. He had taken her down there almost twenty minutes earlier; there was no reason for it to take so long. Unless ... slowly the realisation dawned on him. The fool. He would even pull a stunt like that with her. Did he have any idea who the girl's father was, or from what world she came? Didn't he realise that she was a German, a girl of class and breeding, no matter where her father was or what he'd done? Maybe he could get away with his appalling behaviour with some of the prisoners, but surely not with a girl like this. And whoever the victims were, Hildebrand's outrageous antics made Manfred sick. Without thinking further, he found himself hurrying down the hallways and then clattering down the stairs. Manfred knew it didn't matter in his heart who the hell her father was, not to them. To them she was only a girl. He found himself praying that he was not too late.

He grabbed the key ring from the matron, gesturing to her to stay seated, and barked curtly, 'Never mind. Stay there.' And then with a quick look over his shoulder he asked a question. 'Is Hildebrand down there?' The woman in uniform nodded, and Manfred hurried down the last flight of stairs with the keys, the heels of his boots clicking smartly.

The sounds within told him that Hildebrand was in her cell. Without uttering a single syllable, Manfred turned the key and pulled open the door, and what he saw there was Ariana, almost naked, her clothes in shreds around her, and blood streaming from a cut on the side of her face. Hildebrand stood there also, his face gleaming, his eyes wild with lust, the whip in one hand, the other tearing at Ariana's tangled hair. But from the skirt still barely draped around her middle and from the fight he still saw in her eyes, he knew that the worst had not yet happened. He was grateful that he hadn't been too late.

'Get out.'

'What the hell business is it of yours, damn you? She's ours.'

'She's not "ours", she belongs to the Reich, just as you do just as I do, just as everyone does.'

'The hell she does. You and I aren't sitting in this prison.'

'So you rape her, is that it?' The two men stared at each other in blind fury, and for an instant Ariana, panting and breathless in the corner, wondered if her assailant would also whip the lieutenant who outranked him. But he was not quite that mad. Von Tripp spoke first and stood back from the door. 'I told you to get out. I'll see you upstairs.' Hildebrand snarled as he swept past him, and for an instant in the dark cell neither Manfred nor Ariana spoke. And then, bravely sweeping tears from her cheeks and pushing her hair back from her eyes, she attempted to cover herself decently, as Manfred gazed quietly at the floor. When he sensed that she was calmer, he looked up at her again, and this time he did not avoid her face, or the painfully blue eyes. 'Fräulein von Gotthard ... I'm sorry ... I should have known. I'll see to it that this doesn't happen again. It shouldn't.' And then, 'We're not all like that. I can't tell you how sorry I am.' And he was. He had had a younger sister who was close to Ariana's age, although he himself was thirty-nine. 'Are you all right?' They stood there talking in the dark, with only a small wedge of light peeking through the door.

Her blonde hair flying, she nodded, and he handed her his handkerchief to dab at the blood still dripping down her face. 'I think I'm all right. Thank you.' She was far more grateful than he knew. She had thought that Hildebrand was going to kill her, and when she understood instead that he was going to rape her, she'd hoped that he would kill her first.

Manfred looked at her again for a long moment, and then sighed deeply. As much as he had once believed in it, he had come to hate this war at last. It had become a corruption of everything he had once trusted and defended. It was like watching a woman you once respected become a whore. 'Is there anything else I can do?'

She smiled at him then, holding her sweater wrapped around her torso, with those big, sad, waiflike eyes. 'You've already done everything you can. The only other thing you can do for me is find my father.' And then, suddenly, daring to ask him the truth, her eyes met his. 'Is he here somewhere? In the Reichstag?'

Slowly Manfred shook his head. 'We've had no news 'And then, 'Perhaps he'll still come. Don't give up hope, fräulein. Never do that.'

'I won't. After today.' She smiled at him again, and looking at her gravely, he nodded, stepped outside, and once more locked the door. Slowly Ariana sank to the floor again, thinking of what had happened, and of the officer who had providentially arrived just in time. As she sat in the darkness of her cell, her hatred for Hildebrand dimmed with her gratitude for what Von Tripp had done. They were an odd lot, all of them. She would never understand their kind.

She did not see either man again until the end of the next week. By then she had been locked in the cell in their dungeon for exactly one month. And what she feared most was that her father and Gerhard had been killed. Still, she couldn't accept it. She only allowed herself to think of the present moment. Of the enemy. And of getting back at them.

An officer she had never seen before came to get her and dragged her roughly from her cell. He pushed her up the stairs when she stumbled and cursed her when she tripped and fell. She was barely able to walk now, from fatigue and hunger and the lack of exercise that left her legs eternally stiff and numb. When she reached Dietrich von Rheinhardt's office, she was a different young woman than the one who had sat there so self-possessed and poised only a month before. Von Rheinhardt stared at her with something akin to revulsion, but beneath the filth and tangles he knew precisely what was there. She was a beautiful young woman, well-bred, intelligent, she would have been an enchanting present to give to any man of the Reich. Not for him though, he had other pleasures, other needs. But she would make a handsome gift to someone. He was not sure yet whom.

He no longer wasted time on the 'fräuleins' or on the fancy speeches. She was of no further use to them. 'And so, I'm afraid you've become useless. A prisoner held for ransom when there is no one to pay that ransom is not a valuable possession, but a burden instead. There is no reason why we should feed and house you any longer. Our hospitality, in fact, is at an end.' Then, they were going to shoot her. That was it, she decided. But she no longer cared. It was a better fate than the other possibilities. She didn't want to become a prostitute for the officers and she was no longer strong enough to scrub floors. She had lost her family, her reason for living. If they shot her, it would be over forever. Listening to him, she was almost relieved.

But Von Rheinhardt had more to say. 'You will be driven home for one hour. You may collect your belongings and then you may leave. You may take nothing of great value from the house, no money, no jewels, only whatever personal possessions you may need in the immediate future. After that, you can take care of yourself.'

Then, they weren't going to shoot her? But why not? She stared at him in disbelief. 'You will live in the women's barracks, and you will work like everyone else.

'I'll have someone drive you to Grunewald in an hour. In the meantime, you may wait in the hall.' How could she wait outside, in view of everyone, in her disgraceful condition? Half-naked, in the clothes that Hildebrand had torn off her body a week before. They were truly animals.

'What will happen to my father's house now?' Her voice was a croak in her throat, so seldom had she spoken in the past month.

Von Rheinhardt busied himself with the papers on his desk and at last looked up. 'It will be occupied by General Ritter. And his staff.' His 'staff' consisted of four willing women he had collected carefully over the past five years. 'I'm sure he'll be very happy there.'

'I'm sure.' So had they been. Her father and her brother, and once upon a time her mother, and she. They had all been happy there. Before these bastards had arrived to smash their lives, and now they were stealing the house in Grunewald. For an instant there were tears swimming in her eyes. Maybe – she thought hopefully of the air raids she'd grown so used to – maybe the bombs would come and kill them all.

'That's all, fräulein. Report to your barracks by five o'clock this afternoon. And I might add that the barrack arrangement is optional. You are free to make other ... eh ... living arrangements within the confines of the army ... of course.' She knew what that meant. She could offer to be the general's mistress and he would let her stay in her own home. She felt a stab of indignation as she sat numbly on a lone wooden bench in the hall. Her only consolation was that when she returned to Grunewald, her clothes in tatters, her face scratched and bruised, filthy, hungry, beaten, then Hedwig and Berthold could see what they had done. This was the precious Party that the old fools loved. This was what you got with *'Heil Hitler'*. Ariana was busy with her thoughts and her fury and she didn't see Von Trip approach.

'Fräulein von Gotthard?' She looked up in surprise to see him. They hadn't met since the day he had saved her from Hildebrand and his whip. 'I understand that I'm to take you home.' He didn't smile at her, but he no longer averted his eyes from hers.

'Do you mean that you're to take me to my barracks?' She looked at him icily. And then, regretting her anger, she sighed. It wasn't his fault. 'I'm sorry.'

He nodded slowly. 'The captain said I was to take you to Grunewald to get your things.' She nodded silent assent, her eyes huge in her hungry face. And then, as though he couldn't help it, he seemed to unbend a little, and his voice was kind. 'Have you had lunch yet?' Lunch? She hadn't even eaten breakfast or dinner the night before. Meals in her stinking dungeon had arrived once a day and were never worthy of a name, breakfast, lunch, dinner. It was pigslop no matter what time they served it. Only the prospect of total starvation had in the end forced her to eat. She didn't answer him, but he knew what she was thinking. 'I understand.' And then he gestured her to leave her bench. 'We should go now.' He said it somewhat sternly, and Ariana followed him slowly from the brightly lit hall. Her knees felt weak for a minute, and the sunlight briefly blinded her eyes, but she stood there, breathing deeply, and when she slid into the car beside him, she turned her head away as though to look out at the rows of houses being used as barracks so he wouldn't see her cry.

They drove on for a few minutes, and then he pulled the car over and sat staring for a moment at the back of her head. Ariana only sat there, staring, totally unaware of the tall blond man with the gentle eyes and the aristocratic duelling scar. 'I'll be back in a moment, fräulein.' Ariana didn't answer, she only lay her head back against the seat and pulled the blanket he had given her more tightly around her. She was thinking again of her father and Gerhard, wondering where they were. She hadn't been this comfortable in over a month, and she didn't care what happened now, she was out of that stinking cell at last.

Von Tripp was back in the car again a moment later with a small steaming bundle he extended towards her without words. Two fat bratwurst wrapped in paper, with mustard, and a large hunk of brown bread. She stared at it as he handed it to her, and then at him. What an odd man he was. Like Ariana, he seldom wasted words, yet he saw everything; and again like her, there was a kind of sorrow in his eyes, as though he felt the world's pain in his own flesh, and now her pain as well.

'I thought you might be hungry.'

She wanted to tell him that it was nice of him. Instead she just nodded and took the bundle in her hands. No matter what he did, she couldn't forget who he was or what he was doing. He was a Nazi officer, and he was taking her home to pick up her things . . . her things . . . which things? Which of them was she to take with her now? And after the war, what then? Would she get the house back? Not that it mattered anymore. With her father and Gerhard gone, she didn't care. The thoughts and questions ran maddeningly through her head as they drove along and she took small bites from the bratwurst Von Tripp had bought for her. She wanted to devour them but she didn't dare. After living for so long on bread and meat scraps, she was afraid that she would be sick if she ate the pungent sausage too quickly.

'Is it near the lake in Grunewald?' She nodded. In truth she was surprised that they were letting her come home for anything at all. It was odd how suddenly she was no longer a prisoner.

And horrifying to realise that the house was theirs now. The art, the silver, whatever jewels they found, even her furs would be given to mistresses of the generals, and of course there were all her father's cars. His money and investments had been appropriated by them weeks before. So on the whole they were not unhappy with their profits in the deal. And Ariana – she was merely an extra, a pair of hands to perform whatever work she could, unless of course she struck someone's fancy. Ariana herself had figured that much out. But she would rather have died than become the mistress of a Nazi. She would spend the rest of her life in their stinking barracks rather than do that.

'It's there, a little further down the road, on the left.'

Ariana's eyes widened and once again she turned her head to hide her tears. She was almost home now ... the home that she had dreamed of so desperately in those dark hours, lying in her dark cell, the home where she had laughed and played with Gerhard and waited for her father to return at night, where she had sat and listened to stories for hours, as Fräulein Hedwig read to them by the fire, and where she had stolen glimpses of her mother so very long ago ... the home that now she had lost. To them. The Nazis. In seething hatred she glanced at the man in uniform at her side. To her, he was part of what they represented. Terror, loss, destruction, rape. No matter that he bought her food and had saved her from Hildebrand. In truth he was simply part of a terrifying whole. And given the opportunity, in time he would do the same things to her as the others.

'There it is, there.' She pointed suddenly as they rounded the last bend, and Von Tripp slowed the car as they saw it, as she stared at it with sorrow and regret, and he with respect and awe. He wanted to tell her that it was lovely, and that he, too, had once lived in such a home. That his wife and children had died in the house near Dresden during the bombings, that now he, too, would have nowhere to go. The schloss that had been his parents' had been 'borrowed' by a general at the very beginning of the war, leaving his parents virtually homeless until they had joined his wife and two children at the Dresden home. And all of them were gone now. Dead beneath the Allies' bombs. While the general went on living at their castle, he had been safe there, as would have been Manfred's children, had his parents been allowed to stay.

The Mercedes Manfred was driving crunched along on the gravel, making the sound Ariana had heard ten million times before. If she closed her eyes, it would be Sunday and she and Gerhard and her father would be returning from their drive around the lake after church. She would not be sitting here with this stranger, sitting here in the rags of what had once been her dress. Berthold would be standing at attention. And once inside she would serve tea. '... never again ...' She said the two words softly to herself, stepping down on to the gravel, staring up at the beloved house.

'You have half an hour.' He hated to remind her, but they had to be back, and those had been Von Rheinhardt's orders. They had wasted enough time on the girl already. Von Rheinhardt had been clear about Manfred's spending as little time as possible on the project and then hurrying back. '... and watch her!' he had told him, lest she try to spirit something of value out of the house. Also, it was possible that there were hidden safes and secret panels, and whatever Manfred could discover would be of some help. They had already had teams, skilled in just those pursuits, go over the house, but nonetheless it was possible that Ariana would lead them to something more than they had already found.

Uncertainly, Ariana rang the doorbell, wondering if she would see Berthold's familiar face, but what she saw instead was the general's aide. He looked very much like the man who stood just behind her, but somewhat sterner as he stared down in horror at the girl in rags. He glanced from her to Manfred, the two men saluted, and Lieutenant von Tripp explained.

'Fräulein von Gotthard, sir. She's come to fetch some clothes.'

There was a brief further exchange between the two men.

'There's not much left, you know.' He said it to Manfred, not to Ariana, who was looking up at him in shock. Not much left? Not much, from four closets filled with clothes? How wonderfully greedy they had been, and how quick.

'I don't think I'll be needing much.' There were sparks of anger in her eyes as she stepped inside the front door. Everything looked the same, yet different. The furniture was in the same place, yet, intangibly, some quality of the house had changed. There were no familiar faces, none of the sounds of the people she and the house had always known. Berthold's aging shuffle. Anna's increasing limp, Gerhard's constant slamming and running, her father's dignified progress down the long marble hall. Somehow she expected to see Hedwig – after all her devotion to the Party, surely they would have kept her on – but even Hedwig's familiar face was not among those who stared at Ariana as she made her way upstairs. There were mostly uniforms hurrying in and out of the main study, and several more waiting outside the main salon; there were orderlies carrying trays of schnapps and coffee, and there were several unknown maids. It was like coming back in another lifetime, after everyone you'd known had long since died and another generation had repopulated all the places you had once loved. Her hand touched the familiar banister as she quickened her step and ran upstairs with her eternal shadow still behind her; Lieutenant von Tripp maintained a discreet distance, but he was always there.

She stopped for a moment on the first landing, staring at her father's bedroom door. Oh, God, what could have happened to them?

'In there, fräulein?' Von Tripp's voice was soft behind her.

'I beg your pardon?' She wheeled on him, as though she had just discovered an intruder in her home.

'Is that the room where you are going to fetch your things?'

'I ... it ... my room is upstairs. But I'll have to come back here later.' She had just remembered. But perhaps it was too late. The book may already be gone. Or maybe not. But she didn't really care now. With the loss of Gerhard and her father, and then the house, all was already lost.

'Very well. We haven't much time, fräulein ...' She nodded and ran up the last flight of stairs to the room where Hedwig had betrayed her, the doorway through which the officers had first walked. Hildebrand, with his arrogant gait, strolling into her sitting room as she prayed for her father's return. She pushed open the first door, and then the door to her own room, keeping her eyes averted from Gerhard's doorway across the hall. She didn't have time for nostalgia, and it would have caused her too much pain.

After a moment she hurried out of the room to find a suitcase in a storeroom above them, on the floor where the servants' rooms were, and it was there that she found her, the traitor, hurrying with bent head towards her own room.

Like a dart cast at the woman's retreating back, Ariana hurled the word. 'Hedwig!' The old woman stopped and then hurried on, never turning to face the girl she had raised since birth. But Ariana would not let go of her now. In fact, she never would again. 'Can you not face me? Are you so afraid?' The words a venomous caress, an invitation to drink poison, a machete concealed in a gift of fur. The woman stopped and slowly she turned.

'Yes, Fräulein Ariana?' Calmly, she attempted to face the girl, but her eyes were fearful, and her hands trembled on the stack of linens she had been taking to her room to mend.

'Sewing for them, are you? They must be grateful to you. Just as we were. Tell me, Hedwig.' No more 'Fräulein,' no more respect, only hatred now: Ariana stood with her hands clenched, her fingers tensed like claws. 'Tell me, after you sew their clothes for them, after you take care of their children, if they have any, will you betray them, too?'

'I did not betray you, Fräulein von Gotthard.'

'My, my, how formal. Then it was Berthold and not you who called the police?'

'It was your father who betrayed you, fräulein. He should never have run away as he did. Gerhard should have been allowed to serve his country. It was wrong for him to run away. '

'Who are you to judge that?'

'I am a German. We must all judge each other.' So that was what it had come to. Brother against brother. 'It is our duty, and our privilege, to watch over each other and see that Germany is not destroyed.'

But Ariana spat her answer at her. 'Germany is already dead, thanks to people like you; people like you have destroyed my father and my brother and my country –' she stood there with tears pouring down her face, then, unable to go on as her voice sank to a whisper – 'and I hate you all.'

She turned away from her old nurse, stormed into the storeroom, and took the single valise in which she would pack her remaining belongings from the house. Silently, Von Tripp followed her back to her room and lit a cigarette as he watched her hurriedly stack sweaters and skirts and blouses, underwear and nightgowns, along with several pairs of sturdy shoes. There was no room for frills now. There were no frills in Ariana von Gotthard's life.

But even what she was packing was of a finesse and calibre that was hardly suited to a life in an army barracks – the skirts she had worn to school, the shoes she wore when she went to watch Gerhard play polo or walk slowly with her father around the lake. She cast a glance over her shoulder as she threw a silver and ivory hairbrush into the suitcase. 'Do you suppose they'll mind if I take that? It's the only hairbrush I have.'

Manfred looked momentarily embarrassed and shrugged. For him, it was odd to see her packing. The moment she had walked into the main hallway, it was evident that this was where she belonged. She moved around with an assurance, an authority, that made one want to bow slightly and step aside. But it had been that way for him in Dresden, too. Their house had been only slightly smaller, and in fact even more impressively staffed. The house had been his wife's father's, and when he died two years after they married, it had become theirs. A handsome addition to the schloss he was to inherit when his parents died. So Ariana's lifestyle was not unknown to him, nor was the pain of her fate as she left home. He could still hear his mother crying, when she got the word that she would have to give up the schloss for the duration of the war. 'And how do we know we'll get it back?' she had sobbed to his father.

'We'll get it back, Ilse, don't be silly.'

But now they were all dead. And the schloss would belong to Manfred, when the Nazis finally left it after the war. Whenever that would be. And now Manfred didn't really care. There was no one to go home to. No home where he would care to be. Not without them ... his wife, Marianna, and the children ... he couldn't bear to think of it as he stood there, watching Ariana put another pair of walking shoes into the bag.

'You're planning to take up hiking, Fräulein von Gotthard?' He used a smile to force the pain from his own mind. She had certainly packed a good supply of rugged equipment.

'I beg your pardon? You expected me to wash out bathrooms in a ballgown? Is that what Nazi women do?' Her eyes widened sarcastically as she threw another cashmere sweater on the pile. 'I had no idea they were so formal.'

'Perhaps they're not, but I doubt very seriously that the captain intends to have you scrub floors until the end of the war. Your father had friends, they will invite you. Other officers – '

She cut him off brutally with eyes of stone. 'Like Lieutenant Hildebrand, Lieutenant?' There was a long silence between them and then she turned away. 'I'm sorry.'

'I understand. I just thought ...' She was so young, so pretty, and there would be plenty of opportunity for her to do more than just scrub floors. But she was right and he knew it. She would be better off hiding in the barracks. There would be others like Hildebrand. Even more of them now that she was free. They would see her now, polishing doorknobs, raking leaves, scrubbing toilets ... they would see the huge blue eyes, the cameo face, the graceful hands. And they would want her. She would be accessible to them all now. There was nothing to stop them. She was helpless, not as much as she was in the fetid cell, but almost. She belonged to the Third Reich, a possession, an object, like a bed or a chair, and she could be used accordingly, if someone chose to. And Manfred knew that someone would. At the thought of it, Manfred von Tripp felt sick. 'Perhaps you're right.' He said nothing further, she finished her packing and then lowered her suitcase to the floor. She had left on the bed one heavy brown tweed skirt, a dark brown cashmere sweater, and a warm brown coat, along with suitable underwear and a pair of flat brown suede shoes.

'Do I have time to change my clothes?'

He nodded silently and she disappeared. Officially, he was probably supposed to watch her, but he would have put neither of them through that ordeal. She was not a prisoner to that extent, that she had to be watched every moment. That kind of nonsense was what Hildebrand would have done, forcing her to undress in front of him while he drooled and eventually reached out to pull her towards him. Those were not the games that Manfred von Tripp played.

She returned from the bathroom a moment later, a solemn portrait in brown, with only her pale golden hair providing some sunlight on the sombre scene. She pulled the coat on over her sweater and Manfred had to fight the urge to help. It was painful and confusing standing there beside her. He had to let her carry her own suitcase as well. It fought against everything he had been taught, everything he felt for this tiny, fragile stranger who was leaving her house for the last time. But he had already bought her lunch and saved her once from rape. He could not do much more, not now.

Ariana paused at the top of the last flight of stairs, glancing again at her father's door, and then at Von Tripp standing beside her. 'I'd like to ...'

'What's in there?' His brows knit uncomfortably.

'My father's study.' Oh, Christ, what was she after? Some cash he had hidden somewhere? Some treasure? A tiny pistol she could aim at an assailant's head, or even at his own as they returned to the heart of Berlin? 'Is it purely sentimental? Fräulein, that is the general's study now ... I really ought to ...'

'Please.' She looked so bereft and so helpless, he couldn't force himself to refuse. Instead he nodded slowly, sighed, and cautiously opened the door. An orderly was inside laying out a dress uniform for the general, and Manfred looked at him questioningly.

'Anyone else here?'

'No, Lieutenant.'

'Thank you, we'll only be a moment.'

She walked quickly to the desk, but touched nothing, then more slowly she walked to the window and stared out at the lake. She remembered when her father had stood there talking about Max Thomas, and then telling her the truth about her mother, and when he had stood there again the night before he left with Gerhard. If only she had known it would be their last parting ...

'Fräulein ...' She pretended not to hear him, her eyes rooted to the still blue Grunewaldsee. 'We have to be going.' And then, as she nodded, once again she remembered. The reason why she had wanted to come to the study. The book.

She glanced casually over the bookcase, knowing long before she reached it where it was, and the lieutenant watched her, hoping that she would do nothing desperate that would force him to report her or return her to her cell. But she was only touching one or two of the old leatherbound books that stood in such abundance in the bookcase of her father's room. 'May I take one?'

'I suppose so.' It was harmless after all, and he really had to get back to his office in Berlin. 'But do hurry. We've been here for almost an hour.'

'Yes, I'm sorry ... I'll take this one.' After looking at three or four, she settled on one, a volume of Shakespeare, translated into German, leatherbound and well worn. Manfred glanced at the title, nodded, and opened the door. 'Fräulein.'

'Thank you, Lieutenant.' She glided through it with her head held high, praying that her look of victory would not give her away. In the book she had taken from her father's bookcase reposed the only treasure that she still had. The diamond signet ring was there safely couched by Shakespeare, along with the emerald engagement ring. She slipped the book quickly into the deep pocket of her brown tweed coat, where no one could see it and where she couldn't lose the very last of what she had. Her mother's rings. That and her father's book were all that she had left of her lost life. Ariana's head was filled with memories as she walked sedately down the long hall.

As she did so, the suitcase slapping heavily at her legs, rendering her a refugee where she had once been hostess, a door opened suddenly on her right and a uniform dripping medals instantly appeared.

'Fräulein von Gotthard, how nice to see you.'

She looked at him in astonishment, too startled to be repulsed. It was the aging General Ritter, who was now the master of her father's house. But he held out a hand to her, as though he had met her on the way to tea.

'How do you do.' She responded by reflex and he quickly took her hand, looking into the deep blue eyes, and then smiling as though he had found something with which he was very pleased.

'I'm very happy to see you.' She didn't suggest that he had no reason not to be. He was already the proud possessor of their house. 'It has been a very long time.'

'Has it?' She couldn't ever remember meeting him before.

'Yes, I believe the last time we met you were, oh ... about sixteen ... at a ball at the Opera House.' His eyes glowed.

'You looked lovely.' For a moment she looked absent. It had been her first ball. And she had met that officer she liked so much ... and that Father hadn't quite approved of ... what had been his name? 'I'm sure you don't remember it. It was about three years ago.' She almost expected him to pinch her cheek, and for a moment Ariana felt sick. But she was grateful for the training that made her able to endure as well as pretend. She owed Hedwig a debt after all.

'Yes, I remember.' Her voice was flat, but not quite rude.

'Ah, do you?' He looked immensely pleased. 'Well, you'll have to come back again sometimes. Perhaps for a little party here.' He rolled the words from his tongue in nauseating fashion and for an instant Ariana thought she might throw up. She would die first. In fact, the prospect of death was becoming rapidly more enticing as she began to understand what really was to be her fate. She did not answer him. But the blue eyes shrank from him as he reached out and touched her arm. 'Yes, yes, I do hope we see you here again. We will be having lots of little celebrations, fräulein. You must share them with us. After all, this was your house.' *Is, you bastard, not was!* She wanted to shout the words, but she only dropped her eyes politely, so he could not see the fury that raged in her heart.'

'Thank you.'

The general's eyes shot a cryptic message at Von Tripp, and then he waved vaguely at the aide who stood behind him. 'Remember to call Von Rheinhardt and tell him ... er ... give him an ... er ... invitation for Fräulein von Gotthard. That is if ... er ... there are no other invitations for her already.' He was being careful this time. The last concubine he had added to his pack had been a woman he had stolen from right under yet another general's nose. It had caused a lot more trouble than the woman had been worth. And although this one was pretty, he had enough headaches on his hands just then. Two of the trainloads of paintings he had been waiting for from Paris had just been bombed. So this pretty little virgin was not quite the most pressing affair. Yet he would have enjoyed adding her to his other girls. He smiled at her one last time, saluted, and disappeared.

The suitcase was in the backseat, her head was held high, and the tears streamed down her face. She didn't bother to hide them from the lieutenant. Let him see. Let them all see how she felt about what they'd done. But what Ariana didn't see as she watched the house disappear behind them was that there were tears in Manfred von Tripp's eyes, too. He had all too clearly understood the general's cryptic message. Ariana von Gotthard was about to be added to the lecherous old bastard's harem. Unless someone else put in a claim for her first.

Chapter 17

'All finished with the girl?' Captain von Rheinhardt looked at Manfred irritably as he stalked past his desk later that afternoon.

'Yes, sir.'

'Did you take her out to Grunewald to get her things?'

'Yes, sir.'

'It's a nice house, isn't it? Lucky man, the general. I wouldn't mind having a house like that.' But he wasn't doing badly either. A family whose home had a view of the Charlottenburger Lake and Schloss had been fortunate enough to give up its home for him.

The captain went on to speak to Manfred of other matters. Hildebrand kept busy answering the phones. Time and time again Manfred found himself wondering if one of the calls was General Ritter's aide asking about the girl. Then he would stop his thoughts. What difference did it make to him? She was nothing to him, just a young woman who had fallen on hard times, lost her family and her home. So what? Thousands of others were in the same boat. And if she was attractive enough to catch the eye of a general, then it was just something that she would have to learn to handle herself. It was one thing to protect her from the viciousness of a junior officer planning to rape her in her cell, but quite another to steal her from a general. That would mean trouble. For him.

Manfred von Tripp had been careful to avoid problems with his superiors and other officers during the entire course of the war. It wasn't a war that he approved of, but this was the country that he served. He was a German, first and foremost, and more than many others he had paid dearly for the fervour of the Reich. But still he did not argue, he kept his mouth shut and endured. And one day it would be over, he would go back to the land of his parents, and the schloss would be his. He wanted to restore the castle to its medieval splendour, rent out the farms, and bring the surrounding lands around the castle back to life. And there he would remember Marianna, the little boy and girl, and his parents. He wanted nothing more than to survive the war for that. He wanted nothing further, nothing from the Nazis, no stolen priceless paintings, no misbegotten jewels or cars, he wanted no plunder, no rewards, no gold, no money. What he had wanted and held dear was already gone.

But what troubled Manfred as he sat at his desk and listened was that she was so innocent and so young. In a way their lives were much the same now, but Manfred was thirty-nine and she was nineteen. He had lost everything but he hadn't been helpless the way she was now. He had been agonised, broken, anguished, but not frightened and alone ... Manfred had heard the stories. He knew the kinds of games the old man played, the girls together, he and the girls, a little perversion, a little brutality, a little sadomasochism, a little whip, a little ... Thinking of it made him sick. What was wrong with all of them? What happened to men when they went to war? God, he was tired of it. He was tired of it all.

He threw his pen down on his desk after Captain von Rheinhardt left the office and sat back in his chair with a sigh. It was then that the call came from the general, or rather from his aide, who spoke to Hildebrand, who only grinned. He put the phone back in its cradle after taking the message that the captain should call him back in the morning. 'Something about a woman. Christ, that old fart is going to end this war with his own army – an army of women.'

'Did his aide say who?'

Hildebrand shook his head. 'Just a little matter he would like to arrange with the captain. Unless, as the aide put it, it's already too late. The aide said this is one cookie the general figures will be off the pastry shelves pretty quick. She may already be gone. Knowing Ritter, she'll be lucky if she is. I wonder who he's got his eye on this time.'

'Who knows.' But after the phone call Manfred stirred restlessly in his seat. Hildebrand left for the day, and Manfred found himself sitting there, at his desk, for another two hours. He couldn't get his mind off her and what Hildebrand had said. The general wanted Ariana ... unless the cookie was already off the pastry shelf ... He stood there for a long moment, as though spellbound, and then, hurriedly grabbing his topcoat, he turned off the light in the office and ran down the stairs, out of the building, and across the street.

Chapter 18

Lieutenant Manfred von Tripp found Ariana von Gotthard easily at the barracks. He had been planning to inquire at the desk, but it turned out to be unnecessary. She was outside raking leaves and placing great armloads of them in a barrel, which afterwards she would have to burn. It was easy to see that it was the first time in her life she had done any manual labour.

'Fräulein von Gotthard.' He looked official, his shoulders squared, his head terribly erect, like a man about to make a major pronouncement, and had Ariana known him better, she would have seen, too, that lurking in his blue-grey eyes was also fear. But she didn't know him that well. In fact, she didn't know Manfred von Tripp at all.

'Yes, Lieutenant?' She said it with exhaustion, pushing a long stray lock of blonde hair from her eyes. She was wearing delicate brown suede gloves to work in, they being the only ones she had. She imagined that he had arrived to give her still more orders. Since that afternoon she had scrubbed down two bathrooms, cleaned trays in the cafeteria, carried boxes from the top floor to the basement, and now this. It hadn't exactly been a leisurely afternoon.

'Please be so kind as to collect your bag.'

'My what?' She looked at him in total confusion.

'Your suitcase.'

'Can't I keep it here?' Or what was it, had someone admired the leather, and now they were taking her suitcase, too? She was still carrying the little leather book with the false compartment in her coat. And when she had had to leave it in her room, she had hidden it in a ball of laundry under the bed. It was the only place she had been able to think of in her rush to get to work. The matron in charge was a large bull-shaped woman with a voice better suited to the drill ground than a women's barracks. She had kept Ariana appropriately terrified all afternoon. But now Ariana looked at Manfred with fresh disgust. 'So someone wants my suitcase. Well, let them have it. I'm not going anywhere for a while.'

'You misunderstand.' His voice was gentle, but hers was not. She had to remind herself always that this was the man who had saved her from Hildebrand that night in her cell. Otherwise it was too easy just to think that this man was like the others. Because, after all, he was. He was inextricably woven into the fabric of her nightmare, and she could no longer separate his needs from theirs. She didn't believe in anything anymore, or anyone. Not even this tall, quiet officer who looked at her gently but firmly now. 'In fact, Fräulein Gotthard, you're quite wrong. You are going somewhere.'

'I am?' At first she looked at him in sudden terror. Now what? What were they planning for her now? Some terrible internment in a camp somewhere? Then a sharp stab of joy—Could it be? 'Have they found my father?' His quick look of dismay told her all she needed to know.'

'I'm sorry, fräulein.'

His voice was soothing. He had seen the terror in her face. 'You will be safe.' For a while at least. And that was something these days. A while was better than nothing at all. And which of them were safe? In the past years of never-ending air raids, the bombs never ceased to fall.

'What do you mean, I will be safe?' She eyed him with fear and suspicion, clutching tightly to her rake, but he only shook his head now and spoke softly.

'Trust me.' With his eyes he tried to reassure her but she still looked desperately afraid. 'Now please be so kind as to pack your suitcase. I will wait for you in the main hall.' She looked at him with despair blending into desperation. What did it matter now?

'What should I tell the matron? I didn't finish out here.'

'I'll explain.'

She nodded and walked into the building as, silently, Manfred watched her. He found himself wondering what the devil he was doing. Was he as crazy as the general? But it was nothing like that, he told himself. He was only doing it to protect the girl. Yet he, too, had felt the stirrings. He was not unaware of the beauty that lay only faintly obscured by the drab clothes and her distress. It would take very little to polish the diamond to its old lustre, but that was not what he was doing, it was not why he was taking her to Wannsee that night. He was taking her there to save her from the general, to take the cookie off the bakery shelf. Ariana von Gotthard would be safe in Wannsee, no matter what.

Manfred spoke briskly to the matron, explaining that the girl was being removed. He managed to explain with inferences and subtle nuances that it was a matter of someone's pleasure rather than any military decision regarding the girl. The matron understood perfectly. Most of the girls like Ariana were snatched up by officers within a few days. Only the ugly ones stayed to help her, and when she had first seen Ariana, she had known it wouldn't last. It was just as well really. The girl was too small and delicate to do much work. She saluted the lieutenant smartly and assigned another girl to go outside and rake.

Ariana was back in the main hall not quite ten minutes later, with her suitcase clutched tightly in her hand. Manfred said nothing, but turned on his heel and marched swiftly out of the building, expecting Ariana to follow him, which she did. He opened the door of his Mercedes, took her suitcase from her this time, and tossed it in the back, and then he walked around the car, got behind the wheel, and started the motor. For the first time in a very long time, Manfred von Tripp looked pleased.

Ariana still didn't understand what was happening, and she watched the city around them curiously as they drove off. It took her almost twenty minutes to figure out that they were going in the direction of Wannsee. They had almost reached Manfred's house. But by then she had already figured out what was happening. So this was what he had saved her for, that night in her cell. She wondered if he also used a whip. Perhaps that was how he had got the hairline scar that travelled a short distance along his jaw.

A few moments later they pulled up outside a small house. It looked respectable but not sumptuous in any way, and inside it was dark. Manfred signalled for her to get out of the car, and he grabbed the suitcase from the backseat as she walked towards the front door with her spine ramrod straight and her eyes avoiding his. How charmingly he had arranged things. Apparently she was to be his. For good, she found herself wondering, or just the night?

Without further ceremony he unlocked the front door, waved her in, and stepped inside. He shut the door firmly behind them, flipped on some lights, and looked around. His cleaning woman had been there that morning, and everything looked tidy and clean. There was an unceremonious but friendly living room, with lots of books and plants, and a stack of freshly cut wood next to the fireplace where each night he made a fire. There were photographs, mostly of his children, and a journal of some kind lying closed on his desk. There were big, friendly, country windows that opened out on to a garden filled with flowers, a view shared by the kitchen, a small den, and a tiny, cosy dining room, all of which occupied the main floor of the house. There was a narrow wooden stairway, carpeted with a well-worn but once handsome rug, and all Ariana could see from below was a low-ceilinged upstairs hall.

As though he expected her to understand his intentions, Manfred stalked silently from room to room, throwing open doors and then moving on to the next room, until at last he stood at the foot of the stairs. He looked at her hesitantly for a moment and stared into her deep, angry blue eyes. She still wore her coat and the gloves she'd worn to gather leaves outside the barracks; her hair was falling from its tightly woven golden knot. Her suitcase stood behind them, forgotten near Manfred's front door.

'I'll show you around upstairs.' He said it quietly as he waved her up before him. He didn't quite trust her behind him yet. She was too afraid, too angry, and he knew enough to protect himself, even from a child like this.

Upstairs, there wasn't a great deal to show her. A single bathroom and two ominous-looking doors. Ariana stared at the doors with terror, her huge blue eyes wandering slowly to Manfred's hands and then his face. 'Come, I'll show you.' The words were gentle, but it was useless, he could see from her face that she was so frightened, she could barely hear. What could he do to reassure her? How could he explain what he had done? But he knew that in time she would come to understand.

He threw open the door to his bedroom, a stark and simple room done in browns and blues. Nothing in the house was very fancy, but it was all comfortable and it had been precisely what he wanted when he decided to find his own quarters in Berlin. It was a place where he could escape everything, where he could sit peacefully at night, watch the fire, smoke his pipe, and read. His favourite pipe lay on a table in his bedroom, next to the fireplace where he sat in a well-worn, always welcoming chair. But instead of seeing the harmless surroundings, Ariana stood there, eyes wide, arms down, her feet rooted to the ground.

'This is my bedroom.'

The eyes stared at him in helpless horror, and she nodded. 'Yes.'

And then, touching her arm gently, he walked past her and swung open a door she had assumed would be a closet. But he stepped inside and disappeared. 'Come this way, please.' Gingerly and trembling she followed him, only to discover that it was yet another small room. There was a bed, a chair, a table, a desk so small, it was almost better suited to a child, but there were pretty little curtains and a bedspread covered with roses that matched the wallpaper in the small room. There was something reassuring about it as Ariana stepped inside. 'And this is your room, fräulein.' He looked at her warmly, but still he saw that she didn't understand. Her eyes went to his again, with the same pain, same sorrow, and he smiled at her, and let out a long sigh.

'Fräulein von Gotthard, why don't you sit down, you look exhausted.' He waved her gently to the bed, which she stared at for a moment, and finally rigidly sat down. 'I'd like to explain something to you. I don't think you understand.' He looked suddenly very different as he spoke to her, not like the stern officer who had trotted her up and down those endless halls and stairs, but like the kind of man who came home at night, who ate dinner, sat by the fire, and fell asleep over his paper because he was so tired. He looked like a real person, but still Ariana shrank from him as she watched him from the bed. 'I brought you here tonight because I believed that you were in danger.' He sat back slowly in his chair and prayed that she'd relax. It was impossible to talk to her when she sat there like that, staring at him. 'You're a very pretty woman, Fräulein von Gotthard, or I should say that you're a very pretty girl. How old are you? Eighteen? Seventeen? Twenty?'

'Nineteen.' It was more of a gasp than a word.

'I wasn't so far off, then, but there are those who wouldn't care.' His face grew serious for a moment. 'Like our friend Hildebrand. He wouldn't give a damn if you were twelve. And there are others ...' *If you were a little older, if you had been out in the world for a bit before all this misfortune befell you, you would have some idea how to take care of yourself.* He frowned at her and she stared at him. He sounded more like her father than a man who was going to take her to his bed and rape her. And in his chair he was thinking of her raking the dead leaves outside the barracks; she had looked about fourteen years old. 'Do you understand, fräulein?'

'No, sir.' She looked infinitely pale and wide-eyed. Gone was the young woman who had tried to brazen it out with Von Rheinhardt in the beginning. This was no woman, it was a child.

'Well, it came to my attention this evening that there was a possibility you might be urged to ... er ... join the general ...' Fresh terror flew into her eyes but he held up a hand. 'I felt that that would hardly be a fortuitous beginning to your life on your own. So, fräulein –' he looked around the room that would be hers – 'I brought you here.'

'Will they make me go to him tomorrow?' She stared at him in desperate anxiety as he tried to keep his eyes from noticing the flawless gold of her hair.

'No, that's quite unlikely. The general doesn't ever exert himself over anything. If you had still been there at the barracks, he would have taken you with him to Grunewald, but if you're already gone, then you have nothing to fear.' And then he thought of something. 'Do you mind that? Would it have been worthwhile putting up with him in order to be back in your own house?'

But she shook her head sadly. 'I couldn't have borne to see it like that, with strangers in it, and –' she choked on the words – 'I would have died rather than be with him.' Manfred nodded, and he saw her looking at him appraisingly, as though to see what she'd got herself instead, and he couldn't repress a burst of laughter. He knew exactly why she was looking him over. And at least she had understood that he wasn't going to tear her clothes off halfway through the bedroom door.

'How does the arrangement suit you, fräulein?' He eyed her and she sighed softly.

'I suppose it will do.' What did he expect? Her thanks for making her his mistress instead of the general's?

'I'm sorry these things have to happen. It has been an ugly war ... for all of us.' There was a distant, pensive look on his face. 'Come. I'll show you the kitchen.'

In answer to his question about her cooking, she smiled. 'I've never really cooked before. There was no need.' There had always been servants to do the cooking.

'Never mind. I'll teach you. I won't make you rake leaves or scrub toilets – I have a cleaning woman who comes in to do all that – but it would certainly be pleasant if as part of our exchange you did the cooking. Do you suppose you could do that?' He looked so serious and suddenly she felt so tired. She was his concubine now. Like a bought-and-paid for slave.

She sighed and looked at him. 'I suppose so. And what about the laundry?'

'All you'll have to worry about is your own. That's it really, just the cooking.' It was a small price to pay for her safety. The cooking, and the fact that she was to become his mistress. That much she understood.

She stood quietly by as he taught her how to make eggs, sliced bread, and showed her how to cook carrots and potatoes, and then he left her to wash the dishes in the sink. She heard him put the wood on and start the fire, and then she saw him writing peacefully at his desk. Now and then he would look at photographs of one of the children, and then he'd bow his head again and write some more.

'Would you like some tea, sir?' She felt oddly like one of the maids in her own house, but remembering that she had inhabited the nightmarish cell in the Reichstag only that morning, she was grateful suddenly to be in the lieutenant's house at all. 'Sir?'

'What, Ariana?' And then he blushed faintly. It was the first time, he had called her by her first name. But he had been absentminded. For a moment she hadn't even been sure if he had said Ariana or Marianna. It was hard to tell. 'Sorry.'

'It's all right. I asked you if you would like tea.'

'Thank you.' He would have preferred coffee, but by now it was almost impossible to get. 'Would you like some?' She hadn't dared to pour herself a cup of the precious substance, but at his bidding she ran to the kitchen for a cup and poured herself some tea. For an instant she just sat there enjoying the exotic fragrance. For a month now she had dreamed of just such long-forgotten luxuries as tea.

'Thank you.' For a long moment he wondered about the sound of her laughter. Would he ever hear it? Twice that evening he had won her bedazzling smile. He felt his heart stir as he watched her. She was so desperately serious, so unhappy, her eyes and her face were so marked by her recent trauma. She was looking around the room then, her eyes stopping at the photographs of the children. 'Your children, Lieutenant?' She looked at him curiously, but he didn't smile. It was an odd little tea party they were sharing the two of them with the broken lives. He only nodded in answer to her question and suggested she pour herself another cup of tea, as he lit his pipe and stretched his long legs towards the fire.

They sat there together quietly, until almost eleven o'clock, saying little, simply being there, Ariana growing slowly accustomed to her surroundings, and the lieutenant enjoying having another living, breathing human being in his home. His eyes would stray towards her now and then, and he would watch her, sitting there, dreamily staring into the fire, as though she had drifted back to a world of long ago. At eleven o'clock Manfred stood up and looked down at her, then he began to turn out the lights.

'I have to get up early tomorrow morning.' As though on cue, she rose, too. But there was fresh fear in her eyes now. What would happen next? This was the moment she had dreaded all night.

He waited for her to walk sedately from the room, and then followed her. They reached his door first and stood there. He hesitated for a long moment and then with a small smile he held out a hand. She watched him in amazement, and she had to remind herself to put her hand in his. This was so totally not what she had expected that her jaw almost dropped as he shook her hand. 'I hope that one day, fräulein, we shall be friends. You are not a prisoner here, you know. This just seemed the wisest arrangement ... for your sake. I hope you understand.' Her eyes lit up slowly then and she smiled at him.

'You mean ...'

'Yes, I mean.' His eyes were gentle and she could see that he was a kind man. 'Did you really think that I would stand in for the general? Don't you think that would have been a little bit unfair? I told you, you are not my prisoner. In fact –' he bowed very properly and clicked his heels – 'I shall regard you as my guest.' But Ariana only stared at him, stunned. 'Good night, fräulein.' The door closed softly behind him, and in utter amazement, she walked soundlessly down the hall.

Chapter 19

'Well, where the hell is she?' Von Rheinhardt stared at Hildebrand in annoyance. 'Von Tripp said he took her over there yesterday. Did you ask the matron?'

'No, she was away from her desk.'

'Then go back. I have better things to worry about than this nonsense, for God's sake.'

Hildebrand went back to see the matron and reported to the captain once again an hour later while Von Tripp kept busy with a number of projects he had not completed the day before.

'What did the matron say?' The captain glowered at Hildebrand from across his desk. Everything had been going wrong for him all day. And he didn't give a damn about the general and that damn Von Gotthard girl. They'd finished with her, and what happened to her now was of no interest whatsoever to him. If General Ritter had the hots for her, that was his own problem. He should have sent his own damn aide running around to look for her.

'She's gone.'

'What the hell do you mean, "she's gone."' And then he looked suddenly furious. 'Has she run away?'

'No, nothing like that, Captain. Someone took her. The matron said it was an officer, but she wasn't sure who.'

'Did you check the logbook?' Von Rheinhardt stared at him.

'No. Should I go back?'

'Never mind. If she's gone, she's gone. He'll find half a dozen others he wants by next week. And that little joyride might not have been worth the price of admission. There is always the chance, though admittedly remote, that her father will turn up one day. And there would be hell to pay if Ritter had made her one of his harem.' Von Rheinhardt rolled his eyes and Hildebrand laughed.

'You really think her old man is still alive?' He looked at his captain with interest.

'No, I don't.' The senior officer shrugged then and admonished Hildebrand to get back to work. And it wasn't until late in the afternoon that the captain himself wandered over to the barracks to have a little chat with the matron. A few moments later she quietly produced the logbook, and Von Rheinhardt got the information that he had come for. He read the name on the logbook with interest and mused to himself all the way back across the street. Perhaps Von Tripp was returning to the land of the living after all. It had been his suspicion that Von Tripp would never recover from the loss of his wife and children, nor from the wound he had suffered just the Christmas before. After he was wounded, Manfred seemed to give up life. He was like a shell of a man not ever participating in the freer social scene. But perhaps now ... it was interesting ... He suspected as much, which was why he had gone across the street to check the log. There was very little that escaped Dietrich von Rheinhardt's attention.

'Von Tripp?'

'Yes, sir?' Manfred looked up with surprise. He hadn't seen the captain come in. What's more, he hadn't seen him go out half an hour before. He had been busy across the hall, looking for some files that someone had mislaid.

'I'd like to see you in my office, please.' Manfred followed him with an uneasy feeling. The senior officer wasted no time. 'Manfred, I happened to take a look at that logbook across the street.' But they both knew that the captain never 'happened' to do anything.

'Oh?'

'Yes, "oh." You have her?' It was impossible to read his face, but slowly Manfred nodded.

'Yes, I do.'

'May I ask why?'

'I wanted her, sir.' It was the kind of blunt answer Von Rheinhardt would easily understand.

'I can of course understand that, but were you aware that General Ritter wanted her, too?'

'No, sir.' Manfred felt his skin crawl. 'No, sir, I didn't know. Although we did meet him for a moment in the hall at the house in Grunewald yesterday. However, he gave no indication ...'

'All right, all right, never mind.' The two men eyed each other for a long time. 'I could make you give her up to Ritter, you know.'

'I hope you won't do that, sir.' It was the understatement of a lifetime, and for a long moment neither man spoke.

'I won't, Von Tripp.' And then after another moment, 'It's good to see you alive again.' He grinned broadly. 'It's nice to see you give a damn. I've been telling you for three years that was all you needed.'

'Yes, sir.' Manfred grinned convincingly, wanting to slap his commanding officer across the face. 'Thank you, sir.'

'Not at all.' And then he chuckled to himself. 'Serves Ritter right. He's the oldest man here and he always gets the youngest girls. Don't worry, I've got another one I'll send him. She should keep him happy for weeks.' He laughed raucously to himself and waved Manfred from the room.

So ... he had won her, and by the captain's grace in the end. He felt a long sigh escape him as he looked around the office and realised that it was time to go home.

'Lieutenant?' Her face peered into the hallway, her pretty golden hair looped gracefully on top of her head and her big blue eyes dancing out nervously to see that it was he.

'Good afternoon, Ariana.' He seemed unbearably formal as he gazed into the blue eyes while she stood before him with an anxious look on her face.

'Did ... was ...' She stumbled over the words with a look of terror, and instantly Manfred understood.

'It's all right. Everything's settled.'

'Were they very angry?' The huge blue eyes looked larger than ever as gently he shook his head. Every moment of the terror of the past month was etched in her eyes as she stood there. As brave as she had so often seemed to him, now she seemed like a tiny, defenceless child.

'I told you, it's all right. You'll be safe here now.' She wanted to ask him for how long, but she didn't dare. Instead she only nodded.

'Thank you.' And then, 'Would you like a cup of tea?'

'Yes.' He paused for a moment. 'If you'll have one, too.' She nodded silently and disappeared into the kitchen. She was back a few moments later with a tray and two steaming cups with the precious brew. For her, it was one of the greatest luxuries in his household, after her month in the cell. Being able to be clean again, and to drink tea again. She had actually dared to drink a cup by herself that afternoon as she wandered aimlessly around his living room, glancing at the books and thinking of her father and Gerhard once again. She could barely keep her mind from them. And the ache of worry and sorrow still showed in her eyes. Manfred looked at her gently as she set down his cup. There was so little he could say to her. He knew only too well what it was to cope with the burden of loss. He sighed quietly and picked up one of his pipes as they sat down. 'What did you do today, fräulein?'

She shook her head slowly. 'I ... nothing ... I ... looked at some of your books.' It made him think of the splendid library he had seen in her home the day before, and long before in his own. Thinking back to that made him decide to take the bull by the horns. His eyes carefully sought hers as he lit the pipe.

'It's a beautiful home, fräulein.' She knew instantly which home he meant.

'Thank you.'

'And one day it will be yours again. The war cannot go on forever.' He put the pipe down and his heart reached out to her through his eyes. 'My parents' home was taken over, too.'

'Was it?' There was a flicker of interest in her face. 'Where was it, Lieutenant?'

The sadness came back to his eyes as he answered. 'Outside Dresden.' He instantly read the question in her eyes. 'It wasn't touched by the bombings.' The schloss wasn't ... but everything else was ... everyone else ... everyone ... the children, Theodor and Tatianna ... Marianna, his wife ... his parents, his sister, all of them ... gone. Just like her father and brother. Just as certainly. Forever.

'How lucky for you.' He looked up, startled by her words, and then remembered that they had been speaking of the schloss.

'Yes.'

'And your family?'

He drew a sharp breath. 'Not as lucky, I'm afraid.' She waited, the silence growing heavy between them. 'My children ... my ... wife ... and my parents ... were all in the city.' He stood up and walked to the fireplace. All she could see now was his back. 'They were all killed.'

Her voice was a gentle whisper. 'I'm so sorry.'

He turned to face her then. 'No more so than I am for you, fräulein.' He stood there for a long moment, and their eyes met and held.

'Has ...' She could hardly bring herself to ask him, but she had to know. 'Has there been some news?'

He shook his head slowly. It was time she faced the truth. He had sensed that somewhere in her heart, in her mind, she had refused to face it all along. 'Your father, fräulein, I don't think he just left you ... forgot you. From what I have heard, he was not that kind of man.'

She shook her head slowly. 'No, I know that. Something must have happened to them.' And then she looked up at him defiantly. 'I will find them after ... after the war.'

He looked at her sorrowfully and there was a dampness in his eyes. 'I don't think so, fräulein. I think you should understand that now. Hope, false hope, can be a very cruel thing.'

'Then you've heard?' Her heart raced as she stood there.

'I've heard nothing. But ... my God, think of it. He left to keep the boy from the army, didn't he?' She said nothing. Maybe this was just a cruel trick, to finally get her to betray her father. And she wouldn't. Not even to this man she had almost come to trust. 'All right, don't tell me. But it's what I assume.' And then he shocked her. 'It's what I would have done. What any sane man would have done to save his son. But he must have been planning to come back for you, Ariana. And the only thing that could have kept him from it was his own death. His and the boy's. There's no way they could have got into Switzerland, no way he could have got back. I'm sure that the border patrol got them. They must have.'

'But wouldn't I have heard?' There were tears on her cheek now, rolling slowly down towards her chin as she listened to his words, and her voice was only a whisper when she spoke.

'Not necessarily. They're not exactly the most refined troops we've got out there. If they killed them, and they must have, they would simply have disposed of them. I ...' He looked embarrassed for a moment. 'I already tried to find out. But no one told me anything, fräulein. I think, though, that you must face what happened. They're gone. They must be dead.'

She turned slowly away from him, her head bowed, her shoulder shaking, and on quiet feet he left the room. A moment later she heard his bedroom door close. She stood there, sobbing softly, and at last she lay on the couch and let herself cry. It was the first time since the whole nightmare had happened that she had truly let herself go. And when it was over, she felt numb.

She didn't see Manfred again until the next morning, and when she did, she avoided his eyes. She didn't want to see his pity, his compassion, his own sorrow – it was all she could do to cope with her own.

Often in the next few weeks, Ariana would see him looking at the photographs of the children, and she would feel an ache rise in her own heart as she watched him, thinking of Gerhard and her father, knowing that she would never see them again. And now, as she sat in the living room all afternoon alone, the smiling faces of Manfred's children haunted her, as though they reproached her for being there with their father, when they could be with him no more.

Sometimes she resented them for staring at her, the one with pigtails and white satin bows, the other with such straight blond hair and big blue eyes looking out at her above a smattering of boyish freckles ... Theodor ... But what she resented most about them was that they made the lieutenant human, they made him seem somehow more real. And she didn't want him to be. She didn't want to know about him, or care about him. Despite what he had said when he brought her to Wannsee, he was in a sense her jailer. She didn't want to see him in any other light. She didn't want to know of his dreams or hopes or sorrows, any more than she wanted to tell him of her own. He had no right to know how deeply she felt her grief. He had already seen too much of her life, of her pain and vulnerability. He had seen her at Hildebrand's mercy in the cell at the Reichstag, he had seen her last anguished moments in her own home. He had seen too much, and he had no right to. No one did. She would share no part of herself with anyone ever again. Manfred von Tripp sensed this in her, as he sat silently staring into the fire night after night, smoking his pipe and saying little to Ariana as she sat politely by, lost in her own thoughts, behind a wall of her own pain.

She had been in his house for three weeks when he turned to her suddenly one evening and took her by surprise as he stood up and put down his pipe. 'Would you like to go for a walk, fräulein?'

'Now?' She looked startled and a little bit afraid. Was it a trap? Where was he taking her, and why? The look in her eyes pained him, as he understood all too quickly how great was her fear and her mistrust, still, after all these uneventful days. But it would take a lifetime to blot out the memory of those days in the bowels of the Reichstag. Just as it would take him a lifetime to forget what he'd seen when he'd gone back to Dresden to comb through the ruins of his house ... the dolls lying torn under beams and broken plaster, the twisted silver ornaments of which Marianna had been so proud ... now melted and tarnished ... like her jewellery ... like their dreams. Manfred forced his thoughts back into the present as he looked down into the frightened blue eyes.

'Wouldn't you like some exercise?' He knew that she had never ventured beyond his garden in the weeks that she'd been there. She was still afraid.

'What if there's an air raid?'

'We'll run to the nearest shelter. You don't have to worry. You'll be safe with me.' She felt foolish arguing with the deep, calm voice and the gentle eyes, and slowly she nodded. It would be her first turn out in the world in two months. For a month she'd been in jail, and for almost that long now she'd been in Wannsee, too frightened to stir more than a few feet outside the house. She was haunted by all kinds of terrors, and tonight for the first time Manfred understood to what extent she was afraid. He watched her put her coat on and nodded quietly. Ariana didn't know it, but it was the look he had used on Tatianna, his daughter, when he knew that she was afraid. 'It's all right. The air will do us both good.' All evening he had been warring with his own thoughts.

It had been happening more and more now. Not just the thoughts of the
children or his parents or his wife ... but there were other thoughts now ...
thoughts of Ariana, which had begun to taunt him weeks before. 'Ready?' She
nodded silently, her eyes wide, and as they stepped out into the cool evening,
he slipped her small gloved hand into the crook of his arm. He pretended not to
notice that she absentmindedly clutched his sleeve tightly as they walked
along.

'It's lovely, isn't it?' She glanced up at the sky and smiled again. Her smile
was so rare and so beautiful, it made him smile, too.

'Yes, it is. And you see, no air raid.' But half an hour later, as they had begun
to head back towards his house, the sirens started and people began to rush
from their houses to the shelters nearby. At the first sound of the sirens,
Manfred put an arm around her shoulders and ran towards the shelter with the
others.

Ariana ran with him but in her heart she didn't really care if she was safe or
not. There was nothing for her to live for.

In the shelter there were women crying, babies screaming, and children
playing as they always did. It was always the grown-ups who were frightened.
The children had grown up with this war. One of them was yawning, and two
others were singing a silly song as the shrieking above them continued and in
the distance they heard bombs. Through it all, Manfred watched Ariana, her
face quiet, her eyes sad; and without thinking, he reached out and took her
hand. She said nothing, she only sat there, holding the big smooth hand in her
own and watching those around her, wondering what they lived for, why they
went on.

'I think it's safe now, fräulein.' He still called her that most of the time. He
stood up and she followed him, and they walked rapidly home. It was a
different kind of walk than it had been earlier that evening. He wanted to get
her home again where she was safe. As they walked into the front hallway,
they stood there for a moment, silent, staring at each other, something new and
different in their eyes. But Manfred only nodded and then turned and walked
up the stairs.

Chapter 20

Ariana was standing on a chair in the kitchen when he came home the next
evening, trying desperately to reach a canister that had been put away on a high
shelf. And as he wandered down the hall and saw her, he went quickly to her
side and reached it, handing it to her, and then unthinkingly put his hands

around her waist and lifted her down from the chair. She blushed slightly and thanked him, and then went to make him his usual cup of tea. But it was as though she sensed something different now, too. Some current of electricity that had not been there before, or that had been, but that had lain dormant between these two troubled people who had so much on their minds. This time when she handed him his teacup she had forgotten the sugar and she blushed again as she turned away.

They were both quiet and strained at dinner, and afterwards he suggested another walk. This time everything went smoothly, and there were no air raids until later that night. They both awoke quickly, but too late to flee – they had to take refuge in the cellar, bundled into bathrobes and wearing heavy shoes. Manfred kept a suitcase in the cellar with a change of clothes, in case he had to leave in a hurry, but he realised as he sat there that he had never asked Ariana to bring down some of her things. He suggested it to her now, and she shrugged softly in the light of his pipe. There were pieces of black cloth on the windows, so no one could have seen the tiny speck of light as he smoked. He was puzzled by her gesture, and then he understood.

'Don't you care, Ariana, about surviving?'

Slowly she shook her head. 'Why should I?'

'Because you're still so young. You will build your whole life. When all of this is over, you will have everything ahead of you.' She looked unconvinced.

'Do you care so much?' She had seen the look in his eyes when he looked at those pictures of his children and his wife. 'Does surviving mean so much to you?'

'It means more now than it did.' His voice was oddly soft. 'And in time it will mean more to you again, too.'

'Why? What does any of it matter now? This will never end.' Together they listened to the distant bombs. But she didn't seem afraid, only desperately sad. She wanted the bombs to kill all the Nazis, and then she would be free – or dead.

'It will end one day soon, Ariana. I promise you.' His voice was so soft as they sat in the dark, and as he had the night before, he reached silently for her hand. But this time when he took it, she felt a stirring in her body. He held it for a long time and then she felt him slowly pulling her towards him. She felt unable to resist the gentle motion, and unwilling to push him away. As though it had been what she had always wanted, she felt herself enveloped in the powerful arms, and she felt his mouth come down slowly on hers. The sounds of the bombs in the distance faded, and all she could hear was the pounding in her ears as he held her and kissed her and stroked her, and then breathlessly she pulled away. There was a brief awkward silence and then he sighed. 'I'm sorry ... I'm so sorry, Ariana ... I shouldn't – ' But this time it was Manfred who was astonished as she silenced him with a kiss and then let herself quietly out of the cellar and went upstairs to her room. The next morning neither of them made any mention of what had happened the night before. But each day now there was a drawing closer, a still greater attraction that each found more and more difficult to resist, until at last one morning she awoke to find him standing in her room.

'Manfred?' She looked at him sleepily, unaware that for the first time she had called him by his first name. 'Is something wrong?' Slowly he shook his head and walked towards the bed. He was wearing blue silk pyjamas beneath a dark blue silk robe. For a long instant she wasn't sure what he wanted, and then slowly she understood. She wasn't sure what to say to him as he stood there, but she knew as she looked at him that she wanted this man desperately. She had fallen in love with her captor, Lieutenant Manfred von Tripp. But as he gazed down at her, hungrily, sadly, he realised that he had made a terrible mistake, and before she could say anything he turned away and hurried towards the door. 'Manfred ... what are you doing ... where – '

He turned to look at her. 'I'm sorry ... I shouldn't have ... I don't know what ...' But she held out her arms to him. Not the arms of a child, the arms of a woman. And he turned slowly to face her and walked towards her with a gentle smile and shook his head. 'No, Ariana ... you're only a child. I ... I don't know what happened. I was lying in bed thinking of you for hours and ... I think for a moment I lost my mind.' She slipped quietly from her bed then and stood there, waiting for him to come to her, waiting for him to understand. He looked at her with an air of amazement as she stood there, wearing a white flannel nightgown and a small smile. 'Ariana?' He couldn't believe what he saw in her eyes. 'Darling? ...' It was the merest whisper as he came to her and swept her into his arms, and her mouth found his and she nestled softly into his arms.

'I love you, Manfred.' She hadn't even known until then that she meant that, but as he held her next to his wildly pounding heart, she knew that she did. And moments later they lay together, and he took her with the tenderness of a man very much in love. He loved her expertly and gently and again and again.

It went on like that until Christmas, as Manfred and Ariana revelled in their private world. Ariana spent all day around the house and in the garden, tidying up and reading, and in the evenings they ate quiet dinners and then stretched out for a little while by the fire, but they went upstairs far more quickly now that there was the lure of the wonders Manfred was teaching Ariana in bed. It was a deep romantic love they shared, and in spite of the loss of her father and Gerhard, Ariana had never been so happy in her life. As for Manfred, he had come back to the land of the living with zest and joy and humour. Those who had known him since the death of his children couldn't quite believe that he was the same man. But for the past two months he and Ariana had been infinitely happy, and now only the threat of Christmas worried both of them a little bit, with ghosts from past lives, past years, no longer around them to share in the young couple's new-found joy.

'Well, what are we going to do about Christmas? I don't want either of us to sit around here and get depressed thinking about what isn't anymore.' Manfred eyed her sagely over their morning tea, which they now shared in bed. It had been his turn to bring the tray up that morning. 'Instead I wanted to celebrate what we've got this Christmas, not cry about what we don't. Speaking of which, what do you want for Christmas?' It was still two weeks away, and the weather had been crisp and icy for the past week.

She smiled at him now from her pillows, the look in her eyes a caress. 'You know what I want for Christmas, Manfred?'

'What, my darling?' He could barely keep his hands off her when she looked like that, the golden hair spread around her like a sheet of spun gold, the delicate breasts bare, the look in her eyes one of invitation and loving.

'I want a baby. Your baby.' For an instant he was quiet.

It was something he had thought of more than once.

'Do you mean that, Ariana?' But she was still so young. So much could change. And after the war ... He didn't like to think about it anymore, but it could be that when she no longer had to live under his protection, maybe then someone younger would come along and ... He hated the thought.

But she was looking at him seriously. 'I mean it, my darling. I'd like nothing more than our son.'

He held her tightly for a long moment, unable to speak. It was what he wanted one day. But not yet. Not in these ghastly times. 'Ariana, my darling, I promise you that' – he pulled away to look at her gently – 'when the war is over, we will have a baby. You'll have your gift of a son.'

'Is that a promise?' She smiled happily at him.

'A solemn promise.'

She held tightly to him and laughed the silvery laugh that he loved so much. 'Then I don't want anything else for Christmas. That's all I want in the world.'

'But you can't have that yet.' Her joy was infectious and he was laughing now, too. 'Isn't there something else you'd like as well?'

'No. Except one thing.' She glimmered at him happily.

'What's that?' But she was embarrassed to say it. Talking about having a baby was one thing, but asking a man to get married just wasn't done. So instead she hemmed and hawed and teased and wouldn't answer, and he threatened to get it out of her by that night. But Manfred had his own ideas in that direction. He desperately wanted to marry Ariana, but he wanted to wait until the country was once more at peace. The war couldn't last forever, and it would have meant a lot to him to get married at his family's schloss.

But he had another idea about Christmas, and when Christmas morning came, there were half a dozen boxes under the tree. One was a sweater Ariana had knitted for Manfred, another was a series of poems she had written him and rolled up in a scroll. And third was a box of his favourite cookies, which she had struggled over for several mornings and finally got just the way he loved. Lebkuchen, for Christmas, in all the traditional shapes, some chocolate covered, some not, with little brightly coloured sugar decorations sprinkled on them. He was touched to the core when he saw how hard she had worked.

Manfred's gifts to Ariana were a little less homegrown, and she rattled all the boxes with anticipation and glee.

'What should I open first?'

'The big one.' In fact, he had two other big ones hidden in the closet down the hall, but he hadn't wanted to overwhelm her all at once. The first package she opened held a beautiful ice-coloured blue dress, which hung from her shoulders and danced softly over her bare skin. It was a halter neck with a low

V in the back, and after her winter of rugged skirts, sturdy shoes, and heavy sweaters, Ariana squealed with delight over the beautiful dress.

'Oh, Manfred, I'll wear it tonight to dinner!' Little did she know that that was more or less what he had in mind. The second package yielded a pretty aquamarine necklace to go with it, and the third a pair of absolutely perfect silver evening shoes. Draped in all her finery, Ariana lay across their bed, swilling tea like champagne and singing in a throaty baritone. Manfred laughed happily at her as he went to collect the rest of the boxes, which yielded a white cashmere dress that was a far cry from what she had been wearing, and a simple black wool that was easily worthy of the wardrobe she had had before. He had bought her a pair of plain black pumps, a black alligator bag, and a perfectly simple black wool coat that she slid into with delight, trying on one outfit after the other. 'Oh, I'm going to be so elegant, Manfred!' She hugged him fervently and they both laughed again.

'You already are elegant!' She was wearing the aquamarine necklace, the silver sandals, and the new black coat over white lace underwear. 'In fact, I'd say you look sensational! But there's one thing missing ...' He began fishing in the pocket of his bathrobe for his last gift to her, this one hidden in a very small box. He tossed it into her open hands and sat back against the headboard with a grin.

'What is it?'

'Open it and see.'

She opened it slowly and carefully, and when the box lay open in her hand, there was the joy of one who is loved in her eyes. It was a very handsome engagement ring from Louis Werner on the Kurfustendamm. 'Oh, Manfred, you're crazy!'

'Am I? Somehow I thought that if eventually you wanted to have a baby, it might be a nice touch if somewhere along the way we got engaged.'

'Oh, Manfred, it's so lovely!'

'And so are you.' He slipped the round diamond on to her finger and she lay there grinning at it in the wild costume she had put together from the mountain of gifts he had just bestowed on her.

She propped herself up on one elbow as they sat there. 'I wish we could go out so I could show off all pretty things.' But it was said pensively, without any great urgency. For the past three months they had been content just to go for walks or strolls around Wannsee or one of the other small lakes. They went to an occasional restaurant for lunch, but in effect they had lived like hermits, and they were both happier with each other at home. But he had bought her such pretty things to wear that all of a sudden she was tempted to step out into the world again.

'Would you really like that?' He looked cautious.

She nodded excitedly. 'I would.'

'There's a ball tonight, you know, Ariana.'

'Where?' In fact, there were several. Dietrich von Rheinhardt was having a party, as was General Ritter in her father's old house; then there was one at headquarters, and there were two other big parties being given by the brass. They could have gone to any of the parties they wanted to. Only Ritter's was one Manfred was anxious to avoid. But other than that one, Manfred relayed the list to her and they chose three. 'I'll wear my new blue dress and my necklace ... and my engagement ring.' She grinned at him ecstatically, and then suddenly she remembered something she had never showed him before.

'Manfred?' She looked at him hesitantly.

'What, my love?' Her face had grown serious so rapidly that he wasn't sure what to think. 'Is something wrong?'

'Would you be angry if I showed you something?' He grinned at the question.

'I won't know until you show me.'

'But what if you're angry?'

'I'll control myself.' She went to the room that had been her old room and returned with her father's book. 'You're going to read me Shakespeare now? – On Christmas morning?' He sank back into their bed with a groan.

'No, be serious, Manfred. Listen to me ... I have something to show you. Remember the day you took me to Grunewald, and I got Papa's book. Well, the night my father left with Gerhard and ...' For a moment her eyes were sad, her thoughts turned inwards. She had long ago told him everything, and holding the book in her hand, she went on. 'My father left me these, in case I should ever need them, if something went wrong. They were my mother's.' Without further ado, she flipped open the secret compartment and revealed the two rings, the diamond signet and the emerald. She hadn't dared to include the tiny gun her father had given her. When she had removed the book, she had quietly pushed the gun to the back of the shelf. To have been caught concealing a weapon would have meant instant death. But the rings were her treasures – all she had left. Not expecting what she was about to show him, Manfred gasped.

'My God, Ariana.' And then, 'Does anyone know you have these?' But of course no one did. She shook her head. 'They must be worth a fortune.'

'I don't know. Papa said they might help if I had to sell them.'

'Ariana, I want you to hide the book again. If something ever goes wrong, if the war ends and we do not win, those rings could buy your life someday, or get you somewhere where you could be free.'

'You make it sound like you're going to desert me.' Her eyes looked large and sad.

'Of course not, but anything could happen. We could get separated for a time.' Or he could get killed, but he didn't want to remind her of that on Christmas morning. 'You just hold on to them. And as long as you're so good at keeping secrets, Fräulein von Gotthard – ' he looked at her mock reproachfully – 'I think you should be aware of this.' Without explaining further, he pulled out a drawer and behind it showed Ariana where he had concealed money and a small, efficient-looking gun. 'Should you ever need that, Ariana, you know it's there. Do you want to put the rings there with it?' She nodded and they put her mother's rings away, and she sat gazing happily again at her own. As of Christmas morning, 1944, Ariana Alexandra von Gotthard had become engaged to Lieutenant Manfred Robert von Tripp.

Chapter 21

Their evening began at the Opera House on the broad boulevard Ariana loved so much, Unter den Linden, it's graceful tree-lined expanse interrupted only by the Brandenburg Gate, which lay directly ahead.

Manfred watched with pleasure as she alighted from the car, the pale blue dress hanging from her body like a single sheet of ice, the aquamarines dancing from her neck. It was the first time in months that Ariana had worn clothes that even faintly resembled her old ones, and for just one evening it was lovely to forget the tragedies of the past year.

She clung to him tightly as they made their way through a sea of uniforms, to those of highest rank, to whom Manfred had to pay homage before they joined the others to enjoy the ball. Manfred introduced her sombrely to two generals, several captains, and a handful of colonels whom he knew, each time making a formal introduction as Ariana stood very still, her head held high, her hand outstretched. She would have done any man honour, and Manfred's heart swelled with pride as he watched how poised she was. This was her first time under the scrutiny of half the senior officers of the Reich. Captive princess that she was, they were all a little bit intrigued, and she knew it. Only Manfred knew how frightened she was at the beginning of the evening, as he felt her hand tremble in his, leading her out on to the dance floor to waltz.

'It's all right, darling, you're always safe with me.' He smiled down at her gently and her chin went up just a little higher than before.

'I feel as though they're all staring at me.'

'Only because you look so lovely, Ariana.' But she knew even as she danced with him that she would never feel completely safe again. They could do anything, these people, take her home from her again, kill Manfred, lock her in a cell. But it was absurd to think that way – it was Christmas, and she and Manfred were dancing – and then suddenly, as they whirled around the floor, she remembered and her eyes laughed again as she looked into his.

'Do you know, I came to my first ball here! With my father.' Her eyes glowed, remembering the evening that she had come here, so excited and so filled with awe.

'Aha, should I be jealous, fräulein?'

'Hardly. I was only sixteen.' She looked at him imperiously and he laughed.

'Of course, how foolish of me, Ariana. You're so much older now.' But she was in many ways. She was a lifetime older than the girl who only three years before had danced in this same ballroom, in her layers of white organdy with flowers in her hair. It seemed a thousand years before. And as she thought of it dreamily, someone took their picture. She jumped in surprise and looking, blinking, into his eyes.

'What was that?'

'They took our picture, Ariana. Is that all right?' It was customary to collect dozens of photographs of the officers and their ladies, at each party, every ball. They ran them in the papers, put them up in the officers' clubs, had copies made for relatives. 'Do you mind, Ariana?' For a moment disappointment filled his eyes. Six months before he would have been livid to have his photograph taken with any woman, but now he wanted a photograph of them, as though seeing their faces before him on paper would make it all seem more real. She understood the look in his eyes quickly and inclined her head with a small smile.

'Of course it's all right. I was just surprised. Will I be able to see the pictures?' He nodded and she smiled.

They stayed at the Opera House for over an hour, and then, looking at his watch, he whispered in her ear and went to fetch her wrap. This had been only the first stop of the evening, and the more important stop on their agenda was yet to come. He had wanted to get her accustomed to the sea of uniforms around her, the curious stares, the flashbulbs sending little black dots dancing before her eyes, because at the next stop she would be even more closely watched. As his fiancé she would pass under considerable scrutiny, and he suspected also that the Führer would be there.

When they drove up to the Royal Palace, Manfred immediately spotted Hitler's black 500 K Mercedes. There were dozens of special guards surrounding the palace, and once inside in the splendorous, mirrored gilt and inlay of the old Throne Room, Manfred felt Ariana tighten her grip on his arm. He patted her small hand gently and looked down at her with a warm smile. One by one he made the necessary introductions, wandering slowly through the lines of uniforms, introducing her to the generals and their wives or their mistresses. Watching her incline her head very slightly and hold out the graceful little hand, he felt his heart swell. Until at last they reached a face that was familiar, and General Ritter clutched the delicate young hand.

'Ah, Fräulein von Gotthard ... what a pleasant surprise.' He cast a look of jubilation at her, and then a glance of brief disapproval at Manfred at her side. 'Lieutenant.' Manfred clicked his heels and bowed. 'Would you care to join us later, fräulein? There will be a small supper at my house.' 'His' house. Manfred saw her eyes begin to dance with anger, and he only tightened his pressure on her left hand and then smoothly tucked it into his arm so that the general could easily see the diamond ring.

'I regret, General – ' Manfred's voice was all sugar and cream – 'my fiancée and I have an earlier commitment for this evening, but perhaps – ' he spoke reverently with a hopeful smile – 'another time?'

'Of course, Lieutenant. And ... your fiancée, did you say?' He asked the question of Manfred, but his eyes never left Ariana's as he spoke. She could feel the man's eyes almost undressing her, it made her skin crawl as she pretended not to notice.

But this time Ariana spoke before Manfred, her eyes cast deep into the general's, her tone polite but cold. 'Yes, we are engaged now, General.'

'How nice.' His lip curled. 'Your father would be very pleased.' *Not nearly as pleased as he would be to have you in his house, dear General ... filthy bastard ...* She wanted to hit him as she stood smiling into the repulsive face. 'May I offer my congratulations?' Manfred bowed again, and Ariana nodded demurely before they wandered off.

'I though we handled that rather nicely.' Ariana looked up at Manfred with a small smile.

'We did, did we?' He was amused and, at the same time, madly in love with her. It was lovely taking her out. 'Are you enjoying yourself at all, Ariana?' He looked down at her with concern, his own pride at being with her showing in his eyes.

She returned the look of pleasure and nodded. 'Yes, I am.'

'Good. Then on Monday we're going shopping.'

'Good God, for what? You gave me three dresses and a coat this morning ... and a necklace ... and shoes and an engagement ring.' She ticked it all off on her fingers like a child.

'Never you mind, fräulein. I think it's time that you and I started getting out.' But no sooner had he said it than an odd hush fell over the room, and in the distance they could hear the bombs. Even on Christmas night the war was with them, and he found himself wondering which lovely monument, which home, whose children, had just been destroyed. But they stopped quickly, and no one had to flee to the shelter beneath the building, and the music played on. And they all went on pretending that this was like any other Christmas night. But the Grosses Schauspielhaus had recently been destroyed, and there were other buildings and churches that disappeared now almost every day. For almost a year now many Berliners had gone to bed fully dressed, with suitcases standing next to their beds, ready for a quick trip to the shelters where many of them spent almost every night. The Allies weren't going to let up now, and it frightened Manfred terribly. What if Berlin were another Dresden? What if something should happen to Ariana, too, before the end of the war? But at his side she instantly sensed his feelings, and she reached quickly for his hand, holding it tightly in her own, her deep, lovely blue eyes reaching up towards his to reassure him, her mouth so sensual and gentle. Looking down at her, he could only smile.

'Don't worry, Manfred. Everything will be all right.'

He smiled slowly, looking at her. 'On Monday we go shopping.'

'All right, if that will make you feel better.' And then she stood up on tiptoe and whispered in his ear. 'Now can we go home?'

'Already?' At first he looked surprised and then he grinned, whispered back to his little princess. 'Have you no shame, fräulein?'

'None at all. I'd much rather be home with you than waiting here to see the Führer.' But he put a finger on his lips.

As it turned out, they saw him anyway. He swept into the room surrounded by his henchmen just before they left, a small man with his dark hair and moustache and unprepossessing looks, yet a current of electricity shot through the entire room. Ariana could feel bodies tighten, voices rise, and suddenly there was a wild chanting of Hail to the Führer, and she watched in astonishment as the crowd of men in uniform and women in evening clothes went wild. She and Manfred stayed until the frenzy ended and the crowd had settled down to their entertainment once again, and then slowly they wended their way through the crowd. It was near the doorway that someone touched her, just a quick touch on her arm, and as she turned, she saw Manfred suddenly and ferociously at attention, his right arm held aloft. And she saw then it was Hitler who had touched her, and now he smiled benignly and moved on, as though he had bestowed a blessing. Then, quickly, she and Manfred left. For a long moment they said nothing, and then at last in his car again, she spoke. 'Manfred, they almost went crazy.'

He nodded quietly. 'I know. They always do.' And then he turned to her. 'Have you never seen him before in person?'

She shook her head. 'No, Papa didn't want me involved in all that.' And then she regretted saying it – perhaps Manfred would take it as a reproach of him. But he nodded quickly. He understood.

'He was right. And your brother?'

'He kept him out of it as much as he could. But I think he was afraid in a different way for me.'

'And very rightly.' He drove on for a minute and then turned back to Ariana again. 'Do you know what they're doing at that party at General Ritter's tonight? They're having beauty dancers and transvestites to entertain the guests. Hildebrand tells me that's a regular feature with him.' A look of disgust crossed his face.

'What are beauty dancers and tranvestites?' She sat back with the wide, curious eyes of a child and Manfred grinned.

'Oh, my darling innocent, I love you.' At moments like that he remembered that she was only five years older than his oldest child would have been. 'A beauty dancer is a naked woman who dances in suggestive ways to entertain, and a transvestite is a man masquerading as a woman, usually in evening clothes. They dance and sing, and can also be quite suggestive.'

But Ariana was laughing as she watched his face. 'Aren't they terribly funny?'

He shrugged. 'Sometimes, but generally not. Ritter doesn't have the 'funny' ones, he has the good ones. And when they're all finished performing, everyone ...' Suddenly he remembered that it was she he was talking to. 'Never mind, Ariana. It's all rather disgusting entertainment. I don't want you involved in that.' And there was more and more of it lately. Not just at Ritter's house in Grunewald; the others were all indulging the same whims. As though with each day, with the war around them worsening, they had to indulge their most outrageous fantasies and go to more and more indecent lengths. This was not what he wanted to introduce her to now. But having taken her out that night, he had been reminded of the pleasure of going out into the world with a pretty woman on one's arm, strolling in the midst of admiring glances, seeing her shine in a special kind of way. It made their seclusion in the house in Wannsee still more precious, yet he suddenly liked the idea of going out with her as well.

'You're not disappointed to miss the other parties tonight, Manfred?' Happily, he shook his head.

'There was one at the Summer Palace in Charlottenburg that might have been nice. But actually, there's a much nicer party I know about in Wannsee.' He looked at her lovingly and they both smiled.

They made their way upstairs quickly and fell happily into each other's arms in the large comfortable bed.

The next morning at breakfast Ariana was pensive and Manfred gazed at her quietly. It was Sunday and he didn't have to go to work. This was Hildebrand's Sunday on.

They went for a long walk in the Tiergarten. He induced her to try ice skates on the Neuer See, and together they glided around the ice like smiling children among the pretty women and the men in uniforms. It was difficult to believe that they were still at war.

Afterwards he drove her to a café on the Kurfürstendamm, which always looked to Ariana almost exactly like the Champs-Élysées in Paris, where she had gone before the war with Gerhard and her father on a brief trip. On the Kurfürstendamm they sat down amidst the few artists and writers who were still left in Berlin. There were many men in uniform, but the atmosphere was genial and Ariana stifled a happy yawn as they sat in the cosy café.

'Tired, darling?' He smiled at her, when suddenly in the distance they could hear the screech and wail of bombs. They left and walked quickly back to the car.

As they drove back along the Kurfurstendamm on their way to Wannsee, Ariana moved closer to him and tucked a hand into his arm.

'Do you see that church, Manfred?' She pointed and for an instant he took his eyes from the road. It was the familiar Kaiser Wilhelm Memorial Church on the Kurfïstendamm.

'Yes? Are you feeling religious at this time of night?' He was teasing and they both smiled.

'I just wanted to let you know that is the church where I want to marry you one day.'

'At the Kaiser Wilhelm?'

'Yes.' She glanced again at the pretty little diamond ring.

And he gently put an arm around her houlders. 'I'll remember that, my love. Happy?' He looked over at her in the dark. The bombs had stopped, at least for a while.

'Never happier in my life.'

And when they got the photographs of the Christmas Eve balls, it was easy to see that she was telling Manfred the truth when she said she was happy. Her face beamed out at the camera, her head held high, her eyes bright with love, as just behind her Manfred, in full dress uniform, gazed into the camera with undisguisable pride.

Chapter 22

At the end of Christmas week, at Manfred's insistence they went shopping in downtown Berlin at Grunefeld's. He had to buy her more clothes. Captain von Rheinhardt was pressing him to come out of hiding to rejoin his comrades of the Reich.

'Was he angry, Manfred?' She looked concerned as they drove downtown, but Manfred only patted her hand and smiled.

'No, but I suppose I've got away with being a hermit for as long as I'm going to. We don't have to go out every night, but we should start accepting a few invitations to dinner. Think you can stand it?'

'Sure. Can we go and see General Ritter's transvestites?' She looked mischievous and he couldn't suppress a laugh.

'Ariana, really!'

They staggered out of the store three hours later, so burdened by a stack of boxes, they could hardly get to Manfred's car. Another coat, a little jacket, half a dozen lovely wool dresses, three cocktail dresses and a ballgown, and a divine little dinner suit that looked like a man's tuxedo, except that instead of trousers there was a long narrow skirt with a slit up one side. And in honour of her mother's memory there was also a long, slinky dress in gold lamé.

'My God, Manfred, where am I going to wear it all?' He had spoiled her rotten. He felt as though he had a wife again, a woman to spoil and cherish, to dress and protect and amuse. They were in no way strangers to each other, and she was more at ease with Manfred than she had ever been with anyone in her whole life.

She had many places to wear the clothes. They went to several concerts at Philharmonic Hall, an official reception at the Reichstag for the Parliament and favoured officers stationed in Berlin; there was a party at Bellevue Castle and several small dinners near them in Wannsee, where other officers had sought quieter quarters than they would have found in the heart of town. Little by little, Manfred and Ariana became an accepted couple, and it was understood by everyone that they would marry after the war.

'Why wait, for God's sake, Manfred? Why not do it now?' A fellow lieutenant took Manfred aside at a dinner party one night.

But Manfred only sighed and stared down at the simple gold signet ring that he wore on his left hand. 'Because she's so young, Johann; she's really only a child.' He sighed again. 'And these are special times. She should have the opportunity to make that decision in normal times.' And then, shaking his head slowly, 'If we ever see normal times again.'

'You're right, Manfred. Times are not good. For that reason I think you'd be all the wiser to marry Ariana now.' He lowered his voice conspiratorially. 'We can't hold out forever, Manfred.'

'The Americans?'

Johann shook his head. 'I'm a lot more worried about the Russians. If they get here first, we're dead. God knows what they'll do to us, and if we even survive it, they may ship us all off to camps. But you may have some slim chance of staying together if you're married. Also, practically, the Americans may be nicer to her if she's the legitimate wife of a German army lieutenant instead of a concubine.'

'You think it's that close?'

There was a moment's silence as Johann averted his eyes. 'I think it might be, Manfred. I think even those closest to the Führer think so, too.'

'How much longer do you think we can hold out?'

The other man shrugged. 'Two months ... three ... if a miracle happens, maybe four. But it's almost over. Germany will never again be what you and I have known her to be.' Manfred nodded slowly – in his eyes she had not been for a long time the country he had once loved. Perhaps now, if the Allies didn't totally destroy her, she would have the opportunity to be reborn.

Over the next few days Manfred made discreet inquiries. Johann's information was borne out by everyone of influence whom Manfred knew. It was no longer a matter of if Berlin would fall, but when. Manfred realised he had to make plans.

Some questions in the right ears turned up the first item on his shopping list. He brought it home to Ariana two days later, and she squealed with glee.

'Manfred, I love it! But aren't you keeping your Mercedes?' It was an ugly grey Volkswagen, three years old now, but when it had been made in 1942, it had been one of the first. The man from whom he had bought it insisted that it was reliable and useful. It was just that he no longer needed it, having lost both his legs in an air raid the year before. Manfred did not tell Ariana the reason why the car had been up for sale. He simply nodded quietly and opened the door for her to get inside.

'Yes, I'm keeping my Mercedes.' And then after a moment, 'Ariana, this one is for you.'

They drove around the block, and he was satisfied that she could handle the little car fairly well. For a month now, he had been teaching her to drive his Mercedes, but this was a much easier car to drive. He was looking serious as they pulled back in front of their house. Ariana easily sensed his mood. Quietly she touched his hand.

'Manfred, why did you buy it?' She suspected the truth, but she wanted to know from him. Were they leaving? Were they going to run away?

He turned to her slowly with a look of pain and worry in his eyes. 'Ariana, I think the war will end soon, which will be a relief for us all.'

Before he could go on, he pulled her into his arms and held her tight. 'But before it ends, my darling, things may get very rough for us. Berlin may be taken. Hitler's army isn't going to let go easily. It isn't going to be another Anschluss, or like when we took over France. The Germans will fight to the death, and so will the Americans and the Russians ... This last bit may be one of the bloodiest battles of the war.'

'But we'll be safe here together, Manfred.' She didn't like it when he was afraid, and she could tell now that he was.

'Perhaps, perhaps not. But I don't want to take any chances. If anything happens, if the city falls and is occupied, if something happens to me, I want you to take this car and get out. Go as far as you can.' He said it with an iron determination and there was sudden horror in Ariana's eyes. 'And when you can't drive any more, leave it and start walking.'

'And leave you? Are you crazy? Where would I go?'

'Anywhere you can get to. The closest border. Maybe Alsace, and from there, you could make your way into France. You can tell the Americans you're Alsatian if you have to. They won't know the difference.'

'To hell with the Americans, Manfred. What about you?'

'I'll come and find you. After I've sorted things out here. I can't run, Ariana. I've got a duty to uphold. No matter what – I am an officer.'

But she shook her head emphatically, and then she reached out and clung to him, holding him more tightly than she ever had before. 'I'm not leaving you, Manfred. Never. I don't care if they kill me. I don't care if all of Berlin comes down around my ears, I'll never leave you. I'll stay with you until the end, and they can take us away together.'

'Don't be so dramatic.' He patted her gently and held her close. He knew that what he was saying was frightening her, but it had to be said. It had been three months since Christmas, and the situation had worsened considerably. The British and Canadians had reached the Rhine and the Americans were in Arbrucken. 'But as long as you're so determined not to leave me ...' He smiled down at her gently. He had decided to take Johann's advice. It was possible that for her safety it might make a difference, and for that reason he had decided not to waste any more time. 'As long as you are so hopelessly stubborn, young lady, and we seem to be in this together and for good – ' he grinned down at her – 'do you suppose that I could induce you to marry me?'

'Now?' She stared at him, shocked. She knew how strongly he felt about waiting, but as he nodded, she smiled, too. She didn't look any further for a reason than the look in his eyes.

'Yes, now. I'm tired of waiting to make you my wife.'

'Hurray!' She held him tight and pounded him happily on the back, then she pulled away again, her head tilted, her eyes bright and childlike, her mouth in a broad smile. 'Could we have a baby right away?'

But this time Manfred only laughed. 'Oh, Ariana, darling ... do you suppose that could wait just a few months until after the war? Or do you think I'll be too old to be a father by then? Is that why you're in such a hurry, little one?' He smiled down at her gently and she returned a smile in answer and shook her head.

'You'll never be too old, Manfred. Never.' And then, pulling him tightly into her arms again, she closed her eyes. 'I will always love you, my darling, for the rest of my life.'

'I will always love you, too.' He said the words, praying that they would both survive what lay ahead.

Chapter 23

Ten days later, on the first Saturday in April, Ariana walked slowly down the aisle of the little Maria Regina Kirche just off the Kürfurstendamm on the arm of Manfred Robert von Tripp. There was no one to give her away; there were no bridesmaids, no matron of honour. There was only Manfred and Ariana, and Johann, who had come to witness the event.

As she walked down the aisle of the lovely church towards the elderly priest waiting for them at the altar, Manfred could feel the light pressure of her hand on his arm. She had worn a simple white suit with broad shoulders that set of her own tiny frame. Her golden hair was swept up in a soft roll that framed her face, and she had artfully tucked in a soft cloud of veil behind the roll. She looked prettier than Manfred had ever seen her as she walked down the aisle. Miraculously, he had been able to find a number of white gardenias; she was wearing two on her lapel and one in her hair. Also, on this most special day, she was wearing her mother's intricate diamond signet ring on her right hand, as well as the engagement ring he'd given her on her left.

The wedding ring, which Manfred had bought her at Louis Werner's, was a narrow band of gold. At the end of the ceremony he slipped it on her finger and kissed her with an enormous feeling of relief. It was over, they had done it. Ariana was now Frau Manfred Robert von Tripp, and whatever happened to Berlin, that would offer her some protection. It was only now that it was over that he thought of his first wife, Marianna, who seemed so much older and stronger than this delicate girl. It was as though this were part of another lifetime. He felt bonded to Ariana as he had to none other, and as he looked into her eyes, he could see that she felt the same way.

'I love you, darling.' He said it to her softly as they got back into his car. She turned to him with a smile that lit her face from within, and she knew that they had never been happier as they waved to Johann and drove away towards the Kurfürstendamm in the direction of the restaurant where Manfred had promised to take her for their 'honeymoon' before going home. Ariana glanced back over her shoulder once at the church, just as they reached the Kurfürstendamm and turned. There was an enormous thundering and explosion all around them, and Ariana clutched in desperation and terror at Manfred's arm. She turned just in time to see the church explode in a million pieces behind them, and Manfred stomped hard on the gas, telling her to crouch on the floorboards lest debris from other buildings shatter the windshield and cut her face.

'Stay down, Ariana!' He was driving quickly and lurching terribly to avoid pedestrians and fire trucks streaking by. At first Ariana was too stunned even to react, but then, as she realised that they had escaped death by only moments, she softly began to cry. But they were almost in Charlottenburg before Manfred would pull over. And when he did, he reached down to her gently and pulled her into his arms. 'Oh, darling, I'm so sorry ...'

'Manfred ... we could have ... the church.' She sobbed hysterically.

'It's all right, my darling, it's over ... It's over ... Ariana ...'

'But what about Johann? Do you suppose ...'

'I'm sure he'd got as far from it as we had by then.' But inwardly Manfred wasn't quite as sure as he led her to believe. And as they drove on a few moments later, he felt a wave of exhaustion come over him. He was so desperately tired of the war. All the people one cared about, all the places one had loved, all the homes and the monuments and the cities, wasted.

Silently they drove home, Ariana quiet and trembling next to him in her veil and her pretty white suit, the gardenias wafting their exotic fragrance towards him. He realised then that the smell of gardenias would always remind him of that night, the night of their wedding, and of their escape from death. Suddenly he wanted to cry then, from relief, from exhaustion, from terror, from concern for this tiny, beautiful woman he had just made his own. Instead, he simply held her very tightly, swept her into his arms, and carried her into their house, up the stairs to their bedroom, where this time, thinking only of each other, they abandoned all care, all thought, all reserve, all precaution, and became one.

Chapter 24

'Did you find Johann?' Ariana looked at Manfred worriedly as he came home from the office the next day.

'Yes, he's fine.' He said it curtly, afraid that she would discover that he was lying. In truth, Johann had died outside the church the night before. Manfred had sat trembling in his office for an hour, unable to accept that yet another person he cared about was gone. With a sigh he sat down heavily in his favourite chair.

'Ariana, I want to talk to you about something very serious.' She wanted to tease him, to take some of that terrible earnestness from his eyes, but as she looked at him she knew there was no point. Life in Berlin was very serious these days.

She sat down very quietly and looked into his eyes. 'What is it, Manfred?'

'I want to establish a plan for you, so that you know what to do if something goes wrong. I want you to be prepared at all times now. And, Ariana ... I'm very serious ... you must listen.'

She nodded quietly. 'All right, I will.'

'You know where I keep the money and the gun in the bedroom. If something terrible happens, I want you to take that and your mother's rings and go.'

'Go where?' She looked momentarily overwhelmed.

'Towards the border – there's a map in your Volkswagen. And I always want you to keep the tank filled with gas. I have a spare can in the garage for you. Fill the tank before you go.' She nodded, hating his instructions and explanations. She would never go anywhere. She would never leave him.

'But just how do you think all this would happen? I would just drive off and leave you here, Manfred?' It was a ridiculous suggestion, she never would.

'Ariana, you may have to. If your life is at stake, I want you to go. You have no idea what this city will be like if it is overrun by Allied troops. There will be pillaging, plundering, murders, rapes.'

'You make it sound like the Dark Ages.'

'Ariana, it will be the darkest moment this country has ever known, and you will be totally helpless here if for some reason I cannot reach you. I may get caught at the Reichstag for example, for weeks – or days at the very least.'

'And you really think they'll just let me drive out of here, in that ridiculous little car, with my mother's rings and your gun? Manfred, don't be crazy!'

'Don't you be crazy, dammit. Listen to me! I want you to get as far as you can in the car and then get rid of it. Run, walk, crawl, steal a bicycle, hide in the bushes, but get the hell out of Germany. The Allies are already west of here, all the way to the French border, and I think you'd be safest in France. You can make your way through the Allied lines. I don't think you'll be able to get into Switzerland any more, Ariana. I want you to try to get to Paris.'

'Paris?' She looked stunned. 'That's six hundred miles from here, Manfred.'

'I know. And it doesn't matter how long it takes you to make it, but you have to. I have a friend in Paris, a man I went to school with.' He took out a notebook and carefully inscribed a name.

'What makes you think he's still there?'

'From the reports I've heard for the last six years, I'd say he is. He had polio as a child, so he has been safe from our army and his own. He is the Assistant Minister of Culture in Paris, and he has driven our officers insane.'

'Do you think he's with the Resistance?' She was intrigued.

'Knowing Jean-Pierre, I'd say there was a possibility of that. But if he is, he's smart enough to be discreet. Ariana, if anyone can help you, he will. And I know he'll keep you safe for me until I can get back to you. Stay in Paris if he tells you to, go wherever he thinks you should go. I trust him with my entire being.' He looked at her soberly. 'Which means I trust him with you.' He wrote the name down and handed it to her. Jean-Pierre de Saint Marne.

'And then what?' She looked unhappy as she fingered the note, but she was slowly beginning to wonder if maybe Manfred was right.

'You wait. It won't be long.' He smiled gently. 'I promise.' And then his face hardened again. 'But from now on I want you ready at all times. The gun, the rings, the money, Saint Marne's address, some warm clothes, enough food to carry with you, and a full tank of gas in the car.'

'Yes, Lieutenant.' She smiled softly and saluted, but he didn't smile.

'I hope we never need it, Ariana.'

She nodded, the smile fading, her eyes quiet. 'So do I.' And then after a time, 'I want to try to find my brother after the war.' She still believed Gerhard had got out safely. Time and distance had made her come to realise how much riskier it had been for Walmar, but there was a chance Gerhard had escaped.

Manfred nodded in understanding. 'We'll do our best.'

They spent the rest of the evening quietly, and the next day they went for a long walk on the deserted beach nearby. In summer, the beach at Strandbad on Grosser Wannsee was one of the most popular beaches near Berlin. But now it looked lonely and empty as Manfred and Ariana walked along in the sand.

'Maybe by next summer it will all be over and we can come here and relax.' She smiled at him hopefully and he stooped to pick up a shell. He handed it to her a moment later and she fingered it slowly. It was smooth and pretty and exactly the same blue-grey colour as his eyes.

'I hope that's exactly what we'll do, Ariana.' He smiled as he looked out over the water.

'Can we go to your schloss?'

He looked amused at the matter-of-fact look in her eyes.

'If I have it back by then. Would you like that?'

She nodded at him. 'Very much.'

'Good. Then we'll go there as well.' It was becoming something of a game, as though they could hasten the end of the war and the beginning of their own life by, just wishing the nightmare away and talking of what they would do 'after.'

But the next morning, as she had promised before he went to work, she gathered the things he wanted her to keep in order – the gun, her mother's rings hidden in their hiding place, some food, some money, the address of his French friend – and she went outside to check that the Volkswagen had a full tank of gas. When she went outside, in the distance – but not very distant – she could hear the roar of guns. That afternoon bombs were dropped further into the city. Manfred came home early. As usual during air raids, she was waiting in the cellar with a radio and a book.

'What happened? It said on the radio – '

'Never mind what it said on the radio. You're ready, Ariana?'

She nodded, terrified. 'Yes.'

'I have to go to the Reichstag tonight. They want every available man to defend the building. I don't know how soon I'll be back. You have to be a big girl now. Wait here, but if they take the city, remember all I've told you.'

'How will I get out if they take the city?'

'You will. They'll let refugees out, especially women and children. They always do.'

'And you?'

'I'll find you when it's over.' But then, glancing at his watch, he went upstairs to look for some of his own things, and then he came downstairs again slowly. 'I have to go.' They clung to each other silently for an endless moment, and

Ariana wanted to beg him not to leave. To hell with Hitler, with the army, with the Reichstag, with all of it. She only wanted him there with her, where they would both be safe.

'Manfred ...' From the panic in her voice he knew what was coming. He silenced her with a long tender kiss and shook his head.

'Don't say it, my darling. I have to go now, but I'll be back soon.'

There were tears streaming from her eyes as she walked upstairs with him and stood beside the Mercedes. He turned and wiped her cheeks gently with his hand. 'Don't cry, my darling, I'll be fine. I promise.'

She threw her arms around his neck then. 'If something happened to you Manfred, I would die.'

'Nothing will happen, I promise.' And then, smiling at her through his own pain, he slipped his signet ring from his finger and put it in the palm of her hand, closing his fingers around hers. 'Take care of that for me until I get back.' She smiled softly at him, and they kissed for a long time before he backed out of the driveway, waved, and drove back to the Reichstag in Berlin.

Day after day she heard the reports on the radio, of battles being waged in every corner of Berlin. By the night of 26 April, she knew that every sector had been affected, Grunewald as well as Wannsee. She herself had not left her cellar in days. She had heard the shots and explosions around her and hadn't dared emerge to the main floor. She knew that the Russians were advancing along the Schonhouserallee up to the Stargarderstrasse, but what she did not know was that everywhere in Berlin people like her were blocked in their cellars, most of them without food, water, or air. There had been no plans made for an evacuation. Even the children were condemned to the same fate as their parents, trapped like rats, waiting for it all to end. And what none of them knew was that the High Command had already fled Berlin.

On the night of 1 May Hitler's death was announced on the radio, which the populace listened to in sombre stupefaction as they waited in their black holes, in basements, trapped beneath buildings, as the battle raged and the city burned. The Allies stepped up their fire to a terrific degree. After Hitler's death was announced the sound of Wagner and Bruckner's Seventh Symphony wafted on the radio into the cellar where Ariana hid. It seemed an odd note as she listened to the gunfire and explosions in the distance, remembering the last time she had heard that symphony, with Gerhard and her father, at the Opera House years before. And now she sat, waiting for it all to end, wondering where Manfred was in the holocaust that was Berlin. Later that night she learned that the entire Goebbels family had committed suicide as well, poisoning all six children.

On 2 May she heard the news of the cease-fire given in three languages on the radio. She did not understand it in Russian, and it seemed unreal to her in German, but when an American voice came over the radio, telling her in halting German that it was all over, at last she understood. But still it made no sense to her – she could still hear guns exploding in the distance, and around her in Wannsee she could hear the battle raging on. The skies were still now; the battle was being waged on foot, as looters attacked the houses around her, although in the heart of the city, the Berliners had left their homes. But in

Wannsee, for three more days it continued, and then there was an eerie silence as everything seemed to stop. For the first time in weeks there was no sound at all, except an occasional shout, and then again silence. Ariana sat, waiting, listening, alone in the house, as the sun dawned in the eerie stillness of 5 May.

As soon as it was daylight, she decided to search for Manfred. If the Allies had taken the city, she had to know where he was. He no longer had to defend the Reichstag – there was no longer a Reich to defend.

For the first time in days she climbed the stairs to her bedroom and put on one of the warm, ugly skirts, wool stockings, and her old solid shoes. She pulled on a sweater and grabbed a jacket, shoving Manfred's gun deep into her pocket and concealing it with a glove. She would make no other preparations. She was only going to find Manfred, and if she could not find him, she would come back to the house and wait. A few moments later, outside for the first time in what seemed years, she took a deep gulp of air and was suddenly aware of the acrid smell of smoke. She slipped into her little Volkswagen unseen, turned the ignition, floored the gas.

It took her only twenty minutes to reach the heart of the city, and when she did, she gasped at what she saw. The streets were strewn with debris and rubble, there was no way to get through. At first glance it looked as though there was nothing left. Closer inspection showed that there were still some buildings standing, but none had gone unmarked by the battle that had raged for days. Ariana sat staring with disbelief at what lay around her, and finally she realised how hopeless it would be to try to drive through the mess. Backing her car away slowly, she pulled it into a back alley and as best she could, pulled it out of sight. She pocketed the keys, felt the gun still in its hiding place, pulled her scarf tighter, and got out of the car. All she knew was that she had to find Manfred.

But all she saw as she wandered in the direction of the Reichstag were droves of British and American soldiers hurrying past, and here and there an island of curious Berliners, staring at them from doorways or hurrying away to leave the city as they wondered what would come now. And it was only much later, as she came closer to the Reichstag, that she saw men in German uniforms, huddled together, filthy, exhausted, waiting for buses to come to take them away as Americans stood guarding them, machine-guns pointed, but looking equally filthy and tired. As Ariana watched them and stumbled over the torn sidewalks, she realised to her very soul just how tough a fight it had been. So this was what had happened to her country, this is what the Nazis had brought them in the end. Over 5000 soldiers had attempted to defend the Reichstag and half of them had died. As she stood, not knowing where to turn, a second group of men in German uniforms passed by. Ariana gasped when she recognised Hildebrand, one eye bruised and swollen, his head bleeding through a bandage, his uniform torn, and a vacant look in his eyes. She waved frantically to catch his attention and ran towards him. Surely he would know where Manfred was. She was instantly stopped by two Americans with guns crossed to block her. She pleaded with them in German. But it was obvious that they would not be moved. She shouted at Hildebrand, urgently calling his name until he turned.

'Where is Manfred? ... Hildebrand ... Hildebrand ... Hildebrand! ... Where is – ' His eyes darted to the left and when she followed his gaze, she was overcome by the sight. A stack of broken bodies waiting for trucks to haul them away. The uniforms were besmirched beyond recognition, the faces clenched in the rictus of death. She walked slowly towards them, and then, as though she were meant to find him, she saw the familiar face almost at once.

Her heart knew before her mind, and then she stood, rooted, disbelieving, her mouth open, giving birth to a scream that would not come. Even the American soldier couldn't make her leave him. She knelt beside him and wiped the dirt from his face.

She lay there beside him for almost an hour, until suddenly, terrified, she understood what it meant now, and with a last kiss on the sleeping eyes, she touched his face and ran away. She ran as hard and as fast as she could towards the alley where she had left the funny little car. And when she reached it, she found that two men were already working it over, trying to start it without the key. With eyes narrowed and voice trembling, she pulled out the small gun, pointing it at her fellow Berliners until they stood back with hands raised. Quietly she slid into her car then, locked the door, still holding the gun pointed at them with one hand, and with the other she started the car. And then, pushing the car as hard as it was willing, she shot into reverse out of the alley and drove away.

She had nothing to lose now ... nothing for which to live ... and as she drove along, she could see the looters, other Germans, some soldiers – some even were Russians. Her city was about to be dragged over the coals again. And if they killed her, so be it, she didn't really care now. It didn't matter if they killed her or not. But she had promised Manfred she would try to get to safety. And because of that, she would try to get out.

She drove as quickly as she could back to Wannsee, put the few things she had ready into the car. Some cooked potatoes, some bread, a little bit of stew meat. And then she took the package with the money, the address of the Frenchman, and the book concealing the two rings. Her engagement ring from Manfred she left on her finger – let someone dare to try and take it from her – along with her gold band and his signet. She would have killed them before they'd got the rings off her. Her eyes hard, her mouth set, she set the gun in her lap and once more started the car; and then, with a last look over her shoulder, she glanced at the house where Manfred had first brought her, and great anguished sobs tore at her heart. He was gone now, the man who had saved her ... gone forever. At the pain of that realisation, Ariana thought she would die. She had slipped among her papers the only letter he'd ever written her, a love letter filled with tenderness and promise that he had written after the first time they'd made love. And she had also brought with her some pictures – of them at their first party together at the Opera House, some more from the ball at the Royal Palace, a few others from the Tiergarten, and even those of his children and his dead wife. Ariana would not leave those pictures for anyone else's eyes. They were hers, as would be Manfred, for the rest of her life.

Chapter 25

Along with thousands of others fleeing – on foot, riding bicycles, and now and then in cars – Ariana left the city and headed west. The Allies didn't try to stop the women and children and old people who were leaving the city like frightened rats. Ariana couldn't bear the agony of what she was seeing, and again and again she stopped to give someone a hand, until she knew that she could stop no more. Each time she did, there were attempts to take the car from her, and only at the last did she agree to give two old women a ride. They were silent and grateful, they lived in Dahlem, and all they wanted was to get out of town. Their store on the Kurfürstendamm had been destroyed earlier that morning, their husbands were dead, and now they were afraid for their lives.

'The Americans will kill us all, fraülein', the older of the two women told her, crying. Ariana didn't think so, but she was too tired to argue with either of them. She was too anguished even to talk. But she knew that if the Americans truly wanted to kill them, they had plenty of opportunity, as the refugees thronged the roads. Driving along beside them was also slow going for Ariana, but at last she was able to reach some familiar back roads. And in the end she managed to get as far as Kassel, some 200 miles from Berlin, where she finally ran out of gas.

She had long since dropped off her passengers in Kalbe, where they had cousins and had been received with open arms and tears. As Ariana watched them, she felt a pang of envy. Unlike these old women, she had no one now. And after she had left them, she had driven on mindlessly until the car came to a slow, grinding halt. The jerry can in the back seat was empty. She had come halfway from Berlin to Saarbrücken, the town north of Strasbourg where Manfred had wanted her to try to cross into France. But she had another 200 miles until she reached it. She sat there for a moment thinking of the sea of refugees swarming out of Berlin. She was just another face among them now, shuffling towards nowhere, with no friends and no possessions, and nowhere to go. Fighting back tears as she looked over her shoulder at the lost safety of the little grey car, she tightened her grip on her bundles and began the long walk towards France.

It took her two days to walk the forty miles to Marburg, and from there an old country doctor let her drive with him to Mainz. They made little conversation as they rode along for three hours. The trip covered some eighty miles, and when they reached Mainz, he looked at her sympathetically and offered to take her to Neunkirchen – it was on his way after all. Gratefully she accepted, her mind still whirling from the night before.

In Neunkirchen, Ariana thanked him, staring at him blindly and somehow wanting to say more, but in the endless hours that she had driven and then walked and then finally ridden beside him, something deep inside her had frozen into place, a sense of loss, of broken hope, of deep despair. She was no longer even sure of why she was running, except that Manfred had told her to and she was his wife. He had told her to go to Paris, so she would. Maybe the friend in Paris would have the answers; perhaps he'd tell her that what she had seen in the dawn three days before had been a lie. Perhaps Manfred would be there in Paris, waiting for her to arrive.

'Fraulein?'

The old man had seen the ring but he found it difficult to believe that she was really married. She looked so young. Perhaps she had worn it for protection. Not that it would protect her from the soldiers or that she needed that kind of protection from him. He smiled gently at her as she pulled her little bundle off the seat.

'Thank you, sir.' She looked at him for a long, empty moment.

'You'll be all right?' She nodded in answer. 'Would you like a ride back from Neunkirchen in a few days? I'll be going back to Marburg.' But she would not be going back again. For her it was strictly a one-way journey and her eyes were filled with the tragedy of last goodbyes.

Quietly she shook her head. 'I'm going to stay with my mother. Thank you.' She didn't want to admit to him that she was trying to flee the country. She trusted no one now. Not even this old man.

'Bitte.' She shook his hand politely, stood back, and he drove off. Now all she had to do was to get the twenty miles to Saarbrücken, and then another ten miles to the French border and she'd be all right. But this time there was no old man driving, and it took her three long days to make the trek. Her legs were aching, she was tired and cold and hungry. She had run out of food on the first day. Twice she had seen frightened farmers; one had given her two apples, the other had only shaken his head. But at last she reached the border, six days after her journey had begun. She had done it . . . done it . . . done it . . . All she had to do was crawl through the wire and into France. She did it slowly, with her heart pounding, wondering if someone would see her and shoot her on the spot. But it seemed as though the war was truly over – no one cared if one filthy, exhausted young girl in a torn skirt and sweater crawled through the wire, scratching her face and arms and body. Ariana looked around in exhaustion and murmured, 'Welcome to France,' before she lay down to rest.

She awoke some six hours later, to the sound of church bells pealing, her body aching and agonisingly stiff. For the girl who had lived under her father's kind wing in Grunewald and then under Manfred's protection for the past eight months, this was not what she had been prepared for. She began walking again and it was half an hour later that she fainted on the road. An old woman found her two hours later and thought that she was dead. Only a slight stirring beneath the sweater, as her heart beat softly still, led the old woman to wonder, and she hurried home to find her daughter-in-law, and together they dragged her inside. They touched and they prodded and they held her and when she awoke at last she vomited horribly, and she ran a fever for the next two days. At times they thought that she would die there with them. All the old woman knew about the girl was that she was German, for she had found the German gun and the Reichsmarks among the currency she carried. But the old woman did not hold it against her; her own son had gone to work for the Nazis in Vichy four years before. One did what one had to in wartime, and if this girl was running now, the old woman was willing to help her. The war was over, after all. They nursed her for two more days while she lay and vomited, and then at last Ariana insisted that she was well enough to go. She spoke to them in their own language, and with her cultured accent and fluent knowledge of French, she could just as well have been from Strasbourg as Berlin.

The old woman looked at her wisely. 'Do you have far to go?'

'Paris.'

'That's more than two hundred miles. You can't walk the whole way, you know. Not in the condition you're in.' Already Ariana was showing signs of malnutrition and she figured she must have got a concussion when she'd fallen, else she wouldn't have vomited so violently or had so much pain afterwards in her eyes. And she looked some ten years older than she had when the journey had begun.

'I can try. Someone may give me a ride.'

'In what? The Germans took all our cars and trucks, and what they didn't take, the Americans did. They're all stationed in Nancy, and they've already been up this way to get more cars.' But her daughter-in-law remembered that the old priest was going up to Metz at nightfall. He had a horse he used for his travels. And if Ariana was lucky, he'd give her a ride. As it turned out, Ariana was lucky, and the priest took her along.

They reached Metz by morning, and after the long hours of jolting over the countryside, Ariana was desperately sick again. Too sick to eat, too sick to move, she had to nonetheless. From Metz she had to get another forty miles to Bar-le-Duc. She set out once again, walking, this time praying that someone in a truck would come along, and after the first four miles her prayers were answered – a man with a horse cart happened by. He was neither old nor young. Neither hostile nor friendly. She flagged him down, offered some French money, and climbed into his cart. Four hours she sat beside him, with the spring sun beating down on her head, as the man sat beside her in silence and the horse ploughed on. It was sunset when the man finally halted.

'Are we at Bar-le-Duc? Ariana looked at him in surprise, but he shook his head firmly.

'No, but I'm tired. And so is my horse.' As it so happened, she was also exhausted, but she was anxious to continue on. 'I'll stop for a while and rest, and then we continue. It's all right with you?' She didn't have much choice in the matter. He had already spread his jacket out on the ground and was preparing to devour some bread and cheese. He ate it hungrily and roughly, offering none to Ariana, who felt too tired and sick to eat, let alone watch him eat. She lay down quietly on the grass some distance from him, her head on her precious bundle, and she closed her eyes. The grass was soft and warm beside

her from the bright May sun that had pounded down on it all day, and she felt
herself doze off in exhaustion. It was then she felt the man put his hand up her
skirt. He grabbed her roughly, letting himself down hard on top of her, at the
same time pushing up her skirt and pulling at her pants, while in astonishment
she pushed at him, fighting wildly and flailing at his face with both her hands.
But he was indifferent to her lack of interest in his seduction; he pushed hard at
her with his hands and body, and then with something hard and warm she felt
pulsing between her legs, and then just before he could enter her there was a
stirring, a shout, and a shot fired in the air. The man jumped back, startled and,
much to his chagrin, fully exposed. Ariana quickly leaped to her feet and then
stumbled suddenly as a wave of dizziness overtook her and she almost fell.
Two strongs hands took hold of her shoulders and she was gently set back on
the ground.

'Are you all right?' She hung her head and nodded, not wanting to see his
face, and also not wanting him to see hers. The voice that had saved her spoke
to her in English, and she knew that now she had reached the Americans'
hands. Thinking that she didn't understand him, he spoke to her then in
awkward French. She forced herself not to smile at him when finally she
looked up. It seemed funny that he so easily believed her French.

'Thank you.' He had a friendly face and lots of soft brown hair, curled
beneath a helmet, and in the distance she could see three more men and a jeep.

'Did he hurt you?' he asked her firmly, and she shook her head. Without
discussing matters further, the young American in the helmet took a long
swing and hit the Frenchman squarely in the face. 'That ought to take care of
him.' What pissed him off was that they were always being accused of raping
the locals, when in point of fact the sons of bitches were raping their own. And
then he looked down at the tiny blonde girl again as she stood up and shook the
grass and dust from her fine gold hair. 'Do you need a ride somewhere?'

'Yes.' She smiled weakly. 'To Paris.' It was crazy even to be standing here
talking to him.

'Would you settle for Châlons-sur-Marne? It's about a hundred miles outside
Paris, and from there I ought to be able to find someone to drive you the rest of
the way.'

Was it possible he would help her get to Paris? She stared at him as tears
rolled down her cheeks.

'Okay? Would that help?' His eyes were gentle and his smile widened as she
nodded her head. 'Come on, over here.'

The Frenchman was still dusting himself off as Ariana followed the
American to the jeep. They were young and raucous and happy as they drove
along, the four young men staring curiously at silent Ariana, crushed between
them; their eyes would touch on the gold hair, the delicate face, the sad eyes,
and then they would shrug and go on talking, or now and then break into an off
colour song. The young man who had saved her from the Frenchman wore the
name Henderson on the pocket of his fatigues, and it was he who arranged for
two other soldiers to drive her into Paris, an hour after they arrived at Châlons.
'You'll be okay with them, miss,' he reassured her in his clumsy French and
she put out a hand.

'Thank you, sir.'

'You're welcome, ma'am.' She turned to follow the two soldiers, who were driving to Paris on some mission that involved two colonels who apparently sent each other messages at least three times a day. But it wasn't of the colonels that Henderson was thinking. He was thinking of the look of despair and desperation that he had seen in that tiny pale face. He had seen that look before in wartime. And he knew something else from looking at that face with the sunken blue eyes, the taut skin, the dark circles. That girl was sick as hell.

Chapter 26

The two young American soldiers explained to Ariana that they were going to an address on the rue de la Pompe. Did she know where she was going? She pulled out the paper Manfred had given her. The address was on the rue de Varenne.

'I think that's on the Left Bank, but I'm not sure.' As it turned out, it was. Paris was also showing signs of the war, but it was in no way as shocking as Berlin had been. More than damage by bombs, Paris had suffered at the hands of the Germans, who had attempted to remove everything available and ship it back to the Pinakothek in Berlin.

An old man with a bicycle explained to the two young soldiers where it was Ariana wanted to go and then volunteered gamely to lead the way. It was then that Ariana got her first view of Paris since she'd been there as a child with her father and brother. But she was too tired to appreciate the sights, or even the beauty of the city. The Arc de Triomphe, the Place de la Concorde, the Pont Alexandre III whizzed by her. She simply closed her eyes and rumbled along in the jeep, hearing the old man shout instructions now and then and the young American at the wheel shout his thanks. At last they reached the address and Ariana opened her eyes. She had no choice but to step down then, though she would have preferred infinitely to sleep in the back of their car. In the end her flight from Berlin had taken her a full nine days, and now here she was in Paris, with no idea why she had come or what this man she was looking for would be like. Perhaps he was even dead by now. It seemed to her that everyone was. And as she stood outside his huge ornate doorway, she longed more than ever for the cosy little house in Wannsee she and Manfred had shared. But there was nothing there any longer, she had to remind herself. Nothing at all. Manfred was gone.

'Oui, mademoiselle?' A fat, white-haired old woman swung open the main door, revealing a handsome courtyard on the other side. Across it was a lovely eighteenth-century *hôtel particulier* and a short flight of marble stairs. '*Vous désirez?*' The house lights glowed invitingly in the dark.

'Monsieur Jean-Pierre de Saint Marne.' Ariana answered her in French, and for a long moment the woman stared her down, as though she didn't want to understand. But Ariana persisted. 'Is he away from home?'

'No.' The woman shook her head slowly. 'But the war is over, mademoiselle. There is no need to trouble Monsieur de Saint Marne any more.' She was tired of these people who had come calling and begging and entreating for so long. Let them go to the Americans now. They would kill Monsieur with their exhausting tales, their terrors, their emotions. For how long would this imposition continue to go on? Preying on the poor man like that. Watching her face, Ariana did not understand.

'I ... I'm sorry ... my husband and Monsieur de Saint Marne were old friends. He suggested that I look Monsieur de Saint Marne up when I got here ...' She faltered and the old woman shook her head.

'That's what they all say.' And this one didn't look any better than the others. Sickly, skinny, deathly pale, in torn clothes and worn-out shoes, with only that tiny bundle in her hands. Lord, she looked as though she hadn't bathed in at least a week. And just because Monsieur had money, there was no reason for all this refugee riffraff to prey on him. 'I'll see if Monsieur is at home.' But the handsome Rolls in the courtyard suggested that her master was indeed in. 'Wait here.' Ariana sank down gratefully on a narrow bench in the courtyard, shivering slightly in the chill night air. But she was used to being cold and tired and hungry. Had she ever been otherwise? It was difficult to remember as she closed her eyes. It seemed hours later that someone was shaking her and she looked up to see the old woman, her lips pursed in disapproval, but nodding her head. 'He'll see you now.' Ariana felt a wave of relief overcome her, not at the prospect so much of seeing him, but only because she would have to go no further that night. At least she hoped not. She didn't care if he made her sleep in the attic, but she didn't think she had the strength to go another step before morning. She hoped desperately that he'd let her stay.

Following the old woman, she climbed the short flight of marble stairs to the main doorway, and a sombre-looking butler opened the door and stepped aside. For an instant he reminded Ariana of Berthold, but this man had kinder eyes. He looked down at her for a brief moment and then, without speaking a single word, turned on his heel and disappeared. With that the old woman shook her head again in patent disapproval and muttered to Ariana in the front hall. 'He's gone to get the Master. They'll send for you in a minute. I'll go now.'

'Thank you.' But the old woman cared not two pins for Ariana's thank you.

The butler returned. She was led down a handsomely appointed hallway, draped in velvets and punctuated at regular intervals with portraits of the Saint Marne ancestors. Ariana stared at them blindly as she walked along, until at last they reached a large doorway and the butler flung open a single mirrored door. What she saw inside the room he had thus opened reminded her very much of Berlin's Royal Palace, with cherubs and gilt panels, inlays and marquetries and endless mirrors over white marble mantelpieces, and in the midst of all the splendour was a single serious-looking man, of Manfred's age but slight build, with deep, worried furrows running between his eyes. He sat watching her from a wheelchair in the centre of the room.

'Monsieur de Saint Marne?' She felt almost too tired for the etiquette that seemed required by the circumstances and the room.

'Yes.' He made no move in the wheelchair, but his face bid her approach. He turned welcomingly towards her, his eyes still serious, yet somehow warm. 'That's who I am. Now who are you?'

'Ariana ...' She hesitated for a moment. 'Mrs Manfred von Tripp.' She said it quietly, looking into the gentle eyes that watched her. 'Manfred told me that if Berlin fell, I was to come here. I'm sorry, I hope that ...' The wheels approached her swiftly as she struggled on. He stopped very near to her and held out a hand.

'Welcome, Ariana. Please sit down.' His face had not yet broken into a joyful welcome. He felt certain that this girl had more to tell him, and he wasn't sure at all that it would be good news.

She sat down quietly, looking into the Frenchman's face. In an odd way he was good-looking, though so totally unlike Manfred that it was almost difficult to imagine that they had been friends. As she sat looking at her husband's schoolmate, Ariana found herself lonelier than ever for the man she would never see again.

'How long did it take you to get here?' His eyes searched her face as he asked her. He had seen so many like her before. Sick, tired, broken, afraid.

She sighed. 'Nine days.'

'You came how?'

'By car, by horse, by foot, by jeep ...' *By barbed wire, by prayer, by almost being raped by a disgusting man* ... Her eyes stared emptily at Saint Marne. And then he asked the question he had wanted to ask her from the first.

'And Manfred?' He said it very softly, and she dropped her eyes.

Her voice was nothing more than a whisper in the grandiose room. 'He's dead. He died ... in the ... fall of Berlin.' She looked up at him then squarely. 'But he had told me to come to you here. I don't know why I left Germany, except that now I have nothing left there anyway. I had to go.'

'Your family?' His eyes seemed inured to the bad news he had just had about his friend.

In answer to his question, she sighed jaggedly into the silent room. 'I believe that my father is dead. My mother died before the war. But my brother ... he may be alive still. In Switzerland. My father took him there last August to avoid the draft. My father never returned from Switzerland, and I never heard from Gerhard. I don't know if he's alive or not.'

'Gerhard was to stay?' She nodded. 'And was your father meant to come back?'

'Yes, to get me. But ... our nurse – that is, they called the Nazis. They took me and held me for ransom. They thought my father would be back, too.' She looked up at him quietly. 'After a month, they let me go. Manfred and I ...' She stopped before the tears came.

Jean-Pierre sighed and pulled a piece of paper towards him on the desk. 'I assume this is why Manfred sent you to me.'

Ariana looked confused then. 'I think he only sent me to you because you were his friend and he thought that I'd be safe here.'

Jean-Pierre de Saint Marne smiled tiredly. 'Manfred was indeed a very good friend. But a wise one as well. He knows what I've been up to all during the war. I kept in touch. Discreetly, of course.' He waved vaguely to the wheel-chair. 'As you can see, I am somewhat ... hampered ... but I have managed very nicely in spite of it. I have become something of a philanthropist, shall we say, bringing families back together, sometimes in other countries, and arrang-ing for 'vacations' in warmer climates.'

She nodded at the euphemisms. 'In other words, you've been helping refugees to escape.'

'Mostly. And now I'm going to spend the next few years attempting to reunite families. That ought to keep me busy for a while.'

'Then can you help me find my brother?'

'I'll try. Give me whatever information you have, and I'll see what I can discover. But I'm afraid you have to think of more than that, Ariana. What about you? Where will you go now? Home to Germany?'

She shook her head slowly and then looked up at him blankly. 'I have no one there.'

'You can stay here for a while.' But she knew also that would not be a permanent arrangement, and then where would she go? She hadn't though of it at all, hadn't thought of anything.

Saint Marne nodded quitely with sympathetic understanding and made several notes. 'All right, in the morning I will see what I can do for you. You must tell me everything that you know to help me find Gerhard. And in the meantime – ' he smiled gently – 'you must do something else.'

'What's that?' She tried to return the smile but it was an enormous effort just to look him in the eye and not fall asleep in his intolerably comfortable chair.

'What you must do now, dear Ariana, is get some rest. You look very, very tired.'

'I am.'

They all looked like that when they got to him, exhausted, wounded, frightened. She would look better in a day or two he thought. What a pretty little thing she was, and how unlike Manfred to marry someone so frail, so ethereal, so young. Marianna had been a good deal more solid. First Jean-Pierre was shocked to realise that Ariana was Manfred's new wife. Somehow, he hadn't expected Manfred to marry. He had been so distraught when his wife and children had died. But here was this girl. And he could easily understand Manfred's passion. She was so elfenlike, so pretty, even in her torn, filthy clothes. He would have liked to have seen her with Manfred in better times. And after he was once again alone in the drawing room, he mused to himself about his old friend. Why had he really sent her to him? To wait for him as she had told him, if he had managed to survive the fighting in Berlin? Or did he want something more? Some protection for her? Help in her search for her brother? What? Somehow he felt as though sending her had been a kind of message, and he desperately wanted to decipher what it was. Perhaps, he thought to himself as he sat looking out the window, in time it would become clear.

And in her room, with the view of the pretty cobbled courtyard, Ariana was already fast asleep. She had been put to bed by a kindly middle-aged woman in full skirts and an apron, who had turned back the covers, exposing thick blankets, a comforter, and clean sheets. It seemed a hundred years since Ariana had seen anything so lovely, and without another thought of Jean-Pierre or her brother or even Manfred, she climbed into the bed and slid into a deep sleep.

Chapter 27

The next morning Ariana joined Jean-Pierre after breakfast. It was clear in the light of day that she was ill. She sat in his study, her face tinged a sickly green.

'Were you sick before you left Berlin?'

'No, I wasn't.'

'You may just be worn out from the trip – and your loss. He had seen the reaction to grief too many times before. Sweating, vomiting, dizziness. He had seen grown men faint from the sheer relief of at last reaching the safety of his home. But he was less concerned with her physical state than her emotional state right now. 'Later I'll have a doctor come to see you. But first, I want to find out everything I can about your brother. His description, height, size, weight. Then where was he going, what was he wearing, what were his exact plans. Who did he know?' He faced her squarely and one by one she answered all his questions, explaining in detail the plan that her father intended to follow, walking from the train station at Lörrach across the Swiss border to Basel, where they would take another train to Zurich, and then her father would come back for her. 'And in Zurich, what?'

'Nothing. He was simply to wait.'

'And after that what were the three of you going to do?'

'Go on to Lausanne, to friends of my father.'

'Did the friends know you were coming?'

'I'm not sure. Papa may not have wanted to call them from his house or the office. He may have just planned to call them when he got to Zurich.'

'Would he have left your brother with their number?'

'I'm sure he would.'

'And you never heard from any of them, not the friends, your brother, your father?'

She shook her head slowly. 'No one. And then Manfred said that he was certain that my father was dead.'

He could hear in her voice that she had already made peace, with that. Now it was the losing of Manfred that she couldn't bear.

'But my brother ...' Her eyes looked up pleadingly and he shook his head.

'We'll see. I'll make some calls. Why don't you go back to bed. I'll let you know as soon as I hear anything at all.'

'You'll come and wake me?'

'It's a promise.' But in the end he didn't bother. He found everything there was to learn within the hour, and it wasn't enough to bother waking Ariana up for. As it turned out, she slept through till nightfall, and when Lisette told him she was finally sitting up in bed and looking better, he wheeled himself into her room. 'Hello, Ariana, how do you feel?'

'Better.' But she didn't look it. She looked worse. Paler, green, and it was obvious that she had to fight each moment not to be ill. 'No news?'

He paused only for an instant, but right away she knew. She looked at him more intently and he held up a hand. 'Ariana, don't. There is really no news at all. I will tell you what I found out, but it is less than nothing. The boy is gone.'

'Dead?' Her voice trembled. She had always hoped that he might still be alive. Despite what Manfred thought.

'Maybe. I don't know. This is what I learned. I called the man whose name you gave me. He and his wife were killed in an automobile accident exactly two days before your father and the boy left Berlin. The couple had no children, the house was sold, and neither the new owners of the house nor the man's associates in the bank ever heard from your brother. I talked to an officer of the bank who knew your father of course, but he never heard from him. It's possible that he left the boy and came for you, and that your father got killed somewhere on the way back. In which case, eventually the boy would have called the name your father gave him and discovered that they were both dead, husband and wife. Then I assume he would have either contacted the bank where the man worked or figured he was on his own, rolled up his sleeves, and got to work somewhere, simply to survive. But there is no trace of him, Ariana, not in Zurich, not with the central police, not with the bankers in Lausanne. There is not even a trace of Max Thomas.' She had given him that name, too. He looked at her unhappily. He had tried desperately all day. But there was nothing. No trace at all. 'I tried all the usual routes as well as some of my better contacts. No one ever came across the boy. That may be a good sign or a very bad one.'

'What do you think, Jean-Pierre?'

'That he and your father died together, between Lörrach and Basel.' He knew by her silence that she was paralysed with grief. He kept talking to keep contact with her. To pull her through. 'Ariana, we must go on.'

'But to where? ... To what? ... And why?' She sobbed angrily at him. 'I don't want to go on. Not now. There's no one left. No one but me.'

'That's enough. That's all I have now.'

'You, too?' She stared at him and blew her nose as he nodded quietly.

'My wife was Jewish. When the Germans occupied Paris, they took her and – ' his voice caught strangely and he turned the wheelchair away from Ariana – 'our little girl.' Ariana closed her eyes tightly for a moment. She suddenly felt desperately ill. She couldn't bear it anymore. The endless losses, the immeasurable pain. This man, and Manfred, and Max, and she herself, all of them losing people they loved, children and wives and brothers and fathers. She felt the room spinning, herself spinning; she lay down in a feeble attempt to anchor herself. He wheeled to her side quietly and gently stroked her hair. 'I know, *ma petite*, I know.' He didn't even tell her about the one lead he had had. It would only have made the bitter truth harder to bear. There had been a clerk in a hotel in Zurich who thought he remembered a boy like the one Jean-Pierre described. He had struck up a conversation with the boy and remembered he had said he was waiting for his relatives. He had been at the hotel alone for two weeks, waiting. But then the clerk remembered that he had met up with the relatives and left. It couldn't have been Gerhard. He had no relatives left. Ariana's father would have told her if this had been part of his plan. It was clear he was a very thorough man. The clerk remembered the boy going off with a couple and their daughter. So it wasn't Gerhard after all. And that had been all. There were no other leads, no other hopeful signs. The boy was gone, and like thousands of others in Europe, Ariana had no one left.

After a long time Jean-Pierre spoke to her again. 'I have an idea for you. If you're brave enough. It's up to you. But if I were young enough, I'd do it. To get away from all of these countries that have been destroyed, twisted, broken, bombed. I'd go away and start all over again, and that's what I think you should do.'

She lifted her head and wiped her eyes. 'But where?' It sounded terrifying. She didn't want to go anywhere. She wanted to stay anchored, hiding in the past forever.

'To the States.' He said it very quietly. 'There is a refugee ship leaving tomorrow. It's been arranged by an organisation out of New York. Their people will meet the ship when it docks and help you to relocate.'

'What about my father's house in Grunewald? Don't you think I could get that back?'

'Do you really want it? Could you live there? If you could ever get it back, which I doubt.' The truth of his words struck her with force. And then suddenly as he spoke to her, he understood what had been Manfred's message. This was why Ariana had been sent to her husband's boyhood friend. He had known that Jean-Pierre would come up with a solution. And now he knew that this was the right one.

The one question he had was if she was well enough to travel. But he knew from long experience with the people he had helped in the last six years, it would be months before she was herself again. She had simply lost too much, and the nine days of mad running across Germany, after the shock of seeing Manfred dead, had been the final straw. That was all that ailed her really, fatigue, exhaustion, hunger, too much walking, too much sorrow, too much loss. There was also a problem in that there might not be another ship for a long time. 'Will you do it?' Jean-Pierre's eyes never left hers. 'It could be a whole new life.'

'But what about Gerhard? You don't think that maybe he went to Lausanne after all? Or stayed somewhere in Zurich, that if I got there, maybe I'd find him?' But the hope was gone now from her eyes, too.

'I'm as good as certain, Ariana. There is absolutely no trace of him, and if he were alive, there would be. I think it happened as I told you. He and your father must both have been killed.' She shook her head slowly, letting the finality of it sink in. She had lost them all. She could let herself lie down and die, too – or keep going.

Fighting back the waves of dizziness and nausea, she looked at Jean-Pierre sitting in his wheelchair beside her bed and nodded. Some instinct deep inside her made her say it, and to her ears the voice didn't sound like her own. 'All right. I'll go.'

Chapter 28

Jean-Pierre's large black Rolls pulled sedately into Le Havre harbour. Ariana sat wanly in the back of the car. They barely spoke all the way from Paris. The roads were cluttered with trucks and jeeps and small convoys conveying equipment between Paris and the port. But the situation around Paris had settled down nicely, and apart from the drab colour of the army vehicles, the roads looked almost normal as they drove along.

Jean-Pierre had watched her quietly during most of the journey, and for the first time in his years of assisting the homeless refugees, broken and frightened, he felt at a loss for words that would offer comfort. The look in her eyes said so clearly that nothing anyone could say would ease her terrible burden.

As they drove along, the reality of her situation was hitting her. There was no one left in the world she cherished, no one to turn to; no one could ever share a memory of what had been her past, no one would ever understand without translation, have memories of her brother, her father, the house in Grunewald ... her mother .. Fräulein Hedwig ... the summers at the lake ... or the laughter behind Berthold's back at the table ... No one who would have smelled Gerhard's chemistry set as it burst into flames. Nor would there be anyone who had known Manfred – not in this new world she was going to. There would be no one who understood what it would be like to be caged in that cell. Attacked by Hildebrand ... and then saved by Manfred, spirited away to Wannsee. With whom could she possibly share the memory of the 'stew' she had made from liver sausage, the colour of the bedspread in that first room – or the look in his eyes when he had first made love to her – or the touch of his face when she had found him at last outside the Reichstag in

Berlin. They would never know anything of the past year of her life, or the past twenty, and as she rolled along beside Saint Marne on the way to the ship that would take her away forever, she couldn't believe she would ever share herself with anyone again.

'Ariana?' He called her with his deep voice and French accent. He had barely dared speak to her that morning until they left for Le Harve. She'd been too ill to get up. On the day before, she had fainted twice. Jean-Pierre noticed that now she seemed a little stronger, and he prayed silently that she was well enough to survive the trip to New York. As long as she made it, they'd let her into the States. The United States had opened her arms to the refugees of war. 'Ariana?' He spoke to her again gently, and slowly she returned from her distant thoughts.

'Yes?'

'Were you and Manfred together for very long?'

'Almost a year.'

He nodded slowly. 'I suppose right now that a year must seem to you like a lifetime. But – ' a small smile attempted to offer her hope – 'at twenty, a year seems enormous. Twenty years from now, it won't seem very long.'

Her voice was frigid when she answered. 'Are you suggesting I'll forget him?' She was outraged that Saint Marne would say it, but sadly he shook his head.

'No, my dear, you won't forget him.' For an instant he thought of his wife and daughter, lost only three years before, and the pain of it seared his heart. 'No, you won't forget. But I think in time the pain will be duller. It won't be as unbearable as it is for you now.' He put an arm around her shoulder. 'Be grateful, Ariana, you're still young. For you, nothing is over.' He tried to warm her, but there was nothing hopeful he could read in her great big blue eyes.

When at last they reached Le Havre, he didn't leave the car to accompany her to the boat. It was too complicated to get his wheelchair out of the trunk and have the chauffeur help him get into it. There was nothing more he could do for her now. He had arranged passage to New York, where he knew she would be cared for by the New York Women's Relief Organisation.

He reached out a hand to her through the open window, as she stood there with the small cardboard suitcase his housekeeper had brought up from the basement and packed with some of his wife's clothes, probably none of which fit. She was so tiny and childlike as she stood there, her eyes so huge in the unbelievably finely carved face, that suddenly he wondered if he had done the wrong thing in arranging her passage. Perhaps she was really too frail to make the trip. But she had managed the 600 miles from Berlin, on foot and by car and by horse and cart and jeep, over nine treacherous days – surely she could manage yet another week to cross the ocean. It would be worth it, just to put that much distance between herself and the nightmare, just to find a new life in a new land. 'You'll let me know how you are, won't you?' He felt like a father banishing a treasured child to a school in a foreign land.

Slowly a wintry smile came to her mouth and then to the blue eyes. 'Yes, I'll let you know. And Jean-Pierre ... thank you ... for all that you've done.'

He nodded. 'I only wish … that things could have been different.' He wished that Manfred had been standing there at the side of his bride.

But she had understood his meaning, and she nodded. 'So do I.'

And then in a gentle voice he whispered, *'Au revoir,* Ariana. Travel safely.'

Her eyes thanked him one last time, and she turned towards the gangway to the ship she'd be taking. She turned back one last time, waved solemnly, and whispered, *'Adieu'* with tears streaming from her eyes.

BOOK THREE
ARIANA
NEW YORK

Chapter 29

The SS *Pilgrim's Pride* was appropriately named. She looked as though she had been used by them long before they had switched their business to the *Mayflower*. She was small, narrow, dark, and smelled of mould. But she was seaworthy. And she was filled to the gills. The *Pilgrim's Pride* had been bought jointly by several American rescue organisations and was run primarily by the New York Woman's Relief Organisation, which thus far had overseen four trips of this nature, bringing more than a thousand refugees from war-torn Europe to New York. They had provided sponsors for everyone through their assorted sister organisations across the United States, and they had hired a decent crew to make the journey, bringing men, women, children, and the aged from the wasteland of Europe to their new lives in the States.

The people travelling on the ship were all in fairly poor condition and had reached Paris from other countries as well as other regions of France itself. Some had travelled on foot for weeks and months; others, like some of the children, had been roaming, homeless, for years. None of them had seen real food in longer than they could remember, and many of them had never even seen the sea before, let alone sailed it in a ship.

The Relief Organisation had not been able to find a doctor to sign on with their ship to make these crossings, but they had hired a remarkably competent young nurse. On each crossing so far, her services had been vital. She had already delivered nine babies, assisted at several grim miscarriages, four heart attacks, and six deaths. So Nancy Townsend, as ship's nurse, had to contend with homesickness, fatigue, hunger, deprivation, and the desperate needs of people who had suffered the price of war for much too long. On the last voyage there had been four women who had been held in jail outside Paris for almost two years before the Americans arrived to set them free. But only two of the women had lived through the sea voyage to New York. Each time, as Nancy Townsend watched the passengers boarding, she knew that not all of them would reach New York. Often it was easy to spot which were the strongest and which were those who never should have undertaken the trip. But often, too, there were those who seemed sturdy and then suddenly gave way on this last leg of their escape. It would seem that the tiny blonde woman on the lower deck, in a room with nine other women, was one of those.

A young girl from the Pyrenees had come running to find Nancy, screaming that someone was dying right below her bunk. When Nancy saw the girl, she knew she was dying of seasickness, hunger, dehydration, pain, delirium – it was impossible to tell what had pushed her over the edge, but her eyes were rolled back in her head, and when Townsend touched her, the girl's forehead was hot and parched with a raging fever.

Taking her pulse, the nurse knelt quietly beside her and motioned to the others to stand back. They had been staring at Ariana in discomfort, wondering if she was going to die in their room that night. It had already happened to them two days earlier, on their fourth day out from Le Havre. A small rail-thin Jewish girl who had travelled from Bergen-Belsen to Paris had not survived the last leg of her trip.

Twenty minutes after she had first seen her in the overcrowded cabin, Nurse Townsend had Ariana moved to one of the two isolation rooms. It was there that the fever raged higher and that she developed fierce cramps in her arms and legs. Nancy thought she might go into convulsions, but she never did, and on the last day of their voyage, the fever finally broke. Ariana was vomiting constantly, and each time she had attempted to sit up in bed, her blood pressure dropped so low that she fainted. She was able to remember almost none of her English, and she spoke to the nurse constantly in desperate, frightened German, none of which Nancy understood except the names that had recurred over and over ... Manfred ... Papa ... Gerhard ... Hedwig ... again and again she had shrieked, 'Nein, Hedwig!' when she had unseeingly looked into the eyes of the American nurse. And when she sobbed late into the night, it was impossible to console her. At times Nancy Townsend wondered if this girl was so sick because she no longer wanted to be alive. She wouldn't have been the first.

Ariana looked at her blankly on the last morning; her eyes were less feverish but filled with pain.

'I hope you're feeling better.' Nancy Townsend smiled gently.

Ariana nodded vaguely and went back to sleep. She never even saw the ship pull into New York harbour or the Statue of Liberty with the sun glinting gold on its arm holding the torch. Those who could stood on the decks and cheered wildly, tears streaming down their faces, their arms locked around each other – they had made it at last! But of all this Ariana knew nothing. She knew nothing at all until the special immigration officer came downstairs after they docked. He greeted the nurse quietly and read her reports. Generally they were able to send most of the passengers on to their sponsors, but this was one of those who would have to wait. Given the delirium and the fever, they wanted to be sure that she carried no disease. The immigration official praised the nurse for putting the girl in isolation and then, looking down at the sleeping girl and then at the uniformed woman, he raised an eyebrow in open question.

'What do you think it is?'

The nurse gestured silently towards the corridor and they left her sleeping. 'I can't tell you for certain, but it could be that in some way she's been tortured, or maybe been in one of the camps. I just don't know. You'll have to watch her.' He nodded in answer, sympathetically glancing through the open door.

'No open wounds, infections, obvious lesions?'

'Nothing I could see. But she vomited all the way across the Atlantic. I think you ought to keep an eye on that. There could be some internal damage. I'm sorry – ' she looked at him apologetically – 'I'm just not sure about this one at all.'

'Don't worry, Miss Townsend. That's why you're turning her over to us. She must have kept you pretty busy.' He glanced down at the charts again.

But the nurse smiled a slow smile into the harbour. 'Yes, but she made it.' Her eyes went quietly back to his. 'I think now she'll live. But for a while there ...'

'I can imagine.' He lit a cigarette and glanced below them to watch the others disembarking. He waited while two orderlies came and gently moved the girl on to a stretcher. Ariana stirred slightly, and then with a last look at the nurse who had kept her alive, Ariana left the ship. She didn't have any idea where they were taking her, and she didn't really care.

Chapter 30

'Ariana? ... Ariana ... Ariana ...' The voice seemed to call at her from a great distance, and as she listened, she wasn't sure if it was her mother or Fräulein Hedwig, but whoever it was, she couldn't make herself answer. She felt terribly tired and heavy, she was on a long journey, and it was too much trouble to come back. 'Ariana ...' But the voice was so insistent. Frowning gently in her sleep, Ariana was aware of a sensation of coming back from a long distance. She would have to answer them after all ... but she didn't want to ... what did they want? 'Ariana ...' The voice kept on calling, and after what seemed like a very long time Ariana opened her eyes.

There was a tall grey-haired woman dressed in black. She wore a black shirt and a black sweater, and her hair was pulled back into a heavy knot. And she was smoothing Ariana's hair back from the pillow with strong, cool hands. When at last she took her hand away, Ariana could see a large diamond ring on her left hand.

'Ariana?' The girl found that her voice seemed to have left her and she could only nod in response. But she couldn't remember what had happened. Where was she? Where had she been last? Who was this woman? Everything in her mind was jumbled and out of context. Was she on a ship? Was she in Paris? ... Berlin? 'Do you know where you are?' The smile was as gentle as her hands had been on Ariana's tangled hair, and she spoke English. Now Ariana remembered, or at least she thought so, as she looked questioningly at the woman. 'You're in New York. In a hospital. We brought you here to make sure that you were all right.' And the odd thing was that as far as they could tell, she was.

Ruth Liebman knew full well by now that there was much about these people one never knew and never would know, much that one had no right to ask. 'Are you feeling any better?' The doctor had told Ruth that they could find no reason for the exhaustion, the deep sleep, the weakness, except of course for the vomiting and the fever when she had been on the ship. But now they felt that it was urgent that someone make the effort to pull the girl back from the edge of the abyss where she lingered still. It was their official opinion that the girl was simply quietly giving up the fight to go on living, and it was crucial now that someone step in and pull her back before it was too late. As the head of volunteers of the New York Women's Relief Organisation, Ruth Liebman had come to see the girl herself. This was the second time she had been back to visit. The first time despite the soft stroking of her hair and the persistent calling, Ariana hadn't stirred. Quietly Ruth had looked her over, and stealthily she had looked for the numbers tattooed inside the girl's right arm. But there had been nothing. She had been one of the very lucky ones if she had escaped that fate. Perhaps she had been hidden somewhere by a family, or perhaps she had been one of their special victims, those they left unmarked by numbers but used in other ways. The peaceful, sleeping face of the tiny blonde beauty told her nothing, and all they knew of her was her name and that her sponsorship had been arranged through Saint Marne's refugee organisation in France. Ruth knew of the man slightly, a cripple who had lost his wife and daughter to the war.

She had endured her own tragedies since Pearl Harbor had dragged America into the war. When the war broke out, she had had four healthy, happy children; now she had two daughters and only one son. Simon had been shot down over Okinawa, and they had almost lost Paul in Guam. When the telegram had come, Ruth had almost fainted, but with stern face and trembling hands she had closeted herself in her husband's den. Sam was at the office. The girls had been upstairs somewhere, and in her hands she held the paper that looked so much like the first one ... the paper that would reveal to her her last son's fate. Ruth had decided to face the news alone. But when she read the telegram, the shock was that of relief. Paul had only been injured and he would return stateside in the next few weeks. When she called Sam, there had been the hysterics of rejoicing. She no longer had to maintain her iron calm. For them, the war was over. Her joy had given fresh vigour to her every move, her every thought. She had been distraught over reports of German horrors and stricken with a special kind of guilt, which came of not having suffered as the Jews in Europe had. She threw herself into her volunteer work. She saw these people now with even greater love and compassion, and the gratitude she felt over Paul's survival spilled over into her hours with them – helping them to locate the unknown sponsors, putting them on trains to distant cities in the South and Midwest, and now, visiting this small, frightened girl. Ariana stared at her intently and then closed her eyes.

'Why am I here?'

'Because you were very sick on the ship, Ariana. We wanted to be sure that there wasn't something wrong.' But at this Ariana smiled at her in tired irony. How could they be sure of that? Everything was wrong.

With the older woman's help she sat up slowly and sipped a little of the warm broth the nurse had left, and then Ariana fell back exhausted. Even that small effort had been too much. Gently, Ruth Liebman smoothed the girl's pillows and looked into the troubled blue eyes. And then she understood what the doctors had been saying. There was something terrifying in those eyes that said the girl who lay there had already given up hope.

'You're German, Ariana?' She nodded in answer and closed her eyes. What did being German mean now? She was only a refugee like those others, running away from Berlin three weeks before. Ruth saw the eyelids flutter as the girl remembered, and she gently touched her hand as Ariana once more opened her eyes. Perhaps she needed to talk it out with someone, perhaps she needed to say it, so that the ghosts would not haunt her any more. 'Did you leave Germany alone, Ariana?' Again Ariana only nodded. 'That was very brave of you to do that.' She spoke carefully and precisely. The nurse had told her that Ariana spoke English, but she was not yet sure how well. 'How far did you travel?'

Ariana looked into the kindly face with suspicion, and then she decided to answer. If this woman was with the army or the police or immigration, that didn't matter either any more. For an instant she thought of her endless interrogation at the hands of Captain von Rheinhardt, but that only brought back thoughts of Manfred once again. She pressed her eyes shut for an instant, and then opened them again as two huge tears slid slowly down her cheeks. 'I travelled six hundred miles ... into France.' Six hundred miles? ... And from where? Ruth didn't dare to ask her. It was obvious that just barely touching on the memories, the girl was gripped with fresh anguish.

Ruth Liebman was a woman who never gave up hope. It was an attitude she communicated to others, which was why she was so extraordinary at this kind of work. She had always wanted to be a social worker when she was younger, but as the wife of Samuel Liebman, she had her work cut out for her in other ways.

She sat very still now, watching Ariana, wanting to understand the young girl's sorrow, wanting to know how she could help. 'Your family, Ariana?' The words were spoken very gently, yet it was clear that to Ariana they were words she was not yet ready to hear. Crying more freely, she sat up now and shook her head.

'They're all gone now ... all of them ... my father ... my brother ... my –' She started to say 'my husband,' but she was unable to go on, and without thinking further Ruth took Ariana in her arms. 'All of them ... all of them. I have no one ... nowhere ... nothing ...' Fresh waves of grief and terror overtook her. She felt tormented by all of it as she lay there and prayed for her life to end.

'You can't look back now, Ariana.' Ruth Liebman spoke to her softly as she held her, and for an instant Ariana felt as though she had found a mother as she lay in the woman's arms and sobbed. 'You must look ahead. This is a new life for you, a new country ... and people whom you loved in that other life will never leave you. They are here with you. In spirit, Ariana, you will always take them along.' Just as she did Simon ... just as she would never lose her firstborn son. She believed that, and Ariana caught a glimpse of hope as she clung to the tall, spare woman whose optimism and strength seemed almost tangible as their eyes met and held.

'But what will I do now?'

'What did you do before?' But even Ruth understood quickly that it was a foolish question. Despite the look of added years and fatigue around her eyes now, it was obvious that the girl was probably no more than eighteen. 'Did you work at all?'

Ariana shook her head slowly. 'My father was a banker.' And then she sighed. It was all a joke now. All those shattered unimportant dreams. 'I was to go on to the university after the war.' But even she knew that she would never have used the education. She would have married and had children, given luncheons and played cards, like the other women. Even with Manfred, she would have done nothing more, except travel between their town house and the schloss on weekends and vacations, where she would have had to see that all was in order for her husband ... and then of course there would have been children ... She had to squeeze her eyes shut again. 'But all of that was so long ago. It doesn't matter any more.' Nothing did. And it showed.

'How old are you, Ariana?'

'Twenty.' Paul was only two years older, and Simon would have been twenty-four. Could she really only have been twenty and come so far? And how had she got separated from her family? Why had they killed the parents and brother and spared her? But as Ruth watched her, she understood the answer to the question, and a fresh ache was born in her heart for the girl. Ariana was so devastatingly pretty, even in her present wan condition, with those huge, sad blue eyes. Ruth suddenly felt certain that the Nazis had used her. It was clear to her in an instant what had befallen Ariana during the war. And that was why they hadn't killed her, why they hadn't marked her body, tattooed her arms. As the full realisation came to her, her heart went out to the girl, and she had to fight the tears that pushed from behind her eyes. It was as though they had taken one of Ruth's own beloved girls and used her as they had Ariana, the thought of it almost made Ruth Liebman ill.

For a long moment there was silence between the two women, and then Ruth gently took Ariana's hand. 'You must forget all that's behind you. All of it. You must allow yourself to have a new life.' Otherwise it would taint her forever. She was obviously a girl of good breeding, but if she let it, her nightmare with the Nazis would destroy her life. She could wind up a drunk, a whore, disturbed, in some institution, or she could lie in her bed in Beth David Hospital and choose to die. But as she held Ariana's hand, Ruth made a silent promise – to give this tiny, broken child a fresh chance in life. 'From today, Ariana, everything is new. A new home, new country, new friends, new world.'

'What about my sponsors?' Ariana stared bleakly at Ruth, whose answer to her was vague.

'We still have to call them. First we wanted to make sure you were all right. We didn't want to frighten them by calling before we knew.' But the truth was that they had called them, a Jewish family in New Jersey who had done what they considered their duty, but they were less than thrilled. A young girl was going to be a problem; they ran a business and she would be of little help; besides, they hated Germans. They had told the Women's Relief Organisation that they wanted someone French. And what the hell were they going to do with her if she was lying in a hospital bed in New York? ... Just a precaution, Ruth had assured them, nothing major, we're almost sure. But the people had been curt and unpleasant. And Ruth wasn't sure they'd take her. Unless … A thought suddenly came to her as she sat there – unless she could convince Sam to let Ariana come to them. 'As a matter of fact – ' Ruth Liebman looked pensively down at Ariana and stood to her considerable height. A smile dawned slowly on the large, kindly features and she patted Ariana's hand again. 'As a matter of fact, I have to see them later this morning. I'm sure everything will work out just fine.'

'How long do I have to say here?' Ariana looked around the small bleak room. They had continued to keep her in isolation, mostly because of the endless shrieking nightmares, but they wouldn't keep her there much longer. Ruth had heard them talking that morning of putting her out in the ward.

'You'll probably only be in the hospital for a few more days. Until we know that you're stronger.' She smiled gently at Ariana. 'You don't want to leave too quickly, Ariana you'd just go out and really get sick. Enjoy the rest here.' But as she prepared to leave, she saw a fresh wave of panic over Ariana, who looked in terror around the empty room.

'My God, my things – where are they?' Her eyes flew to Ruth Liebman's, who reassured her quickly with a warm smile.

'They're safe, Ariana. The nurse on the ship gave your suitcase to the ambulance driver, and I understand that they have it locked up here. I'm sure you'll find everything in it that you had there, Ariana. There's no need to worry.' But she was worried – her mother's rings! And with that, she looked down at her own hands. Her wedding band and her engagement ring from Manfred were both gone as well as his signet ring. She looked wildly at the older woman, who immediately understood. 'The nurse put all your valuables in the safe, Ariana.'

'Trust us a little.' And then more softly, 'The war is over, child. You're safe now.'

But was she? Ariana wondered. Was she safe and did it matter?

A few minutes later she rang for the nurse, who came running. She was curious to see the girl they had all been talking about. The one who had escaped the camps in Germany and who had slept for four days straight.

Ariana waited nervously until the woman brought the suitcase.

'Where are my rings? From my hands?' Her English was slightly rusty. She hadn't had her English tutor to give her lessons since before the war. 'I'm sorry … I was wearing rings.'

'You were?' The nurse looked vague and hurried off to check. She was back a moment later with a small envelope, which Ariana took from her and held tightly in her hand, and then she opened it slowly after the nurse had left the room. They were all there, the narrow gold band that had joined her to Manfred, the engagement ring he'd given her at Christmas, and his own signet ring, which she had been wearing behind the rest so it wouldn't fall off. Her eyes filled with tears again as she slipped them on her hands. And when she did, she realised that she had in fact been sicker than she'd realised in the twenty-two days since she had left Berlin. When she pointed her fingers downward, the rings fell swiftly into her lap. Nine days getting to Paris, two days sick with exhaustion and grief and terror there, seven days desperately ill on the ocean, and now four days in this hospital ... twenty-two days ... that seemed more like twenty-two years ... Four weeks earlier she had been in the arms of her husband, and now she would never see him again. She held the rings tightly in the palm of her left hand as, sobbing with determination, she pulled herself together. She opened the suitcase.

The clothes Jean-Pierre de Saint Marne's housekeeper had provided were still packed neatly. After the first two days on the ship, she had been too sick to move or change. Beneath them was an extra pair of shoes, and beneath that the bundle she was desperately seeking, the envelope with the photographs, and the small leather book with the secret compartment in which still rested her mother's jewels. Slowly she brought them out into the open, the large, handsome emerald, and the smaller diamond signet her father had given to her that night before he left. But she didn't put either ring on, she only stared at them as she held them. They were her only possessions, her only security, her only tangible memories of the past. They were all she had of the past. They were all she had of that lost world now. The two rings of her mother's, her rings from Manfred, his simply carved gold signet ring, and a packet of photographs that showed a man in full dress uniform and a happy, smiling nineteen-year-old girl.

Chapter 31

The secretary outside Sam Liebman's private office on Wall Street guarded his presence there like an avenging angel with a sword. No one, not even his wife or children, was allowed to enter unless he had sent for them. When he was at home, he was all theirs, but when he was at work, he considered it a sacred world. Everyone in the family knew that, especially Ruth, who seldom came to his office except on matters of ultimate importance, which was why she sat there now.

'But he may be tied up for hours.' Rebecca Greenspan looked across at her employer's wife with faint exasperation. Ruth Liebman had already been sitting there for almost two hours. And Mr Liebman had left strict orders that he was not to be disturbed.

'If he didn't go to lunch today, Rebecca, he'll have to come out sooner or later to eat. And while he's eating, I can catch a word with him.'

'Couldn't it wait until tonight?'

'If it could, I wouldn't be here. Would I?' She smiled pleasantly but firmly at the girl who was close to half her age – and also close to half her height. Ruth Liebman was an imposing-looking woman, tall, broad-shouldered, but not manly. She had a warm smile and kind eyes. She herself was dwarfed by her husband's overwhelming height. Samuel Julius Liebman stood six feet five in his stocking feet; he was broad-shouldered, had bushy eyebrows and a leonine mane about which his children teased him – his hair was almost the colour of flame. It had dulled now that he was older and had settled down to a kind of coppery bronze, fading ever more as the red hair was dimmed by an increase of grey. Like him, his oldest son, Simon, had been a redhead, but the rest of his children were dark haired like his wife.

He was a man of wisdom, charity, and kindness, and in the world of merchant banking, he was a man of great importance. The house of Langendorf & Liebman had withstood even the crash of twenty-nine, and over the twenty years that he'd built it, it had become an investment house respected by all. And one day Paul would replace his father. That was Sam's dream. He had, of course, always assumed it would be Simon and Paul. Now the entire mantle would fall on his youngest son's shoulders as soon as he was back on his feet.

At last, at three o'clock the door to the inner sanctum opened and the giant with the lion's mane emerged in a dark pin-striped suit and Homburg, his brows knit and his briefcase in his hand.

'Rebecca, I'm going to a meeting.' And then, in astonishment, he saw Ruth waiting patiently in a chair across the room. For an instant terror seized him. What now?

She smiled mischievously at her husband and his worry faded. He returned the smile and kissed her gently as she stood beside him in the anteroom and the secretary discreetly disappeared.

'This isn't the way respectable old people should be behaving, Ruth. And certainly not at three o'clock in the afternoon.'

She kissed him softly and slipped her arms around his neck. 'What if we pretend it's later?'

'Then I miss the meeting I was already late for.' He laughed softly. 'All right, Mrs Liebman, what did you have on your mind?' He sat down and lit a cigar expectantly. 'I'll give you exactly ten minutes, so let's try to get whatever it is settled quickly. Think we can do that?' His eyes danced over the cigar and she smiled. They were notorious for their long-drawn-out battles of will. She had her own ideas on some subjects, and Sam had his, and when the two were not in perfect harmony, the battles could rage on for weeks. 'How about making this a quick one?' The smile broadened to a grin. During the twenty-nine years they had been married, they had learned that in the end it was a compromise that drew on the best from each.

'I'd like to. It's up to you, Sam.'

'Oh, God, Ruth ... not another one of those. The last time you told me something was "up to me," you almost drove me crazy about that car for Paul before he went into the army. "Up to me," my eye, you had already promised him that before you ever asked me. "Up to me."' He chuckled. 'All right, what is it?'

Her face sobered and she decided to come right to the point. 'I want to sponsor a girl we brought into this country a few days ago, Sam. The Women's Relief brought her over on the ship. She's been at Beth David since she got here and the family that sponsored her doesn't want her.' Her eyes showed bitterness and anger. 'They wanted someone French. What, a French maid from a Hollywood movie maybe, or a French whore?'

'Ruth!' He glared at her disapprovingly. It was rare that she ever spoke so sharply. 'What is she, then?'

'German.' Ruth said it quietly and Sam nodded silently.

'Why is she in the hospital? Is she very sick?'

'Not really.' Ruth sighed and walked slowly around the room. 'I don't know, Sam, I think she's broken. The doctors can't find any trace of a specific disease, and certainly nothing communicable.' Ruth hesitated for a long moment. 'Oh, Sam, she's so ... so hopeless. She's twenty years old and she's lost her whole family. It's heartbreaking.' She looked at him, pleading.

'But they're all like that, Ruth.' He sighed softly. For a month now they had been learning daily more of the horrors of the camps. 'You can't bring them all home.' The truth was that with all her work for the Women's Relief Organisation, she had never wanted to bring any of them home before.

'Sam, please ... '

'What about Julia and Debbie?'

'What about them?'

'How will they feel to have a total stranger brought into the house?'

'How would they feel if they lost their whole family, Sam? If they can't at least feel for other people's problems, then I think we've failed as parents. There's been a war, Sam. They have to understand that. We all must share the consequences.'

'They've suffered the consequences.'

Sam Liebman's thoughts turned instantly to his eldest son. 'We all have. You're asking a lot of the family, Ruth. What about Paul when he comes home? It may be hard for him to have a total stranger there while he's coping with whatever problems he may have with his leg, and ...' Sam paused, unable to go on, but Ruth instantly understood. 'He's going to have a number of shocks when he gets home, Ruth, you know. It won't make it any easier for him to have a strange girl in the house.'

The tall, dark-haired woman smiled at her husband. 'It may have just the opposite effect. In fact, I think it may do him a lot of good.' They both understood only too well what Paul had to face when he got home. 'But that isn't the point. The point is this girl. We have the room in our home for her. What I want to know from you is if you'll let me bring her home to live with us, for a while.'

'How long a while?'

'I don't know, Sam. Realistically, six months, a year. She has no family, no assets, nothing, but she seems to be well educated, she speaks English quite well. In time, when she's recovered from the shock of all that's happened, I assume she'll be able to get a job and take care of herself.'

'And if she isn't able to, what do we do with her? Keep her forever?'

'Of course not. Maybe we could discuss that with her. We could offer to take her for six months, and perhaps to extend it for another six months after that; but we could make it clear to her from the beginning that after a year she'd have to go out on her own.'

Sam knew she had won. In her own way, she always won. Even when he thought he'd been winning, somehow she always got her point across. 'Mrs

Liebman, I find you disturbingly persuasive. I'm glad you don't work for any rival firms down here.'

'Does that mean yes?'

'It means I'll think it over.' And then after a moment, 'Where is she?'

'Beth David Hospital. When will you see her?' Ruth Liebman grinned and her husband sighed and put down his cigar.

'I'll try to see her on my way home tonight. Will she recognise the name if I tell her who I am?'

'She should. I was with her all morning. Just tell her you're the husband of the volunteer named Ruth.' And then she saw he was worrying over something. 'What's the matter?'

'Is she disfigured?'

Ruth went to him and touched his cheek gently. 'Of course not.' She loved the weakness and fears that she sometimes saw in him; it made her even more aware of his strengths and reduced him to a scale that seemed more human to her. Catching those glimpses always made her love him more. She looked at him with a small smile and a twinkle. 'In fact, she's very pretty. But she's so . . . so desperately alone now . . . you'll understand when you see her. It's as though she's lost all hope.'

'She probably has after what she's been through. Why should she believe in anyone now? After what they did to those people . . .' There was suddenly fire again in Sam Liebman's eyes. It made him crazy to think of what those sons of bitches had done. When he had read the first reports of Auschwitz, he had sat alone in his study, reading and thinking and praying, and finally crying all night. And then he looked at Ruth again as he reached for his Homburg. 'Does she trust you?'

Ruth thought for a minute. 'I think so. As much as she trusts anyone now.'

'All right, then.' He picked up his briefcase. 'I'll go meet her.'

He looked at her for a long moment, then they walked to the elevator. 'I love you, Ruth Liebman. You're a wonderful woman, and I love you.'

She kissed him gently in answer, and then just before the doors opened for them, 'I love you, too, Sam. So when will you tell me?'

He rolled his eyes as the doors opened and they stepped into the elevator. 'I'll tell you tonight when I get home. Will that do?' But he was smiling at her, and she nodded happily, and then she kissed him quickly on the cheek as he went off to his meeting and she climbed into her new Chevrolet and drove home.

Chapter 32

In her hospital room, Ariana sat quietly on the bed all morning, looking out the window into the bright sunlight and, when that became tiresome, staring at the floor of her room. After a while, a nurse came by to urge her to go walking, and after a few feeble attempts to crawl down the corridor, holding on to railings and doorways, she finally went back to bed. But after lunch they told her she was moving, and by dinnertime she found herself in a bed in the bustling ward. The nurse had told her that it would do her good to see other people, but soon Ariana asked them to put a screen around her; and listening to the laughter and the noises, and smelling the trays of dinner all around her, Ariana lay miserably in her bed overcome by waves of nausea. She was still holding the towel to her mouth, her eyes watering pathetically after another bout of dry heaves, when there was a knock on the screen that shielded her from the others and with a look of panic she put down the towel and looked up.

'Who is it?' Not that it mattered – she didn't know anyone here. Her words were spoken softly and her eyes seemed to grow larger as a huge man loomed at her from around the screen. She had never felt smaller or more frightened than she did at that moment, and as Samuel Liebman looked down at her, she began to tremble visibly and had to fight not to cry out. Who was he? What did he want from her? In his Homburg and dark suit, he looked so official, she was sure he was with the police or immigration. Were they sending her back to France?

But the man looked at her gently, the eyes soft and warm despite his towering height. 'Miss Tripp ... ?' That was the name on her papers. Saint Marne had conveniently dropped the 'von.'

'Yes?' It was barely more than a whisper.

'How are you?' She didn't dare answer. She was shaking so badly that he wasn't even sure if he should stay. She was sick and frightened and alone and he could understand why Ruth's heart had gone out to this girl. She was a lovely child. And it was clear to him as he watched her that she was barely more than a child. 'Miss Tripp, I'm Ruth Liebman's husband.' He wanted to hold out a hand to her, but he was afraid that if he moved towards her, she would leap, trembling, off the bed, so precarious did she seem there, so terrified and poised for flight. 'You know, Ruth Liebman, the lady who was here this morning? The volunteer.' Sam fought to jar her memory. Slowly the light dawned in her eyes. Even in her total state of panic, the name Ruth rang a bell.

'Yes ... yes ... I know ... she was here ... today.' Ariana's English sounded more than adequate, even cultured, but she spoke so softly that Sam could barely hear.

'She asked me to come to see you. So I thought I'd stop in on my way home.' *Did she? Why? As a social visit? Did people still do things like that?* Ariana stared at him in amazement, her eyes a blank stare, and then, remembering her manners, she nodded slowly. 'Thank you.' And then, as though with great effort, she held out a small, wraithlike hand.

'It's a pleasure,' Sam reassured her, though they both knew that that was not quite the word. The ward was perfectly dreadful, and screeches and cries seemed to increase rather than lessen as they attempted to talk. She had waved him to a seat at the foot of her bed, and now he sat there, looking uncomfortable and trying not to stare. 'Is there anything I can get you? Anything you need?' The huge eyes bored into his but all she did was shake her head, while he reproached himself for the stupid question. Her needs could not be easily met.

'My wife and I want you to know that in any way we can, we'd like to help syou.' He sighed jaggedly and went on. 'It's difficult for people in this country to really understand what has happened over there ... but we care ... we care deeply ... and that you have survived it is a miracle we must rejoice in. You and the other survivors will remain something of a monument to these times, and to the others, and you must live well now – for yourself, and for them.' He stood up and walked towards her.

It was a difficult speech for him, and Ariana watched him with round eyes. What exactly was he thinking? Did he know she had escaped from Berlin? Of what 'others' was he speaking? Or did he just mean the Germans who had survived? But whatever he meant, and whomever he was referring to, it was clear that this was a man who cared a great deal. With his great height and wild hair, he looked so different from her father, yet she felt her heart go out to him as though to an old friend. This was a man of dignity and compassion, a man she respected, and whom her father would have honoured, too. She leaned forward then and put her arms gently on his broad shoulders, and kissed him carefully on the cheek.

'Thank you, Mr Liebman. You make me glad that I'm here.'

'You should be.' He smiled tenderly at her, touched by the kiss. 'This is a great country, Ariana.' It was the first time he had called her that, but now he felt he could. 'You'll find out what it's like here. It's a new world, a new life for you, you'll meet new people, new friends.' But her eyes only looked sadder as she listened. She didn't want new people, she wanted the old ones, and they were gone for good. But as though seeing the pain that had returned to her eyes then, Sam Liebman touched her hand. 'Ruth and I are your friends now, Ariana. That's why I came here to see you.' And then, as she understood what he was saying, that he had come to see her, there in the hospital, in that hideous ward, that he had come there because he cared about her, her eyes filled slowly with tears. But behind the tears there was a smile.

'Thank you, Mr Liebman.'

As he watched her, he had to fight back tears, too. He stood up slowly, still holding the small hand, and then he squeezed it for a moment. 'I have to go now, Ariana. But Ruth will be back to see you tomorrow. And I will see you soon, too.' Like a child being deserted she nodded, trying to smile, and desperately fighting the tears that threatened to get out of control. And then, unable to hold himself back any further, Samuel Liebman took her into his arms. He held her that way, bearlike, for almost half an hour, as Ariana gave way to uncontrollable sobs. At last, when she stopped, he handed her his handkerchief and she blew her nose long and hard.

'I'm so sorry ... I didn't mean to ... it was just that ...' 'Sshh ... stop it.' He stroked her head gently. 'You needn't explain Ariana. I understand.' As he looked down at the elflike golden girl, bowing her head into his handkerchief on the big bed, he asked himself how she had survived it. She looked too frail to have survived even one rugged moment, yet he sensed also that beyond the delicately carved features, the thin frame, the little, graceful figure, there was a woman who could have survived almost anything, and still would. Something tough and invincible had allowed her to survive it, and as Sam Liebman looked at the girl who had just become his third daughter, he thanked God that she had.

Chapter 33

The preparations for Ariana's arrival were undertaken with a mixture of rejoicing and awe. Sam had returned to the house after he had met her and all but ordered Ruth to get the child out of that ward by the next day. As long as the doctors felt that she was not ill in any way that endangered his children, he wanted Ariana brought to the house on Fifth Avenue, as quickly as could be arranged. The girls were called to his den after dinner and it was explained to them that Ariana was about to join them, that she was German, had lost her entire family, and that they would have to be gentle with her for a while.

Like their parents, Julia and Debbie were compassionate. They, too, were overcome with the shock of what the news brought daily about Germany. They, too, wanted to lend their support. The next morning they pleaded with Ruth to let them come along on her visit to the hospital. But in this the elder Liebmans held their position firmly. It would be time enough for the girls to meet Ariana at home. And as worn-out as Ariana had been since the disastrous sea voyage, Ruth was afraid that their visits would be too much. In fact, at the doctor's suggestion, she was planning to keep Ariana in bed at home for the first week. After that, if she felt stronger, they could take her out with them for lunch, or dinner, or even a movie or two. But first, it was obvious that she was going to have to build up her strength.

Ruth appeared at the hospital and announced to Ariana that she and her husband wanted her to move into their home, not for the six months she had first told Sam, but for as long as Ariana needed a family. Ariana stared at her in total amazement, sure that her English had momentarily led her astray and she hadn't properly understood.

'I'm sorry?' She had looked at Ruth inquiringly. It was impossible that she had heard what she thought she'd heard. But Ruth had taken both of Ariana's small hands into her larger ones and sat down on the bed in the ward with a smile.

'Mr Liebman and I would like you to come and live with us, Ariana. For as long as you'd like.' After he had seen her it was Sam who had dropped the stipulation of six months to a year.

'At your home?' But why would this woman do that? Ariana already had a sponsor, and this woman had already taken so much time just to be with Ariana. She looked at her benefactress now with nothing less than awe.

'Yes, at our home, with our daughters, Deborah and Julia, and in a few weeks our son will be coming home, too. Paul has been in the Pacific, but he recently took some shell fragments around his kneecap, and soon he will be well enough to travel.' She didn't tell her about Simon. There was really no point. She simply rambled on happily, telling Ariana about the children, giving the girl time to sort out her own thoughts.

'Mrs Liebman ... 'Ariana stared at her. 'I don't know what to say.' For a moment she lapsed into German, but Ruth Liebman's knowledge of Yiddish somewhat helped her out.

'You don't have to say anything, Ariana.' And then suddenly the older woman smiled. 'But if you do, you should try to say it in English, otherwise the girls won't understand.'

'Did I speak German again? I'm sorry.' Ariana blushed and then for the first time in weeks she looked at Ruth Liebman and laughed. 'Are you really taking me home with you?' She looked at her friend in total astonishment, and the two women exchanged a long smile as Ruth nodded and held tightly to the young girl's hands. 'But why will you do this? For what reason? It's so much trouble for you and your husband.' And then suddenly she remembered Max Thomas during the two days he'd stayed with them. He had felt just as she did now ... but that had been different. Max had been an old friend. And her father hadn't offered to house him forever. But as she thought of it, she knew that her father would have. Perhaps this was the same kind of thing.

Ruth was looking at her seriously now. 'Ariana, we want to do this. Because we're sorry about all that has happened.'

Ariana looked at her sadly. 'But it's not your fault, Mrs Liebman. It was just ... the war ...' Ariana seemed so helpless for a moment, and Ruth Liebman put an arm around her shoulders, running a hand over the soft golden hair that hung down her back.

'We've felt the teeth of the war, the unfairness, the horror, the anguish, even here.' As she said it, she thought of Simon, who had died for his country, but truly for what? 'But we have never known what you experienced in Europe. Maybe in some way, if we can, we could make up one tiny bit of what happened to you, just so that you can forget for a moment, just so that you get a fresh start.' And then she gazed at the girl gently. 'Ariana, you're still so very young.'

But Ariana shook her head slowly in answer. 'Not any more.'

Several hours later Sam Liebman's chauffeur-driven Daimler drove Ariana sedately to the Fifth Avenue house. Across the street Central Park beckoned with lush trees and bright flowers, and clipping slowly along the park's paths, Ariana could see hansom cabs and young couples in each other's arms. It was a beautiful spring morning at the end of May. And this was Ariana's first glimpse of New York. She looked like a small child as she sat there, tucked in between Samuel and Ruth.

Sam had left his office to go to the hospital, and he himself had carried Ariana's one pathetic little cardboard suitcase to the car. In it she had once more packed her few treasures, and from it she had planned to pull out whatever she had to wear home when the Liebmans picked her up. But Ruth had stopped briefly at Best & Co, that morning, and the box she proudly handed to Ariana yielded a pretty pale blue summer dress, almost the colour of Ariana's eyes, with a tiny gathered waist and a huge softly flowing full skirt. Dressed in it, Ariana looked more than ever like a fairy princess, and Ruth stood back to look at her with a warm smile. She had also brought her white gloves, a sweater, and a pretty little natural straw cloth hat that tilted to one side and showed off Ariana's face. And miraculously, the pumps she had bought fitted Ariana's tiny feet. When they emerged from the hospital, she looked like a different girl, and sitting in Sam Liebman's handsome maroon car, looking at her first glimpse of the city, she looked more like a tourist than a refugee.

For an instant Ariana found herself wondering if it could be a game of let's pretend ... if she closed her eyes just for a minute, would it feel as though she were back in Berlin, on her way to the house in Grunewald ... but as in testing a too fresh wound, she found that touching it still brought back waves of unwanted pain. It was easier to keep her eyes open, look around her, and drink it all in. Now and then Sam and Ruth smiled at each other over her head. They were happy with the decision they had made. Fifteen minutes after they had left the hospital, the Daimler drew to a halt and the chauffeur got out and held the door. He was a distinguished-looking, careworn black man in a black uniform, a black cap, white shirt, and bow tie.

He touched his cap as Sam alighted and then offered Ruth his arm. She declined it with a warm glance, looking back over her shoulder at Ariana, and then she gently helped her out herself. Ariana had not yet retrieved all her forces, and despite the pretty hat and dress, she was still looking very pale.

'Are you all right, Ariana?'

'Yes, thank you, I'm fine.' But Ruth and Sam watched her with caution. While she had been dressing, she had felt so faint that she had had to sit down, and it was lucky Ruth had been there to help. But it was something else about her that Sam was watching, her finesse, her poise, the calm with which she had moved the moment she got into the car. It was as though she had finally entered a world in which she was entirely at home, and he found himself wanting to ask questions. This was not just a well-brought-up, nicely educated girl; this was a young woman of the uppermost echelons, a diamond of the first water, which made it an even greater tragedy that now she had nothing at all. But she had them now, he consoled himself, as she stood next to Ruth for a moment, looking out at the park with wonder and a long, slow smile. She had been thinking of the Grunewaldsee and the trees and boats. But that might as well have been on another planet as she stood there, feeling far, far from home.

'Ready to go home now?' Ariana nodded and Ruth led her slowly inside, to the main hall, which rose for two floors above them, draped in rich, gem-coloured velvets and filled with antiques they had acquired on trips to Europe before the war. There were medieval paintings, statues of horses, long Persian runners, a small marble fountain, and a grand piano visible in the conservatory at the end of the hall. And in the centre of the entrance a stairway that spiralled skyward, on which stood two wide-eyed, gangling, dark-haired girls.

In silence they stared at Ariana, then their mother, then back at Ariana again, waiting for some silent signal, and then suddenly, not seeming to care about what was expected, they tore down the staircase and threw their arms around Ariana, shouting, giggling, jumping up and down, and dancing with glee.

'Welcome, Ariana! Welcome home!' It was a harmony of shrieking that brought fresh tears to Ruth Liebman's eyes. Gone the solemn moment among the elders – the girls had even obscured Ariana's bittersweet moment and turned it into the celebration that it was. They had a cake waiting, and balloons and streamers, and Debbie had cut a huge bouquet of fresh roses from the bushes in the garden. Julia had baked the cake, and together they had gone out that morning and bought Ariana all the things that they felt a young lady of Ariana's advanced years ought to require, three deep pink lipsticks, several powders and two huge pink puffs, a jar of rouge, several hair ornaments and tortoiseshell hairpins, and even a funny blue hairnet that Debbie insisted was going to be the rage by the fall. They had gift-wrapped each and every item and piled them high on the dressing table of the guest room Ruth had set aside for Ariana the night before.

When Ariana saw the room, she was moved to fresh tears. In some ways it reminded her of her mother's long-closed rooms in Grunewald. This, too, was a paradise of silks and satins done in a spun-candy pink, but this room was even prettier, the bed was larger, and everything was fresh and perfect and cheerful, just as one would have expected a room in America to be. The bed was covered by a huge white organdy canopy, the bedspread a lovely pink and white satin quilt. There was a desk all intricately covered with trompe l'oeil designs and flowers, a huge antique armoire for her clothes, a white marble fireplace topped by a handsome gilt mirror, and an abundance of small, elegantly upholstered chairs covered in pink satin, where the girls could come and sit with Ariana, chatting until the wee hours. Beyond the bedroom was a small dressing room, and beyond that a pink marble bath. And everywhere Ariana looked there were pink roses, and on a table set for five was Julia's cake.

Unable to find the words to thank them, Ariana simply hugged them and continued alternately to laugh and cry. Then she hugged Sam and Ruth again.

What miracle was this that now she should wind up in such a home? It was as though she had come full circle, from the house in Grunewald, to the tiny cell where Von Rheinhardt had left her, to the women's barracks, and then to the safety of Manfred's house, and after that out into the world to nothing, and now back into the luxurious comfort of a world she knew, a world she had grown up in, a world of servants and large cars and pink marble bathrooms, like the one she stared at now in disbelief. But the face she glimpsed briefly in the mirror was no longer the face of the young girl she had known. This was a gaunt and tired stranger, someone who did not really belong in this house. Now she belonged nowhere, to no one, and if they wanted to be kind to her for a while, she would let them and be grateful, but she would never count on a world of pink marble bathrooms again.

In solemn celebration, they sat down to eat Julia's elaborately decorated cake. She had written 'Ariana' in pink rose petals in the frosting, and Ariana smiled as she tried to fight the desperate nausea she never seemed able to escape now as they cut her a slice of the cake. She found that she was barely able to eat it, and although the girls were lovely, she was grateful when at last Ruth shooed them out. Sam had to get back to the office, the girls had to visit their grandmother for lunch, and Ruth wanted Ariana to go to bed now. It was time they left her alone to rest. She laid out the robe and one of the four nightgowns she had bought for her that morning at Best's, and once again, Ariana stared at the gifts in amazement. White lace and satin ... pink lace ... blue satin ... it was all so wonderfully familiar, and yet now it all seemed so remarkable and so new.

'Are you all right, Ariana?' Ruth cast her a searching glance as Ariana sank on to the bed.

'I'm fine, Mrs Liebman ... and you've all been so good to me ... I still don't know what to say.'

'Don't say anything. Just enjoy it.' And then, after a moment of pensive silence, she looked at Ariana. 'In some ways I think it is our way of living with the guilt.'

'What guilt?' Ariana looked at her in confusion.

'The guilt that we were all safe here while all of you in Europe ...' She paused for a moment. 'You were no different than we were, yet you all paid the price for being Jews.'

In a moment of stunned silence Ariana understood. They thought that she was a Jew. So that was why they had taken her in like one of their own children ... that was why they were so good to her – they thought she was a Jew. Bereft and anguished, she stared at Ruth Liebman. She had to tell her. She couldn't let her think ... but what could she tell her? That she was a *German* ... a real one ... that she was one of the race that had killed those Jews? What would they think then? That she was a Nazi. But she wasn't. Nor had been her father ... nor Gerhard. Her eyes filled with tears as she thought of it ... they would never understand it ... never ... they would cast her away from them ... put her on the boat again. A sob broke from her and Ruth Liebman ran to her and held her tightly as they sat side by side on the bed. 'Oh, my God ... I'm sorry, Ariana ... I'm so sorry. There is no need for us to speak of that now.'

But she had to tell her ... had to tell her ... but a little voice inside Ariana silenced her. *Not just yet. Once they know you better, then maybe they will understand.* And she was too exhausted to argue with the voice any further. She just let Ruth Liebman tuck her into the canopied bed beneath the bedspread of pink satin, and with a long, jagged sigh, after a few moments, Ariana slept.

And when she awoke, she once again sat thinking over her problem. Should she tell them now or wait? But by then Debbie had already written her a poem, and Julia knocked softly on the door to bring her a cup of tea and another slice of the cake. It was impossible to tell them. Already she had been woven in among them. Already it was too late.

Chapter 34

'Now what are you three up to?' Ruth looked in on the three girls, giggling together in Ariana's bedroom. Ariana had been showing them how to put on rouge. 'Aha! Painted women!' Ruth looked at the three faces and grinned. Ariana looked even sillier than the two others, with her fair cameo beauty and her long blonde hair falling over her shoulders childlike; the rouge looked ridiculously out of place on her cheeks.

'Can't we take Ariana out tomorrow?' Julia looked at her mother pleadingly, a long-legged, sensual colt with huge brown eyes that somehow made her look more than just sixteen. She was fully as tall as her mother, but there was something more delicate about the cast of her face. Ariana thought her very lovely, and somewhat exotic. And she was so wonderfully honest and open, so bright, and she had such a quick wit.

Debbie on the other hand was more gentle, quieter, but very lovely, too. She was still something of a dreamer, and unlike Julia she was not interested in boys at all. She was only interested in her beloved brother, and in another week he was due home. By then, Ruth had promised, Ariana could be out with the girls, every day if she chose. But in the meantime she still wanted her stay quiet, and she could see, too, that despite Ariana's protests, the girl was often grateful to be left alone to lie down.

'Ariana, is it that you feel ill, dear, or only very tired?' It still troubled Ruth greatly, and she was growing more afraid daily that Ariana had in some way been marked for life. At times she was very lively and rapidly becoming a part of the family's roughhousing and cavorting on weekends and after meals, but still Ruth could see that the girl was not at all recovered from her ordeal. She had made Ariana promise that they would return to the doctor again if she didn't feel a great deal better by the following week.

'I promise you, it's nothing. I'm only tired ... I think it was just from being so seasick on the boat.' But Ruth knew full well that it wasn't the ocean crossing. It was a sickness of the heart. But Ariana never faltered, never complained. She helped the girls each day with their summer studies, tidied her room, sewed for Ruth, and twice now Ruth had found her downstairs helping their housekeeper to rearrange the linen cupboards, sifting through mountains of sheets and tablecloths and napkins, in an effort to put order in areas where Ruth seldom had the time or interest to interfere. The last time she caught her, Ruth had sent her quickly packing to her room, with orders to go back to rest. But instead she had found her in Paul's room, sewing the new curtains Ruth had started but never had time to finish. It was obvious that Ariana wanted to be part of this homecoming. Everyone else in the house was and she wanted to be, too.

And as Ariana sat quietly in Paul's room, sewing, she wondered what kind of young man he was. She knew how infinitely dear he was to his parents, but she didn't know much more than that, except that he was close to her own age and that the high school pictures that lined the room showed a tall, smiling, athletic-looking boy with broad shoulders and a mischievous light in his eye. She liked the look of him, even before they met, and it wouldn't be long now before she met him. He would be home Saturday and Ariana knew now how desperately they had longed for his return, particularly after the death of their eldest son. Ruth had told her gently about Simon, and of course, Ariana knew the loss of Simon had been a severe blow, which made Paul more precious to them now. But Ariana also knew now that Paul's homecoming was not going to be easy for another reason.

Ruth had told her that when he had left two years before, Paul had wanted to be just like his older brother. Everything he did had to be a mirror image of what his older brother did. And when Simon left, he was engaged. So just before Paul shipped out, he got engaged, too. To a girl he'd known all his life. 'She's a very sweet girl,' Ruth had sighed. 'But they were both twenty, and in some ways Joan was a lot more mature than Paul.' As Ariana watched Ruth's eyes, she suddenly understood. 'Six months ago Joan married another man. It's not the end of the world, of course, or it shouldn't be, but ...' She had looked up in agony at Ariana. 'She never told Paul. We thought she'd written to him, but finally she told us that she never told him a thing.'

'He still doesn't know?' Ariana's voice was filled with compassion. Miserably, Ruth shook her head. 'Oh, my God. And you're going to have to tell him when he comes home?'

'We are. And I can't think of anything I less want to do.'

'What about the girl? Do you suppose she'd be willing to come and tell him? She doesn't have to tell him she's married after all. She could just break off the engagement, and then if he found out about it later ... '

But Ruth smiled ruefully. 'I'd love it, but she's eight months pregnant.' Ariana smiled. 'I'm afraid it falls back on me and his father.'

So that was what they had to look forward to. Ariana couldn't help wondering how he'd take the news. She had already heard from his sisters that he had a ferocious temper and that he was a very intense young man. She worried, too, how he would feel about having a stranger there, in his house, when he returned. To him, after all, she would be a stranger, even though before he even came home, Paul was no stranger to her. She had heard dozens of stories about him, his childhood, his jokes, his mischief. She felt that he was already her friend. But what would he feel about this mysterious German girl who had suddenly appeared in their midst? She couldn't help wondering if he wouldn't be put off by her after viewing Germans as the enemy for so long, or if like the rest of his family, he would trust and accept her as one of their own.

It was precisely this trust and acceptance that made her not tell them she was not Jewish. After days of silent torment she had made up her mind. She couldn't tell them, it would destroy everything. They would never understand that a non-Jewish German could be a decent human being. They were too blinded by their own pain and revulsion at what the Germans had done. It was simpler to keep quiet and suffer her twinges of guilt. It didn't matter now. The past was dead and gone. And they would never find out the truth. If they knew, it would only hurt them. They would feel they had been betrayed. And they hadn't. Ariana had lost as much as anyone. She needed the Liebmans just as much as they had known she needed them from the first. There was no reason to tell them. And she couldn't now. She couldn't bear to lose this family, too. She only hoped that Paul would accept her, too. Now and then she worried that he might ask too many questions, but she'd just have to wait and see.

But Ruth's mind was turned in an entirely different direction. It occurred to her that having a young girl as pretty as Ariana afoot would distract him, too. Despite the fatigue that continued to pull her, the girl had blossomed in the brief two weeks. She had the most perfect complexion Ruth had ever seen on another living human being – it was like a perfect peach velvet, her eyes like heather kissed with dew. Her laughter was bright and sunny, her body lithe and graceful, her mind sharp. She would have been a gift to any mother, and the thought of that did not escape Ruth Liebman whenever she worried about Paul. But she couldn't only think of Paul now; she had to consider Ariana too, which reminded her that there had been something she wanted to ask her. She narrowed her eyes now as she looked at Ariana, who felt suddenly like a very small child beneath that gaze. 'Tell me something, young lady, why didn't you tell me that you fainted yesterday morning? I saw you at lunchtime, and you told me you were fine.' The servants had told her that afternoon.

'I was fine by then.' She smiled at Ruth, but Ruth did not look pleased.

'I want you to tell me when those things happen. Do you understand that, Ariana?'

'Yes, Aunt Ruth.' It was the name they had decided was most comfortable.

'How often has that happened?'

'Only once or twice. I think it just happens when I'm very tired or when I don't eat.'

'Which, from what I can see, is all the time. You're not eating enough, young lady.'

'Yes, ma'am.'

'Never mind that. If you faint again, I want to be told immediately, and by you, not by the servants. Is that clear?'

'Yes, I'm sorry. I just didn't want to worry you.'

'So worry me a little. It worries me more if I feel I'm not being told.' And then her face softened again and Ariana smiled. 'Please, darling, I really worry about you. And it's important that in these first few months we take especially good care of your health. If you're careful to recover properly now, you won't have ugly reminders of the past forever. But if you don't take care of yourself, you may pay for it for the rest of your life.'

'I'm sorry, Aunt Ruth.'

'Don't be sorry. Just take care of yourself. And if you continue fainting, I want to take you back to our doctor. All right?' He had already seen her at the hospital before she checked out.

'I promise I'll let you know next time. But don't worry about me, you're going to be busy enough next week with Paul. Will he have to be confined to his bed?'

'No. I think he ought to be able to manage, as long as he's careful. I'll have to follow around after both of you to make sure you take care of yourselves.'

But Ruth didn't have far to follow after her son when he got home. When they told him the news of Joanie's marriage, he was so overwhelmed that he spent two days locked in his room. He let no one in, not even his sisters, and it was his father who at last prevailed and convinced him to emerge. When he did, he looked ghastly, exhausted, unshaven. But the rest of the family looked almost as bad. After the long years of terror and worry, to have him home at last, and so distraught over the broken engagement, made them ache with frustration at his pain. But in a roar of anger his father had finally accused him of self-indulgence and childish pouting, and his own anger at his father's words had at last brought him out of his shell. He appeared at breakfast the next morning, clean-shaven, pale, and red-eyed, and although he spoke tersely to all present, he was at least there. It wasn't until the end of the meal that he addressed anyone. He had been staring angrily at everyone, except Ariana, whom he didn't seem to see at all. And then suddenly, as though someone had hit him on the shoulder, he looked across the table at her with a look of surprise.

For a moment she wasn't sure whether to smile at him or just to sit there. She was almost terrified to acknowledge the look in his eyes. It was a piercing stare that went to the very core of her being, questioning her presence in his home, at his table, silently asking her why she was there. Following her instincts, she nodded and then averted her eyes, but she could feel his gaze on her for endless moments, and when she looked up at him again, there seemed to be a thousand questions in his eyes.

'What part of Germany did you come from?' He didn't say her name, and the question fell strangely into his parents' conversation as he speared her with his eyes.

She looked him straight in the eyes. 'Berlin.'

He nodded, his brows suddenly knit together. 'Did you see it after the fall?'

'Only briefly.' Ruth and Samuel exchanged uncomfortable glances but Ariana didn't waver. Only her hands trembled slightly as she buttered a small piece of toast.

'How was it?' He eyed her with increasing interest. In the Pacific, they had only heard distant rumours of what the fall of Berlin had been like.

But for Ariana the question conjured up a sudden vision of Manfred in the stack of bodies outside the Reichstag, and involuntarily she closed her eyes, as though that gesture could banish the memory, as though anything ever could. For a moment there was a terrible silence at the table, and then Ruth stepped rapidly into the gap.

'I don't think any of us needs to discuss things like that. At least not now, and not at breakfast.' She looked worriedly at Ariana, who had once again opened her eyes, but they were heavily veiled with tears.

Ariana shook her head gently and without thinking stretched a hand across the table to Paul. 'I'm sorry ... it's just ... it's so ...' There was a little catch in her throat '... it is very ... difficult ... for me to remember ...' The tears were rolling openly down her face now. 'I lost ... so much ...' And then suddenly there were tears in Paul's eyes and his hands reached across the table and took hers tightly in their grasp.

'I'm the one who's sorry. I was very stupid. I won't ever ask you anything like that again.' She nodded with a small grateful smile, and then carefully he stood up, walked to her side, and with his linen napkin he wiped the tears from her face. There was total silence in the dining room as he did it, and then quietly the rest of the family collected themselves and went on as before. But a bond seemed to form rapidly between them and she sensed him a friend.

He was as tall as his father but he still had the narrow frame of a very young man. He had the rich dark brown eyes of his mother, and almost raven black hair like the girls', but she knew from photographs that his smile was different from all the others'. It broke across his face with a great splash of excitement, cutting an ivory path of radiance across his otherwise serious face. It was the most serious side Ariana had seen that morning, when he seemed almost sultry, with the black brows knit, the dark eyes angry, like a hurricane gathering and waiting to empty the ire of the heavens on cue. One almost expected thunder and lightning when he looked like that. Thinking of it made her smile as she slipped into a white cotton dress and the cork-soled Wedgie sandals that she and Julia had both bought a few days before. Ruth had insisted that she go shopping and buy a few more things. But Ariana still didn't know what to do about this constant generosity they showered on her. The only solution she could come up with was to keep an elaborate record, and later when she felt well enough to get a job, she would repay them for the hats, the coats, the dresses, the underwear, the shoes. The armoire in her bedroom was rapidly filling with lovely clothes.

As for the rings she still kept hidden, she couldn't think of selling them. Not now. They were the only security she had left. She fingered her mother's rings now and then, and once she had been tempted to show Ruth, but she was afraid that it would seem as though she were showing off. And the rings from Manfred were still much too big for her with all the weight she'd lost. She would like to wear Manfred's rings. In a different way than her mother's, she felt that Manfred's rings were part of her soul, just as Manfred was, and always would be. She would have liked to tell the Liebmans about him, but it was too late. And anyway, to explain to them that she had been married and that her husband had died, too, was more than she could bear to tell them, more than she could stand to think of, and perhaps also more than they cared to hear.

'What are you looking so serious about, Ariana?' Julia had slipped into her room with a small smile. She was wearing the twin pair of sandals, and Ariana looked at the young girl's feet and smiled.

'Nothing special. I like our new shoes.'

'So do I. Do you want to come out with my brother?'

'Wouldn't the three of you rather be alone?'

'No, he's not like Simon was. Paul and I always get into fights, and then he picks on Debbie, and then we all start yelling ...' She grinned at Ariana invitingly, half woman, half girl. 'Doesn't that sound appealing? Come on, you'll have a ball.'

'You know, maybe you're just assuming that's how he'll behave. He's been at war for two years since you last saw him, Julia. He may have changed a lot.' She had already glimpsed that herself at the table that morning.

But Julia only raised her eyebrows. 'Not judging from the performance over Joanie. Gee, Ariana, she wasn't even all that nice. He was just mad that she went off with someone else. And' – Julia giggled unkindly – 'you should see her –' she stuck her arms way out front – 'she looks like an elephant since she got pregnant. Mother and I saw her last week.'

'Did you?' The voice in the doorway was frigid. 'Well, I'll thank you not to discuss it. With me or anyone else in this house.' Paul strolled into the room, looking livid. Julia turned scarlet in embarrassment at being caught gossiping about his affairs.

'I'm sorry. I didn't know you were standing right there.'

'Apparently.' But as he gazed at her haughtily, Ariana suddenly realised the part he was playing. He was only a boy after all, pretending to be a man. And he had been hurt. Perhaps that was why he had attempted to comfort her pain. He looked in an odd way much like Gerhard. And as she watched him then, she couldn't help smiling softly, and when Paul saw her, he looked at her for a long moment, and then he smiled, too. 'I'm sorry if I was rude, Ariana.' And then after a moment, 'I'm afraid I've been rude to everyone since I came home.' He was indeed much like Gerhard, and she felt more kindly to him now because of it. Their eyes met warmly and held.

'You had good reason to. I'm sure it must be very difficult to come home after so long. A lot of things have changed.'

But he only smiled at her in answer, and then he spoke softly. 'Some things even change for the good.'

They drove to Sheepshead Bay out in Brooklyn to eat oysters, down to the tip of Manhattan to glimpse the Statue of Liberty Ariana had been too sick to see a few weeks before; they drove slowly up Fifth Avenue, and then Paul took them over to Third Avenue so he could race along beneath the elevated train. But as they raced across the cobblestones of Third Avenue, Ariana became noticeably green.

'Sorry, old girl.'

'It's nothing.' She looked embarrassed.

Paul was grinning at her good-naturedly. 'It would have been something if you'd got sick in my mother's new car.' Even Ariana had to laugh at that, and the group continued on to Central Park, there they picnicked happily by the boat pond and eventually wandered down to laugh at the animals at the zoo. The monkeys were all cavorting in their cages, the sun was high and warm, it was a perfect June afternoon, and they were all young together. And for the first time since she had lost Manfred, Ariana thought that she felt truly happy again.

'Hey, what are we doing this summer?' Paul broached the subject at dinner that night. 'Are we staying in town?'

The parents glanced at each other quickly. Paul always was the one to get things moving. It took some adjusting to get used to his being at home. 'Well, we weren't sure what your plans would be, darling.' Ruth smiled at him as she served herself some roast beef from the large silver tray being held by one of the maids. 'I had thought about renting something in Connecticut or out on Long Island, but your father and I hadn't made any decisions yet.' After Simon's death they had sold their country house in upstate New York. The memories there had been far too painful.

'Which brings to mind,' his father tossed at him casually, 'that you have a few other decisions to make first. But there's no hurry, Paul. You just got home.' He was referring to the office in his own firm, which was being redecorated for his son.

'I think we have a lot to talk about, Father.' He looked directly at the elder Liebman and the old man smiled.

'Do you? Then why don't you come downtown and have lunch with me tomorrow?' He would have his secretary have special trays sent in from their kitchens just below the boardrooms.

'I'd like that.'

What Sam Liebman wasn't prepared for was that his son wanted to negotiate a Cadillac roadster, and he wanted to have one last idle summer before he went to work for his father in the fall. But even Sam had to admit that it made sense for the boy to do that. He was only twenty-two, and if he had been finishing college, the same rules would have applied. He had a right to one last fling, one summer, and the car wasn't so much to ask. They were grateful to have him home now ... grateful that he had come home at all ...

At four o'clock that afternoon Paul stood in Ariana's open bedroom doorway; he was surprised to find her alone. 'Well, I did it.' He looked quiet but victorious, and for an instant he looked more man than boy.

'What did you do, Paul?' She smiled at him and waved a hand towards a chair. 'Come in and sit down and tell me what you did.'

'I got my father to give me a summer holiday before I go to work for him in the fall. And' – he beamed at her, once more a boy – 'he's giving me a Cadillac roadster. How does it sound?'

'Amazing.' She had only seen one Cadillac in Germany before the war, and she could barely remember it. She was sure it hadn't been a roadster. This was a whole new world. 'What does it look like, this Cadillac roadster?'

'A perfect beauty of a car. Can you drive, Ariana?' He looked at her with a curious smile, and her brow clouded.

'Yes, I can.'

He didn't know what had happened, but he knew that he had revived some old pain. Gently he reached out and took her hand then, and he reminded her more than ever of Gerhard as she fought back tears. 'I'm sorry, I shouldn't have asked you. It's just that sometimes I forget I shouldn't ask you questions about your past.'

'Don't be silly.' She held on to his hand more tightly. She wanted him to know that he had done no harm. 'You can't always treat me like a fragile package. You can't be afraid to ask me things. And in time I will stop hurting ... It's just that now ... some things still hurt very much, Paul ... it's all very fresh.' He nodded, thinking of both Joanie and his brother – they were the only losses he had known. One so real and so forever, the other different but painful nonetheless. As Ariana watched him with his head bowed, she smiled again. 'Sometimes you remind me of my brother.' His eyes reached up to hers then – it was the first time that she had willingly told him of her past.

'What was he like?'

'Outrageous sometimes. He once blew up his room with his chemistry set.' For a moment she smiled, but it was easy to see that her eyes were rapidly filling with tears. 'And once he took my father's new Rolls when the chauffeur wasn't looking and drove it into a tree.' By then he could hear the tears in her voice. 'I used to ...' She closed her eyes for a moment, as though she couldn't bear the pain of what she was about to say. 'I used to tell myself that a boy like him ... like Gerhard ... couldn't be dead. That he would find a way to stay alive ... to ... survive ...' She opened her eyes and the tears poured down her face silently, sorrowfully, and when she turned her eyes to Paul, there was more anguish there than he had ever seen in two years of war. 'But now, for months I have told myself that I have to believe what they told me, that I must give up hope.' Her voice was a fragile whisper. 'I have to believe now that he is dead ... no matter how much he laughed ... or how beautiful and young and strong he was ... no matter how much –' the sobs were jagged in her throat as she whispered the words – 'I loved him. In spite of all that ... he is dead.' There was an endless silence between them, and then quietly he took her in his arms and held her as she cried.

It was a long time before he spoke again, and when he did, he dabbed gently at her eyes with his white linen handkerchief. But though his words were lighthearted and teasing, his eyes told her that he cared a great deal about her pain. There was nothing flip in what he felt for this girl.

'Were you as rich as that, then? Rich enough to have a Rolls?'

'I don't know how rich we were, Paul.' She smiled softly. 'My father was a banker. Europeans don't talk much of things like that.' And then, with a deep sigh, she attempted to speak of the past without crying. 'My mother had an American car when I was very young. I think it was a Ford.'

'A coupe?'

'I don't know.' She shrugged her ignorance. 'I suppose so. You would have liked it. It sat in the garage afterwards for years.' But thinking of that made her think of Max then, and then somehow Manfred and the Volkswagen she had used in the first lap of her escape ... every memory led to another for Ariana. It was still a dangerous game. She felt the weight of loss settle down on her again as she sat there. It was as though she had lived in a universe that was no more.

'Ariana, what were you just thinking?'

She eyed him honestly. He was her friend now. As best she could, she would be honest with him. 'I was thinking how strange it is that it's all gone now, that none of it exists anymore ... none of the people ... none of the places ... everyone is dead, everything has been bombed ... '

'But you aren't.' He eyed her gently. 'Now you're here.' He held tightly to her hand and their eyes held for a long moment. 'And I want you to know how glad I am that you are.'

'Thank you.' There was a long silence between them and then Julia bounded into the room.

Chapter 35

Paul brought home his dark green Cadillac roadster a week later and gave Ariana the first ride. After that he had to give Julia and Debbie each a turn in it, then his mother, and then at last Ariana again. They took a ride around Central Park. The leather upholstery was soft and creamy and the whole car had a brand-new smell to it that Ariana liked.

'Oh, Paul, it's lovely.'

'Isn't it?' He chortled happily. 'And it's all mine. My father says it's a loan until I start working for him, but I know him better than that. The car's a gift.' He smiled proudly down at the new roadster and Ariana was amused. In the past week he had also convinced his mother to rent a house on Long Island, and plans were already under way to find an establishment suitable for all of them for at least a month, if not two. 'And then, the salt mines.' He smiled at Ariana as they drove slowly through the park.

'And then what? Will you get your own apartment?'

'Probably. I'm a little too old to live at home.'

Ariana nodded slowly. He was also a great deal too mature. The apron strings had long since been cut. She had already learned that about him. 'They'll be disappointed if you move out though. Especially your mother and the girls.'

He looked at her strangely then, and Ariana felt something inside her tremble. Then he stopped the car and pulled over. 'And you, Ariana? Will you miss me, too?'

'Of course I will, Paul.' Her voice was very quiet. But she suddenly thought back to their exchange about her past. He had already touched her deeply. And it would hurt to lose him now.

'Ariana ... if I left the house, would you spend some time with me?'

'Of course I would.'

'No.' He looked at her pointedly. 'I don't mean just as a friend.'

'Paul, what are you saying?'

'That I care for you, Ariana.' Paul's eyes never wavered from hers. 'I'm saying that I care for you very, very much. I've been drawn to you, I think, since that first day.' Her mind went back instantly to the breakfast when he had made her cry by asking about Berlin and then wiped the tears from her cheeks. She had felt a strange pull towards him then, and she had felt it since. But she had resisted it from the first. It was wrong for her to feel that way about him, and it was much too soon.

'I know what you're thinking.' He sat back in his seat, but his eyes remained on Ariana, ethereally beautiful as always in a clinging white silk blouse. 'You're thinking that I hardly know you, that until a couple of weeks ago I thought I was engaged to some other girl. You're thinking that it's hasty, that I'm on the rebound ...' He went on matter-of-factly, and Ariana smiled softly.

'Not quite all that.'

'But some of it?'

She nodded. 'You don't really know me, Paul.'

'Yes, I do. You're funny and you're loving and you're kind, you're not bitter in spite of all you've been through. And I don't give a damn if you're German and I'm American. We come from the same kinds of worlds, similar backgrounds, and we're both Jews.' For an instant she looked desperately pained. Every time one of them said something like that, it reminded her again of her lie. But it was so important to them that she be Jewish. It was as though she had to be Jewish to be worthy of their love. She had thought about it often. Everyone they knew, all of the girls' friends, everyone Sam did business with, was Jewish. It was essential. It was a given. An invariable. And the thought that Ariana could be anything but Jewish would have been unthinkable. Worse than that, she knew that it would have been seen as a betrayal, perhaps even the ultimate betrayal. Because she had won their love.

Sam and Ruth hated the Germans, the non-Jewish ones. To them, every German who was not a Jew was a Nazi. Ariana would have been a Nazi to them, if they had known the truth. The realisation of that had come to her quickly, and it still hurt. It was the pain of again realising that that Paul saw once more in her eyes. She turned away from him, with a look of distress on her face. 'Don't, Paul ... don't ... please.'

'Why?' His hand touched her shoulder. 'Is it really too soon? Don't you feel what I do?' The words were hopeful and for a long moment she didn't answer. For her it was and always would be much, much too soon. In her heart she was still married. Had Manfred been alive, they would have been trying to have their first child. She didn't want to think of any other man. Not yet, not now, and not for a very long time.

She turned slowly to Paul, then with a look of sorrow in her eyes. 'Paul, there are parts of my past ... I may never be ready ... it's not fair to let you think ...'

'Do you like me, even as a friend?'

'Very much so.'

'All right, then, let's just give it some time.' Their eyes met and held and she felt a sudden longing for him that frightened her. 'Just trust me. That's all I ask.' And then ever so gently he kissed her on the mouth. She wanted to resist him, she owed that much to Manfred, but she found that she didn't want to make Paul stop, and she was flushed and breathless when he took his mouth from hers.

'Ariana, I'll wait if I have to. And in the meantime –' he kissed her cheek gently and started the car again – 'I'll be content to be your friend.' But as he said the words, she knew she had to say something more. She couldn't just let it go at that.

'Paul –' she put a gentle hand on his shoulder – 'what can I say to you to tell you how much I appreciate your feelings? What can I say to let you know that I feel for you like a brother, but –' He cut her off. 'You didn't kiss me like a sister.'

She blushed. 'You don't understand ... I can't ... I'm not ... I'm not prepared to be a woman to any man.'

And then he couldn't bear it any longer, and before they reached the house where the others waited, he turned to her, with a pain in his eyes she had never seen before. 'Ariana, did they hurt you? ... I mean, the Nazis ... did they?' At the caring in his eyes, her eyes filled with tears and, hugging him tight for how much he truly cared for her, she shook her head.

'No, Paul, the Nazis didn't do what you think to me.' But that night he knew he did not believe her, when he heard her terrible scream. Many nights he had heard her torment, but this time instead of turning over, knowing that the war she still fought was now hers alone to fight, he walked softly on bare feet into her bedroom and found her sitting there at the edge of her bed, a small light burning, her face in her hands, sobbing softly, a small leather book held in her hands.

'Ariana?' He advanced towards her and she turned. He saw then what he had never seen in her before, the raw anguish of torment. He said nothing more. He only sat beside her and held her until at last the sobs subsided and she was calm.

In her dreams she had seen Manfred again ... dead outside the Reichstag. But there was no way she could explain that to this young man. After a long time with her head on his shoulder, he took the small leather book from her and glanced at the spine. 'Shakespeare? My dear, how intellectual for this hour. No wonder you were crying. Shakespeare would do that to me, too.' She smiled through the last of her tears, then shook her head.

'It's not real.' And then, taking the book from him, 'I saved this from the Nazis ... it's all I have left.' She flipped open the secret compartment and for an instant Paul looked stunned. 'They were my mother's'. The tears began to flow again. 'And now they're all I have.'

Paul could see an emerald and a large diamond signet ring among the others, but he dared not ask her anything at all. It was obvious how distraught she was.

Ariana had had the presence of mind to tuck Manfred's photographs into the lining of her purse, but thinking of them now made the tears flow again – thinking that she had to hide him like that.

'Shh ... Ariana, stop.' He held her close and felt her tremble, gazing still at the two rings. 'My God; those are two fairly incredible rocks. You got those out without the Nazis seeing?' She nodded victoriously and he picked up the large emerald ring. 'That's an extraordinary piece of jewellery, Ariana.'

'Isn't it?' She smiled. 'I think it was my grandmother's before her, but I'm not really sure. They say my mother wore it all the time.' She picked up the diamond signet. 'And this one, too. Those are my great-grandmother's in-itials.' But the design was so intricate one had to know that they were there.

Paul looked at her with awe then. 'It's a wonder no one stole them from you coming over on the boat.' Or anywhere else she'd been. He didn't dare say what he was thinking, but it had taken ingenuity for her to bring that little book so far. Ingenuity and guts, but he already knew that she had lots of both.

'I wouldn't have let anyone take them. They were all I had left. They would have had to kill me first.' And as he looked into her eyes, he knew that she meant what she said.

'Nothing is worth dying for, Ariana.' Now his own experiences showed in his eyes. 'I've learned that much myself.' And she nodded her head slowly. Manfred had discovered the same thing. What had there been worth dying over? Nothing. There was winter in her eyes when she looked back at Paul, and this time when he kissed her, she didn't pull away. 'Get some sleep now.' He smiled at her gently and motioned her back under the covers so he could tuck her in. But she was already reproaching herself silently for letting him kiss her. It wasn't right. But once he had left the room, she found her mind drifting back to things he had said, about the war ... about himself ... they were things Manfred might have said. Paul was young, but he was daily becoming more a man in Ariana's eyes.

Chapter 36

'Ariana, are you all right this morning?' Ruth Liebman looked at her over breakfast the next morning and found her looking strangely pale. It had taken hours for her to get back to sleep the night before after Paul and left. She felt guilty about encouraging him. She knew that eventually, after he'd been home for a while and had played for a bit and had run into old friends and made some new ones, she would hold less pull for him. But in the meantime he was like a big, devoted puppy, and she didn't want to hurt his feelings. She was annoyed at herself, but he had been so kind to her when she had had the nightmare, and she was only human after all. She looked up at Ruth Liebman with big sad eyes that morning, and the older woman frowned with concern. 'My dear, is something wrong?'

Ariana shook her head softly. 'No, I think I'm just tired, Aunt Ruth. It's nothing. I'll get some more rest and I'll be fine.' But Ruth Liebman was sufficiently concerned that half an hour later she picked up the phone, and later that morning she appeared in Ariana's room.

Ariana picked her head up off the pillow with a wan smile. The sleepless night had had a dire effect on her. After she had eaten breakfast that morning, she had returned to her bedroom and vomited for half an hour. Now it showed in her pallid face as Ruth pulled up a chair and sat down. 'I think that it might be a good idea for you to see Doctor Kaplan today.' Ruth tried to hide her worry in ordinary words.

'But I'm all right ... really ... '

'Now, Ariana.' She looked reproachfully at the young girl all but hidden by her covers and reluctantly Ariana nodded.

'All right, but I don't want to go to the doctor, Aunt Ruth. There's nothing wrong with me.'

'You sound like Debbie or Julie. Come to think of it,' she grinned, 'you might even sound like Paul.' And then, having thrown one shoe, she decided to throw the other. 'He hasn't been pressuring you, Ariana, has he?' She watched the girl's face intently as Ariana shook her head.

'No, of course he hasn't.'

'I just wondered. He has an awesome crush on you, you know.' Ariana had not heard the word 'crush' before, but she got the message easily.

'I had that feeling, Aunt Ruth.' Ariana perched on the edge of her bed. 'But I've had no intention of encouraging him. He seems like a brother and I miss my brother so much ...' Her voice drifted and Ariana looked once more into the older woman's eyes. 'And I would never do something that would so greatly displease you.'

'That's what I thought I'd tell you, Ariana. It wouldn't displease me at all.'

'It wouldn't?' Ariana looked stunned.

'No, it wouldn't.' Ruth Liebman smiled. 'Sam and I talked about it the other day. And we know the boy is still kind of on the rebound from Joanie, but, Ariana, he's a good boy.'

'I'm not pushing you in any direction. I just wanted to let you know that if the subject should ever come up ...' She gazed softly at the young German girl sitting in their guest room bed. 'We love you very much.'

'Oh, Aunt Ruth.' Her arms went instantly around the woman who had been so good to her since they first met. 'I love you so much.'

'We want you to feel free to do what you want to do. You're a member of the family now. You must do what's right for you. And if he does get that bee in his bonnet, don't let him pressure you if that's not what you want. I know how stubborn he is!' Ariana laughed in answer.

'I don't think it'll ever come to that, Aunt Ruth.' She wouldn't let it. It still didn't seem right to her.

'I couldn't help wondering if that was what was happening, that Paul was pursuing you and you were consumed with guilt because of us.'

'No –' Ariana shook her head tentatively – 'though Paul did say something the other day, but – 'Ariana shrugged and smiled – 'I just think it's his "crush".' She tried out the new word.

'You just follow your heart wherever it takes you.' Ruth smiled at her hopefully and Ariana laughed as she got out of bed.

'Are mothers supposed to play Cupid?'

'I don't know. I've never done it before.' For a moment their eyes met and held. 'But I can't think of anyone we'd rather have as a daughter-in-law, Ariana. You are a very special, lovely girl.'

'Thank you, Aunt Ruth.' With a look of gratitude she turned to the armoire and took out a pink striped sundress and white sandals. The June sun was already warm. And she was about to turn to Ruth again to tell her how foolish it was for them to go to the doctor, when, without any warning, she felt dizzy and slumped slowly towards the floor.

'Ariana!' Ruth was out of her chair instantly and at the girl's side.

Chapter 37

Dr Stanley Kaplan's office was at Fifty-third Street and Park Avenue, and Ruth dropped Ariana off in the doorway of the building and went to park.

'Well, young lady, how are you feeling? I guess that's a stupid question. Not very well obviously, or you wouldn't be here.' The elderly man smiled at her from across his desk as Ariana sat facing him in his office chair. The last time he'd seen her she had been wan, pale, frightened, scraggly. Now she looked like the beautiful girl she was. Almost. There was still that haunted look around her eyes, the look of pain and loss and sorrow that would not be quick to fade. But otherwise her complexion looked good, her eyes bright; her long blonde hair had been shaped into a handsome pageboy. And in the fresh, candy-striped dress she wore that morning, she looked like the daughter of any of his patients, not like a young woman who had fled war-torn Europe some few weeks before. 'So tell me, what's the problem? Still the nightmares, nausea, dizziness, fainting? Tell me.' He smiled warmly and picked up his pen.

'Yes, I still have the nightmares, but not quite as often. Now at least sometimes I can sleep.'

'Yes,' he nodded, 'you look more rested.'

She nodded and then she admitted to him that after almost every meal she was still sick. He looked shocked.

'Does Ruth know?' This time Ariana shook her head. 'You have to tell her. You should be on a special diet. Every meal, Ariana?'

'Almost.'

'No wonder you look so thin. Did you have this before, this stomach problem?'

'Only since I walked most of the way to Paris. Once I didn't eat for two days, and a couple of times I tried to eat some dirt in a field ...' He nodded quietly.

'And the fainting?'

'It still happens a lot.'

And then he did something she wasn't expecting. He put down his pen and looked at her long and hard, but the look was one of kindness and utter compassion, and when he spoke to her, she knew that this man was her friend. 'Ariana, I want you to feel that there is nothing you can't tell me. I want you to tell me anything I need to know about your past life. It is almost impossible for me to help you if I have no idea what you've been through. But I want you to know that what you tell me is sacred. I'm a doctor, and I've taken a sacred oath. Anything you tell me I cannot repeat to anyone else, and I never would. Not Ruth, not Sam, not their children. No one, Ariana. I'm your doctor, and your friend, too. And I'm an old man who's seen a lot in his lifetime, maybe not as much as you've just seen in yours, but I've seen enough. Nothing will shock me. So now, if there's something you need to tell me, for your own sake, about things they did to you that could have led to these problems, I want you to go ahead.' His face was so kind that she wanted to kiss him, but instead she only sighed softly.

'I don't think so, Dr Kaplan. I was in a cell once for over a month, and all they fed me was some potato broth and stale bread and water and once a week they gave us meat scraps. But that was a long time ago, almost a year now.'

'Did the nightmares start then?'

'Some of them. I ... I was terribly worried about my father and my brother.' Her voice dropped painfully. 'I never saw them again after that.'

The doctor nodded slowly. 'And the stomach trouble, that started then, too?'

'Not really.' A smile flashed across her face then, remembering her own first attempts at cooking for Manfred and the liver sausage 'stew'. Perhaps it was that that had destroyed her stomach. But she did not explain the smile.

'Ariana, I feel we know each other a little better now.' He entered the subject slowly. The first time he had seen her, he had not dared to ask.

'Yes?' She looked at him expectantly.

'Were you – ' he thought over how most delicately to put it – '... used?' Judging from her delicate beauty, he had felt sure from the beginning that she had been, but she shook her head now, and he wondered if she was simply afraid to tell the truth. 'Never?'

'Once. Almost. In that same cell.' But she offered no further explanation and he nodded his head.

'Then perhaps we'd just better look at you.' He buzzed for the nurse, who helped her undress.

The doctor had an odd feeling as he went over her body. His brows knit and he examined her more closely, asked for some more information, and then finally; regretfully, suggested a pelvic. He felt sure that she would regard it as an ordeal. But she seemed steeled for the inevitable, and she was oddly quiet as he prodded her and felt at last what he had suspected, the uterus swollen to twice its normal size. 'Ariana, you can sit up now.' She did, and he looked at her sadly. She had indeed been lying. Not only had they assaulted her, they had impregnated her.

'Ariana.' She sat there after the nurse had left the room, so pale, so young, the sheet draped over her. 'I'm afraid I have something to tell you, and then maybe we ought to talk some more.'

'Is something wrong, Doctor?' She looked frightened. She had only assumed that she was exhausted. She had never really believed that she was seriously ill. Even the lack of menses she had attributed to the shock, the trip, and the readjustment.

'I'm afraid so, little one – You're pregnant.' He waited to see the look of grief and horror. What he saw instead was a look of total amazement, and then a small smile.

'You didn't suspect it?' She shook her head, the smile broadening slightly. 'And you're pleased?' Now it was his turn to stare.

Ariana looked as though she had received a priceless gift beyond hope or expectation, and she stared at Dr Kaplan with wide blue eyes filled with love and awe. It had to have happened right after they got married ... some time near the end of April, perhaps on that last time before he'd gone to defend the Reichstag ... which made her about seven weeks pregnant. She stared at the doctor in disbelief.

'Are you quite sure?'

'I'll run a test if you like, but frankly I'm certain. Ariana, do you know ...'

She looked up at him, smiling gently. 'Yes, I know.' She knew she could trust this man. She had to. 'The baby is my husband's. He is the only man I have ever ... known.'

'And where is he now, your husband?'

Ariana's eyes dropped slowly, and two long tears drifted from her lashes to her cheeks. 'He is dead ... like all the others.' She lifted her head again slowly. 'He is dead.'

'But you will have his baby.' Kaplan spoke softly and silently rejoiced with her. 'Now you will always have that. Won't you?' She smiled softly, finally allowing herself to think of Manfred, to see his face in her mind's eyes, to remember his touch. It was as though now she could allow his memory to come back to her, to share in the joy of their child. Until then she had desperately wrestled with the memories, afraid to let them flood her mind. But now, when the doctor left the room, she sat there for a full ten minutes, bathed in the tender memories and the dreams, and now, when the tears came, she was smiling. This was the happiest moment of her life.

When she rejoined the doctor in his office, he looked at her seriously for a time. 'Ariana, what will you do now? You'll have to tell Ruth.' For a long moment there was silence.

Ariana had not yet thought of that. For a moment all the Liebmans had been blotted from her mind. But now she realised she had to tell them, and she knew what they would say. How could they welcome this baby – whose baby? The child of a Nazi officer? She had to defend this unborn child. What would she do now? Silently she thought of her mother's rings. If she had to, she would use them to support herself until the baby was born. She would do anything she had to, but she could not impose on them any longer. In a few months she would leave.

'I don't want to tell Mrs Liebman, Doctor.'

'But why not?' He looked distressed. 'She's a good woman, Ariana, a kind woman, she'll understand.'

But Ariana looked adamant. 'I can't ask her to do more than she's already done. She's done so much for me. And this would be too much.'

'You have to think of the baby, Ariana. You owe that baby a decent life, a decent chance, as good a chance as you've been given, as the Liebmans have given you.'

It was a heavy speech that weighed on her all that evening after she had made the doctor promise that he would not tell Ruth. He simply told her that Ariana was still obviously a bit tired, but that it was nothing to be concerned about. She should not overdo it, she should eat well, she should get lots of sleep, but other than that, she was fine.

'Oh, I feel so much better hearing that,' Ruth had told her on the way home. She seemed even kinder that day than usual, and it tore at Ariana's heart to be deceiving her about the child. But it seemed wrong to ask for still more from them. She had to do this herself, had to take care of this child on her own. It was hers ... her own ... and Manfred's. It was the baby they had both wanted so badly ... conceived amid the ashes of their dreams. He would now return to bloom on greener hillsides, a memory of how bright their love had been. She sat alone in her room that night, wondering, dreaming, would it be a girl or a boy? Would he look like Manfred ... or perhaps like her father? ... It was like expecting a visitor from an old familiar world, as she found herself wondering which of the faces she would never see again would be reborn in this small child. The doctor said that the baby would be born at the end of January, or perhaps even early February. Often, he insisted, first babies come late. And he thought that it would start to show some time in September, perhaps even October, if she was careful of what she wore. So by then she would have to leave the Liebmans. And once she was settled, once she had a job, then she would tell them. When the baby came, Julia and Debbie could come to visit. She smiled to herself as she thought of the tiny bundle in knitted clothes that the girls would come to see ...

'What are you looking so happy about, Ariana?' It was Paul, standing right beside her. She hadn't even seen him come in.

'I don't know. I was just thinking.'

'What about?' He sat down on the floor next to her and looked up into the perfect little face.

'Nothing special.' She smiled slowly at him. Her happiness was almost impossible to hide, and now it touched Paul as well.

'Do you know what I was thinking about today? Our summer. It's going to be wonderful for us out there in the country. We can play tennis and go swimming. We can lie around in the sun and go to parties. Doesn't that sound like fun?' It did but now she had someone else to consider.

She nodded. And then, sobering, she looked at her young friend. 'Paul, I've just made a big decision.'

'What's that?' He smiled in anticipation.

'In September I'm going to get a job and move out.'

'That makes two of us. Want to become room-mates?'

'Very funny. I'm serious.'

'So am I. And what kind of job are you going to get, by the way?'

'I don't know yet, but I'll think of something. Maybe your father can give me some ideas.'

'I've got a better one.' He leaned over and kissed the soft blonde hair. 'Ariana, why won't you listen?'

'Because you're not old enough to make sense.' She was happier than she had been in months, and he laughed in answer. He could sense her good mood.

'You know, if you're serious about getting a job in September, then this will be your "last summer", too. Our last fling before we all settle down.'

'As a matter of fact,' she grinned broadly at him, 'that's exactly what it will be.'

He smiled at her and stood up. 'Then let's make it good, Ariana, the best summer we ever had.' She smiled at him, feeling her heart soar.

Chapter 38

A week later they all moved to the huge house in East Hampton. It had a main building with six bedrooms, three maids' rooms, a dining room large enough to feed an army, a large formal living room, a smaller den, and a family room downstairs. The kitchen was gigantic and friendly, and in the back there was a guest-house, and a beach-house where one could change one's clothes. In the guest-house there were five guest bedrooms, which the Liebmans planned to keep filled all summer with relatives and friends. The vacation was off to a great beginning until Ruth heard from Paul the day after they got there that Ariana planned to move out and get a job in the fall.

'But why, Ariana? Don't be silly. We don't want you to leave.' Ruth Liebman looked at her, crushed.

'But I can't impose on you for ever.'

'You're not imposing. You're one of our children. Ariana, this is absurd. And if you absolutely must have a job, why can't you live at the house?' She looked distraught at the prospect of losing the girl already. 'Go to University if you want to – you said once that you'd wanted to do that. You can do all kinds of things, but there is absolutely no reason for you to move out.'

'Oh, Paul, she looked so hurt.' Ariana looked at him in despair as he drove her into the city in his roadster to pick up some special odds and ends they had promised his mother they would get in New York. There were two more bathing suits for Debbie, some medication for Julia, a bunch of papers relating to the Women's Relief Organisation that Ruth had forgotten on her desk. They gathered it all up quickly, and then Ariana looked at the little gold watch Ruth had given her to wear. 'Do you suppose I have time to do one more errand?'

'Sure, what's up?'

'I promised Dr Kaplan I'd stop by for some vitamins if I had time.'

'Absolutely.' He looked at her sternly. 'We should have done that first.'

'Yes, sir.' She laughed at him and they gathered up all the things they'd promised to return with and headed downtown. It felt good to be young and enjoying the summer. The sunshine smiled down at them, and Ariana stretched out happily in the car.

'Want to try driving on the way back?'

'Your precious roadster? Paul, what have you been drinking?'

He laughed, glad she was feeling light-hearted. 'I trust you. You said that you knew how to drive.'

'I'm very flattered that you'd let me drive your new car.' She was touched by his offer, knowing how much the car meant to him.

'I would trust you with anything I own, Ariana. Even my new car.'

'Thank you.' There was little more she could say until they arrived at Dr Kaplan's office and she prepared to go inside. But he jumped out quickly to help her. He was wearing white linen slacks and a blazer, and with his long, easy stride and his warm smile, he looked youthful and elegant as they went inside.

'I'll come in with you for a minute. I haven't seen him in a while.' There was no longer much reason for him to see Kaplan – the knee that had taken him out of action was almost healed. In fact, one couldn't even see much of a limp, and with the exercise he'd get that summer, by fall the knee would be as good as new.

But Dr Kaplan was delighted to see him, and the threesome chatted for a moment until Dr Kaplan asked if he could see Ariana alone. Paul complied easily and sat down in the waiting room, putting his boater on the chair beside him.

In his office Ariana looked at the doctor with wide eyes.

'How are you feeling, Ariana?'

'Fine, thank you. As long as I watch what I eat, I'm fine.' She smiled at him and he thought that he had never seen her more at peace. She was wearing a summer dress with a big skirt and small waist, and a huge straw hat tied beneath her chin with blue ribbons the same colour as her eyes.

'You're looking wonderful.' And then after an awkward pause, he looked at her more intently. 'You haven't told any of them, have you?'

'No.' She shook her head slowly. 'I made up my mind. You said it would show in September, so when we get back from Long Island this summer, I'm going to move out and find a job. And *then* I'll tell them everything. And I'm sure they'll understand. But I refuse to impose on them any further, or to expect them to support my child.'

'That's noble of you, Ariana. But do you have any idea how you and the baby will eat? Have you thought of the baby at all, or just yourself?' It was an unusually stern speech for him, and Ariana was briefly angry, and then hurt.

'Of course I've thought of the baby. That's all I think of. What do you mean?'

'That you're twenty years old, you have no trade, no profession, that you're going to be alone with a baby in a country you don't know, where people may not hire you simply because you're German. We've just ended a war with Germany and sometimes people hold that kind of grudge for a long time. I'm telling you that you're not giving that baby a decent shake, and you could do it, if you don't wait too long. If you do something about it now.' He looked at her intently and she stared.

'What do you mean?'

'I mean, Ariana – ' his voice gentled – 'get married. Give yourself and the baby a decent chance. I know, it's a hell of a thing to do, but, Ariana, since I saw you last, I've been tormenting myself. I think it's the only answer. I've thought and I've thought and I've thought. I know Paul since he's a baby. I can see what he feels for you. It's hell on my conscience to suggest this – but who will be hurt? If you marry that boy in the waiting room, you'll guarantee your baby's future, and your own.'

'I don't care about me.' She was shocked at what he was suggesting.

'But you do care about the baby. What about that?'

'But I can't do that ... it's dishonest.'

'Don't you think a lot of other girls do the same thing? Girls who have far less reason to do it than you do ... Ariana, the baby won't be born for another seven months. I could say that it came early. No one would have to know. No one. Not even Paul.'

She looked at the doctor, shocked by what he was suggesting. 'Don't you think that I could provide for the baby myself?'

'Of course not. When was the last time you saw a pregnant woman work? Who would hire you? And to do what?'

She sat for a long moment and then nodded pensively. Maybe he was right. She had just assumed she'd be able to get a job in a shop. But what a thing to do ... what a deception ... what a thing to do to Paul ... how could she lie to him like that? He was her friend and in a way she loved him. In fact, she cared for him a great deal.

'How could I do such a thing, Doctor? It's wrong.' She felt guilt and shame rise within her just at the thought.

'You could do it for the sake of your unborn child. What did you do getting to Paris, getting here? Were you always so honest? Wouldn't you have lied or shot or killed to save your life? You must do the same for the baby, Ariana. To provide him with a family, a father, a decent lifestyle, meals in his belly, an education ...' Ariana realised she was naïve to think a few rings tucked away in a box could get her through this. Slowly she nodded her head.

'I'll have to think it over.'

'Do that, but don't think for too long. If you wait much longer, it will be too late. This way, if the baby comes at seven months, I can easily explain it by your frail health, the trip from Europe, all of that.'

'You think of everything, don't you?' She looked at him and realised he was giving her the push she needed to survive. He was teaching her the rules to a game she was getting very good at playing, and in her heart she knew he was right. But where would it end?

He was talking. 'If you do this, Ariana, your secret will always be safe with me.'

'Thank you, Doctor – for my life – and my baby's life.'

He handed her the vitamins and touched her shoulder gently as she left. 'Make your decision quickly, Ariana.'

She nodded quietly. 'Yes, I will.'

Chapter 39

'Ariana, do you want to come swimming?' Julia was pounding on her door at nine o'clock in the morning, and Ariana sleepily opened an eye.

'So early? I'm not up yet.'

'Neither was Paul. And he's coming, too.'

'That's right,' he verified as he sauntered through her doorway, 'and if I have to get up to go swimming with these little monsters, so do you.'

'Oh, I do, do I?' She stretched lazily and smiled as he sat down next to her and kissed the loose blonde hair falling over her face.

'Yes, you do, otherwise, I shall drag you from your bed and pull you screaming down the beach.'

'How charming of you, Paul.'

'Yes, isn't it?' They smiled at each other for a moment. 'By the way, would you like to go to a party in Southampton tonight? My parents are taking the girls somewhere overnight.'

'How come?'

'It's the Fourth of July weekend, my dear. American Independence Day. Wait until you see – it should be quite an event.'

And as it turned out, it was. They went swimming with the girls that morning and on a picnic with the whole family that afternoon. After which Sam and Ruth took the girls off on their excursion and Ariana disappeared upstairs to take her nap. But at seven o'clock she was dressed to go out for the evening, and when she came down the stairs of the big summer home, Paul whistled and grinned.

'Say, lady, nobody ever warned me you'd look like that with a suntan.' She was wearing a turquoise silk dress that highlighted her fresh brown skin. He looked equally dashing in a white linen suit, white shirt, and a wide navy blue tie with tiny white dots, and together they set out for the evening in his new car.

In gala spirit he let Ariana drive it to the party, and once there he immediately brought her a gin fizz. Hesitant about her reactions to the liquor, she only took very small sips. But the party around her was already swinging. There were two bands playing, one in the house and one out on the lawn. Several yachts had pulled up for the occasion and were moored at the long dock where they were tended by a dozen boatsmen, and there was a ripe summer moon hanging overhead.

'Would you like to dance, Ariana?' He was smiling down at her gently, and smoothly she drifted into his arms. It was the first time they had danced together, and in the moonlight it was easy to pretend that it was Manfred, or her father, or anyone at all. 'Has anyone ever told you that you dance like an angel?'

'Not lately, I'm afraid.' She laughed softly at the compliment and they danced on until the end of the set. They walked slowly to a railing where they could look down at the boats bobbing beneath them, and Paul looked at her with a seriousness Ariana had not yet seen.

'I'm so happy when I'm with you, Ariana. I've never known anyone like you before.' She wanted to tease him and ask about Joanie, but she knew that this wasn't the time.

'Ariana – ' he looked at her quietly – 'I have something to tell you.' He reached over slowly, took both her hands in his, and then kissed them gently, one at a time. 'I love you. I don't know how else to tell you. I love you. I can't bear being without you. Being with you, I feel … well … so happy and strong … like I can do anything, like everything I touch is some kind of a gift … like it's all worth it … and I never want to let that feeling go. If you go off on your own after the summer and I do the same thing, we'll lose that.' His eyes misted over as he said it. 'And, Ariana, I can't bear to let you go.'

'You won't have to.' Her voice was a whisper. 'Paul … I – '

And then, as though he had timed it, the first fireworks exploded overhead. He reached into his pocket and took out a large emerald-cut diamond ring. Before she had realised what had happened, he had slipped it on her finger, and his mouth was pressing hard on hers as his urgency and his passion reached towards her. She felt a longing and a stirring in her that she had thought never to feel again. She clung to him almost desperately for a moment, returning his kiss and fighting the longing in her own soul.

At last, after their lips parted, she told him that she was tired and they drove back to his parents' house in East Hampton in a far more subdued state of mind. She was still trying to wrestle with her conscience. How could she go on with this charade? And it wasn't that she didn't love him. She did love him, in a warm, friendly kind of way, but it was wrong to take advantage of his affection, wrong to press on him a child that was not his. When at last they got out of the car in the driveway, Paul put a gentle arm around her and led her inside. And in the front hall he looked down at her sadly.

'I know what you're thinking. You don't want it, not the ring, not what it stands for, not me ... not any of it. It's all right, Ariana. I understand.' But there were tears in his voice as he pressed her to him. 'But, oh, God, I love you so much, please, please, just let me be alone with you here, just this one night. Let me dream, let me imagine what it would have been like if this were our house, if we were married, if all the dreams had come true.'

'Paul.' She pulled away from him gently, but when she did, she saw the handsome young face washed with tears. And then she couldn't bear it any longer; she pulled him close to her and reached her face up to his, offering him a warmth and a loving that she had never thought she would have to give anyone again. Moments later they reached her bedroom, and with a gentleness far beyond his years, Paul carefully peeled away the silk dress. They lay there for a long time in the moonlight, holding, caressing, dreaming, kissing, and saying nothing at all. And at last by the first light of morning, with the last passion spent, they fell asleep in each other's arms.

Chapter 40

'Good morning, my darling.' Ariana squinted in the bright sunlight as she saw him. He had set a breakfast tray down on the bed and was opening several drawers and putting the contents into a small suitcase he had laid out on the bed.

'What are you doing?' She sat up in bed and had to fight a wave of nausea. The coffee was pungent and it had been a long night.

'I'm packing your suitcase.' He smiled at her over his shoulder.

'But where are we going? Your parents will be back tonight. They'll worry if they don't find us – '

'We'll be back by then.'

'Then why the suitcase, Paul? I don't understand.' She felt totally disoriented as she sat there, still naked, as this man with the long legs in a navy blue silk bathrobe packed her bag. 'Paul, will you please stop and talk to me?' There was a faint note of panic in her voice.

'I will in a minute.' And then, when he had finished, he turned, sat down quietly on the bed, and took her hand in his own, the one that still wore the enormous emerald-cut diamond ring. 'All right, now I'll tell you. We're going to Maryland this morning, Ariana.'

'Maryland? Why?'

But this time he faced her squarely. It was as though overnight he had become a man. 'We're going to Maryland to get married, because I'm tired of playing games and acting like we're both fourteen years old. We're not, Ariana. I'm a man and you're a woman, and if something like last night can happen between us once, then it can happen again and again. I won't play games with you, I won't beg you. I love you, and I think you love me, too.' And then his voice softened again slightly. 'Will you marry me, Ariana? Darling, I love you with all my heart.'

'Oh, Paul.' Tears flooded her eyes as she held out her arms to him. Was it possible that she could make him happy? If she did marry him, out of gratitude for what he would be giving her child, she would always be good to him. But all she could do was cry as he held her. It was such a huge decision, and she still wasn't sure what to do.

'Will you stop crying and give me an answer?' He kissed her neck gently, then her face, then her hair. 'Oh, Ariana, I love you ... how I love you ...' He kissed her again, and slowly this time she nodded, and then she faced him, as other faces came to mind ... Manfred ... her father ... briefly she even remembered Max Thomas, kissing her in her mother's room the night he escaped Berlin. What would they all think of her if she married this man? And then she realised that it didn't matter, that it was her decision, her life now. Not theirs. They were all gone. All of them. She was the only one left ... she ... and her baby ... and Paul. He was more real than the others ever could be now. She stretched a hand out to him now with a long, slow smile. She was reaching across a lifetime, reaching out to him with all her heart and soul, and as she did so, she vowed silently never to betray their love.

'Well?' He looked at her, trembling, afraid to take her hand, afraid to move. But she took both of his and brought them slowly to her mouth. And then one by one she kissed his fingers and closed her eyes. When she opened them again, there was a look of tenderness that reached to his very soul.

'Yes.' She smiled at him and pulled him closer. 'Yes, my darling. Yes! The answer is yes.' And then, burying her head in his shoulder, she rejoiced. 'How I will love you, Paul Liebman.' And then she took a step back to look at him. 'What a wonderful man you are.'

'My God.' He grinned at her. 'I think you've gone crazy. But I'm not about to look a gift horse in the mouth. You just stay crazy and let me take care of the rest.'

And so he did. An hour later they were on the road to Maryland, with their suitcases in the back seat and Ariana's temporary identity cards in his pocket. Hours later the wife of a justice of the peace just outside Baltimore snapped their picture as her husband solemnly stared at Paul and nodded, murmuring firmly, 'You may kiss the bride.'

'Mother ... Dad ...' Paul's voice almost trembled as he faced them, but gently he reached out for Ariana's hand. He took it, and he held it proudly, and then he smiled at his parents with a look that said he was a man. 'Ariana and I eloped.' He smiled down at tiny, nervous Ariana. 'I almost had to force her to do it, which is why I didn't want to waste my time waiting around to discuss it with you. So –' he looked at both his parents warmly, and although they were clearly stunned, they did not look displeased – 'may I present to you Mrs Paul Liebman?' He bowed gracefully towards her, and she dropped a curtsy at his feet. And then with one swift, graceful movement, she reached up and kissed him and then reached out quick arms to Ruth. The older woman took her and held her, holding her close for a long moment, remembering the terrifyingly sick girl she had rescued from the ship. Sam watched them for a moment, he then held his arms out to his son.

Chapter 41

As planned, Ariana and Paul stayed in East Hampton until September, and then after Labour Day they went back to the city to begin their search for their own place. Paul began to work with his father at the office, and Ruth joined Ariana in the hunt for the right home. Just after they all celebrated Rosh Hashanah together, a pretty little town house became available in the upper Sixties, and after very little debate Paul decided that it had to be theirs. For the moment they were only renting, but the owner was interested in selling the place to them at the end of their lease. The young couple decided that the arrangement was perfect. It would give them a chance to decide if they really liked the house.

Now all they needed was more furniture, and with the girls back in school, Ruth had more time to help. She was a little less busy with her refugee organisation, and she had been spending almost every day with Ariana, enough so to see that once again the girl wasn't feeling well.

'Ariana, have you been back to see Kaplan?' Ruth looked at her worriedly, and Ariana nodded, trying to decide about a swatch of fabric she'd ordered to match their new rug. 'Well, have you?'

'Yes. I went last Thursday.' She avoided Ruth's eyes for a moment and then looked up at her mother-in-law with a small smile.

'What did he say?'

'That the fainting and the problems with my stomach are going to go on for quite a while.'

'Does he think it's permanent?' Ruth looked at her with greater concern now, but Ariana skook her head.

'Not at all. In fact, he isn't even worried about it any more. He said that before it was from the rigours of my trip to get here. But now it's the price I'm paying for what I did after I arrived.'

'What does he mean by that?' And then suddenly she understood the cryptic message. Her eyes widened and she looked at Ariana with a long, slow smile. 'You mean you're pregnant?'

'Yes, I am.'

'Oh, Ariana!' She looked at her happily and quickly crossed the room to give her a hug. But then she looked at the small young woman with fresh worry. 'Does he think it will be all right for you? It's not too soon after you were so sick ... you're so tiny – you're not a big horse of a woman like me.' But she clung to Ariana's hand tightly, so thrilled with the news. For an instant it reminded her of the joy she had felt when she learned that she was expecting their first child.

'The only thing he wants me to do is start seeing a specialist a little later, when we get closer to the birth.'

'That sounds reasonable, and when will that be, by the way?'

'Early April.' Inwardly, Ariana cringed at the lie, praying that Ruth would never know the truth about the baby, and silently promised herself and Ruth that one day there would truly be a Liebman child. She owed it to Paul to have his baby, and as soon as she was able, she was going to have another, and still more if that was what he wanted. She owed him everything for protecting Manfred's child.

As the months wore on, Paul matured, growing more and more paternal, helping Ariana prepare the nursery and smiling at her as she spent night after night knitting clothes. Ruth had also brought over boxes and boxes of things from her own babies, and there seemed to be little tiny hats and socks and dresses and sweaters everywhere Paul looked.

'Well, from the look of this place, Mrs Liebman, I'd say we were having a baby.' It was two weeks before Christmas. Paul thought she was only five and a half months pregnant, but in truth the baby's birth was only six weeks away. But no one seemed to find her enlarged proportions outrageous. They assumed her impressive bulge was simply due to the fact that it all showed more on a woman of Ariana's size. And by now Paul had grown to like the belly – he called it funny names and said that he had to rub it twice for good luck before he left for work every day.

'Don't do that!' She squealed when he tickled her. 'You'll make it kick me again.'

'It must be a boy.' He said it with great seriousness one night while listening to her stomach. 'I think it's trying to play football.'

Ariana groaned and rolled her eyes as she laughed at her husband. 'It certainly is playing football in there ... with my kidneys, I think.'

The next morning, after Paul had left for the office, something strange happened, and for hours on end Ariana felt overwhelmed by nostalgia for her old life. She sat for hours in a chair thinking of Manfred, got out her jewel box, and tried on his rings. She sat there thinking of their plans and their promises and then found herself wondering what he would have thought of this child. Paul had his heart set on Simon, after the brother who had died. And it was something she felt she should do for him.

As she went through her mementos that morning, she came to the envelope with the photographs of her and Manfred, hidden in a book in a locked drawer at the bottom of her desk. She pulled them out and spread them out in her lap then, staring at the face she had loved, remembering every inch of the uniform, hearing his words at their first Christmas. It was difficult to believe that the photographs of the Christmas Eve balls had been taken only a year before. With two little rivers of tears dripping from her cheeks on to the huge belly, she held the photographs in her hands and never heard her husband come in. A moment later he stood behind her, staring down at the photographs, first in confusion, and then in horror, as the insignia on the uniform finally became clear.

'My God, who is that?' He stared down in fury and amazement, seeing Ariana's smiling face at the man's side. Ariana jumped in terror as she heard him. She had no idea that he was standing there at all.

'What are you doing here?' The tears had stopped and she still held the photographs in her hand as she stood up.

'I came home to check on my wife and see if she wanted to join me for lunch somewhere, but I see that I seem to have interrupted a rather intriguing private time. Tell me, Ariana, do you do this every day, or only on major holidays?' And then after a frozen moment, 'Would you mind telling me who that was?'

'It was ... he was a German officer.' She looked at Paul almost in desperation. This was not the way that she had wanted him to find out.

'I could tell that much from the Nazi armband. Anything else you'd like to tell me? Like how many Jews he killed? Or which camp he ran?'

'He didn't kill any Jews, and he didn't run any camps. In fact, he saved my life. And he kept me from being raped by a lieutenant and made a whore by a general. If it hadn't been for him – ' she began to sob uncontrollably as she held the picture of the man who'd been dead for seven months now – if it hadn't been for him ... I would very probably be dead now.'

For an instant Paul regretted what he had said to her, but then as he looked at the photograph fluttering in her hand, he felt anger overcome him again. 'Then, what the hell are you doing laughing and smiling in these pictures if your life was so much at stake?' He reached for the pictures and then realised with utter fury that she was dancing with the Nazi officer at a ball. 'Ariana, who is this man?' And then suddenly he understood how she had survived the camps after all. His mother had been right. And he had no right to berate her for what she'd done. The girl had no choice. Tenderly, feeling shaken, he reached out to Ariana, and pulled her as close as he could with her huge belly into his arms. 'I'm sorry ... oh, darling, I'm sorry. I think for a moment I forgot what happened. I just saw that face and that uniform and it all looked so German, I think for a minute I lost my mind.'

'But I'm German, too, Paul.' She was still crying, sobbing softly in his arms.

'Yes, but you're not like them, and if what you had to do was to be this man's mistress to survive the camps, Ariana, then I don't give a damn what happened.' But as he said it, he felt her freeze in his arms. And quietly she backed away from him and sat down.

'That's what you think, isn't it, Paul?' She eyed him for an endless moment and he said nothing, and then softly she went on. 'You think I was this man's whore to save my own skin. Well, that's not true and I want you to know the truth. After the death of my father and Gerhard, he – Manfred –took me to his house and he expected nothing from me, nothing. He didn't rape me, he didn't touch me, he didn't hurt me. He only gave me his protection and became my only friend.'

'It's a touching story, but that's a Nazi uniform, isn't it, Ariana?' His voice was like ice as it touched her, but she sat there feeling unafraid – knowing she was doing the right thing.

'Yes, Paul, it is. But there were some decent men wearing Nazi uniforms, and he was one. It's not all just good guys and bad guys. Life isn't always as simple as that.'

'My, my, darling. Thank you for the lesson. But frankly I find it a little hard to stomach when I come home and find my wife crying over pictures of some goddamn Nazi, and then I discover that he was her "friend". The Nazis weren't anyone's friends, Ariana. Don't you understand that? How can you say what you're saying? You're a Jew!' He was raging at her as she sat there, but now she stood to face him and shook her head.

'No, Paul, I am not a Jew. I am a German.' He was shocked into silence, and she went on, afraid that if she if stopped now, words would fail her.

'My father was a good German, and a banker; he was the head of the most important bank in Berlin. But when they drafted my brother after his sixteenth birthday, my father didn't want Gerhard to go.' She tried smiling at him now. What a relief it was to tell him the story, to tell him the truth, no matter what it cost in the end.

'My father's sympathies were never with the Nazis, and when they tried to draft Gerhard, he knew that we had to escape. He devised a plan to get my brother into Switzerland, and then he would come back for me the day after that. Only something must have happened, and he never did return. Our servants turned me in – people I had trusted all my life –' her voice rose – 'and the Nazis came and took me away. They kept me in a cell for a month, Paul, holding me for "ransom", in case my father came back, but he didn't. For a month I lived in a filthy, stinking little cell, half starving and half crazy, in a room half the size of one of the closets of your mother's maids. And then they let me go because I was useless. They took over my father's house, kept all our things, and threw me out in the street. But the general who took over my father's home in Grunewald apparently also wanted me, too. Manfred, this man – ' she pointed at the pictures with trembling hands as tears rolled down her face – 'saved me from him, and from everyone. He kept me safe until the war ended.' Her voice broke then. 'Until the fall of Berlin, when he was killed.' She looked up at Paul then but his face looked as hard as rock.

'And were you lovers, you and this stinking Nazi?'

'Don't you understand? He *saved* me! Don't you care about that?' She eyed him for a long moment, her own anger building.

'I care that you were the mistress of a Nazi.'

'Then you're a fool. I survived, dammit. I survived!'

'And you cared about him?' His voice was frigid and suddenly, as much as she had come to love Paul, she hated him now. She wanted to hurt him as he was hurting her.

'I cared very much. He was my husband, and he would be now, if he weren't dead.'

For an instant they stood there eyeing each other, suddenly aware of all that had been said, and when Paul spoke again, his voice was shaking. He looked and pointed at her stomach and then raised his eyes to her face.

'Whose baby is that?'

She wanted to lie to him, for the child's sake, but she could no longer do it. 'My husband's,' she answered. Her voice was strong and proud, as though she were bringing Manfred back to life.

'I am your husband, Ariana.'

'Manfred's.' She answered softly, suddenly aware of what she had done to Paul. As the full impact hit her, she almost reeled.

'Thank you,' he whispered, and then, turning on his heel, he slammed the door.

Chapter 42

The next morning Ariana received a packet of papers from Paul's attorney. She was being notified that Mr Paul Liebman had the intention of suing her for divorce. She was being formally notified that four weeks after the birth of the baby, she would have to vacate the premises, but that in the meantime she could stay there. She would also continue to be supported for that brief period, and after she left, once the baby was born, the sum of 5000 dollars would be given to her by cheque. No support was going to be forthcoming for the baby, since it apparently was not Mr Liebman's child, nor for her, given the circumstances of their brief and apparently fraudulent marriage. A letter in the same packet from her father-in-law confirmed the financial arrangements, and a note from her mother-in-law berated her for having betrayed them all. How dared she have pretended to be a Jew. It was, as Ariana had always suspected it would be, the ultimate betrayal, not to mention the fact that she was pregnant with 'some Nazi's' child. The war had hit hard. 'Some Nazi' – Ariana flinched at the word when she read it. Further, she forbade Ariana to set foot near the house on Fifth Avenue, and forbade her also ever to come near any of them again. Should she discover that Ariana had attempted to see Deborah or Julia, Ruth would feel no qualms about calling the police.

As Ariana sat in the apartment, reading what they had sent her, she desperately wanted to reach Paul. But he had sought refuge with his parents, and under no circumstances would he take her calls. Instead, he spoke to her through his attorney, the arrangements were begun, the divorce suit was filed, the Liebmans shut her out, and on 24 December, shortly after midnight, one month early, Ariana went into labour all alone.

Her bravado faded then, as, momentarily, did her courage. She was paralysed with fear – of the unknown, and of her aloneness – but she was able to reach the doctor and got to the hospital in a cab.

Twelve hours later Ariana was still in the throes of her labour, and she was almost incoherent with the pain. Frightened, frantic, still shocked by what had happened with Paul and the Liebmans, she was in no condition to deal with what was happening, and time and again she screamed for Manfred, until at last they gave her something for the pain. At ten o'clock on Christmas night the baby was finally delivered, by Cesarean section, but despite the difficulties of the labour neither mother nor baby had come to any harm. They showed him to Ariana briefly, a tiny bundle of wrinkled flesh with the smallest hands and feet that she had ever seen.

He didn't look like her or like Manfred, or like Gerhard or her father. He didn't look like anyone at all.

'What will you call him?' The nurse asked her softly as she held Ariana's hand.

'I don't know.' She was so tired, and he was so little – she wondered if it was all right that he was so small. But through the pain and the anesthetic, she still felt a warm glow of joy.

'It's Christmas, you could call him Noel.'

'Noel?' Ariana thought for a minute, smiling in her drugfilled half-sleep. 'Noel? That's pretty.' And then, turning her face towards where she imagined the baby, she smiled a peaceful smile. 'Noel von Tripp,' she said to herself and fell asleep.

Chapter 43

Exactly four weeks after the birth of the baby, Ariana stood in the front hall with the last of their bags. As per the arrangement, she was vacating the apartment, and she already had the baby all bundled up in the cab. They were going to a hotel a nurse at the hospital had recommended. It was cozy and inexpensive, and the proprietress would serve meals. So soon after the Cesarean, Ariana wasn't really supposed to be up. One more time she had attempted to reach Paul at his office, and then once more she had allowed herself to try him at home. But it was useless. He wouldn't speak to her. It was over. He had sent her the 5000 dollars. All he wanted now was her keys.

She closed the door softly behind them, and with her clothes and her baby, her photographs of Manfred, and her volume of Shakespeare with a compartment for rings, she began her new life. She had already sent back the large diamond Paul had given her, and she was once again wearing Manfred's rings. Somehow they felt more right on her fingers, and she knew now that she would never take them off again. She would be Ariana von Tripp for ever. If it seemed wiser in the States, she would drop the 'von', but she would never betray her old life, she would never lie or pretend any more about who and what she was. She had suffered at the hands of the Nazis, yet she knew better than anyone that the Nazis were only a horde of men, and in the horde somewhere there had been some good ones. She would never betray Manfred again.

He was the husband she would cherish for a lifetime. He was the man she would talk of to her son. The man who had bravely served his country and the woman who had loved him until the very end. She would tell him about his grandfather and sweet Gerhard. Perhaps she would even tell him that she had married Paul, but she wasn't sure. She knew she had been wrong to try to deceive him, but she had paid for that dearly, too, in the end. But, she smiled down at the sleeping baby, she would always have her son.

Chapter 44

When Noel was two months old, Ariana had answered an ad in the paper and gotten a job in a bookshop that specialised in foreign books. They allowed her to bring the baby and paid her a tiny wage on which, at least, she and the baby could survive.

'Ariana ... you really ought to do it.' The young woman was looking at her intensely as Ariana tried to keep an eye on her roving child. She had worked at the bookstore for over a year now and Noel had learned to walk early, and he was already fascinated by the bright books stacked on shelves near the floor.

'I don't think I want anything from them, Mary.'

'Yes, but don't you want something for the baby? Do you want to be doing this kind of work for the rest of your life?' Ariana looked at her hesitantly. 'It won't hurt to ask. And you're not asking them for charity, you're asking them for what's yours.'

'What was mine. That's different. When I left, it was all in the Nazis' hands.'

'At least go to the consulate and ask them.' Mary was insistent, and Ariana decided that maybe she would ask on her next day off. The German government had instated a system whereby the people who had lost goods and property at the hands of the Nazis could now ask the government for some compensation for their loss. She had no proof of what had belonged to her, either the house in Grunewald or Manfred's family schloss, which also, by right, would be hers.

Two weeks later on a Thursday, her day off, she rolled Noel's pram to the consulate. It was a cold, blustery day in March, and she almost hadn't gone out for fear that it might snow. But she bundled the baby into his heavy blanket and walked inside the impressive bronze door.

'Bitte? May I help you?' For an instant Ariana only stared. It had been so long since Ariana had heard her own language, seen a European, or seen things done in the official way she was used to that for a moment all she could do was look around her in astonishment. It was as though in a single instant she had been transported home. Slowly, she began to answer and to explain why she had come. And to her surprise she was treated with the utmost respect and courtesy, given the information she desired and a raft of forms to fill out, and told to come back next week.

When she returned, there was a fairly large crowd in the lobby. She had the forms all filled out in her pocket, and all she had to do now was wait for an interview with some minor consulate official who would process them through. And then who knew how long it would all take? Maybe years if she got anything from them at all. But it was worth a try.

As she stood at the consulate, Noel sleeping in his pram, she couldn't resist the urge to close her eyes and imagine herself at home again. Around her everywhere were Germans, the sounds of Bavaria, of Munich, of Liepzig, of Frankfurt, and then the patter of Berlin. It sounded so sweet and familiar, and yet at the same time it was painful, too. Among all those familiar words and accents and sayings, not a familiar voice could she hear. And then suddenly, as though she were dreaming, she felt someone grab her arm, there was a quick exclamation, an intake of breath, and when she looked up, she was staring into a pair of familiar brown eyes. They were eyes that she had seen before somewhere ... eyes she had known ... and seen for the last time only three years before.

'Oh, my God! Oh, my God!' And then suddenly she was crying. It was Max ... Max Thomas ... and without thinking, she hurled herself into his arms. For what seemed like hours he held her tightly while they both laughed and cried. He hugged her, he kissed her, he held the baby – for both it was a dream they had never thought would come true. And then, huddled in the hallway as they waited, she told him of her father and of Gerhard and of how they had lost their home. And then she told him quietly of Manfred; no longer afraid or ashamed, she told Max that she had loved him, that they had been married, and that Noel was his son. But she discovered quickly that, with the exception of Noel, he knew about all that. He had scoured Berlin for her and her father after the war.

'Did you look for them after the war, Ariana?'

She hesitated for a moment and then shook her head. 'I didn't really know how. My husband said that he was certain my father was dead. And then I contacted a friend of his in Paris, a man who ran a refugee assistance organis-ation of sorts, before I left Europe. He checked out every possible lead, looking for any trace of them, especially of Gerhard.' She sighed softly. 'He even tried to trace you, but there was no sign of you ... or of Gerhard.' And then suddenly the full impact of what she had just said struck her. There had been no trace of Max and he was alive couldn't Gerhard be, too? She looked thunderstruck for a moment and Max gently took her face in his hands as he shook his head from side to side.

'Don't. They're gone, Ariana. I know it. I looked, too.' After the war, I went back to Berlin, to try to reach your father, and ...' He had been about to say 'to see you'. 'I heard from the men at the bank in Berlin what happened.'

'What did they tell you?'

'That he disappeared. And that with hindsight, pretty much everyone knew that he had gone to save Gerhard from the draft. There is absolutely no trace of your father, nor of Gerhard. Once in Switzerland a maid in a hotel recognised a photograph I had of him, thought that he looked like a boy who'd been there a year or so before, but she wasn't sure, and after she looked at the photograph for a while, she was certain it wasn't the same boy. I went back to Switzerland and searched for them for three months.' He sighed deeply and leaned heavily against the wall. 'I think the border patrol got them, Ariana. It's the only answer that makes any sense. If they were alive, they'd have eventually gone back to Berlin. And they never did. I've stayed in touch.' Hearing it from him now made it real once again, and he was right. If they'd been alive, they would have turned up, and if Max had stayed in touch with people at the bank in Berlin, then it was certain. Hearing it made the news seem fresh again and she felt grief tear once more at her heart. He put an arm around her shoulders and with one hand smoothed down her golden hair. 'You know, it's amazing. I knew you had come to the States, Ariana, but I didn't think I'd ever see you again.'

She turned to him in amazement. 'You knew? How?'

'I told you, I looked for all three of you. I had to. I owed your father my life and ...' He looked boyish for a moment. 'I never ... forgot that evening ... tthe night that ...' He lowered his voice. '... I kissed you. Do you remember?'

She looked at him sadly. 'Do you really think that I'd forget?'

'You could have. It's been a long time.'

'It's been a long road for all of us. But you remembered. So did I.' And then she remembered something else. She still wanted to know all the details of the story. 'How did you know I'd come to the States?'

'I don't know. It was just a hunch. I thought that it was safe to assume that if you'd survived the fall of Berlin, you hadn't stayed. As the wife of a German officer ... You see, I knew.' He hesitated for only an instant, his eyes looking deep into hers. 'Were you forced to do that?'

She shook her head. Was her lifetime to be filled with denying that? 'No, Max, I wasn't. He was a wonderful man.' She remembered suddenly Hildebrand and General Ritter ... and Von Rheinhardt and the endless interrogations ... Coming back here, listening to the countless conversations around her in German brought it all back. But now she pulled her attention back to Max. 'He saved my life, Max.' There was a long pause between them, and then he pulled her slowly into his arms. 'I heard from someone that he'd been killed.' She nodded sombrely in confirmation. 'So I tried various possibilities, and France was one. The immigration people in Paris had a record of issuing you temporary travel papers. I knew the date you left France. I traced you to Saint Marne.' She was touched beyond words.

'What made you search so hard?'

'I felt that I owed your father something, Ariana. I hired a detective to look for you all when I got back to Berlin; And of your father and Gerhard – ' he hesitated painfully – 'there was no trace.' And then he smiled softly. 'But you, *Liebchen,* I knew you were alive, and I didn't want to give up.'

'Then why did you? Why didn't you look here? Surely Jean-Pierre must have told you I came to New York.'

'He did. Did you know he died?'

'Jean-Pierre? Dead?' She was rocked by the news.

'He died in a car accident outside Paris.' There was a moment of silence between them and then he went on.

'He gave me the name of some people in New Jersey. I wrote to them and they claimed that they never even met you. They admitted that they were supposed to be your sponsors, but they had changed their minds.' Slowly Ariana recalled the sponsors in New Jersey. They had faded from her life as she had lain half-dead in the hospital.

'They wrote that they didn't know who had become your sponsors, and no one else seemed to know either. The people who took over Saint Marne's files in Paris had no idea. It was only months after I came here myself that someone at the Woman's Relief Organisation told me about the Liebmans. But when I went there to talk to them myself, things became confused.'

Ariana felt her heart race nervously at the sound of the name.

'What did they say?' She looked strangely anxious.

'They said that they'd never seen you either and that they had no idea where you were. Mrs Liebman said she recalled the name but had no further information to give me.' Ariana nodded slowly. She could imagine Ruth doing that. She was so angry at Ariana that she would deny everything now, especially her marriage to their son. Slowly Ariana's eyes rose until she was looking at Max with an expression that told him there was much more.

'I never found any trace of you after that.'

'It doesn't matter, Max.' She touched his arm gently. 'You found me after all.' She hesitated for a moment and then decided to tell him. Why not? 'Ruth Liebman lied to you. I was married to her son.' Max looked astonished as she told him all of it, keeping nothing back, and there were tears in his eyes as he listened. Without realising it, he took her hand and she held it tightly as she told him the story from beginning to end.

'And now?'

'I'm waiting for the divorce. It will be final in July.'

'I'm sorry, Ariana. What more can I say?'

'It was my own fault. I shouldn't have done it the way I did, but I was stupid and foolish. I'm only sorry because now I've lost them all, and they were very special people. Ruth saved my life – and Noel's.'

'Perhaps one day they'll change their minds.'

'I doubt it.'

'And the little one?' Max smiled pensively, remembering his own children at the same age. 'What is his name?'

'Noel.' Ariana returned Max's smile. 'He was born on Christmas.'

'What a nice gift for you.' And then with a tender look at Ariana, 'Was anyone with you?' She shook her head slowly. 'I'm sorry, Ariana.' But she was sorry for them all. How far they had come, and how much they had lost over the past few years. Only she seemed to be lucky as she looked around at the people waiting to make their claims – she had much-treasured Noel, and he had been worth it all.

'And what about you?' Still waiting in the consular hallways, he told her that her father's paintings had kept him alive through the war and not only allowed him to eat, but to go to law school to become an attorney again once he got to the States.

He had remained in Switzerland until the end of the war, working at odd jobs, living hand to mouth, waiting, until V-E Day, when he had finally sold the last of the paintings and shortly thereafter gone to the States, and that had been two years before.

And now he was finally officially once more a lawyer, which was what brought him here. He wanted to establish his own claim and then make an arrangement with the consulate to handle many of the claims that were going to come in droves. He was hoping the consulate would recommend him since he was certified in Germany and the States.

'It won't make me rich, but it's a living. And you? Did you get anything out, Ariana?'

'My skin, a few pieces of jewellery – and Manfred's photographs.'

He nodded slowly, remembering all they had once had, the splendour of her father's house. It seemed incredible that they had all come so far and that there was nothing left of that world. Only memories and trinkets, souvenirs and dreams.

For Max they were memories to which he couldn't have borne to return.

'Do you ever think about going back, Ariana?'

'Not really. I have no more there than I do here. I have no one except Noel now. And here it will be a good life for him.'

'I hope so.' Max smiled at him gently, reminded of his own sons. And then he took Noel carefully from his mother and tousled his hair. Standing there together, they looked like a family, laughing, happy, united; and no one, except others who had been there, would have believed the long road they had come.

BOOK FOUR
NOEL

Chapter 45

The ceremony took place on a brilliantly sunny morning in Harvard Yard between the Widener Library and the Appleton Chapel. There seemed to be a sea of sparkling young faces and tall, lean bodies draped in cap and gown, waiting to receive the diplomas they had struggled towards for so long. Ariana watched them, smiling mistily, as Max sat beside her on the narrow folding chairs, holding her hand and noticing how the large emerald she now wore constantly sparkled in the sun.

'Doesn't he look handsome, Max?' She leaned gently towards the distinguished white-haired gentleman he had become, and he patted her arm and smiled.

'How can you tell, Ariana? I'm not even sure which one is he.'

'Some people just have no respect at all.' They whispered at each other like two children, the laughter still fresh in their eyes. He had been her constant companion now for almost twenty-five years, and they still enjoyed each other's company after all this time.

She smiled up at him, her golden beauty not yet faded and only slightly quieter with time. The features were still perfect, her hair a softer gold, the eyes still enormous and the same deep blue. It was Max who had changed greatly, still tall, spare, almost lanky, but with a full mane of white hair now. Nineteen years older than Ariana, he had just turned sixty-four.

'Oh, Max, I'm so proud of him.'

This time his arm went gently around her and he nodded. 'You should be. He's a good man.' And then he smiled again. 'And a good lawyer. It's a damn shame he wants to work for that high-falutin fancy firm. I would be proud to have an associate like him.' But although Max's law practice in New York had grown to considerable proportions, it was still a relatively small show compared to the firm that had already made Noel an offer the summer before. He had clerked for them for one summer, and they were quick to offer him a job the moment he would graduate from Harvard Law. And now that moment had come.

By noon it was all over, and he returned to hug his mother warmly and shake hands with Uncle Max.

'Well, you two, surviving? I was afraid that by now you'd both be cooked by the sun.' The huge blue eyes danced as he looked down at his mother, and she smiled up into the face that was so exactly Manfred's that it still startled her at times. He had the tall, lean frame of his father, the broad shoulders, the graceful hands, yet oddly, now and then there was a look ... an expression ... some vague hint of Gerhard, and she would smile as she looked at Noel ... yes, they did live on in her son.

'Darling, it was a lovely ceremony. And we're both so proud.'

'So am I, you know.' He bent the broad shoulders lower to speak to her softly, and she touched his face with the hand that wore her mother's signet ring on her little finger and the ring Manfred had given her, which had never left her hand since her son had been born. In all those early years after Paul had left her, she had never given up the treasured rings. They were not only her last security, but they remained the only reminder of the past. In time Max had won her the restitution, both for the house in Grunewald and some of its contents and Manfred's schloss. The amount was not an overwhelming fortune, but it was nonetheless very handsome and had been enough to invest well and provide herself and the child with a healthy income, at least for the rest of Ariana's life. She needed no more than that. For her the days of glory now were gone. She was able to quit the bookshop. She bought a small town house on the East Side, in the upper Seventies, invested all her money, and spent every living, waking moment caring for her only child.

For the first years Max had tried to talk her into getting married, but after that he stopped. Neither of them wanted any more children, and in their own way they were both still too tied to those they had loved in the past. Instead, for a while Max rented a small apartment, and eventually at Ariana's urging he bought a small but handsome co-op across the street from her house. They went to the opera, theatre, dinner, disappeared occasionally together on weekends, but in the end, they went home to their separate retreats. For a long time Ariana did so because of Noel, but eventually it just became a habit. And now, even in the seven years he had been at Harvard, Ariana still spent much of her time in her own place.

'You have every right to be proud, darling.' She gazed at him from under her straw hat and he wondered for an instant, as Max did so often, if she would ever show the signs of age. She was still as spectacularly pretty as she had been when she was a girl.

But Noel was shaking his head and smiling. 'I didn't mean that I was proud of me,' he whispered. 'I meant that I was proud of you.' She laughed at him softly in amusement, touched his face, and tucked her arm into Max's.

'I don't think you're supposed to say things like that to your mother, Noel.'

'That's right: Besides – ' Max smiled at them both – 'I might get jealous.' They both laughed and Ariana took hold of Max's hand. 'So when do you start work, Noel?'

'The hell I'm going to work now, Uncle Max. Are you kidding? I'm taking a vacation!'

Ariana turned to look at him with surprise and pleasure. 'Are you? Where are you going?' He hadn't said anything to her yet. But he was a man now. She didn't expect him to share all his plans. Wisely, with Max's help, she had learned to let go slowly when he had first left for Harvard in the fall of 1963.

'I thought I'd go to Europe.'

'Really?' She looked at him in amazement. On their trips together they had gone to California, Arizona, the Grand Canyon, New Orleans, New England ... everywhere except Europe, because neither Max nor she had ever been able to go back. What was the point of returning to old places, seeing the homes and haunts and hideouts of the people they had loved, people who were gone but not yet forgotten? Max and she had both agreed long before never to go back. 'Where in Europe, Noel?' For an instant she paled.

'I haven't decided.' And then he looked at her gently. 'But I'll probably stop in Germany, Mother, I have to ... I want to ...' She nodded slowly. 'Can you understand that?'

She smiled gently up at the son who was so suddenly a man. 'Yes, darling, I do.' Yet she was surprised to realise that it hurt her. She had wanted so to give him everything American, to create a world where there would be no room for Germany in his life, where the boy would be content with what he had here, and never want to go back to her old world.

'Don't look so unhappy, Ariana.' Max looked at her gently while Noel went off to get their lunch. 'For him it isn't going "back". It's simply going, to see something he's heard about, read about. It doesn't have all the deeper meaning you want to give it. Trust me.' She looked up at him and smiled slowly.

'Maybe you're right.'

'It's just a healthy curiosity, believe me. Besides, it's not just your country, Ariana, it was his father's.' And they both knew that to Noel that was sacred. To Noel, Manfred had always been something of a god. Ariana had told him all about his father, how he had saved her from the Nazis, how good he'd been, how much they'd cared for each other. He'd seen the photographs of his father in uniform. Nothing had been hidden from him, nothing spared.

Max looked at her again as they sat there, and patted her hand in the warm Cambridge sun. 'You did a good job with him, Ariana.'

'You think so?' She peered at him mischievously from beneath her hat.

'Yes, I do.'

'And you had no hand in it at all, did you?'

'Well, just a little ...'

'Max Thomas, you're such a fibber. He's as much your son as mine.' For a long moment Max didn't answer, and then he kissed her softly on the neck.

'Thank you, my darling.'

They both jumped, startled as Noel towered above them, carrying two trays and wearing a broad smile. 'I mean really, everyone will know you're not married if you sit around here necking.' The three of them laughed and Ariana blushed.

'Really, Noel!'

'Don't look at me like that, Mother. I wasn't sitting here behaving like a teenager ... and in *broad daylight!*' He emphasised it again and all three of them laughed together, and then he smiled at them very gently. 'It's nice to see you two so happy.'

'Weren't we always?' Ariana looked at Max in surprise, and then at her son, who nodded slowly.

'Yes, amazingly, you always were. I think that's fairly rare though.' He smiled again. And this time Ariana quietly kissed Max.

'Perhaps it is.'

The three of them settled down to lunch then, and it was almost time for the guest speaker when suddenly Noel stood up and waved to a friend. For a minute the gown billowed as he signalled and tried to urge whoever it was to approach, and then he sat down smiling broadly, with a look of victory he shared with his mother and Max.

'She's coming over.'

'Is *she*?' Max teased, and this time it was Noel who blushed. And a moment later they were joined by a young lady. Noel instantly stood up. She had huge green eyes, and olive complexion, and a long, straight sheaf of shining black hair. She had long, thin legs and Ariana noticed that she wore sandals.

'Max, Mother, this is Tamara.' It was a congenial introduction. The girl smiled, showing perfect teeth. 'Tammy, my mother and Uncle Max.'

'How do you do.' She shook hands politely, casting a great shaft of the raven hair over her shoulder, and then she looked into Noel's eyes. For an instant there seemed to be a kind of secret, a message of some kind, an exchange. And Max found himself smiling at them. That kind of look between two people only meant one thing.

'Are you also at the law school, Tamara?' Ariana looked at her politely, trying not to feel awed by the presence of this girl in her son's life. But there was very little awesome about her; she seemed like a very open, friendly girl.

'Yes, I am, Mrs Tripp.'

'Yes, but she's still a baby lawyer,' Noel teased as he touched a lock of the shining hair. 'Just a fledgling greenie,' he teased, and her eyes shot friendly daggers.

'I still have two more years to finish,' she explained to Max and Ariana. 'Noel is all pleased with himself today.' As she said it, it was as though there was an understanding between them. As though Noel was more hers than theirs. Ariana understood the message and smiled.

'Maybe we're all a little impressed with him, Tamara. But your turn will come. Will you be staying on at Harvard?'

'I think so.' But again there was a quick look between the two.

Noel treated the matter casually and glanced quietly at Tamara. 'You'll be seeing her in New York sometime. If she ever does her homework. Right, little one?'

'Oh! Look who's talking!' Suddenly as Ariana and Max watched in amusement, they were both forgotten by the youngsters. 'Who finished your last paper for you? Who did all your typing for the last six months?' But they were both laughing and he quickly put a finger to his lips.

'Sshh, that's a secret, for chrissake, Tammy! You want them to take back my diploma?'

'No.' She grinned at him. 'I just want them to give it to me, so I can get out of here, too.' But at that moment the guest speaker was ready to address them; Noel shushed Tamara, who shook hands again with Max and his mother and then disappeared to rejoin her friends.

'She's a very pretty young lady,' Max whispered to Noel with a smile. 'Quite a striking beauty in fact.'

Noel nodded. 'And one day she'll be a hell of a good lawyer.' He glanced into the distance admiringly, and looking at her son, so young, so tall, so golden, Ariana just sat back and smiled.

Chapter 46

That night they had dinner at Locke Ober's, but all three of them were exhausted, and the subject of Tamara did not come up again. Max and Noel talked law while Ariana half listened, watched the people, and thought once or twice of the girl. For some reason she had an impression that she'd already seen her, but she wondered if that was because Noel had had a snapshot of her somewhere in the apartment in New York. Anyway, it didn't seem too important. However taken with each other they seemed to be, their paths were now going to take very different turns.

'Don't you think so, Ariana?' Max looked over at her with a raised eyebrow and then grinned. 'Flirting with the younger men, darling?'

'Oh, my, he caught me. I'm sorry, darling. What did you say?'

'I asked you if you didn't think he'd prefer Bavaria to the Black Forest.'

Her face clouded at the question. 'Maybe. But frankly, Noel, I think you ought to go to Italy instead.'

'Why?' He faced her squarely. 'Why not Germany? What are you afraid of, Mother?' Privately, Max was glad that the boy had the courage to to bring it out.

'I'm not afraid of anything. Don't be silly.'

'Yes, you are.'

She hesitated for a long moment, looked at Max, and then dropped her eyes. The three of them had always been so honest, but now suddenly it hurt her to say what she was thinking. 'I'm afraid that if you go back, you'll find some piece of you that belongs there. You'll feel at home.'

'And then what? You think I'll stay there?' He was smiling gently at his mother and quietly reached out and took her hand.

'Maybe.' She sighed softly. 'I don't really know what I'm afraid of, except that ... I left there so long ago, and it was such an ugly time. For me, all I can think of is what I lost ... the people I loved.'

'But don't you think I have a right to know something more about them, too? To see the country where they lived? Where you lived as a child? To see the house where you lived with your father, where my father lived with his parents? Why can't I see it, just so I know it's there, somewhere, a part of me the way it has stayed a part of you?'

There was a long silence at the table and Max spoke first. 'The boy is right, Ariana. He has a right to that.' And then he looked at Noel. 'It's a beautiful country, son. It always was and I'm sure it always will be. And maybe one of the reasons we don't go back is because we still love it so much and it hurt us so deeply to know what happened.'

'I understand that, Max.' And then he looked at his mother again gently, with compassion. 'It can't hurt me, Mother. I never knew it as it was. I'm just going there to see it, that's all, and then I'll come back to you and my own country, a little richer for what I understand about you and myself.'

She sighed softly and looked at them both. 'You're both so eloquent, you should be lawyers.' And then the three laughed softly, finished their coffee, and Max signalled for the cheque.

Noel's plane was to leave Kennedy Airport two weeks later, and he planned to stay in Europe for about six weeks. He wanted to be back in New York by mid-August, so he would have time to find his own apartment and start work on 1 September.

The weeks before he left for Europe were hectic. He had friends he wanted to see, parties to go to, and almost every day now he sat down and went over his travel plans with Max. The trip still bothered Ariana, but she made her peace with it. And she was amused by Noel's constant running. She thought, as she saw him drive off with friends one night, that in twenty years young men had not changed very much after all.

'What were you thinking just then?' Max had seen the glimmer of nostalgia in her eyes.

'That nothing changes.' She smiled tenderly at her beloved.

'Doesn't it? I was just thinking that it does. But maybe that's because I'm almost twenty years older than you are.'

They both thought back to her mother's deserted apartment in the house in Grunewald, when he had first kissed her, while he was hiding from the Nazis. His eyes asked her if she remembered.

Slowly, Ariana nodded. 'Yes, I do.'

He smiled back. 'I told you then that I loved you. And I did, you know.'

She kissed his cheek softly. 'I loved you then, too, as best I knew how in those days.' And then she smiled into the rich brown eyes. 'You were the first man I had ever kissed.'

'And now I hope to be the last. In which case I shall have to live to be at least a hundred.'

'I'm counting on it, Max.' They smiled at each other for a long moment and then purposely he took her hand, the heavy emerald as always on her finger.

'I have something to say to you, Ariana ... or rather, something I would like to ask.'

Suddenly she knew. Was it possible? Did it still matter, after all these years?

'Yes, it's very important. To me. Ariana, will you marry me?' He said it so gently, with such a look of love and pleading in his eyes.

For a moment she didn't answer, and then she looked at him with her head tilted to one side. 'Max, why now, my love? Does it really make so much difference now?'

'Yes. To me. Noel is gone now. He's a man, Ariana. When he gets back from Europe, he's moving into his own apartment. And what about us? We maintain appearances, as we always have? For what? My doorman and your maid? Why don't you sell your house, or I'll sell the apartment, and let's get married. It's our turn now. You've devoted twenty-five years to Noel. Now let's devote the next twenty-five to us.' She couldn't help but smile at his argument. In a way she knew that he was right, and she liked what he had in mind.

'But for that we have to be married?'

He grinned at her. 'Don't you want to be respectable at your age?'

'But, Max, I'm only forty-six.' She had smiled at him then, and he had known that finally, he had won her. And he kissed her once more, twenty-eight years after the first time.

They told Noel the next morning, and he was delighted. He kissed his mother, and this time he kissed Max as well.

'Now, I'll feel better going. And especially moving out in September. Are you keeping the house, Mom?'

'We haven't worked that out yet.' She was still a little flustered by their decision. And then Noel suddenly grinned as he kissed her on the cheek again.

'Just think, not every couple gets married to celebrate their silver anniversary ...'

'Noel!' She still felt a little odd getting married at her age. Getting married, as far as Ariana was concerned, was something one did at twenty-two or twenty-five, not two decades later, with a son who was already a man.

'So when's the wedding?'

Max answered for her. 'We haven't decided. But we'll wait till you get back.'

'I should hope so. Well, do we get to celebrate?' It seemed that that was all they had done for weeks since he'd left Harvard, and he was leaving for Europe the next day.

But Max took them both to dinner at Côte Basque that evening. It was a sumptuous meal, and a wonderful occasion. They celebrated Noel's flight into the past and their venture into the future, and as always, Ariana shed a few tears.

Paris was everything he'd hoped. He visited the Eiffel Tower, the Louvre. He stopped in cafés, read the paper, and wrote a postcard home addressing it. 'Dear Engaged Couple,' and signing it, 'Your Son.' That night before dinner, he called a friend of Tammy's whom he had promised to call, Brigitte Goddard, daughter of the noted art dealer and proprietor of the Galerie Gérard Goddard. Noel had known Brigitte only slightly during her brief stint at Harvard, but she and Tammy had become good friends. She was an intriguing girl with an odd family, a mother she hated, a father she claimed was obsessed with his past, and a brother whom she laughingly insisted was crazy. She was always teasing and cavorting. She was beautiful and funny.

But there had been something tragic about her as well, as though there was something missing. And when Noel had questioned her seriously about it once, she had said, 'You're right. My family is missing, Noel. My father lives in his own world. None of us matter to him ... only ... the past ... the others ... the people he lost in another lifetime ... We, the living ... we don't count. Not to him.' And then she had said something cynical and funny, but he had never forgotten the look in her eyes – it was an expression of sorrow and loss and desolation well beyond her years. And now Noel wanted to see her, and he was bitterly disappointed when he learned that she was out of town.

As a consolation he took himself out for a big dinner, with drinks at La Tour d'Argent, and dinner at Maxim's. He had promised himself he'd do that before he left Paris, and now he wasn't going to be able to do it with Brigitte. But now he had the extra leisure time for the fancy dinner, and he enjoyed it thoroughly as he watched the elegant French women and their rather dapper-looking men. He noticed how different the styles were here, how much more cosmopolitan people seemed. He liked the looks of the women, the way they moved, the way they dressed, the way they did their hair. In a way, they reminded him of his mother. There was a finished quality about the way they put themselves together that pleased the eye, an extra touch, a something subtle but sexy, like a flower hidden in a garden; it didn't assault the senses, but one sensed instantly that it was there. Noel liked the subtlety of these women; it evoked something in him that he had never known was really there.

The next morning he left for Orly very early, caught his flight to Berlin, and landed at Tempelhof airport, his heart beating with excitement and anticipation. It wasn't a sensation of homecoming, but of discovery, of finding the answers to secrets long unspoken, of tracing people who had long since vanished, where they had been, where they had lived, what they had been and meant to each other. Somehow, Noel knew that the answers would all be there.

He left his things at the Hotel Kempinski, where he had made a reservation, and as he walked out of the lobby, he looked up and down the Kurfürstendamn for a long time. This was the street Max had told him about where writers and artists and intellectuals had congregated for decades. Around him he could see cafés and shops, and swirls of people walking along arm in arm. There was a festive feeling around him, as though they had all been waiting, as though it had been time for him to come.

With a map and a rented car he set out slowly. He had already seen the remains of the Maria Regina Kirche where he knew his parents had been married. What was left of it still stood there, pointing emptily at the sky. He remembered his mother's description of when they had bombed it, and now it remained, a shattered memory of another time. Most of Berlin showed none of the scars, the damage had all been repaired, but here and there were shells of buildings, monuments to that troubled time. He drove slowly past the Anhalter Station, which also stood in ruins, too, then on to the Philharmonic Hall, and then he walked through the Tiergarten to the Victory Column, which stood as it always had, and Bellevue Palace just beyond it, which was as beautiful as Max said it was. And then beyond that Noel came to a sudden halt. There it stood, gleaming in the sunlight, the Reichstag, which had been Nazi headquarters, located on what they now called the Strasse des 17 Tury, the building his father had died defending. Around him, other tourists also gazed at it in silent awe.

To Noel this was no monument to the Nazis; this had nothing to do with history, or politics, or a little man with a moustache who had had an insatiable desire to control the world. This had to do with a man whom Noel had always suspected had been very much like him, the man who had loved his mother, and whom Noel had never known. He remembered his mother's description of that morning ... the explosions, the soldiers, the refugees, and the destruction of the bombs ... and then she had seen his father dead. As Noel stood there, a quiet path of tears coursed down his face. He cried for himself and for Ariana, feeling her pain as she had stood there, looking into his father's lifeless face lying in a stack of bodies on the gutted street. How in God's name had she survived it?

Noel quietly walked away from the Reichstag, and it was then that he caught his first glimpse of the Wall; solid, intransigent, determined, it wended its way across Berlin, to one side of the Reichstag and cutting right through the Brandenburg Gate, turning the once flourishing Unter den Linden into a dead end. He looked at it in interested silence, curious about what lay beyond. This was something that neither Max nor his mother had ever experienced, the wall that had left a divided Berlin. Later in his stay he would go there, to see the Marienkirche, the City Hall, and the Dom. He understood that there were many untouched ruins there, too. But first there were other places he wanted to visit, places he had come to see.

With his map on the seat of the Volkswagen he'd rented, he drove from the heart of the city around the Olympic stadium, out to Charlottenburg, where he stopped for a moment by the lake and looked at the schloss. And though he could not know it, this was exactly the place where thirty-five years before his grandmother Kassandra von Gotthard had stood with the man she loved, Dolff Sterne.

From Charlottenburg he drove to Spandau, staring at the great citadel in fascination and getting out to inspect the famous doors. There, the helmets of countless wars were carved in great detail, from the Middle Ages until the last panel, which bore the legend '1939'. The prison held only one prisoner, Rudolf Hess, who was costing the city government more than 400,000 dollars a year to keep. And from Spandau he drove to Grunewald, driving along the lake, looking carefully at all the houses, and searching for the address he had gotten from Max. He had wanted to ask his mother, but when the time had come, he hadn't dared. Max had given him the directions and told him briefly how lovely the house had been, and once again he had told him the story of how Noel's grandfather had saved Max's life when he was fleeing the country, how he had cut the two priceless paintings from the walls where they hung, rolled them up, and handed them to his friend.

At first Noel thought he had missed it, but then suddenly he saw the gates. They had changed not at all from Max's description, and as Noel got out of the car and peered in, a gardener waved.

'Bitte?' Noel's German was very rusty. He knew only what he had learned at

Harvard in three semesters several years before. But somehow he managed to explain to the old man tending the gardens that long ago this had been his grandfather's house.

'*Ja?*' The man eyed him with interest.

'*Ja*. Walmar von Gotthard.' Noel said it proudly and the man smiled, shrugging. He had never heard the name. An old woman appeared, admonishing the gardener to hurry, the madam would be back from her trip the next evening.

Smiling, the old man explained to his wife why Noel had come there, and looking at him with suspicion, she then stared back at the old man. At first the woman hesitated, but after a moment she grudgingly nodded her head and gestured towards Noel. He looked at the old man questioningly, not sure he had understood them.

But the old man was smiling as he took Noel's arm. 'She will let you look around.'

'Inside the house?'

'Yes.' The old man smiled gently. He understood. It was nice that this young American cared enough about his grandfather's country to come back. So many of them had forgotten where they came from. So many of them knew nothing of what had happened before the war. But this one seemed different, and it pleased the old man.

In some ways the house looked very different than he had expected, and in others it looked precisely like Ariana's memories of when she was a child, memories she had shared with him constantly through the years. The third floor, where she had lived with her nurse and her brother, still looked as she had described it. The large room that had been their playroom, the two bedrooms, the large bathroom the children had shared. Now it stood made into guest rooms, but Noel could still see exactly where his mother had lived. On the floor beneath that, much seemed to have changed. There seemed to be lots of smaller bedrooms, sitting rooms, libraries, a sewing room, and a small room filled with toys. Obviously the house had been remodelled, and there was little trace of the past. The downstairs still remained impressive and somewhat stuffy. But Noel could more easily imagine his grandfather presiding over the large dining room table in the huge hall. He thought fleetingly of a Nazi general cavorting there with his girls, but quickly dismissed the image from his mind.

He thanked the old couple profusely before he left them, and took a photograph of the house from the spot where he had left his car. Maybe he could get Tammy to do a sketch from the photograph, and he could give it to his mother sometime. The thought pleased him as he drove along to the Grunewald cemetery, where it took him a long time to find the family plot. But there they were, the aunts and the uncles, the great-grandparents; all with names and histories he did not know. The only one that was familiar was that of his grandmother Kassandra von Gotthard. It touched him that she had been only thirty and he wondered briefly how she had died.

There were things that his mother still had not told him things that he did not need to know. Like the truth about her mother's suicide, which was something that had always disturbed Ariana a great deal. And the fact that she herself had briefly been married to Paul Liebman. She didn't feel Noel needed to know that either. By the time he was old enough to understand things, she and Max had decided that it was a closed chapter in Ariana's life, and one of which her son did not need to be apprised.

Noel wandered slowly through the cemetery, looking at the peaceful green mounds, and then at last he got back into his car and drove out towards Wannsee, but this time he struck out. The house whose address he still vaguely remembered from his mother's stories was no longer there. Instead, there were neat rows of modern buildings. The house where she had lived with Manfred was gone.

He stayed on in Berlin for another three days then, journeying back to Grunewald once, and to Wannsee, but spending most of his time on the other side of the Wall. The eastern side of Berlin fascinated Noel – how different the people were, how barren their faces, how bleak their stories. It was his first and only view of communism, and this was far more real to him than the faded ghosts of the Nazis, which some had attempted to keep alive.

After Berlin he went to Dresden, and went to the few places he knew of there. Mostly he was interested in the schloss for which his mother had been given restitution. He knew only that it was used now as a small country museum where they gave occasional tours. On the day that he reached it, it was all but deserted, blessed with only one sleeping guard. It was dark and somewhat dreary, the furnishings sparse, most having been removed, a plaque said, during the war. But here again, as he had in Grunewald, he could reach out and touch the same walls that his father had touched as a boy. It was a strange, thrilling feeling to look out the same windows, stand in the same doorways, touch the same doorknobs, breathe the same air. This might have been the house of his boyhood, if he had not lived instead on East Seventy-seventh Street in New York. And as he left the house, the guard smiled at Noel from the chair where he sat watching.

'Auf Wiedersehen.'

Without thinking, Noel smiled at him and murmured, 'Goodbye.'

But instead of being depressed by his visits, in an odd, wonderful way, he felt finally free. Free of the questions, of the empty places that they had seen and he hadn't. Now he had seen them all, too. He had seen them as they were now, as part of the present, as part of his times, not of theirs, not as they had been. Now they were a part of his life, and he felt he understood them, and now he felt freer than ever to be himself.

He had the time he needed to put the past into perspective, to understand his mother even more, how much she had endured, how strong she was. He vowed he'd do all he could to make her proud of him for the rest of his life.

He got off the plane at Kennedy Airport, looking relaxed and happy, and for a long moment held his mother tightly in his arms. No matter what he had seen, or how much some of it had meant to him, there was no doubt in his mind whatever, this was home.

Chapter 47

'Well, guys, when's the wedding?' On his return Noel had found his own apartment, in the east Fifties, overlooking the East River, and cozily located near an assortment of friendly neighbourhood bars. He still liked to go drinking with his law school buddies, and his playtime hadn't entirely come to an end, even with his first job. But he was not quite twenty-six yet, and Max and Ariana knew he had time to settle down. 'Have you set a date yet?' It was the first dinner they had shared since he had moved out, and Max's bathrobe had been appearing more regularly on the back of Ariana's bedroom door.

'Well.' She smiled at Max and then at Noel. 'We were thinking about Christmas. How does that sound to you?'

'Wonderful. We can do it before my birthday.' And then he smiled shyly. 'Will it be a big wedding?'

'No, of course not.' Ariana shook her head, laughing. 'Not at our age. Just a few friends.' But as she said it, there was a faraway look in her eyes. For the third time in her life, she was getting married and the memories of her lost family flashed across her heart and her mind. Noel looked at her and seemed to sense her thoughts. Since his trip to Europe they had been even closer than before. It was as though now he *knew*. They seldom spoke of it, but the new bond was there.

'I was wondering if I could bring a friend to the wedding, Mother. Would that be all right?'

'Of course, darling.' Ariana was instantly smiling. 'Anyone we know?'

'Yes. You met her this summer, at my graduation. Remember Tammy?' He tried so desperately to look nonchalant, but instead looked so nervous as he said it that Max couldn't suppress a laugh.

'The ravishing Rapunzel with the long black hair, if I'm not mistaken. Tamara, yes?'

'Yes.' He looked gratefully at Max and his mother smiled.

'I remember her, too. The young law student – she was just finishing her first year.'

'Right. Well, she'll be down to see her parents over Christmas, and I just thought ... I mean ... she'd enjoy the wedding.'

'Of course, Noel. Of course.' Max got him off the hook quickly by changing the subject, but the look on Noel's face had not escaped Ariana. That night she turned to Max before they went to bed.

'You don't suppose he's serious, do you?' She looked worried, and Max smiled gently and sat down on the edge of the bed.

'He might be, but I doubt it. I don't really think he's ready to settle down.'

'I hope not. He isn't even twenty-six.' Max Thomas grinned at the woman he was soon to marry.

'And how old were you when you had him?'

'That was different, Max. I may only have been twenty, but that was war-time, and – '

'Do you really think you would have stayed single until you were twenty-six if there hadn't been a war? On the contrary, I think you'd have married in no time at all.'

'Oh, Max, that was another world. Another life!' For a long moment they said nothing and then quietly she joined him in the bed and took him in her arms. She needed him now, to ward off the memories and the pain. And he knew it too. 'Tell me, Ariana, after all these years, will you take my name?'

She looked at him in astonishment. 'Of course I will. Why wouldn't I?'

'I don't know.' He shrugged. 'These days women are so independent. I thought maybe you'd prefer to stay Ariana Tripp.'

'I'd prefer to be your wife, Max, and to be Mrs Thomas.' And then she smiled slowly. 'It really is time.'

'What I like about you, Ariana,' he said gently as his hands caressed her body beneath the sheets, –' is that you make such quick decisions. It's only taken you twenty-five years.' But then she laughed softly at him. The tinkling laugh of crystal had not changed since she was a girl, nor had the passion with which she received him, startled as always by the thrust of his desire as he took her and held her and filled her with his love.

Chapter 48

'And do you, Maximilian, take this woman to be ...' The ceremony was brief and lovely, and Noel watched them with tears in his eyes, grateful that, as tall as he was, few people could notice if his lashes were damp. 'You may kiss the bride.' They kissed for a long moment, obviously enjoying it more than they should. The friends they had invited giggled, and Noel tapped Max on the shoulder and smiled.

'Okay, you two, break it up. The honeymoon is in Italy. This is only the reception.' Max turned to him with a long smile of amusement and Ariana grinned and smoothed a hand over her hair.

They had decided to hold the wedding and the reception at the Carlyle. It was close to the house and there was a lovely room available that was just the right size. They had, in the end, invited almost forty people for the ceremony and a formal luncheon, and a small quartet was already playing for those who wanted to dance.

'May I, Mother? I think the first dance is supposed to be between the bride and her father, but maybe you'll accept this modern variation on the theme.'

'I'd be delighted.' He bowed and she took his arm and slowly they moved on to the floor for a graceful Waltz. He danced as impeccably as had his father, and Ariana wondered if it was simply in his genes. The boy had a fluid grace of movement that was irresistible to almost any female watching him make his way smoothly around the floor. As she looked happily past him at her new husband, Ariana saw Tammy, standing quietly in a corner, her black hair wound neatly in a knot, wearing small diamond earrings and a pretty black wool dress.

'Will you look at those two?' Noel was smiling at his mother as Tammy stood by. She felt faintly uncomfortable in the crowd of strangers, but she was always happy at Noel's side. It was odd to see him here though. She was so used to seeing him in blue jeans and turtleneck sweaters, playing touch football with his friends in Harvard Yard. He had already been up to see her twice this winter, and she had just told him what she had in mind.

'What do you think, Noel?'

'About what?' He was smiling distractedly at his mother from where he stood.

'You know about what.'

'About your transferring to Columbia? I think you're out of your mind. You have a chance at a Harvard Law degree, kiddo. That's quite a piece of paper to throw away for a piece of ass.'

'Is that all it is to you?' Her eyes narrowed and she looked both angry and hurt. But he was quick to take her hand and kiss it softly.

'No, and you know it. But what I'm trying to point out to you is that because you're so goddamn horny – ' he grinned at her gently – 'you're not willing to sit it out at Harvard for the next two years while I commute.'

'But that's silly. It's hard on you and on me. You're going to be having more briefs to write, more research to do, now that you're working. How much time do you think you'll be able to spend coming up to Cambridge? And with law school getting as tough as it has this year, I can hardly get away. If I'm here, then we can just both do what we're doing and be together.' The huge eyes looked at him, pleading, and he had to fight himself not to beg her to do what she said.

'Tammy. I just don't want to influence your decision. It's too important. You're talking about a major change that could affect your whole career.'

'Oh, don't be such a snob, for chrissake, I'm talking about Columbia, not Backwater U.'

'How do you know they'll accept you as a transfer?' He was desperately trying to do his duty, but he equally desperately wanted her to make the switch.

'I already asked, and they said I could start next term.' He looked at her pointedly without commenting. 'Well?' She looked at him expectantly.

He drew a long, slow breath. 'I think this is where I'm supposed to discourage you and be noble.'

'Is that what you want to do?' She searched his face and his eyes met hers squarely.

'No. I want to live with you. Right here. Right now. But that's awfully selfish. You should be aware of that.' He moved closer to her and their bodies touched lightly as they stood side by side. 'I love you and I want you with me.'

'Then let me do what I want to do.' She smiled up at him and he smiled in return just as Max and Ariana approached them, watching them with appreciative smiles.

They were so young and so good-looking, so happy and so free, one wanted just to stand near them, to be a part of what they had before them. It was like looking down a long, long stretch of open road.

'You remember Tammy, Mother?'

'I do.' Ariana gazed warmly at the girl. She liked her. She liked her looks and her spirit. She just wasn't so sure about that tender, earnest look in her son's eyes.

'Maybe I should renew the introductions. After all, my mother has a new name.' This time it was Ariana who blushed gently, as Max stood proudly by and grinned. 'My mother, Mrs Maximilian Thomas, my stepfather, Max Thomas, and my friend, Tamara Liebman.'

'Liebman – ' Ariana was taken by surprise but managed to rein in her emotions quickly. 'Are you related to Ruth and Samuel Liebman?' She hadn't dared mention Paul's name. Tammy nodded quietly, her eyes puzzled by what she saw and did not understand in the other woman's face.

'They were my grandparents, but they died a long time ago. I never knew them.'

'Oh.' Ariana was struck mute for a while. 'Then you're ...'

'Paul and Marjorie Liebman's daughter. And my Aunt Julia lives in London. Maybe you knew her, too.'

'Yes ...' Ariana was almost choking and she was suddenly very pale.

Tammy couldn't know what was behind Ariana's shock. She only knew the anguish of rejection as a few minutes later they spun slowly on the dance floor and tears rolled slowly down her face.

'Tammy? Are you crying?' Noel looked down at her tenderly and she shook her head. But her denials were useless. 'Come on, let's get out of here for a minute.' He took her downstairs to the lobby and slowly they walked the halls. 'What's the matter, baby?'

'Your mother hates me.' A little sob escaped her as she said it. And she had so wanted everything to be all right. She knew how close Noel was to his mother, and it was essential that she fit in from the start. She had known that. But now it was already over.

'Did you see her face when she heard my name? She almost fainted in her tracks because I was Jewish. Didn't you tell her before now?'

'I didn't think I had to, for chrissake. Tammy, this is the Seventies. Being Jewish is no big thing.'

'Maybe not to you, but it is to her. Just like your being German was a shock to my parents. But at least I warned them! How can you not understand that about your mother? She's anti-Semitic, for chrissake, and you don't even know!'

'No, she isn't! Next you'll be calling my mother a Nazi.' That wasn't likely, but it was exactly what her father had called him.

'Noel, you don't understand anything.' She stood shivering in the lobby, watching people hurry down the street.

'I do. I understand perfectly that you're buying into their bullshit and all their old games. It's not our fight, Tammy. It wasn't our war. We're people, black, white, brown, yellow, Jewish, Irish, Arab. We're Americans – that's the whole beauty of this country. That other stuff doesn't matter any more.'

'It does to them.' She looked heartbroken as once more she thought of his mother, but firmly he pulled her into his arms.

'But it doesn't matter to me, do you believe that?' She nodded. 'And I'm going to talk to my mother tonight before she leaves for the airport to see if you're right.'

'I know I'm right, Noel.'

'Don't be so sure.' But she refused to go back to the party. They went upstairs briefly so she could retrieve her coat, and after politely saying good-bye to his mother, Tammy went back downstairs and he put her into a cab.

'Your friend looked very pretty, Noel.' Ariana said it stiffly as they sat down in her living room after they got back from the reception at the hotel. They had three hours until she and Max had to leave for the airport. They were going back to Europe for their honeymoon, but only to Geneva and Rome. 'She seems like a lovely girl.' But there was an odd silence in the room after she said it. She had already discussed it with Max when they had a few moments alone.

Noel stood facing her from where he stood near the fireplace with a look in his eyes that said he didn't understand her tone. 'She thinks you don't like her, Mother.' There was no answer. 'Because she's Jewish. Is that true?' It was a quiet accusation as he stood there, and slowly Ariana lowered her eyes.

'I'm sorry she thinks that, Noel.' And then she looked up at her son again. 'But no, that isn't why.'

'Then she's half right – you don't like her?' He looked angry and hurt by what he was hearing and it killed Ariana to go on.

'I didn't say that. She seems like a very nice person. But, Noel ...' She looked at him bluntly. 'You have to stop seeing that girl.'

'What? Are you kidding?' He left the fireplace and stalked the room. 'No, I'm not.'

'Well, just exactly what is going on here? I'm twenty-six years old and you're telling me whom I can and can't see?'

'I'm telling you for your own good.' The excitement of the past few hours seemed to have faded, and suddenly Ariana looked tired and old. Max reached out and touched her hand gently, but even Max couldn't comfort her for having to hurt her own son now.

'It's none of your damn business.'

She winced slightly. 'I'm sorry to hear you say that. But the fact is that when her father learns all about you, you're going to be hurt, Noel. You might as well know that now.'

'Why?' It was an agonised wail. 'And what the hell do you know about her father anyway?'

There was a long silence in the room, which Max was going to interrupt to save Ariana, but she quietly held up a hand. 'I was married to him, Noel, when I first came to the States.' This time it was her son who looked shocked. He sat down heavily on a chair.

'I don't understand.'

'I know.' Her voice was gentle. 'And I'm sorry. I just didn't think you'd ever need to know.'

'But weren't you really married to my father?'

'Yes, but when I got here, widowed and frightened, I was terribly sick. I had come over on a boat sponsored by the Women's Relief Organisation here. I don't think they even exist now, but they were very important then. And I was befriended by a lovely woman –' she thought quietly of her for a moment, sorry that she had heard from Tammy that Ruth was dead – 'Ruth Liebman. She was Tammy's grandmother. And they decided to take me into their home. They were wonderful to me. They nursed me back to health, they gave me everything, and they loved me. But they also believed I was Jewish. And I was foolish enough not to correct that belief.' She stopped for what seemed like a long time. And then she looked straight at her son.

'They had a son. He had come back from the Pacific because he was wounded, and he had a crush on me. I was twenty then and he was only twenty-two. And after your father, he seemed ... well, like a little boy. But he was sweet, and he had just been jilted by the girl he'd been engaged to during the war. And –' she swallowed hard – 'I discovered that I was pregnant with you, Noel. I was just going to leave them and have you, but ... something ... I don't know what happened ... Paul kept asking me to marry him, and it seemed so simple. I had nothing at all to give you, and if I married Paul Liebman, I could do everything for you.' She wiped a tear from her cheek sadly. 'I thought that ... he'd give you everything I couldn't, and I would always be grateful to him.' She wiped the tears away with one hand. 'But two weeks before you were born, he came home one afternoon and found me looking at the photographs of your father and it all came out. I couldn't lie to him any more. I told him the truth. And then he knew that the baby was Manfred's and not his.' Her voice seemed very distant as she stared into space. 'He left the house that day, and I never saw him again. He only communicated with me through his lawyers.' Her voice grew softer still. 'I never saw any of them again. To them, I was a Nazi.'

Noel left his chair then and went to his mother, and he knelt beside her, softly stroking her hair. 'They can't do anything, Mama, not to me and not to Tammy. Times are different now.'

'It doesn't matter.'

He pulled her chin up gently with one hand. 'Yes, it does. To me.'

'I agree with you entirely, Noel.' Max stood up and spoke for the first time in half an hour. 'And now, if you will forgive me for being selfish, I would like to have your mother to myself until we leave.' He knew that Ariana had had enough.

'Of course, Max.' Noel kissed them both and stood in the doorway for a long moment.

'You're not angry that I didn't tell you, Noel?' She eyed him with regret as they stood in the door, but he shook his head slowly.

'Not angry, Mother, just surprised.'

'He'll be all right,' Max reassured her as he walked her back inside. 'You don't owe anyone any explanations, darling. Not even him.' And with that he kissed her gently and she followed him inside.

Noel had already gotten into a cab, and he was at his own apartment minutes later, the phone in his hand. She was on the line a moment later, sounding unusually subdued.

'Tammy? I have to see you.'

'When?'

'Now.'

Twenty minutes later she was there.

'I've got a few surprises for you, kiddo.'

'Like what?'

He didn't know where to begin. So he decided to take a dive. 'Like your father was almost my father.'

'What?' She stared at him in confusion and slowly he began to explain. It took almost half an hour to sort it all out, after which they sat and stared at each other. 'I don't think anyone in the family knows he was married before.'

'Well, his parents obviously did, and his sisters. I wonder if your mother does.'

'Probably.' She thought about it for a moment. 'He's so scrupulous about honesty and revealing everything, he probably told her when they met.'

'It's no reflection on him really. It was my mother who tried to pull the wool over his eyes.' But Noel said it kindly, he had nothing but tenderness and compassion for what she had tried to do. He imagined the twenty-year-old pregnant refugee, and his heart reached out to her.

The tragedy that had belonged to another generation had once more become just another piece of history with the passage of time. It made no real difference to them now, it only mattered to those who had participated in the drama long before. 'Are you going to tell him about us, Tammy?'

'I don't know. Maybe.'

'I think you should tell him now. Let's not wait to unveil any secrets till later. I'd like to get all our cards out on the table now. Our parents have had enough surprises in their lives.'

'Does that mean you want to live with me, Noel?' Her deep green eyes were filled with hope, and he nodded solemnly.

'Yes. It does.'

Chapter 49

When the winter term ended, Tammy had already made her decision. She had long since organised the paperwork for her transfer to Columbia Law School, and all that remained was for her to pack her bags and vacate the tiny apartment she had rented in Cambridge with four other girls. Noel appeared bright and early on a Saturday morning, and together they made the brief trip to New York.

At his apartment he had made space for her in every cupboard, and there were flowers and balloons and a cooler of champagne waiting in the fridge. That had been three months earlier, and there had been no problems between them, except one. Neither her parents nor Ariana knew about the arrangement. Contrary to his usual principles of total honesty with his mother, Noel hadn't told his mother that he was living with Tammy. And Tammy had simply installed her own phone on the desk, and when it rang, Noel knew not to touch her line. It would be her father calling to see if she was in.

But in late May the game halted abruptly one day when Ariana came by to drop off some mail that had come to her house by mistake. She had been about to leave it with the doorman when Tammy came flying out of the building, carrying their laundry and her law books, on her way to school.

'Oh ... oh ... hello, Mrs Tripp – I mean Mrs Max ... Mrs ...' Her face had been one bright red flame as Ariana greeted her coolly.

'Visiting Noel?'

'I ... yes ... I had to check some things in his old law books ... research ... a paper ...' She wanted to lie down on the spot and die. Noel had been right. They should have told them months before. Now Ariana looked disappointed and betrayed.

'I'm sure he's very helpful.'

'Yes, yes ... very ... and how've you been?'

'Very well, thank you.' And then with a polite greeting she was off to the nearest phone booth to call her son. In the end he was just as glad it had happened. It was high time they knew. And if Tamara didn't plan to tell her father, Noel had made up his mind that he would. With a steady hand he dialled Information and then called Paul Liebman's office and made an appointment for two forty-five.

The building where the cab stopped was the same building where Sam Liebman had established his offices almost fifty years before, and the office where Paul Liebman ran the firm's investments was the same office in which

Sam had sat for so long. It was the office where Ruth had visited her husband and begged him to take the tiny blonde German girl into his home. It was the office that the German girl's son walked into with his long, confident stride; he shook hands with Tamara's father and quietly sat down.

'Do we know each other, Mr Tripp?' He had looked Noel over carefully and there was something familiar about the young man. His business card showed him to be associated with a very reputable law firm, and Paul Liebman was wondering if the young man was there on the firm's business or his own.

'We've met once, Mr Liebman. Last year.'

'Oh, I'm sorry.' The older man smiled pleasantly. 'I'm afraid my memory is not quite at its peak these days.'

Noel smiled gently. 'With Tamara. I graduated from Harvard Law last year.'

'Oh, I see.' And then suddenly he remembered, and the smile began slowly to fade. 'I assume, however, Mr Tripp, that you are not here to discuss my daughter. In what way may I assist you today?' They had only given the boy the appointment on the strength of his law firm's name.

'I'm afraid that your assumption, sir, is not quite correct. I am indeed here to talk to you about Tamara. And myself. I'm afraid I have some difficult things to tell you, but I want to be forthright with you from the first.'

'Is Tamara in some kind of trouble?' The man blanched. He remembered who the boy was now. He remembered perfectly. And he already hated his guts.

But Noel was quick to reassure him. 'No, sir. She is not in any kind of trouble. In fact, she's in something very nice.' He smiled and tried to look less nervous than he was. 'We've been in love with each other, Mr Liebman, for quite some time.'

'I find that difficult to believe, Mr Tripp. She hasn't mentioned you in months.'

'I think she hasn't because she's been afraid of your reaction. But before I go any further, there's something I must tell you, because if I don't, sooner or later it will come out. And we might as well get it out right now.' He looked away from the older man for a moment and wondered if he'd been mad to come at all. This was crazy. And it was also the hardest thing he'd ever done. 'Twenty-seven years ago I believe your mother was involved in a refugee organisation here in New York.' Paul Liebman's face tightened and Noel pushed ahead. 'She befriended a young woman, a German girl, a refugee from Berlin. Whom, for whatever reasons, you married shortly thereafter, only to discover that she was pregnant by her husband who had died in the fall of Berlin. You left her, and divorced her, and – ' he paused for only an instant – 'I am her son.' There was an electrifying moment of silence and then Paul Liebman stood up.

'Get out of my office!' He pointed savagely towards the door, but Noel didn't move.

'Not until I tell you that I love your daughter, sir, and that she loves me. And that – ' he rose to his full height, towering over even Paul Liebman – 'my intentions towards her are entirely honourable.'

'Do you dare to tell me that you wish to marry my daughter?'

'Yes, sir, I do.'

'Never! Do you understand me? Never! Is your mother promoting this arrangement?'

'Absolutely not, sir.' For an instant Noel's eyes flashed, too, but then the fire left Paul's gaze. Whatever had passed between them, Liebman would not malign Ariana now. He let the matter of Ariana drop.

'I forbid you to see Tamara again.' There was rage in his face, based on an old, old pain he had never quite been able to forget.

But Noel spoke calmly. 'I'm telling you now, to your face, that neither she nor I will obey you. Your only choice is to make peace with what is.' And then, without waiting to hear the remainder of Liebman's anger, Noel walked directly to the door and left. He heard a huge pounding on the desk behind him, but by then the door to the office was already closed.

As Tamara came to know Noel's mother, she came to love her almost as her own, and it was at Christmas, when Noel decided to announce their engagement, that Ariana gave Tammy the gift that so deeply touched her heart. Noel already knew what was coming and for an instant the mother and son exchanged a secret smile as slowly Tammy unwrapped the bright paper, and then suddenly the brilliant ring fell into her hand. It was the signet ring set in diamonds, which had been Kassandra's so many years before.

'Oh, my God ... oh ... oh, no!' She looked around her in amazement, first at Noel, then at Ariana standing by, and then at Max smiling broadly, and then, reaching blindly for Noel, she began to cry.

'It's your engagement ring, my darling. Mother had it sized for you. Come on, let's try it on.' But as she slipped it on her finger, all she did was cry more. She knew the history of that diamond ring so well now ... and now the ring that had been worn by four generations before her was hers. It fit perfectly on the third finger on her left hand, and it sat there, beautifully wrought and skilfully woven, the diamonds sparkling brilliantly as she stared.

'Oh, Ariana, thank you.' But holding Noel's mother tightly only brought fresh tears.

'It's all right, darling. It's all right. It's yours now. May it bring you much joy.' Ariana looked at the girl gently; she had been completely won over. And now she had decided to take matters into her own hands.

Three days after Christmas, with trembling hands, she looked up the number and dialled the phone. She identified herself only as Mrs Thomas, got an appointment, and the next day quietly took a cab downtown. She said nothing to Max or Noel; she didn't feel they had to know, but it was time that, these many years later, she faced him, and also time that he faced her.

The secretary announced her, and Ariana, wearing a black dress and a dark mink coat, walked sedately into the room. On her hand she wore only her large emerald now. The diamond signet was Tamara's.

'Mrs Thomas?' But as Paul Liebman stood to greet her, he opened his eyes wide with shock. Even in his surprise it flashed through his mind how little she had changed, even in almost thirty years.

'Hello, Paul.' She stood there bravely and waited for him to ask her to sit down. 'I thought that I should come to see you. About our children. May I sit down?' He waved her into a chair and then, still staring, sat down himself. 'I believe my son has already been to see you once.'

'It served no purpose.' His face hardened still more. 'And your visit will be useless, too.'

'Perhaps. But the point, I think, is not how we feel, but how our children feel. At first I felt the same way you did. I was violently opposed to their getting together. But the fact is that whether or not we like it that's what they want.'

'And may I ask why you'd have any objection?'

'Because I assume you're bitter about me and equally so about Noel.' And then she paused and her voice was softer when she went on. 'What I did was terribly, terribly wrong. Afterwards I understood that, but in the desperation of the moment, wanting the right things for the baby ... the things you could have given him, and I couldn't ... what can I say to you, Paul? I was wrong.'

He sat looking at her for a long, long time. 'Did you have other children, Ariana?'

She shook her head with a small smile. 'No. And I never remarried until last year.'

'Not because you pined for me, I might assume.' But there was less anger in his voice now and the hint of an old warmth in his eyes.

She sighed briefly. 'No, because I knew that I had been married, that I had cast my lot for good or bad with what happened. I had my son, and I never wanted to marry again.'

'Who changed your mind?'

'An old friend. I gather though that you remarried very quickly.'

He nodded. 'As soon as the divorce became final. She was a girl I had gone to school with.' And then he sighed across his desk, across his lifetime, at Ariana. 'In the end, those are the best kind. And that is why I've been so opposed to Tamara and your boy. Not so much because he's your son.' He sighed again. 'He's a fine boy, Ariana. A good man. He had the courage to come here to see me, to tell me the whole story. I respect that in a man.' And then he growled softly. 'It was more than Tamara had the decency to do. But the real issue here is not whether or not you and I were married, but what kind of people they are. Look at what he comes from, at his heritage. Look at your family, Ariana, what I know of it now. And we're Jewish. Can you really justify joining the two?'

'If they can. I don't think it really matters if I'm a German and you're a Jew. Maybe that only mattered so much then, after the war. I'd like to think that now it doesn't matter quite so much.'

But Paul Liebman shook his head with determination. 'It still does. Those things will never change, Ariana. Long after you and I are gone, those things will go on.'

'Won't you at least give them a chance?'

'To do what? Convince me that I'm wrong? So that they can quickly have three children then come back five years from now to tell me they're getting a divorce because I was right and it didn't work out?'

'Do you really think you can prevent that?'

'Maybe.'

'And what of the next man? And the one after that? Don't you realise that she'll do what she wants anyway? No matter what. She'll marry whom she pleases, lead her life, go her own way. She's been living with Noel for a year now, no matter how you feel about it. The only one who will lose in the end is you, Paul. Maybe it's time you ended that war between us and took another look at this generation. My son doesn't even want to be a German. And maybe your daughter doesn't want to carry any more banners that proclaim her a Jew.'

'What does she want to be, then?'

'A person, a woman, a lawyer. They have ideas these days that I don't really understand. They're a lot more independent and free-thinking.' She smiled at him slowly. 'Maybe they're right. My son tells me that the war we talk about is our war, not theirs. To them, it's only history. I guess to us, sometimes, it's still real.'

'I looked at him, Ariana – ' his voice dropped painfully low – 'and I still saw those pictures that you held that day. I could imagine him in a uniform ... A Nazi uniform like his father's ...' He squeezed his eyes tightly shut, and then he looked at her bleakly. 'He looks just like him, doesn't he?'

She smiled gently and nodded. 'But Tamara doesn't look very much like you.' There was nothing else she could say to him, but at least he smiled.

'I know, she looks just like her mother. Her sister looks like Julia though ... and my boy ...' He said it so proudly. '... he looks like me.'

'I'm glad.' And then after a long, empty silence, 'Have you been happy?'

He nodded slowly. 'And you? I wondered about you sometimes, what had happened, where you'd gone. I wanted to reach out and just let you know that I was thinking of you, but I was afraid to – '

'Why?'

'I was afraid to seem a fool. At first I was so hurt. I thought you'd just laughed at me all along. It was my mother who eventually understood it. She knew you'd done it for the baby, and she suspected that perhaps you loved me, too.' At the mention of his mother, Ariana's eyes filled slowly with tears.

'I did love you, Paul.'

He nodded slowly. 'After she thought it over, she knew.' And then they sat there for an instant, united after so long. 'What do we do now, Ariana, about our children?'

'We let them do what they have to. And we accept.'

She smiled and stood up hesitantly, holding out a hand. But he didn't take her hand, he walked slowly around his desk and for an instant took her in his arms.

'For what happened so long ago, I'm sorry. I'm sorry I wasn't big enough to understand it or let you explain.'

'It was the way it had to be, Paul.' He shrugged and nodded, and then she kissed his cheek and left him with his own thoughts, staring out at the Wall Street view.

Chapter 50

The wedding was scheduled for the following summer, after Tamara had duly finished law school, and the two looked around for an apartment, picked out what they wanted, and Tamara landed a job that was to begin in the fall. 'But first we're going to Europe!' She had announced it to Ariana and Max with a happy smile.

'Where to?' Max looked at her with interest.

'Paris, the Riviera, Italy and then Noel wants to take me to Berlin.' But this time there was no shadow in Ariana's eyes.

'It's a beautiful city. At least it was.' But she had seen Noel's pictures from his trip two years before, and she cherished the photograph of the house in Grunewald – now she no longer had to strain to remember some fading detail. She could simply look at the photograph and see it all. He had even given her photographs of the schloss she'd heard about from Manfred and never seen. 'How long will you two be gone?'

'About a month.' Tammy sighed happily. 'This is my last free summer, and Noel really had to fight to get four weeks off.'

'What will you be doing on the Riviera?'

'Stopping by to see a girl I knew from school.' They had decided to visit Brigitte. 'But first – ' Tammy grinned at Ariana – 'we have to survive the wedding.'

'It's going to be lovely.' For months now Ariana had listened to the plans. At last Paul had softened, and he had to admit that he liked Noel, and they had begun to plan the wedding in February, for June.

When at last the day came, Tamara looked overwhelmingly beautiful in a dress made entirely of cream-coloured satin and covered by an overdress of priceless Chantilly lace. The cap she wore over her dark hair covered all but her chignon with the flawless lace, and the clouds of veil that floated around her created even more of an impression of ethereal splendour. Even Ariana was impressed.

'My God, Max, she looks gorgeous.'

'Of course she does.' He smiled at his own wife proudly. 'But so does Noel.' In his cutaway and striped trousers, he looked more elegant than ever, with the brilliant blue eyes and the shaft of blond hair. Ariana had to admit, as she smiled to herself, that he did look very German, but somehow even that didn't seem to matter any more. Paul Liebman was smiling at the young couple benignly, having disbursed fortunes on the wedding of his wife's somewhat extravagant dreams. Ariana had finally met her, a pleasant woman who had probably been a good wife to him over the years.

Debbie was married to a Hollywood producer. Julia was the loveliest and had the most spirit, and her children looked as though they were both intelligent and fun. But the two women only spoke to Ariana briefly. They had been too deeply wounded by the past. For all of them, Ariana had ceased existing the day that Paul had left her.

Paul glanced at her once or twice during the wedding, and once for a long moment, their eyes held, and for the first time in a long time she remembered him with love. And as she stood there, she felt a pang of sorrow over the loss of Ruth and Sam.

'Well, Mrs Tripp, we made it.' Noel grinned at Tammy and she nuzzled his neck with her soft lips.

'I love you, Noel.'

'So do I, but if you do a lot of that here ... I'm going to start our honeymoon right here on the plane.' She smiled coyly at her husband and retreated to her seat with a happy sigh. She glanced at the large, handsome diamond signet on her finger. She would never get over Ariana's giving it to her as her engagement ring. She had truly come to love Noel's mother, and she knew that Ariana loved her, too.

'I want to buy your mother something gorgeous in Paris, Noel.'

'Like what?' He smiled at her over his book. The nice thing about having lived together for almost two years was that it had taken the frenzy out of finally being married at last. They were comfortable with each other, and they both felt at home together wherever they were. 'So what do you want to buy her?'

'I don't know. Something exciting. Like a painting or a Dior dress.'

'Good God, that is exciting. How come?' She flashed her ring at him in answer and he smiled.

As a gift from Tammy's father, they stayed at the Plaza Athénée in an elaborate suite. They went downstairs after their first candlelit honeymoon dinner in their rooms, to meet Brigitte at the famous bar. When they got there, the Relais Plaza was jammed with exotic-looking people, men in open shirts with chests covered with neck chains, and women in long slashes of red satin pants or little mink jackets with jeans.

Tammy barely recognised the girl she'd known at Radcliffe. Her face was white, her lips were rouged, and her blonde hair had been frizzed out wildly on either side; but the blue eyes still danced as mischievously as ever, and she was enchantingly tiny, and wearing a full tuxedo and a black satin top hat with only a red satin bra.

'My dear, I had no idea you'd gotten so conservative.' All three of them grinned. Brigitte Goddard had become even more outrageous than before.

'You know, Noel, you've gotten better looking too.' She grinned mischievously and Tammy laughed.

'Too late, you two, we're married, remember? Sorry, guys ...' But Noel looked at her warmly and Brigitte only laughed.

'He's too tall for me anyway. Not my type.'

'Watch out, he's sensitive.' Tammy put her finger to her lips and the three laughed again. Together they enjoyed a pleasant evening, and for the next week Brigitte took them from one end of Paris to the other, from lunch at Fouquet's to dinner at the Brasserie Lipp in the Latin Quarter, to dancing at Castel's and Chez Regine, then on to the Halles for breakfast, and off to dinner at Maxim's the next day. And on and on and on it went, from bars to restaurants to parties, where everyone knew her and she knew everyone and men practically begged her for attention as she jumped from one crazy costume to another and Tammy and Noel stared in frank admiration.

'Isn't she divine?' Tammy whispered it to Noel as they wandered through the boutique at Courrèges.

'Yes, and a little crazy. I think I like you better, kid.'

'That's good news.'

'I'm not looking forward to meeting her family.'

'Oh, they're all right.'

'I don't want to stay with them for ever. Two days and that's it, Tammy. I want to be alone with you for a while. This is our, honeymoon, after all.' He looked at her petulantly and she kissed him and laughed.

'I'm sorry, darling.'

'Don't be. Just promise me, no more than two days with them on the Riviera and then we go on to Italy. Got that?'

'Yes, sir.' She saluted smartly, and Brigitte returned to them to drag them on to Balmain, Givenchy, and Dior.

At Dior, Tammy found exactly what she wanted for Ariana, a delicate mauve silk cocktail dress that she knew would look incredible with Ariana's huge blue eyes. It had a matching scarf, and Tammy threw in a pair of earrings. The whole shebang cost her over 400 dollars and Noel almost gasped. 'I'll be employed by September, Noel. Don't look like that.'

'You'd better be if you plan to buy those kinds of presents.' But they both knew that this was special. It was Tammy's way of saying thank you for the ring. Brigitte had noticed it almost immediately when she'd met them that first night at the Plaza; she had ogled it and then admitted to Tammy that she couldn't take her eyes off her hand. Apparently her father's gallery now had a section just for antique jewellery, but they had nothing as remarkable as Tamara's new ring.

On the last afternoon before they left Paris, Brigitte took them to the Galerie Gérard Goddard on the Faubourg-St-Honoré, and they wandered around it in wonder for more than an hour, admiring the Renoirs, the Picassos, the Fabergé boxes, the priceless antique diamond bracelets, the little busts and statues. It really was extraordinary. Noel looked at Brigitte with sheer delight and pleasure as they left.

'It's like a tiny museum, only better.'

She nodded proudly. 'Papa has some nice things.' It was rather a severe underestimation, and behind her Noel and Tammy smiled. It had been why her father had sent her to Radcliffe, hoping she would get a solid background in history and art, but Brigitte had other leanings, like football games and parties, med students, and grass. And at the end of two years of disaster, her father had brought her home to amuse herself more simply in France. At the moment she was talking vaguely about studying photography or making a film, but it was obvious that she had no burning ambitions, yet she was really a lot of fun. She was kind of a sprite that ran off madly in all directions, always amusing, but never lighting anywhere for very long. There was a restlessness about her that was rapidly becoming the *mal du siècle.*

'The odd thing about her is that she never seems to grow up,' Tammy mused about her as Noel shrugged.

'I know. But some people just don't. Is her brother like that?'

'Yeah. Only more so.'

'How come?' Noel looked puzzled.

'I don't know, spoiled, maybe unhappy. I don't know. You have to see the parents to understand better. Mama is kind of a nasty Lady Bountiful, and her father is just very withdrawn, as though he's haunted by ghosts.'

Chapter 51

The flight to Nice only took a little over an hour, and Bernard Goddard was waiting for them at the gate. He was as fair and beautiful as his sister as he stood there barefoot, wearing a silk shirt and silk slacks. He had an air of being totally absent, as though he had been deposited there without his knowledge. He seemed to come to when his sister threw her arms around his neck. The large silver box of marijuana in the glove compartment of his Ferrari explained something about his vague aura.

But when pressed into conversation with Tammy and Noel, he seemed able to spring back to life.

'I'm planning to come to New York in November.' He smiled at them sweetly, and for an odd moment Noel had the feeling that he resembled photographs he'd seen somewhere a long time before. 'Will you be there then?'

'Yes, we will.' Tammy answered for Noel.

'You're going when?' Brigitte looked at her brother in surprise.

'November.'

'I thought that was when you were going to Brazil.'

'That's later, and I don't think I'll go to Brazil anyway; Mimi wants to go to Buenos Aires.' Brigitte nodded as though it all made sense, and Tammy and Noel exchanged a silent look of awe. Somehow Tammy hadn't remembered them as quite that racy, and suddenly she wished they hadn't planned to stop at St-Jean-Cap-Ferrat before driving on to Rome.

'Do you want to leave tomorrow morning?' Tammy whispered it to Noel as they followed the two into a huge French Provincial house.

'Perfect. I'll tell them I have to see a client of the firm on the way.' She nodded conspiratorially and they went on to their bedroom, a huge room with endless ceilings, an antique Italian bed, and a view that included a vast expanse of sea. The floor was a pale beige marble, and on the terrace was a wonderful antique sedan chair, in which Brigitte had conveniently left their phone.

Lunch was served downstairs in the garden, and despite their somewhat zany lives and plans, Brigitte and Bernard both managed to be fun. Knowing that they were leaving the next morning, Tammy and Noel felt better, less like prisoners in a strange science fiction colony, and more like guests.

But they felt a great deal more like guests that evening when they entered the formal dining room and Noel was introduced to Brigitte and Bernard's parents for the first time. Before him stood a somewhat heavyset but still strikingly beautiful woman with enormous flashing green eyes. She had a dazzling smile and long, lovely legs, but there was also something very tough about her. As though she were used to commanding, as though she had always run her own show. She was not particularly amused by her children, but she seemed to find Tammy and Noel charming, and she made a great effort to be a good hostess, overseeing everything, including her husband, who was a tall, handsome blond man with quiet, but sad, blue eyes. Again and again through the evening, Noel found himself drawn to the older man. It was almost as though he knew him, or had seen him, and eventually he decided that it was only because he looked so much like his son.

When at one point Madame Goddard took Tammy out of the drawing room after dinner to show her a small Picasso, Gérard Goddard turned to Noel, and it was then that the American noticed his accent for the first time. It wasn't entirely like the others, not quite as rich or quite as French. For a moment Noel wondered if maybe he was Swiss or Belgian. He wasn't sure, but more than ever he was intrigued by the sorrow he could see amid the lines in the man's face.

When Tammy returned from her errand, the group began its aimless chatter once again, until Tammy put her hand on the table and the diamond signet ring sparkled in the candlelight. For an instant Gérard Goddard stared at it and simply stopped mid-sentence. And then, without asking for permission, he reached for her hand, held it, and stared.

'Pretty, isn't it, Papa?' Brigitte was quick to admire the ring again, and Madame Goddard looked disinterested as she made conversation with her son.

'It's lovely.' Monsieur Goddard still held Tammy's hand in his own. 'May I see it?' Slowly, she slipped it off and handed it to him with a smile.

'It's my engagement ring from Noel.'

'Is it really?' He stared at his young guest. 'Where did you get it? In America?' He seemed to have a thousand questions.

'From my mother. It was hers.'

'Really?' For an instant Gérard Goddard's eyes searched inwards.

'It has a long family history that she could tell you better than I could, if you ever come to New York.'

'Yes, yes ...' He looked vague for a moment, and then smiled at his young friends. 'I do that sometimes – I'd like to call her.' And then, quickly, 'You know we've just opened a whole space for jewellery at the gallery. I'd be very interested in anything else she might have.'

Noel smiled at him gently. The man was so persistent. In a way so desperate, and so sad. 'I don't think she'd sell anything, Monsieur Goddard, but she does have another of my grandmother's rings.'

'Really?' His eyes were wide.

'Yes.' Tammy smiled at him. 'She has a fabulous emerald.' She showed him with her fingers. 'About this size.'

'You really must tell me how to reach her.'

'Of course.' Noel took out a pad and little silver pencil and began to write. He put down her address and phone number. 'I'm sure she'd be happy to hear from you whenever you're in New York.'

'Is she there this summer?'

Noel nodded, and the older man smiled.

The conversation then moved on to other subjects, and at last it was time to go to bed. Tammy and Noel wanted to retire early so that they would be fresh for their long drive the next day. They were going to rent a car in Cannes and leave from there. And Brigitte and Bernard had a party to go to, which they insisted wouldn't even start till twelve or one o'clock. So in a moment only Gérard and his wife were left in the salon, staring at each other and what remained of their life.

'You're not starting again with that nonsense, are you?' As she looked at him in the soft light from the candles, her voice was harsh. 'I saw you with the ring the girl was wearing.

'It would be a good piece for the gallery, if her mother-in-law has others. I have to be in New York anyway this week.'

'You do?' She looked at him with suspicion. 'What for? You hadn't mentioned it before.'

'There's a collector selling a very fine Renoir. I want to see him before he officially puts it up for sale.' At that she nodded wisely. Whatever his failings as a man, he had certainly done well for the gallery, better than her father had ever dreamed, which was why eventually she had let Gérard change the gallery's name to his own. But it had been an arrangement from the beginning, when they'd taken him in, given him a home, a job, and then an education in the world of art. It was when she and her father had escaped to Zurich during the war.

They had met him then, given him shelter, employment, and a home. And when they'd gone back to Paris when the war was over, they'd brought him along. And by then Giselle was pregnant and the old man had not given Gérard any choice. But in the end it was he who had prevailed over the two wily Parisians, he who had learned the métier so well that he had made the gallery a huge success. And as for Giselle, it didn't matter. For twenty-four years now, he'd played the part. They had given him what he wanted, a home, a life, success, money, and the means he needed for his search. But it was the search that had kept him going for all these years.

For twenty-seven years now he'd been looking for his father and his sister, and he had known long since that he would never find them. Still, he kept on looking, when he thought he had a lead to something, when someone thought they knew someone who ... He had made over sixty trips to Berlin. And it was all fruitless. Useless. In his heart Gérard knew that they were gone. If they weren't, he would have found them or they would have found him. His name was not so different. From Gerhard von Gotthard, he had become Gérard Goddard. But to wear the name of a German after the war in France had been to invite ridicule, assault, anger, beatings. After a while he had been unable to take it any more. It had been the old man's idea to change his name, and at the time it seemed a wise one. Now, after all these years, he was more French than German. And it didn't matter. Nothing did. His dreams were gone.

Sometimes he wondered what he would have done if he had found them. What, in reality, would it have changed? In his heart he knew that it would have changed everything for him. He would have had the courage finally to leave Giselle, and maybe even take his children more firmly in hand and maybe even sell the gallery and enjoy his money for a change. He smiled at the endless options, knowing secretly that to find them would be not the end, but the beginning of his whole life's dream.

The next morning Tammy and Noel said goodbye to Brigitte and her brother, and just before they left, Gérard Goddard came hurriedly downstairs. He looked deep into the eyes of Noel, wondering if ... but that was crazy ... he couldn't be ... but maybe this Mrs Max Thomas would know ... it was a kind of madness Gerard Goddard had lived with for almost thirty years.

'Thank you so much, Mr Goddard.'

'Not at all, Noel ... Tamara ... we hope to see you here again.' He said nothing of the address they had given him, but simply waved as they shouted their goodbyes again, and drove away.

'I like your friends from New York, Brigitte.' He smiled at his daughter warmly and for once she returned the smile. He had always been so vague, so distant, so unhappy. It had made him an absentee father all her life.

'I like them too, Papa. They're very nice.' She watched him then as he walked pensively back towards his bedroom, and later that morning she heard him on the phone to Air France. She wandered casually into his bedroom. Her mother was already out. 'Are you going somewhere, Papa?'

He nodded slowly. 'Yes, New York. Tonight.'

'Business?' He nodded. 'Could I come with you?' He was startled as he watched her. Suddenly she looked almost as lonely as he. But this was one trip he had to make without her. Maybe next time ... if ...

'How about if I take you with me next time? This is going to be a little rocky. Kind of a tight deal I'm making. And I don't think I'll be gone for long.'

She eyed him quietly from the bedroom door. 'Will you really take me next time, Papa?'

He nodded slowly, awed that she would ask him. 'Yes, I will.'

He was vague when he talked to Giselle later that morning. And then he went quietly back to his room and packed his bag. He didn't plan to be gone for more than a day or two, scarcely longer. After hastily kissing Giselle and the children, he hurried to the airport to make the flight. His long stride allowed him to reach the gate in time, and the flight went from Nice to Paris and then directly to New York. From Kennedy he took a taxi, and then with trembling hands he had the cab stop at a phone booth very near to her address.

'Mrs Thomas?'

'Yes.'

'I'm afraid you don't know me, but my daughter is a friend of Tammy's – '

'Is something wrong?' She was suddenly frightened but her voice held nothing familiar for the man who listened. It was probably another wild-goose chase. He had been on so many before.

'No, not at all.' He was quick to reassure her. 'They went to Italy this morning and everything was fine. I just thought ... I had some business to do here ... a Renoir ... and I was impressed with your daughter-in-law's ring. She mentioned that you had another, an emerald, and I had a spare moment, I thought ...' He faltered, wondering why he had come all this distance.

'My emerald ring is not for sale.'

'Of course, of course. I understand that.' Poor man. He sounded so boyish and so shy. She realised then that this was probably the Gérard Goddard Tammy had mentioned and suddenly Ariana felt bad about sounding unwelcoming and unkind.

'But if you'd just like to see it, perhaps you'd like to come over in a little while?'

'I'd like that, very much, Mrs Thomas ... Half an hour? That would be fine.' He didn't even have a hotel room; all he had was a taxi and a suitcase, and he still had to waste another half hour. He had the driver drive him around in circles, up Madison Avenue and down Fifth and finally into the park. And then at last it was time to meet her. With trembling knees, he got out of the cab.

'Do you want me to wait here?' the cabbie offered. The fare was already forty dollars. Hell, why not? But the Frenchman shook his head, handed the man a fifty-dollar bill he had changed at the airport, and took his briefcase and his bag. He rang the doorbell beside the brass knocker and waited for what seemed like a very long time. His well-cut grey suit hung well on his thin frame and he was wearing a dark blue Dior tie, his white shirt looked sadly crumpled from the trip, and his shoes were handmade in London, like his shirts. But for all the expensive trappings, Gérard felt like a very young boy again, waiting for a father who never would return.

'Yes? Mr Goddard?' Ariana swiftly pulled the door open and looked into his face with a gentle smile. The emerald ring was on her finger. Their eyes met – they had the same deep blue eyes. For a moment she did not know him and she did not understand, but as he stood there, the man who had been Gerhard von Gotthard knew that he had at least found one of them at last. He stood there crying softly, making not a single sound. She was the same girl who had haunted his memories ... the same face ... those same laughing blue eyes ...

'Ariana?' It was a whisper, but it called to her mind the sounds of so long ago ... the shouts in the stairwell ... the shrieks from his laboratory ... the games they had played outside ... Ariana ... she could still hear it ... Ariana! ...

'Ariana!' It was like an echo as a sob tore through her and she flew into his arms.

'My God ... my God ... it's you ... oh, Gerhard ...' She held him with the anguish of a lifetime, as in her arms the tall, handsome, blue-eyed man held her close and sobbed.

They stood there for endless moments, holding tightly to the present and the past, and when at last she brought her brother inside with her, she smiled up at him, and he smiled, too ... two people who had carried lonely burdens for half a lifetime and who had finally found each other, and were free at last.

CHANGES

To Beatrix, Trevor, Todd,
Nicky, and especially John,
for all that you are, and
all that you have given me.

With all my love,
d.s.

And with special thanks to Dr Phillip Oyer

Chapter 1

'Dr Hallam ... Dr Peter Hallam ... Dr Hallam ... Cardiac Intensive, Dr Hallam ...' The voice droned on mechanically as Peter Hallam sped through the lobby of Center City Hospital, never stopping to answer the page since the team already knew he was on his way. He furrowed his brow as he pressed six, his mind already totally engaged with the data he had been given twenty minutes before on the phone. They had waited weeks for this donor, and it was almost too late. Almost. His mind raced as the lift doors ground open, and he walked quickly to the nurses' station marked Cardiac Intensive Care.

'Have they sent Sally Block upstairs yet?' A nurse looked up, seeming to snap to attention as her eyes met his. Something inside her always leapt a little when she saw him. There was something infinitely impressive about the man, who was tall, slender, grey-haired, blue-eyed, soft-spoken. He had the looks of the doctors one read about in women's novels. There was something so basically kind and gentle about him, and yet something powerful as well. The aura of a highly trained racehorse always straining at the reins, aching to go faster, farther ... to do more ... to fight time ... to conquer odds beyond hope ... to steal back just one life ... one man ... one woman ... one child ... one more. And often he won. Often. But not always. And that irked him. More than that, it pained him. It was the cause for the lines beside his eyes, the sorrow one saw deep within him. It wasn't enough that he wrought miracles almost daily. He wanted more than that, better odds, he wanted to save them all, and there was no way he could.

'Yes, Doctor.' The nurse nodded quickly. 'She just went up.'

'Was she ready?' That was the other thing about him and the nurse marvelled at the question. She knew instantly what he meant by 'ready'; not the I.V. in the patient's arm, or the mild sedative administered before she left her room to be wheeled to surgery. He was questioning what she was thinking, feeling, who had spoken to her, who went with her. He wanted each of them to know what they were facing, how hard the team would work, how much they cared, how desperately they would all try to save each life. He wanted each patient to be ready to enter the battle with him. 'If they don't believe they have a fighting chance when they go in there, we've lost them right from the beginning,' the nurse had heard him tell his students, and he meant it. He fought with every fibre of his being, and it cost him, but it was worth it. The results he'd got in the past five years were amazing, with few exceptions. Exceptions which mattered deeply to Peter Hallam. Everything did. He was remarkable and intense and brilliant ... and so handsome, the nurse reminded herself with a smile as he hurried past her to a small lift in the corridor behind her. It sped up one floor and deposited him outside the operating rooms where he and his team performed bypasses and transplants and occasionally more ordinary cardiac surgery, though not often. Most of the time, Peter Hallam and his team did the big stuff, as they would tonight.

Sally Block was a twenty-two-year-old girl who had lived most of her adult life as an invalid, crippled by rheumatic fever as a child, and she had suffered through multiple valve replacements and a decade of medication. He and his associates had agreed weeks before when she'd been admitted to Center City that a transplant was the only answer for her. But thus far, there had been no donor. Until tonight, at two thirty in the morning, when a group of juvenile delinquents had engaged in their own private drag races in the San Fernando Valley; three of them had died on impact, and after a series of businesslike phone calls from the splendidly run organisation for the location and procurement of donors Peter Hallam knew he had a good one. He had had calls out to every hospital in Southern California for a donor for Sally, and now they had one – if Sally could just survive the surgery, and her body didn't sabotage them by rejecting the new heart they gave her.

He peeled off his street clothes without ceremony, donned the limp green cotton surgery pyjamas, scrubbed intensely, and was gowned and masked by surgical assistants. Three other doctors, two residents and a fleet of nurses did likewise. But Peter Hallam seemed not even to see them as he walked into the operating room. His eyes immediately sought Sally, lying silent and still on the operating-room table, her own eyes seemingly mesmerised by the bright lights above her. Even lying there in the sterile garb with her long blonde hair tucked into a green cotton cap she looked pretty. She was not only a beautiful young woman but a clever human being as well. She wanted desperately to be an artist ... to go to college ... to go to a prom ... to be kissed ... to have babies ... She recognised him even with the cap and mask and she smiled sleepily through a haze of medication.

'Hi.' She looked frail, her eyes enormous in the fragile face, like a broken china doll, waiting for him to repair her.

'Hello, Sally. How're you feeling?'

'Funny.' Her eyes fluttered for a moment and she smiled at the familiar eyes. She had come to know him in the last few weeks, better than she had known anyone in years. He had opened doors of hope to her, of tenderness, and of caring, and the loneliness and isolation she had felt for years had finally seemed less acute to her.

'We're going to be pretty busy for the next few hours. All you have to do is lie there and snooze.' He watched her and glanced at the monitors nearby before looking at her again. 'Scared?'

'Sort of.' But he knew she was well prepared. He had spent weeks explaining the surgery to her, the intricate process, and the dangers and medications afterwards. She knew what to expect now, and their big moment had come. It was almost like giving birth. And he would be giving birth to her, almost as though she would spring from his very soul, from his fingertips as they fought to save her.

The anaesthetist moved closer to her head and searched Peter Hallam's eyes. He nodded slowly and then smiled at Sally again. 'See you in a little while.' Except it wouldn't be a little while. It would be more like five or six hours before she was conscious again, and then only barely, as they watched her in the recovery room, before moving her to intensive care.

'Will you be there when I wake up?' A frown of fear creased her brows and he was quick to nod.

'I sure will. I'll be right there with you when you wake up. Just like I'm here with you now.' He nodded to the anaesthetist then, and her eyes fluttered closed briefly from the sedative they had administered before. The sodium pentathol was administered through the intravenous tube already implanted in her arm; a moment later, Sally Block was asleep, and within minutes, the delicate surgery began.

For the next few hours, Peter Hallam worked relentlessly to hook up the new heart, and there was a wondrous look of victory on his face as it began to pump. For just a fraction of a second, his eyes met those of the nurse standing across from him, and beneath the mask he smiled. 'There she goes.' But they had only won the first round, he knew only too well. It remained to be seen if Sally's body would accept or reject the new heart. And as with all transplant patients, the odds weren't great. But they were better than they would have been if she hadn't had the surgery at all. In her case, as with the other people he operated on, it was her only hope.

At nine fifteen that morning, Sally Block was wheeled into the recovery room, and Peter Hallam took his first break since four thirty a.m. It would be a while before the anaesthetic wore off, and he had time for a cup of coffee and a few moments of his own thoughts. Transplants like Sally's drained everything from him.

'That was spectacular, Doctor.' A young resident stood next to him, still in awe, as Peter poured himself a cup of black coffee and turned to the young man.

'Thank you.' Peter smiled, thinking how much the young resident looked like his own son. It would have pleased him no end if Mark had had ambitions in medicine, but there were other plans: business school, or law. He wanted to be part of a broader world than this, and he had seen over the years how much his father had given of himself and what it had cost him emotionally each time one of his transplant patients died. That wasn't for him. Peter narrowed his eyes as he took a sip of the inky brew, thinking that maybe it was just as well. And then he turned to the young resident again.

'Is this the first transplant you've seen?'

'The second. You performed the other one too.' And performed somehow seemed the appropriate word. Both transplants had been the most theatrical kind of surgery the young man had witnessed. There was more tension and drama in the operating room than he had ever experienced in his life, and watching Peter Hallam operate was like watching Nijinsky dance. He was the best there was. 'How do you think this one will do?'

'It's too soon to tell. Hopefully, she'll do fine.' And he prayed that what he said was true, as he covered his operating-room garb with another sterile gown and headed towards the recovery room. He left his coffee outside, and went to sit quietly in one of the chairs near where Sally lay. A recovery-room nurse and a battery of monitors were watching Sally's every breath, and so far all was well. The trouble, if it arose, was likely to come later than this, unless of course everything went wrong from the beginning. And that had happened before too. But not this time ... not this time ... please God ... not now ... not to her ... she's so young ... not that he would have felt any differently if she had been fifty-five instead of twenty-two.

It hadn't made any difference when he lost his wife. He sat looking at Sally now, trying not to see a different face ... a different time ... and yet he always did ... saw her as she had been in those last hours, beyond fighting, beyond hope ... beyond him. She hadn't even let him try. No matter what he said, or how hard he had tried to convince her. They had had a donor. But she had refused it. He had pounded the wall in her room that night, and driven home on the motorway at a hundred and fifteen. And when they picked him up for speeding, he didn't give a damn. He didn't care about anything then ... except her ... and what she wouldn't let him do. He had been so vague when the police stopped him that they made him get out of the car and walk in a straight line. But he wasn't drunk, he was numb with pain. They had let him go with a stiff warning, and he had gone home to wander through the house, thinking of her, aching for her, needing all that she'd had to give, and would give no more. He wondered if he could bear living without her. Even the children seemed remote to him then ... all he could think of was Anne. She had been so strong for so long, and because of her he had grown over the years. She filled him with a kind of strength he drew on constantly, as well as his own skill. And suddenly that wasn't there. He had sat terrified that night, alone and frightened, like a small child, and then suddenly at dawn, he had felt an irresistible pull. He had to go back to her ... had to hold her once more ... had to tell her the things he had never said before ... He had raced back to the hospital and quietly slipped into her room, where he dismissed the nurse and watched her himself, gently holding her hand, and smoothing the fair hair back from her pale brow. She looked like a fragile porcelain doll, and once, just before morning burst into the room, she opened her eyes ...

'... Peter ...' Her voice was less than a whisper in the stillness.

'I love you, Anne ...' His eyes had filled with tears and he had wanted to shout, 'Don't go.' She smiled the magical smile that always filled his heart, and then with the ease of a sigh she was gone, as he stood in bereft horror and stared. Why wouldn't she fight? Why wouldn't she let him try? Why couldn't she accept what other people accepted from him every day? He stood and he stared at her, sobbing softly, until one of his colleagues led him away. They had taken him home and put him to bed, and somehow in the next days and weeks he had gone through all the motions that were expected of him. But it was like an ugly underwater dream, and he only surfaced now and then, until at last he realised how desperately his children needed him. And slowly, he had come back, and three weeks later he returned to work, but there was something missing now. Something that meant everything to him. And that something was Anne. She never left his mind for very long. She was there a thousand times a day – as he left for work, as he walked in and out of patients' rooms, as he walked into surgery, or back out to his car in the late afternoon. And when he reached his front door, it was like a knife in his heart again every time he went home, knowing that she wouldn't be there.

That was over a year ago now, and the pain was dimmer, but not yet gone. And he somehow suspected that it never would be. All he could do was continue with his work, give everything he could to the people who turned to him for help ... and then of course there were Matthew, Mark, and Pam. Thank God, he had them. Without them he would never have survived. But he had. He had come this far, and he would live on ... but so differently ... without Anne ...

He sat in the stillness of the recovery room, his long legs stretched out before him, his face tense, watching Sally breathe, and at last her eyes opened for an instant and fuzzily swept the room.

'Sally ... Sally, it's Peter Hallam ... I'm here, and you're fine ...' For now. But he didn't say that to her, nor did he even let himself think that. She was alive. She had done well. She was going to live. He was going to do everything in his power to see to it.

He sat at her bedside for another hour, watching her, and speaking to her whenever she came round, and he even won a small, weak smile from her before he left her shortly after one in the afternoon. He stopped in the cafeteria for a sandwich, and went back to his office briefly, before coming back to the hospital to see patients at four o'clock, and at five thirty he was on the motor-way on his way home, his mind once again filled with Anne. It was still difficult to believe that she wouldn't be there when he got home. When does one stop expecting to see her again? he had asked a friend six months before. When will I finally understand it? The pain he had come to know in the past year and a half had etched a certain vulnerability into his face. A visible hurt of loss and sorrow and pain. There had only been strength before, and confidence, the certainty that nothing could ever go wrong. He had three perfect children, the perfect wife, a career he had mastered as few men do. He had climbed to the top, not brutally but beautifully, and he loved it there. And now what? Where was there left to go, and with whom?

Chapter 2

As Sally Block lay in her room in intensive care at Center City in LA, the lights in a television studio in New York shone with a special kind of glare. There was a bright whiteness to them, reminiscent of interrogation rooms in B films.

Outside their intense beam, the studio was draughty and chill, but directly beneath their intense gaze, one could almost feel one's skin grow taut from the heat and glare. It was as though everything in the room focused on the object of the spotlight's beam, all points came together as one, intensifying moment by moment, as even the people in the room seemed drawn to its centre, a narrow ledge, a shallow stage, an unimpressive desk, and a bright blue backdrop with a single logo on it. But it wasn't the logo that caught the eye, it was the empty chair, thronelike, waiting for its king or queen. Hovering about were technicians, cameramen, a makeup man, a hairdresser, two assistant producers, a stage manager, the curious, the important, the necessary, and the hangers-on, all of them standing ever nearer to the empty stage, the barren desk, on which shone the all-revealing spotlight beam.

'Five minutes!' It was a familiar call, an ordinary scene, yet in its own remote way, the evening news had an element of 'show biz' to it. There was that faint aura of circus and magic and stardom beneath the white lights. A mist of power and mystery enveloping them all, the heart beating just a shade faster at the sound of the words, 'Five minutes!', then 'Three!', then 'Two!'. The same words that would have rung out in a backstage corridor on Broadway, or in London, as some grande dame of the stage emerged. Nothing here was quite so glamorous, the crew standing by in running shoes and jeans, and yet, always that magic, the whispers, the waiting, and Melanie Adams sensed it herself as she stepped briskly onto the stage. As always, her entrance was timed to perfection. She had exactly one hundred seconds to go before they went on the air. One hundred seconds to glance at her notes again, watch the director's face to see if there was any last-minute thing she should know, and count quietly to herself just to calm down.

As usual, it had been a long day. She had done the final interview on a special on abused kids. It wasn't a pretty subject, but she had handled it well. Still, by six o'clock, the day had taken its toll.

Five ... the assistant director's fingers went up in the final count ... four ... three ... two ... one ...

'Good evening.' The practised smile never looked canned, and the cognac colour of her hair gleamed. 'This is Melanie Adams, with the evening news.' The President had given a speech, there was a military crisis in Brazil, the stock market had taken a sharp dip, and a local politician had been mugged that morning, in broad daylight, leaving his house. There were other news stories to relate as well, and the show moved along at a good clip, as it always did. She had a look of believable competence about her, which made the ratings soar and seemed to account for her enormous appeal. She was nationally known, and had been for well over five years, not that it was what she had originally planned. She had been a political science major when she dropped out of school to give birth to twins at nineteen. But that seemed a lifetime ago. Television had been her life for years. That, and the twins. There were other pastimes, but her work and her children came first.

She collected the notes on her desk as they went off the air, and as always the director looked pleased. 'Nice show, Mel.'

'Thanks.' There was a cool distance about her, which covered what had once been shyness, and was now simply reserve. Too many people were curious about her, wanted to gawk, or ask embarrassing questions, or pry. She was Melanie Adams now, a name that rang a certain magic bell ... I know you ... I've seen you on the news! ... It was strange buying groceries now, or going shopping for a dress, or just walking down the street with her girls. Suddenly people stared, and although outwardly Melanie Adams always seemed in control deep within it still felt strange to her.

Mel headed towards her office to take off some of the excess makeup and pick up her handbag before she left, when the story editor stopped her with a sharp wave. 'Can you stop here for a sec, Mel?' He looked harried and distracted as he always did, and inwardly Mel groaned. 'Stopping for a sec' could mean a story that would keep her away from home all night. Normally aside from being the anchor on the evening news she only did the major stories, the big newsbreaks, or the specials. But God only knew what they had in store for her now, and she really wasn't in the mood. She was enough of a pro now that the fatigue rarely showed, but the special on abused kids had left her feeling drained, no matter how alert and alive she still looked, thanks to her makeup.

'Yeah? What's up?'

'I've got something I want you to see.' The story editor pulled out a reel of tape and flicked it into a video machine. 'We did this on the one o'clock. I didn't think it was big enough for the evening news, but it could make an interesting follow-up for you.' Mel stared at the video machine as the tape began to roll, and what she saw was an interview with a nine-year-old girl, desperately in need of a heart transplant, but thus far her parents had been unable to get her one. Neighbours had started a special fund for Pattie Lou Jones, an endearing little black girl. And as the interview came to an end, Mel was almost sorry she had seen the film. It was just one more person to hurt for, to care about, and for whom one could do nothing at all. The children in her child abuse special had made her feel that way too. Why couldn't they give her a good political scandal on the heels of the other piece? She didn't need this heartache again.

'Yes.' She turned tired eyes to the man removing the reel. 'So?'

'I just thought it might make an interesting special for you, Mel. Follow her for a while, see what you can set up. What doctors here would be willing to see Pattie Lou.'

'Oh, for chrissake, Jack ... Why does that have to fall to me? What am I, some kind of new welfare bureau for kids?' Suddenly she looked tired and annoyed, and the tiny lines near her eyes were beginning to show. It had been a hell of a long day, and she had left her house at six o'clock that morning.

'Listen,' he looked every bit as tired as she, 'this could be a hot piece. We get the station to help Pattie Lou's parents find a doctor for her, we follow her through the transplant. Hell, Mel, this is news.'

She nodded slowly. It was news. But it was ghoulish too. 'Have you talked to the family about it?'

'No, but I'm sure they'd be thrilled.'

'You never know. Sometimes people like taking care of their own problems. They might not be so crazy about serving Pattie Lou up to the evening news.'

'Why not? They talked to us today.' Mel nodded again. 'Why don't you check out some of the big-wheel heart surgeons tomorrow and see what they say? Some of them like being in the public eye, and then you could call the parents of that kid.'

'I'll see what I can do, Jack. I have to tie up my child abuse piece.'

'I thought you finished that today.' He scowled instantly.

'I did. But I want to watch them edit some of it at least.'

'Bullshit. That's not your job. Just get to work on this. It'll be an even tougher piece than the child abuse thing.' Tougher than burning a two-year-old child with matches? Cutting off a four-year-old's ear? There were still times when the business of news made her sick. 'See what you can do, Mel.'

'Okay, Jack. Okay. I'll see what I can do.' ... Hello, Doctor, my name is Melanie Adams and I was wondering if you'd like to perform a heart transplant on a nine-year-old girl ... possibly for free ... and then we could come and watch you do it, and blast you and the little girl all over the news ... She walked hurriedly back to her office, with her head down, her mind full, and collided almost instantly with a tall dark-haired man.

'My, don't you look happy today. Being on the news must be fun.' The deep voice, trained long ago as a radio announcer, brought her eyes up from the floor and she smiled when she saw her old friend.

'Hi, Grant. What are you doing here at this hour?' Grant Buckley had a talk show that went on every night after the late news, and he was one of the most controversial personalities on the air, but he was deeply fond of Mel, and she considered him one of her closest friends, and had for years.

'I had to come in and check out some tapes I want to use on the show. What about you? It's a little late for you, isn't it, kid?' She was usually gone by then, but the story of Pattie Lou Jones had kept her around for an extra half hour.

'They saved an extra treat for me today. They want me to set up a heart transplant for some kid. The usual, no big deal.' Some of the clouds lifted from her face as she looked into his eyes. He was incredibly bright, a good friend, an attractive man, and women all over the network envied the obvious friendship they shared. They had never been more than just friends, although there were rumours from time to time. They only amused Grant and Mel.

'So what else is new? How'd the special on child abuse go?'

Her eyes were serious as they met his. 'It was a killer to do, but it was a good piece.'

'You have a way of picking the heavy ones, kid.'

'Either that, or they pick me, like this heart transplant I'm supposed to arrange.'

'Are you serious?' He had thought she was kidding at first.

'I'm not, but apparently Jack Owens is. You got any bright ideas?'

He frowned for a minute as he thought. 'I did a show on that last year, there were some interesting people on. I'll look at my files and check the names. Two of them instantly come to mind, but there were two more. I'll see, Mel. How soon do you need the stuff?'

She smiled. 'Yesterday.'

He ruffled her hair, knowing she wasn't going back on the air. 'Want to go out for a hamburger before you go home?'

'I'd better not. I should be getting home to the girls.'

'Those two.' He rolled his eyes, knowing them well. He had three daughters of his own, from three different wives, but none of them twins, or quite as adventurous as Mel's two girls. 'What are they up to these days?'

'The usual. Val has been in love four times this week, and Jess is working on straight A's. Their combined efforts are defying all my efforts to remain a redhead, and giving me grey hair.' She had just turned thirty-five, but looked nowhere near her age, despite the responsibilities she bore, the job which weighed heavily on her at times, but which she loved, and the assorted crises that had come through her life over the years. Grant knew most of them, and she had cried on his shoulder more than once, about a disappointment at work, or a shattered love affair. There hadn't been too many of those, she was cautious about whom she saw, and careful too about keeping her private life out of the public eye, but more than that she was gunshy about getting involved after being abandoned by the twins' father before they were born. He had told her he hadn't wanted kids, and he had meant every word he said. They had married immediately after school and gone to Columbia at the same time, but when she told him she was pregnant, he didn't want to hear.

'Get rid of it.' His face had been rock hard, and Mel still remembered his tone.

'I won't. It's our child ... that's wrong ...'

'It's a lot more wrong to screw up our lives.' So instead he had tried to screw up hers. He had gone to Mexico on holiday with another girl, and when he came back he announced that they were divorced. He had forged her signature on the forms, and she was so shocked that she didn't know what to say. Her parents wanted her to fight back, but she didn't think that she could. She was too hurt by what he'd done, and too overwhelmed at the prospect of being alone for the birth of her child ... which then turned out to be two. Her parents had helped her for a while, and then she had gone out on her own, struggled to find a job, and done everything she could from secretarial work to door-to-door sales for a vitamin firm. At last she had wound up as a receptionist for a television network, and eventually in a pool of secretaries typing up pieces for the news.

The twins had thrived through it all, though Mel's climb hadn't been easy or quick, but day after day, typing other people's words made her realise what she wanted to do. The political pieces were the ones that interested her most, reminiscent of her college days before her whole life had changed. And what she wanted was to become a writer for the news. She applied countless times for the job, and eventually understood that it wouldn't happen for her in New York. She went first to Buffalo, then Chicago, and at last back to New York, finally succeeding. Until a major strike, when suddenly management looked at her and someone jerked a thumb towards the set. She was horrified, but she had no choice. It was either do what they said, or lose her job, and she couldn't afford that. She had two little girls to support, their father had never contributed ten pence and had gone on his merry way, leaving Mel to cope alone. And she had. But all she wanted was enough for them, she had no dreams of glory, no aching desire to deliver the stories she wrote herself, and yet suddenly there she was, on TV, and the funny thing was, it felt good.

They farmed her out to Philadelphia after that, and back to Chicago again for a while, Washington DC, and at last home. In their estimation, she had been properly groomed, and they weren't far wrong. She was damn good. Powerful and interesting, strong, and beautiful to watch on the air. She seemed to combine honesty with compassion and brains to such an extent that at times one actually forgot her striking looks. And at twenty-eight she was near the top, co-presenting the evening news. At thirty, she broke her contract and moved to another show, and suddenly there she was. Sole presenter, delivering the evening news. The ratings soared and they hadn't stopped since.

She had worked like a dog after that, and her reputation as a top newswoman was well deserved. What's more, she was well liked. She was secure now. The hungry days were long gone, the juggling, the struggling – her parents would have been desperately proud, had they still been alive, and she wondered now and then what the twins' father thought, if he regretted what he'd done, if he even cared. She had never heard from him again. But he had left his mark on her, a mark that had dulled, but never quite been erased over the years. A mark of caution, if not pain, a fear of getting too close, of believing too much, of holding anyone too dear ... except the twins. It had led her into some unfortunate affairs, with men who were taken with who she was, or used her cool distance to play around, and the last time around with a married man. At first, to Mel, he had seemed ideal, he didn't want anything more than she did. She never wanted to marry again. She had everything she wanted on her own: success, security, her kids, a house she loved. 'What do I need marriage for?' she had said to Grant, and he had maintained a sceptical view.

'Maybe you don't but at least get yourself someone who's free.' He had been insistent and firm.

'Why? What difference does it make?'

'The difference it will make, my friend, is that you'll wind up spending Christmas and holidays and birthdays and weekends alone, while he sits around happily with his wife and kids.'

'Maybe so. But I'm special to him. I'm the caviar, not the sour cream.'

'You're dead wrong, Mel. You'll get hurt.' And he had been right. She had. Eventually it all began to cause her pain for just the reasons he had feared and there had been a terrible parting in the end, with Melanie looking gaunt and drawn for weeks. 'Next time, listen to Uncle Grant. I know.' He knew a great deal, mostly about how carefully she had built walls around herself. He had known her for almost ten years, meeting while she was on the way up, and he had known then that he was watching a bright new star rise in the heavens of television news, but more than that, he cared about her, as a human being and a friend. He cared enough not to want to spoil what they had. They had both been careful never to get involved with each other. He had been married three times, had a stable of 'temporaries' he enjoyed spending his nights with, but Mel was much more than that to him. She was his friend, and he was hers, and with Mel it was important not to betray that trust. She had been betrayed before, and he didn't want to be the second one to hurt her. 'The truth is, love, most men are shits,' he had confessed to her late one night after interviewing her on his show, which had been fun. And afterwards they had gone out for a drink, and sat around at Elaine's until three a.m.

'What makes you say that?' There had suddenly been something distant and cautious in her eyes. She knew one who had been, but it was grim to think that they all were.

'Because damn few want to give as good as they get. They want a woman to love them with her whole heart and soul, but they keep an important piece to themselves. What you need is a man who'll give you as much love as you have to give.'

'What makes you think I have that much love left?' She tried to look amused, but he wasn't convinced. The old hurt was still there, distant, but not gone. He wondered if it ever would be.

'I know you too well, Mel. Better than you know yourself.'

'And you think I'm pining to find the right man?' This time she laughed and he smiled.

'No. I think you're scared to death you will.'

'Touché.'

'It might do you good.'

'Why? I'm happy by myself.'

'Horseshit. No one is. Not really.'

'I have the twins.'

'That is *not* the same thing.'

She shrugged. 'You're happy alone.' She searched his eyes, not sure what she'd find, and was surprised to see a trace of loneliness there. It came out at night, like a werewolf he hid by day. Even the illustrious Grant was human too.

'If I were so happy alone, I wouldn't have married three times.' They both laughed at that, the evening wore on, and eventually he dropped her at her front door with a fatherly peck on the cheek. Once in a while she wondered what it would be like to get involved with him, but she knew that it would spoil what they had, and they both wanted to avoid that. It was too good like this.

And in the corridor outside her office, she looked up at him now, tired, but relieved to see his face at the end of a long day. He gave her something no one else did. The twins were still young enough to take from her, they had a constant need for attention, for love, for discipline, limits, new ice skates, designer jeans. But he put something back in her soul, and there was really no one else who did.

'I'll take a rain check on that hamburger tomorrow night.'

'Can't.' He shook his head with regret. 'I've got a hot date with a sensational pair of boobs.'

She rolled her eyes and he grinned. 'You are without a doubt the most sexist man I know.'

'Yup.'

'And proud of it too.'

'You're damn right.'

She smiled and looked at her watch. 'I'd better get home, or Raquel will lock me out, tyrant that she is.' She had had the same housekeeper for the last seven years. Raquel was a godsend with the girls, but she ran a tight ship. She was inordinately fond of Grant, and had tried to press Mel into a relationship with him for years.

'Give Raquel my love.'

'I'll tell her it was your fault I'm late.'

'Fine, and I'll give you that list of cardiac surgeons tomorrow. Will you be around?'

'I'll be here.'

'I'll call.'

'Thanks.' She blew him a kiss, and he went his way. She stepped into her office and picked up her bag with a quick look at her watch. It was seven thirty and Raquel was going to have a fit. She hurried downstairs and hailed a cab and in fifteen minutes the driver turned into Seventy-ninth Street.

'I'm home!' She called out into the silence, passing through the front hall. It was done in delicate flowered wallpaper and there was a white marble floor. From the moment one walked in, one sensed the friendly, elegant mood of the place, and from the bright colours, big bouquets of flowers, and touches of yellow and pastel everywhere, one had an instant feeling of good cheer. The house always amused Grant Buckley. It was so obviously a woman's house. One would have had to begin decorating from scratch were a man to make his home there. There was a big antique hat rack in the front hall, covered with Mel's hats and the favourites left there by the two girls.

The living room was done in a soft peach, with silky deep couches that invited one to be swallowed up, and delicate moiré curtains that hung in lush folds with French tiebacks, and the walls were painted the same delicate peach shade, with creamy trim on the mouldings and delicate pastel paintings everywhere. As Melanie sank down now into the couch with a contented sigh, it was the perfect setting for her with her creamy skin and her flaming red hair. Her bedroom was done in soft blues, in watered silks, the dining room was white, the kitchen orange and yellow and blue. Melanie's home had a happy feeling that made one want to wander around and hang out. It was elegant, but not too chic and not so much so that one was afraid to sit down.

It was a small house, but perfect for them, with the living room, dining room, and kitchen on the main floor, Mel's bedroom, study, and dressing room were one flight up, and above that were two big sunny bedrooms for the two girls. There wasn't an inch of unused space, and even one extra body in the house would have seemed like too much. But just for them, it was exactly the right size, as Melanie had known it would be when she'd first seen it and fallen in love with it the same day.

She walked hurriedly up the stairs to the girls' rooms, faintly aware of an ache in her back. It had been a hell of a long day. She didn't stop in her own room, knowing already what would be there, a stack of mail she didn't want to see, mostly bills relating to the girls, and an assortment of other things. But that didn't interest her now. She wanted to see the twins.

On the third floor, she found both their doors closed, but the music was so loud, she could already feel her heart pound halfway up the stairs.

'Good God, Jess!' Melanie shouted above the din. 'Turn that thing down!'

'What?' The tall, skinny redheaded girl turned towards the door from where she lay on her bed. There were school books spread all around, and she had the telephone pressed to her ear. She waved to her mother, and went on talking on the phone.

'Don't you have exams?' A silent nod, and Melanie's face began to look grim. Jessica was always the most serious of the twins, but lately she had been losing ground in school. She was bored, and the romance she'd had all year had just gone down the tubes, but that was no excuse, and she still had to study for her exams. 'Come on, hang up, Jess.' She stood leaning against the desk, arms crossed, and Jessica looked vaguely annoyed, said something unintelligible into the phone, and hung up, looking at her mother as though she were not only overly demanding but rude. 'Now turn that thing down.'

She unwound the long, coltlike legs from the bed, and walked to the stereo, flinging her long coppery mane over her shoulders. 'I was just taking a break.'

'For how long?'

'Oh, for chrissake. What do I have to do now? Punch a time clock for you?'

'That's not fair, Jess. You can have all the leeway you need. But the fact is, your last grades ...'

'I know, I know. How long do I have to hear about that?'

'Until they improve.' Melanie looked unimpressed by her daughter's speech. Jessica had been testy since the end of the romance with a young man named John. It was probably what had affected her grades, and for Jessica that was a first. But Melanie already sensed that things were on their way back up. She just didn't want to let Jessica off the hook yet, not till she was sure. 'How was your day?' She slipped an arm around her daughter's shoulders and stroked her hair. The music had been turned off, and the room seemed strangely still.

'It was okay. How was yours?'

'Not bad.'

Jessie smiled, and when she did, she looked very much as Melanie had when she was a little girl. She was more angular than her mother was, and already two inches taller than Mel in her bare feet, but there was a lot of her mother in her, which accounted for the rare bond the two women shared; there were times when it didn't even require words. And other times when their friendship exploded because of the similarities that made them almost too close. 'I saw the piece you did about the legislation for the handicapped on the evening news.'

'What did you think?' She always liked to hear what they said, especially Jess. She had a fine mind, and was very direct with her words, unlike her twin, who was kinder, less critical, and softer in a myriad ways.

'I thought it was good, but not tough enough.'

'You're mighty hard to please.' But her sponsors were too. Jessica met her eyes with a shrug and a smile. 'You taught me to question what I hear and be demanding of the news.'

'Did I do that?' The two women exchanged a warm smile. She was proud of Jess, and in turn Jessica was proud of her. Both twins were. She was a terrific mother to them. The three of them had shared some damn tough years. It had brought them closer, in respect, and attitudes.

Mother and daughter exchanged another long look. In a way, Melanie was just a shade gentler than her oldest child. But she was of another generation, another lifetime, a different world. And for her time, Melanie had already come far. But Jessica would go farther, move ahead with even more determination than Mel had. 'Where's Val?'

'In her room.'

Melanie nodded. 'How are things in school?'

'Okay.' But she thought Jessica sagged a little as she asked, and then sensing her mother's thoughts, she once again sought Melanie's eyes. 'I saw John today.'

'How was that?'

'It hurt.'

Melanie nodded and sat down on the bed, grateful for the openness that they always shared. 'What did he say?'

'Just "hi." I don't know, I hear he's going out with some other girl.'

'That's rough.' It had been almost a month now, and Melanie knew that it was the first real blow Jessica had suffered since she had started school. Always near the top of her class, surrounded by friends, and chased by all the best boys in school since she'd turned thirteen. Just shy of her sixteenth birthday, she had experienced her first heartbreak, and it hurt Melanie to watch it, almost as much as it hurt Jess. 'But you know, what you've forgotten by now is that there were times when he really got on your nerves.'

'He did?' Jessica looked surprised.

'Yes, ma'am. Remember when he showed up an hour late to take you to that dance? When he went skiing with his friends instead of taking you to the football game? The time he ...' Melanie seemed to remember them all, she knew her girls' lives well, and Jessica grinned.

'Okay, okay, so he's a creep ... I like him anyway ...'

'Him, or just having someone around?' There was a moment's silence in the room, and Jessica looked at her with surprised eyes.

'You know, Mom ... I'm not sure.' She was stunned.

The uncertainty was a revelation to her.

Melanie smiled. 'Don't feel alone. Half the relationships in the world go on because of that.'

Jessica looked at her then, her head turned to one side; she knew how difficult her mother's standards were, how badly she'd been hurt, how careful she was not to get involved. Sometimes it made Jess sorry for her. Her mother needed someone. Long ago, she had hoped it would be Grant, but she knew long since that was not destined to be. And before she could say anything more, the door opened and Valerie walked in.

'Hi, Mom.' And then she saw their serious looks.

'Should I go?'

'No.' Melanie was quick to shake her head. 'Hello, love.' Valerie bent to give her a kiss and a smile. She looked so different from Melanie and Jess that one almost wondered if she were related to the other two. She was smaller than both Melanie and her twin, but with a voluptuous body that made men drool as she walked by, large, full breasts, a tiny waist, small, rounded hips, shapely legs, and a curtain of blonde hair that fell almost to her waist. There were times when Melanie saw men's reactions to her child and almost visibly cringed. Even Grant had been taken aback when he'd seen her recently. 'For God's sake, Mel, put a bag over the child's head until she turns twenty-five, or you'll drive the neighbourhood mad.' But Melanie had responded with a rueful smile, 'I don't think putting it over just her head would do the trick.' She watched Valerie with a careful eye, more so than Jess, because one sensed instantly that Valerie was almost too open and very naïve. She was bright, but not as sharp as her twin and part of her charm was that she was almost totally unaware of herself. She breezed in and out of a room with the happy-go-lucky ease of a child of three, leaving men panting in her wake, as she unconcernedly went on her way. It was Jessica who had always watched over her in school, and even more so now. Jessica was well aware of how Valerie looked, so Valerie had two mothers watching over her.

'We watched you tonight on the news. You were good.' But unlike Jessica, she didn't say why, didn't analyse, didn't criticise, and in a funny way, what went on in Jessica's head made her almost more beautiful than her dazzling twin. And together, they were quite a pair, the one redheaded and long and lean, the other so voluptuous and soft and blonde. 'Are you having dinner with us tonight?'

'I sure am. I turned down dinner with Grant to have dinner with you two.'

'Why didn't you bring him home?' Val looked instantly chagrined.

'Because I enjoy being alone with you sometimes. I can see him some other time.' Val shrugged, and Jessica nodded, and that instant Raquel buzzed them from downstairs on the intercom. Val picked it up first, said 'Okay,' then hung up, and turned to her mother and twin.

'Dinner's on, and Raquel sounds pissed.'

'Val!' Melanie didn't look pleased. 'Don't talk like that.'

'Why not? Everyone else does.'

'That's no reason for you to.' And with that, the threesome went downstairs, bantering about their day, Mel told them about the special on child abuse, she even told them about Pattie Lou Jones, desperate for a heart transplant which Mel had been assigned to find.

'How are you supposed to do that, Mom?' Jess looked intrigued. She loved stories like that, and thought that her mother did them exceedingly well.

'Grant said he'd give me some names, he did a show on four big heart-transplant specialists last year, and the network research people will give me some leads.'

'It should be a good piece.'

'Sounds disgusting to me.' Val made a face as they walked into the dining room and Raquel glared.

'You think I gonna wait all night?' She grunted loudly and whisked through the swinging door as the threesome exchanged a smile.

'She'd go crazy if she couldn't complain,' Jessica whispered to them both, and they laughed, sobering their faces for her benefit as she returned with a platter of roast beef.

'It looks great, Raquel!' Val was quick to offer praise as she helped herself first.

'Hrmph.' She whisked out again, returning with baked potatoes and steamed broccoli, and the three of them settled down to a quiet evening at home. It was the only place in Mel's life where she could totally, completely free herself of the news.

Chapter 3

'Sally? ... Sally? ...' She had been drifting in and out of consciousness all day, and Peter Hallam had been to see her five or six times. It was only her second postoperative day, and it was still difficult to tell how she would do, but he had to admit to himself that he wasn't entirely pleased. She opened her eyes at last, realised who he was, and greeted him with a warm smile, as he pulled up a chair, sat down, and took her hand. 'How're you feeling today?'

She spoke to him in a whisper. 'Not so good.'

He nodded. 'It's still pretty soon. Every day you'll feel stronger.' He seemed to will his strength into her through his words and his voice, but slowly she shook her head. 'Have I ever lied to you?'

She shook her head again, spoke again, despite the uncomfortable naso-gastric tube scratching the back of her throat. 'It won't work.'

'If you want it to, it will.' Everything inside him went tense. She couldn't afford to think like that. Not now.

'I'm going to reject.' She whispered again. But he doggedly shook his head, a muscle tensing in his jaw. Dammit, why was she giving up? ... and how did she know? ... It was what he had feared all day. But she couldn't give up the fight ... couldn't ... dammit, it was like Anne ... why did they suddenly lose their grasp? It was the worst battle he fought. Worse than the drugs, the rejections, the infections. They could deal with them all, at least to a point, but only if the patient still had the will to live ... the belief that they would live. Without that, all was lost.

'Sally, you're doing fine.' The words were determined and firm, and he sat by her bedside for over an hour, holding her hand. And then he went to make rounds, in each room, turning his full attention to the patient he saw, spending as much time as was needed to explain either surgical procedures that were going to be conducted soon, or what had already happened, what they felt, why they felt it, what the medications and steroids had done. And then at last, he went back to Sally's room. But she was asleep once again, and he stood for a long time watching her. He didn't like what he saw. She was right; he sensed it in his gut. Her body was rejecting the donor's heart, and there was no reason why it should. It had been a good match. But he instinctively sensed that it came too late for her, and as he left the room, he had a sense of impending loss which weighed on him like a lead balloon.

He went to the small cubicle he used as a surgery when he was there, and called his office to see if they needed him there.

'Everything's fine, Doctor,' the efficient voice said. 'You just had a call from New York.'

'From whom?' He didn't sound overly interested in the call, it was probably from another surgeon wanting to consult on a difficult case, but his mind was filled with Sally Block, and he hoped it could wait.

'From Melanie Adams, on Channel Four news.' Even Peter knew who she was, as isolated as he sometimes was from the world. He couldn't figure out why she had called him.

'Do you know why?'

'She wouldn't say, or at least not in detail. She only said that it was urgent, something about a little girl.' He raised an eyebrow at that. Even television newswomen had kids and maybe this had to do with her own child. He jotted down the number she had left, glanced at his watch, and dialled.

They put him through at once, and Melanie ran halfway across the newsroom to pick up a phone.

'Dr Hallam?' She sounded breathless.

'Yes. I had a message that you called.'

'I did. I didn't expect to hear from you so soon. Our research department gave me your name.' She had heard it often too, but as he was on the West Coast it hadn't occurred to her to call, and the four names she'd got from Grant had done no good at all. Not one of them would do the surgery for the little black child – the publicity frightened them too much and the surgery had to be performed. Melanie had also called a surgeon of some note in Chicago, but he was in England and Scotland doing a lecture tour. She explained to Hallam quickly about the little girl, and he asked her a number of pertinent questions. She had learned a lot in one day, talking to the other four.

'It sounds like an interesting case.' And then he spoke bluntly. 'What's in it for you?'

She took a quick breath, it was hard to say. 'On the surface, Doctor, a story for my network, about a compassionate doctor, a desperately sick little girl, and how transplants work.'

'That makes sense. I'm not sure I like the publicity angle though. And it's damn hard to find a donor for a child. Most likely we'd try something a little more unusual with her.'

'Like what?' Mel was intrigued.

'It depends on how severe she is. I'd like to see her first. We might first repair her old heart and put it back in.' Mel knit her brows. 'Does that work?'

'Sometimes. Do her doctors think she'd survive the trip?'

'I don't know. I'd have to check. Would you actually do it?'

'Maybe. For her sake, not yours.' He sounded blunt again, but Mel couldn't fault it. He was offering to do the surgery for the child, not make a spectacle of himself on the news. She respected him for that.

'Would you give us an interview?'

'Yes.' He spoke up without qualm. 'I just want to make it clear why I'd do it at all. I'm a physician, and a surgeon, committed to what I do. I'm not looking to turn this into a circus, for any of us.'

'I wouldn't do that to you.' He had seen her stories on television before, and suspected that that was true. 'But I would like to interview you. And if you do the transplant on Pattie Lou, it would provide an opening for a very interesting piece.'

'On what? On me?' He sounded shocked, as though he'd never thought of that before, and at her end Mel smiled. Was it possible that he didn't realise how well known he was? Maybe he was so involved in his work that he really didn't know. Or care. The possibility of that intrigued her.

'Heart surgery and on transplants in general if you prefer.'

'I would.' She heard a smile in his voice, and went on.

'That could be arranged. Now what about Pattie Lou?'

'Give me her physician's name. I'll call and see what I can find out from here. If she's operable, send her out, and we'll see.' And then he had another thought. 'Will her parents agree to this?'

'I think so. But I'd have to speak to them too. I'm kind of the matchmaker in all this.'

'Apparently. Well, at least it's all for a good cause. I hope we can help the child.'

'So do I.' There was an instant's silence between them, and Mel felt as though miraculously she had fallen into the right hands, and so had Pattie Lou. 'Shall I call you back, or will you call me?'

'I've got a critical case here. I'll get back to you.' And suddenly he sounded desperately serious again, as though he were distracted. Mel thanked him again, and a moment later he was gone.

That afternoon she went to see the Jones', and their desperately ill child, but Pattie Lou was a game little thing, and her parents were thrilled at even the faint shred of hope Mel offered them. There was enough in their meagre fund to pay for the plane fare to LA, for one of the parents at least, and the child's father was quick to urge his wife to go. There were four other children at home, all older than Pattie Lou and Mr Jones felt sure that they could all manage on their own. Mrs Jones cried, and her husband's eyes were damp when they said goodbye to Mel, and two hours after she returned to her office, Hallam called again. He had spoken to Pattie Lou's physicians and in their estimation it was worth taking the risk of the trip. It was the only hope she had. And Peter Hallam was willing to take the case.

Having seen Pattie Lou that afternoon, tears instantly filled Mel's eyes, and her voice was husky when she spoke again. 'You're a hell of a nice man.'

'Thank you.' He smiled. 'How soon do you suppose you could arrange to have her on the plane?'

'I'm not sure. I'll have the network work out the details. When do you want her there?'

'From what her doctors said, I don't think tomorrow would be too soon.'

'I'll see what I can do.' She checked her watch, it was almost time to do the evening news. 'We'll call you in a few hours ... and Dr Hallam ... thank you ...'

'Don't. It's part of what I do. And I hope we understand each other about all this. I will do it gratis for the child, but there will be no cameras in surgery with us. And what you get is an interview after it's all done. Agreed?'

'Agreed.' And then she couldn't resist stretching it a bit. She had an obligation to the network and her sponsors too. 'Could we interview you about some other cases too?'

'In what regard?' He sounded faintly suspicious of her now.

'I'd like very much to do a story on heart transplants as long as I'll be out there with you, Doctor. Is that all right?' Maybe he had some preconceived prejudice about her. She hoped not, but one never knew. Maybe he hated the way she did the evening news. It was broadcast to California after all, so she couldn't be totally unknown to him, and of course she was not. But her fears were ill founded, as he nodded at his end.

'Of course. That's fine.'

There was a moment of silence between them, and then he spoke up, his voice thoughtful. 'It's odd to think of a human life in terms of a story.' He was thinking of Sally, hovering on the verge of a massive rejection. She wasn't a 'story', she was a twenty-two-year-old girl, a human life, as was this child in New York.

'Believe it or not, after all these years, it's hard for me to think of it that way too.' She took a deep breath, wondering if she seemed callous to him. But the news business was that way sometimes. 'I'll get in touch with you later, and let you know when we're coming out.'

'I'll make arrangements here to receive her.'

'Thank you, Doctor.'

'This is what I do, no thanks necessary, Miss Adams.'

To Mel it seemed a far more noble task in life than reporting news 'stories', and as she hung up, she thought of what he had said as she went about making arrangements to get Pattie Lou Jones and her mother to California. In less than an hour she had taken care of everything from the ambulance from their home to the airport, special service on the flight, a nurse to travel with them, to be paid for by the network, a camera crew to join them from point of departure all the way to California, a similar crew to continue with them in LA, and hotel accommodation for herself, the crew, and Pattie Lou's mother. All that remained was to let Peter Hallam know, and she left a message with his service. He was not available when she called him several hours later, and that night she told the twins that she was going to California for a few days.

'What for?' She explained the story to both girls.

'Boy, Mom, you're turning into a regular paramedic.' Val looked amused, and Mel turned to her with a tired sigh.

'I feel like it tonight. It ought to be a good story though.' That word again, a 'story', as weighed against a human life. What if it were Valerie or Jessie? How would she feel then? How much of a 'story' would it be to her? She cringed inwardly at the thought, and understood again Peter Hallam's reaction to the term. She wondered too what it would be like to meet him, if he would be pleasant, easy to work with, or terribly egocentric. He didn't sound it on the phone, but she knew that most surgeons had that reputation. Yet he had sounded different. She had liked him, sight unseen, and she had deeply respected his willingness to help Pattie Lou Jones.

'You look tired, Mom.' She noticed that Jessica had been staring at her.

'I am.'

'What time do you leave tomorrow?' They were used to her comings and goings, and were comfortable with Raquel in her absence.

'I should leave the house by six thirty. Our flight's at nine, and I'm meeting the camera crew outside the Jones house. I'll be up by five, I guess.'

'Urghk.' Both girls made a face, and Mel smiled at them.

'Exactly. Not always as glamorous as it seems, eh girls?'

'You can say that again,' Val was quick to answer. The girls knew what hard work Mel's career was, how often she had stood outside the White House, freezing in snow storms, covering hideous events in distant jungles, political assassinations and other horrendous moments. Both of them respected her more for it, but neither of them envied what she did, or longed for the same career. Val thought she'd just like to get married, and Jess had her heart set on becoming a doctor.

Mel went upstairs with them after dinner, packed her bag for the trip to the West Coast, and went to bed early. Grant called her just after she turned the light out, and asked her how his lists of doctors had worked out that morning.

'None of them would help, but research gave me Peter Hallam's number. I called him in LA and we're all flying out tomorrow.'

'You and the kid?' He sounded surprised.

'And her mother and a nurse, and a camera crew.'

'The whole circus.'

'I think that's what Hallam felt about it.' In fact he had even used the same word.

'I'm surprised he agreed to do it.'

'He sounds like a nice man.'

'So they say. He certainly doesn't need the publicity, although he keeps a lower profile than the others. But I think that's by choice. Will he let you film the surgery on the kid?'

'Nope. But he promised me an interview afterwards, and you never know, he may change his mind once we get there.'

'Maybe so. Call me when you get back, kiddo, and try to stay out of trouble.' It was his usual warning and she smiled as she turned off the light again a few minutes later.

At the opposite end of the country, Peter Hallam wasn't smiling. Sally Block had gone into massive rejection, and within an hour, she had slipped into a coma. He stayed with her until almost midnight, emerging from her room only to speak to her mother, and at last, he allowed the sorrowing woman to join him at Sally's side. There was no reason not to. The fear of infection no longer mattered, and at one o'clock that morning, LA time, Sally Block died without ever regaining consciousness to see her mother or the doctor she had so greatly trusted. Her mother left the room in bereft silence, with tears pouring down her cheeks. Sally's war was over. Peter Hallam signed the death certificate, and went home to sit in his study in total darkness, staring out into the night, thinking of Sally, and Anne, and others like them. He was still sitting there two hours later when Mel left her apartment to go to the Jones apartment in New York. Peter Hallam wasn't even thinking of Pattie Lou Jones at that moment, or Mel Adams ... only of Sally ... the pretty twenty-two-year-old blonde girl ... gone now ... gone ... like Anne ... like so many others. And then, slowly, slowly, feeling the weight of the world on his shoulders, he walked up to his bedroom, closed the door, and sat on his bed in the silence.

'I'm sorry ...' the words were whispered, and he wasn't even sure to whom he spoke them ... to his wife ... his children ... to Sally ... to her parents ... to himself ... and then the tears came, falling softly as he lay down in the darkness, sorrowing in his soul for what he hadn't been able to do this time ... not this time ... but next time ... next time ... maybe next time ... And then at last, Pattie Lou Jones came to mind. There was nothing to do but try again. And something deep within him stirred at the prospect.

Chapter 4

The plane left Kennedy airport with Mel, the camera crew, Pattie Lou, the nurse, and Pattie's mother all safely ensconced in a segregated first-class section. Pattie had an IV, and the nurse seemed highly skilled in the care of cardiac patients. She had been recommended by Pattie's own physician, and Mel found herself praying that nothing untoward would happen before they reached Los Angeles. Once there she knew that they would be in the competent hands of Dr Peter Hallam, but before that, Mel's idea of a nightmare was having to land in Kansas with a dying child, suffering from cardiac arrest before they could reach the doctor in California. She just prayed that that wouldn't happen, and as it turned out, they had a peaceful flight all the way to Los Angeles, where Hallam had two members of his team and an ambulance waiting, and Pattie Lou was whisked off to Center City with her mother. By previous agreement with Dr Hallam, Melanie was not to join them. He wanted to give the child time to settle in without disruption, and he had agreed to meet Mel in the cafeteria at seven o'clock the following morning. He would brief her then on Pattie Lou's condition, and how they planned to treat her. She was welcome to bring a notepad and a tape recorder, but there was to be no camera crew at that meeting. The official interview would come later. But Mel found that she was grateful for the reprieve from the medical tension, and she went to her hotel and called the twins in New York, showered, changed, and walked around her hotel area in the balmy spring air, her mind constantly returning to Peter Hallam. She was desperately curious to meet him, and at six the next morning, she rose swiftly and drove her rented car to Center City.

Melanie's heels clicked rhythmically on the tiled floor as she turned left down an endless hall, and passed two maintenance men dragging wet mops behind them. They watched her back recede into the distance with an appreciative glance, until she stopped outside the cafeteria, read the sign, and pushed open the double doors. Her nostrils were assailed with the rich aroma of fresh coffee. And as she looked around the brightly lit room, she was surprised at how many people were there at that hour of the morning.

There were tables of nurses having coffee and breakfast between shifts, residents taking a break, interns finishing a long night with a hot meal or a sandwich, and one or two civilians sitting bleakly at tables on the sidelines, undoubtedly people who had been up all night waiting for news of critically ill relatives or friends. There was one woman crying softly and dabbing at her eyes with a hankie as a younger woman dried her own tears and tried to console her. It was an odd scene of contrasts, the silent fatigue of the young doctors, the mirth and chatter of the nurses, the sorrow and tension of people visiting patients, and behind it all the clatter of trays and steaming water being splashed on dirty dishes in efficient machines. It looked like the operations centre of a strange modern city, the command post of a spaceship floating through space, totally divorced from the rest of the world.

As Melanie looked around, she wondered which white-coated figure was Peter Hallam. There were a few middle-aged men in starched white coats, conferring solemnly at one table over doughnuts and coffee, but somehow none of them looked the way she expected him to, and none of them approached her. At least he would know what she looked like.

'Miss Adams?' She was startled by the voice directly behind her, and she wheeled on one heel to face it.

'Yes?'

He extended a powerful, cool hand. 'I'm Peter Hallam.' As she shook his hand, she found herself looking up into the sharply etched, handsome, well-lined face of a man with blue eyes and grey hair and a smile that hovered in his eyes but didn't quite reach his lips. Despite their conversation on the phone, he wasn't at all what she had expected. He was much taller, and powerfully built, his shoulders were pressed into the starched white coat he wore over a blue shirt, dark tie, and grey trousers, and one instantly guessed he had played football in college. 'Have you been waiting long?'

'Not at all.' She followed him to a table, feeling less in control than she would have liked. She was used to having a certain impact on her subjects, and here she had the impression of simply being dragged along in his wake. There was something incredibly magnetic about him.

'Coffee?'

'Please.' Their eyes met and locked, each one wondering what they would discover in the other, friend or foe, supporter or opponent. But for the moment they had one thing in common. Pattie Lou Jones, and Mel was anxious to ask him about her.

'Cream and sugar?'

'No, thanks.' She made a move as though to join him on the food line, but he waved a hand towards an empty chair.

'Don't bother. I'll be right back. You keep an eye on the table.' He smiled then and she felt something gentle wash over her. He looked like a kind man, and a moment later he returned with a tray bearing two steaming cups, two glasses of orange juice, and some toast. 'I wasn't sure if you'd had breakfast.' There was something so basically decent and thoughtful about him, she found herself instantly liking him.

'Thank you.' She smiled at him and then couldn't hold back any longer. 'How's Pattie Lou?'

'She settled in nicely last night. She's a courageous little kid. She didn't even need her mother to stay with her.' But Mel somehow suspected that had to do with the comforting welcome she got from Peter Hallam and his team, and she was right on that score. His patient's mental well-being was of major importance to him, which was extremely rare for a surgeon. He had spent several hours with Pattie Lou after she arrived, getting to know her, as a person, not just an accumulation of data. With Sally gone, Peter had no other major crisis to attend to and now he wasn't thinking of Sally, only Pattie.

'How do her chances look, Doctor?' Mel was anxious to hear what he thought, and hopeful that the prognosis would be good.

'I'd like to say good, but they aren't. I think fair is a more accurate assessment of the situation.' Mel nodded sombrely and took a sip of coffee.

'Will you do a transplant on her?'

'If we get a donor, which isn't very likely. Donors for children are very rare, Miss Adams. I think my first thought was the right one – repairing her own heart as best we can.'

'When?'

He sighed and narrowed his eyes, thinking about it as she watched him. 'We'll run a battery of tests on her today, and we might do the surgery tomorrow.'

'Is she strong enough to survive it?'

'I think so.' Their eyes met and held for a long moment. There were no guarantees in this business. There were never sure wins, only sure losses. It was a tough thing to live with, day by day, and she admired what he was doing. She felt a strong urge to tell him that, but somehow it seemed too personal a statement to make, so she didn't, and kept the conversation to Pattie Lou and the story. After a while, he looked searchingly at Mel. She was so interested, so human. She was more than just a reporter. 'What's your interest in all this, Miss Adams? Just another story or something more?'

'She's a special little girl, Doctor. It's difficult not to care about her.'

'Do you always care that much about your subjects? It must be exhausting.'

'Isn't that true of you? Do you care about them all, Doctor?'

'Almost always.' He was being very honest with her and it was easy to believe him. The patient he didn't care deeply about would be a very, very rare exception. She had already sensed that about him. And then he looked at her with a curious smile: her hands were folded in her lap as she watched him. 'You didn't bring a notebook. Does that mean you're taping this?'

'No.' She quietly shook her head and smiled. 'I'm not. I'd rather we get to know each other.'

That possibility intrigued him, and he couldn't resist asking another question. 'Why?'

'Because I can do a better job of reporting what you do here if I learn something about you. Not on paper, or on tape, but by watching, listening, getting to know you.' She was good at what she did, and he sensed that. It was just that she was well known in the business, a star actually, she was in truth a real pro, and an unusually good one. Peter Hallam liked that. It was like being perfectly matched to your opponent in a competitive sport, and it gave him a feeling of excitement, which suddenly led to an offer he hadn't planned to make her.

'Would you like to follow me on rounds this morning? Just for your own interest.'

Her eyes lit up. She was flattered by the unexpected offer, and hoped that it meant that he liked her, or better yet, was already beginning to trust her. That was important for the smooth flow of any story.

'I'd like that very much, Doctor.' She let her eyes convey to him how touched she was by the offer.

'You could call me Peter.'

'If you call me Mel.' They exchanged a smile.

'Agreed.' He touched her shoulder as he stood, and she leapt up, excited by the prospect of following him on rounds. It was a rare opportunity and she was grateful for it. He turned to her again, this time with a smile, as they left the cafeteria. 'My patients will be very impressed to see you here, Mel. I'm sure they've all seen you on TV.' For some reason, the remark surprised her and she smiled.

'I doubt that.' There was a modesty about her that those who knew her well always teased her for, especially Grant and her daughters.

But this time he laughed at her. 'You're hardly an anonymous figure, you know. And heart patients watch the news on TV too.'

'I just always assume that people won't recognise me off camera.'

'But I'll bet they do.' He smiled again and Melanie nodded in answer. It was intriguing to him that she hadn't let her success go to her head over the years. He had expected someone very different.

'In any case, Doctor Hallam,' she went on, 'you're the star here, and rightly so.' Her eyes shone with frank admiration, but this time a similarly humble side turned up in him.

'I'm hardly a star, Mel.' He was serious as he said it. 'I just work here, as part of a remarkably good team. Believe me, my patients will be a lot more excited to see you than me, and rightly so. It'll do them good to see a new face.' He pressed the button for the lift, and when it came, he pressed six, and they entered amidst a group of whitecoated doctors and fresh-faced nurses. The shifts were just changing.

'You know, I've always liked your views, and the way you handle a story.' He spoke softly as the lift stopped at each floor, and Mel noticed two nurses staring discreetly at her. 'There's something direct and honest about your approach. I suppose it's why I agreed to do this.'

'Whatever your reason, I'm glad you did. Pattie Lou needed you desperately.' He nodded, he couldn't disagree with her on that score. But now there was more to it. He had opened himself up to an interview on network news, and as they sat in his cubicle on the sixth floor, a few minutes later, he looked with honesty at Mel and tried to explain to her the risks and dangers of transplants. He warned her that she might even come away from the story with negative feelings about them. It was a possibility he'd thought of before agreeing to the interview, but he was willing to take that risk. There was more to be gained by telling all than by hiding from the press, and if she handled it right, she could warm up public opinion considerably, but she seemed startled by the risks he described and the odds he gave.

'Do you mean I could possibly decide that heart transplants aren't a good idea? Is that what you're saying, Peter?'

'You might, although that would be a very foolish view. The fact is that transplant patients are going to die anyway, and quite soon. What we give them is a chance, and sometimes not a very good one at that. The risk is high, most of the time the odds are poor, but there is that chance, and the patient makes up his own mind. Some people just don't want to go through what they'd have to, and they opt not to take the chance. I respect that. But if they let me, I try. It's all anyone can do. I'm not advocating transplant for all patients, that would be mad. But the fact is that for some it's ideal, and right now we still need to open new doors. We can't just operate with human heart donors, we need more than there are, so we're groping for new paths, and it's that process that the public resists. They think we're trying to play God, and we're not, we're trying to save lives, and doing our best, it's as simple as that.' He stood up, as she followed suit, and he looked down at her from his considerable height. 'You tell me what you think at the end of today, and tell me if you disagree with the means we pursue. In fact' – he narrowed his eyes as he looked at her – 'I'd be particularly interested in what you think. You're an intelligent woman, yet relatively uneducated in this field. You come to it with fresh eyes. You tell me if you're shocked, if you're appalled, or if you approve.' And as they left his cubicle, he had another thought. 'Tell me something, Mel, have you formed any kind of preconceived opinion at all?' He watched her face intently as they walked and she furrowed her brow.

'Honestly, I'm not entirely sure. Basically, I think that everything you're doing makes sense, of course. But I must admit, the odds you're talking about frighten me. The chances of survival, for any reasonable length of time, are so slim.'

He looked long and hard at her. 'What may seem unreasonable to you may be the last straw of hope to a dying woman or man or child. Maybe to them, even two months ... two days ... two hours longer sounds good. Admittedly, the odds frighten me too. But what choice do we have? Right now, that's the best we've got.' She nodded and followed him into the hall, thinking of Pattie Lou, and she watched him as he began to read through his patients' charts, face intent, brows knit, asking questions, looking at the results of tests. Again and again, Melanie heard the names of the drugs given to heart-transplant patients to allay rejection of the new heart. And she began to make a few notes herself, of questions she wanted to ask him when he had time, about the risks of these drugs, their effects on the patients' personalities and minds.

Suddenly she saw Peter Hallam get up, and walk quickly down the hall. She followed him a few steps, and then stopped, unsure of whether or not he wanted her with him, and as though sensing her indecision, he suddenly turned to her with a wave.

'Come on.' He waved to a stack of white coats on a narrow stainless steel cart and indicated to her to grab one, which she did on the run, and caught up with him as she struggled to put it on. He had his arms full of charts, two residents and a nurse were following respectfully behind. Peter Hallam's day had begun. He smiled once at Mel and pushed open the first door, which revealed an elderly man. He had had a quadruple bypass two weeks before and said that he felt like a boy again. He didn't look much like a boy, he still looked tired and pale and a little wan, but after they left his room, Peter assured her that he was going to be fine. They moved on to the next room, where suddenly Melanie felt a tug at her heart. She found herself staring down into the face of a little boy. He had a congenital heart and lung disease, and nothing surgical had been done for him yet. He wheezed horribly and was the size of a five- or six-year-old child, but a glance at his chart told Mel that he was ten. They had been contemplating a heart-lung transplant on him, but thus far, there had been so few done that they felt it was too soon to attempt it on such a young child, and intermediary measures were being taken to keep him alive. Melanie watched as Peter sat down in a chair next to his bed and talked at great length to him. More than once, Melanie had to fight back tears, and she turned so the boy wouldn't see her damp eyes. Peter touched her shoulder again as they left the room, this time in comfort.

They moved on to a man who had been given a plastic heart, which Melanie learned was powered by air. The patient was suffering from a massive infection, which apparently was often a problem. And then there was another patient, comatose, and after speaking briefly to the nurse, Peter didn't linger in the room. There were two moon-faced men who had undergone heart transplants within the year, and Melanie already knew from the material she'd read that often the steroids they took had that side effect, but eventually it would be controlled. Suddenly these people came alive to her. And what was even more real to her now was how poor the odds were. Peter answered some of her questions now, as they sat in his cubicle again. And as she looked at her watch, she was amazed to discover that it was almost noon. They had been doing rounds for four hours, had probably been to twenty rooms.

'The odds?' He looked at her over his coffee cup. 'Heart-transplant patients have a sixty-five per cent chance of living for one year after the surgery is performed. That's roughly two chances in three that they'll make it for a year.'

'And longer than that?'

He sighed. He hated these statistics. They were what he fought every day. 'Well, the longest we can give anyone is about a fifty-fifty chance for five years.'

'And after that?' She was making notes now, appalled by the statistics, and sympathetic to the defiance in his voice.

'That's about it right now. We just can't do better than that.' He said it with regret, and simultaneously they both thought of Pattie Lou, willing her better odds than that. She had a right to so much more. They all did. One almost wanted to ask what was the point except that if it were one's own life, or one's child, wouldn't one take any chance at all, for a day, or a week, or even a year?

'Why do they die so soon?' Mel looked grim.

'Rejection mostly, in whatever form. Either a straight across-the-board rejection, or they get hardening of the arteries, which will lead to a heart attack. A transplant will kind of step things up. And then the other big problem we face is infection, they're more prone to that.'

'And there's nothing you can do?' As though it all depended on him. She was casting him in the role of God, just as some of his patients did. And they both knew it wasn't fair, but it all seemed to be in his hands, even if it was not. In a way, she wanted it to be. It would have been simpler like that. He was a decent man, he'd make things all right ... if he could.

'There's nothing we can do right now. Although some of the new drugs may change that. We've been using some new ones lately that may help. The thing you have to remember,' he spoke gently to her, almost as though she were a child, 'is that these people would have no chance at all without a new heart. So whatever they get is a gift. They understand that. They'll try anything, if they want to live.'

'What does that mean?'

'Some don't. They just don't want to go through all this.' He waved at the charts and leaned back in his chair, holding his coffee cup. 'It takes a lot of guts, you know.' But she realised something else now. It took a lot of guts for him too. He was a matador of sorts, going into the ring with a bull named Death, trying to steal men and women and children from him. She wondered how often he'd been gored by dashed hopes, by patients who had died whom he cared about. Somehow one sensed about him that he was a man who really cared. As though he heard her thoughts, his voice suddenly grew soft. 'My wife decided not to take the chance.' He lowered his eyes as Mel watched, feeling suddenly rooted to her chair. What had he said? His wife? And then he looked up, sensing her shock, and his eyes looked straight into Mel's. They weren't damp, but she saw a grief there that explained something to her about him. 'She had primary pulmonary hypertension, I don't know if that means anything to you or not. It damages the lungs, and eventually the heart, and it requires a heart-lung transplant, but at the time there had only been two done anywhere in the world, and neither of them here. I wouldn't have done it myself of course' – he sighed and leaned forward again in his chair – 'she would have been operated on by one of my colleagues and the rest of the team, or we could have taken her to any of the great men around the world and she very quietly said no. She wanted to die as she was, and not put herself, or me, or the children through the agonies she knew my patients go through, only to die anyway in six months, or a year, or two years. She faced it all with terrific calm' – and now Mel saw that his eyes were damp, – 'I've never known anyone like her. She was perfectly calm about it, right up until the end.' His voice cracked and then he went on, 'It was a year and a half ago. She was forty-two.'

He looked deep into Mel's eyes then, unafraid of what he felt, and the silence was deafening in the tiny room. 'Maybe we could have changed all that. But not for long.' He sounded more professional now. 'I've done two heart-lungs myself in the last year. For obvious reasons, I have particularly strong feelings about that. There's no reason why it can't work, and it will.' It was too late for his wife. But in his heart he would never give up the fight, as though he could still convince her to let him try. Mel watched him with a pain in her soul for what he'd been through, and the helplessness he felt which still showed in his eyes.

Her voice was very soft when she spoke. 'How many children do you have?'

'Three. Mark is seventeen, Pam will be fourteen in June, and Matthew is six.' Peter Hallam smiled then as he thought of his children and looked at Mel. 'They're all great kids, but Matthew is the funniest little kid.' And then he sighed and stood up. 'It's been hardest on him, but it's hard on all of them. Pam is at an age when she really needs Anne, and I can only give her so much. I try to get home early every day, but some crisis or other always comes up. It's damn hard to give them everything they need when you're alone.'

'I know.' She spoke softly. 'I have that problem too.'

He turned and looked at Mel, seeming not to have heard what she said. 'She could at least have given us a chance.'

Mel's voice was soft. 'And she'd most likely still be gone now. It must be very hard to accept.'

He nodded slowly, looking sorrowfully at Mel. 'It is,' and then as though suddenly shocked at all he had said he picked the charts up in his arms, as though to put something between them again. 'I'm sorry. I don't know why I told you all that.' But Melanie wasn't surprised, people often opened their hearts to her, it had just happened a little more quickly this time. He tried to brush it off with a smile. 'Why don't we go down the hall and visit Pattie now.' Mel nodded, still deeply moved by all he'd said. It was difficult to find the right words to say to him now, and it was almost a relief to see the child she'd brought out from New York. Pattie Lou was obviously thrilled to see both of them, and it reminded Mel of why she was there. They spent a comfortable half hour chatting with the child and as Peter read the results of her tests, he seemed pleased. He turned to her at last with a fatherly look in his eyes.

'Tomorrow is our big day, you know.'

'Is it?' Her eyes grew wide, she seemed at the same time both excited and unsure.

'We're going to work on your old heart, Pattie, and make it as good as new.'

'Can I play baseball then?' Mel and Peter both smiled at the request.

'Is that what you want to do?'

'Yes, sir!' She beamed.

'We'll see.' He explained the procedures of the following day to her, carefully, in terms she could understand, and although she seemed apprehensive, she was obviously not desperately afraid. It was easy to see that she already liked Peter Hallam, and she was sorry when they both left her room. Peter glanced at his watch, as they left. It was after one thirty.

'How about some lunch? You must be starved.'

'Getting there,' she smiled. 'But I've been too engrossed to think of food.'

He looked pleased. 'Me too.' And then he led her outside and it was suddenly a relief to be out in the fresh air. Peter suggested a quick lunch, and Mel agreed, as they strode in the direction of his car.

'Do you always work this hard?' she asked him and he looked amused.

'Most of the time. You don't get much time off from something like this. You can't afford to turn your back on it even for a day.'

'What about your team? Can't you share the responsibility of all this?' Otherwise the burden would be too much to bear. 'Of course we do.' But something about the way he said it made her doubt his words. One had the feeling that he took most of the responsibility on himself, and that he liked it like that.

'How do your children feel about your work?'

He seemed to think for a moment before he spoke. 'You know, I'm not really sure. Mark wants to go into law, and Pam changes her thoughts on the subject every day, especially now, and of course Matthew is too little to have any idea what he wants to be when he grows up, other than being a plumber, which he decided last year.' And then Peter Hallam laughed. 'I suppose that's what I am, isn't it?' He grinned at Mel. 'A plumber.' They both laughed in the warm spring air. The sun shone down on them both, and Melanie noticed that he looked younger here. Suddenly, she could almost imagine him with his children.

'Where shall we go to lunch?' He smiled down at her from his great height, obviously comfortable in his kingdom, but it wasn't just that. There was something more. There was a new bond of friendship between them now. He had bared his soul to her, and told her about Anne. And as a result, he felt suddenly freer than he had in a long time. He almost wanted to celebrate the lightness he felt in his heart, and Mel sensed his mood as she smiled at him. It was remarkable to think that he dealt in life and death, and she had come to Los Angeles to deliver a desperately sick child to him. And yet, in the midst of it all, they were still alive, still young, and slowly coming to be friends. And not so slowly at that. Something about him reminded her of the instant openness she had felt when she met Grant, and yet she realised that she felt something more for this man. He was potentially enormously attractive to her, his strength, his gentleness, his vulnerability, his openness, his modesty coupled with his enormous success. He was an unusual man, and as he watched her, Peter Hallam was thinking many of the same things about her. He was glad he had asked her out to lunch. They had earned the break. They were both people who worked hard and paid their dues, and it didn't seem out of place to take a little time together now. Mel told herself that it would help the interview.

'Do you know LA well?' he asked.

'Not very. I always come here to work and dash from one place to the next until I leave. I never have much time for relaxed meals.' He smiled, neither did he, but today it felt right. He also felt as though he had made a new friend. And she smiled up at him now. 'I suspect you don't usually go out to lunch, do you?'

He grinned. 'Once in a while. Usually, I eat here.' He waved at the hospital behind them, and stopped at his car. It was a large, roomy silver-grey Mercedes sedan, which surprised her. The car didn't really look like him, and he read her thoughts.

'I gave this to Anne two years ago.' He said it quietly, but there was less pain in his voice this time. 'Most of the time I drive my own car, a little BMW, but it's in the garage. And I leave the station wagon at home for my housekeeper and Mark to drive.'

'Do you have someone good with your kids?' They were just two people now as they drove in the direction of Wilshire Boulevard.

'Terrific.' He looked over at Mel briefly with a smile as he drove. 'I'd really be lost without her. She's a German woman we've had since Pam was born. Anne took care of Mark herself, but when Pam was born she was already having cardiac problems and we hired this woman to take care of the baby. She was to stay for six months' – he smiled at Mel again – 'and that was fourteen years ago. She's a godsend for us now' – he hesitated only slightly – 'with Anne gone.' He was getting used to words like that now.

And Mel was quick to pick up the conversational ball and keep it rolling. 'I have a wonderful Central American woman to help me with my girls.'

'How old are they?'

'Almost sixteen. In July.'

'Both of them?' He looked surprised and this time Mel laughed.

'Yes. They're twins.'

'Identical?' He smiled at the idea.

'No, fraternal. One is a svelte redhead, whom people say looks like me, but I'm not sure she does. And the other one I know doesn't look like me at all, she's a voluptuous blonde who gives me heart failure every time she goes out.' She smiled and Peter laughed.

'I've come to the conclusion, in the last two years, that it's easier to have sons.' His smile faded as he thought of Pam. 'My daughter was twelve and a half when Anne died. I think that the loss compounded with the onset of puberty has been almost too much for her.' He sighed. 'I don't suppose adolescence is easy for any child, but Mark was so easy at her age. Of course he had us both.'

'That makes a difference, I guess.' There was a long pause as he searched her eyes.

'You're alone with the twins?' She had said something about that, hadn't she?

Mel nodded now. 'I've been alone with them since they were born.'

'Their father died?' He looked as though he hurt for her. He was that kind of man.

'No.' Mel's voice was calm. 'He walked out on me. He said he never wanted kids, and that's exactly what he meant. As soon as I told him I was pregnant, that was it. He never even saw the twins.'

Peter Hallam looked shocked. He couldn't imagine anyone doing a thing like that. 'How awful for you, Mel. And you must have been very young.'

She nodded with a small smile. It didn't really hurt any more. It was all a dim memory now. A simple fact of her life. 'I was nineteen.'

'My God, how did you manage alone? Did your parents help you out?'

'For a while. I dropped out of Barnard when the girls were born, and eventually I got a job, a whole bunch of jobs' – she smiled – 'and eventually I wound up as a receptionist for a television network in New York, and a typist in the newsroom after that, and the rest is history, I guess.' She looked back on it now with ease, but he sensed what a gruelling climb it had been, and the beauty of it was that it hadn't burned her out. She wasn't bitter or hard, she was quietly realistic about the past, and she had made it in the end. She was at the top of the heap, and she didn't resent the climb.

'You make it sound awfully simple now, but it must have been a nightmare at times.'

'I guess it was.' She sighed, and watched the city slide by. 'It's actually hard to remember it now. It's funny, when you're going through it, there are times when you think you won't survive, but somehow you do, and looking back it never seems quite so hard.' He wondered, as he listened, if one day he would feel that way about losing Anne, but he doubted that now.

'You know, one of the hardest things for me, Mel, is knowing that I'll never be both a mother and a father to my kids. And they need both, especially Pam.'

'You can't expect that much of yourself. You're only you, and you give the best you have to give. More than that you can't do.'

'I guess not.' But he didn't sound convinced. And he glanced over at her again. 'You've never thought of remarrying for the sake of the girls?' It was different for her, he told himself, she didn't have the memory of someone she had loved to overcome, or perhaps she had loved him but there was anger she could hang on to and in that way she was far freer than he, and for her, also, it had been a much longer time.

'I don't think marriage is for me. And I think the girls understand that now. They used to bug me about it a lot, when they were younger. And yeah, there were times when I felt guilty too. But we were better off alone than with the wrong man, and the funny thing is' – she smiled sheepishly at him – 'sometimes I even think I like it better like this. I'm not sure how I'd adjust to someone sharing the girls with me now. Maybe that's an awful thing to admit, but sometimes that's what I feel. I've got very possessive about them I guess.'

'That's understandable if you've been alone with them for all this time.' He sat back against his seat and looked at her.

'Maybe. Jessica and Val are the best things in my life. They're a couple of terrific kids.' She was all mother hen as they exchanged a smile and he got out of the car to open her door. She slid off the seat and looked up at him with a smile. They were in posh Beverly Hills, only two blocks from the illustrious Rodeo Drive. And Melanie looked around. The Bistro Gardens was a beautiful restaurant that seemed to combine art deco and a riot of plants leading to the patio outside, and everywhere she looked were the chic and the rich and the fashionably dressed. Lunch was still in full swing. She saw faces she knew at several tables, movie stars, an ageing television queen, a literary giant who made the bestseller lists every time, and then suddenly as she looked around, she noticed that people were looking at her, she saw two women whisper something to a third, and when the headwaiter approached Peter with a smile, his eyes took in Melanie too.

'Hello, Doctor. Hello, Miss Adams, it's nice to see you again.' She couldn't remember ever seeing him before, but it was obvious that he knew who she was and wanted her to know. She was amused as she followed him to a table beneath an umbrella outside and Peter looked at her with a questioning glance.

'Do people recognise you all the time?'

'Not always. It depends on where I am. I suppose that in a place like this they do. It's their stock in trade.' She glanced at the well-filled tables all around, the Bistro Gardens catered to the moneyed, the chic, the celebrated, the successful, a host of important names. And then she smiled at Peter again. 'It's like being around Dr Hallam at the hospital where everyone was staring at you. It depends on where you are.'

'I suppose.' But he had never noticed people staring at him. He could see a number of people watching Melanie now, and she handled it very well. She didn't seem aware of the curious stares at all.

'This is a wonderful place.' She breathed a sigh in the balmy air, and turned so that she would get the sunshine on her face. It really felt like summer here, and one didn't have the feeling of being trapped in a city, which could happen in New York. She closed her eyes, enjoying the sun. 'This is just right.' And then she opened them again. 'Thank you for bringing me here.'

He sat back in his seat with a smile. 'I didn't think the cafeteria was quite your style.'

'It could be, you know. Most of the time, it is. But that's what makes something like this such a treat. When I'm working I don't have much time to eat, or to bother with the niceties of a delightful place like this.'

'Neither do I.'

They exchanged a grin, and Melanie raised an eyebrow with a smile. 'Do you suppose we both work too hard, Doctor?'

'I suspect we do. But I also suspect we both love what we do. That helps.'

'It sure does.' She looked peaceful as she looked at him, and he felt more comfortable than he had in almost two years.

As she watched him, she realised again that she admired his style. 'Will you go back to the hospital again today?'

'Of course. I want to do some more tests on Pattie Lou.' Mel frowned at his words, thinking of the child.

'Is it going to be very rough for her?'

'We'll make it as easy as we can. Surgery is really her only chance.'

'And you're still going to take her old heart out, repair it and put it back?'

'I think so. We haven't had any suitable donors for her in weeks, we may not in months. There are few enough donors for the adults, for whom it's easier to find matches. On the average we do twenty-five to thirty transplants a year. As you saw from our rounds today, most of what we do is bypass surgery. The rest is very special work and we don't do very much of it, although of course that's all you hear about in the press.'

Mel looked puzzled and took a sip of the white wine the waiter had brought. She found that she was growing fascinated by his work, and regardless of the story she was here to do, she wanted to learn more. 'Why are you using a pig valve?'

'We don't need blood thinners with animal valves. And in her case, that's a real plus. We use animal valves all the time and they don't reject.'

'Could you use the whole animal heart?' He was quick to shake his head.

'Not a chance. It would reject instantly. The human body is a strange and beautiful thing.'

She nodded, thinking of the little black girl. 'I hope you can fix her up.'

'So do I. We've got three others waiting for donors right now too.'

'How do you determine which one gets the first chance?'

'Whoever is the best match. We try to come within thirty pounds from donor to recipient. You can't put the heart of a ninety-pound girl in a two-hundred-pound man, or vice versa. In the first case, it wouldn't support the man's weight, and in the second, it wouldn't fit.'

She shook her head, more than a little in awe at what he did. 'It's an amazing thing you do, my friend.'

'It still amazes me too. Not so much my part in it, but the miracle and mechanics of it all. I love my work, I guess that helps.' She looked carefully at him for a moment, and then glanced around the glamorous crowd at the restaurant and back at him. He was wearing a navy blue linen blazer over his light blue shirt, and she decided he had a casual but distinguished air.

'It feels good to like what you do, doesn't it?' He smiled at her words. Obviously her own work made her feel that way. And then Melanie suddenly found herself thinking about Anne.

'Did your wife work?'

'No.' He shook his head, remembering back to the constant support she'd given him. She was a very different breed of woman from Mel, but he had needed her to be that way at the time.

'No, she didn't. She stayed home and took care of the kids. It made it even harder on them when she died.' But he was curious about Mel now.

'Do you think your daughters resent your work, Mel?'

'I hope not.' She tried to be honest with him. 'Maybe once in a while, but I think they like what I do.' She grinned and looked like a young girl. 'It probably impresses their friends, and they like that.' He smiled too. It even impressed him.

'Wait till my kids hear I had lunch with you.' They both laughed and he paid for their lunch when the bill came. They stood up regretfully, sorry to leave, and to end the comfortable exchange. She stretched as they got in the car.

'I feel so lazy.' She smiled happily at him. 'It feels like summer here.' It was only May, but she would have enjoyed lounging at the pool.

And as he started the car, his own mind drifted ahead. 'We're going to Aspen, as usual this year. What do you do in the summer, Mel?'

'We go to Martha's Vineyard every year.'

'What's that like?'

She squinted her eyes, with her chin in her hand. 'It's a little bit like being a little kid, or playing Huckleberry Finn. You run around in shorts and bare feet all day, the kids hang out at the beach, and the houses look like the kind of place where you'd visit your grandmother, or a great-aunt. I love it because I don't have to impress anyone if I don't want to, I can just lie around and hang out. We go there for two months every year.'

'Can you leave your work for that long?' He seemed surprised.

'It's in my contract now. It used to be one month, but for the last three years it's been two.'

'Not bad. Maybe that's what I need.'

'Two months at the Vineyard?' She looked enchanted at the idea. 'You would adore it, Peter! It's an absolutely wonderful, magical place.'

He smiled at the look on her face, and suddenly noticed the texture of her hair. It shone like satin in the sun and he suddenly wondered to himself how it felt to the touch. 'I meant a contract for my work.' He tried to pull his mind and his eyes away from her shimmering copper hair. And her eyes were of a green he had never seen before, almost emerald with gold flecks. She was a beautiful woman, and he felt something deep within him stir. He drove her back to the hospital then, and tried to keep the conversation centred on Pattie Lou. They had come close enough in the past few hours, almost too close, and it worried him. He was beginning to feel as though he had betrayed Anne by what he felt for Mel. And as they walked back into the hospital, Mel wondered why he was suddenly cool.

Chapter 5

The next morning, Mel left her hotel at exactly six thirty, and drove to Center City, where she found Pattie Lou's mother seated in a vinyl chair in the corridor outside her daughter's room. She was tense and silent, as Mel slipped quietly into the seat beside her. The surgery was scheduled for seven thirty.

'Can I get you a cup of coffee, Pearl?'

'No, thanks.' The soft-spoken woman smiled at Mel, and she looked as though she had the weight of the world on her frail shoulders. 'I want to thank you for everything you've done for us, Mel. We wouldn't even be here if it weren't for you.'

'That's not my doing, that's the network.'

'I'm not so sure of that.' Her eyes met Mel's. 'From what I know, you called Peter Hallam for us, and you got us out here.'

'I just hope he can help her, Pearl.'

'So do I.' The black woman's eyes filled with tears, and she turned away, as Mel gently touched her shoulder.

'Is there anything I can do?' Pearl Jones only shook her head in answer, and dried her eyes. She had already seen Pattie Lou that morning, and now they were prepping her for surgery. It was only ten minutes later when Peter Hallam came down the hall, looking businesslike and wide awake despite the early hour.

'Good morning, Mrs Jones, Mel.' He said nothing more, but disappeared inside Pattie Lou's room. A moment later they heard a soft wail from within and Pearl Jones stiffened visibly in her chair, and spoke almost to herself.

'They said I couldn't go in there while they prep her.' Her hands were shaking and she began to twist a hankie, as Mel firmly took one of her hands in hers.

'She's going to be fine, Pearl. Just hang in there.' Just as she said the words, the nurses wheeled the child out on a stretcher, with Peter Hallam walking beside her. They had already begun the intravenous, and inserted the ominous-looking nose and gastric tube. Pearl steeled herself as she walked quickly to her daughter's side and bent to kiss her. Her eyes were bright with tears, but she spoke in a strong, calm voice to he daughter.

'I love you, baby. I'll see you in a little while.' Peter Hallam smiled at them both and patted Pearl's shoulder, glancing quickly at Mel. For an instant, something rapid and electric passed between them, and then he turned his full attention back to Pattie. She was faintly groggy from the shot they had just given her, and she looked wanly at Peter, Mel, and her mother. Hallam signalled to the nurses, and the stretcher began to roll slowly down the hall, with Peter holding Pattie's hand, and Mel and Pearl walking just behind him. A moment later she was wheeled into the lift to the surgery on the floor above, and Pearl stood staring blankly at the doors, and then turned to Mel, her shoulders shaking. 'Oh, my God.' And then the two women clung to each other for a long moment, and returned to their seats to wait for the news of Pattie.

It was a seemingly endless morning, with silence, spurts of conversation, countless cardboard cups of black coffee, long walks down the corridor, and waiting, waiting ... endless waiting ... until finally Peter Hallam reappeared, and as Mel held her breath, she searched his eyes, as the woman beside her froze in her seat, waiting for the news. But he was smiling as he came towards them, and as he reached Pattie Lou's mother, he beamed.

'The operation went beautifully, Mrs Jones. And Pattie Lou is doing just fine.' She began to tremble again, and suddenly slipped into his arms as she burst into tears.

'Oh my God ... my baby ... my God ...'

'It really went very well.'

'You don't think she'll reject the valve you put in?' She looked worriedly up at him.

Peter Hallam smiled. 'Valves don't reject, Mrs Jones, and the repair work went very well indeed. It's too soon to be absolutely sure of course, but right now everything looks very good.' Mel's knees felt weak as she watched them both, and she fell limply into a chair. They had waited for four and a half hours – the longest in her life. She had really come to care about the little girl. She smiled up at Peter then, and he met her eyes. He seemed ebullient and jubilant as he took a seat beside her.

'I wish you could have watched.'

'So do I.' But he had forbidden her to, and he had been adamant about not wanting a camera crew there.

'Maybe another time, Mel.' He was slowly opening all his private doors to her. 'What about doing our interview this afternoon?' He had promised to do it after the surgery on Pattie Lou, but he hadn't said how soon.

'I'll line up the crew.' And then she looked suddenly concerned. 'But are you sure that's not too much for you?'

He grinned. 'Hell, no.' He looked like a boy who had just won a football game. It made up for all the other times. And Mel just hoped that Pattie Lou didn't begin to fade and dash all their hopes again. Her mother had just gone to call her husband in New York, and Mel and Peter were left alone. 'Mel, it really went very well.'

'I'm so glad.'

'So am I.' He glanced at his watch then. 'I'd better do rounds, then I'll call my office, but I could be free for you by three. How would that be for the interview?'

'I'll see how fast the camera crew can be here.' They had been waiting in the wings for two days, and she was pretty sure it could all be arranged. 'I don't think it'll be a problem though. Where do you want to do it?'

He thought for a minute. 'My office?'

'That sounds fine. They'll probably come at two and start to set up.'

'How long do you think it'll take?'

'As long as you can spare. Does two hours sound like too much?'

'That's fine.'

She thought of something else then. 'What about Pattie Lou? Any chance we can get a few minutes on her today?'

He frowned and then shook his head. 'I don't think so, Mel. Maybe a couple of minutes tomorrow though, if she does as well as I think she will. The crew will have to wear sterile gowns, and it'll have to be short.'

'That's fine.' Mel jotted down a few quick notes on a pad she always kept in her bag. She would get an interview with Pearl Jones that afternoon, then Peter, then Pattie Lou the following morning, and the camera crew could shoot some more general footage the following day, and that would wrap it up. She could catch the 'red-eye' flight to New York the following night. End of story. And maybe in a month or so, they could do a more lengthy interview with Pattie Lou, as a follow-up, about how she had felt, how she was doing by then. It was premature to think of that. The crux of the story could be done now and it was going to be powerful stuff to show on the evening news. She looked up at Peter then. 'I'd like to do a special on you one day.'

He smiled benevolently, still basking in their success with the child. 'Maybe one day that could be arranged. I've never gone in for that kind of thing much.'

'I think it's important for people to know what transplants and heart surgery are all about.'

'So do I. But it has to be done in the right way, at the right time.' She nodded in agreement and he patted her hand as he stood up. 'See you in my office around two, Mel.'

'We won't bother you until three. Just tell your secretary where you want us to set up, and we will.'

'Fine.' He hurried to the nurses' station then, picked up some charts, and a moment later he disappeared. Mel sat alone in the hall, thinking back on the long wait they'd all been through and feeling relief sweep over her. She made her way to a bank of pay phones then, and waved at Pearl, crying and laughing in an adjoining phone booth.

She got the camera crew set up for an interview with Pearl at one o'clock. They could do it in a corner of the hospital lobby, so she wouldn't have to be far from Pattie Lou. Mel looked at her watch, and mentally worked it all out. At two o'clock they would go over to the complex where Peter's offices were, and set up for the interview with him. She didn't expect any problem with the interviews, and she began to think about going home to the twins the following night. It had been a good story, and she would have only been gone for three days, though it felt more like three weeks.

She went downstairs to wait for the crew. They arrived promptly and interviewed a deeply grateful and highly emotional Pearl Jones. The interview went very well, sketched out beforehand by Mel as she gobbled a sandwich and gulped a cup of tea. And at two o'clock they moved on, and were ready for Peter promptly at three. The office where he sat for the interview was lined with medical books on two walls, and panelled in a warm rose-coloured wood. He sat behind a massive desk, and spoke earnestly to Mel about the pitfalls of what he did, the dangers, the realistic fears, and the hope they were offering people as well. He was candid about both the risks and the odds, but since the people they did transplants on had no other hope anyway, the risks almost always seemed worthwhile, and the odds were better than none at all.

'And what about the people who choose not to take that chance?' She spoke in a soft voice, hoping that the question wasn't too personal and wouldn't cause him too much pain.

He spoke softly too. 'They die.' There was a moment's pause and he went back to talking specifically about Pattie Lou. He drew diagrams to explain what had to be done, and he seemed very much in command as he described the surgery to both the camera and Mel.

It was five o'clock when they finally stopped, and Peter seemed relieved. It had been a long day for him, and he was tired by the two-hour interview.

'You do that very well, my friend.' She liked the term he used, and smiled as the cameramen turned off the lights. They were pleased with what they'd got too. He presented well, and Mel instinctively knew that they had got exactly what she needed for the extended piece for the news. It was to be done as a fifteen-minute special report, and she was excited now about seeing what they had on tape. Peter Hallam had been both eloquent and remarkably at ease.

'I'd say you're pretty good at that stuff too. You handled it very well.'

'I was afraid I'd get too technical or too involved.' He knit his brows and she shook her head.

'It was just right.' As had been, in its own way, the interview with Pearl. She had cried and laughed, and then soberly explained what the child's life had been like for the past nine years. But if the surgery was as successful as he thought it would be, Peter's prognosis for her was very good. And viewers' hearts would undeniably go out to her as Mel's had, and Peter's too. Sick children were impossible to resist anyway, and Pattie Lou had a magical kind of light to her, perhaps because she had been so sick for so long, or maybe that was just the way she was. And over the past nine years, a great deal of love had been lavished on her.

Peter watched Mel as she instructed the crew, and there was frank admiration in his eyes, much as there had been in hers whenever she watched him. But his train of thought was interrupted as one of his nurses came in. She spoke to him in a low voice, and he immediately frowned, just as Mel turned, and she felt her heart sink. She couldn't stop herself from walking toward them and asking if something had happened to Pattie Lou.

But Peter was quick to shake his head. 'No, she's fine. One of my associates saw her an hour ago, this is something else. Another transplant case just came in. A red hot. She needs a donor now, and we don't have anything for her.' He was instantly enveloped by the new problem to solve. He glanced quickly at Mel. 'I have to go.' And then, on impulse he turned to Mel. 'Do you want to come?'

'To see the patient with you?' She was pleased that he would ask, and he was quick to nod.

'Sure. Just don't explain who you are. I can always explain you as visiting medical personnel from a hospital in the East.' He smiled briefly. 'Unless they recognise you. I just don't want the family to get upset, or think that I'm exploiting the case.' It was one of the reasons why he had always been gun-shy about publicity.

'Sure. That's fine.' She grabbed her handbag, said a few words to the crew, and hurried out to his car with him. And moments later, they were back at Center City, on the sixth floor, hurrying down the hall to the new patient's room.

As Peter opened the door for Mel, she was startled at what she saw. A remarkably beautiful twenty-nine-year-old girl.

She had pale, pale blonde hair and huge sad eyes, the most delicate milky blue-white skin that Melanie had ever seen, and she seemed to take in each one of them as they were introduced, as though she had to remember each face, each pair of eyes. And then she smiled, and suddenly she seemed younger than she was, and Melanie's heart went out to her. What was this lovely girl doing in this terrifying place? She already had a thick bandage on one arm, covering where they had had to cut down to reach her veins to take extensive amounts of blood, and the other arm was black and blue from an intravenous she had received only a few days before. And yet somehow one forgot about all that as one listened to her speak. She had a soft lilting voice, and it was obviously hard to breathe, yet she seemed happy to see them all, said something funny to Mel when they were introduced, and she bantered easily with Peter as they all stood around. Melanie suddenly found herself praying for a heart for her. How could all these people be in such desperate need, and what was wrong with the world to strike all these people down, dying slowly with their weak hearts, while others dug ditches, climbed mountains, went dancing, skied? Why had they been so cheated, and while still so young. It didn't seem fair. And yet there was no resentment in the girl's face. Her name was Marie Dupret, and she explained that her parents had been French.

Peter smiled. 'It's a beautiful name.' But more than that, she was a beautiful girl.

'Thank you, Dr Hallam.'

And on those words, Mel noticed that she had a slight Southern drawl, and a moment later Marie mentioned that she had grown up in New Orleans, but she had been in LA now for almost five years. 'I'd like to go back to N'Orleans someday' – the way she said the words delighted the ear as she smiled up at Peter again – 'after the good doctor here patches me up.' And then she looked searchingly at him as her smile faded and one began to glimpse her worry and pain. 'How long do you think that will be?' It was a question no one had an answer to, save God, as they all knew, including Marie.

'We hope soon.' Just the tone of his voice was reassuring, and he went on to reassure her about other things, and to explain to her about what they would be doing to her that day. She didn't seem frightened about the endless tests, but she kept wanting to come back to the big questions again, her enormous blue eyes turned up to him in a pleading way, like a prisoner on death row, seeking a pardon for a crime she did not commit. 'You're going to be very busy for the next few days, Marie.' He smiled again and patted her arm. 'I'll stop in again to see you tomorrow morning, Marie, and if there's anything else that comes to mind, you can ask me then.' She thanked him, and he and Mel left the room, but once again Melanie was struck with the enormity of each circumstance, the terrors that each one faced, alone, in the end. She wondered who Marie would have to hold her hand, and she somehow sensed that the young woman was alone in life. If not, wouldn't her husband or her family have been there? In other rooms there was evidence of spouses or at least friends, but not here, which was why she seemed so much more dependent on Peter than the others had, or perhaps it was because she was new. But as they walked slowly down the hall, somehow Melanie felt as though they were abandoning her. And Mel looked sadly up at Peter as they went downstairs.

'What'll happen to her?'

'We have to find a donor. And soon.' He seemed preoccupied as well as concerned, and then he remembered Mel. 'I'm glad you came along.'

'So am I. She seems like a nice girl.' He nodded, to him they all were, the men, the women, the children. And they were all so desperately dependent on him. It would have frightened him if he had dwelled on it too much. But he seldom did. He just did what he could for them. Although sometimes there was damn little he could do. Mel had wondered for days how he bore the burden of it. With so many lives with so little hope in his hands, and yet there was nothing dismal about the man. He seemed almost a vehicle of hope himself, and once again Melanie was aware of how much she admired him.

'It's been quite a day, hasn't it, Mel?' He smiled at her as they walked outside, still side by side.

'I don't know how you do this every day. I'd be dead in two years. No' – she smiled up at him – 'make that two weeks. My God, Peter, the responsibility, the strain. You go from operating room to sickbed to office and back again, and these aren't just people with bunions, each one is a matter of life and death ...' She thought of Marie Dupret again. '... like that girl.'

'That's what makes it worthwhile. When you win.' They both thought simultaneously of Pattie Lou, the last report of the day had still been good.

'Yeah, but it's incredibly rough on you. And on top of everything else, you gave me a two-hour interview.'

'I enjoyed that.' He smiled, but his mind was still half engaged with Marie. He had checked the charts, and his colleagues had her well in hand. The main issue was whether or not they would find a donor in time, and there was nothing he could do about that, except pray. Mel found herself thinking of that too.

'Do you think you'll find a donor for Marie?'

'I don't know the answer to that. I hope we do. She doesn't have much time to spare.' None of them did. And that was the worst of it. They sat waiting for someone else to die and give them the gift of life, without which they were doomed.

'I hope so too.' She took a deep breath of the spring air and glanced over at her rented car. 'Well' – she stuck out her hand – 'I guess that's it for today. For me anyway. I hope you get some rest after a day like this.'

'I always do when I go home to my kids.'

She laughed openly at that. 'I don't know how you can say that, if they're anything like mine. Invariably, after an absolutely bitching eighteen-hour day, I crawl home, and Val is torn between two boys she absolutely has to discuss with me, and Jess has a fifty-page science project I have to read that night. They both talk to me at once, and I explode and feel like a total bitch. That's the hard part of being alone, there's no one else to share the load, no matter how tired you are when you get home.'

He smiled. It had a familiar ring. 'There's some truth to what you say, Mel. At my house, it's mostly Matt and Pam. Mark is pretty independent by now.'

'How old is he?'

'Almost eighteen.' And then he suddenly had an idea. He looked at Melanie with a small smile as they stood in the parking lot. It was six fifteen. 'How about coming home with me now? You could have a quick swim, and eat dinner with us.'

'I couldn't do that.' But she was touched by the thought.

'Why not? It's no fun going back to a hotel room, Mel. Why not come home?

We don't eat dinner late, and you could be home by nine o'clock.' She wasn't sure why, but she was tempted by the idea. 'Don't you think your kids would rather have you to themselves?'

'No. I think they'd be very excited to meet you.'

'Don't overestimate that.' But suddenly, the idea really appealed to her. 'You're really not too tired?'

'Not at all. Come on, Mel, it would be fun.'

'It would for me.' She smiled. 'Shall I follow you in my car?'

'Why not just leave it here?'

'Then you'll have to drive me back. Or I could take a cab.'

'I'll drive you. Then I can have another look at Pattie Lou.'

'Don't you ever stop?' She smiled as she slid into his car, pleased to be going home with him.

'Nope. And neither do you.' He looked as pleased as she as they pulled out of the parking lot and headed for Bel-Air.

Melanie leaned back against the seat with a sigh as they drove through the huge black wrought-iron gates leading into Bel-Air.

'It's so pleasant here.' It was like driving around in the country as the road swooped and turned, giving glimpses of secluded but palatial homes.

'That's why I like it here. I don't know how you can stand New York.'

'The excitement makes it all worthwhile.' She grinned.

'Do you really like it, Mel?'

'I love it. I love my house, my job, the city, my friends. I'm sold on the place, and I really don't think I could live anyplace else.' And as she said the words, she suddenly realised that it wouldn't be so bad after all to go home the next day. New York was where she belonged, however much she liked LA and admired him. And when he glanced at her again, he saw that she looked more relaxed, and with that he made one final left turn, into a well-manicured drive, which led to a large, beautiful, French-style house, surrounded by neatly trimmed trees and flower beds. It looked like something on a French postcard and Melanie looked around in surprise. It wasn't at all what she'd expected of him. Somehow she had thought he would live in something more rustic, or a ranch house. But this was actually very elegant, she noticed as he stopped the car.

'It's beautiful, Peter.' She looked up at the mansard roof, and waited to see children but there were none in sight.

'You look surprised.' He laughed.

'No.' She blushed. 'It just doesn't look like you.'

And then he smiled again. 'It wasn't at first. The design was Anne's. We built it just before Matthew was born.'

'It's really a magnificent house, Peter.' It was, and now she was seeing a whole other side of him.

'Well, come on.' He opened his door and looked over his shoulder for one last instant. 'Let's go in, I'll introduce you to the kids. They're probably all around the pool with fourteen friends. Brace yourself.' And with that they both stepped out of the car, and Melanie looked around. It was so totally different from her town house in New York, but it was fun to see how he lived. She followed him inside, with only a slight feeling of trepidation about meeting his children, wondering if they would be terribly different from her twins.

Chapter 6

Peter unlocked the front door and stepped into a front hall whose floor was inlaid with black and white marble in a formal French diamond pattern, with crystal sconces on the wall. There was a black marble console table with gold Louis XVI legs and on it was set a magnificent crystal bowl filled with freshly cut flowers that sent a spring fragrance into the air as Melanie looked around. It was somehow so totally different from what she had expected. He seemed so relaxed and so unassuming in his ways, that she had never imagined him in a home furnished in elaborate French antiques. But indeed this was. Not in a vulgur, opulent way, but in an obviously expensive way, and as she glimpsed the living room, she saw that there, too, was more of the same, the fabrics on the delicate fauteuils were mostly cream-coloured brocades. The walls were beautifully done in several shades of cream, with the mouldings in lighter shades and the detailing on the ceiling intricately highlighted in beige and white and a soft creamy grey. There was still a look of surprise on her face as she looked around and Peter led her into his study and invited her to sit down. Here, everything was in deep rich reds, with antique English chairs, a long leather couch, and hunting scenes on the walls, all handsomely framed.

'You look so surprised, Mel.' He was amused and she laughed and shook her head.

'No, I just saw you in something very different from this. But it's a magnificent home.'

'Anne went to the Sorbonne for two years, and then stayed on in France for two years after that. I think it made a permanent impression on her taste.' He looked around, as though seeing her again. 'But I can't complain. The house is less formal upstairs. I'll give you a tour in a little while.' He sat down at his desk, checked the messages on the pad, spun around to face her, and then clapped a hand to his head. 'Damn. I forgot to have you stop at your hotel and pick up a bathing suit.' And then he squinted as he looked at her. 'Maybe Pam can help out. Would you like to swim?' It was amazing. They had spent the whole day at the hospital and in the interview, he had operated on Pattie Lou, and suddenly they were talking about taking a swim, as though they'd done nothing else all day. It was mind boggling, and yet somehow everything seemed normal here. Maybe that was the way he survived it all, she thought.

Peter stood up and led the way outside to an enormous stone patio surrounding a large oval pool, and here Mel felt more at home. There were at least a dozen teenagers and one little boy running around, dripping wet, shrieking at the top of his lungs. Remarkably, she hadn't been aware of the noise before but she was now, and she began to laugh as she watched their antics and the boys showed off, pushing each other in, playing water polo at one end, riding on each other's shoulders and falling in. Several well-endowed young girls watched. Peter stood to one side, getting splashed as he clapped his hands, but no one heard, and suddenly the little boy ran up and threw his arms around Peter's legs, leaving his wet imprint where his arms had been, as Peter looked down at him with a grin.

'Hi, Dad. Come on in.'

'Hi, Matt. Can I change first?'

'Sure.' The two exchanged a warm look that passed only between them. He was an adorable impish-looking child, with fair hair bleached by the sun.

'I'd like to introduce you to a friend of mine.' He turned to Mel, and she approached. The little boy looked just like him, and when he smiled, she saw that he had lost both front teeth. He was the cutest child she had ever seen. 'Matthew, this is my friend, Melanie Adams. Mel, this is Matt.' The child frowned and Peter grinned. 'Excuse me, Matthew Hallam.'

'How do you do.' He proffered a wet hand, and she formally shook his, remembering briefly when the twins were that age. It had been ten years before, but there were times when it seemed only a moment ago.

'Where's your sister, Matt?' Peter looked around. There seemed to be only Mark's friends around the pool, but he had been unable to catch the attention of his eldest son, who was throwing two girls in at once, and then dunking another friend. They were having a grand time as Mel watched.

'She's in her room.' A look of disgust crossed Matthew's face. 'Probably on the phone.'

'On a day like this?' Peter looked surprised. 'Has she been inside all day?'

'Pretty much.' He rolled his eyes then, and looked at both his father and Mel. 'She's so dumb.' He had a rough time with Pam, as Peter knew. At times they all did, but she was going through a difficult stage, particularly in a male family.

'I'll go inside and see what she's up to.' Peter looked down at him. 'You be careful out here, please.'

'I'm okay.'

'Where's Mrs Hahn?'

'She just went inside, but I'm okay, Dad. Honest.' And as though to illustrate the point, he took a running leap into the pool, splashing them both from head to foot. Melanie jumped back with a burst of laughter, and Peter looked at her apologetically as Matthew surfaced again.

'Matthew, will you please not ...' But the little head disappeared beneath the surface of the pool and he swam like a little fish underwater to where the others were, just as Mark caught sight of them and gave a shout and a wave. He had his father's build, his height and grace and long limbs.

'Hi, Dad!' Peter pointed at his youngest son, swimming towards Mark, and the older boy gave an understanding nod, and caught the child in his arms as he surfaced and said something to him, sending him towards the edge of the game, to where he wouldn't get hurt. Peter decided that all was well, and as they walked back into the house, he turned to Mel.

'Are you soaking wet?' She was, but she didn't mind. It was a relief from the seriousness of the earlier part of the day.

'I'll dry off.'

'Sometimes I'm sorry as hell that I put in that pool. Half the neighbourhood spends their weekends here.'

'It must be great for the kids.'

He nodded. 'It is. But I don't very often get a swim, except when they're in school. I come home for lunch once in a while, when I have time.'

'And when's that?' She was teasing him now. It suddenly felt as though everyone was in a lighthearted mood as he laughed.

'About once a year.'

'That's what I thought.' And then she remembered Matt and the toothless smile. 'I think I'm in love with your little boy.'

'He's a good kid.' Peter looked pleased, and then thought of his older boy. 'So is Mark. He's so responsible, it's frightening sometimes.'

'I have one like that too. Jessica, the oldest twin.'

'Which one's that?' Peter looked intrigued. 'The one that looks like you?'

'How did you remember that?' Mel was surprised.

'I remember everything, Mel. It's important in my field. A little forgotten detail, a hint, a clue. It helps when you're constantly balancing life against death. I can't afford to forget anything.' It was his first open admission to his extraordinary skill, and Mel watched him with interest again as she followed him into the house, into a large sunny room filled with large white wicker chairs, wicker couches, a stereo, an enormous TV, and ten-foot palms that swept the ceiling with their fronds. It looked like a nice room to be in on a sunny day. And here suddenly, Melanie saw half a dozen pictures of Anne scattered around in silver frames, playing tennis, with Peter in a photograph in front of the Louvre, with a tiny baby, and one with all the children in front of the Christmas tree. It was as though all at once everything stopped, and Melanie found herself mesmerised by her face, her blonde hair, her big blue eyes. She was an attractive woman, with a long, lanky athletic frame. And in some ways she and Peter looked alike. In the photographs, she seemed like the perfect mate for him. And Melanie realised suddenly that Peter was standing at her side, looking down at one of the photographs too.

'It's hard to believe she's gone.' His voice was soft.

'It must be.' Melanie wasn't sure what to say. 'But in some ways, she lives on. In your heart, in your mind, through the children she left.' They both knew that wasn't the same thing, but it was all that was left of her. That and this house, which was so much to her taste. Melanie looked around the room again. It was an interesting contrast to the formal living room and study that she had seen when she came in. 'What do you use this room for, Peter?' Melanie was curious. It was so much a woman's room.

'The kids use it to hang around in. Even though it's mostly white, there isn't too much damage they can do in here.' Melanie noticed a wicker desk then, looking out at the pool. 'She used to use this a lot. I spend most of my time at home in my den, or upstairs.' And then he gestured towards the hall. 'Come on, I'll show you around. We'll see if we can find Pam.'

Upstairs everything was formal and French again. The hall floors were done in a pale beige travertine, with matching console tables at either end, and a beautiful French brass chandelier. And here there was another smaller but equally formal sitting room done in soft blues. There were velvets and silks, and a marble fire-place, and wall sconces and a crystal chandelier, pale blue silk curtains with pale yellow and blue trim, tied back with narrow brass arms that allowed one a view of the pool. Beyond it was a little office done in dusty pinks, but Peter frowned as they passed that room and Melanie instantly sensed that it was unused. Not only that, but that it had been Anne's.

And beyond that was a handsome library done in dark greens. There were walls and walls of books, a small mountain of chaos on the desk, and on one wall an oil portrait of Anne, and double French doors leading into their bedroom, which Peter now slept in alone. It was all done in beige silk, with French commodes, a beautiful chaise longue, and the same rich curtains and sconces and another beautiful chandelier. But there was something about the place that made one want to take off one's clothes and dance around, and defy the formality of it all. It was almost too much, no matter how beautiful it was, and the more Melanie saw, the more she felt that it just didn't look like him.

They took another staircase upstairs then, and on this floor everything was brightly coloured and fun, and the open doors showed three large, sunny children's rooms. The floor of Matt's was littered with toys, Mark's half-closed door showed total chaos within, and the third door was ajar and all Mel could see was a huge white canopied bed, and a girl's back as she lay on her side on the floor near the bed. At the sound of their footsteps in the hall, she turned and stood up, whispering something into the phone and then hung up. Melanie was astonished at how tall and grown up she looked. If this was his middle child, it was difficult to believe that she was just fourteen. She was long and lanky and blonde, with a shaft of wheat-coloured hair like Val's, and big wistful blue eyes. But most of all she looked like the photographs of Anne that Mel had just seen.

'What are you doing inside?' Peter searched her eyes and Mel felt them both grow tense.

'I wanted to call a friend.'

'You could have used the phone at the pool.'

She didn't answer him at first and then she shrugged. 'So?'

He ignored the remark and turned to Mel. 'I'd like you to meet my daughter, Pam. Pam, this is Melanie Adams, the newswoman from New York I told you about.'

'I know who she is.' Pamela didn't extend a hand at first, but Mel did, and she shook it at last. Her father had begun to seethe. He never wanted it to be like this between them, but she always did something to upset him, to be rude to his friends, to make a point of not cooperating when there was no reason for her not to. Why, dammit, *why*? They were all unhappy that Anne had died, but why did she have to take it out on him? She had for the last year and a half, and was even worse now. He told himself that it was the age, a passing phase, but sometimes he wasn't so sure.

'I was wondering if you could lend Mel a bathing suit, Pam. She left hers at the hotel.'

There was a fraction of a moment of hesitation again. 'Sure. I guess I could. She's' – she hesitated on the word, Mel was by no means large, but she wasn't as rail thin as Pam – 'she's bigger than me though.' And there was something else too, a look that had passed between them that Pam didn't like. Or more exactly the way her father looked at Mel.

And Mel quickly understood. She smiled gently at the girl. 'It's all right if you'd rather not.'

'No, that's okay.' Her eyes searched Melanie's face. 'You don't look the same as on TV.' There was no smile in the girl.

'Don't I?' She smiled at the slightly uncomfortable but very attractive young girl. She looked nothing like Peter, and there was still an undefined childishness about her face, despite the long legs and full bust, and body that had already outstripped her chronological age. 'My daughters always say I look more "grown up" on TV.'

'Yeah. Sort of. More serious.'

'I think that's what they mean.'

The three of them stood in the pretty white room, as Pam continued to stare at Melanie, as though looking for an answer to something in her face. 'How old are your daughters?'

'They'll be sixteen in July.'

'Both of them?' Pam was confused.

'They're twins.' Melanie smiled.

'They are? That's neat! Do they look alike?'

'Not at all. They're fraternal twins.'

'I thought that just meant they were boys.'

Mel smiled again and Pam blushed. 'That means they're not identical twins, but it is a confusing term.'

'What are they like?' She was fascinated by Mel's twins.

'Like sixteen-year-old girls.' Mel laughed. 'They keep me on my toes. One's a redhead like me, and the other one is a blonde. Their names are Jessica and Valerie, and they love to go out to dances and they have lots of friends.'

'Where do you live?' Peter was watching the exchange intently but he said nothing at all.

'In New York. In a little town house.' She smiled at Peter then. 'It's very different from this.' And then she turned back to Pam. 'You have a beautiful house, and it must be nice to have a pool.'

'It's okay.' She looked unenthused as she shrugged. 'It's either full of my brother's obnoxious friends, or Matthew's peeing in it.' She sounded annoyed and Mel laughed but Peter was not amused.

'Pam! That's not something to say, and it's not true.'

'It is so. The little brat did it an hour ago, as soon as Mrs Hahn went inside. Right from the edge of the pool too. At least he could do it while he's swimming around.' Mel had to suppress the laughter she felt and Peter blushed.

'I'll say something to Matt.'

'Mark's friends probably do it too.' It was obvious that she didn't enjoy either of the boys. She went to hunt for a suit for Mel, and came back with a white one-piece bathing suit she thought might fit. Mel thanked her and looked around again.

'You really have a lovely room, Pam.'

'My mom did it for me just before ...' Her words trailed off and there was something desperately sad in her eyes and then she looked at Peter defiantly. 'It's the only room in this house that's all mine.' It seemed an odd thing to say and Mel felt for her. She seemed so unhappy and so much at odds with them all. It was as though she couldn't show them her pain, only the anger she felt instead, as though they were all responsible for taking Anne from her.

'It must be a nice room to share with your friends.' Mel found herself thinking of her own girls, and their friends who sat around on the floor of their rooms, listening to records, talking about boys, laughing and giggling and sharing secrets with each other, which they eventually always shared with Mel. They seemed very different from this awkward, hostile girl, with the body of a woman and the mind of a child. It was obviously a very difficult time for her, and Mel could see that Peter had a lot on his hands. No wonder he tried to come home early every day. With a six-year-old child hungering for love, a teenager of the older boy's age to watch over, and an adolescent girl as unhappy as this one was, the household needed more than just a housekeeper's care, it needed a father and a mother too. She understood now why Peter felt such a desperate need to be there for them all, and why he felt at times that he was inadequate to the task. Not that he was, but they all needed a great deal from him, and even something more than that, at least this child did. Melanie found herself wanting to reach out to her, to hold her close, to tell her that eventually everything would be all right. And as though sensing Mel's thoughts, Pam suddenly stepped back from her.

'Well, I'll see you downstairs in a while.' It was her invitation to them to leave. And Peter walked slowly to the door.

'Are you coming downstairs, Pam?'

'Yeah.' But she didn't sound too sure.

'I don't think you ought to spend the afternoon in your room.' He sounded firm but she looked as though she were inclined to argue with him, and Melanie didn't envy him his role with her. She wasn't an easy child to deal with, at least not at the present time. 'Will you be down soon?'

'Yes!' She looked more belligerent still and Mel and Peter left the room. She followed him back downstairs to his room and he opened a door across the hall from him, to reveal a pretty blue and white guest room.

'You can change in here, Mel.' He didn't say anything to her about Pam, and when she came out again ten minutes later, he looked more relaxed. He led the way back downstairs to the big white wicker garden room. There was a refrigerator concealed behind white lacquered doors and he took out two cans of beer and handed one to her, reached for two glasses from a shelf with one hand and then waved for her to sit down. 'We might as well wait a few more minutes for the kids to wear themselves out.' They were already beginning to leave the pool. Melanie noticed then how good-looking Peter was in his dark blue swimming trunks and a French T-shirt and bare feet. He didn't even look like the same man she had interviewed for the past two days, but rather like someone else. Just an ordinary mortal now. She smiled the thought to herself as he watched her eyes, and then his face sobered as he thought of the child upstairs. 'Pam isn't an easy child. She was while her mother was alive. But now she runs the gamut from being intensely possessive of me to hating us all. She thinks nobody understands what she's going through, and most of the time these days she acts as though she's living in an enemy camp.' He sighed with a tired smile as he sipped his beer. 'It's hard on the boys at times too.'

'I think she probably just needs a lot of love from all of you, especially you.'

'I know. But she blames everything on us. And well ...' He seemed embarrassed to say what was on his mind. 'Sometimes she makes herself difficult to love. I understand it, but the boys don't. At least not all the time.' It was the first time that he had admitted to Mel what a problem he had with her.

'She'll come round. Give her time.'

Peter sighed again. 'It's been almost two years.' But Melanie didn't dare say what she thought to him. It had been almost two years, and yet Anne's photographs were still everywhere in sight, and Mel sensed nothing in the place had been touched since Anne died, and Peter himself acted as though she had only died that week. How could the child be expected to adjust if he himself had not? He was still reproaching himself for what he hadn't been able to convince Anne to do, as though any of it could be changed now. Mel said nothing, but he didn't avert his eyes when she looked at him. 'I know. You're right. I'm still hanging on too.'

'Maybe when you close the door to the past, she will too.' Mel spoke in a gentle voice, and without thinking, Peter's eyes drifted to the nearest photograph of Anne, and Mel suddenly asked something she had promised herself not to say. 'Why don't you move?'

'From here?' He looked shocked. 'Why?'

'To give everyone a fresh start. It might be a relief to all of you.' But he was quick to shake his head.

'I don't think it would. I think it would be more disruptive than helpful, to be in a new house. At least we're all comfortable and happy here.'

'Are you?' Mel didn't look convinced and she knew that he was hanging on, and so was Pam, and she wondered if the others were too. Just as the thought crossed her mind, a stocky woman in a white uniform entered the room, and looked at them both, particularly Mel. She had a face that was well worn by time, and her hands were gnarled from long years of hard work, and yet her eyes were bright and alive and she seemed to take everything in.

'Good afternoon, Doctor.' She seemed to say 'doctor' as though she were saying 'God', and Mel smiled. She knew instantly who she was, and Peter stood to introduce Mel to her. She was the invaluable housekeeper he had spoken of before, the precious Mrs Hahn, who shook Mel's hand with an almost brutal shake, her eyes combing the pretty redhead in the borrowed white bathing suit she instantly recognised as Pam's. She knew everything that happened in the house, who came, who went, where they went, and why. She was particularly careful about Pam. There had already been enough trouble with her the year of her mother's death, with that business of scarcely eating a mouthful of food for six months, and then making herself throw up after every meal for months after that. But now at least that problem was in control, and she was much better than she had been. But Hilda Hahn knew that the girl had had a hard time, and she needed a woman's eye on her, which was why Mrs Hahn was there. She looked Mel over carefully now, and decided that she looked like a nice woman after all. She knew who she was, and that she was doing a story on the doctor's work, but she had expected her to be somewhat arrogant and she didn't seem to be. 'It's nice to meet you, ma'am.' She was both formal and tight-lipped and did not return Melanie's smile, as Mel almost laughed thinking of the contrast to Raquel. In fact, just about everything was different about their two homes, from their maids to their decor, to their kids, and yet she felt as though she had a great deal in common with him. It was funny how differently they lived. 'Would you care for some iced tea?' She looked disapprovingly at their beers, and Mel felt like a wayward child.

'No, thank you very much.' She smiled again, to no avail, and with a curt nod, Hilda Hahn disappeared to her own domain behind the swinging doors that led to the kitchen and breakfast room, pantry, and her small apartment in the rear. She was extremely comfortable here. When Mrs Hallam had built the house she had promised Hilda her own suite of rooms, and that was what she had now. Mrs Hallam had been a fine woman, she always said, and would say so again, many times, and did later on in plain hearing of Mel, before she brought the dinner in. Melanie had noticed Pam's eyes seem to glaze over as Hilda mentioned her mother's name. It was as though they were all still fighting to recuperate. One almost wanted to put away the pictures for them, pack them up, and move them to another house. They were all still so devoted to her, as though they were waiting for her to come home, and it made you want to tell them that she never would. They had to get on with their lives, every one of them. The two boys seemed better adjusted to their mother's death. Matthew had been so young when she died that his memories of her were already dim, and he climbed willingly into Mel's lap after they had a swim, and she told him about the twins. Like Pam, he was fascinated by the idea of twins and wanted to know what they looked like. Mark seemed like a bright easygoing boy of seventeen; there was a look of greater wisdom in his eyes than his years would suggest, and yet he seemed happy as he chatted with both Peter and Mel. He only got annoyed when Pam arrived and complained that his friends were still hanging around the pool. A fight between them seemed imminent until Peter stepped in.

'All right, you two. We have a guest. Several in fact.' He glanced severely at Pam, and then his eyes took in Mark's remaining friends. There were only two boys and one girl left and they were sitting quietly on the cement nearby chatting and drying their hair. But it was as though Pam resented anyone in her home, except Peter and the boys and Mrs Hahn. She had solved the problem of Mel by almost totally ignoring her since she'd arrived at the pool, except for furtive, curious glances from time to time, mainly when Peter was talking to Mel. It was as though she wanted to be sure there was nothing special going on, but some instinct deep within told her that danger lurked there.

'Isn't that right, Pam?' Peter had been talking about her school, but she had been staring intently at Mel and hadn't heard what he said.

'Huh?'

'I said that the athletics programme there is outstanding, and you won two awards for track events last year. And they have access to some fabulous stables too.' Again, it was very different from the school in which she had her girls, which was very much a sophisticated urban school. The life-style in LA was much more geared to the outdoors than what they had back East.

'Do you like your school, Pam?' Mel gently spoke to her.

'It's okay. I like my friends.'

At that, Mark rolled his eyes, quick to show that he disapproved, and Pam took the bait at once. 'What's that supposed to mean?'

'It means that you hang around with a bunch of dumb uptight, anorexic girls.' It was a word that still made her scream.

'I am not anorexic, damn you!' She jumped to her feet, her voice shrill, and Peter began to look tired.

'Stop it, you two!' And then he addressed Mark. 'That was unnecessarily cruel.'

Mark nodded, subdued. 'I'm sorry.' He knew that the very word was now taboo, but he still wasn't convinced that she was totally cured. She looked unnaturally thin to him, no matter what she and her father said. He looked apologetically at Mel and sauntered off to talk to his friends, and Pam went back into the house, followed by Matthew who was in search of something to eat. For a long moment, Peter sat quietly staring into the pool and then he turned his eyes to Mel.

'Not exactly a peaceful home scene, I guess.' He looked hurt by his children's actions and words, as though he held himself responsible for all their turmoil and pain. 'I'm sorry if it was awkward for you, Mel.'

'Not at all. It isn't always smooth sailing with mine either.' Although she couldn't even remember the last time she'd seen the twins have a fight, but this family still seemed in crisis and Pam seemed like a very unhappy girl.

He sighed and laid his head back against the chair, looking out at the pool. 'I suppose eventually they'll all settle down. Mark will be going away to college next year.' But the problem was not Mark, as they both knew, it was Pam. And she wasn't going anywhere for a long time. Peter glanced at Mel again then. 'Pam took her mother's death the hardest of all.' That much was easy to see, but Peter had taken it harder still, and still was. And what he needed, she sensed, was a woman to replace Anne, and for him to share his burdens with. He needed it as much for him as for the kids. It hurt to think of him so much alone. He was intelligent and attractive, capable and strong, he had a lot to offer anyone. And as she sat there beside him, she smiled to herself, thinking of Raquel and the girls. She could almost hear them ask: 'What about you, Mom? ... Was he cute? ... Why didn't you go out with him? ...' He didn't ask. And suddenly she wondered if she would go out with him on a date, if she had the chance. It was funny to think about as they sat side by side at the pool. He was totally different from the other men she knew. The men she had chosen before were all ineligible in some subtle way. And she had liked it that way. But Peter was different from all of them. He was open and real, and an equal match for her. And more important than that, he appealed to her a great deal. It would actually have frightened her if she weren't leaving the next day.

'What were you thinking just then?' His voice was soft in the late-afternoon sun, and she pulled her thoughts back to him with a smile.

'Nothing much.' There was no reason to tell him about the men in her life, or even what she thought of him. There was nothing personal between them, and yet there was, some intangible presence that she felt when she was near him. It was almost like an illusion that she knew him better than she really did. But there was something very vulnerable about this man, which she liked. Considering who and what he was, he had remained very human, and now that she saw him here at home, she liked him even more.

'You were a million miles away just then.'

'No, not quite that far. I was thinking of some things in New York ... my work ... the girls ...'

'It must be rough having to go away for your work.'

'Sometimes. But they understand. They're used to it by now. And Raquel keeps an eye on them while I'm gone.'

'What's she like?' He was constantly curious about her, and Melanie turned to him with a grin.

'Nothing like Mrs Hahn. In fact, before I was thinking how totally different our lives are, externally at least.'

'How?'

'Our houses for instance. Yours is much more formal than mine.' She laughed then. 'I guess mine is a hen house of sorts. It looks like a woman's house.' She glanced at his home. 'Yours is much larger and more formal than mine. And so is Mrs Hahn. Raquel looks like she has never learned to comb her hair, her uniform is always buttoned wrong, and she talks back all the time. But we love her, and she's wonderful with the girls.' He smiled at her description of Raquel.

'What's your house like?'

'Bright and cheery and small, and just right for me and the girls. I bought it a few years ago, and it scared me to death to take it on at the time, but I've always been glad that I did.' He nodded, thinking of the responsibilities she tackled alone. It was one of the things he admired about her. There was a lot about her he liked. And he was intrigued because she was so different from Anne. And then Melanie smiled at him. 'You'll have to come and see me in New York sometime.'

'Someday.' But he instantly found himself wishing that it would be soon, and he wasn't sure why, except that she was the first person in a long time that he had opened up to. And before he could say anything more, Matthew returned with a plate of fresh cakes, and without a second thought, he plonked himself down beside Mel and offered to share them with her. There were crumbs all over his face and his chubby little hands, and he dropped the rest all over himself and her, but she didn't seem to mind. Little boys were a novelty to her. They got into a serious discussion about his school and his best friend while Peter watched, and then left them to go for a swim. When he returned, they were still deeply engrossed in their talk, and Matthew had climbed into her lap and was nestled against her. He seemed totally happy there.

When Peter climbed out of the pool, he stopped at the top of the ladder for a moment and looked at them with a sad smile. The boy needed someone like her, they all did, and for the first time in almost two years he realised how much had been missing from his life. But as the thought crossed his mind, he pushed it from him, and rejoined them with a quick step, grabbing a towel from a table as he approached and drying his hair, as though to chase the new thoughts he'd had from his head. At that moment Mark's friends left, and he joined Melanie and Matthew, and sat down in Peter's empty chair.

'I hope my friends didn't drive you nuts.' He smiled shyly at her. 'They get a little unruly at times.'

She laughed thinking of Val and Jessie's friends, who came near to destroying her house from time to time, and seemed no less unruly than Mark's friends. 'They seemed fine to me.'

'Tell my dad that.' Mark smiled appreciatively at her, and tried not to notice how sexy she looked in his sister's bathing suit.

'What's that? Taking my name in vain again?'

Mark looked victoriously at him. He liked his father's new friend, and the girls had been tremendously impressed that Melanie Adams was just 'hanging out' at their pool.

'Miss Adams thinks my group's not so bad.'

'She's just being polite. Don't believe a word of it.'

'That's not true. You should see Val's and Jessie's friends. They gave a party once, and someone accidentally set fire to a chair.'

'Oh my God.' Peter cringed and Mark smiled. He liked her. She was so easy and open and natural, not like a TV star at all, and if Mel could have heard his thoughts she would have laughed. She never thought of herself that way, nor did the twins. 'What happened after that?'

'I put the girls on restriction for two months, but I let them off the hook after one.'

'They're lucky you didn't send them to reform school.' Mark and Mel exchanged a conspiratorial grin in the face of Peter's tough stance, and Matthew, indifferent to it all, leaned a little closer to her, so she wouldn't forget him. She gently stroked his hair, and he didn't seem to mind having lost her ear. He knew that in her own way she was still paying attention to him. And at exactly that moment she happened to look up at the house, and saw Pam, standing almost hidden at her bedroom window, looking down at them. Their eyes met and held, and then a moment later Pam disappeared. Melanie wondered why she didn't come back to the pool. It was almost as though she wanted to be left out. Or maybe she wanted Peter to herself, and didn't want to share him with her, or the two boys. She wanted to say something about it to Peter, but she didn't want to interfere. Instead the banter between them rambled on, until a slight breeze came up and they all began to feel the chill. It was after six o'clock by then, and Mel looked at her watch, and realised that she'd have to go soon. It was almost dinnertime and Peter had seen her look at her wrist.

'You haven't swum yet, Mel. Why don't you go in for a minute. And then we'll eat. Mrs Hahn will go berserk if we're late.' It all seemed so mechanised, so perfectly run, and without being told, Mel knew it was all the legacy of Anne, who had run her home like a well-oiled machine. It wasn't Mel's style, but it was impressive to see. And it was part of what had kept them all going after she was gone, even though it would probably have done them all good to change now, if they could. But old habits were hard to break, especially for Peter and Mrs Hahn. A moment later, the children left, and Mel dived neatly into the pool as Peter watched. She was so easy to have around and so good to see. He felt an enormous hunger well up within him again as she glided through the water with expert ease, and at last she returned to the side, her hair wet, her eyes bright, with a happy smile on her face, just for him. 'You were right. This was just what I needed.'

'I'm always right. You needed dinner here too.'

She decided to be honest with him. 'I hope the children don't mind too much.' She had already seen a great deal in Pam's eyes. More than Peter would have wanted to see.

'I don't think they quite know what to make of my being here.'

Their eyes met and held and he approached the pool and sat down, unable to stop what he felt, or had to say. 'Neither do I.' He was stunned by his own words, and Mel suddenly looked scared.

'Peter ...' She suddenly felt that she should tell him something more about herself, her old scars, her fears of getting too deeply involved with men. And yet they both sensed that there was something strange happening to them.

'I'm sorry. That was a crazy thing to say.'

'I'm not sure it was ... but ... Peter ...' And then, as she looked away from him, searching for her words, she glimpsed Pam at the window again, and an instant later she disappeared. 'I don't want to intrude into your life.' She forced her eyes back to his.

'Why not?'

She took a deep breath and pulled herself out of the pool and he almost gasped as he saw the long, lean limbs and the white suit. This time he looked away, but he felt a wave of emotion wash over him. Her voice was almost too gentle as she spoke again. 'Has there been anyone here since Anne?'

He knew what she meant and shook his head. 'No. Not in that sense.'

'Then why upset everyone now?'

'Who's upset?' Peter looked surprised and Mel decided to be blunt.

'Pam.'

And with that Peter sighed. 'That has nothing to do with you, Mel. The last couple of years have been hard on her.'

'I understand that. But the reality is that I live three thousand miles away and it's not very likely we'll see each other again for a long time. And what we're doing with the interview about you is exciting for both of us. And funny things happen to people when they go through something like that. It's like being cast adrift on a ship, you grow amazingly close. But tomorrow the interview will be complete and I'm going home.' Her eyes were almost sad as she said the words.

'So what harm will one dinner do?'

She sat pensively beside him for a long time. 'I don't know. I just don't want to do anything that doesn't make sense.' She looked into his eyes again and saw that he looked sad too. It was crazy. They liked each other, but what was the point?

'I think you're making too much of all this, Mel.' His voice was deep and almost gruff.

'Am I?' Her eyes never wavered from his and this time he smiled.

'No. Maybe I am. I think I like you a lot, Mel.'

'I like you too. There's no harm in that, as long as we don't get carried away.' But she wished they would. And it was crazy really, sitting there at the side of the pool talking of something that had never been and would never be, and yet there was something there. And Mel couldn't decide if it was illusion created by working so closely side by side for two days or if it was real. There was no way to know, and by the next day she'd be gone. Maybe there was no harm in one dinner after all, and she was expected to stay.

Peter looked down at her again and spoke softly to her. 'I'm glad you're here, Mel.' He sounded like Matt, and she smiled.

'So am I.' For a long moment their eyes met and held and Mel could feel cold chills run up her spine. There was something magical about this man, and he seemed to feel it too. He stood up with a happy smile on his face and held out a hand to her. He looked almost shy, and she smiled and followed him inside, glad that she had decided to stay. She went back to the guest room, and changed her clothes, rinsed out the bathing suit and went upstairs to return it to Pam, her wet hair pulled back into a knot, and her face lightly tanned with only mascara and lipstick on. There weren't many women her age who looked as well with almost no makeup on.

She found Pam sitting in her room, listening to a tape with a dreamy look on her face. She seemed almost startled to see Mel, who knocked on the open door and stepped in.

'Hi, Pam. Thanks for the suit. Shall I put it in your bathroom?'

'Sure ... okay ... thanks.' She stood up, feeling awkward with Mel, and Mel suddenly felt the same overwhelming urge to take athe young girl in her arms, however tall and grown-up she was. Inside, she was still a lonely, unhappy little girl.

'That's a nice tape. Val has that too.'

'Which one is she?' Pam looked intrigued again.

'The blonde.'

'Is she nice?'

Mel laughed. 'I hope so. Maybe someday if you come east with your dad, you could meet them both.'

Pam sat down on her bed again. 'I'd like to go to New York someday. But we hardly ever get to go away. Dad can't leave his work. There's always someone he has to be around for. Except for a couple of weeks in the summer, when he goes nuts, leaving the hospital, and calls back there every two hours. We go to

Aspen.' She looked unimpressed, and Mel watched her eyes. There was something broken there. Everything about her looked as though it needed some pep, some excitement, some joy. But Mel had a feeling that a woman could work wonders for the girl. Someone to love her and take her mother's place. The child was keening for Anne, and no matter how much she would resist someone new, it was what she needed most. That dry stick of a German woman downstairs couldn't give her love. Peter did his best, but she needed something more.

'Aspen must be nice.' Mel was fighting to open a closed door between herself and the girl. And once or twice she thought she could see a glimmer of hope, but she wasn't sure.

'Yeah, it's okay. I get bored going there though.'

'Where would you rather go instead?'

'The beach ... Mexico ... Europe ... New York ... someplace neat.' She smiled hesitantly at Mel. 'Someplace where interesting people go, not just nature lovers and people who hike.' She made a face. 'Yuck.'

Mel smiled. 'We go to Martha's Vineyard every summer. That's the beach. It's not too exciting, but it's nice. Maybe someday you could visit us there.' But at that, Pam looked suspicious again, and before Mel could say anything more, Matthew bounded into the room.

'Get out, squirt!' She leapt quickly to her feet, protecting her domain.

'You're a creep.' Matthew looked more annoyed than hurt, and he looked possessively at Mel. 'Dad says dinner's ready and we should all come downstairs.' He stood waiting to accompany her down, and she had no further time alone with Pam, to reassure her that the invitation was just a friendly thought on her part, and not an omen of things to come between her father and herself.

Mark joined them on the stairs and he and Pam gnawed at each other all the way down, while Matthew kept up a running patter with Mel. Peter was already waiting in the dining room. Mel saw a haunting expression cross his face as they entered the room en masse, but he quickly recovered himself. There must have been a familiar look to it all, something he hadn't seen in a long time.

'Were they holding you hostage upstairs? I was afraid of that.'

'No. I was talking to Pam.'

He looked pleased at that, and everyone took their chairs. Mel hesitated, not quite sure where to sit. Peter quickly pulled out the chair to his right, and Pam looked shocked and half rose from her seat. She sat at the foot of the table, facing Peter, with both boys on one side.

'Never mind!' His voice was firm, and Mel knew instantly what he had done. He had put her in his late wife's chair, and she wished that he had not. There was a long, heavy silence in the room, and Mrs Hahn stared as she came in. Mel looked at Peter imploringly. 'It's all right, Mel.' He looked reassuringly at her, and took the others in with one glance. The conversation began again. A moment later the dining room was filled with the usual chatter, as everyone started with Mrs Hahn's cold watercress soup.

As it turned out, it was a pleasant meal, and Peter had been right. There was no need to make a major event of it. He and Mel shared coffee in the den when they were through, and the children went upstairs. Mel didn't see them again until she was ready to leave. Pam rather formally shook her hand, Mel sensed she was relieved to see her go, Mark asked for her autograph, and Matthew threw his arms around her neck and begged her to stay.

'I can't. But I promise I'll send you a postcard from New York.'

Tears filled his eyes. 'That's not the same.' He was right, but it was the best she could do. She held him for a long moment and then gently kissed his cheek and stroked his hair.

'Maybe you'll come to see me in New York one day.' But when he looked into her eyes, they both knew that it wasn't likely to happen for a long time, if at all, and she felt desperately sorry for him. When she finally left, and they drove away from the house, Matthew kept waving as the car pulled down the block. Mel was almost in tears. 'I feel like such a rat leaving him.' She looked at Peter and he was touched by what he saw in her eyes. He reached out and patted her hand. It was the first time he had actually touched her, and he felt a thrill run through his arm. He quickly withdrew his hand and she looked away. 'What a super kid he is ... they all are ...' Even Pam. She liked them all, and felt for what they'd been through, and Peter too. She sighed softly then. 'I'm glad I stayed.'

'So am I. You did us all good. We haven't had a happy meal like that in ... years.' And she knew just how many too. They had been living in a tomb, and again she found herself thinking that he should sell the house, but she didn't dare say that to him. Instead she turned to him, thinking of his children again.

'Thank you for inviting me over this afternoon.'

'I'm glad you came.'

'So am I.'

The hospital parking lot came too soon, and they were standing awkwardly outside her car uncertain of what to say. 'Thank you, Peter. I had a wonderful time.' She made a mental note to send flowers the next day, and maybe something special for the children if she had time to shop before she left. She still had to shop for the twins too.

'Thank you, Mel.' He looked into her eyes for a long time and then held out a hand to shake hers. 'I'll see you tomorrow then.' She would briefly be filming Pattie Lou before she left and it would be her last chance to see him. He walked her to her car, and they stood there for another moment before she slid in.

'Thanks again.'

'Good night, Mel.' He smiled and turned to walk into the hospital for a last look at Pattie Lou.

Chapter 7

The filming of Pattie Lou in intensive care went smoothly the next day. Despite the surgery and the tubes, she already looked infinitely healthier than she had before and Melanie was amazed. It was almost as though Peter had wrought a miracle cure, and she didn't let herself dwell on how long it would last. Even if it was only a few years, it was better than a few days. With the living example of Pattie Lou, Peter Hallam had totally won her over.

She saw him in the hall, shortly after she left Pattie Lou. The crew had already left, and she had been about to say goodbye to Pearl. She had to check out of her hotel, and there were a few errands in Beverly Hills she wanted to do, including bringing a little something back for the girls. It was a tradition maintained over the years, so now she was going to steal an hour to do a little shopping on Rodeo Drive.

'Hello there.' He looked handsome and fresh, as though he hadn't worked all day. 'What are you up to today?'

'Winding up.' She smiled. 'I just saw Pattie Lou. She looks great.'

'Yes, she does.' He beamed, a proud rooster. 'I saw her this morning too.' In fact he had seen her twice, but he didn't mention that to Mel, not wanting to make her worry that anything was wrong.

'I was going to call you this afternoon, to thank you for dinner last night. I had a wonderful time.' She carefully sought his eyes, wondering what she would see there.

'The children loved meeting you, Mel.'

'It was nice meeting them.' But she couldn't help wondering if Pam had reacted badly when he returned home again.

She noticed then that he was looking wistfully at her, and she wondered if something was wrong. He seemed to hesitate, and then he spoke up. 'Are you in a rush?'

'Not really. My flight isn't until ten o'clock tonight.' She didn't mention her shopping on Rodeo Drive for the girls, it seemed far too frivolous here, amidst the battle for human life. 'Why?'

'I wondered if you wanted to stop in and see Marie Dupret again.' She could see that the girl already meant something to him. She was his latest little wounded bird.

'How is she today?' Mel watched his eyes, wondering how any one man could care so much. But he did. It was obvious in everything he did and said.

'About the same. We're getting down to the wire on that donor heart for her.'

'I hope you get one soon.' But again, that seemed a ghoulish thought, as she followed Peter to Marie's room.

The girl seemed paler and weaker than she had the day before, and Peter sat quietly with her and talked, in an almost intimate way, that excluded everyone else in the room save themselves. It was as though there was a special communion between them, and for a fraction of an instant Mel found herself wondering if he was attracted to her. But his style with her had no sexual overtones, it was just that he seemed to care so much, and one had the feeling that they had known each other for years, which Mel knew wasn't the case. It was a striking case of there being an extraordinary kind of rapport between them. After a little while Marie seemed more peaceful than she had been before, and her eyes reached out to Mel.

'Thank you for coming by to see me again, Miss Adams.' She seemed so weak and pale, one sensed that she wouldn't live much longer without the transplant she so desperately needed. She seemed to have worsened since the day before, and Mel felt a tug at her own heart as she walked towards the young woman.

'I'm going back to New York tonight, Marie. But I'll be looking forward to hearing good news about you.'

For a long moment the young woman with the translucent pallor said nothing, and then she smiled almost sadly. 'Thank you.' And then, as Peter watched, she let her fears overwhelm her and two tears slid down her cheeks. 'I don't know if we'll find a donor in time.'

Peter stepped forward again. 'Then you'll just have to hang in there, won't you?' His eyes were so intense in their grasp of the girl that it was almost as though he were willing her to live, and Mel felt as though she could almost touch the magnetic force between them in the room.

'It'll be all right.' Melanie reached out and touched her hand, and was surprised at how cold it was. The girl had practically no circulation, which accounted for the bluish pallor. 'I know it will.'

She turned her eyes to Mel then, and seemed almost too weak to move. 'Do you?' Melanie nodded, fighting back tears. She had the terrifying feeling that the girl was not going to make it, and she found herself silently praying for her as they left the room, and in the safety of the hall, she turned to Peter with worried eyes.

'Can she hold out until you find a donor?' Mel doubted it now, and even Peter looked unsure. He suddenly seemed exhausted by it all, which was rare for him.

'I hope so. It all depends on how soon we find a donor.' Melanie didn't ask the obvious question, 'And if you don't?' because the answer to that was too easily guessed from the condition of the girl. She was the frailest, most delicate girl Melanie had ever seen, and it seemed miraculous that she was still alive at all.

'I hope she makes it.'

Peter looked at her intently, and then nodded. 'So do I. Sometimes the emotional factors help. I'll come back and see her again later, the nurses are keeping a very close watch on her, not just through the monitors. The problem is that she has no family or relatives at all. Sometimes people so alone have less reason to hang on. We have to give them that reason as best we can. But in the end, what happens is not our decision.' Was it hers then? Was it up to this frail girl to will herself to live? It seemed a lot to expect of her, and Melanie was silent as she followed Peter, almost dragging her feet. There was no further reason to linger here. Peter had his work to do and she had to move on, no matter how little the prospect appealed to her. Somehow she wanted to stick around now, to watch Pattie Lou, talk to Pearl, pray for Marie, drop in on the others she'd seen. But the issue was none of them, as she suspected now. It was Peter himself. She really didn't want to leave him. And he seemed to sense that too. He left the nurses and the charts and walked to where she stood.

'I'll take you downstairs, Mel.'

'Thank you.' She didn't decline. She wanted to be alone with him, but she wasn't even sure why. Maybe it was just his style that had got to her, the bedside manner, the warmth, yet she knew that it was something more. She was remarkably drawn to the man, but to what end? She lived in New York and he lived in LA. And if they had lived in the same town? She wasn't even sure of that as he walked her to her car in the parking lot, and she turned to face him again. 'Thank you for everything.'

'For what?' He smiled gently down at her.

'For saving Pattie Lou's life.'

'I did that for Pattie Lou, not for you.'

'Then for everything else. Your interest, your time, your cooperation, dinner, lunch ...' She was suddenly at a loss for words and he looked amused.

'Anything else you want to add? Coffee in the hall?'

'All right, all right ...' She smiled at him and he took her hand.

'I should be thanking you, Mel. You did a lot for me. You're the first person I've opened up to in two years. Thank you for that.' And then, before she could respond, 'Could I call you in New York sometime, or would that be out of line?'

'Not at all. I'd like that very much.' Her heart pounded in her chest, and she felt like a very young girl.

'I'll call you then. Have a good trip back.' He squeezed her hand once more, and then turned, waved, and was gone. As simple as that. And as she drove towards Rodeo Drive, she couldn't help wondering if she would ever see him again.

Chapter 8

While Mel finished her shopping that afternoon, she found that she had to push Peter Hallam from her head again and again. It wasn't right that she should think so much about him. What was he to her after all? An interesting man, the subject of an interview, nothing more, no matter how appealing he was. She tried to fill her mind with thoughts of Val and Jess, and suddenly he would crop up. She was still thinking of him as she threw her suitcase into the back of a cab and headed for the airport at eight o'clock that night, and suddenly in her mind's eye, she saw a crystal-clear vision of Pam, a troubled, brokenhearted, lonely little girl.

'Shit.' She muttered out loud, and the driver glanced at her.

'Something wrong?'

She had to laugh at herself, and shook her head. 'Sorry. I was miles away.'

He nodded, nonplussed. He had heard it all before anyway and as long as she gave him a decent tip, that was all he cared about.

Once they had reached the airport she checked in, bought three magazines, and sat down near the gate to wait for her flight. It was already nine o'clock, and in twenty minutes they would board. She looked around and realised that the flight would be full, but as usual, she would be travelling first class, so it probably wouldn't be too bad. She flipped through the magazines waiting for the flight to be called, keeping one ear alert for the flight number. It was the last flight of the day headed for New York, familiarly termed 'the red eye', because that was how one would arrive at six o'clock the next morning, red-eyed and exhausted, but at least one didn't lose an entire day flying.

As she listened, she suddenly started. She thought she had heard her name, but decided that she had been mistaken. They called the flight, and she waited for the first crush of passengers to get on board, and then picked up the briefcase and handbag she was carrying and got in line with her ticket and her boarding pass in her hand, and again she heard her name. But this time, she was certain it was not her imagination.

'Melanie Adams, please come to the white courtesy phone ... Melanie Adams ... white courtesy phone, please ... Melanie Adams ...' Glancing at her watch to see how much time she had, she dashed for a white phone on the far wall and picked it up, identifying herself to the operator who answered.

'Hello, this is Melanie Adams. I believe you were paging me a moment ago.' She set her bags down on the floor next to her feet and listened intently.

'You had a call from a Dr Peter Hallam. He wants you to call him back immediately if you can.' And with that, she gave Mel his home number. She repeated it to herself, as she ran to the nearest phone booth, digging in her bag for a dime, and keeping one eye on the large clock hanging above. She had five minutes left to board her flight, and she couldn't afford to miss it. She had to be in New York by the next morning. The dime found, she slipped it into the slot in the phone and dialled the number.

'Hello?' Her heart pounded as he answered, wondering why he had called her.

'Peter, it's Mel. I only have a couple of minutes to catch my flight.'

'I don't have much more than that either.' His voice sounded terse. 'We just got a donor for Marie Dupret. I'm leaving for the hospital now, and I just thought I'd let you know on the off-chance that you'd want to stay.' Her mind raced as she listened, and for only the flash of a second she was disappointed. She had thought he had called her to say goodbye, but now she felt the adrenaline course through her system as she thought of the transplant. Now Marie had a chance. They had found a heart for her. 'I didn't know if you'd want to change your plans, but I thought I'd let you know, in case. I wasn't even sure what airline you were on and I took a wild guess.' His guess had been a good one.

'You just caught me.' And then she frowned. 'Could we film the transplant?' It would be a sensational addition to the story, and it would give her justification for staying another day.

There was a long pause. 'All right. Can you get a camera crew there right away?'

'I can try. I have to get clearance from New York to stay.' And the time it would take to call could cost her her flight. 'I don't know what I can do. I'll leave a message at the hospital for you either way.'

'Fine. I've got to go now. See you later.' His voice was businesslike and brusque and he hung up without saying more. Melanie stood in the phone booth for a second gathering her thoughts. The first thing she had to do was talk to the ground supervisor at the gate. She had done this before, and with any luck at all, they would hold the flight for five or ten minutes, which would give her time to call New York. She just hoped that she could reach someone of sufficient rank in New York to get clearance. Grabbing her briefcase and handbag, she took off at a run for the gate, where she found a supervisor, and explained who she was, flashing her press card from the network.

'Can you hold the flight for me for ten minutes? I've got to call New York on a big story.' The supervisor didn't look pleased, but for people of Mel's rank they often did special favours, like finding them seats on fully booked flights, even if it meant bumping some unsuspecting passenger off the plane, or holding a flight just before takeoff, like this one.

'I'll give you ten minutes, but I can't give you much more than that.' It cost the airlines a fortune to pull stunts like that and delay on the ground. She turned away from Mel and then spoke into the small walkie-talkie she carried as Mel ran back to the pay phone, and put the call on her credit card. They got her through to the newsroom right away but it took four precious minutes to find an assistant producer and a story editor, who conferred with Mel on the phone.

'What's up?'

'A real break. One of the people I interviewed was a patient waiting for a transplant. And I just got a call from Hallam. They've got a donor, and they're going to operate now. Can I stay and take a camera crew back out to Center City to film the operation?' She was breathless from the excitement and from running to the phone.

'Didn't you shoot him in surgery before?'

'No.' She held her breath, knowing that that could decide it all.

'Then stay. But get home tomorrow night.'

'Yes sir.' She grinned as she hung up the phone, and hurried back to the gate. She told them she wasn't taking the flight and then called the local network for a camera crew. She hurried outside for a cab then, hoping that the airline would hold on to her bag in New York, as they'd promised to.

The camera crew was waiting for her in the lobby when she arrived, and they went straight upstairs to surgery. They all had to scrub, don masks and gowns, and they had been assigned a minuscule corner of the room to which they had to confine their equipment. Mel was vehement about following the rules because she was grateful that Peter let them be there at all and she didn't want to abuse the privilege.

At last, wheeled into the room on a stretcher with the side rails up, Marie appeared. Her eyes were closed, and she looked deathly pale. She didn't stir at all, until Peter walked in, in mask and gown, and spoke to her. He didn't even seem to see Mel then, although he glanced once at the camera crew, and seemed satisfied at where they stood. Then everything got underway, and Mel watched in fascination.

Peter frequently glanced at the monitors and gave a constant series of orders to his team. They moved in total unison like an intricate ballet of hands, with instruments being passed to him from an enormous tray.

Melanie looked away when they made the first incision, but after that she was drawn to the intensity of the scene, and hour after hour she stood by and watched, praying silently for Marie's life, as they worked endlessly to replace her dying heart with the new one of the young woman who had died only hours before. It was fascinating to watch as they lifted the old one from her chest and placed it on a tray, and Melanie didn't even gasp as she watched them lower the new one into the cavity they had left. Valves, arteries and veins were hooked up and his hands moved ceaselessly over the woman's chest. Melanie held her breath, then suddenly the monitors came to life again, and the sound of the monitored heart beat leapt into the room like a drum in everyone's ears, and the cardiac team gave a cheer. It was truly amazing. The heart so lifeless since the death of its donor sprang to life again in Marie's body.

The surgery continued for another two hours, and at last the final incision was closed. Peter stood back, his back and chest drenched, his arms sore from the precise work, and he watched carefully as they slowly pushed her bed from the room again, into a nearby cubicle where she would be watched for several hours. He would remain close by for the next six or eight hours himself to make sure that all went well, but for the moment everything seemed to be under control. He walked out into the hall and took a deep breath of air, and Melanie followed him, feeling her legs shake. It had been an extraordinary experience watching him work, and she was deeply grateful for his call. He chatted for a few moments with the others, still in his cap and gown, his mask cast aside on a desk, and for a few minutes Mel conferred with the camera crew. They were ready to go home, and enormously impressed with what they'd seen.

'Christ, that guy's good.' The man in charge peeled off his blue gown and lit a cigarette, wondering at the wisdom of it as he did, but all he could think of was what they'd got on film: the constantly moving hands of the doctors, working in pairs, sometimes two pairs together, never stopping, picking up tiny slivers of tissue to be repaired and veins barely thicker than hairs. 'It really makes you believe in miracles to see something like that.' He looked at Mel in awe, and he shook her hand. 'It was nice working with you.'

'Thank you for getting here so fast.' She smiled, and they glanced over some notes. He told her he'd have the film in New York the next day to add to the rest and then he and his crew left. She changed her clothes and was surprised to see Peter emerge in his street clothes too. Somehow she had assumed that he'd be sticking around in his operating-room garb, but she didn't know why she'd assumed that. It was strange to see him as just an ordinary mortal again. 'How did it go?' she asked him as they walked outside together into the hall. Something deep inside her leapt to see him again.

'Okay so far. The next twenty-four hours will be crucial for her though. We'll have to see how she holds up. She was terribly weak when we went in. Did you see that heart? It was like a piece of rock, it didn't have any give left at all. I don't think she'd have made it another twenty-four hours. She was damn lucky we got that donor in time.' Donor ... donor ... no face ... no name ... no past ... just 'donor', an anonymous heart in a body one knew, with a face like Marie's. It was still difficult to absorb. Even after watching the operation performed for four hours.

Mel looked at her watch then and was surprised to see that it was well after six o'clock, and when she glanced outside she saw that the sun had come up. The night was gone, and Marie was alive. 'You must be beat.' He looked her over carefully and noticed the dark shadows under her eyes. 'Just standing there watching is a lot harder than doing the work.'

'I doubt that.' She yawned in spite of herself, and wondered how Marie would feel when she woke up. That was the worst of all and Melanie didn't envy her. She would have a lot to go through now, even more than she'd gone through before. She had the drugs to absorb, the rejection and infections to fight, and she would have the pain of having been cut almost in half as they worked. Mel almost shuddered at the thought, and Peter saw her grow pale, and without further ado, pushed her into the nearest chair. He'd seen the symptoms before, even before Mel herself knew she was growing faint. He gently pushed her head down towards her knees with his powerful hands and Mel was too surprised to speak.

'Take slow, deep breaths, and exhale through your mouth.' She was about to say something flip to him but suddenly found that she felt too sick to speak, and when she'd recovered again, she looked up at him in surprise.

'I didn't even feel that coming on.'

'Maybe not, my friend, but for a minute there, you turned an interesting shade of green. You ought to have something to eat downstairs, and go back to your hotel to sleep.' Then he remembered that she had checked out, and no longer had a room, and he thought of something. 'Why don't you go back to my place for a while? Mrs Hahn can put you in the guest room, and the kids won't even know you're there.' He looked at his watch, it was a few minutes before seven. 'I'll give her a call.'

'No, don't, I can go back to my hotel.'

'That's silly. Why go through all that, when you can sleep at my place? No one will bother you all day.' It was a generous offer, but she wasn't sure it was quite right. But she found that when she stood up, she was too tired to argue or even call her hotel for another room. He walked to a desk and picked up a phone and she sat watching him like an exhausted child. He came back to her looking as fresh as he had the morning before, although he had lost a night's sleep too, but he seemed to be used to it, and he was still exhilarated by his success. 'She'll be waiting for you when you arrive. The kids won't even be up till eight, except Mark who's already gone.' He glanced around and spoke rapidly to a nurse and then returned to Mel. 'Marie's doing fine, I'll take you downstairs and put you in a cab myself, and then I'll come back here to check on her.'

'You really don't have to... it's silly...' It was ridiculous, she had covered everything from mass murders to minor wars, and suddenly now she felt as though her entire body was going to melt, and she was grateful for his strong arm nearby as he led her downstairs. 'I must be getting old.' She smiled ruefully as they waited for the cab. 'I shouldn't be this tired.'

'It's the letdown. We all feel it eventually. It just hasn't hit me yet.'

'What'll you do?'

'Stay close, and catch a few hours of sleep here if I can. I called my secretary last night after I called you, and she'll cancel all my appointments today. Someone else on the team will cover for me this morning, and I'll do rounds myself this afternoon.' But she knew that he had to be dead on his feet now, not that it showed. He was as dynamic and alive as he had been hours before. He looked down at her gently as he put her in the cab. 'When are you going back to New York?'

'I'll have to go back tonight. They won't let me stay another day.'

He nodded, pleased that he'd caught her the night before. 'There won't be anything else for you to film anyway, Mel. From now on, we watch, and we juggle the doses of the medication to something she can tolerate. You saw everything there was to see last night.' She looked into his eyes again.

'Thank you for letting us be there.'

'It was good to have you there. Now go and get some sleep.' He gave the driver his address and closed the door before the cab disappeared into the Los Angeles traffic and headed in the direction of Bel-Air. As he watched her drive away, he was suddenly grateful that she was still there, and that he would see her again in a few hours. He was as confused as Mel about what he felt. But he felt something for her. That was for sure.

Chapter 9

At the house in Bel-Air, Mrs Hahn was standing near a window, waiting for her, and with barely more than a hello, she led Mel upstairs to the guest room. Mel thanked her and looked around, starving and exhausted all at once, and longing for a hot bath, but too tired to do anything about any of it. She dropped her briefcase and her handbag beside the bed, wondering if she'd catch up with her suitcase again in New York, but right now she didn't really care. She lay down on the bed fully clothed and began to drift off to sleep thinking of Peter and Marie, just as she heard a soft knock on the door. She turned over in surprise, and pulled herself back to consciousness again. 'Yes?'

It was Mrs Hahn with a small wicker tray. 'The doctor thought you should have something to eat.' She felt like a patient as she eyed the plate of steaming scrambled eggs and toast, and a cup of chocolate that she could smell halfway across the room. 'I didn't bring you coffee so you would sleep.'

'Thank you so much.' It was embarrassing to be waited on, but the food looked wonderful to her as she sat up on the edge of the bed, her jacket rumpled, her shirt creased, her hair dishevelled from the way she had lain. And without another word, Mrs Hahn set the tray down on a small table beside the bed, and left the room again.

And as Mel devoured the eggs and toast, suddenly ravenous, she heard soft bumping sounds upstairs, and wondered if it was Matthew or Pam, getting ready for school. But she didn't have the strength to be polite and go upstairs to see them. She downed the hot chocolate, ate the last of the toast, and lay down again, sated, exhausted, pleased with her night's work. She closed her eyes and it was three o'clock in the afternoon when she awoke again. She looked at her watch in shock, and jumped off the bed, but she suddenly realised there was nowhere she had to go. She wondered what Mrs Hahn would think of her sleeping all day, and any minute the children would be home. And when she'd gone to sleep they had just been getting up to go to school. And then as she walked around the room, she began wondering how Marie had fared for the past seven hours. She saw a phone on a desk across the room, and walked to it in stockinged feet, looking down at the wrinkled clothes she wore. She dialled the hospital at once, asked for the cardiac floor, and then for Peter himself, and the woman who answered told her that he could not be called to the phone. Melanie wondered if he was asleep too.

'I was calling to see how Marie Dupret, the transplant patient, is.' There was a silence at the other end. 'This is Melanie Adams. I was in the operating room last night.' But she didn't need to say more. Everyone in the hospital knew who she was, and that she was doing a story on Peter Hallam and Pattie Lou Jones.

'Just a moment please.' The voice was crisp and she was put on hold, and then an instant later she heard a familiar voice.

'You're awake?'

'Barely, but I am. And mortified to have slept all afternoon.'

'Bull. You needed it. You were ready to pass out when you left here. Did Mrs Hahn give you something to eat?'

'She certainly did. This is the best hotel in town.' She smiled as she looked around the comfortable, well-decorated room, and imagined that here again all had been arranged by Anne. 'How's Marie?'

'She's doing great.' He sounded pleased. 'I couldn't take the time to explain it to you last night, but we tried a new technique, and it worked. I'll draw you a few sketches later, but suffice it to say for now that so far, so good. We won't know about rejection for at least a week.'

'How long before she's out of the woods?'

'A while.' The rest of her life, Mel knew. 'We think she'll do fine. She met all our criteria for a potential success.'

'I hope she keeps it up.'

'So do we.' She was struck again by how little of the credit he took for himself, and couldn't help but admire him again.

'Did you get any sleep?'

He sounded vague. 'Some. I decided to do rounds myself this morning, and I lay down for a while after that. I'll probably come home tonight for dinner with the kids. I can leave someone else in charge here by then.' And then he had a thought. 'I'll see you then, Mel.' He sounded so friendly and warm, and she was suddenly anxious to see him again.

'Your children are going to get awfully tired of me.'

'I doubt that. They'll be thrilled that you're still here, and so am I. What time's your plane, or have you thought about that yet?'

'I guess I'll take the same flight tonight.' She felt rested enough to tackle the red eye, after sleeping all day. 'I should leave here at eight o'clock.'

'That works out fine. Mrs Hahn feeds us at seven as a rule, and I'll be home by six if all goes well here. If anything comes up, I'll give you a call.' For a moment, she could almost imagine him saying the same thing to Anne; and it felt strange to listen to him, as though she were trying to take the dead woman's place, but she chided herself for being foolish as he said goodbye. There was nothing unusual about what he had said, and she was irritated with herself for fantasising again. And as though to wash away her thoughts of him, she walked into the shower and turned it on full blast, dropped her clothes on the bed, and stood beneath the steam. It occurred to her then that she could also swim in the pool but she didn't want to go outside yet. She needed time to wake up and clear her head. It had been a long night, and when she got out of the shower she realised that she had to call the studio in New York, and then Raquel. She had asked the story editor to call her home the night before, and she hoped they had. Raquel confirmed that to her when she reached her home number. The girls were disappointed that she hadn't come home that day, but she promised that the following morning she'd be there. And then she called the newsroom and told them that all was well. She reassured them that the transplant had been an enormous success, and they had got every moment of it on film.

'It's going to be a great piece, guys. You'll see.'

'Agreed. It'll be good to see you back, Mel.' But she didn't entirely agree. She wasn't anxious to leave LA, or Peter, and there seemed to be so many reasons to stay here: Pattie Lou, Peter, Marie ... all excuses, she knew, but she just didn't want to go.

She put down the phone and dressed and then left her room to find Mrs Hahn. She found her in the kitchen, making pot roast for that night. She thanked her again for the breakfast she'd brought her when she arrived and apologised for sleeping all day.

Mrs Hahn looked unimpressed. 'The doctor said that was why you were coming here. Would you like something to eat?' She was efficient but not warm, and there was something intimidating about the way she spoke and moved. She was definitely not the kind of woman Mel would have wanted around her kids, and wondered that Peter did. He seemed warmer to her than that, and with no mother around ... but again Mel remembered that she had been hired by Anne. Sacred Anne.

Mel settled for a cup of black coffee and made herself a piece of toast. She sat in the bright garden room filled with white wicker chairs.

To Mel, it seemed the sunniest room in the house, and the one she was most comfortable in. The formality of the other rooms put her off, but this one did not, and she lay down on a chaise longue and ate her toast, looking out at the peaceful view of the pool. She didn't even hear footsteps and had no idea she wasn't alone until she heard the voice.

'What are you doing here?'

She jumped up with a start, spilling some of her coffee on her leg, but thanks to her black gabardine pants, she didn't get burned. She turned, she saw Pam. 'Hello. You surprised the hell out of me.' She smiled, but Pam did not.

'I thought you were in New York.'

'I almost was. But I stayed to watch your father do a transplant last night. It was fabulous.' Her eyes lit up again as she remembered Peter's deft hands, but his daughter looked unimpressed and disgruntled.

'Oh yeah.'

'How was school, Pam?'

She stared at Mel. 'This was my mother's favourite room.'

'I can understand that. I like it too, there's so much sunshine here.' But the comment had increased the awkwardness between them, just as Pam had intended.

Pam sat down slowly across the room from Mel, and glanced outside. 'She used to sit here every day and watch me play in the pool.' It was well set up for that and just a pleasant place to be. Mel watched the girl's face and the sadness she saw there and she decided to take the bull by the horns.

'You must miss her a lot.'

Something hardened in Pam's face, and she didn't answer for a long time. 'She could have had an operation, but she didn't trust my dad to do it.' It was a brutal thing to say, and inwardly Mel cringed if that was what she thought of Anne's decision.

'I don't think it was as simple as that.'

She jumped to her feet. 'What do you know about it, except what *he* told you?'

'It was a choice she had a right to make.' But Mel knew she was treading on delicate ground. 'Sometimes it's difficult to understand why other people do things.'

'He couldn't have saved her anyway.' She walked nervously around the room as Mel watched. 'She'd have been dead by now, even with a transplanted heart.' Mel nodded slowly, most likely it was true.

'What would you have liked her to do?'

Pam shrugged and turned away and Mel saw her shoulders shake. Without giving it a second thought she went to her. 'Pam ...' She turned her slowly around and saw the tears running down the young girl's face, she gently took her in her arms and let her cry. She stood there for a few minutes leaning against Mel, as Mel gently stroked her hair. 'I'm so sorry, Pam ...'

'Yeah. Me too.' She pulled away at last and sat down again, wiping her face on her sleeve. She looked at Mel with misery in her face. 'I loved her so much.'

'I'm sure she loved you too.'

'Then why didn't she try? She'd have at least been here till now.'

'I don't know the answer to that, maybe no one does. I think your father asks himself the same thing all the time, but you have to go on. There isn't anything else you can do, as much as it hurts.' Pam nodded silently, and looked at Mel.

'I stopped eating for a while. I think I wanted to die too.' At least it was what the psychiatrist had said. 'Mark thinks I did it just to bug Dad, but I didn't. I couldn't help it.'

'Your father understands that. Do you feel better about things now than you did then?'

'Sometimes. I don't know ...' She looked so desperately sad, and there was so little Mel could say to help. All one could do was be there for her. She had two brothers, neither of whom could be of much help to her, a hard–boiled German housekeeper who offered no warmth at all, and a father who was busy saving other people's lives. There was no doubt that this child needed someone else, but who? For a minute Mel wished that she could be there for her, but she had her own life to live three thousand miles away, her own children, problems, job.

'You know, Pam, I wish you'd come to visit me in New York sometime.'

'Your daughters would probably think I was dumb. My brothers do.' She sniffed loudly again and looked like a little girl.

Mel smiled gently at her. 'I hope they're smarter than that, and boys don't always understand. Mark is going through his own adjustments growing up, and Matt is too young to be much help.'

'No, I'm not,' a small voice piped up. Neither of them had seen him walk into the room. He had just come home from school, dropped off by the car pool he rode in every day. 'I make my bed, I take a bath myself, and I can cook soup.' Even Pam laughed at that, and Mel smiled at him.

'I know, you're a terrific kid.'

'You came back.' He looked pleased as he walked towards her and sat down.

'No, I just left a little later than I thought. How was your day, my friend?'

'Pretty good.' And then he stared at Pam. 'How come you're crying again?' And before she could answer he turned to Mel. 'She cries all the time. Girls are dumb.'

'No, they're not. Everyone cries. Even big men.'

'My dad never cries.' He said it with enormous pride, and Mel wondered if Peter played a macho game with him.

'I'll bet he does.'

'Nope.' He was firm, but Pam intervened.

'Yes he does. I saw him once. After ...' But she didn't say the words. She didn't have to. They all understood, and Matt glared at her.

'That's not true. He's tough. So's Mark.' And with that, Mrs Hahn came into the room, and dragged Matthew away to wash his hands and face. He did his best to resist, but there was no swaying her, and Mel and Pam were alone again.

'Pam' – she reached out and touched her hand – 'if there's ever anything I can do for you, if you need a friend, call. I'll leave you my number when I go. Call me collect any time. I'm fairly good at listening, and New York isn't all that far away.' Pam looked at her with watchful eyes and then nodded her head.

'Thanks.'

'I mean it. Any time.'

Pam nodded and stood up. 'I'd better do my homework now. Are you leaving soon?' It was half hopeful, half not, as mixed as the rest of her feelings about Mel.

'I'm leaving for New York tonight. I'll probably hang around here till about eight o'clock.'

'Are you eating with us?' She looked annoyed, and Mel remembered what she had said.

'Maybe. I'm not sure. Would you mind that very much?'

'No, that's okay.' And as she stood in the doorway she turned back to ask, 'Do you want to borrow my bathing suit again?'

'I think I'll pass on that today, but thanks anyway.'

'Sure.' She nodded again and was gone, and a few minutes later Matthew bounded back into the room, bringing with him two books for her to read. It was obvious that they were both starved for attention as well as love, and he kept her busy and amused until Peter came home, and she saw that the day had finally taken its toll. He looked pale and tired, and she was sorry for him. There was so much for him to do here, as well, the children had such different needs, and his work used up so much of his energy and time. It was a wonder there was anything left for the children at all, but there was, whatever he could spare of himself at least.

'How's Marie?' Her eyes were full of concern and he smiled tiredly.

'Doing very well. Did Matthew drive you crazy all afternoon?'

'Not at all. And I had a nice talk with Pam.' He looked surprised.

'Well, that's something anyway. Want to come into the den for a glass of wine?'

'Sure.' She followed him across the house, and when they reached the den, she apologised again for taking advantage of his home.

'That's ridiculous. You put in a tough night last night. Why shouldn't you stay here for a day?'

'It was awfully nice.'

'Good.' He smiled at her and handed her a glass of wine. 'So are you.' He seemed warmer to her again. Like his daughter, he seemed to run hot and cold towards Mel, but she had the same conflicting emotions too, and she wasn't at all sure how to handle them. She just looked into his eyes and sipped her wine, and they reverted to small talk about the hospital which almost felt like her second home now, and before they had finished their second glass, Mrs Hahn knocked smartly on the door.

'Dinner is served, Doctor.'

'Thank you.' He stood up and Mel followed suit and walked beside him into the dining room, where they were rapidly joined by Pam, Matt and Mark, who came home just a few moments before. Mel found herself caught up in their banter once more. She felt surprisingly comfortable with them all and when it came time to leave to catch her plane, she was sorry to go. She gave Pam a hug, Matt a goodbye kiss, shook Mark's hand, thanked Mrs Hahn, and actually felt as though she were leaving old friends. She turned to Peter then, and shook his hand too.

'Thank you again. Today was really the best day of all.' She looked at his children standing nearby, and then back at him. 'And now I'd better call a cab, or you'll be stuck with me again.'

'Don't be ridiculous. I'll drive you to the airport myself.'

'I wouldn't think of it. You were up all night too. And you didn't sleep all day like me.'

'I slept enough. Come on, no nonsense now.' His voice was almost sharp. 'Where's your bag?'

Mel laughed. 'In New York, waiting for me, I hope.' He looked baffled and she explained. 'It was already checked on to the plane last night when you called.' And then he laughed too.

'You really are a good sport.'

'Wrinkled, but a good sport and I wouldn't have missed that opportunity for anything in the world.' She looked down at the rumpled silk shirt and she had forgotten for the past few hours. The state of her dress didn't seem very important here. 'Anyway, don't be stubborn. Let me call a cab.' She looked at her watch. It was eight fifteen. 'I really have to go.'

He pulled his car keys out of his pocket and waved them at her. 'Come on, let's go.' He turned to the children and Mrs Hahn. 'If the hospital calls, I'll be home in an hour or two. I have my pager on me, so they can catch me if they have to.' Just to be safe, he called to check on both Marie and Pattie Lou again before they left, and the resident in charge said they were fine, and with that he escorted Mel to the door. She waved at the children for a last time, and they got into the car. She had the feeling that all her decisions were being made for her, but it was a pleasant change from constantly looking out for herself.

'There's something about you, Doctor. You seem to make up my mind for me and I can't even say I object.'

He laughed. 'I guess I'm used to giving orders most of the time.' He smiled at her. 'And being obeyed.'

'So am I.' She grinned. 'But it's kind of pleasant taking orders from someone else for a change, even about something so simple as not taking a cab.'

'It's the least I can do. You've been my shadow for the past four days, and done something absolutely marvellous, I suspect.'

'Don't say that until you see the finished film.'

'I can just tell from the way you work.'

'That's a lot of faith. I'm not sure I deserve all that.'

He looked at her again. 'Yes, you do.' And then he frowned. 'By the way, how was your talk with Pam?'

Mel sighed. 'Touching. She's not a very happy child, is she?'

'Unfortunately, that's all too true.'

'She's tormenting herself about Anne.' It seemed strange to say his wife's name, it felt awkward on her lips. 'I think she'll be all right in time. Mostly she needs someone to talk to.'

'I send her to a psychiatrist.' He said it defensively.

'She needs more than that. And ...' She hesitated and then decided to go ahead. 'Mrs Hahn doesn't seem very warm.'

'She's not, at least not outwardly, but she loves those kids. And she's extremely competent.'

'She needs someone she can talk to, Peter, and so does Matt.'

'And what would you suggest?' He sounded bitter now. 'That I find a new wife just for them?'

'No. If you lead a normal life, you'll find one for yourself in time.'

'That's not what I have in mind.' She saw his jaw clench, and realised that they were both more tired than they knew.

'Why not? You were happily married before, you could be happily married again.'

'It would never be the same.' He looked sadly at Mel. 'I really don't want to get married again.'

'You can't stay alone for the rest of your life.'

'Why not? You never remarried. Why should I?' It was a good point.

'I'm not the marrying kind. You are.'

He laughed aloud at that. 'Well, that's a crock. Why not?'

'I'm just not. I'm too involved in my work to get tied down again.'

'I don't believe that. I think you're scared.' She almost flinched as he said the words; he had hit a nerve.

'Scared?' She sounded surprised nonetheless. 'Of what?'

'Commitment, love, being too close. I'm not sure. I don't know you that well.' But he had certainly seen into her. She didn't answer for a long time; she just stared into the night as they drove along and then she turned to him.

'You're probably right. But I'm too old to change now.'

'At thirty-two, four, five, whatever you are? That's crap.'

'No, it's not. And I'm thirty-five.' She smiled. 'But I like my life just as it is.'

'You won't when your daughters are gone.'

'That's something you should think of too. But in your case, your children need someone now, and so do you.' And then suddenly she began to laugh as she looked at him. 'This is crazy, here we are practically shouting at each other, that we should each get married. And we hardly know each other.'

He glanced over at her with a funny look on his face. 'The odd thing is that I feel as though we do. It seems as though you've been out here for years.'

She grew pensive then. 'I feel that way too, and it really doesn't make sense.' And then they were cast into the crowds and bright lights. He had tipped a porter so he could leave his car at the kerb, and he followed Mel inside, sorry that they hadn't had more time to talk alone. After last night he felt even closer to her than before. It was as though they had shared something special, the saving of a woman's life. It was like being combat buddies, or something more, and he was even sorrier now to see her go than he had been the day before.

'Well, let me know how the film looks.' They stood awkwardly at the gate as the flight was called, and she found herself itching to be held in his arms.

'I will. Take care. And give my love to the kids.' There was a feeling of *déjà vu* to the scene, but it was more poignant than before. 'And Marie and Pattie Lou.' Her voice was soft.

'Take care of yourself. Don't work too hard, Mel.'

'You too.' His eyes reached out to her, but there were no words for the confusion that he felt and he wasn't sure what to do. There was no privacy here, and he still wasn't sure what he felt for her.

'Thank you for everything.' And with that she shook him off guard by kissing his cheek, and walking through the gate, giving him a last wave, and then she was gone. He stood and stared, and then his beeper went off at his side, and he had to hurry to a phone. He couldn't wait for the plane to take off. He called the hospital, and the resident had a question about Marie. She was running a slight temperature, and he wanted to know if Peter wanted any of the doses of her medications varied. He made the necessary changes and walked back to his car, thinking not of Marie, but of Mel, just as her plane took off. The giant silver bird rose into the air and Mel stared down at the endless parking lots below, wondering where he was, and if she would ever see him or his children again. This time, there was no doubt in her mind. She was sad to leave, and sadder still to be going home. Tonight she didn't even try to convince herself that it wasn't true. She just sat staring out the window, thinking of him and the past four days, knowing that she liked him too much and it would get her nowhere. They led separate lives, in separate worlds, in cities three thousand miles apart, and that was just the way things were. And none of that would ever change.

Chapter 10

The flight to New York passed uneventfully. Mel took out a notebook and jotted down notes about the past few days while they were still fresh in her mind. There were a number of things she wanted to touch on in her commentary on the piece. Then at last, feeling drained, she closed the book and laid her head back against the seat and closed her eyes. The stewardess had offered her cocktails, wine, or champagne several times, but she had declined. She wanted to be left alone with her own thoughts, and after a while she drifted off to sleep for the last few hours of the flight. The trip from west to east always went too quickly to get much rest. With tail winds pushing the plane along, they made it to New York easily in just under five hours. She woke again with the sound of the landing announcement in her ears, and a stewardess touching her arm, asking her to fasten her seat belt before landing.

'Thank you.' She looked up at the stewardess sleepily and stifled a yawn, as she fastened her seat belt and then opened her bag to take out a comb. She felt as though she had been wearing the same clothes for days, and wondered again if she would find her suitcase waiting for her in New York. It seemed aeons since she had almost got on the plane in LA some thirty hours before, and been stopped by Peter's call. Then her mind drifted back to him again. His face seemed to come alive before her as she closed her eyes, and then forced herself to open them again as she felt the plane land on the runway in New York. She was home. And she had a mountain of work to do for the news and on the film she had done of him and Pattie Lou, and she had lots to do with the girls as well. She had her own life to lead, and yet there was the oddest feeling of regret to be back. She wished she could have stayed longer in LA, but there was no need, and she could never have explained it to the network in New York.

She found her bag waiting for her in the special-services area of baggage claim, picked it up, walked outside, hailed a cab, and headed for New York City at full speed. There was no traffic at all at six thirty in the morning, and the sun shot darts of gold across the sky, which was reflected on the windows of the skyscrapers that lined the view. As they came across the bridge and headed south on the East River Drive, she felt something stir in her again. New York always did that to her. It was a splendid town. And suddenly it wasn't so bad to be home again. This was where she belonged. As she smiled to herself, she noticed the driver watching her in his rearview mirror with a curious look. As she often did to strangers, she looked familiar to him, and he wasn't sure why. Maybe he had had her in the cab before, he thought to himself, or she was the wife of some important man, a politician or a movie star and he'd seen her in the news. He knew he'd seen that face somewhere before, but he wasn't quite sure where.

'Been away long?' He continued to search his mind as he looked at her.

'Just a few days, on the West Coast.'

'Yeah,' he nodded, turning right at Seventy-ninth and heading west. 'I been out there once. But there ain't no place like New York.'

She smiled. New Yorkers were a breed unto themselves, loyal to the end, despite dog mess, debris, crime in the streets, pollution, overpopulation, and the city's myriad failings and sins. Nonetheless, it had a quality one found nowhere else, a certain electricity that touched one to the very core. And she could feel it even now, as she watched the city come alive, as they sped through its streets.

'It's a great town.' He voiced his passion for his hometown again, and Mel nodded her head.

'It sure is.' It really was good to be back, and a happy feeling stirred her soul, as they pulled up in front of her house. She was excited about seeing the girls again, paid the cab, carried her bag inside, set it down in the front hall, and bounded upstairs to see them. They were both asleep, and she walked quietly into Jessica's room and sat down on the bed, looking at her. Her flame-coloured hair was spread out on the pillow like a dark red sheet, and she stirred as she heard her mother's voice and opened one eye. 'Hi, lazybones.' She bent down and kissed her cheek, and Jessie smiled.

'Hi, Mom. You're home.' She sat up and stretched and then hugged her mother with a sleepy smile. 'How was the trip?'

'Okay. It feels good to be back.' And this time she meant what she said. It did feel good. She had left California behind, along with Peter Hallam, and Marie Dupret and Center City Hospital, and all that she had done since she left New York. 'We did a terrific film.'

'Did you watch them operate?' Jessie was instantly intrigued. She would have given anything to have seen that, although her twin would have blanched at the thought.

'I did. I stayed to watch them do a transplant last night ... no, the night before ...' The time was all confused now in her head and she smiled. 'Whenever it was, it was a success. It was extraordinary, Jess.'

'Can I see the film?'

'Of course. You can come down to the station before we air the piece.'

'Thanks, Mom.' She climbed slowly out of bed, her long legs seeming longer beneath a short pink nightshirt, and Melanie left the room to see the other twin. In her room, Valerie was buried in her bed, fast asleep, and it took several gentle shoves and taps to move her at all. Melanie finally had to pull the blanket away from her and tug at the sheets, until at last Val woke up with a sleepy growl.

'Cut it out, Jess ...' And then she opened her eyes and saw Melanie instead. She looked surprised and confused, forgetting that her mother was due back. 'How come you're home?'

'That's a nice welcome home. Last I heard, I live here.'

Valerie grinned sleepily and turned over on her side. 'I forgot you were coming back today.'

'So what were you planning to do? Sleep all day and cut school?' She didn't really worry about that, about either of them, although Valerie was sometimes the less conscientious of the two.

'That's a nice idea. After all, school's almost out.'

'Then what do you say you hang in for a couple more weeks?'

'Awww Mom ...' She tried to go back to sleep and Melanie tickled her instead. 'Stop that!' She sat up with a shriek, defending herself against Mel's nimble hands. She knew all the places that tickled Valerie most, and a minute later they were laughing and Val was still shrieking as Jessica wandered into the room. With a single bound, she leapt into the bed, and helped Mel out, and then there was a pillow fight, which Valerie started in her own defence, and the three of them lay on the bed after a while, laughing and breathless. Mel felt her heart soar. Whatever she did, wherever she went, it was always so good to come home to them. And almost as soon as the thought crossed her mind, she found herself thinking of Pam in Los Angeles, and how different her life was from all this. How much she would have benefited from a life like the twins', and how lonely she was. Over breakfast, once the twins were dressed, she told them about the Hallam kids, especially Pam, and they seemed sorry for her when Mel explained to them about Anne's death.

'That must really be rough on her.' The more compassionate of the two, Val was the first to express concern, and then she grinned. 'And what's her brother like? I'll bet he's cute.'

'Val ...' Jessie said it with a disapproving glance. 'That's all you think about.'

'So what? I'll bet he is.'

'Who cares? He doesn't live here. There are probably a lot of cute boys in LA. What's that going to do for you in New York?' Jessie looked annoyed and Mel was amused.

She addressed her youngest daughter as she finished her tea. 'Does that mean you've exhausted the supply in New York?'

Val laughed. 'There's always room for one more.'

'I don't know how you keep their names straight.'

'I don't think she does,' Jessica was quick to add. In that one area, she disapproved of Val's style. She was more like Mel that way, independent, cool, cautious about getting involved with boys – too cautious at times – and it even worried Mel. Her life-style had clearly left its mark on the oldest twin. Maybe even on both. Perhaps that was why Val was always so anxious *not* to be without a beau. She didn't want to end up like Mel. 'She just oohs and smiles at them all in the halls at school, and I don't think they even care if she forgets their names.' It was more disapproval than jealousy at times like this, Mel knew. Val's passion for the opposite sex seemed trivial to Jess, who frequently had more important projects of an intellectual or scientific bent on her mind, but she had her share of boyfriends too. Mel reminded her of that when Val left the room to get her books for school. 'I know. But she acts like she doesn't have any sense. It's all she thinks about, Mom.'

'She'll get over it in a few years.'

'Yeah.' Jessie shrugged. 'Maybe.' And then they hurried off to school on Ninety-first Street, off Fifth, ten blocks away, and Melanie was left to gather her thoughts and unpack. She wanted to get to the station early that day to sort through her notes, and she had just stepped out of the shower at ten o'clock, when the phone rang, and she picked it up, still dripping wet. It was Grant, and she smiled to hear his voice. 'So you're back. I was beginning to think you'd left for good.'

'Nothing quite so dramatic as that. Although the last day was fairly dramatic, in a different way. They found a donor for a transplant patient that was barely hanging on, and I missed my plane and went back to watch the surgery.'

'Your stomach is infinitely stronger than mine.'

'I'm not so sure about that, but it was fascinating to watch.' And again a vision of Peter flashed into her mind. 'It was a good trip all in all, and how are you?'

'No change. I called the girls a few times to make sure they were all right, and they were fine. I can't keep up with their social lives, I'm afraid.'

'Neither can I. But you were nice to call.'

'I told you I would.' He sounded happy to hear her voice, and she was equally so to hear his. 'How'd the little girl do?'

'Great. She looked brand-new the last time I saw her at the hospital. It's just amazing, Grant.'

'And the good doctor who did it all? Was he amazing too?' It was as though he already sensed what she felt, but she felt foolish admitting her feelings to him. She was too old for that. Sudden attractions like that were better left to Val.

'He was an interesting man.'

'That's all? One of the foremost cardiac surgeons in the country, and that's all you have to say?' And then suddenly he grinned. He knew her too well. 'Or is it that there's more?'

'There isn't more. I just had a very hectic few days.' She wanted to keep her feelings about Peter Hallam to herself.

There was no point sharing them with anyone, not even Grant. Most likely she would never see him again and the words were better left unsaid.

'Well, when you settle down, Mel, give me a call, and we'll go have drinks sometime.'

'You're on.' But she didn't even feel like doing that right now. She was in her own private haze and she didn't feel like emerging from it yet.

'See you later, kid.' And then after a moment's pause. 'I'm glad you're back.'

'Thanks, me too.' But it was a lie. Even the excitement of being back in New York didn't woo her this time.

As she left the house, she glanced at her watch, and saw that it was eleven o'clock. Peter would be in surgery by then. And suddenly she had an overwhelming urge to call the hospital and inquire about Marie, but she had to retreat back into her professional life now. She couldn't take on all their problems as though they were her own, Marie's heart, Peter's kids, Pam's empty, lonely life, little Matthew with the big blue eyes ... suddenly she found herself longing for them again. Pushing them determinedly from her head, she hailed a cab and sailed downtown, looking at the city that she loved: people scurrying into Bloomingdale's and down into the ground to catch the subway, hailing cabs, or rushing in and out of skyscrapers on their way to work. It was like being part of a film just being there, and she felt buoyant and alive, even with almost no sleep, and she walked into the newsroom with a happy smile.

'What's with you?' The story editor growled at her as she rushed past, carrying two cans of films.

'I'm happy to be back.'

He shook his head, muttering, as he disappeared. 'Fool.'

She found a stack of mail on her desk, memos, summaries of major news items she'd missed while she was gone, and went out into the hall to watch the teletypes coming in for a while. There had been an earthquake in Brazil, a flood in Italy that had killed a hundred and sixty-four people, the President was going down to the Bahamas for a long weekend to fish. The news of the day didn't look overwhelmingly bad or good, and when her secretary came to tell her that there was a call for her, she went back into her office and picked up the phone without sitting down. She answered absentmindedly, glancing at the memos on her desk.

'Adams here.'

There was a moment's pause, as though she'd thrown someone off with the brusque words, and she heard a long-distance purr. But she didn't even have time to wonder who it was. 'Is this a bad time?' She recognised the voice instantly and sat down, surprised to hear from him. Maybe, with some time to think in her absence, he was getting worried about the piece.

'Not at all. How are you?' Her voice was soft and at his end he felt the same mysterious stirring he'd felt in his soul since they met.

'I'm fine. I finished surgery early today and thought I'd call to make sure you got back all right. Did you find your bag in New York?' He sounded nervous, and she was pleased by the call.

'I did. How's Marie?' Maybe he had called to give her bad news.

'She's doing beautifully. She asked for you today in fact. And so did Pattie Lou. She's the real star around here.'

Mel felt tears sting her eyes, and once again she felt the same ache she'd felt on the plane, of wanting to be in LA and not New York. 'Tell her I send my love. Maybe when she's feeling a little better, I'll give her a call.'

'She'd love that. And how are your girls?' He seemed to be groping for something to say and Mel was both confused and touched.

'They're fine. I think Valerie fell in love a few more times while I was gone, and Jessica is desperately jealous that I got to watch the transplant. She's the more serious of the two.'

'She's the one who wants to go to med school, isn't she?' Melanie was surprised that he'd recalled and she smiled.

'That's the one. She read her sister the riot act this morning, about falling in love six times a week.'

Peter laughed from his little cubicle in the hospital on the West Coast. He

had billed the call to his home phone. 'We used to have the same problem with
Mark when he was about Pam's age. But in the last few years he's settled down.'

'Ah, but wait for Matt!' Mel laughed. 'That one's going to be the lady's man of
all time.'

Peter laughed too. 'I have a sneaking suspicion that you're right.' There was a
comfortable pause and then Mel filled the gap.

'How's Pam?'

'She's all right. Nothing new.' He sighed into the phone. 'You know, I think
it did her good to talk to you. Just to be able to relate to someone other than Mrs
Hahn.' Mel didn't dare tell him what she thought of the icy woman. She didn't
feel it was her place to speak up.

'I enjoyed talking to her too.' Her emotional needs seemed so desperate, and
there seemed to be a lot of anger to vent too. Mel couldn't resist asking him
then. 'Did they get the little packages I sent yet?'

'Packages?' He sounded surprised. 'Did you send them gifts? You shouldn't
have done that.'

'I couldn't resist. I saw something perfect for Pam, and I didn't want to leave
Matthew and Mark out. Besides, they were very tolerant about letting me hang
around. As you said, you haven't seen people much since ... in the past year
and a half' – she hastened to fill the awkward gap – 'so it must have seemed
strange to them to have me appear. The least I could do was send them a little
surprise to thank them for their hospitality.'

He was touched by the thought and his voice was soft. 'You didn't have to do
that, Mel. We enjoyed having you here.' His words almost caressed her and she
blushed. There was something deeply intimate about this man, even by phone,
with three thousand miles in between, and she found herself thinking of him
again in ways she hadn't wanted to. It was almost impossible not to be drawn to
him. He was at the same time vulnerable and strong, humble and kind and yet so
full of the miracles he wrought. It was a combination which, for Mel, had
enormous appeal. She had always liked strong men, and yet too often she had
shied away from them. It was easier to get involved with lesser lights than he.

'I really enjoyed working with you, you know.' She wasn't sure what else to
say, and still wasn't sure why he'd called.

'You stole my lines. That's what I was calling to tell you. I'd been very
apprehensive about doing the interview. And you made me glad I decided to go
through with it. Everyone here is.' But not as much as he was, though he didn't
tell her that.

'Well, wait until you see it all on film. I hope you like it as much then.'

'I know I will.'

'I'm grateful for your faith in me.' And she truly was, but there was something more to what she felt as well, and she wasn't quite sure what it was.

'It's not just a matter of that, Mel. I ...' He didn't quite know how to put his
feelings into words, and suddenly wondered if he should have called. She was a
woman who signed autographs and appeared on national TV. 'I just like you a
hell of a lot.' He felt as awkward as a fifteen-year-old boy and they both smiled,
in LA and New York.

'I like you too.' Maybe it was just as simple as that, and there was no harm in it. Why was she fighting so hard against what she felt? 'I liked working with you, meeting your kids, seeing your home.' And then she understood something else. 'I think I was especially touched that you let me into your private life.'

'I think I felt safe doing that with you. I didn't plan it that way. In fact, I told myself before you came that I wasn't going to tell you anything personal about myself ... or Anne ...' His voice grew very soft again.

Mel was quick to respond. 'I'm glad you did.'

'So am I. I thought you handled the piece on Pattie Lou beautifully.'

'Thank you, Peter.' She liked what he had said. The trouble was that she liked too much about him. And then she heard him sigh softly at the other end. 'Well, I guess I should let you go back to work. I wasn't sure you'd be in after taking the red eye last night.'

She laughed softly at her end. 'The show must go on. And at six o'clock I have the news to do. I was just watching the teletypes come in when you called.'

'I hope I didn't interrupt.' He sounded contrite.

'No, it's kind of like watching the ticker tapes. After a while, you stop seeing what you read. And there's nothing major happening today, so far.'

'That's about the way it is here. I'm going to the office now. I have a lot of catching up to do, after keeping an eye on Marie and Pattie Lou for the past few days.' They were both back to their usual lives, their work, their kids, their responsibilities on separate coasts, and again she felt how much she had in common with him. He had as much resting on his shoulders as she on hers, in fact more. And it was comforting to know that there were other people in the world, carrying burdens and obligations as demanding as hers.

'You know, it's kind of nice knowing someone who works as hard as I do.' And he felt odd as she said the words. He had thought the same thing about her from the first. Even with Anne, it had bothered him sometimes that all she had to do was redecorate the house and buy antiques, work on the PTA and chauffeur children from here to there. 'I don't mean to sound presumptuous because my work doesn't include saving lives, but still, it's demanding as hell and most people don't understand that. Some nights I finish here and my brain is absolutely mush. I couldn't say an intelligent word to a living soul if my life depended on it when I got home.' It was one of the many reasons why she had never been tempted to marry again. She wasn't sure she could live up to the demands of it any more.

But he felt as relieved as she. 'I know exactly what you mean. But on the other hand, sometimes it's difficult not to have someone to share it with.'

'I never really have. As long as I've done well at my work, I've been alone, or more or less. I think it's easier like this.'

'Yes' – but he didn't sound convinced – 'but then there's no one to share the victories with.' Anne had always been good at that, and good at sharing the heartbreaks and tragedies too. It was just that her life had never been as full as his, but on the other hand maybe that had left her freer to support him. It was difficult to imagine a working wife, and yet he had always admired hardworking teams, doctors married to other doctors, lawyers married to bankers, professors and scientists. The combinations seemed to feed on themselves, giving each one a new impetus, although at times it could also be a double drain. 'I don't know the answers to all this, my friend. I just know it isn't always easy being alone.'

'Neither is being together.' She was convinced.

'No. But it has its rewards.' Of that he was sure. Especially when he looked at his kids.

'I guess that's true. I don't know the answers myself. I just know it's good talking to someone who understands what it's like to work like a mule, and then have to come home and be two parents instead of just one.' There had been times over the years when she thought she couldn't pull it off, but she had, and she had done well. Her job was secure, her success immense, her children happy and they were good kids. 'You've done a good job, Mel.' They were words that meant more to her than anything else.

'So have you.' Her voice was like silk to his ears.

'But I've only done it alone for a year and a half. You've been alone for fifteen. That really means something.'

'Only a few more grey hairs.' She laughed softly into the phone. Just then one of the editors signalled to her from the door. And she signalled back that she'd be with him in a few minutes, so he disappeared again. 'Well, it looks like they want me to go to work around here. One of the editors just showed up. I hope that means our film is in from LA.'

'So soon?'

'It's complicated to explain, but they do it all by computers. We get it here within a day. I'll let you know how it looks.'

'I'd like that.'

And she had liked hearing from him. 'Thank you so much for calling me, Peter. I really miss you all.' The 'all' kept it safe. It meant she didn't just miss him. It was like listening to Val and Jess on the phone, fencing with their boyfriends, she chided herself and then smiled. 'I'll talk to you soon.'

'Good. We miss you too.' 'We' instead of 'I'. They were playing the same game and neither of them could figure out why, but they weren't ready for more. 'Take care.'

'Thanks. You too.' They rang off and Mel sat at her desk for a long moment, thinking of him. It was crazy, but she was excited that he'd called. As excited as a little girl. She hurried down the hall to the editing labs with a grin on her face that she just couldn't erase. A grin that stayed there until she saw the film. She saw herself looking at him, and Pattie Lou and Pearl and even Marie and her transplant done at two a.m., and she felt her heart race each time he spoke, each time the camera looked into his eyes and saw the decency and caring there. She felt almost breathless when at last they turned on the lights. It was a sensational piece of film.

In its pre-cut stake it went on for hours, it would need much cutting and editing. But all she could think of as she left the room, was him . . .

Chapter 11

That night, Melanie did the news again for the first time since she'd been back, and everything went as smoothly as it always did. She signed off with the pleasant, professional smile that people recognised everywhere across the entire United States, and as she walked off the set, she had no idea that Peter Hallam had been watching her intently in his den in LA. Halfway through it Pam had walked into the room and stood there and stared. Peter hadn't even known she was there.

'Someone shoot the President or something, Dad?'

He looked at her, annoyed, it had been a long day and he wanted to see Mel before she went off the air. He had watched her before, but it had never been quite like this. He knew her now, and suddenly it seemed terribly important to see her after their call that day. 'Pam, I'll come upstairs in a little while. I just want to be alone to watch the news.'

For a long moment, Pam stood there in the doorway, torn by her own feelings of anger and attraction to Mel. She had liked her when they met, but she didn't like the way her father looked when he saw her. 'Yeah, sure . . . okay . . .' But he didn't see the look on her face as she left the room and he sat staring at the set as Mel wound up for the day. He sat there for a little while longer, and then he turned off the set and went upstairs to see his children. He was truly exhausted. He had spent two hours with Marie that afternoon at the hospital. She seemed to be developing an infection, and was having a reaction to the medication. It was expected, but difficult anyway.

In New York, Mel hurried home after doing the news, and had dinner with the girls, and then went back to the studio to do the eleven-o'clock show. It was after that that Mel saw Grant again for the first time. He was waiting for her on the set when she came off the air.

'You did a nice job tonight.' He looked down at her with a warm smile and could see how tired she was. But he saw something else too. Something that hadn't been there before, a kind of glow. 'How are you holding up with no sleep?'

'I'm beginning to fade,' she admitted with a tired smile, but she was glad to see him.

'Well, go home and get some rest.'

'Yes, Dad.'

'I'm old enough to be, so watch your step.'

'Yes, sir.' She saluted smartly, and a few minutes later she left, dozing sleepily in the cab.

She climbed the stairs to her room, peeled her clothes off and dropped them on the floor beside her bed. Five minutes later, she was sound asleep between her cool sheets, naked and peaceful, her mind empty at last of anything at all. And she didn't stir again until early next afternoon, when the phone rang and it was Peter again.

'Good morning. Is it too early to call?'

'Not at all.' She stifled a yawn and glanced at the clock. It was ten fifteen for him on the Coast. 'How's life in LA?'

'Busy. I've got two triple bypasses scheduled today.'

'How are Marie and Pattie Lou?' She sat up in bed and looked around her room in New York.

'They're both fine. Pattie Lou more so than Marie.' She really had been a victory for him. 'More importantly, how are you?'

'Honestly?' She smiled. 'I'm dead.'

'You ought to get some rest. You work too hard, Mel.'

'Look who's talking.' She tried to pretend that it was normal for him to call, but secretly she was thrilled. 'I'm going on holiday soon anyway.'

'You are?' He sounded surprised, she hadn't mentioned it before, but when had there been time during her few days in LA. 'Where?'

'Bermuda.' She sounded pleased. She'd been looking forward to it for a long time. A television producer she knew had offered to rent her her house for a few days, and because it didn't coincide with any school holiday for the twins, she had just decided to go alone anyway.

He sounded nervous when he next spoke. 'Are you going with friends?'

'No. By myself.'

'You are?' He sounded both stunned and relieved.

'What an independent lady you are.' He admired her for that. He wasn't ready for a holiday alone yet. He would have been lost without the children, now that Anne was gone. But Mel had been alone for a lot longer than he.

'I just thought it might be fun. The girls are jealous as hell. But they have friends and a big prom that week.'

'I'm jealous too.'

'Don't be. It'll probably be very quiet.' But it wouldn't have been with him. She forced the thought from her mind. 'But it'll do me good.'

'Yes, it will.' He didn't begrudge her that. He just wished he could have been there with her, as crazy as the thought was. They were almost strangers to each other, although not nearly as much as they had been. They talked on for a little while, and then he had to go off to surgery, and Mel wanted to go to the network to watch them edit some more of her film.

Chapter 12

The phone rang just as she was leaving the house the following Wednesday morning. She was in a hurry to get to Bloomingdale's because she desperately needed some more bathing suits for the trip to Bermuda that week. She had looked over the ones from the summer before and they were all badly worn and stretched and faded. She lived in her bathing suits for two months, and every year they took a beating.

'Hello?'

'It's me.' It was Grant.

'What's up? I was just running out to buy some new bathing suits for my trip.' She was finally beginning to look forward to it. And she was leaving in two days. 'Do you want me to pick anything up for you? I'm going to Bloomie's.'

'No, thanks. I forgot you were going down there. Need a butler or a male secretary while you're there?'

'No thank you.' She smiled at the phone, and he realised he'd hardly seen her since she got back from LA.

'I just wanted to ask you a question about Marcia Evans.' She was the grande dame of legitimate theatre and Mel had done an intimate interview with her six months before. 'I'm having her on the show tonight.'

Mel cringed. 'Good luck. She's a dragon.'

'Shit. That's what I thought. And the producer told me I had nothing to worry about. Any tips for my survival?'

'Bring along a snake-bite kit. She's the most venomous woman I've ever met. Just watch out that you don't piss her off. You'll see her coming.'

'That's a big help.' He didn't sound pleased, and he was furious with his producer for setting him up.

'I'll give it some more thought while I'm out shopping, and I'll call you when I get home.'

'Do you want to have dinner tonight, to give me courage?'

'Why don't you drop by to see the girls?'

'I'll try' – he grinned – 'if nothing else interferes.'

'You and tits, Grant.' She laughed.

'I can't help it if I'm weak. I'll call you later, kid.'

'Okay.' He hung up, and she looked in the mirror and picked up her handbag. She was wearing a white linen dress with a black silk jacket and black and white patent leather shoes she had bought in Rome the year before. She looked very chic and she felt good. They had worked like demons for a week, editing the film on Peter Hallam and Pattie Lou Jones and she was just loving what they got as they went along. As she reached the front door, the phone rang again, and she was tempted not to answer. It was probably the damn editor wanting her to come in, and for once she wanted some time to herself to do her shopping. But it rang so persistently that she gave in and walked into the living room and picked up the white phone she had concealed in a nook there.

'Yes?' She waited, afraid she'd hear the editor's voice again. He had already called twice that morning. But it wasn't the editor at all. It was Peter Hallam again. He called her often.

'Hello, Mel.' He sounded hesitant after her gruff response when she picked it up and she was embarrassed.

'Hi, Peter, I'm sorry if I barked. I was just running out, but ...' She felt young again, and nervous, just as she had when he'd called before. He had a funny effect on her, which seemed to cancel out her success and her self-confidence. She was just a young girl again when she talked to him ... or maybe 'just' a woman. '... it's nice to hear from you.' He hadn't called in a few days. 'How's Marie?' Suddenly she was afraid that he had called to give her bad news, but he was quick to reassure her.

'Much better. We had a problem last night, and I thought she was going into a major rejection, but everything's under control again. We switched her medication. We think she might even be ready to go home in a few weeks.' It was something Melanie would have liked to see, but it didn't justify a trip West and her producer would never have let her go just for that.

'And the children?'

'They're fine. I just wondered how you were. I called you at the office but they said you weren't there.'

'I'm playing hooky.' She laughed and felt lighthearted and happy. 'This is the weekend I'm going to Bermuda, and I needed to shop for a few things.'

'That sounds like fun. We're staying here for a long weekend. Mark is playing in a tennis tournament and Matthew's going to a birthday party.'

'The girls are going to that prom I told you about, and then to Cape Cod with a friend and her parents.' They seemed to hide a lot in talk of their children, and Mel found herself wondering how *he* was, not Pam and Mark and Matthew. And then she decided to ask him. 'Are you all right, Peter? Not working too hard?'

'Of course I am,' he laughed, but he was pleased at the question. 'I wouldn't know how to do anything else, and neither would you.'

'That's true. When I get old and wrinkled and have to retire, I won't know what the hell to do with myself every morning.'

'You'll think of something.'

'Yeah, brain surgery maybe.' They both laughed, she sat down as Bloomingdale's and the bathing suits slipped her mind completely. 'Actually, I'd like to write a book then.'

'What about?'

'My memoirs.' She teased.

'No, really.'

It wasn't often that she confessed her dreams to anyone, but he was easy to talk to. 'I don't know, I think I'd write a book about being a woman in journalism. It was tough at first, although it's a lot easier now, but not always. People resent it like hell when you make it. They're half glad, and half pissed. It's been interesting coping with that, and I think it's something a lot of women could relate to. It doesn't matter if you do what I do, or you do something else. The issue is crawling to the top, and I know what that's like, how much work it takes and what happens when you get there.'

'It sounds like an instant best seller.'

'Maybe not, but I'd like to try it.'

'I've always wanted to write a book about heart surgery for the layman, what it's like, what to expect, what to demand of your doctor, what the risks are in specific situations. I don't know if anyone would give a damn, but too many people are unprepared, and get screwed over by their doctors.'

'Now, that sounds like a good one.' She was impressed, there was a need for a book like that and it would be interesting to see what he did with it.

'Maybe we should run away to the South Pacific together, and write our books. When the kids grow up,' he added.

'Why wait?' It was an amusing fantasy, but it suddenly reminded her of the trip to Bermuda. 'I've never been to the South Pacific.' And she had been to Bermuda. It was tropical and it wasn't too far away but it was definitely not exciting. Or maybe it was that going alone didn't excite her. And Peter did? That question was frightening to answer.

'I've always wanted to go to Bora Bora,' he confessed, 'but I can never get away from my patients for long enough to make it worthwhile.'

'Maybe you don't want to.' It was something Anne had accused him of too, and it was probably true.

'You may be right.' Somehow it was easy to be honest with her. 'I'll have to save it till I retire.' There was a lot he had saved for that, and now that Anne was gone it would never be shared after all. He had put off so much for 'later' that he regretted now. There was no later. At least not for them. And he wondered at the wisdom of continuing to save things for 'later'. What if he had a stroke, if he died, if ... 'Maybe I'll go sooner than that.'

'You ought to. You owe yourself something.' But what? All he wanted lately was her.

'Are you excited about your trip, Mel?'

'Yes and no.' She had been to romantic spots alone before. It had its drawbacks.

'Send me a postcard.'

'I will.'

And then, 'I'd better let you go. Call me when you get back from your trip. And rest!'

'You need it as much as I do. Probably more.'

'I doubt that.'

She looked at her watch then, wondering where he was. It was nine thirty in the morning in California. 'Aren't you in surgery today?'

'No. The last Wednesday of every month we have conferences to bring the whole team up to date on new techniques and procedures. We discuss what's being done all over the country, and what we've each tried to accomplish in surgery that month.'

'I wish I'd known. I would have loved to have that on film.' But she had enough without it.

'We start at ten o'clock. And I finished my rounds early.' He sounded boyish too then. 'Calling you is a treat I've been promising myself for days.' It was easier to say things like that on the phone, and he was suddenly grateful for the distance between them.

'I'm flattered.' He wanted to tell her that she should be, that he had never called another woman, in that sense, since marrying Anne, but he didn't say it. 'I've thought about calling you a few times too, to see how Marie was, but the time difference was always off.'

'That happened to me too. Anyway, I'm glad I called. Have a nice weekend in Bermuda.'

'Thank you. You have a nice one too. I'll call you when I get back.' It was the first time she had promised that in just that way, and she was already looking forward to it. 'Our film is looking sensational, by the way.'

He smiled warmly. 'I'm glad.' But that wasn't why he had called. 'Take care of yourself, Mel.'

'I'll call you next week.' And suddenly she knew that a bond had formed between them that hadn't been there before, and as she left to go to Bloomingdale's, she felt young and excited and carefree.

She tried on two blue bathing suits, a black one, and a red one, but red had never been a good colour with her hair, and she bought a rich royal-blue one and the black one. They were a bit risqué, but she felt exotic today. As she stood at the counter smiling to herself, holding her charge card and the two bathing suits, waiting to be helped, she saw a woman in tears rush towards her. 'The President's been shot!' she screamed to anyone who would listen. 'He's been shot in the chest and the back, and he's dying!' The entire store seemed shot with an electric current as people shouted the news to each other and began running, as though their frenzied activity would help. But Mel, operating by reflex, dropped the bathing suits on the counter, and ran down three flights of stairs and out of the door. She climbed into the first cab she saw, breathlessly gave the studio address, and asked the driver to turn on the radio as they drove. Both she and the cabbie sat frozen in silence as they listened to the news. No one seemed to know yet for certain if the President was alive or not. He had been in Los Angeles for a day, conferring with the governor and assorted civic leaders in LA. He was rushed to the hospital in an ambulance moments before, critically wounded, as two Secret Servicemen lay dead on the pavement next to where he had stood. Mel's face was pale as she threw a ten-dollar bill into the driver's hands and hurtled through the double doors leading into the network building. Everything was already in total chaos there from the lobby to the newsroom, and as she flew towards the bureau chief's desk, he looked at her with relief.

'Christ, I hoped you'd get here, Mel.'

'I practically ran all the way from Bloomingdale's.' At least, she felt like she had. She knew that the one place she had to be was here.

'I want to put you on with the special bulletins right away.' He looked at what she was wearing and she looked fine, but he wouldn't have given a damn if she'd been stark naked. 'Get some makeup on and can you close your jacket a little? The dress is too white for the camera.'

'Sure. What's new now?'

'Nothing yet. He's in surgery, and it looks bad, Mel.'

'Shit.' She ran to her office, and where she kept her makeup, and five minutes later she was back, ready to go on the air. The producer followed her into the studio, and handed her a stack of papers for her to read quickly. She looked at him a moment later, with grim eyes. 'It doesn't look good, does it?' He'd been hit in the chest three times, and his spine seemed to have been affected, from the early reports. Even if he lived, he could be paralysed or worse yet, a complete vegetable. He was in Center City, undergoing surgery right then. And Mel suddenly wondered what Peter Hallam knew about it that the press didn't, but she didn't have time to call before she went on the air.

She went quickly to her desk, and began ad-libbing soberly into the camera as she went on beneath the hot lights and she delivered the news bulletins as they came on. All normal programming had been stopped to give the public the news as it came, but there wasn't a great deal to say yet. She had to wing it for most of the afternoon, and she didn't get a break for three hours, when she was relieved by one of the other anchors, the man who did the weekend news. They had all been called in, and there was endless discussion and surmise on the air between reports from the West Coast, and moments when they switched to the reporters in LA, standing in the lobby of Center City, so familiar now to Mel. She only wished that she were there, as she listened to the news. But by six o'clock there was still no news, except that he was still alive and had survived surgery. They would have to play a waiting game, as would the First Lady, who was in the air on her way to LA now, and due to arrive at LA within the hour.

Mel did her usual show at six o'clock, and of course covered almost exclusively the news from LA and when she came off the air, the producer was waiting to confer with her.

'Mel.' He looked at her sombrely and handed her another sheaf of papers. 'I want you out there.' For a moment, she was stunned. 'Go home, get your stuff, come back and do the eleven o'clock, and we'll run you out to the airport. They're going to hold a flight for you, and you can start reporting from out there first thing tomorrow morning. By then, God only knows what will have happened.' The man who had shot him was already in custody, and lengthy profiles of his chequered past were on the air constantly, interspersed with interviews with major surgeons giving their opinions of the President's chances. 'Can you do it?' They both knew it was a rhetorical question. She had no choice. This was what they paid her for, and the coverage of national emergencies was part of it. She mentally ran over the list of what she had to do. She knew from experience that Raquel would take care of the girls, and she would see them when she went home between shows to pack.

At home, she found the twins and Raquel in tears in front of the TV, and

Jessica was the first to approach her. 'What's going to happen, Mom?' Raquel loudly blew her nose.

'We don't know yet.' And then she told them the news. 'I have to go to California tonight. Will you guys be okay?' She turned to Raquel, knowing her answer would be yes.

'Of course.' She almost looked insulted.

'I'll be back as soon as all of this is over.'

She kissed them all and left for the network to do the late news, and as soon as she came off the air, she left in the wake of two cops who had been waiting to escort her to their car downstaioirs. They all listened intently to the radio as they sped to the airport with the sirens shrieking. It was a favour the police occasionally did for the station. They made it to JFK by twelve fifteen and the plane took off ten minutes after she boarded. Several times the stewardesses came to give her bulletins, transmitted by the pilots, as they got the news from towers and air controllers as they crossed the country. The President was still alive, but there was no way of telling for how long. It seemed an endless night and Mel finally disembarked feeling truly exhausted. She was met again by a police escort there, and she decided to go to Center City before going to her hotel and sleeping for a few hours. She would have to go to work at seven o'clock the next morning, and it was already four o'clock in the morning in LA. But when she reached Center City, there was no further news, and she got to her hotel just before five a.m. She figured that she could sleep for an hour or so before reporting for work. She was just going to have to drink a lot of black coffee, and she requested a wake-up from the hotel operator so she wouldn't oversleep. They had booked her into a hotel where she had never stayed, but it was close to Center City. And suddenly she realised how strange it was that she was back in LA again so soon, and wondered if she would have time to see Peter. Maybe when it was all over. Unless, of course, the President died. She might have to fly back simultaneously with *Air Force One* to attend the funeral in Washington, in which case she would never see him. But she hoped for the President's sake that wouldn't happen. And she desperately wanted to see Peter in the next few days. She wondered if he'd know she was there.

She woke up instantly when the operator called, all her senses alert, although her limbs ached and she felt as though she hadn't slept at all. But she would have to operate on black coffee and nervous energy and stay on her feet somehow. She had done it before, and she knew she could do it this time. Dressing quickly in a dark grey dress and high-heeled black shoes, she was out of the hotel and in the police car at six thirty and at the hospital ten minutes later, to get the latest details and go on the air. It was already almost ten o'clock in New York by then and the eastern portion of the country had been hungry for news for hours.

She saw the camera crew she had used before in the fray along with at least fifty other cameramen and two dozen reporters. They were camping out in the lobby and a hospital spokesman was giving them bulletins every half hour. And finally at eight o'clock, an hour after Mel went on the air, looking grave and impressive, the first bit of good news reached them. The President was conscious, and his spinal cord had been neither damaged nor severed. If he survived he would not be paralysed, and there had been no brain damage from what they could tell so far. But he was still critically ill and hovering between life and death. His survival was not yet assured, and three hours later the First Lady joined them and spoke a few words to the nation. Mel was able to get three minutes of her time. The poor woman looked grief-stricken and exhausted, but she stood speaking to Mel with dignity and a firm voice. One's heart went out to her as tears filled her eyes, but her voice never wavered. Mel let her speak, asked only a few questions, and assured her of the nation's prayers, and then miraculously was able to get a few moments later on with the President's surgeon. By six o'clock that night there was no additional news, and Mel was relieved by a local anchor, going on for the network. She was given five hours to go to her hotel and sleep, if she could. But by then she was so wound up, she couldn't sleep. She lay in the dark, thinking of a thousand things, and suddenly she reached for the phone, and dialled a local number.

Mrs Hahn answered the phone, and without friendly preamble Mel asked for Peter, and he was on the line a moment later.

'Mel?'

'Hi. I don't even know if I make sense, I'm so cross–eyed, but I just wanted to call and tell you I was here.'

He smiled gently then. She sounded exhausted. 'Remember me? I work at Center City too. Not to mention the fact that we do have a television set here. I saw you twice today, but you didn't see me. Are you holding up all right?'

'I'll do. I'm used to this. After a while, you just have to put your body on automatic pilot, and hope that you don't crash into a wall somewhere looking for a bathroom.'

'Where are you now?' She gave him the name of her hotel, and it struck him as remarkable that she was so near again. He had to admit that in spite of the horrendous circumstances, he liked it, although he wondered if he'd be able to see her. 'Is there anything I can do for you?'

'Not right now. But if there is, I'll let you know.'

He felt like a complete idiot asking her the next question, but he had to. 'Is there any chance that ... I can see you sometime? I mean other than across a crowded lobby full of reporters?'

'I don't know yet.' She was honest with him. 'It depends on what happens.' And then she sighed. 'What do you think will happen, Peter? What are his chances really?' She should have asked him before, but she was so tired she didn't think of it till just now.

'Fair. Depends on what kind of shape he's in. His heart's not involved or they would have called me in. I was in the operating room when they operated, just in case. But they didn't need me.' She hadn't known that from the reports, but she suspected that there was a lot of information held back. The only thing they knew everything about was the assailant, a twenty-three-year-old man who had spent the last five years in a mental hospital and had told his sister two months before that he was going to kill the President. No one took him seriously since he thought that his roommate at the hospital was God and the head nurse was Marilyn Monroe. No one even thought he knew who the President was, but he did. He knew well enough to almost kill him, and maybe succeed after all. 'We'll know a lot more tomorrow, Mel.'

'If you get any inside leads, will you call me?'

'Sure. But why don't you get some sleep before you become the next patient?'

'I will, but I'm so damn keyed up I can't sleep.'

'Try. Just close your eyes and rest, don't think of sleeping.' His voice was soothing and she was glad she had called him. 'Do you want a ride to the hospital tomorrow?'

'Tomorrow?' She laughed. 'I have to be back at eleven o'clock tonight.'

'That's inhuman!' He was outraged.

'So is shooting the President.' They both agreed and she hung up, glad she had called. Melanie just hoped they could get together before she left LA. It would kill her to have been there and to leave without even seeing him once, but they both knew it could happen. And as Mel rolled over on the bed in her hotel room, she prayed that it wouldn't.

Chapter 13

On Friday, Mel and the rest of the press crew spent a long anxious day in the lobby of Center City. There were half a dozen people assigned to bring them sandwiches and coffee, and periodically they went on the air to give their assorted news stations the latest bulletins on the President's condition. But on the whole, nothing changed much from six in the morning until seven that evening. After coming back on duty at eleven o'clock on Thursday night, Mel didn't leave the hospital until eight o'clock Friday night, so exhausted that her head was throbbing and her eyes burning. She walked out into the parking lot and as she slid behind the wheel of the car that had been rented for her the previous night, her vision was so blurred that she was afraid to turn the key in the ignition and drive back to her hotel. The voice that she heard seemed to be coming at her out of the thick fog, as she turned to see who was standing beside the car and speaking to her.

'You're in no condition to drive, Miss Adams.' At first she thought it was a cop, but as she squinted she saw a familiar face, and she smiled and leaned her head back against the seat. The window was rolled down all the way. She knew she had needed as much air as she could get so she wouldn't fall asleep at the wheel on the way home.

'Well, I'll be damned. What are you doing here?' Even in her state of near collapse, she could see that his eyes were a deep blue, and it was wonderfully comforting just seeing him there.

'I work here, or did you forget?'

'But isn't it late for you to be here?'

He nodded and watched the look in her eyes. She was happy to see him too, but she was too exhausted to move. 'Move over. I'll drive you back to your hotel.'

'Don't be silly. I'm fine. I just have to . . .'

'Look, be practical, Mel. With the President here, when you wrap yourself around a tree in this car, they won't even give you a Band-Aid in the emergency room. Everyone in the whole place is rallying around him. So let's save ourselves a big headache, and let me drive you home. Agreed?' She didn't have the strength left to argue with him. She just smiled like a tired child, nodded her head, and slid over. 'That's a good girl.' He glanced at her to see if she'd object to the term and was relieved that she didn't. She just sat there looking glazed and didn't seem to object to his taking over. He drove expertly through the LA traffic, which was still heavy at that hour, and glanced over at her from time to time. At last he spoke again. 'You okay, Mel?'

'I'm just beat. I'll be okay with a little sleep.'

'When do you have to go back?'

'Not till six o'clock tomorrow morning, thank God.' And then she sat up a little straighter in her seat. 'Do you know anything I should know about the President's condition?' But he only shook his head. 'I hope he makes it.'

'So does everyone else in the country, so do I. You feel so helpless with something like this. But actually, you know, he was damn lucky. It could have been over right away. In fact, from the X-rays I saw it was very close. He came within a hair of losing his life, or his mind, or at best his ability to ever move from the neck down. If the bullet had ricocheted a little differently than it did . . .' He didn't have to finish the sentence. The surgeons working on the President were his friends, and he was painfully up to date.

'I feel so sorry for his wife. She's being brave, and she looks as though she's just barely hanging on to her last shred of hope.' She wasn't a young woman, and the last two days had been a terrible strain on her.

'She has a heart problem, you know. Only a slight one. But this is not exactly what the doctor ordered for her.'

Mel looked at him with a tired smile. 'At least you're around in case she has a problem.' And she was suddenly very grateful that he was around for her too. She realised now that she would never have made it across the obstacle course of the freeway. She said as much to him as they pulled up in front of her hotel.

'Don't be silly. I wouldn't have let you drive like that.'

'I'm just lucky you were there when I came out.' She felt slightly revived, but only barely. And she hadn't figured out that he'd been waiting for her, having foreseen the problem. It was something he had wanted to do for her, and he was glad that he had. 'Thanks so much, Peter.' They both got out of the car and he looked down at her.

'Will you get into the hotel all right?'

She smiled at the care he took of her. No one had been that preoccupied with her in years, if ever. 'I'm fine. I can walk. I just can't drive.' But she would have, if she'd had to.

'I'll pick you up tomorrow morning. Quarter to six?'

'I can't let you do that.'

'Why not? Normally, I'd be there by six thirty. What difference does half an hour make?'

'Really, I can drive myself.' She was almost embarrassed by the attention, but he held firm.

'I don't see why you should have to.'

And suddenly she had a thought. 'How are you going to get home from here?'

'Don't worry about that. I'll grab a cab back to the parking lot and pick up my car. Me, I'm wide awake. You're the one who's dead on your feet.'

'Oh, Peter, I didn't mean to ...' But she yawned and cut off her own words and he laughed.

'Yes? Is there anything else you'd like to say to your public?' He was teasing and she was sorry she was so dazed by her long day.

'Just thank you.' Their eyes met and held for a moment outside the hotel. 'And it's nice to see you again.'

'No, it isn't, you can't even see. For all you know, a perfect stranger just drove you home.' He guided her gently towards the door of her hotel and walked her into the lobby.

'All strangers should be so nice.' She mumbled softly.

'Now be good, and go up to your room and get some sleep. Have you eaten?'

'Enough. All I want now is my bed. Come to think of it, any bed will do.' The floor was even beginning to look good. He pressed the lift button for her and propelled her gently inside and before she could say more, he stepped back.

'See you in the morning.'

She would have objected, but the doors closed, and the lift deposited her on her floor. All she had to do was walk to her room, open the door, close it again, and make it to her bed. All of which she did, feeling like a zombie. She didn't even bother to take off her clothes, she called the operator before she passed out, and left a wake up for five o'clock in the morning, and the next thing she knew she was asleep, and the phone was ringing.

'Five o'clock, Miss Adams.'

'Already?' Her voice was hoarse and she was still half asleep. She had to shake herself awake, as she sat up with the phone in her hand. 'Have you heard any news? Is the President still alive?'

'I believe so.' But if he weren't, they would have called her from the hospital, or the network in LA.

Mel hung up and dialled the local station. The President was still alive, and there was no news since the night before. His condition was stable but still critical. She headed for the shower after that. It was too early to even order coffee. And then she went downstairs to stand outside the hotel at twenty to six, feeling that she should have insisted the night before that Peter not pick her up. There was no reason for him to chauffeur her around. It was silly really. But at exactly five forty-five, he picked her up, and opened the car door for her (he looked wide awake) and as she slid beside him, he offered her a thermos of coffee.

'Good God, this is the best limo service I've ever had.'

'There are sandwiches in that bag.' He pointed to a brown paper bag on the floor and smiled at her. 'Good morning.' He had correctly guessed that she hadn't eaten the night before, and he had made some sandwiches himself to bring to her.

'It sure is nice having a friend in LA.' She took a big bite of a turkey sandwich on white toast, and sank back gratefully against the seat of the Mercedes with a cup of coffee in her hand. 'This is the life.' And then she looked over at him with a shy smile. 'Somehow, when I left here two weeks ago, I didn't really think we'd see each other again. Or at least not for a long time.'

'That's what I thought too. I'm sorry it has to be over something as serious as this. But I'm glad you're here, Mel.'

'Know something?' She took another swig of the steaming coffee. 'So am I. That's awful to say, given why I'm here. But I don't know...' She looked away for a moment and then back at him. 'You've been on my mind a lot since I went back, and I wasn't sure why. Maybe coming back here will help me sort that out.'

He nodded. He had had the same problem. 'It's difficult to explain to you what I've been feeling. I keep wanting to call you to tell you things, to give you the latest news about Marie ... or a surgery we just did ... or something one of the children said.'

'I think you've just been terribly lonely and I opened a door. Now you don't know what to do with it.' He nodded, and Mel looked thoughtful. 'But the funny thing is that neither do I. You opened a door for me too, and I kept thinking of you when I went home. I was so glad when you called me that first time.'

'I didn't have any choice. I felt that I had to.'

'Why?' They were both looking for answers they didn't have.

'I don't know, Mel. It was actually a relief to know you were back. Maybe this time I'll find what I'm trying to say.' ... or maybe I won't dare say it ...

'But Mel dared to ask the most difficult question. 'Does it scare you?'

'Yes.' His voice almost trembled and he didn't look at her as he drove. 'It scares me a lot.'

'If it's any consolation, it scares me too.'

'Why?' He glanced at her in surprise. 'You've been out there on your own for years. You know what you're doing. I don't.'

'That's the whole point. I've been out there alone for fifteen years. No one has ever come too close. If they did, I ran off. But there's something about you ... I don't know what to make of you, and I was so damn drawn to you when I was here before.'

He stopped the car in the parking lot of Center City and turned to face her. 'You're the first woman I've been attracted to in twenty years, other than my wife. That scares the hell out of me, Mel.'

'Why?'

'I don't know. But it does. I've been hiding since she died. And all of a sudden

I'm not sure I want to any more.' They sat in silence for a long time, and Mel broke the silence first.

'Why don't we just wait and see what happens. Not push anything. Neither of us has risked anything yet. You've made a couple of phone calls, and I'm out here because the President was shot. That's all there is to it for now.' She was trying to reassure herself as much as him, but neither of them was convinced.

'Are you sure that's all there is to it?' His eyes were gentle and she smiled at him.

'No, I'm not. That's the trouble. But maybe if we take it slow, we won't scare ourselves half to death.'

'I hope I don't scare you, Mel. I like you too much to want to frighten you away.'

'I scare myself more than you ever could. I never wanted to get hurt again, or to depend on anyone but myself. I've built a fortress around me, and if I let anyone in, they might destroy what I've built, and it took me so long to put it all together.' It was the most honest thing she could have told him, and there were tears in her eyes as he watched her.

'I won't hurt you, Mel, ever, if I can help it. If anything, I would want to take some of that load off your shoulders.'

'I'm not sure I want to give it up.'

'And I'm not sure I'm ready to take it on.'

'That's okay. It's better that way.' She sat back against the seat for one more moment before she had to leave him. 'The only thing that's too bad is that we're so far apart. You live here. I live there. We'll never find anything out like this.'

'Maybe we will while you're here.' He sounded hopeful, but she shook her head.

'That's not very likely while I'm working this hard.'

But he wasn't willing to be discouraged. Not yet. He needed to find out what he felt for this woman who appealed to him so much. He looked at the big green eyes he had remembered so well. 'The last time you were here, you followed me around while I was working. This time let me put myself at your disposal, as much as I can. Maybe we'll find a little spare time to talk.'

'I'd like that. But you see what it's like. I'm working day and night.'

'Let's just see. I'll see if I can ferret you out in the lobby later when I finish surgery and rounds. Maybe we can grab a sandwich.' She liked the idea, but she had no idea if she could get free.

'I'll do what I can to get away. But Peter, you have to understand that I may not be able to.'

'I understand that.' And then for the first time, he reached out and touched her hand. 'It's all right, Mel. I'm here. I'm not going anywhere.' But maybe she would. They both silently hoped that it wouldn't be too soon.

She smiled at him, enjoying the feel of his hand on hers. 'Thanks for the ride to work, Peter.'

'At your service, Ma'am.' He slid out and opened the door for her, and a moment later they were swallowed up by the crowd in the lobby. He turned back to glance at her once, but she was already deep in conversation with the other less important members of the press who had spent the night in the lobby, and the lift doors closed on him before she saw him again.

The news that Mel got was hopeful. The President was still alive, and half an hour before, a hospital spokesman had told them that there was some improvement in his condition.

At eight o'clock the First Lady returned. She was staying at the Bel-Air Hotel, and she was surrounded by Secret Servicemen who forced their way through the lobby. It was impossible to approach her although Mel and a host of others tried. The poor woman looked haggard and wan, and again Mel felt for her. At eight thirty she went on the air to New York, and again at nine for the noon news. All she could tell the nation was that the President was still alive. And she continued gathering bulletins throughout the day, without a moment to think of her own life, or Peter Hallam.

She didn't see him again until three o'clock, when suddenly he appeared beside her, looking impressive in his starched white coat and suddenly there was a surge of press around him. They thought he had arrived to give them news and it was almost impossible to shout above the din and explain that he was there to see a friend purely as a civilian. At last he and Mel escaped to a corner, although several members of the press thought she was getting a scoop on them. And finally in desperation, he pulled off the white coat and shoved it behind a waste bin in the lobby.

'Christ, I thought they would maul me.'

'They would, given half a chance. I'm sorry.' She smiled tiredly at him. She had worked for nine hours straight and the only food she'd had was the sandwich he'd given her in the car, although she had drunk gallons of coffee all day.

'Have you eaten?'

'Not yet.'

'Can you get away?'

She looked at her watch. 'I have to go on in ten minutes for the six o'clock in New York. But I should be able to get free after that.'

'How long do you have to stay?'

'A few more hours. I should be able to leave by six o'clock. I can always come back at eight if I have to, to cover the eleven o'clock in New York. In fact, I probably will have to. But after that, I hope I'm through, unless something new develops.'

He was thinking and then said, 'Why don't I leave here now, and come back for you at six o'clock. We can go somewhere quiet for dinner, and I'll get you back in here in time for you to do the bulletin for the eleven o'clock news in New York, and right after that I'll take you back to your hotel.'

'I'll probably be a zombie by then, and I may fall asleep in my dinner.'

'I don't mind. I've put people to sleep over dinner before. At least this time I can tell myself there might be an excuse.' He smiled at her, and felt an urge to pull her into his arms.

She smiled too. 'I'd like to see you tonight.'

'Good. See you at six then.' He hurried off to his office then, and he returned exactly three hours later. By then, Mel had dark circles under her eyes, and he could see when she got into his car that she was absolutely exhausted. She looked over at him with a tired smile.

'You know, Peter, any attraction you may feel for me right now practically amounts to necrophilia.'

He laughed at the horrifying suggestion and made a face. 'That was disgusting.'

'That's how I feel. How was work?'

'Fine. How's the President tonight?' He figured that now she knew more about it than he did. He was too busy with his own patients to worry about anyone else.

'He's holding his own. I'm beginning to think that he'll make it if he's held up for this long. What do you think?'

'I think you may be right.' And then he smiled. 'I just hope he doesn't spring to his feet in the morning, so that you have to fly home tomorrow.'

'I don't think there's any danger of that for the moment. Do you?'

'Honestly, no.' He looked pleased and glanced over at her as he drove her to a restaurant nearby.

'How are the kids, by the way?'

'Fine. They know you're here from what they see on the news, but I haven't had time to tell them I've seen you.'

She was quiet for a moment. 'Maybe you shouldn't.'

'Why not?' He looked surprised.

'Maybe it would make them nervous. Kids have remarkable antennae. I know mine do. Especially Jess. You can put something over on Val for a while, because she's always so wrapped up in herself. But Jessica almost senses things before they happen.'

'Pam's like that sometimes too. But the boys are different.'

'That's my point. And she has enough to contend with in her life, without worrying about me.'

'What makes you think she'd worry?'

'What makes you think she wouldn't? I mean, think of it, her whole world has been turned upside down in the last two years, but at least she knows she has you. And there have been no women for her to compete with, in her mind at least. And then I come on the scene, and I'm an instant threat.'

'What makes you think that?'

'I'm a woman. She's a girl, and you're her father. You belong to her.'

'My being interested in someone wouldn't change that.'

'Subtly, in some ways, it might. I'm sure your relationship with Pam was different when your wife was alive. You had less time for her, you had other things to do. Now suddenly you're all hers, or almost. Changing that back again, and for a stranger, won't be very welcome.'

He looked pensive as he stopped the car in front of a little Italian restaurant. 'I never thought of it that way.' And then he smiled slowly at Mel. 'But I never had to. Maybe I should be a little cautious about what I tell her.'

'I think so.' She grinned. 'Hell, you may never want to see me again after the next few days. You're about to see me at my worst. After enough days of no sleep, I start to fall apart.'

'Don't we all.'

'I didn't think you did. You seem to hold up miraculously with all that you do.'

'I have my limits too.'

'Me too, and I hit mine about two days ago.'

'Come on, let's get you fed. That'll help.' They walked inside, and the headwaiter gave them a quiet table. 'Wine, Mel?' But she quickly shook her head.

'I'd pass out in my plate.' She laughed and ordered a small steak. She wasn't even hungry any more, but she knew that the protein would do her good. However, they enjoyed the dinner and the small talk, and she was amazed at how comfortable she was with him. He seemed interested in her work, and she already knew a great deal about his. It was a relaxing but stimulating conversation, and she sat back with her cup of coffee at the end, feeling content and sated. 'You are an absolute godsend. Do you know that?'

'I'm enjoying it too.'

'This is not at all what I expected when I came to LA.'

'I know.' He smiled. 'By now, you thought you'd be in Bermuda.'

'Is that what day this is?' She had lost track of time and she hadn't even talked to the girls since she'd arrived, but she knew they'd all understand. And the girls were in Cape Cod anyway for the long weekend. She hadn't even realised it had begun, but it had. It felt as though she had already been in LA for weeks. And in a way, she wished she had been. She had never felt that way before. Her whole life centred around New York, as a rule, but not right now. Her life was here.

'I'm sorry you missed the trip to Bermuda, Mel.'

'I'm not.' She looked frankly into his eyes. 'This is where I'd much rather be.' He wasn't quite sure how to respond, so he reached out and took her hand.

'I'm glad. I'm happy you're back, Mel. I'm just sorry you have to work so hard.'

Her eyes were deadly earnest as they looked into his. 'It's a small price to pay to see you.'

But Peter couldn't repress a sad thought. 'I'm sure the President doesn't feel that way.' They shared a serious moment and then Mel regretfully looked at her watch. It was time for her to go back to work. He offered to take her back to the hospital and wait but she protested for his sake. 'I can take a cab after I do the eleven o'clock,' which was only eight o'clock in LA.

'I told you. For as long as you're here, I'm your chauffeur.' He looked embarrassed then. 'Unless you'd rather not . . .'

This time she reached out and touched his hand. 'I love it.'

'Good.'

He paid the bill and they left and went back to Center City in time for her to announce to the viewers in New York that the President had a slight fever, but it was to be expected. And then half an hour later, Peter drove her back to her hotel, and dropped her outside, promising to be back early the following morning. Once again, she went inside and climbed into bed, but tonight it took her longer to fall asleep, and she was still awake when he called her half an hour later.

'Hello?' She was afraid it was bad news about the President.

'It's me.' It was Peter and she breathed a sigh of relief and told him why. 'I'm sorry if I scared you.'

'That's okay. Is something wrong?'

'No.' He hesitated and she could almost hear him breathing. 'I just want to tell you that I think you're terrific.' He had startled himself and could feel his heart beat faster. Melanie sat up in bed, feeling nervous and pleased all at once.

'I came to the same conclusion about you the last time I was here.'

He blushed, feeling silly and she smiled and they chatted for a little while, and then hung up at last, feeling both excited and scared and happy, like two kids. They were both taking tiny baby steps out on a limb, and it wasn't too late to turn back yet, but the balancing act got more delicate each day, and neither of them could figure out what would happen when she went back to New York, but it was too soon to worry about that. For the moment they were content.

Chapter 14

The next morning Peter picked her up again, and dropped her off at the hospital where she was told that the President was doing a little better. For the first time in days she found that she had a few minutes to herself in the middle of the day, and on a sudden whim, she called the cardiac unit, and asked if she could visit Marie. She took the lift to the sixth floor, and found her sitting up in bed looking pretty but pale, and her face had a new fullness to it. Melanie realised with sorrow that the unnatural bloating from the drugs was already setting in, but her eyes were bright and she looked happy to see Mel.

'What are you doing here?' She looked up at Melanie in surprise as she entered the room. There were still intravenous tubes in her arms, but she looked healthier than she had before the transplant.

'I came to see you. But not from New York, I'm afraid. I've been in the lobby for days, because of the President.' Marie nodded with a serious look in her eyes.

'What a terrible thing. Is he any better?'

'A little today. But he's not out of the woods yet,' and then suddenly she realised that it was a tactless thing to say, because Marie wasn't out of the woods yet either. She smiled gently at the young woman who was only a few years her junior, and whose life was held in such a delicate balance. 'He's not as lucky as you are, Marie.'

'That's because he's not a patient of Peter Hallam's.' There was a warm glow in her eyes as she said his name, and Mel watched her as understanding dawned. Peter Hallam had become a god of sorts to this girl. And Mel suspected that she had a crush on him. It was not an unnatural occurrence, given her dependence on the man, and the fact that he had saved her life by performing the transplant. But it was only when Peter himself came into the room a little while later, and blushed as he saw Mel, that she saw something more. The remarkable communication between doctor and patient. He sat down beside Marie's bed, and talked to her in his quiet, soothing voice, and it was as though everyone in the room disappeared except them.

Mel suddenly felt like an intruder and left a little while later, returning to the mass of press still milling around the lobby. She didn't see Peter again until he drove her back to the hotel that night. As she had the night before, she had a two-hour break, and then she had to return to the hospital at eight o'clock to do a live report for the eleven o'clock news in New York. And it was on the way to dinner that she mentioned Marie to him.

'She absolutely worships you, Peter.'

'Don't be silly. She's no different from any other patient.' But he knew what Melanie meant, there was a special bond between him and each of his patients and may be particularly with Marie, who had no one to stand beside her. 'She's a nice girl, Mel. And she needs someone to talk to while she goes through all this. You lie there all day and you think, sometimes too much. She needs someone to vent all that with.'

'And you are so eternally patient.' She smiled, wondering how he did it. He gave and he gave and he gave, almost beyond measure, of his skill, his heart, his time, his patience. It seemed incredible to her.

Halfway through dinner his pager went off, and he had to return to the hospital for an emergency.

'Marie?' Mel asked worriedly as they hurried to the car.

He shook his head. 'No, a man who came in last week. He needs a heart badly and we don't have a donor yet.' It seemed to be a never-ending problem for him, the absence of a heart when it was desperately needed.

'Will he make it?'

'I don't know. I hope so.' He wove his way expertly through the traffic and they were back at the hospital in less than ten minutes. It was the last she saw of him that night. She got a message in the lobby before she went on the air that Dr Hallam would be in surgery for several hours, and she wondered if that meant they had found a donor, or if Peter was trying to do whatever repair work he could in the meantime. She went back to her hotel alone in a cab, and she was surprised to find how much she missed him. She took a hot bath, and sat staring at the tile wall, sorry that she had questioned him about Marie. There had just been something in the woman's face when she said his name, and his tone with her had been so intimate. It almost made Mel jealous. She was in bed by nine thirty and slept soundly until her five o'clock call the next morning, and at five forty-five he was downstairs as always. But he looked tired this morning.

'Hi.' She slid into the car quickly and for an instant there had been almost a reflex reaction. She had been about to lean over and give him a kiss on the cheek, but at the last minute she didn't. She searched his eyes, and suddenly realised that something was wrong. 'You okay?'

'I'm fine.'

But she didn't believe him. 'How was last night?'

'We lost him.' He started the car and Mel watched his profile. There was something hard and lonely in his eyes. 'We did our best, but he was just too far gone.' And Mel suddenly understood something.

'You don't have to convince me.' Her voice was soft. 'I know how hard you tried.'

'Yeah. Maybe I just need to convince myself.'

She reached out and touched his arm then. 'Peter ...'

'I'm sorry, Mel.' He glanced over at her with a tired smile, and she wished there were something she could do for him, but she wasn't sure what.

'Don't do that to yourself.'

'Yeah,' and then five minutes later, 'He had a young wife and three small kids.'

'Stop blaming yourself.'

'Who should I blame?' He turned to her with a flash of sudden anger.

'Has it ever occurred to you that you're not God. That you aren't to blame? That you don't give the gift of life?' They were harsh words, but she could see that he was listening. 'It's not in your hands, no matter how skilled you are.'

'He would have been a perfect candidate for a heart transplant, if we'd had a donor.'

'But you didn't. And it's over. Close the door.' They stopped in the hospital parking lot then, and he looked at her.

'You're right and I know it. After all these years, I shouldn't punish myself, but I always do.' He sighed softly. 'Do you have time for a cup of coffee?' There was something so comforting about her presence and he needed to be comforted.

She looked at her watch and frowned. 'Sure. I'll just check in. There's probably nothing new.' But when she walked in, there was news. A bulletin was due to be delivered on the air in three minutes. The President had just come off the critical list. When the news was announced, a cheer went up in the lobby. For most of the members of the press, it would mean that they would go home soon, and could stop camping in the lobby of Center City.

Mel went on the air to deliver the news to the East as Peter watched. While the whole country would rejoice, she and Peter felt strangely depressed. Their eyes met when she went off the air.

'Will you have go go home now?' It was a worried whisper.

'Not yet – I just got a memo. They want an interview with his wife today, if I can get it.' At that moment, Peter was paged, and he had to leave her.

Mel sent a note upstairs to the President's wife who had been sleeping in a room adjoining the President's for the past two days. A response came back a little while later. The first lady would grant Mel an exclusive interview at noon, in a private room on the third floor – which ruled out any hope of having lunch with Peter, but the interview went well and Mel was pleased, and that afternoon another encouraging bulleting was delivered. The President was out of the woods. By that evening when Peter drove her out for a bite to eat, the atmosphere of tension had greatly abated.

'How was your day?' She collapsed against the seat and looked over at him with a smile. 'Mine was a killer, but things are looking up.'

'I didn't stop all day. And Marie said to say hello.'

'Say hi for me.' But her mind was on other things. She was beginning to wonder how soon she would have to leave. There was a rumour that in a few days the President would be moved to Walter Reed Hospital in Washington DC, but the First Lady had been unable or unwilling to confirm it.

'What are you thinking about, Mel?' She noticed that he looked less depressed than he had that morning.

She smiled. 'Ten thousand things at once. We're hearing that they're going to send the President home soon. Do you think they can really move him?'

'Right now they'd be taking a chance, but if he continues to improve they could. And they can take all the equipment they'd need on *Air Force One*.' He didn't seem cheered by the thought and neither was Mel, but over dinner they forgot about it, and Peter began to tell her funny stories about Matt when he was two or three years old, and ridiculous episodes that had happened in the hospital when he was in training. From sheer exhaustion, they found themselves laughing like two kids, and when he drove her back to the hospital shortly before eight, she was in no mood to do the news with a serious face. Surprisingly they were both still in high spirits when they left Center City again half an hour later. There was something about being together that always buoyed them both and made life worth living.

'Do you want to come home with me for a drink?' He really didn't want to leave her yet, and suddenly he realised that she might be gone in a few days. He wanted to savour every moment of her presence.

'I don't think I should. I still think your kids would be upset.'

'What about me? Don't I have a right to see a friend?'

'Sure, but taking someone home can be a heavy trip. How do you think Pam would react to seeing me again?'

'Maybe that's an adjustment she'll just have to make.'

'Is it worth if for a few days?' Mel didn't think so. 'Why don't you come to my hotel for a drink instead? It's ugly as sin but the bar looks halfway decent.' Neither of them was interested in drinking. They just seemed to want to sit and talk for hours until they were ready to fall over from exhaustion.

'You know, I could sit here and talk to you all night.' He was still amazed at the range of conflicting emotions he felt for her, excitement, attraction, respect, trust, fear, distance, and closeness all at once. But whatever it was, he couldn't seem to get enough of it. The presence of Mel Adams in his life was apparently addictive. He was hooked, and he didn't know what to do about it.

'I feel the same way and the funny thing is that we hardly know each other, and I feel as though I've known you for years.' She had never enjoyed talking to anyone as much, and that still frightened her a little when she allowed herself to think of it. It was a subject neither of them discussed but both of them thought of. She was the brave one tonight, as she looked at him over their second Irish coffee. The drinks seemed to pick them up, while putting a soft edge on things. It was the mixture of coffee and whisky that did it, enhanced by the heady effect each of them had on the other. 'I'm going to miss you like crazy when I go back.'

He watched her carefully over his drink. 'So am I. I was thinking of it this morning after I dropped you off. What you said about the patient last night made a lot of sense. You kind of took my day out of the ditch and picked me up again. I was headed for a real tailspin. It's going to be strange when I'm not picking you up at your hotel at six o'clock every morning.'

'You might even get some time to yourself again, and to spend with your kids. Are they complaining yet?'

'They seem to be wrapped up in their own lives.'

'So are the twins.' They were due back from Cape Cod that night.

'I'll have to call them if I can get the hour difference worked out right. When I wake up, they've left for school, and when I come home they're asleep.'

'You'll be home soon.' But he said the words with sorrow and she didn't answer for a time.

'It's a crazy life I lead, Peter.' She looked him straight in the eye as though asking him how he felt about it.

'But fulfilling, I suspect. We both seem to go nonstop, but it's not so bad if you like what you do.'

'That's how I've always felt.' She smiled, and he reached across the table for her hand. It was the only contact they ever had, but it was a comfortable gesture now. 'Thank you for everything you've done for me, Peter.'

'What? Drive you back and forth to the hospital a few times? That's hardly a monumental favour.'

'It's been nice though.' She smiled and he smiled in return.

'It has been for me too. It'll be strange when you're not here any more.'

She laughed. 'I'll probably be standing outside my house in New York at quarter to six every morning, waiting for you to come around the corner in your Mercedes.'

'I wish ...' They fell silent then, and the bill arrived. He paid it, and they walked slowly into the lobby. It was late and they both had to get up early the next morning, and as they said good night to each other, Melanie found herself wishing they didn't have to.

'I'll see you tomorrow, Peter.' He nodded, and waved as the lift doors closed. He went home, thinking about Mel, and wondering what life would be like again without her. He didn't even want to think of it. In her hotel room, Mel stood for a long time staring out the window, thinking of Peter, and the things they had said to each other in the past few days, and suddenly she felt an ache of loneliness well up in her, unlike any she had felt before. Suddenly she didn't want to go back to New York at all. But that was crazy. It was just what she had felt when she was in LA before, only more so. She went to bed with the uneasy feeling that night that Peter Hallam was deeper under her skin than she wanted him to be. And yet when she was with him, she didn't think of that. She just talked to him with the ease usually born of years of knowing someone. He made her feel that way each time she saw him, and she wondered for a moment, if that was only his bedside manner. She fell into an uneasy sleep that night, and was relieved to see him the next morning. She slipped quickly into the car, and they made the familiar drive to the hospital, chatting easily, and then suddenly Peter laughed and turned towards her.

'It's kind of like being married, isn't it?'

She felt herself go pale. 'What is?'

'Going to work together every day.' He looked sheepish. 'I have a confession to make. I like routine. I'm a creature of habit.'

'So am I.' She smiled back, feeling better again. For a moment she had been frightened. She settled back against the seat and watched the hospital loom towards them. 'I wonder what news awaits me today?' The President had been making steady progress, and they were just waiting for news of his being moved.

Nonetheless, when the announcement came that morning that the President was leaving for Washington the next day with a team of doctors, on *Air Force One,* she was stunned, and felt as though someone had delivered a blow to her solar plexus. The air whooshed out of her in one gasp – a barely audible 'No'. But it was true. He was leaving. And once again, all was chaos in the lobby. Bulletins went on the air, interviews with doctors, Mel had to make a dozen calls to New York. They were asking for clearance for her for *Air Force One,* but thus far the only news was that six members of the press would be allowed on the plane. Silently, Mel found herself praying all day not to be among the lucky six, but at five o'clock she got a call from New York. She was among them. They were leaving at approximately noon the next day and she was expected to be at the hospital at nine o'clock, to cover all the preparations. When she met Peter in the parking lot that night, her whole body sagged as she got into the car.

'What's the matter, Mel?' He could see instantly that something was wrong. He had had a long day himself, in surgery for four hours, putting in a plastic heart, which he hadn't wanted to do in the first place. But in this particular case, there had been no other solution. They had already tried everything else, and there was no donor in sight for a transplant. But he knew how great a risk they ran now in regard to infection. And Marie had had a number of problems today too. But he didn't say anything to Mel as she turned to him with an unhappy look on her face.

'I'm leaving tomorrow.'

'Blast.' He stared at her for a long moment, and then nodded. 'Well, we knew you wouldn't be here forever.' It took him a few minutes to regain his composure and then he started the car. 'Do you have to come back tonight?'

She shook her head. 'I'm finished until nine o'clock tomorrow morning.'

At that he smiled more gamely and looked over at her with gentle eyes. 'Then I'll tell you what, why don't I drop you off at your hotel, let you relax for a while, and change if you want, and we'll go somewhere nice for dinner. How does that sound?'

'Lovely. You're sure you're not too tired?' She noticed now that he looked exhausted.

'Positive. I'd love it. Do you want to go back to the Bistro?'

'Yes'– she smiled finally – 'the only place I don't want to go back to is New

York. Isn't that awful?' She would have been gone for only a week, but it felt like a year, and suddenly her life in New York loomed into perspective. The six- and eleven-o'clock news, the twins, her daily routine. At that precise moment, none of it was appealing, and she was still depressed when she went upstairs to change. The only thing that cheered her was when she saw Peter again, at seven thirty. He was wearing a dark grey flannel double-breasted suit, and she had never seen him look as handsome. All she had to wear was a beige silk dress with a heavy cream silk jacket that she had brought to wear on the air, but hadn't taken out yet.

They looked like a very distinguished pair as they walked into the Bistro, and the headwaiter gave them a lovely table. Peter ordered their drinks, and the waiter brought the chalkboard to the table, showing them the menu. But Mel wasn't even hungry. All she wanted to do was talk and be near Peter, and she found herself wanting to cling to him numerous times during the evening. Finally after the chocolate soufflé and the coffee, he ordered brandy for them both and looked at her sadly.

'I wish you weren't leaving, Mel.'

'So do I. It sounds crazy, but it's been a wonderful week, in spite of all the hard work.'

'You'll be back.' But God only knew when. She hadn't been to LA for over a year before she'd come to interview him. It was just a fluke that she had come back again so soon.

'I wish we didn't live so far away from each other.' She said it mournfully, like a little girl with a new best friend, and he smiled and put an arm around her shoulders.

'So do I.' And then, 'I'll call you.' But then what?

It was impossible to find the answers, they had lives at opposite ends of the country, with children, homes, careers, friends. None of it could be stashed into a suitcase and moved. The phone calls and occasional visits would have to be enough for Mel and Peter. It was almost more than she could bear to recognise that fact. They walked along Rodeo Drive after dinner, chatting.

'I wish our lives were different, Peter.'

'Do you?' He seemed surprised. 'How?'

'At least we could live in the same city.'

'I agree with you there. But otherwise, I'd say we're pretty lucky, now that we know each other. It's added a lot to my life.'

'Mine too.' She smiled and their hands knit tighter as they walked, each lost in thought for a little while.

He looked down at her, his hand still in hers. 'It's going to be damn lonely around here without you.' He heard the echo of his own words and couldn't believe he had said them, but he had, and he was less frightened of what he felt now. The brandy helped, and a week in her company had been like a gift he had never expected. He had grown fonder of her each day, and the prospect of seeing her go really depressed him, much more than he had expected.

Eventually they made their way slowly back to the car, and he took her back to her hotel, until at last they sat outside, and looked at each other in the lamplight. 'Will I see you tomorrow, Mel?'

'I don't have to be there until nine.'

'I'll be in surgery at seven. What time does the President's plane leave?'

'At noon.'

'Then I guess this is it.' They both sat sadly, looking at each other and then, without saying a word, he leaned towards her and gently took her face in his hands and kissed her. She closed her eyes and felt her lips melt into his, and she felt as though her insides trembled. She was almost dizzy when he stopped and she clung to him for a long moment. Then she looked at him and let her fingers touch his face, and then his lips, as he kissed the tips of her fingers. 'I'm going to miss you, Mel.'

'Me too.'

'I'll call you.' But then what? Neither of them had any answers. And without saying anything more he pulled her close to him again and held her for a long time, and at last he walked her back into the lobby and kissed her one last time before she disappeared into the lift. Slowly, he walked back to his car, and drove away, feeling something heavy in his heart that he hadn't felt since he'd lost Anne. And he had never wanted to feel that again. It frightened him that he had come to care about her so much. It would have been so much easier if he hadn't.

Chapter 15

When Mel arrived at the hospital the next day, she was allowed to go upstairs with a two-man crew and speak to the First Lady briefly, while preparations were being made for the President's removal. They would be leaving the hospital at ten o'clock, arriving at Los Angeles International Airport shortly before eleven, and they would take off as soon as possible after that. The President was doing well, but the First Lady was obviously extremely worried. His condition was stable, but it was difficult to predict what might happen in the air. Nonetheless, he wanted to go back to Washington, and his physicians had approved the plan.

Mel completed the interview and waited in the hallway until forty-five minutes later when the President appeared on a stretcher. He waved his arm to the nurses and technicians lining the hall, and he smiled gamely and murmured greetings, but he still looked deathly pale, was heavily bandaged and there was an intravenous tube running into his arm. There was a fleet of Secret Service-men surrounding the stretcher, interspersed with doctors and nurses who would be returning to Washington with him. Mel fell into step at a respectful distance, and took another lift to the lobby, where she joined up with the handful of other select reporters flying east on *Air Force One*. A separate limousine had been reserved for them, and she stepped into it with one glance back over her shoulder at Center City. She would have liked to have left a message at the desk for Peter before she left, but there was neither the opportunity nor the time, and a moment later they sped away towards the airport.

'How'd he look to you?' the reporter next to her asked briefly, checking some notes while lighting a cigarette with one hand. They were a relaxed group of pros, but nonetheless there was a faint hint of electricity and tension in the air. It had been an endless week for them all, and it would be good to get home and unwind. Most of them were returning to their home bases as soon as they reached Washington, and the network had already booked a seat to New York for Mel at ten o'clock that night. She would be picked up at LaGuardia at eleven and taken home. In a way, she felt as though she were returning from another planet. But she was not at all sure she wanted to go home now, and her mind lingered on Peter's words, and his face, the night before.

'Hm?' She hadn't heard the reporter's question.

'I said how did he look?' The older reporter looked annoyed and Mel narrowed her eyes, thinking of the President as he lay on the stretcher.

'Lousy, but he's alive.' And unless something drastic happened on the flight east, or he met with severe complications, it was unlikely that he would die now. He was a very lucky man, as they had all said again and again on the air. Other presidents had not been as lucky with assassination attempts as this one.

There was the usual banter between them on the way to the airport, dirty jokes, exchanged bits of gossip and old news. No one ever gave anything important away, but this was not as tense a trip as the one to LA had been for all of them. Mel thought back to the week before, and to seeing Peter again for the first time. She wondered now when she would see him next. She couldn't imagine another opportunity presenting itself in the near future, and the realisation of that depressed her.

The reporter sitting next to her glanced her way again. 'You look like the last week got you down, Mel.'

'No.' She shook her head, her eyes averted. 'I'm just tired, I guess.'

'Who isn't?'

And half an hour later they boarded the plane and sat in the passenger area in the rear. A sort of hospital-room arrangement had been made for the President towards the front, and none of them was allowed near it. Every hour or so, during the flight, the press secretary would join them and tell them how the President was doing, but it was an uneventful flight for them all and they reached Washington in four and a half hours and had the President settled at Walter Reed Hospital within an hour after that, and suddenly Mel realised that it was all over for her. The network's Washington correspondent had met them at the airport, and after accompanying the President to Walter Reed along with the others who had come from LA and glimpsing the First Lady once more, Mel stepped outside to the limousine waiting for her and went back to the airport. She had an hour left before her flight to New York, and she sat down, feeling as though she were in shock. The last week was beginning to seem like a dream and she wondered if she had imagined Peter and the time she had spent with him.

She walked slowly to a telephone booth at an adjacent gate, put a dime in the slot, and called her home collect. Jessie answered and for a moment, Mel felt tears fill her eyes, and she suddenly realised how exhausted she was.

'Hi, Jess.'

'Hi, Mom. Are you home?' She sounded like a child again as her voice filled with excitement.

'Almost, sweetheart. I'm at the Washington airport. I should be at the house by eleven thirty. God, I feel like I've been gone a year.'

'We've missed you like crazy.' She didn't even reproach her mother for not having called. She knew how impossible her schedule had been. 'Are you okay?'

'Wiped out. I can't wait to get home. But don't wait up. I'm going to crawl in and pass out.' It wasn't just the fatigue that was getting to her now. A kind of depression was setting in, as she realised how far away she was from Peter. And that was foolish too. But she couldn't seem to stop the feelings any more.

'Are you kidding?' Jess sounded outraged at her end.

'We haven't seen you in a week! Of course we'll wait up. We'll carry you upstairs if we have to.'

Tears filled Mel's eyes as she smiled at the phone. 'I love you, Jess.' And then, 'How's Val?'

'She's okay. We've both missed you.'

'I've missed you too, sweetheart.' But something important had been happening to her in California. There was a lot she needed to sort out, or at least absorb and the only people she wanted to see or talk to right now were the twins.

They were waiting in the living room when she got home, and fell into her arms one by one, delighted to have her home again. As Mel looked around, her house had never looked as good to her as it did now, or her children.

'Boy, it's good to be back, you guys!' But a tiny part of her said it wasn't. A tiny part of her said she wanted to be three thousand miles away, having dinner with Peter. But that was all behind her now and she had to forget it, at least for now.

'It must have been awful, Mom. It looked like you almost never left the hospital lobby from what we saw on the news.'

'Hardly ever except for a few hours' sleep here and there ...' And time spent with Peter ... She looked into their eyes, almost expecting them to see something different about her. But they didn't. There was nothing to see, except what she felt deep inside, and she kept that well hidden. 'Have you two been behaving all week?' Val brought her a Coca-Cola and she smiled gratefully at the voluptuous twin. 'Thanks, love.' And then she grinned. 'Are you in love again, young lady?'

'Not yet.' She laughed into her mother's eyes. 'But I'm working on it.' Mel rolled her eyes and they sat and chatted for a long time, and it was one o'clock in the morning by the time they all went upstairs. They kissed their mother goodnight outside her bedroom and went up to their own floor as Mel went to unpack her bag and take a hot shower. When she looked at the clock again, it was two o'clock in the morning ... eleven o'clock on the West Coast ... suddenly all that seemed to matter was where he was and what he was doing. It was like being constantly torn in two. She had a life to lead here in New York, and yet she had left a part of her three thousand miles away. It was going to be a difficult way to live, at least for now, and she still had to sort out what it all meant to her ... what Peter Hallam meant to her ... but, secretly, she already knew.

Chapter 16

The next morning, Grant called her just before noon, and woke her up, and his voice made her smile as she rolled over in bed and looked out at the brilliantly sunny June day.

'Welcome home, old girl. How was LA?'

'Oh, charming.' She smiled and stretched. 'I just sat around by the pool and soaked up the sun.' They both laughed, knowing what a rat race she'd been in. 'How've you been?'

'Busy, crazy, the usual. What about you?'

'What do you think with that insanity out there?'

'I think you must be dead on your feet.' But she didn't sound so bad.

'You're right. I am dead.'

'Are you coming in today?'

'Tonight, to do the six o'clock. I don't think I'll make it in before that.'

'Good enough. I'll keep an eye out for you. I've missed you, kid. Will you have time for a drink?' Time, yes, but the inclination, no. She still wanted some time to herself to sort things out. And she didn't feel like saying anything to Grant about it yet.

'Not tonight, love. Maybe next week.'

'Okay. See you later, Mel.'

As she got out of bed and stretched, she thought of Grant and smiled to herself. She was lucky to have a friend like him, and just as she went into the bathroom to turn on the shower, she heard the phone ring, and wondered if he was calling her back again. Not many people called her at home at noon, and hardly anyone knew she was back from the Coast yet. They wouldn't know that until they saw her on the news that night. Mel picked up the phone with a puzzled frown, hovering naked at her desk, looking out at the garden behind the house.

'Hello?'

'Hi, Mel.' He sounded faintly nervous and her heart seemed to give an enormous jerk as she heard his voice. It was Peter, and she could hear the hum of long distance. 'I wasn't sure if you'd be home, and I only had a few minutes, but I thought I'd call. Did you get home all right?'

'Yes ... fine ...' Her words seemed to tangle on her tongue and she closed her eyes, listening to his voice.

'We took a little break between surgeries today, and I just wanted to tell you how much I miss you.' And with one short sentence, he turned her heart upside down again and she didn't answer. 'Mel?'

'Yes ... I was just thinking ...' And then she threw all caution to the winds and sat down at her desk with a sigh. 'I miss you too. You sure turn my life topsy-turvy, Doctor.'

'I do?' He sounded relieved. She did the same to him. He had barely slept the night before, but he hadn't dared call and wake her up. He knew how exhausted she was when she left. 'Do you realise how crazy this is, Peter? God knows when we'll see each other again, and here we are like two kids, having a mad crush on each other.' But she felt happy again as they talked. All she had wanted was to hear him.

He laughed at her choice of words. 'Is that what this is? A crush? I wonder.'

'What do you think?' She wasn't sure what she was fishing for, and she was a little bit frightened of what she would get. She wasn't ready for declarations of passionate love from him, but he wasn't ready to give them either. She was still safe. But the worst of it was that she didn't even know if she wanted to be safe from him.

'I think that's about right. I'm in crush with you, Mel, is that how you say it?' They both laughed and Mel felt like a little girl again. He did that to her every time, and he was only nine years older than she was. 'How are the girls, by the way?'

'Fine. And your troupe?'

'They'll do. Matthew was complaining last night that he never sees me. We're going to go fishing or something this weekend if I can get away. But it depends on how this next surgery goes.'

'What are you doing?'

'A triple bypass, but there shouldn't be any complications.' And with that he glanced at the clock in the little room from which he'd called. 'Speaking of which, I'd better get back and scrub again. I'll be thinking of you though, Mel.'

'You'd better not. You'd better think of the patient.' But she was smiling. 'Maybe I should start ending the news with "And good night, Peter, wherever you are".'

'You know where I am.' His voice was so gentle it made her ache for him.

'Yeah. Three thousand miles away.' She looked sad.

'Why don't you come out for a weekend?'

'Are you crazy? I just left there.' But she loved the idea, as impossible as it was.

'That was different, you were working. Take some time off and come out for a visit.'

'Just like that?' She was amused.

'Sure. Why not?' But she suspected that it would have terrified them both if she'd done that, and she wasn't ready to take such a major step towards him.

'It may come as a shock to you, Dr Hallam, but I have a life here, and two children.'

'And you take July and August off every year. You told me that yourself. Take the girls to Disneyland or something.'

'Why don't you come visit us at Martha's Vineyard?' They were playing a game with each other and they both knew it, but it felt good to do it.

'First, my friend, I have to do a triple bypass.' End of round. 'Good luck. And thanks for calling.'

'I'll call you later, Mel. Will you be home tonight?'

'I'll be home, between shows.'

'I'll call you.' And he did, and her heart leapt again. She had finished dinner with the girls, and he had just got home from his office. It threw her into a tizzy until she left to do the eleven o'clock show, and she told herself it was crazy. She forced her mind back to the news and again as she delivered it, and she managed to keep her concentration until she went off the air, but when she saw Grant outside his studio she looked totally distracted.

'Hi, Mel. Something wrong?' He was going on in fifteen minutes and they didn't have much time to talk.

'No. Why?'

'You just look funny. You okay?'

'Sure.' But there was a dreamy look in her eyes and he felt as though she wasn't really there. And then suddenly he understood. He had seen a look faintly like it in her eyes once before, although she hadn't seemed as intensely stricken as she did now. He wondered who it was and couldn't figure out when she had found the time. Or where. New York or LA? He was somewhat intrigued, and Mel looked as though she was in a different world.

'Go home and get some sleep, kid. You look like you're still half out of it.'

'I guess I am.' She smiled at him and watched him walk into the set and then she left, but she realised that Peter's calls that day had set her back again. How on earth was she going to concentrate on her work? She could barely think straight.

She went home in a cab and let herself into the house. The girls were already in bed and Raquel had taken a few days off to make up for the previous week. Mel sprawled out on the living room couch, thinking of her life. She thought of Peter's suggestion to come out to LA, but that was crazy. The only answer was to hang in for the next few weeks in New York, and get to Martha's Vineyard. Maybe then she could sort out her head as she did every year. Things would get back to normal with the sun and the sea and the totally relaxed life she led there.

Chapter 17

'Is everybody ready?' Melanie called upstairs from the hall, and looked around for a last time. She was closing the house in New York for the summer, and her two large suitcases were already in the hall, along with all three tennis rackets, two large straw hats belonging to the girls, (Mel was wearing hers), and Raquel's small green vinyl suitcase. She came with them every year for six weeks, and took the last two weeks off and returned to New York alone for her holiday. 'Come on, you guys! We have to be at the airport in half an hour!' But they were only going to LaGuardia, so she knew they would make it.

There was a wonderful upbeat feeling to their departure every year and she always felt like a young girl again as they left for Martha's Vineyard. She had signed off on the news the night before and she and Grant had gone out for a drink after his show to celebrate her temporary release, and things had been relaxed between them, but he could see in her eyes that she was still confused, and lately she had been tired and nervous. She had worked long hours at the station, finished the piece on heart surgery in California and done two major interviews and a feature before she left, so they'd have them to use during the summer. She was, as always, conscientious about her work, and lately it seemed to be taking more of a toll than it had before, but Grant had suspected that it was because of the emotional whirl she was in, although he still knew none of the details. In fact, Peter was still calling her every day, and Melanie had no idea what would ever come of it, if anything. Lately, she'd even been worrying about her contract which had to be renewed in October. There were a lot of political changes at the station, and there was talk of a new owner, and God only knew what that would mean. But Grant reassured her when they went out that she had absolutely nothing to worry about. Peter said the same when she confessed her concern to him. But nonetheless it had been on her mind, and now all of it could be packed up and put away for two months. She wouldn't think of work, or even Peter or Grant. She was just going to Martha's Vineyard, to relax with her daughters. But not if they didn't come soon, she told herself as she waited in the front hall with Raquel. Finally they came thundering down the stairs with assorted games and books and bags in their arms. Valerie was carrying an enormous stuffed bear.

'Val ... for God's sake ...'

'Mom, I have to. Josh gave him to me last week and his parents have a house in Chappaquiddick, he'll be coming over to see us and if I don't ... '

'All right, all right. Just get all this junk put together please, and let's get in a cab or we'll never get there.' Going on a trip with the girls was always a challenge, but the cabdriver actually managed to get almost all of it squashed in his boot, and they finally took off with Mel and the girls in the back seat, Val carrying the enormous teddy, and Raquel in the front with the hats and the tennis rackets. As they sped along towards LaGuardia, Mel mentally ticked off a list, making sure that she had locked the garden door, and all the windows, turned on the burglar alarm, turned off the gas ... there was always that sinking feeling that you'd forgotten something. But they were all in high spirits by the time they got on the plane, and as they left the ground, Mel had a feeling of relief that she hadn't had in weeks, as though she were leaving all her confusion behind in New York, and she would find peace in Martha's Vineyard.

Peter had been calling her once or twice a day, and as much as she enjoyed their conversations, she tormented herself about them. Why was he calling? When would they see each other again? And finally, what was the point? He admitted to the same confusions as she, but they seemed unable to stop moving inexorably forward on this path towards an unseen goal that still frightened them both and that they did their best not to talk about. They stuck to safe subjects, and now and then admitted how much they missed each other. But why, Mel asked herself too often, why do I miss him? She still didn't know the answer, or didn't want to.

'Mom, do you think my bike got rusty?' Valerie was staring into space on the plane, hugging her bear, and looking totally happy, as a man across the aisle stared at her in lustful fascination. Mel was just glad she hadn't let her wear the little blue French short shorts she had worn to breakfast, and threatened to wear on the trip to Martha's Vineyard.

'I don't know, love. We'll have to see when we get there.' The woman they rented the house from every year allowed them to leave a few things in the basement.

In Boston they rented a car and drove to Woods Hole where they took the ferry across to Vineyard Haven. The ferry was the part of the trip they all liked best. It gave one the impression of leaving the real world behind, and all its responsibilities with it. Melanie stood alone at the railing for a few minutes, letting the wind whip her hair, and feeling freer than she had in months. She realised suddenly how desperately she needed a holiday. And she enjoyed the few moments alone before the girls came to find her. They had left Raquel talking to some man on the lower deck, and when she joined them at last they teased her about it. Mel suddenly laughed at a mental image she had of Peter's Mrs Hahn, she could hardly imagine anyone teasing her, or her flirting with a man on a ferry. But for all Raquel's independent ways, they loved her, and she was pleased to see Jess give her a hug once before they landed. Even Raquel smiled. The Vineyard was a haven for them all, and when they reached the familiar house in Chilmark, the girls went running barefoot down on the beach, and chased each other as far as they could, while Mel watched them.

It was as easy settling in as it was every year, and by nightfall the four of them looked and felt as though they had been there for a month. They had got pink cheeks from the few hours they spent on the beach that afternoon, they were unpacked, and the teddy bear was ensconced in the rocking chair in Val's room. The house was comfortably furnished but there was nothing fancy about it. It looked like a grandmother's house, with a porch and a wicker swing, and flowered chintzes in all the rooms. At first it always had a musty smell which went away in a few days, and they no longer noticed. It was just part of the familiarity of Chilmark. The girls had been coming here since they were little, and, as Mel explained to Peter when he called that night, Chilmark was part of home.

'They love it here and so do I.'

'It sounds very New England, Mel.' He tried to envision it from her description. Long beaches, white sand, a casual life-style of shorts and sweat shirts and bare feet, and a smattering of intellectuals who came from New York, and gathered from time to time for lobster dinners and clambakes. 'We go to the mountains every year, to Aspen.' It was totally different from Martha's Vineyard, but sounded intriguing too as he described it. 'Why don't you come and bring the girls? We're going for the first ten days in August.'

'You couldn't pry them away from here for a million dollars or a date with their favourite rock star. Well ...' She reconsidered the last and they both laughed. They had an easy telephone relationship going, but it seemed so unreal at times. They were disembodied voices lodged in the phone night after night, but never getting any nearer.

'I don't suppose I could pry you away.'

'I doubt it.' There was a strange silence then and Mel listened, wondering what was on his mind, but when he spoke again, he sounded as though he were teasing.

'That's too bad.'

'What is?' He wasn't making sense, and she was wonderfully relaxed after dinner. She didn't want to play games on the phone, but he was obviously in a playful mood.

'That you don't want to leave there.'

'Why?' Her heart began to thump. He was making her oddly nervous.

'Because there's a conference I've been asked to attend in New York, to speak to a group of surgeons from all over the East Coast. They'll be gathering at Columbia Presbyterian.' She didn't answer for a moment as she held her breath and then she spoke in a rush.

'They will? And you're going?'

'I could. Normally I'd refuse, particularly at this time of year. New York in July is no treat, but I thought that maybe under the circumstances ...' He was blushing furiously at his end, and Mel gasped. He continued, 'I told them yes at three o'clock this afternoon. Now what about you and Martha's Vineyard?'

'Shit' – she looked around the room with a grin – 'we just got here.'

He was quick to ask, 'Would you rather I not come? I don't have to.'

'For chrissake, don't be an ass. How long do you think we can go on like this? Calling each other twice a day and never seeing each other?' It had only been three and a half weeks since she'd left California, but it felt more like three years to them both, and they needed to get together again to resolve at least some of their feelings.

'That's what I thought too. So ...' He laughed again, pleased with the prospect.

'When do you arrive?'

'Next Tuesday.' And then he added softly, 'I wish it was tomorrow.'

'So do I.' Her face sobered. And then she whistled. 'That's only six days away.'

'I know.' He grinned, he was as excited as a child. 'They took a reservation for me at the Plaza.' But as he spoke, Mel had a thought. She was hesitant to voice it, for fear of putting them both in an awkward spot, but if they could handle it, it might work out well.

'Why don't you stay at the house? The girls won't be there, and you could have their whole floor to yourself. It would be a lot more comfortable for you than a hotel.'

He was silent for an instant, weighing the pros and cons as she had before she asked. Staying under one roof could prove to be very awkward, and it was quite a commitment ... but on a separate floor ... 'You wouldn't mind? It would be easier, but I wouldn't want to put you out, or ...' He bumbled over the words and she laughed and stretched out on her bed, still holding the phone to her ear.

'It makes me just as nervous as it makes you, but what the hell, we're grown-ups, we can handle it.'

'Can we?' He smiled at the phone. He wasn't sure he could. 'And can you leave the girls alone?'

'No, but Raquel is here, so that'll be fine.' She was suddenly wildly excited that he was coming. 'Oh, Peter, I can't wait!'

'Neither can I!'

The next six days dragged unbearably for them both. They spoke on the phone two or three times a day, and Raquel finally caught on that there was someone important calling Mel but the girls seemed not to see it. On Sunday night, Mel casually mentioned that she had to go to New York for a few days, and she'd be leaving on Tuesday morning, but the news was met with dropped jaws and staring eyes. She had never gone back to New York for anything, except the year Jess broke her arm and Mel wanted her to see an orthopaedic man in New York. But they had only stayed for two days, and that was important. This time Mel said she'd be back on Friday afternoon, which meant four days away. They found it hard to believe that she was going, but she insisted that there was a problem with one of her features at work and she had to go back and watch them edit. The girls were still amazed when they went back to the beach that night to meet some friends and build a fire, but Raquel eyed her shrewdly as they cleared the table.

'It's serious this time, huh?'

Mel avoided her eyes, and carried a stack of plates into the kitchen. 'What is?'

'You can't fool me. You got a new man.'

'That's not true at all. The man is a subject I did an interview with.' But she couldn't meet Raquel's eyes, and she knew that if she did, she couldn't convince her. 'Just keep an eye on the girls while I'm gone, especially Val. I notice that the Jacobs boy is all grown-up, and drools every time he sees her.'

'He won't do no harm. I'll watch them.' And then she watched Mel retreat into her room and walked into the kitchen with a grin and a cigarette. She was certainly no Mrs Hahn, but she was a sharp old woman and she loved them.

And on Tuesday morning, Mel took the ferry back, and flew from Boston to New York. She reached the house at four o'clock in the afternoon, which gave her plenty of time to air the place out, turn the air conditioning on, go around the corner to buy fresh flowers and whatever groceries they might need, and then come back and get ready to pick him up. His plane wasn't due in until nine, and she left for the airport at seven thirty to be cautious, which was just as well, because the traffic was heavy and cars were overheating left and right and it was eight forty-five when they got there. She had just enough time to check the gate at which he would arrive, hurry out there, and then stand tapping her foot nervously for the next half hour, as they were fifteen minutes late. At nine fifteen exactly, the big silver bird drew up at the gate, and passengers began disembarking. She stood watching intently as the people poured off, with Californian tans, and straw hats, and bare golden legs, and silk shirts open to the waist with gold chains, and then suddenly she saw a man who looked nothing like any of them, in a beige linen suit and a blue shirt and navy tie, his hair only slightly bleached from the sun, and his face tanned. But there was a serious air about him, as he walked towards Mel and looked down at her where she stood. Then without further ado he bent to kiss her. They stood there for what seemed like a very long time as people eddied around them like a river cascading past rocks, and then he looked at her and smiled.

'Hello.'

'How was the flight?'

'Not nearly as nice as this.' He grinned, and with that they walked hand in hand to pick up his baggage, and then went to find Mel's car in the enormous garage. But time and time again they stopped to kiss as they stood between the cars, and Mel wondered how she had ever survived without him. 'You look wonderful, Mel.' She had a deep tan which set off her green eyes and copper hair and she had worn a white silk dress with a flower in her hair and white high-heeled sandals. She looked summery and healthy and happy, and her eyes seemed to drink his as though she had waited for him for a lifetime.

'You know, I haven't been to New York in years.' He looked at the ugly scenery passing by as they drove into town, and shook his head. 'I always turn them down, but I figured this time . . .' He shrugged and leaned over to kiss her again as she drove. She hadn't expected him to be as bold, or herself to be as comfortable with it. But the endless conversations on the phone seemed to have given them an ease with each other they might otherwise not have had. They had only known each other for two months now, but it felt like two years, or twice that.

'I'm glad you didn't turn them down this time.' She smiled at him and then returned her gaze to the road. 'Are you hungry?'

'Not very.' For him it was only quarter to seven, but it was shortly before ten in New York.

'I've got food at the house, but we can go somewhere for a bite to eat, if you like.'

'Whatever makes you happy.' He couldn't take his eyes off her. All else slipped his mind as he reached for her hand. 'I'm so happy to see you, Mel.' It almost seemed unreal that they should be together again.

'It's a little like a dream, isn't it?' She smiled as she asked.

'It is. Best dream I've had in years.' They fell silent again as they drove into town.

He smiled at her, and touched her neck with his hand. 'I figured I owed you at least one trip east, after all you've been to LA twice.' But still he had needed an excuse, a reason to come. He hadn't just got on a plane and come to see her. But it was easier for both of them this way, they could advance towards each other as they had been, by inches. 'The President's certainly made a remarkable recovery.'

'It's only been five weeks and he's on his feet and in the office a few hours a day.' Mel shook her head, still amazed at all that, and then she remembered something. 'How's Marie, by the way?'

'Fair.' A frown crossed his face, but he shook off the worry. 'I left two other men in charge while I'm gone. She's all right, but she had a terrible time with the steroids. Her face is bloated like a full moon now, and there isn't a damn thing we can do. We've juggled everything we could. But she never complains.' He looked unhappily at Mel. 'I wish it weren't so difficult for her.' For an instant, Mel tried to focus on Marie in her mind, but all she could really think of now was him. Everything else in their lives seemed unreal to them both. Children, patients, war, TV shows. All that mattered was Peter and Mel.

She drove down the FDR Drive and turned off at Seventy-ninth Street, and Peter watched the city streets drifting past them, curious about where she lived, about what her house would be like, about everything. In some ways, he knew so much, of what she felt and thought, and in other ways, he knew so little, mostly about her environment.

Mel smiled to herself, remembering the first time she had seen the house in Bel-Air, and been struck by its air of formality. She knew that he would find her house very different and she was right. He was enchanted as he stepped inside, and smelled the flowers she had bought, looked around at the bright colours everywhere, and out into the pretty little garden. He turned to her then with a delighted smile. 'This house is so you. I knew it would look like this.' He put his arms around her waist and she smiled.

'Do you like it?' But it was obvious that he did, even before he nodded.

'I love it.'

'Come on, I'll show you the rest.' She took his hand and led him upstairs, standing in the doorway of her own room, and den, and then taking him up to the girls' rooms, where she had prepared everything for him. Fresh flowers on the desk and near his bed, a silver thermos filled with ice water, stacks of thick towels next to the tub, and the lights were on invitingly as they came up the stairs. She had put him in Jessica's room, because Jessie was neater, and it was easier to make him comfortable there.

'This is absolutely lovely.' He sat down at the desk and looked around with delight, and then at Mel again. 'You have such a loving touch.' She thought the same of him, although it wasn't as apparent in his home, which still bore the chill trace of Anne, but as he reached out to her now there was such a gentle look in his eyes. She walked slowly towards him and he took her hand from where he sat. 'I'm so happy to see you again, Mel.' And then he pulled her down on his lap and kissed her again, and she was still breathless when they went back downstairs. They sat at the kitchen table, not caring to eat anything, and talked for hours, as they had for weeks now on the phone, and it was almost two o'clock when they finally went back up and said goodnight outside Mel's room with another endless kiss, and then with a smile and a wave he disappeared up the stairs to her daughter's room. Mel went into her own room, and thought of every word he had said to her that night. She realised again how happy she was with him. As she brushed her teeth and took off her dress, she couldn't stop thinking of him and she slid into her bed, glad that he had stayed at the house. Apparently, they could handle it with ease, and she liked hearing him walking around upstairs. With the time difference he wasn't tired yet, and the odd thing was that neither was she. All she could do was lie there and think of him, and it seemed hours later when she heard him padding softly down the stairs and past her room. She listened and heard the kitchen door close, and with a grin she got out of bed and followed him down. He was sitting at the kitchen table eating a ham and cheese sandwich and drinking beer.

'I told you we should eat!' She smiled and got a 7-Up for herself.

'What are you doing up, Mel?'

'I can't sleep. Just excited I guess.' She sat across from him and he smiled.

'Me too. I could sit here and talk to you all night, but then I'll fall asleep tomorrow when I have to speak.'

'Do you have a prepared speech?'

'More or less.' He explained to her what it was about. He was using slides of several surgeries, including Marie's. 'What about you? What are you doing this week?'

'Absolutely nothing. I don't have to work for two months, so I'll just hang around and play while you're here. Can I come and hear you speak?'

'Not tomorrow. But on Friday you can. Would you like to come?'

'Of course.' He looked surprised and she laughed. 'Remember me? I'm the lady who did the interview on you at Center City.'

He clapped a hand to his head with a look of surprise. 'So that's who you are! I knew we'd met before but I couldn't remember where.'

'Dummy.' She nibbled his ear and he swatted her behind. It was so comfortable sitting there together in the middle of the night, and at last they walked up the stairs again side by side, holding hands, as though they had lived together for years, and when she stopped outside her room, he bent to kiss her again.

'Goodnight, little friend.'

'Goodnight, my love.' The words just slipped out, and she looked up at him, her eyes wide, and with that he gently enfolded her in his arms again, and she felt so safe there.

'Goodnight.' He whispered the word, kissed her lips once more, and disappeared upstairs. She went into her room, turned off the light, and climbed into bed, thinking of him again and what she had just said. And the amazing thing was that she knew it was true. And as he lay in bed upstairs, he knew he loved her too.

Chapter 18

When Mel awoke the next day, Peter was already gone. She got up slowly and went upstairs to make his bed for him, but she found the room perfectly neat and when she went into the kitchen, she found a note he had left for her.

'Meet you here at six. Have a nice day. Love, P.' She smiled at the simple words, but it felt so good to read them. And she felt as though she were floating all day. She went to Bloomingdale's, and bought some things for herself and the house and the girls, and when she came home, there was that amazing feeling that in a few hours she wouldn't be alone.

She sat in the living room, cooling a bottle of wine, waiting for him, and at last he arrived, looking rumpled and tired and excited to see Mel. She rushed to her feet and quickly went to him. 'Hi, love, how was your day?'

'Wonderful now.' He walked into the living room with a smile. There were no lights on yet, and the room was filled with daylight and sun. 'How was yours?'

'Endless without you.' It was a very honest thing to say and she sat down again and patted the couch next to her. 'Come and sit down and tell me what you did today.' It was fun having someone to talk to at the end of the day, other than the girls. She told him what she had bought, where she had gone, and then sheepishly, she told him that she had literally counted the hours until she saw him again, and he looked pleased.

'I felt the same way. All I could think of was you. It does sound crazy, doesn't it?' And with that he put an arm around her shoulders and pulled her close. Their lips met and they kissed until they were both breathless. There seemed to be nothing to say when they stopped. All they wanted was to kiss again.

'Maybe I should start dinner or something?' Mel laughed, as though they needed a distraction from what they both felt.

'How about a cold shower, à deux?'

She smiled again. 'I'm not sure the "à deux" would help.' She got up and walked around but he pulled her into his arms again.

'I love you, Mel.' And then it was as though the whole world stood still for them both. He had never said that to any woman except Anne, and Mel had told herself for years that she never wanted to hear or say those words again. But this time it meant something to them both, and when he kissed her again she felt it sear her very soul, and she clung to him as though she would drown if she let go. He kissed her face, her lips, her neck and her hands, and then suddenly, without thinking about it, Mel stood up and gently led him upstairs, to her room. And then she turned to him.

'I love you too.' She spoke so softly that had he not been watching her, he would never have heard.

'Don't be afraid, Mel ... please ...' He walked to her and carefully unzipped her dress as she slowly unbuttoned his shirt, and when she was undressed he carefully laid her on the bed, and ran his hands slowly over her silky flesh, until at last she arched towards him, aching for his body on hers, and they pressed themselves close to each other, savouring each moment before he finally entered her and she gasped, and then it was almost as though he could hear her purr until at last she screamed and he groaned, and they lay in silence as the sunlight streamed across the floor. And when Peter looked down at her, there were tears coursing silently from her eyes. 'Oh baby, I'm sorry ... I ...' He was aghast, but she shook her head and kissed him again.

'I love you so much, it scares me sometimes.'

'It scares me too.' But he held her so close that night as they lay side by side, that it was impossible to believe that they would ever know anything except joy.

At nine o'clock they went downstairs, naked and hand in hand. She made sandwiches and they came back upstairs and watched TV and laughed. 'Just like married folk,' he teased, and she rolled her eyes and pretended to faint and he held her comfortably in his arms. And Mel realised that she had never been so happy with any man. They slept together in her bed that night, and awoke to make love several times. When he got up to go to his conference again, she got up with him, and made him coffee and scrambled eggs before he left. And when he was gone, she sat naked and alone, aching for the moment when he would return again.

Chapter 19

On Friday Mel went to the conference with Peter and listened to him speak, fascinated by what he said, and pleased for him by the reaction from the audience. His comments and slides and explanations of their latest techniques were met with continuous applause, and he was surrounded by his colleagues afterwards for almost an hour, as Mel stayed at a discreet distance and watched him with pride.

'Well, what did you think?' he asked her when they were finally alone again that night. They had opted for a quiet dinner at home, since he was leaving the next day, and they wanted some time to themselves.

'I think you're sensational.' She smiled happily at him as they shared a bottle
of white wine. She had bought great big Maine lobsters that day, reminiscent
of the dinners they would have eaten at Martha's Vineyard. She was going to
serve them cold, with salad and garlic bread and chilled Pouilly Fumé. 'And I
also thought their reaction was extremely good.'

He looked satisfied, and smiled. 'I thought so too.' He leaned towards her
and gently kissed her lips. 'I'm glad you were there.'

'Me too.' And then a shadow crossed her eyes, thinking of the next day when
he'd be gone. They were leaving for the airport together the next day at eight
a.m. His flight was at ten, and he would be back in Los Angeles by one o'clock
their time, in time to see Pam and spend some time with her before she left for
camp the next day. And when she dropped him off, Mel was heading back to
Martha's Vineyard and her girls.

'What's wrong, love?' He took her hand in his. 'You looked so sad just then.'
He wondered for the hundredth time since they'd first made love if she regretted getting involved with him. He would be leaving after all, and neither of
them knew when they would meet again. It seemed to be an uncertainty they
constantly had to bear.

'I was just thinking of tomorrow when you leave.'

'So was I.' He put his wineglass down and took her hand in his. 'It's a crazy
life we lead, you and I.' She nodded and they smiled. 'But we'll figure something else out.' And then he decided to pursue an idea he'd had before. 'What
about coming to Aspen with your girls? We go in about three weeks, and
Valerie and Jessica would love it, Mel. It's a wonderful place for kids ... for us
... for anyone, in fact.' His eyes lit up at the thought. 'And it would give us a
chance to be together again.'

'But not like this.' She sighed and met his eyes with a rueful smile. 'Our
children would probably all go nuts if they realised what was going on.' At
least his daughter would, but she knew that it would startle hers as well. There
had been no time to prepare them at all. Peter was a stranger to them, a name
they'd almost never heard, except in the context of her work. And then
suddenly, 'Zap! Guess what, girls, we're going to Aspen with him and his kids!'
Melanie knew they'd have a fit.

'They'll adjust. And they don't have to know all the details.' He sounded so
assured that Mel sat back and looked at him with a long, lazy, happy smile. For
a man who had known no woman but his wife for the past twenty years, and
no one at all since she had died, he seemed remarkably confident about things
now, and Mel wasn't sure if it was indicative of what he felt for her, or simply a
result of his constant poise.

'You're awfully relaxed about all this, beloved sir.'

He smiled at what she said. 'I've never felt like this before, Mel. But it all feels
so right.' At least it did there, in New York, in her pretty little sun-filled house,
alone with her. Perhaps it would be different when they were surrounded by
kids, but he didn't think it would. 'I think our children will be able to handle it.
Don't you?'

'I wish I were as sure. What about Pam?'

'She liked you when she met you in LA. And in Aspen, everyone has something to do, hiking, walking, swimming, tennis, fishing, the music festivals at night. The kids always seem to meet friends and have their own things to do.' But it sounded too easy to Mel, and she wondered how realistic he was. 'Besides' – he moved closer to her and held her tight – 'I don't think I can survive for more than a few weeks without you.'

'It seems like forever, doesn't it?' Her voice was soft and sad as she leaned her head against his chest and felt his warmth envelop her. 'But I don't know if we should come to Aspen, Peter. That's a lot to push at them all at once.'

'What? That we're friends?' He sounded both surprised and annoyed. 'Don't read something into it that they won't see.'

'They're not blind, Peter. They're all practically adults by now, except for Matt. They won't be fooled.'

'Who's fooling them?' He pulled away from her for a moment to look into her eyes. 'I love you, Mel.' It was all he could think of each time he saw her face, every time she entered a room ... whenever he thought of her.

'Do you want them to know that?'

He smiled. 'Eventually.'

'And then what? We go our separate ways, living our separate lives three thousand miles apart, and they know we've had an affair? Think of how they'll feel about it.' She thought for a moment, her mind filled with a picture of Pam's haunted face. 'Especially Pam.'

She sounded sincere and he sighed. 'You think too much.'

'I'm serious.'

'Well, don't be. Just come to Aspen and let's have some fun, without worrying about the kids. They'll be fine. Trust me.'

Mel was bemused by his innocence. Sometimes she was surprised at how naïve he was about his kids. But she had to admit that in spite of her reservations about the trip she was anxious to see him again, and Aspen would provide a golden opportunity, if she could convince the twins to leave Martha's Vineyard for a week or two. She frowned as she considered what she would tell them when she went back.

'Don't worry so much, Mel. Just come.'

She smiled at him and they kissed and afterwards she sat pensively sipping her wine. 'I just don't know what to tell the girls about leaving Martha's Vineyard.'

'Tell them the mountains are better for their health.'

She laughed and looked at him with her head tilted to one side. 'Don't you like the beach?'

'Sure. But I love the mountains. All that good air, splendid views, good hikes.' She had never thought of him as being the outdoor type, but after the intensity of his work, it was easy to understand that he needed an outlet, and one on a grand scale. The mountains would provide that for him, but she had loved the beach since she was a child, and Martha's Vineyard was exactly what she wanted for her holidays with the girls.

'I could remind them about Mark;' – she grinned –'that would convince Val anyway, but that headache we don't need.' He laughed at that.

'Maybe I should tell him about the twins before we go.' He didn't dare to ask her again that night if she was convinced, but the next morning, as they sat over coffee, he had to know. They were leaving the house in an hour for the airport, and his bags were already packed, and her little bag was too. She didn't plan to come back to the house in the city again until September. 'Well, Mel, are you coming?'

'I wish I were.'

He set down his cup and leaned over to kiss her. 'Will you come to Aspen at the end of the month, Mel?'

'I'll try. I have to think it out.' She had turned it over in her mind several times, and was still undecided. But if they didn't go, she might not see him again for months, and she didn't want that to happen either.

She set down her cup with a sigh, and looked him in the eye. 'I just don't know if it's a good idea for us to involve the children in what we feel.'

'Why not?' He looked upset.

'Because it may be too much for them to handle.'

'I think you're underestimating our children.'

'How are you going to explain our coming out there?'

'Does it have to be explained?'

'Oh, for God's sake, what do you think? Of course it does. How could you not explain it to them?'

'All right, all right. So we'll explain it. We'll tell them we're old friends.'

'Which they know damn well isn't true.' She seemed to be getting upset. He looked at his watch. It was seven thirty, and they had half an hour left. There wasn't much time to convince her. And if she didn't come, God only knew when he'd see her again.

'I don't give a damn what you tell them, Mel, your children or mine. But I want you to come to Aspen.' He was beginning to sound bullheaded about it and it annoyed her.

'I have to think it over.'

'No, you don't.' He towered over her, looking as immovable as a marble column. 'You've been making your own decisions for so damn long, that you don't know how to let yourself go and trust someone else.'

'That has nothing to do with this.' Their voices were rising. 'You're being naïve about how the children will react.'

'So what, for chrissake. Don't we have a right to a life too? Don't I have a right to love you?'

'Yes, but we don't have the right to screw up our kids for something that can't go anywhere, Peter.'

'And what makes you think that?' He was shouting now. 'Do you have other plans?'

'I happen to live in New York, and you live in LA, or don't you remember?'

'I remember perfectly, which was why I wanted to meet you halfway three weeks from now, or is that too much to ask?'

'Oh for chrissake . . . all right!' She shouted the words 'All right! I'll come to Aspen.'

'Good!' He glanced at his watch then. It was five minutes after eight, and he suddenly reached out and pulled Mel towards him. Time was moving too fast.

They were supposed to have left five minutes before, but he couldn't leave her now. He kissed the top of her head and stroked her hair, smiling at his own thoughts. 'I think we just had our first fight. You're a damn stubborn woman, Mel.'

'I know. I'm sorry.' She looked up at him and they kissed. 'I just want to do the right thing, and I don't want to upset our kids.'

He nodded. 'I know. But we have to think of ourselves now.'

'I haven't done that in a long time. Except to be sure I didn't get hurt.'

'I won't hurt you, Mel.' His voice was sad, it depressed him to think that she would defend herself against him too. 'I hope to hell I never do that.'

'You can't help it. When people care about each other, they get hurt. Unless you stay at a safe distance all the time.'

'That's not living.'

'No, it's not. But it's safe.'

'Screw safe.' He looked down at her seriously. 'I love you.'

'I love you too.' She still trembled when she said the words. 'I wish we didn't have to leave yet.' They were going to have to run like hell to catch his plane, and he looked at his watch and then at her.

'I have a suggestion.'

'What's that?'

'I'll call home and get someone to cover for me for another day. If they survived this long without me, they can hang on for another day. What do you think?'

She smiled like a little girl and let her whole body sag against him. 'I think it sounds wonderful.' And then she thought of something. 'What about Pam? Don't you want to see her before she goes to camp?'

'Yes, but maybe for the first time in almost two years, I'll do what I want to do for a change. I'll see her in three weeks when she comes home. She'll survive without me.'

'Are you sure?'

He looked very serious as he held her. 'What about you? Can you go back to the Vineyard tomorrow?'

'Are you serious, Peter?' She turned to face him, amazed at his decision. But she could see instantly that he was serious about staying.

'Yes. I don't want to leave you. Let's spend the weekend together.' A smile dawned slowly in her eyes and she hugged him to her.

'You are the most remarkable man.'

'In love with the most extraordinary woman. I'd say we make quite an impressive couple, wouldn't you?'

'Yes, I would.' Her voice was soft as they stood together in her kitchen. And then she looked up at him with a small smile. 'As long as you're not leaving right away, what do you say we go upstairs for a while, Doctor Hallam?'

'Excellent idea, Miss Adams.' She went upstairs and he followed her a moment later. He stayed in the kitchen, just long enough to call the doctor who was covering for him in LA and ask if he would mind staying on for two more days. His colleague teased him about it, but didn't seem to mind at all, and two minutes later Peter bounded up the stairs, taking them two at a time with his long legs and he burst into Melanie's bedroom with a boyish grin. 'I can stay!'

She didn't say a word in answer. She only walked towards him and took his clothes off one by one, and they fell onto her bed with an abandon that came from having taken one more step closer to each other.

Chapter 20

'But how come you're not coming home?' Pam's voice approached a whine when Peter called her before lunch. 'You don't have any patients in New York.' She sounded both angry and hurt and her voice was filled with accusation.

'I got delayed at the conference here, Pam. I'll be home tomorrow night.'

'But I'm leaving for camp tomorrow morning.'

'I know. But Mrs Hahn can take you to the bus. It's not like it's the first time you've gone.' It was odd how one had to defend oneself to one's children, Mel thought as she listened. 'This is your fourth year. You should be an old pro by now, Pam. And you'll be home in three weeks.'

'Yeah.' She sounded distant and gloomy and guilt pulled at his heartstrings, more so now that the decision was made and he had made love to Mel for the past two hours. Now it seemed less urgent that he stay, and Pam was bringing his responsibilities at home back into focus again. 'Okay.' She was shutting him out and he felt bad about it.

'Sweetheart, it couldn't be helped.' But it could have, which made him feel worse. Had he been wrong to stay? But dammit, didn't he have a right to his own life, and some time with Mel?

'It's okay, Daddy.' But he could already hear how despondent and depressed she sounded, and he knew from experience how unwise it was to upset her.

'Look, I'll come up to see you next weekend.' The camp was near Santa Barbara, and he could drive up easily from LA, and then he remembered that he would be on call all weekend. 'Damn, I can't. The next weekend then.'

'Never mind. Have a nice time.' She seemed suddenly anxious to get off, and in New York, Mel watched Peter's face, easily reading the emotions there. When he hung up, she came and sat beside him.

'You can still catch a plane this afternoon, you know.'

But he shook his head with a dogged air. 'I don't think I should, Mel. What I said before is true. We have a right to some time together.'

us 'But she needs you too, and you feel torn.' It didn't take a psychic to see how he felt, and he nodded.

'Somehow she always makes me feel guilty. She's been doing it ever since Anne died. It's almost as if she holds me responsible for her death, and for the rest of time I'll have to atone for my sins and I'll never quite make it.'

'That's a heavy burden to bear. If you're willing to accept it.'

'What choice do I have?' He looked unhappy. 'She's had every emotional problem in the books since her mother died, from anorexia to skin problems and nightmares.'

'But traumas happen to everyone sooner or later. She's going to have to accept what happened, Peter. She can't make you pay for it forever.' But it looked like she was going to try. At least that was how it looked to Mel, but she didn't say anything further to Peter. He was determined to stay, and let her make the adjustment. And a little while later Mel called the twins and Raquel at the house in Chilmark.

The twins were both obviously disappointed that she wasn't coming home, Jessica more than Val, but they both said they'd see her the following night, and then turned the phone over to Raquel, who waited until they left the room before she made comment.

'Boy, he must be somethin' else!'

'Who?' Mel's face looked blank as Peter watched.

'The new boyfriend in New York.'

'What boyfriend?' But now she was blushing. 'Raquel, you're oversexed. How are the girls?'

'They're okay. Val has a new boyfriend she met on the beach yesterday, and I think there's someone who's interested in Jessica, but she doesn't look too excited.'

Mel smiled. 'Sounds like everything there is normal. How's the weather?'

'Gorgeous. I look like a Jamaican.' The two women laughed and Mel closed her eyes, thinking of the Vineyard. She wished that she and Peter were there, and not stuck in New York on a Saturday in July. She knew that, even mountain lover that he was, he would love it.

'See you tomorrow, Raquel. And I'll be in and out of the house here if you need me.'

'We won't.'

'Thanks.' It was always so comforting to know that the girls were in good hands, and as she hung up she smiled to herself, trying to imagine that exchange with Peter's housekeeper, Mrs Hahn. It was beyond even Mel's imagination, and she laughed as she told him.

'You like your housekeeper a lot, don't you?'

Mel nodded. 'I'm damn grateful to her for all she's done. She's an ornery old bitch at times, but she loves those kids, and she even loves me.'

'That's not hard to do.' He kissed Mel full on the mouth and sat back to look at her. She handled her children differently than he did, spoke to her help in a way he never would, and her life seemed to run remarkably smoothly. For a minute, he asked himself if he would only disrupt it, and she saw the look in his eyes as she got up and stretched. They had had a wonderful morning, and it was like an extra gift, since they hadn't expected to be together, and it made them appreciate the time even more.

'What were you thinking then, Peter?' She was always curious about his thoughts, and always intrigued by what he told her.

'I was thinking how well organised your life is, and how long it's all been running on the same track. I was wondering if I'm more of a disruption than an asset.'

'What do you think?' She sprawled on the chaise longue in her room, naked, and he found himself longing for her again. It was amazing how constantly his body hungered for her.

'I think I can't think straight when I see you without your clothes on.'

'Neither can I.' She grinned and beckoned to him with one finger, as he approached and lay down on the chaise beside her, and a moment later he rolled slowly over her, pulling her long thin figure on top of his body.

'I'm crazy about you, Mel.'

She could hardly breathe she wanted him again so badly. 'Me too ...' And then they made love again, and forgot their troubles and guilts and responsibilities, and even their children.

It was one thirty before they had showered and got dressed and Melanie looked like a contented cat as they strolled out of the house into the hot sunshine. 'We sure are lazy.'

'Why not? We both work so damned hard, I can't remember ever having a weekend like this.' He smiled down at her and she laughed.

'Neither can I. Or I'd be too tired to work.'

'Good. Maybe I need to keep you too tired to work, so you don't think of that fancy job of yours all the time.'

She was surprised at his comment. 'Do I do that?' She wasn't aware of thinking of work all the time, and wondered what he meant by it.

'Not really. But there's a certain awareness that you have another life, not just your kids and your house, and a husband.'

'Ah.' Understanding was beginning to dawn. 'You mean I'm not just a housewife. Do you mind that?'

'No.' He shook his head slowly, thinking about it, as they wandered down Lexington Avenue with no particular destination in mind. It was just a hot, sunny day, and they were happy to be together. 'I respect who you are. But it's different than if you were just ...' He looked for the words and smiled down at her. 'An ordinary mortal.'

'Bullshit. What's different about it?'

'You couldn't just leave for Europe with me for six months, could you?'

'No, my contract wouldn't exactly melt into thin air, not without a hefty lawsuit. But you couldn't do that either.'

'That's different. I'm a man.'

'Oh, Peter!' She hooted. 'You are a rotten chauvinist.'

'Yes' – he looked down at her proudly – 'I am. But I still respect your job. So long as you stay as feminine as you are and can manage all the womanly stuff too.'

'What does that mean?' She was suddenly vastly amused by him. From anyone else it might have annoyed her, but it didn't from him. 'You mean like wax floors and bake cheesecake?'

'No, be a good mother, have babies, care about the man in your life, without putting your work first. I was always happy that Anne didn't work because it meant she was there for me. It would bother me if the woman I loved weren't.'

'No one's there all the time, Peter. No woman and no man. But if you care enough about someone you can juggle things most of the time, so you're there when they really need you. It's a question of good organisation, and a sense of priorities. I've been there for the girls most of the time, in fact almost always.'

'I know you have.' He had sensed that about her from the first. 'But you haven't wanted to be there for a man.'

'No, I haven't.' She was honest with him.

'And now?' He looked worried as he asked the question, like a little boy who was afraid he wouldn't find his mommy.

'What are you asking me, Peter?' There was a sudden silence between them. There was a potential which they both sensed, which still frightened them both, but Peter was bravest about pointing to it, and now he suddenly wanted to know where Mel stood, but he didn't want to scare her off. Maybe it was too soon to be asking these questions. She sensed his concern and leaned towards him. 'Don't worry so much.'

'I just wonder what all this means to you sometimes.'

'The same thing it means to you. Something beautiful and wonderful that's never happened to me before. And if you want to know where it's going, I can't tell you.'

He nodded. 'I know. And that bothers me too. It's like in surgery, I don't like to wing it, I like to know where I'm going, what's the next step.' He smiled at her. 'I'm a planner, Mel.'

'So am I. But you can't plan these things.' And she smiled at him, the mood lightened between them.

'Why not?' He was teasing now and she grinned.

'What do you want, a contract from me?'

'Sure. A contract for that gorgeous body of yours any time I want it.'

They held hands and swung their arms, and Mel looked at him happily. 'I'm so glad you stayed for the weekend.'

'So am I.'

They went to Central Park and wandered around until five and then walked up Fifth Avenue to the Stanhope Hotel and had a drink at the outdoor café. Then they walked the few blocks back to her house again, ready to sequester themselves in her comfortable little house. They lay on the bed and made love, and sat watching the sunset at eight o'clock, and then they showered and went to Elaine's for dinner. The place was full and Mel knew half the people there, even though most of the people she knew left town for the weekend in summer. One instantly sensed how much a part of her life this was; the celebrities whom she knew and who knew her, the recognition, and the whole electricity of New York seemed to suit her. There was a milieu like that in LA too but it had never been a part of his life. He was too busy with his own doings, his family, and his patients.

'So, Doctor, what do you think of New York?' They were walking arm in arm down Second Avenue, back towards her house.

'I think you love it, and it loves you.'

'I think you're right.' She smiled happily. 'But I happen to love you too.'

'Even though I'm not a talk show host, or a politician or a writer?'

'You're better than all that, Peter. You're real.'

He smiled at the compliment. 'Thank you. But so are they.'

'It's not the same thing with them. They only touch half my life, Peter. There's another part they never come near. I've never really found anyone who understood both halves of my life before. My family life and my professional life are both important to me, and they're so diametrically different.'

'You seem to manage both.'

She smiled, and nodded. 'It's not always easy though.'

'What is?' He was suddenly thinking of his daughter's reaction to his staying in New York, and he suspected that she'd make him pay for it when she saw him again. She always did.

But Mel looked at him then with a smile and they turned west on Eighty-first Street, and went back to her house to lie in bed and talk until two in the morning.

The next morning, they had brunch at the Tavern-on-the-Green, and then they went down to Greenwich Village for a street fair. There wasn't a great deal to do in New York in the summertime, but neither of them seemed to care. They just wanted to be together, and they walked for hours, talking of their pasts, their lives, their work, their children, themselves. It was as though each couldn't get enough of the other, and at five o'clock they regretfully went back to Mel's house, and made love for a last time. At seven o'clock they took a cab to the airport. And suddenly the time moved all too quickly. It seemed only minutes later when they had to say goodbye and they clung to each other at the gate for their final moments.

'I'm going to miss you so much.' He looked down at her, infinitely glad he had come to New York. He sensed that it had changed the course of his whole life and he wasn't even afraid any more. He put a finger under her chin and tipped her face up to his. 'You promise, you're coming to Aspen?'

She smiled and fought back the tears she felt welling up in her throat. 'We'll be there.' But she still didn't know how she'd tell the twins.

'You'd better.' He held her close and kissed her one last time before boarding the plane with a wave, and as he left, Mel felt as though he had taken her heart with him.

It was a long lonely trip back to Martha's Vineyard that night and she didn't arrive at the house in Chilmark until after midnight, and everyone was asleep. She was relieved that they were. She didn't want to talk to a soul in the world except Peter Hallam, and he was still on a plane heading west to Los Angeles.

Mel sat for a long time on the porch of the house that night, listening to the sound of the ocean, and feeling the gentle breeze on her face. There was a wonderful, peaceful feeling just being there, and she was sorry he hadn't been able to be there with her. But for now, it was just as well. They had needed to be alone. And being in Aspen with his children and hers was going to be enough of a challenge. She still hadn't decided when or how to tell the girls, but she decided the next morning at breakfast that it would be best to give them all the time she could to get used to the idea. They had never left the Vineyard in the middle of the summer before, and she knew they would find it strange. More than that, they would find it suspicious.

'Aspen?' Jessica stared at her in amazement. 'Why would we be going to Aspen?'

Mel attempted to look nonchalant, but she could feel her heart beating faster. Partly because they were putting her on the spot, and partly because she was about to tell a lie. 'Because it's a very exciting invitation, and we've never been there.' Raquel snorted as she went back to the kitchen for the maple syrup, and Val looked at her mother in horror.

'But we can't leave. Everything's happening here, and we don't know anybody in Aspen.'

Mel looked at the youngest twin calmly. She would be easier to convince than her sister. 'Relax, Val, they have boys in Aspen too.'

'But that's different. And we know everyone here!' She looked as though she were going to cry, but Mel held firm.

'I just think it's an opportunity we shouldn't miss.' Or did she mean 'I'? She felt guilty for what they didn't know.

'Why?' Jessica was watching her every move. 'What's in Aspen?'

'Nothing ... I mean ... oh, for chrissake, Jess, stop acting like the official investigative team. It's a fabulous place, the mountains are wonderful, there are loads of kids and things to do, pack trips, horses, hiking, fishing ...'

'Blyearghk!' Valerie interrupted with disgust. 'I hate all that stuff.'

'It'll do you good.'

But this time Jessica intervened, ever practical. 'But that means we'll miss part of the summer here. And we rented the house for both months.'

'We'll only be gone for two weeks. You'll still have six weeks here.'

'I just don't understand it.' Jessica left the table in obvious annoyance and Val burst into tears and hurried to her room.

'I won't go! It's the best summer I've ever had, and you're trying to wreck it!'

'I am not trying to –' But the door slammed before she could finish, and she looked at Raquel in obvious irritation as she cleared the table.

'It must be serious.' She shook her head wisely and Mel got up with a groan of aggravation.

'Oh, for chrissake, Raquel.'

'All right, all right. Don't tell me. But wait and see, six months from now you gonna get married. I never seen you leave the Vineyard before.'

'This will be a fabulous trip.' She was trying to convince them all, including herself, and wishing it were a little bit easier.

'I know. And what about me? Do I have to go too?' She didn't look any more thrilled than the girls.

'Why don't you take your holiday then instead of waiting until the end of the summer?'

'Sounds good to me.'

At least that was one worry behind her. Val didn't come out of her room for two hours, and then emerged, red-eyed and red-nosed, to meet her friends on the beach, and she was obviously not speaking to her mother. Jessica came to find Mel alone on the porch half an hour later, answering some letters. She sat down on the steps near Mel's feet, and waited until her mother looked up from what she was writing.

'How come we're going to Aspen, Mom?' She looked Mel straight in the eyes and it was difficult not to tell her the truth ... because I've fallen in love with this man and he goes there in the summer.

'I thought it might be a nice change for us, Jess.' But she didn't quite look Jessica in the eyes, and didn't see how carefully she was watching her mother.

'Is there another reason?'

'Like what?' She was stalling for time, her pen poised over her paper.

'I don't know. I just don't understand why you'd want to go to Aspen.'

'We were invited by friends.' At least it was a half-truth, but this was turning out to be as difficult as Mel had feared, and if Peter thought his group was going to be any easier, he was crazy.

'What friends?' Jessica looked at her more intently, and Mel took a deep breath. There was no point lying to her, she'd find out soon enough.

'A man named Peter Hallam and his family.'

Jessica looked shocked. 'The doctor you interviewed in California?' Mel nodded. 'Why would he invite us to Aspen?'

'Because we're both alone with our children, and he was very nice to interview and we got to be friends. He has three children more or less your ages.'

'So what?' Jessica sounded even more suspicious now.

'So it might be fun.'

'For whom?' Touché. She was outraged now, and Mel felt suddenly exhausted. Maybe it was stupid to push to go to Aspen.

'Look, Jess, I just don't want to argue about this with you. We're going and that's it!'

'What is this?' She stood up with her hands on her hips, glaring at her mother. 'A dictatorship or a democracy?'

'Call it what you like. We're going to Aspen in three weeks. I hope you'll enjoy it, if not, call it two weeks out of a very long pleasant summer. I might remind you that you're going to have one hell of a nice time here, get to do everything you want for almost two months, and you and Val are having quite an elaborate birthday party next week. I don't think you have much to complain about.' But apparently Jessica did, as she stomped off in a huff without saying another word to her mother.

Things didn't improve much in the next two weeks despite the clambake on the beach for seventy-five kids for Jessie's and Val's sixteenth birthday. It was a wonderful party and everyone had a great time, which made them even more resentful that they had to leave the following week. By then, Mel was sick to death of hearing them complain about it.

'What about you, love?' She lay on her bed talking to Peter one night. They were still talking to each other twice a day, and dying to see each other, in spite of the children.

'I haven't told them yet. There's time.'

'Are you kidding? We're meeting you next week.' She sounded aghast. She had taken two weeks of abuse from the twins, and he hadn't even started dealing with it at his end.

'You have to be casual about these things.' He sounded extremely nonchalant and Mel thought he was crazy.

'Peter, you've got to give them time to adjust to the idea that we're meeting you there, or else they're going to be awfully surprised and probably very angry.'

'They'll be fine. Now tell me about you.' She told him about what she'd been doing, and he reported on the technique he had tried in surgery that morning. Marie was doing extremely well, despite a minor setback and she was due to leave the hospital in a few days, later than expected but in high spirits.

'I can't wait to see you, love.'

'Me too.' He smiled at the thought, and they chatted on for a little while. But he wasn't smiling when he faced Pam four days later.

'What do you mean we've invited friends to Aspen this year?' She looked livid as she faced him across the dinner table. He had told Mark the night before, just casually, as he was going out, and Mark had looked surprised but he hadn't had time to discuss it. And he was going to tell Matthew after he told Pam. But Pam looked as through she were about to go through the roof as she looked at her father. 'What friends?'

'A family I thought you'd enjoy.' He could feel sweat drip slowly down his sides, and was annoyed with himself for it. Why did he let her make him so nervous? 'There are two girls almost your age.' He was stalling, and they both knew it but he was terrified to tell her it was Mel. What if he went off the deep end again?

'How old?'

'Sixteen.' He looked hopeful, but his hopes were quickly dashed.

'They're probably creeps and they'll snub me because I'm younger than they are.'

'I doubt that.'

'I won't go.'

'Pam ... for heaven's sake ...'

'I'll stay here with Mrs Hahn.' She seemed as movable as granite.

'She's taking her holiday.'

'Then I'll go with her. I won't go to Aspen with you unless you get rid of these people. Who are they anyway?'

'Mel Adams, and her twins.' It had to be said, and Pam's eyes opened wide.

'*Her?* I won't go!' Something about the way she said it finally got to him, and before he could stop himself, he slammed a fist into the dining table.

'You'll do what I tell you, do you understand? And if I say you're going to Aspen, that's exactly what you'll do! Is that clear? But she said not a single word in answer; she took her empty plate and threw it against the wall, where it shattered in a dozen pieces on the floor. She flew from the room and he watched her. If Anne had been alive, she would have forced her to come back and clean up the mess, but he didn't have the heart to do that to her. She was a child without a mother. Instead, he sat in the dining room, staring at his plate, and then a few moments later, he left the room and closed himself in his den. It took him half an hour to get up the courage to call Mel. He just needed to hear her voice, but he didn't tell her anything of what had happened.

The next morning, Pam did not come down to breakfast and Matthew quizzed him with a look of interest. He had returned from his grandmother's house the night before after dinner.

'Who's coming to Aspen with us, Dad?'

With a belligerent air, Peter looked at him straight in the eye. 'Miss Adams. The lady who had dinner with us here one night, and her two daughters.' He sat braced for war since that was what he'd met in the first round, but Matthew's face exploded with joy at the news.

'She is! Wow! When is she coming?'

Peter relaxed in his chair with a smile and looked at his youngest child in relief. Thank God one of them was decent about it. He still hadn't heard from Mark, but maybe he would behave as strangely as Pam, although that was unlikely. Mark was too involved in his own life these days to be much trouble. 'She's meeting us in Aspen, Matt. All three of them are.'

'Why don't they come here and we can fly together?'

'Fly where?' Mark entered the room with a sleepy scowl. He had been out late the night before and had to get to work in a hurry now, but he was starving. He had already asked Mrs Hahn for fried eggs, bacon, toast, orange juice, and coffee.

'We were talking about Aspen.' Peter looked defensively at Mark, and waited for the now-expected explosion. 'He was thinking that Mel Adams and her daughters should meet us here.' There was no immediate reaction and he turned back to Matt. 'But they're coming from the East and it's easier for them to fly to Denver and then Aspen.'

'Are they cute?'

'Who?' Peter looked blank. He couldn't keep up with them all these days and he was still unnerved by Pam's reaction the night before. She had yet to emerge from her room, and the door had been locked when he tried it the night before and there had been no answer when he called her name. He decided to leave her alone to cool off for a day. He'd talk to her tonight after he came home from the office.

'Are her daughters cute?' Mark looked at his father as though he were extremely stupid, and Peter sat back in his chair and laughed, just as Mark's gargantuan repast arrived.

'Good God, who's all that for?'

'Me. Well, are they?'

'Are they what? Oh ... oh ... sorry ... I don't know. I assume so. She's a good-looking woman, her daughters must be too.'

'Hmmm ...' Mark was torn between attending to his breakfast and discussing the prospects of Mel's daughters. 'I hope they're not dull.'

'You're a jerk.' Matt looked at him in disgust. 'They're probably gorgeous.'

And with that, Peter stood up with a grin. 'And on that note, gentlemen, I bid you good morning. If you see your sister, give her my love. I'll see you all tonight. Mark, will you be home?'

He nodded, gobbling half a piece of toast, one eye on the clock, worried about being even later for work. 'I think so, Dad.'

'Don't forget to tell Mrs Hahn your plans.'

'I won't.' With that, Peter left them and went to the hospital to do rounds. They weren't doing any surgeries that morning. Another special meeting had been called to discuss techniques, among them Peter's newest which he explained in great detail to Mel later that afternoon when he called her. And when he had finished, he decided to be honest with her about Pam's reaction.

'She'll be all right. I think it's just very threatening to her.'

'Do you still want us to come?'

'Are you kidding?' He sounded horrified that she would even ask. 'I wouldn't even consider going without you. What about your brood? Are they adjusting?'

'Grudgingly.'

The 'casual' reception he had hoped for had vanished into thin air. Mel had been right, about Pam at least. 'Matt is thrilled. And I'm afraid that Mark is already contemplating the twins with a somewhat eager eye. But he's harmless.'

'Don't tell me that!' Mel laughed. 'Wait till you see Val!'

'She can't be as exotic as all that.' Mel was always talking about the girl's voluptuous figure and sex-kitten allure. But she was probably viewing the child with a far from objective eye, as the girl's mother.

'Peter.' Mel's voice was firm. 'Valerie is not exotic. She's just downright sexy. You'd better start putting saltpetre in Mark's food right now.'

'Poor kid. I think he's still a virgin, but working really hard to change his status. He turns eighteen next month, starts college in September, and the last thing he wants to be is a virgin.'

'Well, tell him to practise on someone other than my daughter.'

'That's a deal, as long as I can practise on her mother.' They both laughed then, and said they were looking forward to Aspen in spite of their children.

'Think we'll survive it, Peter?'

'I have not a single doubt, my love. We're all going to have a great time.'

'You think Pam will be okay?'

'I'm certain of it. And the fact is we have to think of ourselves too. I love you, Mel.' She responded in kind and they hung up at last.

But his diagnosis seemed to be a trifle optimistic as they boarded the plane to Denver from LAX a few days later.

'Come on, sourpuss, it's time to board.' Mark found Pam unbearable when she sulked, as she had been for days. She wasn't speaking at all to their father. 'You're going to make it a great holiday for all of us, aren't you?'

'Up yours.' She spoke to her older brother in a tone that would have curled anyone's hair, and Mark looked as though he would have liked to hit her.

'Come on, you two.' Peter was wearing chino slacks, a plaid shirt, and a red sweater over his shoulders, carrying a small back-pack. He had everyone's boarding passes in one hand, and was holding on to Matt's hand with the other. Matthew was in such high spirits that he amply made up for Pam, who found a

seat by herself across the aisle when they boarded. The men sat three abreast
with Matthew on the window side so he could look out, and Peter on the aisle
so he could keep an eye on Pam, but she turned her face away, and looked out
the window for the first half of the flight and then she read a book until lunch
was served, but she did no more than pick at her food before the tray was
picked up again. Peter concealed his worry. Later, when Peter broke out the
candy he had brought for the kids, he passed some to her too, but she declined
it without looking at him.

'She's really being stupid, Dad.' Mark said it sotto voce to his father before
they landed in Denver.

'She'll be all right. Mel's girls will distract her. She's probably just feeling
threatened because she won't be the queen bee for a while. She's used to being
the only girl around the three of us, and here come three new ones. It's bound
to be a bit of a jolt at first.'

'She just likes getting her way. She has ever since Mom died.' He looked
reproachfully at their father. 'Mom would never have let her get away with
this.'

'Maybe not.' But even that reproach hurt Peter. He tried so damn hard, and
why did they always think Anne had done it all better?

But then Matthew reclaimed his attention as they landed, and they had to run
to change planes, and catch the flight to Aspen. It was a short bumpy ride over
the mountains and they made a spectacular landing, dipping in between the
mountains to the tiny airport filled with Lear jets and small private planes.
Aspen was a magnet to the very rich, and also to a more varied, interesting
crowd. There seemed to be everything there, all kinds of people, which was
one of the reasons why Peter liked it. It was one of the many traditions he had
shared with Anne, that he still kept up now, because they had shared happy
times during their holidays there, in winter and summer.

'We're here!' He said it with joy in his voice and the four of them disembarked and rented a car at the airport, to go to a condo much like the one they had
rented for the past five years. It seemed time for a new one this time, and even
Pam seemed more excited as they approached town. As usual, nothing had
changed, including the spectacular view of the mountains. They had just
enough time to settle in and unpack, and go to the supermarket for some food,
before Peter had to go to the airport to meet Mel's plane. He looked around
the group unpacking the food before he left and made one of his seemingly
'casual' offers. 'Anyone want to come?'

'I'll come.' Mark was quick to drop what he was doing, and put his Topsiders
on his bare feet. He was wearing khaki shorts and a red T-shirt, and with his
deep tan from LA and his hair bleached from the sun, even Peter had to notice
that the boy was strikingly handsome. Mel's twins would melt, and if they
didn't there was something wrong with them, he grinned to himself, proud of
his oldest son.

'Me too!' Matt piped up, grabbing his favourite space gun.

'Do you need that thing?' Peter glanced at the gun, it made a noise that drove
him crazy.

'Sure, we might be invaded by creatures from outer space.'

'They're coming in on the next flight?' Pam asked pointedly and Peter glared.

'That's enough! In fact' – he looked angrily at Pam – 'I think you should come too. We're a family, and we do things together.'

'How touching' She stood firmly in the kitchen. 'I think I'll stay.'

'Come on, idiot.' Mark pushed her towards the door and she pushed him back. Peter roared.

'God damn it! I want you to behave, now!' Pam seemed suddenly mollified by the roar from her father, and the four of them drove to the airport in silence. Peter worried about what Pam would say to Mel and her daughters. But as he saw Mel step off the plane, all he could think of was how much he loved her and how desperately he wanted to pull her into his arms. But they had to remain in control in front of the kids. She came towards him, with her red hair tied in a loose knot, a straw hat shielding her eyes, and a pretty cream-coloured linen dress and sandals. 'It's good to see you, Mel.' He took her hand as the children watched, and she kissed his cheek lightly and turned at once to his children. It took every ounce of self-restraint she had not to kiss him full on the mouth.

'Hi, Pam, it's nice to see you again.' She lightly touched her shoulder and bent to kiss Matt who threw his arms around her neck, and then at last she turned to say hello to Mark, but he was staring intently at a young woman behind her. 'Let me introduce my daughters to you. This is Jessica.' It was easy to see that they were mother and daughter from the red hair, but it was Valerie who had riveted Mark's attention. 'And this is Valerie.'

Both girls said hello quietly, and Mel introduced them both to Peter, who had to fight not to burst into laughter. His oldest son looked as though he were going to fall into a dead faint at Val's feet, and as he and Mel went to gather their bags he looked at her with a grin and shook his head.

'You were right. I'm not even sure that saltpetre would have made a difference.' The girl had a voluptuous quality that almost defied description, even more so because she appeared so fresh and naïve. 'You ought to keep her off the streets, Mel.'

'I try, love, I try.' She turned to him then. 'How are you? Did the trip go okay?'

'Fine.'

'How's Pam?' She glanced at her out of the corner of her eye and saw that Jessie was talking to her. Matt stared up at Jess in blatant adoration. 'I'd say some of the dynamics are going to work out okay.' Val and Mark were talking animatedly and Pam seemed to be answering Jess, as Jessica took Matt's small hand in her own, and admired the space gun between spurts of conversation with his sister. 'They're all good kids, that should help.'

'So is their mother.'

'I love you,' she mouthed silently to him, with her back turned to the children, and he longed to take her in his arms.

'I love you too.' He said it close to her ear, and a porter helped them with their bags. It was a good thing they had a station wagon. With seven of them and the Adams' bags, the car was crammed to the gills on the way back to the condo. Everyone seemed to be talking at once – even Pam seemed to be slowly coming out of her shell, with Jessica devoting her attention to her.

She didn't even seem to object as vehemently as Peter had feared when he explained the sleeping arrangements. Pam, Jess, and Val would share the room with two sets of bunk beds. It was cramped, but the girls didn't seem to mind it. Pam was actually laughing by then, as Jessica teased her about something. The two boys shared a room with twin beds, and Peter and Mel took the two smallest rooms, with a single bed in each. Usually, Peter's children had their own rooms, but this year it had taken a little creative arranging to fit them all in and manage separate bedrooms for himself and Mel, but that was crucial on this first trip with the children.

'Everybody all set?'

'We're fine,' Valerie was quick to answer, looking admiringly at Peter, and later she whispered to her mother, 'He's cute,' as Mel laughed. Unfortunately, she also clearly thought his son was. But Mel had already warned her that another romance would only complicate everyone's life for the next two weeks. Val had dutifully agreed on the flight to Denver, but by the time they were all cooking dinner that night, she and Mark were in charge of the salad and baked potatoes, and Mel was beginning to lose hope of dashing a potential romance. She only hoped they'd get good and tired of each other in the next two weeks. 'Val wasn't known for the length of her romances,' Jessica said to Pam with a laugh as they sat near the fire, after she had helped Pam put Matthew to bed. She seemed sensitive to Pam's threatened feelings.

'I don't think Mark has uncrossed his eyes since you two got here.' Peter grinned, appreciating the efforts of the older twin to put his daughter at ease. She seemed like a very special girl, and he remembered much of what Mel had said about her. It was funny to see them now after hearing so much about them, but they were very much as Mel had described, especially Val, whom one would almost imagine as a centrefold in *Playboy*, instead of a junior in high school. But there was a pleasing innocence about the girl, despite her spectacular body. 'I hear you're interested in going to medical school, Jess.' Her eyes lit up at his question and Pam looked bored.

'How disgusting.'

'I know.' She looked placatingly at Pam. 'Everyone thinks that. I want to be a gynaecologist or a paediatrician.'

'They're both good specialities, but very demanding.'

'I want to be a model,' Pam assumed an aloof stance and Jess smiled.

'I wish I could be, but I don't have your looks.' It was not true, but Jessica genuinely believed it. She had lived too long in Val's shadow.

'You can be anything you choose to, Jess.' Mel was sitting by the fire, relaxed, and happy just to be near Peter again. It seemed a thousand years since she had last seen him.

'Anyone for a walk?' Mark bounded into the room with the suggestion and after working on them all for a while, the whole group agreed, except Matt who was sound asleep in his bed. 'Will he be all right here alone?' Mel looked concerned, and Peter nodded with a smile.

'He'll be fine. He sleeps like a rock. Mountain air does that to him. Anne always said ...' He stopped, visibly pale. Mel felt a tremor up her spine. It was odd to be following in Anne's footsteps, to be here with her children now that his wife was no longer alive. She wondered if that was part of Pam's reaction, and made a point of trying to talk to her as they wandered in the cool mountain air, but Pam seemed much more interested in chatting with Jessie, and they walked in three comfortable pairs for about half an hour, Val and Mark, Jessie and Pam, and Melanie and Peter.

'See? It all worked out fine, didn't it?' He sounded supercilious and Mel laughed. 'Don't count your chickens yet. We just got here.'

'Don't be silly. What could happen now?'

She pretended to shield her head from the wrath of the gods, and then glanced at Peter. 'Are you kidding? Anything. Let's just hope there are no murders, broken bones, or unwanted pregnancies after this little adventure.'

'Such an optimist you are.' And with that he pulled her behind a tree and kissed her quickly, unseen by the children, and they giggled softly as they began walking again. It felt so good just to be together again, and there was something nice about seeing their children together, no matter what horrors Mel predicted.

They returned at last to the condo, happy, relaxed, tired from their trip and from settling in, and everyone went to their assigned rooms, apparently without problem. Each room had its own basin, so there was no massive lineup to brush teeth, and Mel could hear the girls giggling in their room after the lights were turned out. She was dying to tiptoe down the hall to Peter, but she didn't think it was wise. Not yet. Not with the children so close. Just as she lay in bed, thinking of their time together in New York, she saw her door open and a shadow cross the room. She sat up in bed in surprise, just as he slipped beneath her covers.

'Peter!' She was startled to see him.

'How do you know?' He was smiling in the dark and she put her arms around his neck and kissed him.

'You shouldn't ... what if the children ...'

'Never mind the children ... the girls are too busy thinking we don't hear them, and Mark is probably as dead to the world as Matt by now ... it's time for us now, kiddo.' He put his arms around her and let his hand slip beneath her nightgown as she fought not to make a sound. 'God, how I've missed you.'

But Mel said not a single word, and what she showed him told him that she had missed him too. Their bodies blended in exquisite pleasure for hours, and then, reluctantly, he left her. She tiptoed to the door to kiss him goodnight and watched him pad softly down the hall. There was no sound from the children's rooms. They were all sound asleep, and she couldn't remember ever being so happy. She tiptoed back to her bed, which still bore the sweet smell of their passion, and drifted off to sleep, holding her pillow.

Chapter 21

The next day they went on a five-mile hike, and picnicked on the way. They stopped beside a small stream, and went wading and Matt caught a snake for Mark, which sent all three of the girls screaming back to Peter and Mel, who laughed at them. But eventually Matthew let the snake go, and they continued their hike until the late afternoon, when they went back to the condo for a swim in the pool, and the kids cavorted like old friends, but Mel noticed that whenever Jessica wasn't talking to Pam, Pam was watching her with Peter.

'They make a nice group, don't they, Mel?'

There was no denying that. A handsome one too. They were all beautiful children, but there was still that unhappy light in Pam's eyes, particularly whenever she saw Mel with her father. Mel was particularly grateful to Jessie for keeping her distracted. And of course Valerie and Mark had been inseparable since breakfast that morning. 'They do make a nice group,' Mel agreed with a tired smile. 'But one that bears watching.'

'There you go again. What are you worrying about now?' He was amused by her reactions. She seemed to be ever watchful over their joint brood, but he liked that about her too. He could easily see that she was a wonderful mother.

'I'm not worried about anything. But I'm keeping an eye on things.' She grinned, and Peter glanced at Val and Mark.

'I think they're harmless. All that energy and young flesh, but fortunately neither of them is quite sure what to do about it all yet. Next year we might not be as lucky.'

'Oh, Christ' – Mel rolled her eyes – 'I hope that's not true. I wish I had married that child off when she was twelve. I don't think I can stand watching her for another four or five years.'

'I don't think you really have to. She's an awfully nice girl.'

Mel nodded, but she looked cautious. 'But much too trusting. She's an entirely different character from Jessie.'

He nodded in agreement. He had seen that already. 'Pam seems to be very fond of Jess.'

'She's good with younger kids.'

'I know.' He smiled happily, it was the happiest he had been in two years. 'Matt adores her.' And then he lowered his voice and bent near Mel's ear. 'And I adore you. Do you suppose we could stay here forever?'

'I'd love it.' But that wasn't entirely true either. She missed their time alone in New York. Here, she was not free to be herself. She had to keep an eye on the children, and she wasn't afraid to put her foot down when she had to. She let the four older ones go to the cinema that night, while she and Peter stayed home with Matt, but when Mark and Val wanted to go out alone after they'd brought Jessie and Pam home, Mel vetoed the idea without question. 'It wouldn't be nice to the others, you two. We're here as a group.' And there were other reasons, which she didn't go into. Reasons why she kept a close vigil every day, as they went for walks, and rode horses, and had picnics in fields full of flowers. There was something so natural and sensual about it all, in their tight T-shirts, and short shorts, and skimpy bathing suits, with the fresh mountain air, and the constant proximity in the condo. She had never seen Val quite so taken with any boy, and it worried her more than she admitted to Peter. She said something to Jess about it when they were alone one day, and Jessie had noticed it too.

'You think she's okay, Mom?' There was a strong bond between the twins, and Jessica always worried about her sister.

'I do. But I think she bears watching.'

'Do you think she ...' Jessie felt uncomfortable accusing her sister to her mother. 'I don't think she'd ...'

Mel smiled. 'I don't think she would either, but I think it's easy to get carried away in fields of wild flowers, with snow on the mountains, or at night if you're alone. I think Mark is more intense than a lot of boys she's used to. And I just want to be sure that she doesn't do anything foolish. I don't really think she would though, Jess.'

'She's not saying much to me this time, Mom,' and that was very unusual for Val. Usually she told Jess everything that happened in her life, particularly what concerned boys. But about Mark she was strangely quiet.

'Maybe she thinks it's more serious than it is. First love.' Mel smiled again.

'Just so she doesn't do anything stupid.'

'She won't.' Mel looked confident in both her own vigil and her daughter's wisdom. 'What about Pam? How do you think she is, Jess?' She trusted her daughter's judgment almost more than anyone else's, except now maybe Peter's, and he was hardly objective about his only daughter.

'I don't think she's a really happy kid, to say the least. We've talked about a lot of stuff, and she opens up a lot sometimes, and other times she's all locked up. I think she really misses her mother. Maybe more than the others. Mark is older, and Matthew was pretty little when she died, but Pam feels ripped off. She gets angry at her father sometimes about it.'

'Is that what she said, Jess?' Mel's voice was soft and filled with concern.

'More or less. I think mostly she's confused. It's not an easy age, Mom.' Jessica looked older and wiser than her years as she spoke and Mel was touched by it.

'I know. And you've been nice to her. Thank you, Jess.'

'I like her.' She said it honestly. 'She's a real bright kid. A little mixed up sometimes, but smart as hell. I invited her to come and see us in New York sometime, and she said yes.' Mel looked surprised. 'Would you mind that?'

'Not at all. All the Hallams are welcome any time they'd like.'

Jess fell silent for a moment and then looked at her mother. 'What's happening with you and Dr Hallam, Mom?'

'Not much. We're good friends.' But she felt as though Jessica already knew much more. 'I like him, Jess.'

'A lot?' Jessica searched Mel's eyes, and she knew she had to be honest with the child.

'Yes.'

'Are you in love with him?'

Mel held her breath. What did those words mean? What did Jess want to know? The truth, Mel told herself. Only that. She had to tell her the truth. 'Yes, I think I am.' Jessica looked as though she had received a physical blow.

'Oh.'

'Are you surprised?'

'Sort of yes and sort of no. I suspected it before, but I wasn't sure. It's different when you actually hear someone else say it.' And then she sighed and looked at Mel. 'I like him.'

'I'm glad.'

'Do you think you two will get married?'

But this time Mel shook her head. 'No, I don't.'

'Why not?'

'Because our lives are too far apart. I can't quit my job and move to LA and he can't move to New York. And we both have too much keeping us where we are.'

'That's sad.' Jessica searched her eyes. 'If you lived in the same town, do you think you'd get married?'

'I don't know. It can't be an issue for us. So it's nice to enjoy whatever time we have.' Mel reached out and touched her daughter's hand. 'I love you, Jess.'

She smiled. 'I love you too, Mom. And I'm glad we came after all. I'm sorry I gave you such a hard time before.'

'That's okay. I'm glad it all worked out.'

'Am I interrupting anything?' Peter wandered into the room and saw them both, and the two of them holding hands, but Mel shook her head.

'We just had a nice talk.'

'That's nice.' He seemed pleased and smiled at Jess. 'Where's everyone else?'

'I don't know.' It was about five o'clock and Mel had just come back from the store when she started talking to Jess. She assumed the other kids were at the pool as they had been at that hour, every day for the past week.

'Val and Mark took a walk with Matt.'

'They did?' Mel was surprised. 'Then where's Pam?'

'In our room, asleep. She had a headache this afternoon. I thought you knew.' But Mel still looked surprised, and Peter patted her arm.

'Mark will take care of Val and Matt. Don't worry about them, Mel.' But when they weren't back at seven o'clock, Mel was seriously concerned, and Peter didn't look as confident as he had before.

He stopped in to see Jess and Pam in their room. 'Do you know where they went?' Jessica shook her head and Pam looked blank.

'I was asleep when they left.'

He nodded and went back to Mel. It was still light outside but he wanted to have a look around. 'I'll be back in a little while.' But when he didn't come back in an hour either, Mel was as frightened as the girls.

'What do you suppose happened, Mom?' Jessica whispered. Pam was sitting white-faced in their room.

'I don't know, love. Peter will find them.' But on the hillsides behind the house, he was wandering aimlessly, having abandoned the trails, calling out their names. And it was dark when he found Val and Mark at last, scratched and frightened and alone.

'Where's Matt?' He spoke directly to his son, with fear and tension in his voice, as he noticed that Val's face was covered with tears and scratches.

Mark looked as though he were about to cry too. 'We don't know.'

'When did you see him last?' Peter felt his jaw go tense.

'About two or three hours ago. We were just walking along and then all of a sudden we turned around, and he wasn't there.' Val began to cry incoherently giving her version of the tale, and Peter saw that Mark was still holding her hand and he began to suspect what had happened and why they had lost track of Matthew.

'Were you two making out?' He was blunt with the words, which only made Val cry more, and sheepishly Mark hung his head, but not before his father's hand cracked across his face. 'You little sonofabitch, you had a responsibility to your brother if you took him out with you!'

'I know, Dad.' Tears began to slide down his face now, but the next hour of their search yielded nothing more, and Peter led them back to the trail they had left, and back to the condo far down the mountainside. They had to call the sheriff and begin the search for Matthew. He found Mel pale-faced with the girls, and when he returned with only Val and Mark, the three girls burst into tears. He went quickly to the phone with Mel at his side, and the search party arrived in less than half an hour, with ropes and stretchers, a paramedic team, and enormous search-lights.

'We'll take helicopters up tomorrow, if we don't find him tonight.' But Peter didn't want him out alone all night, and he was already terrified that the child might have fallen into a ravine, and broken a leg or worse. He could be unconscious somewhere. Peter left with the other man, and the girls stayed with Mel and Mark below. Mark was crying openly now, as Mel tried to reassure him, but there was no way of soothing the guilt he felt and Mel had managed to say almost nothing to Val. It was well after ten o'clock by now, and there was still no sight of the child, as suddenly Pam exploded at Val and shrieked at her.

'It's all your fault, you horny bitch, if you hadn't been out kissing Mark, my little brother wouldn't have got lost.' To which Val found no response, and she collapsed in Jessie's arms, sobbing hysterically. It was only then that Mel heard a shout and a bleat of horns well up the mountainside; lights were flashed and it seemed moments later when the entire crew came down, victorious, with Matthew in their arms, and Peter fighting back tears of relief as he waved at them.

'Is he all right?' Mel ran to Peter's side, and the tears escaped his eyes at last. He stood there for a long time, holding her, as he sobbed. Matthew was still a little way behind in the arms of one of the sheriff's men. They had found him just outside a cave, frightened and cold and unharmed. He said he had wandered off by himself for a little while, and got lost. And he claimed to have seen a bear.

'Oh, Mel' – Peter couldn't let go of her – 'I thought we'd lost him.'

She nodded, tears pouring down her own face. 'Thank God he's all right.' She saw him being carried into their midst, filthy dirty, his face scratched and his clothes torn, and she could see that he had fallen a few times, but he looked very excited to be with the sheriff's men and he was wearing someone's hat. Mel scooped him into her arms and held him there. 'You scared us to death, Matt.'

'I'm okay, Mel.' He looked suddenly very grown-up and brave.

'I'm glad.' She kissed his cheek and handed him to his father then, who thanked all the sheriff's men, and at last they all went back inside and collapsed in the living room. Mark was hugging his little brother to his chest, and Valerie was still crying but she was smiling now as well, and even Pam had cried with relief. Everyone fussed over him, and it was midnight before they all settled down, and Pam had apologised to Val, and Mark had sworn that they would never go off alone again. As they all sat by the fire, finishing the hamburgers that Mel had made for them all, Peter spoke to them.

'I want one thing clear right now. I think tonight has taught us all something.' He looked pointedly at Val and Mark. 'We can all have a wonderful time while we're here. But you can't kid around, you can get lost in the woods, you can get bitten by snakes and God knows what. And I want you each to feel responsible for the rest of the group. From now on, I want to see all five of you together or not at all. If anyone goes somewhere, the rest of you go too. Is that clear?' He looked at his oldest son again, who nodded his head shamefacedly. He had been so intent on Val that he had entirely forgotten about Matthew. And when they had caught their breath again, he had gone. 'If I see anyone paired off here, they're going home that day, and I don't care who it is.' But they all knew he meant Val and Mark. 'Now I want everyone to go to bed and get some sleep, it's been a tough night for everyone.' They were quick to disband and go to their rooms, but there was a new camaraderie between them now.

'Christ, Mel, I thought I'd die out there on that hill with no goddamn sign of him.' He lay in her bed that night, thinking of it all again and she held him again and felt him tremble in her arms.

'It's all over, my love. He's safe, and it won't happen again.'

They didn't even make love that night. They held each other close, and Mel lay awake beside him for most of the night, watching him sleep until the sky lit up with the first light of dawn. She woke him gently then, and he went back to his own bed, and then she slept at last. But all she thought of all night was how much she loved him – loved them all – and how desperately she wanted nothing awful to happen to any of them again. It was the first time she had realised how *much* she loved them and how deeply they were lodged in her heart. When they all awoke the next day, they truly seemed like one family. The five children became inseparable from that moment on, and although Mel frequently saw Mark holding Val's hand, or looking into her eyes with that special glance that lit up her face, they never went off alone again and the remaining week slid by them much too quickly.

On their last night there, Peter took them all out, and they had a wonderful time, laughing and talking like old friends. To look at them one would never have known that they hadn't grown up under one roof, and no one would have believed the extent to which they had fought the trip at first. Peter smiled at Mel several times. It had been a perfect holiday, despite that one ghastly night of looking for Matt, but even that seemed to be forgotten now.

They sat by the fire until late that night, even Matt, who finally fell asleep on Jessica's lap, and she put him in his bed with Pam's help. When they all parted at last, it was with regret to end their happy time, and Mel and Peter lay awake for hours, both of them sad to be leaving.

'I can't believe I'm leaving you again.' He was leaning on one elbow, looking down at her, after they'd made love.

'It can't be helped.' And then suddenly she had a thought, and she looked at him with a hopeful smile.

'Why don't you all spend the Labor Day weekend at Martha's Vineyard with us?'

'That's a hell of a long trip for three days, Mel.' He looked dubious, but he wanted to cling to any hope he could.

'Then stay a week.' Stay a month ... stay a year ...

'I can't.'

'But the kids could.' It seemed like a great idea to her. 'Pam and Matt could. Mark will be through his job around then too. He could fly back for the weekend with you. The other two could come ahead.'

'It's a thought.' He smiled at her; not really thinking of the kids just then, but only of her. He wanted desperately to stay with her, but there was no way they could. 'I love you so much, Mel.'

'I love you too.' And they lay back in each other's arms again and made love on and off until the dawn. They both looked depressed the next morning when they got up in their separate rooms. There would be no lovemaking again that night, no long walks in the woods or in the fields of flowers. It was time to go home again. Back to reality, and clinging to him on the phone. But she brought up her idea for Labor Day and the kids cheered. 'That does it then.' She looked victoriously at Peter and he laughed. He looked happy about the holiday too.

'All right. You win. We'll come.'

'Hurray!' You could hear their shouts halfway up the mountainside, and they chattered all the way from Aspen to Denver on the flight. The kids sat in one row straight across, and Peter and Mel sat alone for the last time. And in Denver, everybody cried, and Peter looked into Mel's eyes and whispered to her.

'I love you, Mel. Don't ever forget that.'

'Remember that I love you too.' The kids pretended not to watch, but Val and Mark smiled, and Pam turned away so as not to see, but she and Jessica were holding hands, which gave Pam some comfort. And Matt gave Mel a great big goodbye kiss.

'I love you, Mel!'

'I love you too.' She tore her eyes from his, and kissed each of the children, and told Pam, looking into her eyes. 'Take good care of your dad.' She wanted to add 'for me'.

'I will.' There was a new gentleness in Pam's voice, and they were all subdued as they went their separate ways and Matthew cried openly as his father led him to their plane.

'I want them to come with us.'

'You'll be seeing them again soon.'

'When?'

'In a few weeks, Matt.' Peter glanced at Mark then and saw a dreamy expression on his face. He wondered just how much had happened between him and Val but figured it couldn't be much. On the plane they left for Boston at the same time as the flight to LA, Jessica and Val barely spoke, and Mel looked out the window seeing nothing there except a vision of Peter's face. Three weeks till Labor Day seemed endless to her, and then what? An endless year until Aspen again? It was madness they had inflicted on themselves, but Mel knew, as well as Peter did on the flight to LA, that for them it was too late to turn back now.

Chapter 22

The weeks at Martha's Vineyard seemed to drag by for them all once they returned from Aspen. It was nothing like their time there in July, when they threw themselves wholeheartedly into the amusements of the summer. Instead, once they got back, Val seemed to spend all her time staring into space, and Mel spent most of hers on the phone, and Jessica teased them both.

'Boy, you two sure are a lot of fun.' Valerie almost killed herself getting to the mailbox every day to check for letters from Mark, and each time Mel left the house she would come back and casually ask, 'Anyone call?' and both girls would laugh. Only Raquel seemed to treat it all like a serious illness that had descended on their home. She warned them all that in six months ... they'd see! She never finished her warnings, but they sounded ominous to everyone, and Mel always listened to her with amusement.

'Now, Raquel, relax!'

'This time it's serious, Mrs Mel.'

'Yes, it is. But serious and terminal aren't the same.'

Grant called too to say hello. He was madly in love with the weather girl on Channel 5, and there was also a cute little redheaded female jockey in White

Plains, not to mention some staggeringly sexy Cuban girl. Mel teased him about it and told him to act his age, and she finally told him about Peter, or rather the girls did. He sounded hurt when Mel got back on the phone.

'You couldn't have told me yourself? I thought we were friends.'

'We are, but I needed time to think this thing out.'

Grant sounded surprised. 'Is it as serious as that?'

'It could be, but we haven't solved the problem of distance yet.'

'Distance?' And then suddenly, all the pieces fell into place. 'You little minx, it's the heart surgeon on the West Coast, isn't it?'

She grinned like a little kid and giggled into the phone.

'You jerk. Now what are you going to do? You're here, he's there.'

'I haven't figured that out yet.'

'What's to figure out, Mel? You've done it again, found yourself the "Impossible Dream". Neither of you is going to quit your job for chrissake, and you're both anchored where you are. My friend, you've done it again. You're playing it safe.'

His words depressed her long after she got off the phone, and she spent days wondering if what he said was true. Was she really involved in just another impossible romance?

As if to validate her feelings she dialled Peter in California.

He was excited about Marie's progress, having seen her that day and she was doing very well. Mel found herself praying that no new transplant patient would come on the scene in the next week, or he wouldn't be able to fly east for the Labor Day weekend.

He reported that Pam and Matt were ready for the trip east, and Matthew was so excited he could hardly see straight.

'What about Pam?'

'She's more outwardly subdued than Matt, but she's just as excited as he is.'

'So are the girls. They can hardly wait until they get here.' They had made dozens of plans to include Pam, and Mel was going to take charge of Matthew. Even Raquel was excited about the prospective visits, although she pretended to complain about the extra work. They had spent hours trying to work out the sleeping arrangements and finally decided that Mark would sleep on a sleeping bag on the living room couch, Pam would sleep on a rollaway bed in the twins' room, Matt would sleep in the twin bed in Raquel's, and when he came, Peter would have the guest room. It had taken some doing, but the house could accommodate them all.

When Pam and Matthew arrived, there was an aura of festivity throughout the whole house, and all the children went down on the beach as Mel watched them join the others they met there every day. The boy Val had discovered at the beginning of the summer no longer held an interest for her, and there were half a dozen madly in love with Jess, who wouldn't give any of them the time of day. One or two of them thought Pam a remarkably attractive girl, and no one could believe she was only fourteen. She was so tall and looked so much older, and for the whole week, Mel was happy with her brood of four and reported to Peter twice a day.

'I wish you'd hurry up and get here.'

'So do I. Mark is practically catatonic with anticipation.' But the night before they were due to leave LA the whole trip almost went down the drain. A young woman came in with rejection of the transplant that had been done four months before, and a severe infection. Mel heard the news with a sinking feeling in the pit of her stomach, but she didn't press Peter about the trip, or urge him to leave the woman in the care of his very capable colleagues. As it turned out, the poor woman died before morning. He called Mel about it the next day and was very depressed.

'There was nothing we could do.' But it always got him down anyway.

'I'm sure there wasn't. It'll do you good to get away now.'

'I guess it will.' But it took some of the shine out of the trip for him, and he was quiet as he and Mark flew to Boston. But on the second leg of the trip, he seemed to revive and he and Mark chatted about Mel and her daughters.

'They're really nice, Dad.' Mark blushed as he tried to sound nonchalant, and Peter smiled at his son.

'I'm glad you think so, I think so too.' It was going to be wonderful to see her again, and suddenly it was all he could think of as the small plane landed on the narrow airstrip, and he hastened off the plane behind Mark, who was practically jet propelled out of the door, and down the rickety metal stairway. He came to a screeching halt in front of Val, not sure whether to shake hands or kiss her or just say hi. He stood there stumbling over his own feet and blushing furiously as Val did the same, and Peter pulled Mel into his arms with a ferocious grip and held her, and then he dutifully kissed Pam, and Jess and Val, and then Matt. Val and Mark headed towards the baggage claim together, and Peter saw Mark stealthily take her hand and he grinned at Mel.

'There they go again.'

She smiled, glancing at the two lovebirds far ahead. 'At least here they can't get lost in the mountains.' But they seemed to go off in a sailboat much of the time over the Labor Day weekend, and Peter had to remind them again about the group rules he had insisted on in Aspen.

'The same rules apply here.'

'Oh, Dad.' It was Mark who objected, almost whining as he hadn't in years, but he wanted so much to be alone with Val. They had so much to tell each other. 'We just want to talk.'

'Then do it with the others.'

'Yuck.' Pam rolled her eyes and held her nose. 'You should hear the junk they say to each other.' But Mel had noticed that there was a fourteen-year-old boy from down the beach whom Pam had not found particularly 'yucky'. Only Jess and Matthew seemed to have maintained their sanity by the end of the weekend. Jessica was already thinking ahead to the first day of school, and Matt was so happy with Mel and his father that he was no trouble at all. He had longed for that kind of security for years, without actually understanding what was missing. And Peter chuckled at Raquel, who obviously approved of him and spent a lot of time telling him how lucky he was to have Mel, how all she'd needed was a good man, and what she needed now was to get married. Mel was horrified when he told her as they lay on the beach on Sunday.

'Are you kidding? She said that?'

'She did. Maybe she's right. Maybe that is what you need. A good husband, to keep you barefoot and pregnant.' He seemed amused by it all, and even more so to watch the children living out their end-of-summer madness. He was keeping a good eye on Mark. He didn't want him getting out of line with Val, and he could see that their hormones were pumping furiously throughout the weekend. Peter turned back to Mel then, remembering what Raquel had said. 'What do you say to that?'

'I'm sure the network would be thrilled.' She was amused at the suggestion, but didn't consider it a real threat. All she cared about right now was being with him for the weekend. She'd think about the future later, about what they would do about seeing each other again, and when. And then she remembered something else. 'You just reminded me, I have to call my lawyer after the Labor Day weekend.'

'How come?'

'My contract is up in October, and I like getting started nice and early outlining what I want for the next one.' He admired the way she handled her work. In fact, there was a lot more than that he admired about her.

'You must be able to call your own shots by now.'

'To some extent. Not entirely. But anyway, I want to sit down with him some time in the next couple of weeks and see what he thinks.'

Peter grinned, in a silly mood, the end-of-summer madness was beginning to touch them all. 'Why don't you just quit?'

'And do what?' she didn't find the idea quite as funny as he did.

'Move to California.'

'And sell tacos on the beach?'

'No, this may come as a shock to you, but we have television there now too. We even have news.' He was smiling and she thought he had never looked more handsome.

'Do you? How intriguing.' But she didn't take the suggestion seriously for a moment until he reached out and touched her arm, and she saw that he was looking at her strangely.

'You know, you could do that.'

'What?' A chill ran down her spine despite the brilliant sunshine and hot weather.

'Quit and move to California. Someone would put you on the air there.'

She sat up very straight and stared down at him lying in the sand. 'Do you have any idea how many years it took me to get where I am here at the network? Do you have even the remotest idea of what Buffalo was like at twenty below, or Chicago? I worked like hell for this job, and I'm not giving it up now, so please don't joke about it, Peter. Ever.' She was still upset when she lay down in the sand beside him again. She didn't find the suggestion even remotely amusing. 'Why don't you give up your practice and start fresh in New York?'

She saw that he was looking at her intently, and she was sorry her tone had been as sharp. He looked hurt. 'I would if I could, Mel. I'd do anything to be near you.' And the accusation was that she wouldn't, which wasn't fair.

'Do you understand that it's no easier for me?' Her voice was gentler now. 'Leaving New York would be a step down for me now, wherever I went.'

'Even to LA?' He looked suddenly depressed. Their situation was hopeless.

'Even to LA.' And then after a moment's silence when they both stared out to sea licking their wounds, 'We'll just have to find some way to be together.'

'What do you suggest? Weekends in Kansas City?' This time it was Peter who sounded angry and bitter, and he looked down at her now with fire in his eyes. 'What do you think this will be when it grows up, Mel? A holiday romance? We meet for long weekends with our kids?'

'I don't know what to suggest. I can fly to LA, you know, and you can come here.'

'You know how rarely I can leave my patients.' And she couldn't leave the girls all the time, and they both knew it.

'So what are you telling me? That I should give up now? Is that what you want?' Suddenly, she was frightened by the gist of their conversation. 'I don't have the answers, Peter.'

'Well, neither do I. And something tells me you don't want to find them.'

'That's not true. But the reality is that we both have important jobs at opposite ends of the country, and neither one of us can just dump what we're doing and move, nor would we want to. And we're not ready to yet, anyway.'

'Aren't we?' He looked angry again. 'Why not?'

'Because we've only known each other for four months, and I don't know about you, but that doesn't seem like very long to me.'

'I'd have atmarried Anne five minutes after I met her and I was right.'

'That was Anne.' She was shouting at him now, but they were alone on the beach. The children had all gone to play volleyball somewhere else and Matt was with Raquel looking for seashells. 'I'm not Anne, Peter, I'm me. And I'm not going to follow in her goddamn footsteps. Even if you did take me to Aspen, which is where you went with her every year.'

'So what, dammit. Didn't you like it?'

'Yes, I did. But only after I overcame the creepy feeling I had every time I thought that you'd been over every inch of that place with her, and probably even slept in the same bed.'

He was on his feet now and so was she. 'It may interest you to know that this time I ordered a different condo. I'm not as totally insensitive as you seem to think, Miss Adams.' And after that they both stood very still, and suddenly Mel hung her head.

'I'm sorry ... I didn't mean to hurt you ...' She looked up at him again then. 'It's difficult, sometimes, knowing how attached you were to her.'

Peter pulled her slowly towards him. 'I was married to her for eighteen years, Mel.'

'I know ... but I feel like I'm always being compared to her. The perfect wife. The Perfect Woman. And I'm not perfect. I'm me.'

'Who compares you?' He looked shocked. He had never said anything like that. But he hadn't had to.

Mel shrugged as they sat very close on the sand again. 'You ... the children ... maybe Mrs Hahn.'

Peter was watching her closely. 'You don't like Mrs Hahn, do you? Why?'

'Maybe because she was Anne's. Or because she's so cold. I don't think she likes me either.' Mel smiled, thinking of Raquel, and Peter laughed, knowing what she was thinking.

'No, she certainly isn't Raquel, but no one is. Except Raquel herself.' He had come to like her too, but he wasn't sure he could live with her loose tongue in his household. He liked Mrs Hahn's restraint and the way she controlled the children. Raquel was more like a friend with a mop in one hand, and a microphone in the other.

'Were you serious about me moving to California, Peter?' She looked worried as she asked, and slowly he shook his head.

'I guess not. Just dreaming. I know you can't give up your job here. I wouldn't want you to anyway. But I wish there were a way we could be together. This is going to be a terrible strain commuting back and forth.' Grant's words echoed in her ears ... dead end ... dead end ... And she didn't want it to be.

'I know it's a strain to come here. I'll do my best to come to LA as much as I can.'

'So will I.' But they both knew that she would do most of the commuting. There was just no other way. She could leave the twins more easily than he could leave his patients, and sometimes she could bring them too. As though to illustrate the point, he got a call late Sunday night. One of his old transplant patients had had a major heart attack. He gave all the suggestions he could over the phone, but the transplant had been two years before, and the man's chances weren't great, whether Peter was there or not. He stayed awake all night, worrying about his patient, and feeling that he should have been there with him. 'I have a responsibility to these people, Mel. It doesn't just end when I pull off the mask and gown after the surgery. It goes on, as long as they live. At least that's how I feel.'

'That's why you're good at what you do.' Mel sat next to him on the porch, hugging her knees as they watched the sun come up, and an hour later they got the call from LA that his patient had died. They took a long walk on the beach then, saying little, and Mel held his hand, and when they came back to the house he felt better. It was all that he would miss when he went back to LA again. He needed her with him.

Monday was their last day together at the Vineyard. The kids had plans for the entire day, and Raquel was busy cleaning up before they closed the house. Mel had encouraged everyone to pack the day before so they didn't have to waste their last day packing. And they had already decided that they wouldn't leave until Tuesday morning. Peter and his children would leave as they had come, on a seven a.m. flight out of the Vineyard, which coordinated with a nine a.m. flight to Los Angeles from Boston, which arrived in the morning in LA. The time difference worked in their favour, and Peter could go straight to the hospital and do rounds, after dropping the kids off at home. Pam and Matthew didn't start school until the following week and Mark had three weeks before he started college.

Mel and the twins would take the ferry to Woods Hole, drive to Boston, return their rented car, and then fly to New York, getting to their home actually later than the group flying to LA. But as they contemplated leaving on

Monday night, there was silence. It was sad to be leaving each other again, they were really a group now. Pam was the first to express her sorrow to be leaving, and Mark quickly seconded his sister's view, holding tightly on to Valerie's hand, a sight they were all beginning to get used to.

'Can't you ever prise those two apart?' Peter was still mildly worried, but Mel was beginning to relax about it as they lay in bed on their last night.

'They're all right. I think the less fuss we make, the quicker they'll get bored with it.'

'Just so no one gets pregnant.'

'Don't worry, I'm keeping an eye on Val, and so is Jess. And frankly, I think Mark is a very responsible boy. I don't think he'd take advantage of Val. Not even if she tempted him, which I'm praying she won't.'

'I hope you're not overestimating him, Mel.' He put an arm around her shoulders and thought back over the weekend. And then he looked at her with a tender smile. 'So when do you come to LA?'

'I go back to work in two days, let me see what's happening there and we'll talk about it. Maybe weekend after next, or the weekend after that?' She sounded hopeful, but he looked depressed.

'That's practically October.'

'I'll do my best.'

He nodded, not wanting to argue with her, but her best still wasn't going to be what he wanted. He wanted her there all the time and he couldn't see how he was going to get that. He wasn't ready to give her up either. Suddenly in the last month he had come to feel that he couldn't live without her. He knew that was crazy, but it was how he felt. He needed her near him to share the joys and burdens of his daily life, the funny things said by Matt, the patients who died, the tears shed by Pam, the beauty, the traumas, all of it. It meant nothing without her, but there was no way that he could take her to LA with him. And as they made love that night he wanted to drink her spirit and swallow her soul and remember every nook and cranny of her body.

'Sure you won't come with me?' he whispered before he boarded the plane to Boston.

'I wish I could. But I'll be there soon.'

'I'll call you tonight.' But just the idea of having to call her again, and not see her, depressed him. He had finally found the woman he wanted and he couldn't have her, not because another man did, but because a network thought they owned her, and worse yet, she liked it. Yet he knew that she loved him. It was a lousy situation, but he hoped that in time something would happen to resolve it. He smiled to himself. Maybe she would decide that she couldn't live without him. 'I love you, Mel.'

'I love you more,' she whispered, and out of the corner of their eyes they saw Val and Mark kissing and holding each other tight, and Pam made a horrible face.

'Yuck. They're disgusting.' But the boy she had liked on the beach had come to say goodbye to her, and she blushed furiously as she said goodbye to him. Only Matt was left out of the romantic scene, and everyone kissed him goodbye half a dozen times.

'Come out soon,' Peter said to Mel.

'I promise.'

The two tribes waved as the Californian contingent boarded the small plane, unsuccessfully trying not to shed tears en masse, and then the Adams got into their car and drove toward the ferry, the twins waving handkerchiefs and crying openly, as Mel tried to conceal her aching heart.

Chapter 23

The interview that Melanie had done of Peter when they met aired the first week in September and was hailed as one of the most extraordinary documentaries that had been done in the history of television. Everyone felt sure that Mel would win an award for it, and suddenly everyone seemed to be talking about Dr Peter Hallam. And better yet, since the surgery, Pattie Lou Jones had bloomed. There was a brief film clip of a follow-up on her.

Everyone in LA called to tell Peter again and again what a marvellous interview it was, and what a breakthrough for heart transplants and greater public acceptance of them. But repeatedly, Peter gave Mel the credit, and said what a remarkable job she'd done. So much so that when she finally came out to Los Angeles for the last weekend in September, everyone in the hospital seemed to treat her like an old friend, as did Matthew and Mark; Pam still showed a little reserve, and Mrs Hahn was no friendlier than she had been before.

'It's almost like coming home, Peter.' She smiled happily as he drove her to her hotel. She was staying at the Bel-Air, because it was close to his house and she liked the seclusion. He was spending the night with her and they could hardly wait. They felt like two kids sneaking off to a hotel, and Mel giggled at the thought. He was going to tell the children the next day that he had stayed at the hospital with a patient, but all his medical contacts knew where he was, in case he was needed during the night. 'It's so good to be back.' She strutted around the large, cheerful room, peeled off her dress, and sat happily in her slip looking at Peter. It had been three and a half weeks since she'd seen him, but she just hadn't been able to come out sooner, no matter how lonely she'd been for him. And she was. There had been one emergency at the station, Jessica had got sick, and it had taken more time than she had thought to reorganise their life in the autumn. It always did, but this year she was in more of a hurry than usual. She was absolutely desperate to get to LA to be with him.

'It's so good to see you, Mel. It's awful being three thousand miles apart.'

'I know.' But there was no solution to that, and they both knew it. They ordered room service and enjoyed staying in their room alone, and they had already made love once when Peter asked her how the sketching of the new contract was going. 'We know what we want at least. The question now is will we get it.' It was a bit like his own plight with her and he smiled, and kissed her softly on the lips.

'They're crazy if they don't give you everything you want. You're the best thing they've got and they know it.'

Mel smiled at the lavish praise. 'Maybe I should have you negotiating this instead of my lawyer.'

'When do you start actually negotiating this?'

'In about two weeks.'

He looked sad, but almost resigned now. 'That means I don't see you for another month, I imagine.'

She couldn't deny that. Contract negotiation was a tense time for her, and she wanted to be on hand every moment. She wouldn't be in the mood to go anywhere, not even to see him. 'Can you come east?'

He shook his head. 'I doubt it. We've done two heart transplant patients in the last month' – she knew that much already –'and we're waiting to do another heart-lung. I'm not going to be able to go anywhere for quite a while.'

'Able,' she reminded him, 'but not willing. There's a difference.' But she understood the reasons why. They were both trapped by their jobs and their lives and their children. It was crazy, almost like being married to separate people, and they had to take what they could while they could get it.

Mel didn't even see his children again until Sunday afternoon, the night before she took the red eye. They had stayed almost in hiding at the Bel-Air. They wanted to be alone every moment they possibly could, and Mel thought it was best if they didn't see too much of the children. She could already sense that now that Pam was back on her own turf, she was not as warm to Mel. She felt more secure here, and she had her father to herself again. But the boys hadn't changed. Mark pumped her for every possible bit of news of Val, and all Matthew wanted to do was sit on her lap and hug her. The afternoon and evening went too quickly, and it seemed only hours after she arrived that she was back at the airport with Peter, waiting for her plane, with tears in her eyes. She didn't want to leave him, but she had to.

'It's a crazy life we lead, isn't it?'

'It is.' His pager went off then and he rushed to a nearby phone. There was a problem with one of his transplants, and he had to leave at once. For a second, it reminded him of the night he had operated on Marie, and had called her at the airport just before she got on the plane. But this time she wasn't invited, and she wasn't on a story, and she had to get back to New York by the next morning. He couldn't even wait for her flight. He had to kiss her then, and run down the long terminal hall, turning to wave once or twice before he disappeared, and she was left alone. It was awful having two careers as demanding as theirs, she thought to herself as she boarded the plane in the first class section, and she decided that if anyone asked for an autograph she would break their arm. She wasn't in the mood to be nice to anyone, but fortunately no one spoke to her from Los Angeles to New York, and she walked into her house at six thirty the next morning, feeling tired and depressed. When she called Peter at the hospital, at seven a.m, his time, she was told that he had just gone back into surgery. It was a lonely existence for both of them, but it couldn't be helped.

And as it turned out, she didn't get back out to see him at all in October. The negotiations for the new contract were hard going.

'Have you forgotten me entirely, or is there any hope for the coming month?' Peter was beginning to complain daily on the phone, and Mel thought that if she saw another flowery envelope from Mark to Val she would scream. He must have bought her every corny card in the state of California by then, and it drove her crazy, but Val loved it.

'I promise, I'll be out this month.'

'That's what you said last month.'

'It's the damn contract, besides which, you know I worked two weekends.' This was when the Soviet premier and his wife had arrived for an unexpected visit, and Mel had been dispatched to Washington, D.C., to interview the Russian counterpart of America's First Lady. She had actually liked her. The following weekend she had done a follow-up interview on the President's recovery. 'I can't help it, Peter.'

'I know, but I have no one else to moan to.'

She smiled. There were times when she felt the same way about his patients. 'I promise. I'll be out next weekend.' And she kept her word, but he spent most of it in surgery with Marie, who was suddenly failing. They had operated on her twice in the past month, but she was having every possible complication typical of transplants. Mel spent most of the weekend shopping and taking his children out. She took Pam with her when she shopped for the girls, and they had lunch at the Polo Lounge at the Beverly Hills Hotel, which Pam loved although she didn't admit it. Her eyes grew as wide as saucers whenever someone approached Mel for an autograph, which they did four or five times before lunch was over. After that she took Matt to a film. And finally on Sunday, she got some time with Peter, but he was distracted, listening for the phone with one ear, and thinking about Marie the entire time.

'You know, if she weren't so damn sick, I'd be jealous.' She tried to joke with him about it, but neither of them was really in the mood. 'She's a very sick girl, Mel.'

'I know she is. But it's hard sharing you with her, when we wait so long between visits.' But that reminded him of something he'd been meaning to ask her.

'What about Thanksgiving?'

'What about it?' She looked blank.

'I've been wanting to ask you if you and the girls would come out here. We do a traditional Thanksgiving every year, and we'd all love to have you. It would make it a real family event for us.'

'That's about three weeks away, isn't it?' He consulted his calendar and nodded. 'Then we should have closed the contract by then.'

'Is everything determined by that, Mel, even Thanksgiving?' He looked upset and she tried to soothe his ruffled feathers with a kiss.

'It puts a lot of pressure on me, that's all. But we should have wrapped it up by then.'

'Then you'll come?'

'Yes.' He looked first thrilled, then worried.

'What if the contract doesn't close before Thanksgiving?'

'Then I'll come anyway. What do you think I am? A monster?'

'No, a damn busy woman. And too important by half.'

'Do you love me in spite of that?' Now and then she worried that it would get to him and he'd throw in the towel. It was something she had always worried about, that success would cost her the love of a decent man like him.

But he put his arms around her now and held her close. 'I love you more than ever.' And tonight when he took her to the plane he stayed until it took off.

When she told Jess and Val the next morning, Valerie gave a squeal of delight and rushed upstairs to dash off a note to Mark before she left for school. Mel stared at the stairs in annoyance and then addressed herself to her oldest daughter.

'Doesn't she think of anything else any more?'

'Hardly ever,' Jessica answered honestly.

'I can't wait to see her grades at half-term.' Jessica didn't say a word, she knew just how bad they were going to be. The constant letter writing to Mark had taken its toll on her sister's homework.

'It'll be fun to go to California for Thanksgiving.'

'I hope so.' Mel smiled tiredly, and kissed the girls when they went to school. Before she unpacked from the weekend, she called her lawyer. She knew he went to the office before eight o'clock every morning. But the news he gave her wasn't good. The network was still stalling on the contract, hoping she'd give up some of what she wanted. But he reminded Mel that she didn't have to, that they'd probably give in to her demands, and if they didn't, a dozen other offers would come in a matter of moments, if she even hinted that she was open to offers.

'But I'm really not, George. I want to stay where I am.'

'Then hang tough.'

'I intend to. Any chance we get it wrapped up before Thanksgiving?'

'I'll do my best.'

But as it turned out, his best didn't do it. And when they took the plane to LA three weeks later, nothing was settled. Mel's lawyer insisted that they were at the eleventh hour, but nothing was signed yet, and it was driving her crazy. Peter could see just from the nervous way she walked off the plane that it was all getting to her, but they would have four days together now, and he hoped she would unwind. He just prayed that the President didn't get shot and no one needed a heart transplant over Thanksgiving. His prayers were answered. They spent a peaceful Thanksgiving, with all five children happy to be together again. Mrs Hahn outdid herself nobly with a Thanksgiving feast which left everyone barely able to leave the table.

'My God, I can't move.' Val stared down at her stomach in despair. Mark came to her rescue, and pulled her out of her seat, as Pam and Jess went upstairs to play chess. Matthew curled up near the fire with his favourite blanket and his teddy bear and went to sleep. Peter and Mel repaired to his den to relax and talk. There was a feeling of homecoming about it all, and Peter had insisted that they not sleep at a hotel, but stay there at the house, in the guest room. Because Jess was there Mel felt that Pam wouldn't be as upset at their staying there. She was in effect Mel's guarantee of safe passage.

'It was a beautiful dinner, Peter.'

'I'm glad you're all here.' He looked at her searchingly and saw the tired lines around her eyes. They didn't show on camera with her makeup, but he knew they were there, and it bothered him to see them. She shouldn't have been working that hard, or been under that much pressure. 'You've been pushing too hard, my love.'

'What makes you say that?' She stretched her legs out towards the fire.

'You've lost weight and you look tired.'

'I suppose I do ... It's a tough business.' She smiled at him. She knew he'd had a rough time too, with two new transplants and Marie, who was developing problems with the steroids again, but she was doing better.

'Nothing new on the contract?'

'George says it's a matter of hours. They ought to sign it on Monday when I go back.'

Peter didn't say anything for a long time and then he looked at Mel. He didn't know how to begin to approach it, but the time was now or never. It might be his last chance forever, or at least a year. He had to. 'Mel ...'

'Hmm?' She had been staring into the fire in the silence, and now she looked up with a smile, relaxing at last after weeks of tension. 'Yes, Doctor?'

He wanted to move closer to her, but he didn't. 'I've got something to ask you.'

'Something wrong?' Maybe something about Pam, but she had been all right lately. Better than Val surely, whose grades, Mel had discovered, had never been lower. But she was going to speak to Peter about that later in the weekend. They were going to have to put some kind of restrictions on the two lovebirds before Val flunked out of school completely, and Mel wanted Peter's support. But there was no rush to talk about that yet. 'What's up love?'

'Something I've been wanting to discuss with you for a long time. About your contract.'

She looked surprised. So far he'd stayed away from advising her about her work, and she thought it just as well. He didn't know her field any better than she knew his, and all they could offer each other was moral support, which was what they both needed. 'What about it?'

'What if you don't sign it?'

She smiled. 'The problem isn't me, it's them. I'd sign it in a minute, if the bastards would give us all the conditions we want. And I think they will. But it's been a war of nerves till now.'

'I know it has. But what if you don't sign it ...' He held his breath and then went on a moment later, 'And sign with someone else instead?'

'I may have to if I don't get what I want.' But she hadn't got the point yet. It was the farthest thing from her mind. 'Why? what did you have in mind?' He was obviously telling her something but she wasn't sure what yet.

He looked her straight in the eye and said it in a single word. 'Marriage.' There was a total blank on her face and then a look of shock as she went pale, staring at him.

'What do you mean?' Her voice was no more than a whisper.

'I mean I want to marry you, Mel. I've been trying to get up the guts to ask you for months, but I didn't want to screw up your career. But with your contract taking this long to get signed, I just thought ... I wondered ...' She got up and stalked across the room, to stand near the fire with her back to him, and then at last she turned slowly.

'I don't know what to say to you, Peter.'

He tried to smile, but he was so desperately afraid he couldn't. 'A simple yes will do.'

'But I can't do that. I can't give up everything I've built in New York. I just can't ...' Her eyes filled with tears. 'I love you, but I can't do that ...' She started to tremble all over and he went to her and took her in his arms, with tears that she could not see filling his eyes as he held her.

'It's all right, Mel. I understand. But I had to ask you.' She pulled away from him so she could see him, and there were tears pouring down her cheeks as well as his now. 'I love you ... oh God, don't ask me to do that, Peter. Don't make me prove something I can't prove to you.'

'You don't have to prove anything to me, Mel.' He wiped his cheeks and sat down on the couch. There was no kidding themselves either, they couldn't go on flying across the country to see each other forever. The end was inevitable, and they both knew that. He looked at her now, his eyes boring into hers and shook his head slowly. 'I used to think we were both such lucky people, good kids, good careers, and we found each other.' He smiled ruefully. 'Now I don't think we're so lucky.'

Mel didn't answer and at last she blew her nose and wiped the tears from her cheeks. 'I don't know what to say to you, Peter.'

'Don't say anything. Just know that if you change your mind I'm here and I love you. I want to marry you. I'll support everything you do, within reason. You could work as hard as you want and as much as you want at any of the LA networks.'

'But LA's not New York.' He wanted to ask her then if New York meant more to her than he did, but it wasn't a fair question and he knew it.

'I know that. We don't need to discuss it. I just had to ask you.'

'It looks like I'm choosing work instead of you, and that's so ugly.'

'Sometimes the truth is ugly.' It had to be faced between them.

'Will you still want to continue ... with ... us ... with me ... if I sign my new contract and stay in New York?' She trembled at the question. What would she have now if she lost him? Nothing.

'Yes, we'll continue for as long as we can both stand it. But it can't go on forever and we both know that. And when it ends, Mel, we're both losing something wonderful, something that we both need desperately. I've never loved anyone more than I love you.' Tears spilled down her cheeks again then and she couldn't bear it any longer. She went outside for some air, and a little while later Peter joined her. 'I'm sorry I asked you, Mel. I didn't mean to make you unhappy.'

'You didn't. It's just that sometimes' – her eyes filled with tears and her voice broke – 'life is full of such tough choices. All I wanted was a better contract and now I feel like I'm breaking your heart if I sign it.'

'You're not.' He held her close to him. 'You're doing what you have to do for you, Mel, and that's terribly important. I respect that.'

'Why the hell did we have to be so unlucky?' She was openly sobbing. 'Why couldn't we both have lived in the same city?'

He smiled, accepting their fate now. She was what she had been from the beginning and he had been wrong to try to change that. 'Because life is full of challenges, Mel. We'll make it. Hell, if I had to travel five times that distance, I would still want to see you.' And then he looked at her again in the soft darkness. 'Will you come back out here for Christmas?'

'Yes, if I'm not working.'

'Okay.' He tried to feel satisfied with that, but he wasn't. He had no choice though, and as they lay side by side that night they were both thinking, and the heavy mood was still on them the next day and the day after.

And the children didn't help them. Val and Mark seemed to have plans for every moment of the weekend, and Jess and Pam and Matthew went to films, visited friends, did errands. Peter didn't even insist this time that they all stick together, he had too much on his own mind. And Mel looked even more upset when they left than she had when they'd arrived, and her lawyer's call the next morning did nothing to soothe her.

'Well, we got it.' He almost crowed with victory when he called at eleven o'clock that morning. She had been quietly pacing her room, thinking of Peter's face when she left him. He looked devastated and she felt worse, but there had been no choice to make and he knew it.

'Got what?' Mel was almost too nervous this morning to think straight. And she had sent the girls off to school despite their return on the red eye.

'Good God. What did you do in California, Mel? Spend the whole weekend on dope or LSD? You got your *contract!*' He was as nervous and exhausted as she was. It had been a long fight this time, but it was worth it. She had had the guts to hold out, and had got everything she wanted. Not too many of his clients had the gall to do that, but she did. 'We sign at noon today. Can you be there by then?'

'Hell, yes.' She grinned, it was what they had waited two months for, but somehow when she hung up the phone, she found that the thrill was gone. The victory was empty now, thanks to Peter. When she signed the contract, she would feel that she had betrayed him.

But at noon she was at the network and George and all of the officials were waiting. There were ten people in the room, and Mel was the last to arrive, dressed in a black Dior suit, with a mink coat over her arm and a black hat with a veil, which suited her humour. She looked like a widow in an old film, going to the reading of a will. She made a dramatic entrance and the network men seemed pleased. They always got their money's worth with Mel Adams, and even they respected her for the long battle. She cast smiles around the room and sat down with a look at George, who nodded. He could hardly wait to call the press and announce this one. It was a knock-out contract for Mel and everyone in the room knew it, including Mel herself. She glanced over the conditions, pen in hand. The network officials had already signed it, and all that was missing was her signature on the dotted line. She picked up her pen, and held it, feeling her palms damp, her face grow white, as suddenly she seemed to see Peter's face before her. She stopped, silent, pale, thinking, and looked at George. He nodded again.

'Everything's just fine, Mel.' He was smiling, looking ghoulish and suddenly she knew that she couldn't do it. She stood up, the pen still clutched in her hand, and shook her head at them, looking at the men she had worked for.

'I'm sorry. I can't do it.'

'But what's wrong?' They were stupefied. Was she crazy? She would have told them that she was if they had asked her. 'It's all there, Mel. Everything you asked for.'

'I know.' She sat down again, looking broken. 'I can't explain it. But I can't sign the contract.'

As a single body, they began to look ugly, and George with them. 'What the hell ...'

She looked up at each one of them, still shaking, and tears stung her eyes, but she couldn't cry now. She wanted it so badly she could taste it, but there was something else she wanted more and which she knew would last a lifetime, not just a year. And he was right. She could work in LA. Her career wouldn't be over just because she left New York. She stood up again and said in a strong voice, 'Gentlemen, I'm moving to California.'

The room was stunned into silence. 'You signed with the network there?' Now they knew she was crazy. They couldn't have offered her more money. Or had they? The flashy creeps. But Mel had always had more class than that. No one understood what had happened, least of all her own lawyer. She gulped then, and spoke to no one in particular.

'I'm getting married.' And then without another word, she strode from the room, rushed into the lift, and left the building before anyone could stop her. She walked all the way home, and when she got there she found that she felt a little better. She had just thrown her whole career out of the window, but she thought that he was worth it. She just hoped she wasn't wrong, as she picked up the phone and dialled his number. The operator in the hospital paged him, and found him. He was on the phone in less than a minute, busy and distracted, but happy to get the call.

'Are you okay?' He was only half listening to her answer.

'No. I'm not.'

And then he heard her, and the strangeness of her voice. God, something had happened. He had sounded like that when Anne died. ... the twins ... 'What is it?' His heart pounded as he waited.

'I went to sign the contract ...' She sounded numb. 'And I didn't.'

'You didn't what?'

'I didn't sign it.'

'You what?' His legs turned to jelly beneath him. 'Are you crazy?'

'That's what they said.' And suddenly she panicked, terrified that he had changed his mind and now it was too late. She had thrown everything out the window. She almost whispered. 'Am I?'

And then he understood what she had done and why, as tears came to his eyes. 'Oh, baby, no you aren't . . . yes, you are . . . oh God, I love you. Do you mean it?'

'I think so. I just threw away a million bucks for the year. I think maybe I must mean it.' She sat down and started to laugh, and suddenly she couldn't stop laughing and he couldn't stop either. She took off her hat and veil and tossed them in the air. 'Doctor Hallam, as of the thirty-first of December, which happens to be New Year's Eve, I'm unemployed. Practically a vagrant.'

'Terrific. I've always wanted to marry a vagrant.'

The laughter at her end died into silence. 'Do you still?'

His voice was very gentle. 'Yes. Will you marry me, Mel?' She nodded and he waited, terrified. 'I can't hear you.'

'I said yes.' And then, desperately nervous, 'Do you think they'll hire me in LA?'

'Are you kidding?' He laughed again. 'By tonight, they'll be beating your door down.' But there were other things on his mind. 'Mel, let's get married at Christmas.'

'Okay.' She was still in a kind of stupor, and everything he said sounded fine to her now. 'When at Christmas?' It was all like a dream, and she wasn't sure yet how long she'd been dreaming. She remembered a room full of men in dark suits, and her refusing to sign a contract, but after that everything was a blur except this phone call. She could hardly remember how she had got home now. Had she walked? Taken a cab? Flown?

'How about Christmas Eve?'

'Sure. When's that?'

'In about three and a half weeks. Is that okay?'

'Yes.' She nodded slowly. And then, 'Peter, do you think I'm crazy?'

'No, I think you're the bravest woman I've ever met, and I love you for it.'

'I'm scared.'

'Don't be. You'll get a great job out here, and we'll be happy. Everything is going to be wonderful.' She hoped he was right. All she could think of now was what she had done by refusing to sign the contract, but if they had asked her again, she would have refused again. She had made her decision, and now she would have to live by it, whatever that took, and of that she wasn't sure yet.

'What'll I do with my house?'

'Sell it.'

'Can't I rent it?' She felt sick at the thought of giving it up forever. She had to take such giant steps now.

'Are you planning to move back there?'

'Of course not, unless you do.'

'Then why keep it? Sell it, Mel. You can use the money to invest in something out here.'

'Will we be buying a new house?' She felt confusion begin to sweep over her as she sat staring into space and she heard the doorbell ringing in the distance but she didn't answer. It was Raquel's day off and there was no one she wanted to see now, particularly reporters, if they'd heard the news.

'We don't need a new house, Mel. We have this one.' He sounded so happy, but as she listened she knew she didn't want to live there. It was Anne's house ... their house ... not her house ... but maybe just in the beginning ... 'Look, you just relax. Have a drink or something. I've got to get back to work here. I'll call you later. And remember. I love you.'

'I love you too.' But her voice was only a whisper, and she didn't move from the chair for an hour as she contemplated what she'd done, and when George called she attempted to explain it. He told her that he thought she was crazy, but it was an intensely personal decision. He agreed to sound out the LA networks, and by that night she had three offers, and by the following week she had a contract, for the same money she had wanted in New York, and had had to wait two months for. But of course this was LA, and not New York. But the furore she had created was beyond measure, and it was an agony to go into work now. They had asked her to stay until December 15, and then she could leave two weeks before the end of her contract. But everywhere she was treated like a traitor, even Grant came to see her to tell her that she was crazy, that it would never work, that she was meant for the big time in New York, not the LA market, and marriage wasn't her life-style. She felt as though she were drifting through a nightmare, and the twins kept looking at her as though she had betrayed them.

'Did you know you were going to do it?' Jess asked when she told them, meaning accept Peter's proposal. But it sounded as though she were asking her if she knew she was going to commit murder.

'No, I didn't.'

'When did he ask you?'

'On Thanksgiving.' The reproach she felt was in her eyes each time she looked at her mother, and Valerie was so nervous that she seemed ready to throw up each time Mel looked at her. Even she wasn't totally pleased to be moving. They had to change schools mid-year, leave their home, their friends. And when Mel put the house on the market, she thought it would kill her. It sold on the first weekend, and when she got word, she sat down on the stairs and cried. Everything was happening much too quickly. Only Raquel seemed to know what was going on, as she packed endless boxes for California.

'I tole you, Mrs Mel ... I tole you last summer ... in six months ... '

'Oh, for chrissake, Raquel, shut up.' But halfway through the packing, Mel realised that she didn't know what she was going to do with Raquel. There was no room for her at Peter's, and the woman had been with her for years. She called him in a panic one night at midnight in California, 3 a.m, in New York.

'What am I going to do with Raquel?'

'Is she sick?' He had been half asleep when she called him. But Mel was wide awake.

'No. I mean about bringing her.'

'You can't bring her, Mel.'

Why not?' She bridled.

'There's no room, and Mrs Hahn would kill her.'

'Personally, I'd prefer it if Raquel killed Mrs Hahn.'

'Mrs Hahn is devoted to my children.' It was the first time he had spoken to her in that tone of voice and Mel didn't like it.

'Raquel is devoted to mine. Now what?'

'Be reasonable.' How reasonable did she have to be? She had given up a job, a house, her children had given up friends and schools, just how much more did he want her to leave behind her? Raquel too?

'If she doesn't come, Peter, neither do I, or the children.'

'Oh, for God's sake.' And then he decided it was too late to argue. 'All right. We'll rent her a flat.'

'Thank you.' Mel announced the news to Raquel the next morning, still feeling annoyed at Peter, but this time Raquel surprised her.

'To California? You crazy? I live here, in New York.' She smiled at Mel and kissed her cheek. 'But thank you. I gonna miss you. But I just don' want to move to California. You gonna have a good life now. You got a good husband. But me, I got a boyfriend here. Maybe sooner or later I'll get married too.' She looked hopeful, and determined not to go to California.

'We're going to miss you too.' They would have nothing familiar except each other. Even her furniture was going into storage. There was no room for it in his house. And as the days progressed, Mel realised that this was not going to be easy.

On the fifteenth of December, two weeks earlier than her contract required, she did the eleven o'clock news for the last time, from New York. And she knew that approximately two weeks later, she would be coming on the air, on another network, from LA, but this era in her life was over. Gone forever. She cried as she put down her mike, and walked out of the studio, and outside Grant was waiting. He hugged her, and she cried in his arms, as he shook his head, like an astonished father, but he was proud of her too. She had done something good for herself, and he was glad. Peter Hallam was a fine man. Grant just hoped that everything would work: the careers, the kids, the move. It was a lot to ask. But Mel could handle it, if anyone could.

'Good luck, Mel. We'll miss you.' They had wanted to give her a party, but she had refused. She couldn't bear it. Her emotions were too raw now. She promised to come back and visit, and introduce everyone to Peter. To them it was a fairy story. She had gone to do an interview and fallen in love with the handsome doctor, but it all hurt so much now. Leaving them, closing the house, leaving New York.

'Goodbye, Grant. Take care.' She kissed his cheek, and walked away with tears running down her face. She was leaving all that was familiar to her and all her old friends, and five minutes later she left the building, the building where she had aspired to so much and gone so far. Now she was leaving, and when she got home that night, all she saw was a mountain of boxes. The movers were coming the next morning, and it would be Raquel's last day as well. They would stay at the Carlyle Hotel for the weekend, and on Monday they would close the house, she would pick up the white wool Bill Blass dress she'd bought at Bendel's, and the day after, on December 19, they'd fly to LA, five days before the wedding ... her wedding ... she sat up in the dark, feeling it all close in around her. Her wedding. She was getting married ...

'Oh my God.' She sat in bed and looked at the chaos around her, and the tears slid slowly down her face, as she wondered what madness had overtaken her life. Even the thought of Peter waiting for her in LA didn't console her.

Chapter 24

On Saturday the sixteenth of December, Mel stood in her bedroom on East Eighty-first Street for the very last time. The moving men had ransacked the house, and the last truck had just rumbled down the street, to carry her 'goods', as they called them, to California, where everything but her clothes and a few small treasures she loved would go into storage. The rest simply wouldn't fit into Peter's house, he had told her.

The girls were waiting downstairs for her with Raquel, in the front hall, but she had wanted to see the view from her bedroom one last time. Never again would she lie in bed in the morning, looking out the window, listening to the birds in the small garden. There would be other birds in California, another garden, a whole different life. But it was impossible not to think of how much it had meant to her when she bought this house. It was a lot to give up for a man she loved, and yet it was only a house after all.

'Mom?' Val shouted up to her from the front hall. 'You coming down?'

'I'll be right there,' she shouted back, her eyes dragging across the room for a last time, and then she ran quickly down the stairs, and found them waiting for her, their arms loaded with the gifts they had exchanged with Raquel, standing next to the cases they were taking to the hotel. When Mel went outside to hail a cab she saw that there was a light snowfall settling on the ground. It took her almost half an hour to find a cab, and when she came back to get the girls, she found them in tears, locked in Raquel's arms.

'I gonna miss you guys.' Raquel looked into Mel's eyes and smiled through her tears. 'But you did okay, Mrs Mel. He's a nice man.'

Mel nodded, unable to speak for a moment, and then she kissed Raquel's cheek and looked at the twins. 'The cab's outside, girls, why don't you put your stuff in the front seat?' They trundled outside in their boots and parkas and jeans and warm scarves, and Mel found herself thinking that those days were over too, except when they went skiing somewhere, from now on.

'Raquel' – Mel's voice was hoarse from the emotion she felt – 'we love you, remember that. And if ever you need anything, or if you change your mind about coming to LA ...' Her eyes filled with tears, and the two women embraced.

'It's gonna be okay, *hija* ... you gonna be happy out there ... don' cry ...' But she was crying too. They had shared so many years, and together they had raised the girls. And it was all over now. Mel had given everything up for her new life, even Raquel.

'We're going to miss you so much.' A horn honked outside, and Mel hugged Raquel once more and looked around the darkened house. The sale would be completed on Monday, and the new people were moving in the following day, and everything would be different. They would paint and paper the whole house, redo the kitchen, knock out some walls. She shuddered at the thought as Raquel watched her.

'Come on, Mrs Mel, let's go.' She gently took Mel by the hand and they walked outside. Mel turned to lock her front door for the last time, feeling everything inside her go taut. But this was what she had wanted, and there was no turning back now.

They stood on the pavement side by side, Raquel in the new coat they had bought her as a Christmas gift that she had decided to open early this year, and Mel walked towards the cab. Mel had also given her a cheque that would tide her over for a month or two, and a reference that would win her any job. She pulled open the door of the cab and slid in beside the girls, and waved to Raquel as they drove away, all three of them crying in the back seat and Raquel crying and waving as she stood in the falling snow.

Once they got to the hotel, the girls were excited by the elaborate suite. They ordered room service, turned on the TV, got on the phone to their friends; Mel finally had a little time to herself. She called Peter from the separate phone in her room.

'Hi, love.'

'You sound beat. Are you all right?'

'Yeah, it was awful saying goodbye to Raquel and selling the house.'

'You'll be out here soon and that'll all bnse behind you, Mel.' He told her that he had got a stack of papers for her from the station in LA that day. She was due to start on the first of January, and they wanted to see her briefly at the station the minute she arrived.

'I'll call them on Tuesday when I come out.'

'That's what I told them too. Are you all right, sweetheart?' He knew how hard it was for her to leave New York, and he admired her for the courageous thing she had done. Even though he had asked her to marry him, he had had almost no hope of her doing that. It had all seemed like a dream to him, and now the dream was coming true.

'I'm okay, love. Just tired.' And depressed, but she didn't want to tell him that. It would be better once she was with him again, then the anguish of the change wouldn't be quite as sharp as it was now. 'How's work?'

'Intense just now. We seem to have a house full of patients needing transplants, and no hearts. It's like a juggling act keeping ten balls in the air at once.' But she knew how well he did that, and she smiled to herself, and realised again how much she missed him. She hadn't seen him since their

Thanksgiving trip to LA, she hadn't even seen him since she accepted his proposal.

'How's Marie?'

'Doing better again. I think she'll be fine.' He was obviously in high spirits, and Mel felt better again when she got off the phone. That night she and the girls ordered dinner in their rooms, and they went to bed early, and when they woke up the next day there was a foot of snow outside.

'Look, Mom!' For once, Jessica forgot her serious thoughts and she squealed like a little child. 'Let's go to the park and have a snowball fight.' Which was exactly what they did, and afterwards Mel suggested they rent skates, and they skated at Wollman Rink, laughing and teasing, gliding, and falling down. Val didn't seem as enchanted with the plan as her mother and her twin, but in the end she was game and they all had a wonderful time, and they walked slowly back to the hotel, and had steaming cups of hot chocolate and whipped cream.

'I guess we're just tourists now.' Mel smiled. And the three of them went to the cinema that night. The girls had plans to see their friends the next day, but they had nothing planned for that night. And on Monday morning, Mel gave in the keys for the house, and then stopped at Bendel's to pick up her wedding dress, as planned. It was a simple white wool dress with a jacket that matched, in a beautiful textured wool by Bill Blass. The girls came with her and picked out dresses for themselves in a pale blue, and at Mel's suggestion, they bought an identical dress for Pam.

They were getting married on Christmas Eve at St Albans Church in Beverly Hills on Hilgard Avenue across from UCLA, and there would be only a handful of guests, all of them Peter's friends, since Mel knew no one in LA.

'It's going to be weird with none of our friends there, isn't it, Mom?' Val looked concerned and Mel smiled.

'It's going to be that way for a while, until Peter's friends are our friends too.' Val nodded, and Jessica looked downcast. It reminded her again that they didn't know a soul in LA and had to go to a new school. She wasn't looking forward to that. Only Val didn't mind quite so much, it was easier for her because of Mark.

And on Monday night, Mel took them both to 21 for their last dinner in New York, and a limousine took them back to the hotel for their last night. The three of them stood looking out at the skyline before they went to bed, and Mel felt tears sting her eyes again. 'We'll be back to visit, you know.' But she wasn't sure if she was reassuring herself or the girls. 'And maybe you'll want to come to college here.' That was only two years away for them, but for her ... except for visits, there would be no coming back. She had made an enormous step in every way.

The next day, leaving the Carlyle was not as painful as leaving the house had been. There was a sense of an adventure begun as they left, and the girls were in high spirits as they left for the airport in a limousine, and then boarded the plane. Two college students going home to LA had already spotted Jess and Val, and once the plane took off Mel hardly saw them again until they landed.

'Where have you two been?' She wasn't particularly concerned as they came back to their seats to land. There wasn't very far for them to go on a plane.

'Playing bridge in the back with two kids from LA. They go to Columbia and they're going home for Christmas and they invited us to a party tomorrow night in Malibu.' Val's eyes shone and Jessica laughed and looked at Mel.

'Yeah, and I bet Mom will really let us do that.' She was wise to her mother's rules, and Mel laughed.

But Val tried again. 'We could take Mark.'

'I think we're going to have some settling in to do.'

'Oh, Mom ...'

But the plane touched the ground then, and it was bright and sunny outside, and the three of them looked around anxiously as they came off the plane, wondering which Hallams had come to the airport, but then Val gave a whoop as she saw Mark, and Mel saw that they were all there, even Matthew. She rushed into Peter's arms and he held her tight, and in that single moment she knew that she had done the right thing. She knew that with every ounce of her being, she loved him.

Chapter 25

Mel and the girls stayed at the Bel-Air until December twenty-fourth, and at five in the afternoon, a rented limousine came to pick them up, and drove them to the church. She looked beautiful in the white wool dress, and the girls looked lovely in their blue ones. Mel was carrying a bouquet of white freesia mixed with white cymbidium orchids and baby's breath, Jess and Val had small bouquets of white stephanotis, mixed in with tiny spring flowers, and there were tiny knots of the same flowers woven into their shining hair.

Mel looked at them one last time before they got out of the car, and approved of what she saw. 'You look beautiful, girls.'

'So do you, Mom.' Jessica's eyes shone as she searched her mother's eyes. 'Are you scared?'

She hesitated and then grinned. 'To death.'

Jessica smiled, and then a worried look crossed her eyes, maybe they would go home again. 'Are you going to chicken out?'

But at that, Mel laughed. 'Hell no. You know what they say, "You can't go home again."' But as she said the words, a shadow crossed Jessie's eyes, and Mel was sorry she had been flippant. She reached out and touched the pretty young redhead's hand. 'I'm sorry, Jess.' And then in a soft voice, 'This will be home to us soon.' But she knew that of all of them, the move had been hardest on Jess, and yet the girl never seemed to complain. She had spent the last five days helping Pam reorganise her room, and helping Val move their things into the guest room. She and her twin were going to share the guest room, and it would be strange to no longer have their own rooms.

'I wouldn't mind if she weren't such a slob,' Jess confided to Pam, and then shrugged. There simply wasn't enough room in the house to give them separate rooms, and Jessica accepted that. She accepted everything. Even the chilly reception by Mrs Hahn, who continually looked into their suitcases and the closets with discerning glances. And the last of their things waited now in suitcases at the Bel-Air Hotel, where they would be picked up that night and moved to the Hallam house. Mel hadn't wanted any of them to move in until the wedding day.

'Well' – Jess glanced out the car window at the pretty little church – 'I guess this is it.'

Mel fell silent and simply looked and Val gasped as she saw Mark go into the church, he looked so handsome and young and strong. Peter and Matt were already inside, and Pam was waiting for them in the vestibule. She was going to go up the aisle first in her blue dress that matched the girls', carrying a similar bouquet and then Valerie would follow Pam, and Jessica behind her, and after a moment's pause, Mel. Peter and the boys would be waiting at the altar for them, and on the way out, Pam and Matt would hold hands, leading the entourage down the aisle, and Mark would walk behind them, and then Peter and Mel. They had planned it all in a matter of weeks, Mel had ordered the invitations she liked in New York, and Peter's secretary had sent them out to his closest friends.

Mel looked around the church as she walked down the aisle, she realised that there was not a single soul there she knew. Here she was getting married, with not a single friend there, only her twins. And as she approached the altar, she looked deathly pale, anticipation and excitement were draining her, and her eyes went to Peter's, as he stepped forward and quietly took her arm. Suddenly nothing mattered in the world, except him, and a soft rose glow brought life to her face. He whispered softly to her before the ceremony began.

'I love you, Mel. Everything's going to be fine.'

'I love you, too.' It was all she could say.

And then the minister reminded the congregation of why they were there. 'Dearly beloved, we are gathered here today, on Christmas Eve, on this holy day' – he smiled – 'to join this woman and this man in the bond of holy matrimony ...' Mel could hear her heart pound, and every minute or two Peter would gently pat her hand, and then the moment came to exchange their vows and their rings. He had ordered hers without her being there, a simple circlet of diamonds in a narrow band. She had insisted that she didn't want an engagement ring. As she looked down at the ring now she felt tears fill her eyes, so that she could barely see him as she slipped on a simple gold wedding band.

'To have and to hold from this day forward ... for better or worse ... until death do you part ...' A shiver ran down her spine. After all this she couldn't bear losing him. And yet he had survived losing Anne, and now here they were. She looked into his face, looking up at the man who was her husband now. 'I now pronounce you man and wife.' The organ sprang to life, and a choir sang 'Silent Night', and as Mel looked into Peter's eyes she felt as though she were going to melt. 'You may kiss the bride,' the portly minister said to the groom, and smiled at Mel. Peter did, and then they seemed to float down the aisle, and for the next hour she shook hands with dozens of people she had never seen, their faces all strange to her, but she found a minute to kiss Mark, Matthew and Pam and tell them how happy she was, and in the distance she glimpsed Mrs Hahn. Even on their wedding day, Mel thought the woman looked sour, but Peter made a point of going to shake her hand, and then Mel saw her smile. And she wondered if Mrs Hahn disapproved of her. Perhaps she still missed Anne. Seeing her there suddenly brought back visions of Raquel, and Mel wished she were there to see her wedding day. With no family of her own, Raquel had been almost a mother to her.

The seven of them hopped in a limousine afterwards to go to the Bel-Air Hotel, where the reception was being held, and Mel suddenly became aware that her wedding party was larger than she had thought it would be. The invitations to the reception had been for six o'clock, with dinner scheduled for seven thirty, and as they entered the enormous facilities of the club, Mel realised that there were at least a hundred people there. A seven-man band began to play 'Here Comes the Bride' and Peter stopped her right there and kissed her full on the mouth.

'Hello, Mrs Hallam.' Suddenly it all felt crazy and wonderful to Mel, and it didn't matter who the people were, strangers or not, or even people she would never see again. They were all sharing in the happiest moment of her life. People came up to her constantly and shook her hand, told her how much they enjoyed seeing her on TV, and how lucky Peter was. So they didn't seem so much like strangers any more.

'No, I'm the lucky one,' she insisted again and again, and there was only one moment to mar the fun, when she thought she glimpsed Val talking to Mark, crying softly in the corner of the dining room. By the time she got to where they sat, Val seemed to have recovered, and she smiled and hugged Mel. Jessica watched, and then took her mother in her arms too.

'We love you, Mom. And we're so happy for you.' But she could see in Jessie's eyes that there was pain there too. It was going to take them all time, even Mel with Peter at her side. But she felt certain that she had done the right thing for all of them, especially Peter and herself, and the girls would have to adjust to that. But she knew that to them it still seemed brutal, and she was just grateful that they hadn't taken it out on Peter. That could have been a possibility with children less supportive than hers.

She had noticed once or twice how snappy Pam was with her. But she would take care of that slowly, when Pam was used to the idea of her father being married again. All in good time, Mel reminded herself again and again.

The romance between Val and Mark still seemed to be on, although they didn't seem quite as happy as they had been before. Mel suspected that living together would take the bloom off the rose for both of them. Once he saw what a 'slob' she was, as Jess said, and she had him around all the time, the romance was bound to cool. At least Mel hoped it would. She turned her thoughts from them to Matt, who bowed and invited her to dance. She did a sort of little jig with him as people smiled and watched, and at the very end, Peter cut in, and swept her off in a waltz.

'Do you have any idea how beautiful you are?'

'No, but do you know how happy I am?' She beamed at him.

'Tell me. I want to hear.' He looked as happy as she. But the changes had been easier for him. They were all happening to Mel, giving up her job, pulling her kids out of school, selling her house, letting Raquel go, leaving New York . . .

'I've never been happier in my life.'

'Good. That's how it should be.' He glanced around the room as they twirled. 'Our kids look pretty happy too.' Pam was laughing at something Jess had said, and Mark was dancing with Val, as Matthew entertained the guests.

'I think they are. Except Mrs Hahn, she doesn't look too thrilled.'

'Give her time. She's a little stiff.' That was the understatement of the year, but Mel didn't comment on it.

'She loves you too, and so do all my friends.'

'They look nice.' But they could have been members of a wedding anywhere, sent by central casting to eat, dance, and beam.

'Later, when things settle down, I'll arrange some quiet evenings so you can meet people in small groups. I know how hard this must be.'

'It isn't really.' She smiled into his eyes. 'Because of you. You're all I care about here, you know, except the kids.'

He looked pleased, but he wanted her to like his friends too. They already knew who she was, but now she needed to meet them. 'You'll get to like them, too.' The dance ended, and one of Peter's colleagues cut in, and they spoke of the interview she had done of Peter earlier in the year. He had been in the operating room when they did the transplant on Marie, and Mel remembered him.

She danced with dozens of people she didn't know, laughed at jokes, shook hands, tried to remember names and then gave up, knowing she never would, and at last at eleven o'clock they all went home. The limousine took them to Peter's house on Copa de Oro Drive in Bel-Air and the children filed in. Mark was carrying Matt who had fallen asleep in the car, and the girls were still chatting between yawns, as Peter took Mel's arm and stopped her from walking in the door.

'Just a minute, please.'

'Something wrong?' She looked surprised. The chauffeur was going in with their bags, but Peter was smiling at her, and then he suddenly swept her into his arms, and carried her over the threshold, depositing her inside near the Christmas tree.

'Welcome home, my love.' They stood and kissed and the kids tiptoed upstairs, but the only one who really smiled was Mark. All three girls looked tense as they tried not to think what this day meant. It was no longer a game. It was for real. Pam and the twins quietly said goodnight, and went upstairs to their rooms, and closed their doors. Pam didn't like seeing Mel in Peter's arms, any more than the twins liked realising that their mother was no longer solely theirs. The lines had been drawn.

Peter and Mel lingered downstairs for a while, talking about their wedding day. It had been a lovely party and they'd had a good time. He poured her another glass of champagne from his bar, some Cristal he had saved, and he toasted her as the clock on the mantelpiece chimed. 'Merry Christmas, Mel.' She stood up and set down her glass, and they kissed for a long, long time and then he swept her into his arms, wedding dress and all, and carried her upstairs.

Chapter 26

Peter and Mel spent Christmas with their children in the house on Copa de Oro Drive, and Mrs Hahn cooked them a wonderful Christmas dinner, of goose and wild rice, a chestnut purée, little peas and onions, and mince pie and plum pudding for dessert.

'No turkey this year?' Jessica looked surprised as they came down to dinner, and when she got one whiff of the goose, Val burst into tears and ran upstairs, but when Mel started to go to comfort her, Mark stopped her.

'I'll do it, Mel.' He seemed strangely quiet, but no one except Jessica noticed. Val seemed to cry a lot lately, or Jess thought so at least, and she had heard her crying in her bed the night before, but Val wouldn't tell her what was wrong, and Jessie didn't want to upset her mother, who hadn't seemed to notice anything wrong with Val.

'Thanks, Mark.' And then she turned to Peter, 'I'm sorry. I think everyone's tired.'

He nodded, not looking worried. Their traditions were new to the twins. They had goose every year, thanks to Mrs Hahn in recent times and Anne before that. They only ate turkey on Thanksgiving. And on Easter they had ham.

But when Mrs Hahn served the mince pie Jessie and Val only picked at it, longing for the hot apple pie they always had in New York at Christmas. Even the tree looked strange to them. There were tiny flashing lights on it and only large gold balls. All of their antique Christmas decorations they had spent years collecting and loved, and multi-coloured lights, had gone into storage with the rest of their things.

'I'm full.' Mel looked at Peter in despair as they left the table. The only good thing she could say about Mrs Hahn was that her cooking was superb. It had been a lavish meal, and they all felt full as they went to sit in the living room. And then, as Mel looked around at her new home, she realised that there were still all the same pictures of Anne around, and one oil portrait over a narrow French table. Peter noticed her looking at the photos of Anne, and he tensed for a moment, wondering if she would say something. But she didn't. She silently made a mental note to put them away when they came back from their honeymoon on the morning of New Year's Eve.

Peter had suggested Puerto Vallarta, one of his favourite places, and they were taking all five children with them, although Mel was nervous about taking Matt to Mexico, in case he got sick. The others were old enough to be careful, but she'd have to watch Matt. They had decided that it wouldn't be diplomatic to leave the children so soon. They could take a trip alone later, maybe to Europe, or Hawaii, depending on when they could get away. Under her new contract, Mel no longer had two months off as she had in New York. She had only one and a maternity leave. She had been amused when they insisted in putting it in the contract. She had had all the babies she was going to have, and all at once too. She had laughed again when she told Peter about it, and he teased her about getting pregnant if she didn't behave. In answer to which she had teasingly menaced him with pinking shears.

As they sat in the living room on Christmas night, Mel groaned at the thought of packing again. It seemed as though she had done nothing but for the past month. At least she wouldn't need much in Puerto Vallarta, and all the children were excited about going. That night there was much scurrying between rooms as they giggled and teased and took things from each other. Matt bounced on Val's bed, and Pam tried on some of Jessica's sweaters, at her new sister's invitation.

Peter and Mel could hear the racket from their room and Mel smiled. 'I think they're going to make it.' But she was still aware of a certain mild tension between the two groups. there was something very real about all this, and there was no escaping it now.

'You worry about them too much, Mel. They're fine,' he told her with a smile as he answered the ringing telephone. Then he sat down at his desk with a frown, with the phone still in his hand as he asked a series of rapid-fire questions. He set the phone down again and grabbed his jacket from a chair, explaining quickly to Mel what had happened. 'It's Marie. She's rejecting again.'

'Is it serious?'

He nodded, his face pale. 'She's in a coma. I don't know why they didn't call me earlier today. They gave me some bullshit story about it being Christmas and not wanting to disturb me since I wasn't on call. God damn it.' He stood in the doorway looking unhappily at Mel. 'I'll be home when I can.'

As he left, she saw their trip to Mexico going out the window. When the children came to say goodnight a while later, she didn't say anything, not wanting to upset them. She said only that he'd gone to the hospital to check on a patient. But once they'd left the room again, she found herself thinking about Marie, and praying for her. Peter never called to give her any news. At two thirty Mel gave up and went to bed, hoping he'd be able to leave on the trip. Otherwise they would have to cancel it. She didn't want to leave without him. This was their honeymoon.

She felt him slip into bed beside her just after five o'clock, and when she reached out to him he felt distant and stiff. It was so unlike him that she opened an eye, and then moved closer to him.

'Hi, sweetheart. Everything all right?' He didn't answer, and she opened both eyes. Something was wrong. 'Peter?'

'She died at four o'clock. We opened her up and she was just too far gone. She had the worst case of hardening of the arteries I've ever seen, and with a new heart, dammit.' It was obvious that he blamed himself. They had given her seven months and no more, but it was seven months more than she would have had without it.

'I'm sorry.' There seemed to be so little she could say, and he was shutting her out. He resisted all her efforts to console him. And finally at six o'clock he got out of bed. 'You should try to get some sleep before we leave.' Her voice was gentle and she was obviously worried about him. But she felt it too. Marie had been someone important to them both, right from the first. Mel had watched the transplant. And she felt the girl's loss now. But she was not prepared for what Peter said next. He sounded like an angry unhappy child.

'I'm not going. You take the children.' He looked petulant and upset as he sat down heavily in a chair in their bedroom, and as it was still dark outside, Mel turned on a light to see him better. He looked exhausted and there were dark circles under his eyes. It was a hell of a final note to their wedding and a rotten beginning for their honeymoon.

'There's nothing you can do here. And we won't go without you.'

'I'm not in the mood, Mel.'

'That's not fair. The children will be so disappointed, and it's our honeymoon.' He was being unreasonable, but she knew that he was too tired to make much sense. 'Peter, please ...'

'Dammit' – he leapt to his feet, glaring at her – 'how would you feel? Seven lousy months, that's all ... that's all I gave her.'

'You're not God, Peter. You did what you know how to do, and you did it brilliantly. But God makes those decisions, you don't.'

'Bullshit! We should have done better than that.'

'Well, you didn't, dammit, and she's dead.' Now Mel was shouting too. 'And you can't stay here and sulk about it, you have a responsibility to us too.' He glared at her and stalked out of the room, but he came back half an hour later with two cups of coffee. They didn't have to be at the airport until noon so there was still time to convince him. He handed Mel a cup of the steaming brew with a sour look and she looked into his eyes as she thanked him.

'I'm sorry, Mel ... I just ... I can't ever feel good about it when I lose a patient, and she was such a sweet girl ... it's not fair ...' His voice drifted off and Mel set down her cup and put her arms around his shoulders.

'You're not in a fair business, sweetheart. You know that. You know the odds each time you go in. You try to forget them, but they're still there.' He nodded, she was right. She knew him well. He turned to her with a sad smile.

'I'm a lucky man.'

'And a brilliant surgeon. Don't ever forget that.' She didn't ask him about Mexico again until after he'd had breakfast with the children; he was strangely subdued and Mark asked Mel about it as they walked back upstairs side by side.

'What's wrong with Dad?'

'He lost a patient last night.'

Mark nodded, understanding. 'He always takes that hard, especially if they're transplant patients. Was it?'

'Yes. The one he did when I interviewed him in May.' Mark nodded again and looked questioningly at Mel.

'Are we still leaving for Mexico?'

'I hope so.'

Mark didn't look too sure. 'You don't know how he gets with this kind of thing. We may not be going.'

'I'll do my best.'

He looked at her then and seemed about to say something else but Matt came along and interrupted them. He couldn't find his flippers and wanted to know if Mel had seen them.

'No, I haven't, but I'll look around. Did you check out at the pool?' He nodded, and Mel went on to her own room after he went his way and she found Peter there, sitting in a chair and staring into space, looking suddenly older than his years. His oldest son knew him well. He was taking Marie's death very hard, and Mel was beginning to doubt that they would be going anywhere that day. 'Well sweetheart' – she sat down near him on the edge of the bed – 'what'll we do?'

'About what?' He looked blank, he was thinking of how her heart had looked when they'd opened her up.

'The trip. Shall we go or stay?'

He hesitated for a long moment, looking into Mel's eyes. 'I don't know.' He seemed incapable of making that decision at the moment.

'I think it would do you good, and the kids too. We've all been through a lot lately, a lot of adjustments, a lot of changes, and there are more to come. It seems to me that a trip might be just what the doctor ordered.' She smiled and didn't point out to him that she was starting work at the new network in a week and would be under tremendous pressure herself. She needed a holiday even more than he did.

'All right. We'll go. I guess you're right. We can't disappoint the children, and I've already arranged for someone to cover for me.' She put her arms around him and hugged him tight.

'Thank you.' But he barely responded, and he spoke to no one on the way to the airport. Once or twice Mel's and Mark's eyes met, but they said nothing until they were alone for a moment on the plane, after take-off.

Mark filled her in on what to expect. 'He could be like this for a while, you know.'

'How long does it usually last?'

'A week, sometimes two. Sometimes even a month, it depends on how responsible he feels and how close he was to the patient.'

Mel nodded. It didn't give her much to look forward to, certainly not on their honeymoon. And Mark was right. They landed in Puerto Vallarta and piled into two jeeps to take them to their hotel where they had three rooms reserved, which looked out over the beach and water. There was an enormous open-air bar downstairs just below their windows, and three swimming pools filled with laughing, shouting people. Above all the other noises were the sounds of a steel band, interspersed from time to time with mariachis. It was a festive atmosphere and the children were thrilled, especially Jessica and Val who had never been to Mexico before. Mark took them all downstairs to swim and have a soda in the bar, but Peter insisted on staying in their room. Mel tried to woo him out of his mood.

'How about a walk on the beach, love?'

'I don't feel like it, Mel. I'd really like to be alone. Why don't you join the children?' She wanted to snap at him that it was their honeymoon, not the children's, but she decided that it was wisest to say nothing at all. Maybe he would snap out of it quicker. So she left him.

But as the days rolled on, he didn't seem to improve. She went shopping in town with Pam and the twins and they bought beautiful embroidered blouses and dresses to wear in LA at the pool, and Mark took Matthew fishing twice. She took everyone except Matt to Carlos O'Brien's for Cokes and people-watching several times and she even took the older ones to a disco one night, but Peter never joined them at all. He was obsessed with what had happened to Marie, and several times a day he would spend an hour in the room trying to get a line to LA to check on his current patients.

'It really wasn't worth coming, for you to sit in your room all week long, calling Center City,' Mel finally snapped at him towards the end of their stay, but he only looked at her with empty eyes.

'I told you that at home, you didn't want to disappoint the children.'

'This is our honeymoon, not theirs.' She had finally said it. She was bitterly disappointed. He had made no effort all week, and they hadn't even made love since Marie had died. A honeymoon to remember it was not.

'I'm sorry, Mel. It was just rotten timing. I'll make it up to you later.' But she wondered if he ever could. And suddenly she realised that she didn't even have her own home to return to when the trip was over. She missed the house in New York more than ever, and thinking of it reminded her of the photographs of Anne she wanted to put away when they returned. She wondered what Peter would do with her portrait. It was her house now too, and she didn't want to look at Anne every time she turned around. That seemed normal, at least to Mel, but she wasn't going to broach the subject until they returned to Los Angeles. She still called it LA whenever she spoke of it, and never home, because it wasn't home yet. New York was. She noticed that with the twins too; when they were at Carlos O'Brien's, some boys asked Jessica where they were from and she answered 'New York' without thinking and then Mark teased her and she explained that they had just moved to LA. But other adjustments came more quickly. Mel noticed that they referred to each other as brothers and sisters, except for Mark and Val who had reason not to adopt those titles.

The only one to get sick was Valerie, on the last day. She bought an ice cream on the beach, and when Mel heard what she'd done she groaned as she stood by Val, while she threw up for hours and then had diarrhoea all night. Peter wanted to give her something but she absolutely refused to take it, and when Mel finally came to bed at four in the morning, he awoke, his medical instincts alert.

'How is she?'

'Asleep at last. Poor child. I've never seen anyone so sick. I don't know why she wouldn't take the Lomotil you offered her, she isn't usually that stubborn.'

'Mel, is she all right?' He was frowning and thinking of something.

'What do you mean?'

'I don't know. I don't know her that well. But she looks different than she did in Aspen, and at Thanksgiving.'

'Different how?'

'I'm not sure what I mean, to tell you the truth. Just a feeling. Has she had a checkup lately?'

'You're making me nervous. What are you suspecting?' She expected nothing less than the threat of leukaemia, but he shook his head.

'Anaemia maybe. She seems to sleep a lot, and Pam says she threw up after Christmas dinner.'

Mel sighed. 'I think it's nerves. Jess looks lousy to me too. I think the move was a big change for them, and they're at a tough age for that. But maybe you're right. I'll take them both to the doctor when we get back.'

'I'll give you the name of the doctor we use. But don't worry about it.' He kissed her for the first time in days. 'I don't think it's serious, and I think you may be right. Girls at that age tend to nervous upsets. It's just that ever since Pam had anorexia last year, my antennae go up every time something seems off to me. It's probably nothing.'

But in Pam's room, Mark was sitting beside her bed. He had waited for hours for Mel to leave, and Val was awake now, and terribly weak from her bout with tourista. She was crying softly and Mark was stroking her hair, as they both whispered so as not to wake Jessie or Pam.

'Do you think it'll hurt the baby?' Val whispered to Mark, and he looked at her miserably. She had found out two days after she arrived from New York. He had taken her for a pregnancy test. And they both knew when it had happened. When they finally made love for the first time, on Thanksgiving. Val looked terrified now. They hadn't decided what to do about it yet, but if they decided to have it, she didn't want to have a deformed baby.

'I don't know. Did you take any medicine?'

'No,' she whispered. 'Your dad tried to give me some, but I wouldn't take it.' Mark nodded, but that was the least of their problems. She was only five weeks pregnant, but that meant that they had less than two months to do something about it, if she would.

'Do you think you can sleep now?' She nodded, her eyes already half closed and he bent to kiss her, and then tiptoed out of the room. He had wanted to tell his dad, but he couldn't with Christmas and the wedding and everything, and Val had begged him not to. He had to take her to a good doctor, if she was going to get an abortion, not to some crummy clinic, but he was waiting to talk to her about it until they got back to LA. There was no point discussing it here. There was nothing they could do, and it would just make her more nervous.

'Mark?' Jessica turned in her bed as he was about to leave the room. His departing noises had awoken her. 'What's wrong?' She sat up and glanced from him to her sister.

'I just came to see how Val was.' Val was already sleeping and he didn't approach from the doorway.

'Is something wrong?' She must have been totally out of it, Mark decided, if she didn't remember how sick Val had been all day with the tourista.

'She got sick from something she ate.'

'I mean, more than that.'

'No, she's okay.' But he was shaking when he got back to his own room. Jessica sensed something, and he knew what they said about twins, that they were practically psychic about each other. All he needed was for her to say something to his dad, or their mother and all hell would break loose. He wanted to take care of it himself. He had to. There was no other way.

Chapter 27

They left for LA the morning of New Year's Eve with Val still weak, but well enough to go home. And they got back to the house at four in the afternoon, tired and suntanned and happy with their trip. Peter had finally consented to come out of seclusion for the last day, and a good time was had by all. Even Mel. Although it hadn't been much of a honeymoon for her, to say the least. He apologised to her on the flight home, and she told him she understood. At least she had got some rest before she started work at the network in LA. She had to report at noon the next day, on New Year's Day, and at six o'clock that night she would begin co-anchoring with Paul Stevens. He had been at the station for years, and although he had some devoted fans, his ratings were starting to slip, and they were bringing Mel in to pull him up again. The network felt that together they should make an unbeatable team. He was tall, grey-haired, and blue-eyed, with a resonant deep voice, and a style which appealed to the ladies, according to the surveys. Mel had a strong female draw too, and the surveys all showed that men loved her as well. With the two of them on the air, the network knew that they had a prize show, and even if Stevens slipped farther, Mel could carry him. But it was the first time Paul Stevens had ever co-anchored, and he was less than thrilled, and for Mel it was a step down too, as she had been sole anchor now for years. It was going to be a humbling experience for both, she knew, and a lesson in diplomacy, working with him.

Peter and Mel decided to stay home on New Year's Eve, and drink champagne by the fire. Mark took Val and Jessie out to a party he'd been invited to.

Mel was pleased that he had included Jessie as well, although she didn't look too thrilled to go and Val wasn't on top form yet. Mel suggested that they not stay out too late, and warned them to be careful driving, and then she went upstairs to check on Pam, who had a friend sleeping over. Matt was asleep in his bed with a noisemaker beside him. He wanted someone to wake him up at midnight so he could blow his horn, but Mel correctly assumed that there would be no one awake in the house by midnight to wake him up. She was half tempted to wait up for Mark and the twins but she and Peter were exhausted. As he sat in bed reading some of his medical journals, Mel wandered around the house, trying to make herself feel as though it were her home too, but it just didn't feel like it yet. She saw the photographs of Anne in the silver frames, and began gathering them up one by one. There was a grand total of twenty-three, and she put them all in a drawer in Peter's study, and as she crossed the living room with the last batch in her arms, she saw Pam standing in the doorway.

'What are you doing?'

'Putting some pictures away.' There was a strange exchange of looks and Mel saw that Pam was rigid as she stood there.

'Of who?'

'Your mother.' Mel's voice didn't waver.

'Put them back!' Her voice was almost a snarl, and Mel saw that the friend who was sleeping overnight was standing just behind her.

'Excuse me?'

'I said, put them back. This is my mother's house, not yours.' If Mel didn't know her better she would have said she was drunk. But she wasn't. She was just extremely angry and upset, so much so that she was shaking where she stood.

'I think we can discuss this some other time, Pam. When we're alone.' Mel was determined not to lose her cool, but she found that she was shaking too.

'Give me those!' And then suddenly, Pam lunged at her, but Mel saw her coming and dropped the pictures into a chair and grabbed Pam's arms before she could do any damage. She held her fast and spoke to her in a stern voice.

'Go to you room. Right now!' It was nothing different than she would have said to the twins. But Pam ignored her and frantically picked up all the framed photographs Mel had dropped into a chair. And she stood glaring at Mel with her arms full.

'I hate you!'

'You're welcome to all the photographs you like. I put the rest in your father's study.'

Pam ignored her. 'This is our house, *ours*, and my mother's, and don't you forget it!' Mel's palm itched to slap her, but it seemed unwise in the presence of her friend. Instead, she took a firm grip on Pam's shoulder and propelled her to the door.

'Go upstairs to your room right now, Pam. or I'm going to call your friend's mother and ask her to pick her up. Is that clear?' Pam said not a word, she trundled upstairs with the photographs of her mother, and her embarrassed friend Joan trailing behind her, as Mel stayed long enough to turn off the lights downstairs and then went up to her bedroom, where Peter was still happily reading his journals. Mel stood staring at him for a long moment, aware that at least some of what Pam had said was true. It was their house. Mel hadn't even been allowed to put her furniture in it. And it still had Anne's mark on it everywhere. Still trembling from her encounter with Pam, Mel stared at Peter as he looked up. 'I want that portrait taken down tomorrow.'

'What portrait?' He looked at her as though she were crazy, and she almost looked it.

'The one of your late wife.' She spoke through clenched teeth and he was totally baffled. Maybe the champagne had gone to her head.

'Why?'

'Because this is my house now too, not hers. And I want it taken down. Immediately!' She was almost shouting at him.

'It's by a very famous artist.' He started to stiffen too. Her attitude seemed totally uncalled for and he knew nothing of the exchange with Pam.

'I don't care who it's by. Get rid of it. Throw it out. Burn it. Give it away. Do whatever the hell you want with it, but get it out of my living room!' She was suddenly on the verge of tears as he stared at her in disbelief.

'What in hell is wrong with you, Mel?'

'What's wrong with me? What's wrong with me? You move me into a house where not so much as a hat pin is mine, where everything belongs to you and your children and you've got photographs of your first wife all over the house, and I'm supposed to feel at home?'

He was beginning to understand, or so he thought, but she still sounded irrational. And why now? 'Then put the photographs away if you want to. But you didn't object to them before.'

'I didn't live here before. But I do now.'

'Apparently.' He was getting annoyed. 'I suppose you don't find the decor adequate for you?' There was suddenly a nasty tone in his voice.

'It's perfectly adequate, if you don't mind living in Versailles. Personally, I'd rather live in a house, a home, something a little warmer and on a slightly more human scale.'

'Like that dollhouse you had in New York, I suppose?'

'Precisely.' They stood across the room from each other as each one steamed.

'Fine. Then put the photographs away if you want. But the portrait stays.' He said it just to annoy her, because he didn't like the way she'd broached the subject at all, and Mel's mouth almost fell open.

'The hell it does.' And then, 'It goes or I do.'

'Doesn't that sound ridiculous to you? You're behaving like an idiot, or aren't you aware of that?'

'And you're selfish. You expect all the adjustments to be mine, and you don't change a thing, not even the photographs of your wife.'

'Then have some photographs taken of yourself and we'll put those around too.' He was being nasty now and he knew it, but he was tired of hearing her bitch about Anne's pictures. He had thought of putting them away once or twice himself, but the thought depressed him and he didn't want to upset the children. He reminded her of that now. 'I don't suppose you've thought of what reaction you'd get if you threw that portrait out.'

'Oh, yes, I already know that.' She advanced on him with a vicious look. 'I was just putting the photographs in question in your study, and your daughter informed me that this is your house and not mine, or more exactly, her mother's.'

And suddenly Peter understood it all. He sat down with drooping shoulders and looked up at Mel. He could just imagine the scene with Pam, and that explained Mel's behaviour to him. It hadn't made any sense before. He didn't think she was given to rages. 'Did she say that, Mel?' His voice was kinder now, and his eyes were too.

'She did.' Mel's eyes filled with tears and she still did not approach her husband.

'I'm sorry.' He beckoned to her but she didn't approach and she was crying openly now. He went to her and put his arms around her. 'I'm so sorry, love. You know this is your home too.' He held her and she began to sob. 'I'll take the portrait down tomorrow, it was stupid of me.'

'No, no, it's not that ... it's just ...'

'I know ...'

'It's so hard to get used to living in someone else's house. I'm so used to having my own.' He sat her down beside him on the bed.

'I know ... but this is your home now too.'

She looked up at him and sniffed. 'No, it's not. Everything is yours and Anne's ... I don't even have any of my own things around.' Peter looked pensive as he listened to her.

'Everything I have is yours, Mel.' But she wanted her own, not his.

'Just give me time. I'll get used to it all. I'm just tired, and there's been so much going on, and Pam upset me with what she said just now.' Peter kissed his wife and stood up.

'I'll go up and talk to her.'

'No! Let me handle that. If you intervene, she'll just resent me more.'

'She loves you. I know she does.' But there was worry in his eyes.

'But it's different now. I was just a guest before, and now I'm an intruder in her house.'

Peter looked even more upset at that. Was that how she felt?

'You're not an intruder. You're my wife. I hope you remember that.'

She smiled through her tears. 'I do! There's just a lot going on at once, and tomorrow I start my new job.'

'I know.' He understood, but it made him sad to see her cry, and he vowed to himself to take Anne's portrait down the next day. She was right. 'Why don't we both go to bed early tonight? We're both tired and it's been a rough week.' Mel didn't disagree. Moving from New York, their wedding, honeymoon, Marie's death ... They brushed their teeth and went to bed and he held her close to him in the dark, feeling her warm flesh next to him. This was what he had longed for in the past six months ... more than that, the last two years ... and even before that, it had never been like that with Anne. She had been so much more distant than Mel. Mel seemed almost like a part of him, and for the first time in a week he felt something deep inside him stir, and as he held her close, he wanted her as never before. And when the old year became the new, he was making love to her.

Chapter 28

As per her new contract, negotiated while she was still in New York, the car arrived for Mel in the early afternoon, and drove her to the station where she would work. She walked inside, aware of a hundred stares. There was incredible curiosity about her. Mel Adams was starting work. She was introduced to the producers, assistant producers and directors and cameramen and editors and grips, and suddenly despite the new surroundings, Mel felt as though she were in a familiar world. It was no different for New York or Chicago or Buffalo before that. A studio was a studio, and as she looked around the office she was assigned, she suddenly sighed and sat down. In a way, it felt like coming home. She spent the entire afternoon familiarising herself with the people who came and went, the features and interviews recently done. She had a glass of wine with the producer and his crew, and at five thirty Paul Stevens arrived. The producer introduced them at once, and Mel smiled as they shook hands.

'It'll be nice working with you, Paul.'

'Wish I could say the same.' He shook her hand and walked away, as the producer attempted to fill the awkward gap and Mel raised an eyebrow and turned away.

'Well, at least I know where I stand.' She grinned ruefully. But it wasn't going to be easy working with him. He was furious to have a female share his spot, and he was going to make Mel pay for it in every way he could. She discovered that the instant they went on the air that night. He was saccharine sweet whenever he spoke to her, but he undercut her and upstaged her in every way he could, trying to make her nervous, throw her off, and generally drive her insane. It was obvious to her that his outrage was so acute that when they went off the air, she stood in front of Paul's desk and looked down at him. 'Is there anything we ought to talk about right now, before this thing gets out of hand?'

'Sure. How would you like to split your pay cheque with me? I'm splitting my spot with you, that seems only fair.' His eyes glittered evilly, and Mel understood what the problem was. The papers had long since leaked what her contract was, and it was probably three times what they paid him, but that wasn't her fault.

'I can't help the arrangements the network made with me, Paul. It was a price war with New York. You know what that's like.'

'No, but I'd like to try.' He had been trying to get to New York for years,

and she had just thrown it away, and come to breathe down his neck. He hated
the bitch, no matter how good they said she was. He didn't need her co-
anchoring with him. He stood up now and almost snarled at her. 'Just stay out
of my face, and we'll do okay. Got that?'

She looked at him sadly and turned and walked away. It wasn't going to be
easy working with him, and she thought about it all the way home. She only
had to do the six o'clock here, for the same money she'd been offered to do the
six and eleven in New York. LA had really done well by her. And Paul Stevens
hated her for it.

'How'd it go? You looked great.' Peter looked proud of her when she came
home, and everyone was still gathered around the set, but Mel didn't look
pleased.

'I've got a co-anchor who hates my guts. That ought to make work fun.' That,
and Pam reminding her that she lived in Peter and Anne's home, she thought, as
she hung up her coat.

'He'll mellow out.'

She didn't look as sure. 'I wouldn't bet on that. I think he's hoping I drop dead
or go back to New York.' Mel's eyes drifted to Pam, wondering what she'd see
there, but the girl's eyes were blank. And when Mel glanced at the living room
wall, she saw that the portrait was gone, and she was thrilled. She threw her
arms around Peter's neck, feeling better after all, and whispered in his ear.
'Thank you, my love.' Pam knew what they were talking about. She got up and
left the room as the others watched, and Peter spoke in a normal voice.

'I hung Anne's portrait in the hall.'

Mel froze. 'You did? I thought you said you'd put it away.'

'It won't bother anybody there.' Oh, no? Their eyes met and held. 'You don't
mind, do you?'

She spoke in a very quiet voice. 'As a matter of fact, I do. That wasn't what we
agreed.'

'I know . . .' And then he turned to her, 'It's a little rough on the kids to do
everything at once. All the photographs are gone.' Mel nodded and didn't say a
word, she went upstairs to her room to wash her face and hands, and then joined
them at dinner, and afterwards she knocked on Pam's door.

'Who is it?'

'Your wicked stepmother.' She smiled at the door.

'Who?'

'Mel.'

'What do you want?'

'I've got something to give you.' And when Pam cautiously opened the door
to her, Mel handed her a dozen photographs of Anne in silver frames. 'I thought
you'd like these for your room.'

Pam glanced at them and then took them from her. 'Thanks.' But she said
nothing more. She simply turned and closed the door in Mel's face and Mel
went back downstairs.

'Were you upstairs with Pam?' Peter was pleased as she walked into their
room. He was reading his medical journals again. He had to keep abreast of
what was new.

'Yes. I took her some of the photographs of Anne.'

'You know, that really shouldn't be such an issue with you, Mel.'

'Oh, no?' He really didn't understand and she was too tired to argue about it with him. 'Why not?'

'Because she's gone.' He said it so quietly, Mel had to strain to hear.

'I know. But it's difficult living here with her photographs staring at me all the time.'

'You're exaggerating. There weren't that many around.'

'I put twenty-three of them in your study last night. That's not bad. I just gave a dozen of them to Pam. And I thought I'd put some in Matt's and Mark's rooms. That's where they belong.' Peter didn't answer and went back to the journals on his lap, as Mel stretched out on the bed. The producer had suggested she do as many special features as she could in the next month. They were desperate to pull their ratings up, and historically her interviews had worked miracles for the news show in New York. She had promised to do her best, and had already made notes about half a dozen subjects that interested her. But she could just imagine what Paul Stevens was going to say when he got wind of that. Maybe all she could do was ignore the man, but the following night, he was rude to her as she came on the set, and despite his charm while they were on the air, she had the feeling that he would have liked to punch her out when they went off. It was really an untenable way to work, and not what she was used to at all. But she submitted her list of possible interviews to the producer that night, and he loved almost all of them, which was both good news and bad. It meant that she would be working overtime for the next month or two, but maybe that was one way to settle in. It was always strange working for a network at first. It was just a little stranger for her this time because she was feeling her way around at home as well.

'Busy day today?' Peter looked at her distractedly as he came in and she smiled. She had got home at seven fifteen, and he was even later than that. It was almost eight o'clock.

'Pretty much.' She was in a quiet mood. The hassles with Paul Stevens wore her out.

'Is that guy behaving any better than before? Paul What's His Name?'

She smiled. Everyone in LA knew his name, whether they liked him or not. 'No. I think he was a little worse.'

'Sonofabitch.'

'What about you?' The kids had gone back to school, and had eaten dinner at six. Mel and Peter were eating at eight.

'Three bypasses in a row. It wasn't a very exciting day.'

'I'm doing an interview with Louisa Garp.' She was the biggest star in Hollywood.

'You are?'

'I am.'

'When?'

'Next week. She accepted today.' Mel looked pleased and Peter was obviously impressed. 'Hell, I even did Dr Peter Hallam once.' She smiled and he reached out and took her hand. They were both so busy now, both had such hectic jobs. He hoped it didn't mean they'd never be able to spend time with each other. That wasn't the kind of life he liked. He liked knowing that his wife was there for him. And he wanted to be there for her too.

'I missed you today, Mel.'

'I missed you too.' But she also knew what the next two months would be like. She was going to scarcely see him at all. But maybe after that things would settle down.

They sat in the living room after dinner and talked for a while and Pam came down. Peter stretched an arm out to her. 'How's my girl?' She came to him with a smile. 'Did you know that Mel is doing an interview with Louisa Garp?'

'So?' She seemed to be bitchy all the time now, as though Mel were a real threat to her, and Peter looked annoyed.

'That's not a very pleasant thing to say.'

'Oh yeah?' She was asking for it, but Mel didn't say a word. 'So what? I got an A on my art history paper today.'

'That's great!' Peter let the second comment slide by. Mel was furious and when the girl left she told him so. 'What did you want me to say? Last year the kid was flunking out, now she tells me she has got an A.'

'Terrific. But that doesn't cancel out her being rude to me.'

'For chrissake, Mel, give her time to adjust.' He was tired now. He'd had a long day. And he didn't want to come home to argue with Mel. 'Let's go upstairs to our room and close the door.' But as soon as they did, Jess came in, and Mel gently asked her to leave.

'Why?' She looked shocked.

'Because I haven't seen Peter all day, and we want to talk.'

I haven't seen you either.' She was clearly hurt.

'I know. But we can talk in the morning, Jess. Peter will be at the hospital by then.' He left the room to take a shower and Mel kissed her cheek but Jess drew away.

'Never mind.'

'Jess, come on ... it's hard cutting myself into pieces for everyone. Give me a chance.'

'Yeah, sure.'

'How's Val?'

'How do I know? Ask her. She doesn't talk to me any more, and you don't seem to have time to talk to us.'

'That's not fair.'

'Isn't it? It's true though. I take it he comes first.' She nodded towards the bathroom door.

'Jess, I'm married now. If I'd been married all these years, it would have been different than it was.'

'So I gather. Personally, I preferred it before.'

'Jessie ...' Mel felt agonised as she looked at her oldest child. 'What's the matter with you?'

'Nothing.' But tears filled her eyes, and she sat down on her mother's bed, trying not to cry. 'It's just ... I don't know ...' She shook her head in despair and looked up at Mel. 'It's everything ... a new school, a new room ... I'll never see any of my friends again ... I have to share a room with Val and she's such a pig. She takes all my stuff and she never gives it back.' They were big problems to her and Mel's heart went out to her. 'And she cries all the time.'

'She does?' And just saying it made Mel think. She realised that Val had been crying a lot in the last few weeks. Maybe Peter had been right, and Val was sick. 'Is she all right, Jess?'

'I don't know. She acts weird. And she's always with Mark.' Mel made a mental note to say something again about that.

'I'll talk to them again.'

'It won't change anything. She's in his room all the time.'

Mel frowned. 'I specifically told her not to do that.' But there were other things that Mel had also specifically told her not to do, and Jess knew perfectly well that she did, but she would never have told her mother that. Mel put her arms around Jessica then and kissed her cheek and Jessie looked at her with a sad smile.

'I'm sorry if I was a bitch.'

'It's hard on all of us at first, but we'll get used to it. I'm sure it's hard on Pam and Mark and Matt to have us in the house too. Let's give everyone a little time to settle down.'

'What's all this?' Peter came out of the shower with a towel wrapped around his waist and smiled at Jess. 'Hi, Jess. Everything okay?'

'Sure.' She smiled and stood up. She knew she should leave them alone. She turned to Mel. 'Goodnight, Mom.' And as she left the room, it tore at Mel's heart to see her so sad. She didn't say anything to Peter about their exchange but it was one more burden on her heart as she went back to work the next day, and had to deal with Paul Stevens again, and that night when she came home, Peter called. There was an emergency he had to take care of himself, he'd be home in a 'while', and a while turned out to be eleven o'clock.

They never seemed to get off the merry-go-round any more, and for the next three weeks she was constantly out doing interviews, fighting with Paul Stevens before or after the show, or listening to Jessie's and Val's complaints when she got home. Mrs Hahn wouldn't let them in the kitchen for a snack. Pam was taking their clothes, Jess said that Val and Mark were locked in his room all the time, and to top it off at the end of January, Mel got a call from Matt's school. He had fallen out of a swing in the playground and broken his arm. Peter met them in the emergency room with an orthopaedist friend, and Mel joked tiredly that it was the first time they'd seen each other in weeks. He had had emergencies almost every night, endless bypasses to do, and two potential transplant patients had died for lack of donors' hearts.

'Do you think we'll survive, Mel?'

She collapsed on their bed in exhaustion one night. 'Some days I'm not sure. I've never done so many goddamn interviews in my life.' And she still felt as though she were living in someone else's home, which didn't help, but she hadn't had time to do anything about it yet. And she hadn't even had time to tackle the frozen Mrs Hahn. 'I wish you'd get rid of her,' Mel finally admitted to Peter one afternoon.

'Mrs Hahn?' He looked shocked. 'She's been with us for years.'

'Well, she's making life very tough for Val and Jess, and she certainly isn't pleasant to me. This might be a good time for a change.' There were a lot of changes she wanted to make around the house, but she didn't have time.

'That's an insane idea, Mel.' He looked angry at the mere thought. 'She's part of this family.'

'So was Raquel part of ours, and I had to leave her in New York.'

'And you resent me for that?' He was wondering if in transplanting Mel, he had asked too much. She was testy with him now all the time, and he knew that she wasn't crazy about her job. The money was fabulous, there was no denying that, but the conditions weren't as good as those she had known before, there was the endless problem with Paul Stevens, she said. 'You blame everything on me, don't you?' He was looking for a fight. For no reason he could explain, that morning a perfectly decent bypass patient had died.

'I'm not blaming anything on you.' She looked desperately tired as they talked. 'But the fact is that we both have enormous jobs that make tremendous demands on us, five kids, and a very demanding life. I want to make things easier in every possible way. And Mrs Hahn is complicating things.'

'Maybe for you, but not for the rest of us.' He looked stubbornly at Mel and she wanted to scream.

'And don't I live here too? Christ, between you and Pam ...'

'Now what?' The remark didn't miss its mark.

'Nothing. She just resents our being here. I expected that.'

'And you don't think your daughters resent me? You're crazy if you think they don't. They're used to having a hundred per cent of your time, and every time we close our bedroom door now, they get pissed off.'

'I can't help that, any more than you can change Pam. They all need time to adjust, but Jess and Val have had the biggest change in their lives.'

'The hell they did. Pam lost her mom.'

'I'm sorry.' There was no talking about it with him, or touching the sacred subject of Anne. Mel had noticed that a few of Anne's pictures had gone back up, but she hadn't brought up the subject again, and her portrait was still in the hall.

'So am I.'

'No, you're not.' Mel wouldn't let the argument die, which was not wise. 'You expect us to make all the adjustments around here.'

'Is that right? Well, just exactly what do you think I ought to do? Move to New York?'

'No.' She looked him straight in the eye. 'Move to a new house.'

'That's absurd.'

'No, it's not, but changes scare you to death. When I came along, you were still sitting around with everything the same, waiting for Anne to come home. And now you've moved me into her house. It's okay for me to turn my whole life upside down, but you want everything just the way it was. And guess what? That doesn't work.'

'Maybe it's the marriage you want to move out of, Mel, and not the house.'

She stood staring at him from across the room, in total frustration and despair. 'Are you ready to quit?'

He sat down heavily in his favourite chair. 'Sometimes I am.' He looked up at her honestly. 'Why do you want to change everything, Mel? Mrs Hahn, the house, why can't you leave things as they are?'

'Because everything here is changed, whether you want to admit that or not. I'm not Anne, I'm me, Mel, and I want a life that's ours, not borrowed from someone else.'

'This is a new life.' But he didn't sound convinced.

'In an old house. Jess and Val and I feel like intruders here.'

'Maybe you're just looking for an excuse to go back to New York.' His face was grim, and Mel wanted to cry.

'Is that what you think?'

'Sometimes.' He was being honest with her.

'Well, let me explain something to you. I have a contract here. If you and I called it quits tonight, I'd still be stuck here for two years, like it or not. I can't go back to New York.'

'And you hate me for that.' It was a statement of his view of the facts.

'I don't hate you for anything. I love you.' She came and knelt beside his chair. 'And I want this to work, but it isn't going to happen by itself. We both have to be willing to change.' She reached up and gently touched his face.

'I guess ...' Tears suddenly began to fill his eyes and he turned his head away and then looked back again. 'I guess I thought ... we could keep a lot of things ... the same ...'

'I know.' She reached up and kissed him. 'And I love you so much, but there's so much going on that my head spins sometimes.'

'I know.' Somehow they always found each other after the fights, but there were so many fights these days. 'I should have made you sign the contract in New York, Mel. It wasn't fair to drag you out here.'

'Yes, it was.' She smiled through her own tears. 'And you didn't drag me anywhere. I didn't want to stay in New York. All I wanted was to be here with you.'

'And now?' He looked frightened of what she would say.

'I'm glad we came. And in a while, it'll all fall into place.'

He took her hand then and led her gently to the bed and they made love as they had before, and Mel knew she had found him again. She didn't regret any of what she had done, but it had taken its toll, and there were pressures on all of them. She just hoped they'd all survive it, but with Peter strong at her side, she knew they would.

The only misery he couldn't seem to protect her from was at work, and in February he looked at her one night as she came home almost in tears.

'My God, if you only knew what a creep that man is.' Paul Stevens was driving her insane. 'One of these nights I'm going to kill him right on the set, when we're on the air.'

'Now that would be news.' He looked sympathetically at her. For once, things were a little quieter for him at work. 'I have an idea.'

'A hit man. That's the only thing I want to hear.'

'Better than that.'

'Cement shoes.'

Peter laughed. 'Let's all go skiing this weekend. It'll do everyone good. I'm not on call, and I hear the snow is great.' Mel looked wan at the thought. Just the idea of packing them all up exhausted her. 'What do you think?'

'I don't know.' She hated to be a spoilsport and for once Peter was in such a good mood. She smiled at him and he put his arms around her. 'Okay.' At least they'd get away from the problems in the house.

'Is it a deal?'

'Yes, Doctor.' She grinned, and went upstairs to tell the kids, but she found that Val was in bed with what looked like a bad case of flu. She was deathly pale, half asleep in bed, and when Mel touched her forehead, she felt terribly hot. And Mark was sitting worriedly near her bed. It didn't look any different from the flu's she had got so frequently in New York. She was made of much less rugged stuff than Jess. 'I've got good news,' she told Mark and the twins in the girls' room. 'Peter's taking us all skiing this weekend.' They all looked pleased but their reaction was subdued. Mark seemed terribly involved with Val, and Jessie seemed vague as she glanced at her twin.

'That's nice.' Val was the first to speak, but her voice sounded terribly weak.

'You okay, love?' She sat down on Val's bed, and the girl winced.

'I'm fine. Just the flu.'

Mel nodded, but she was still worried about Val. 'You think you'll be okay by this weekend, Val?'

'Sure.'

Mel went down the hall then to tell Pam and Matt and then came back with some aspirin and juice for Val, and then she went back downstairs.

'Everyone pleased?'

'I think so. But Val's sick.'

'What's she got?' He looked concerned. 'Should I go have a look?'

Mel smiled, but she knew her daughter better than that. 'I think she'd be embarrassed if you did. It's just the flu.'

He nodded. 'She'll be all right by the end of the week.'

'I still have to get her to that doctor you mentioned to me.' But every time she had suggested it to Val, she had burst into tears and insisted she was fine. When they flew to Reno at the end of the week, and piled into a van for Squaw Valley, Val still looked terribly pale, but all of her other symptoms seemed to be gone, and Mel had other worries by then. Paul Stevens had made a major scene on the set just before they went on the air the night before she left for Reno. It was becoming an agony to go to work, and she dreaded each day more, but she was determined to stick it out no matter what. The weekends were a blessed relief now, especially this ski trip to Squaw Valley.

Peter had rented a van for them at the Reno airport, and they piled into it in high spirits, singing songs, helping each other with skis and bags. Peter stopped to kiss Mel before they climbed in the van, and the kids all hung out of the windows and hooted and cheered. Even Pam seemed in better spirits than she had been in over a month, and Val had a little colour in her cheeks, as they took off for Squaw Valley, and by the time they got there, everyone was laughing and joking and Mel was delighted that they had come. It would do them all good to leave LA and the house which was becoming such a source of contention between her and Peter.

He had found them a pleasant little condo, in a place where he and his children had stayed before. It was small but adequate for them. They slept as they had in Mexico, the girls in one room, the boys in another, and Mel and Peter in a third. And by lunchtime they were on the slopes, whooping and laughing and chasing each other down the mountain. As usual, Mark stayed close to Val, but there seemed to be less frivolity between them than there had been before, and Jess and Pam raced down the steepest trails with Matt just behind them.

At the end of their first run, Mel stopped breathlessly at the foot of the mountain and stood beside Peter as they waited for the others. It was exhilarating just to be there in the fresh mountain air, and Mel felt younger than she had in a long, long time. She looked at Peter with joy, and watched their children coming down the hill from over his shoulder.

'Aren't you glad we came up, Mel?'

She looked happily into his eyes. He was handsomer than ever, his blue eyes bright, his cheeks pink, his whole body filled with life. 'You know, you make me so damn happy.'

'Do I?' He looked hopeful, he loved her so much. He had never wanted to make her unhappy, but now and then he feared that he had, just by the very fact that he had brought her west and indirectly forced her into another job. Sort of like a mail-order bride. He smiled at the thought. 'I hope so. There's so much I want to do with you, and give you.'

'I know.' She understood him better than he knew. 'But we have so little time. Maybe as time goes on, we'll get better at juggling it all.' But there would always be interviews and features and news reports she had to do, and there would always be people who needed new hearts, or their old ones repaired. 'At least the children will settle down.'

'I wouldn't bet on that.' He laughed as he watched the five of them zoom towards them, with Matthew bringing up the rear, but not by much. He was almost as swift as the others. 'Not bad, you guys. Shall we try it one more time? Or do you want to stop for lunch now?' They had eaten on the plane, and bought sandwiches to eat in the van in Reno, but Jess was quick to speak up.

'I think Val should eat.' Mel was touched at how she still looked after her twin, and then noticed how pale the child was. She moved towards her, still on skis, and touched her forehead. She had no fever.

'You feeling okay, Val?'

'Sure, Mom.' But her eyes seemed a little vague, and on their way back up the mountain, Mel mentioned it to Peter again on the chair lift.

'I've got to get her to the doctor when we get home, no matter how much she cries and screams. I don't know why she's so dead set against going to a new doctor.'

Peter smiled as they floated through the air, past the enormous pine trees on the way up the mountain. 'Two years ago I had to take Pam to her paediatrician for a checkup for school, and she ran all around the room, screaming so he couldn't give her her tetanus booster. The truth is that no matter how tall they are, or how adult they think they are, they're all kids. It's easy to forget it sometimes, because they seem so sophisticated. But it's all veneer. Underneath, they're no more mature than Matthew.'

Mel smiled her agreement as their skis dangled crazily in midair. 'You're right about Val, but I don't think that's true of Jessie. That kid has been an old soul from the day she was born, and she's always looked out for her sister. Sometimes I think I rely on her too much.'

Peter looked at her and spoke very gently. 'Sometimes I think you do too. She's been looking upset since you got out here. Is it me, or is she jealous of Val and Mark?' She hadn't been aware of the tension emanating from Jessie like barbed wire, and Mel was surprised that he had noticed. He was amazingly perceptive, particularly considering how little he saw of them because of his long hours in the hospital and in his office.

'I think it may be a little bit of both. She's used to having me to herself more than she does now. And I've been trying to iron things out with Pam, and Matthew needs me more than the others. He's been hungry for some loving for two years.'

Peter looked hurt. 'I tried.'

'I know you did. But you're not ...' She leaned over and kissed him, and they sped off the lift at the top of the mountain. It was nice having time to talk to her husband. They had too little of it in LA, and they were both always exhausted. But here, even in a few hours, she felt as though they had made contact again. And she glanced back once or twice as they skied down the slopes, to make sure that the others were all there. She recognised them all by their colour combinations and their outfits. Jessica and Val in matching yellow ski suits, Mark in black and red, Pam in red from head to toe, and Matthew in royal blue and yellow. She had worn a fur jacket and hat and black ski pants, and Peter was entirely clad in a navy blue stretch suit. They were a colourful bunch.

Towards the end of the afternoon, they all went inside for cups of hot chocolate, and then they went back out to the slopes. And this time the young people took a different trail from Mel and Peter, but by then Mel was confident that they were all good skiers and could take care of themselves, even Matthew, and she knew that Jessie would keep an eye on him, if Pam didn't. It was heavenly skiing beside Peter in the crisp mountain air, and on their last run they raced each other down the trail. Peter won by several yards and Mel was breathless and laughing when she joined him at last.

'You're terrific!' She gazed at him with admiration. He seemed able to tackle anything he wanted, and to do it well.

'Not any more. I was on the ski team in college, but it's been years since I took it seriously.'

'I'm glad I only met you now. I could never have kept up.'

'You're not bad.' He smiled and swatted her behind with a leather glove, and she giggled and they kissed, and then they left the slopes and took off their skis, and waited for the kids at the bottom. It seemed a long wait, but eventually, they all came down, Val in the rear this time. She seemed much slower than the others, and Jess turned back several times to watch her, as Mel narrowed her eyes and watched them.

'Is she all right?'

'Who?' He had been watching Matt. The boy was making amazing progress. 'Val.'

'Right behind Mark?' He couldn't see the colour of her hair in the white woolly hat, and he had mistaken Jess for her sister.

'No, she's the last one, still a little ways up, in the same suit as Jess.' He looked and they both saw that she faltered once or twice, stumbled, caught herself, and then continued downhill, narrowly missing two skiers and flying between them. 'Peter ...' Instinctively Mel grabbed his arm as they watched. 'Something's wrong.' But almost as she said it, Val seemed to loop crazily for a moment, regain her balance, and then she began weaving as all of them watched, and suddenly she fell just before the end of the slope; she fell sideways and her bindings released, but she lay face down in the snow, as Mel rushed to where she lay and Peter followed. He knelt quickly beside the unconscious girl, pulled her eyelids up, looked at her eyes, felt her pulse, and looked at Mel, unable to comprehend what had happened to her.

'She's in shock.' Without saying more, he unzipped his jacket and put it on her, and by reflex Jess did the same and handed hers to Peter, as the others stared at her in disbelief and Jess knelt beside her and held her hand. Peter looked around the group, hoping that the ski patrol would see them soon. 'Does anyone know what happened? Did she have a bad fall, hit her head? Could she have broken something? Even a bad sprain?' Mark was strangely silent and Pam shook her head as Matt began to cry and clung to Mel. And then suddenly Mel gave a shout as she watched her daughter's inert form; there was a huge red stain spreading up from where her trouser legs met, and even the snow around her was red.

'Peter, oh my God ...' She pulled off her gloves and touched Val's face; it was like ice, but it was a cold that came from within.

Peter looked at his wife, and then down at his stepdaughter. 'She's having a haemorrhage.' Mercifully at that moment the ski patrol arrived, and two powerful young men wearing red and white arm bands knelt beside Peter.

'Bad fall?'

No, I'm a doctor. She's having a haemorrhage. How fast can you get a stretcher for her?' One of them pulled out a small walkie-talkie and gave a red alert and their exact location.

'It should be here pretty quickly.' And almost before he had finished speaking, a stretcher on a sled appeared in the distance, with two men skiing with it. Mel was kneeling beside Val, her own jacket on top of the unconscious girl now, and she could see that in spite of their efforts her lips were turning blue. Mel eyed Peter frantically.

'Can't you do anything?' They were eyes filled with tears and accusations, and he looked at Mel almost with desperation. If they lost her, Mel would never forgive him. But he was absolutely helpless.

'We have to stop the bleeding, and get her a transfusion as quickly as we can.' He turned to the boy from the ski patrol then. 'How close is the nearest first-aid station?' The patrolman pointed to the very foot of the hill. It was barely more than a minute from where they stood. 'Have you got plasma?'

'Yes, sir.' Val was already on the sled, and she had left a huge puddle of blood in the snow behind her, as the whole family followed the sled to the little shelter.

Peter turned to Mel again. 'What's her blood type?'

'O, positive.'

Jessie was crying softly by then, as was Pam, and Mark looked as though he would be the next one in need of the sled. They unloaded Val as quickly as they could and carried her inside. There was a trained nurse there, and a doctor had been called. He was out on the slopes, bringing down a man with a broken leg, but Peter quickly propped Val's hips higher than her head, and the nurse helped him pull off her clothes as the others stood by. They began the plasma and an I.V., but Val showed no sign of coming round, and Mel's face was grim and filled with terror.

'My God, Peter ...' There seemed to be blood everywhere and she turned to Jess suddenly, remembering Matthew, staring wide-eyed at his stepsister. 'Pam, take your brother outside.' She nodded dumbly and left as Mark and Jessica stood by, clinging to each other with a vicelike grip, as Peter and the nurse fought to save Val's life and Mel watched.

The doctor arrived only minutes later, and added his efforts to Peter's. An ambulance had been called, and they had to get her to the hospital at once, it was obviously a gynaecological haemorrhage, but there was no way of knowing how it had started or why.

'Does anyone know ...' The doctor began, and Mark stunned them all by stepping forward and speaking in a trembling voice.

'She had an abortion on Tuesday.'

'She what?' Mel felt the room spin around her as she stared at Mark and then Peter. He caught her just before she fell. The nurse brought smelling salts, and the doctor continued to work on Val. But it was obvious that only surgery would stop the bleeding, and even that wasn't sure now. She had lost massive amounts of blood, and Peter looked at his son in horror.

'Who in God's name did this?'

Tears stood out in Mark's eyes and his voice trembled hideously as he faced his father. 'We didn't want to go to anyone you knew, and that ruled out just about everyone in LA. Val wanted to go to a clinic. We went to one in West LA.'

'Oh, for chrissake ... do you realise they may have killed her?' Peter was shouting in the tiny room and Mel began to sob as Jess clung to her mother.

'She's going to die ... oh my God ... she's going to die ...' Jessica had totally lost control at the sight of her dying twin, and it brought Mel to her senses to see what was happening around her.

She spoke to Jess in a brutal voice, and hers was the only voice one heard in the tiny shelter. 'She's not going to die, do you hear me? She's not going to die!' She said it as much to God as to those in the shelter. And she glanced from Mark to Jess in sudden fury. 'Why in hell didn't any of you tell me?' There was only silence as she looked at Mark. It would have been too much to expect of them, to tell her, and then she turned to Jess. 'And you! You knew!' It was a vicious accusation.

'I guessed. They never told me.' But her tone was as filled with fury as her mother's. 'And what difference would it have made if we had told you? You're always too busy with your job and your husband, and Pam and Matt. You might as well have left us in New York, you might as well – ' But she was silenced by a sharp crack across the face from her mother which sent her sobbing into the corner. The shriek of the ambulance suddenly echoed in the distance, and a moment later they were busy bundling Val into it, with two attendants and Mel beside her.

Peter spoke quickly to his wife. 'I'll follow you in the van.' He ran outside, leaving all their skis at the shelter. They could come back later, that was the least of their problems now. He started the engine, and the others silently hopped in. Jess and Mark beside him in the front, and Pam and Matthew in the back. No one said a word as they drove to the hospital in Truckee. It was Peter who first broke the silence.

'You should have told me, Mark.' It was a quiet voice in the silent car, and he could only begin to imagine what his son was going through.

'I know. Dad, will she make it?' His voice trembled and there were tears pouring down his face.

'I think so, if they get her there quickly. She's lost a lot of blood, but the plasma will help.' Jessica sat between them in stony silence, the mark of her mother's hand still on her face, and then Peter looked down at her, and touched her knee with one hand. 'She'll be all right, Jess. It looks worse than it is. It's impressive as hell when you see a lot of blood like that.' Jessica nodded and said nothing. And when they reached the hospital in Truckee, they all piled out of the car, but the young people got no farther than the waiting room. Peter and Mel went inside with Val while they prepped her, and Peter opted not to scrub and watch the surgery so he could stay with Mel while they waited. A gynaecological surgeon had been called, and Peter assumed he knew what he was doing. They were told only that she was in grave danger, and that there was a possibility that a hysterectomy would have to be performed. They wouldn't know till they got inside how bad the damage was. Mel nodded dumbly and Peter led her outside to wait with the others. She stayed noticeably away from Mark, and Jess kept her distance from her, and after a while, Peter went to his oldest son and gave him twenty dollars and told him to take the others to the cafeteria and get something to eat. Mark nodded and left, with the rest of the group in tow, but none of them was hungry. All they could think of was Val on the operating-room table. When they were gone, Mel turned to Peter with tears streaming from her eyes and sank onto his chest with a wail of despair. It was a scene he saw every day in the halls of Center City, but now it was happening to them ... to Mel ... to Val, and he had the same feeling he had had when Anne had died, of being utterly helpless. At least now he could help Mel. He held her tight in his arms, and made soft soothing noises.

'She'll be all right, Mel ... she'll be –'.

'What if she can never have babies?' Mel was sobbing uncontrollably in his arms.

'Then at least she'll be alive and we'll have her.' That would be something to be grateful for at least.

'Why didn't she tell me?'

'They were afraid to, I guess. They wanted to work it out for themselves.' It had been admirable but foolish.

'But she's only sixteen.'

'I know, Mel ... I know ...' He had suspected a while before that she and Mark had finally made love, but he hadn't wanted to say anything to upset Mel. And he realised now that he should have had a talk with Mark. He sat thinking about it all as they came back from the cafeteria and Mark slowly approached Mel and his father. Mel looked up at him miserably and continued to cry and he sat down and looked at her in as much pain as she.

'I don't know what to say ... I'm sorry ... I ... I never thought ... I would never have let her ...' He bowed his head in lonely grief as the sobs racked him, and Peter's heart went out to him as he took him in his arms with Mel, and suddenly Mel and Mark were clinging to each other and crying, and then Jessica was there too, and Pam and Matthew. It was a hideous scene, and the doctor came out and looked at them with a groan. Peter saw him first and disengaged himself from the others. He went to speak to the surgeon quietly, as Mel watched with terrified eyes.

'How did it go?'

The surgeon nodded, and Mel held her breath. 'She was lucky. We didn't have to remove her uterus. She just had a monstrous haemorrhage, but there's no permanent damage. I wouldn't suggest she try an abortion again though.' Peter nodded. Hopefully not.

'Thank you.' He extended a hand, and the two surgeons shook hands.

'I was told you're a doctor.'

'I am. Cardiac surgery. We're from LA.' The other surgeon narrowed his eyes, clapped a hand to his head and grinned.

'Oh, yes. I know who you are. You're Hallam!' He was so excited he could hardly stand it. And then he laughed. 'I'm glad I didn't know that before we went in. I'd have been a nervous wreck.'

'You shouldn't. I couldn't have done what you just did.'

'Well, I'm glad to have helped.' He shook Peter's hand again. 'Honoured.' Peter knew then that there would be no bill, and he was sorry, the man had done a fine job and he had saved Val's life and the lives of her future children, and maybe even Mark's. He wondered if this would end the romance now, or if it would pull them together closer. It had certainly pulled the family together in the last hour, and as they sat and waited for Val to come out of the anaesthetic, they began to come alive again. They talked and joked a little, but the atmosphere was generally subdued. It had been a heavy dose of reality for them all to live through. And before Val ever woke up, he took Pam and Matthew back to the condo. Mark and Jess had insisted on staying with Mel, and they wanted to see Val, but the other two looked worse than Val by then. Peter had insisted on taking them home no matter how much they protested.

'We want to see Val,' Matthew whined.

'They won't let you, and it's late, Matt.' His father was gentle but firm. 'You'll see her tomorrow, if it's allowed.'

'I want to see her tonight.' He led him outside and Pam followed with a last look at the others, and when Peter returned Val had just woken up and was back in her room, but she was too groggy to understand what they said to her. She just smiled and drifted off and when she saw Mark, she reached for his hand and whispered, 'I'm sorry ... I ...' And then she went back to sleep, and an hour later they all left and went back to the condo. It was almost midnight and everyone was exhausted.

Mel kissed Jessie goodnight and held her close for a long moment before she went to bed, and Jessica looked at her mother with sad eyes. 'I'm sorry I said what I did.'

'Maybe some of it was true. Maybe I have been too busy with the others.'

'There are a lot of us now, and there's a lot of pressure on you. I know that, Mom ...' Her voice drifted off, remembering another time, another place ... when they didn't have to share quite as much as they did now.

'That's no excuse, Jess. I'll try to do better from now on.' But how much better could she do? How many more hours were there in a day? How could she give each one what they needed, do her job, and even have time to breathe? She was a mother of five now, and the wife of an illustrious surgeon, not to mention co-anchor-woman on a TV news show. It barely left her time to breathe. And her daughter had accused her of being more interested in her stepchildren than in her own. Maybe she was trying too hard to please them all. She kissed Mark goodnight too, and then fell into bed with Peter, but as tired as she was, she couldn't sleep. She lay awake for hours thinking of what Jess had said, and of Val lying in the snow covered with blood. Peter felt her shudder beside him.

'I'll never forgive myself for not knowing what was going on.'

'You can't know everything, Mel. They're almost grown-up people now.'

'That's not what you said today. You said they were as grown up as Matthew.'

'Maybe I was wrong.' It had shocked him to realise that his son had almost become a father. But Mark had turned eighteen in August. In truth, he was a man. 'I know they're young, and they're too young to be doing what they are, making love, and getting pregnant and having abortions, but it happens, Mel.' He sat up on one elbow and looked down at his wife. 'They tried to work it out, you have to give them credit for that.' She wasn't ready to give them credit for a damn thing, nor herself.

'Some of what Jessie said was true, you know. I've been so involved with you, and Pam and Matthew, I haven't had much time for them.'

'You have five children now, and a job, and a bigger house to run, and me. Just how much can you expect of yourself, Mel?'

'More, I guess.' But she was exhausted at the thought.

'How much more can you do?'

'I don't know. But apparently I'm not doing enough, or this would never have happened to Val. I should have seen what was going on. I should have known, without being told.'

'What do you want to do? Play policeman? Give up your job, so you can drive car pools?'

It wasn't a very appealing thought, and they both knew it, but a little while later Mel answered in a small voice. 'That's what Anne did though, isn't it?'

'Yes, but you and she are different women, Mel. And I don't think she ever really felt fulfilled, if you want to know the truth. The difference is that you do. It makes you a happier person.' It was a nice thing to have said, and she turned to him with a smile as they lay in the dark, with only the moonlight outside, casting soft shadows on them.

'You know, you make me feel better, Peter. About a lot of things. Most of all myself.'

'I hope I do. You make me feel better about me. I always feel that you respect what I do.' He took a deep breath. 'Anne never really approved of what I did.' He looked at Mel with a small smile. 'She thought transplants were disgusting and wrong. Her mother had been a Christian Scientist, and she always had a basic distrust of the medical profession.'

'That must have been hard on you.' He had never told her before, and she was intrigued by the information.

'It was. I never fully felt I had her approval.'

'You have mine, you know, Peter.'

'I know that. And it means a lot to me. I think that was one of the first things I liked about you. I respected you, and I could feel that you respected me.' He smiled and kissed the tip of her nose. 'And then I fell in love with your sexy legs and here we are.'

She laughed softly in the darkness, amazed at how strange life was at times. Only hours before she had been hysterical, sure that she was about to lose her daughter, and now they were lying in the dark exchanging confidences and talking. But she realised something that she hadn't been aware of before. She and Peter had become friends over the past few months, best friends, and she had never been as close to anyone, woman or man. He had broken through the walls she had built over the years, and she hadn't even noticed. 'I love you, Peter Hallam, much, much more than you know.' And with that, she yawned, and fell asleep in his arms, and when he looked down at her, he saw that she was smiling.

Chapter 29

Peter took Mark and Jess and Matthew home on Sunday night, and Mel stayed in Truckee with Val. They gave up the condo and she took a room in a motel, and walked to the hospital every day, and on Wednesday the doctor said Val could fly home with her mother. Surprisingly, it was a nice time for both of them, and they talked to each other as they hadn't in years, about life, about boys, about Mark, about sex, about marriage and Peter, and Mel's life. When they landed in Los Angeles on Wednesday night, Mel felt that she knew Val as she never had before. And she only wished that she had that kind of time with them more often, without having to go through the trauma that they had just endured.

Val seemed in pretty good shape mentally as well. She felt terrible about having done away with an unborn child, but she had decided that having a baby at sixteen would have ruined her life and Mel couldn't disagree with her. It would have changed her whole life, and forced her into a lasting relationship with Mark, which may not have been what she would want later. She had admitted to her mother that she was ready to let go of him for a while, and see other boys. The intensity of their relationship scared her, and she didn't want the same thing to happen again. Mel was pleased with her conclusions, and maybe it had been a costly lesson that would serve her well for the rest of her life. She would never be cavalier about birth control, or getting involved in a sexual relationship without giving it serious thought. But she was sorry that she had to go through such misery. She had described the abortion to Mel, and Mel was astounded by her courage, and she told her as much.

'I don't think I could have done it.'

'I didn't feel like I had a choice. And Mark was there.' She tried to shrug it off, but they both knew she never would. Mel had held her close and they had cried, as Val told her.

'I'm sorry, baby.'

'Me too, Mom ... I'm sorry ...' She returned to LA contrite, and Mel noticed that night at dinner that she treated Mark more like a brother now, and he didn't seem to mind. There had already been a subtle change between them, and it was for the best. Peter had noticed it too, and mentioned it to Mel that night. 'I know.' She nodded. 'I think the big romance is over.'

'That's just as well.' Peter smiled tiredly. He had had a long day, and been in surgery for five hours that morning. He had come back to real life and a mountain of work waiting for him at Center City. 'We can let him loose on the neighbourhood now and wish him luck. I never realised what an agony it was to have daughters.' Even though he had done his share of worrying about Pam, but not in quite the same way as one worried about Val. It was that damn body of hers that worried one so. 'It's a damn shame she's not ugly.'

Mel grinned. 'Tell me about it. I've been getting grey hair over it for years.'

But by the next day she was back to getting grey hair in the newsroom. Paul Stevens had created all kinds of chaos while she was gone. She had called in sick for three days, and when she came back on Thursday morning, he had done everything he could to sabotage her. Fortunately, the producer knew what Stevens had in mind, that he hated Mel with a passion, so he hadn't done any real damage. But it was depressing to hear the gossip he had circulated about her, and to hear the trouble he had tried to create, by claiming she was hailed as a royal bitch in New York, and everyone there had hated her guts, that she had slept her way to the top, and any other bit of filth he could think of. Mel reported it all to Peter that night, and he was livid for her.

'Why, that little sonofabitch ...' He had clenched a fist and Mel smiled tiredly at his reaction.

'He really is a bastard.'

'I'm sorry you have to go through that.'

'So am I. But there it is.'

'Why does he hate you so much?'

'Mainly, the difference in money, and also because he doesn't want to share the limelight. He hadn't had a co-anchor in years and he doesn't want one. Neither have I, but I figure you have to adapt to the situation. I'd like nothing better than to get rid of him, but I figure that it's not worth the aggravation.'

'Too bad he doesn't figure the same thing.'

'Isn't that the truth.'

And on and on it went for the next month, so much so that Mel began to feel ill most of the time. She had headaches, and a knot in her stomach that never went away, and she began to dread going to the station. She did as many interviews as she could, just to get away, but nowadays she was also trying to spend more time with the girls, particularly the twins. Jessica's speech hadn't gone unheeded at the time of Val's abortion. She had accused her mother of being more interested in Peter's children than them and now she was trying to shift the balance. But she sensed that Pam seemed to feel put aside, and she noticed her ganging up on her with Mrs Hahn whenever she could, and to alleviate that, Mel attempted to include Pam with the twins whenever possible, but it was difficult to keep everyone happy, and lately she had been feeling so lousy that it was difficult to meet their needs and hers too. She was out shopping with Matt one day when she actually had to sit down and catch her breath. She was so dizzy and nauseous that she thought she was going to faint in Safeway. She made him promise not to tell his father, but he was so upset he told Jess, who immediately told Peter when he came home. He glanced thoughtfully at Mel over dinner and then questioned her about it that night.

'You sick, Mel?'

'No, why?' She turned away so he wouldn't see her face.

'I don't know. A little bird told me that you didn't feel so hot today.' He was looking worriedly at her when she turned around.

'And what did the little bird say?' She wanted to feel out how much Peter knew.

'That you almost fainted at the grocery store.' He pulled her down on the bed next to him and looked closely at her. 'Is that true, Mel?'

'More or less.'

'What's wrong?'

She sighed and stared at the floor and then back at him. 'That Paul Stevens has been driving me crazy. I think I might have an ulcer, and I've been feeling lousy for the past few weeks.'

Peter looked at her unhappily. 'Mel, will you promise me you'll have it checked out?'

'Yeah,' she sighed, but she didn't sound sure. 'I really don't have time though.'

He grabbed her arm. 'Make time then.' He had lost one wife, and couldn't bear the thought of losing another. 'I mean it, Mel! Either that or I'll check you in the hospital myself.'

'Don't be silly. I just got dizzy.'

'Had you eaten?'

'Not in a while.'

'Then it might have been that. But I want you to check it out anyway.' And he noticed now that she had lost weight, her face was drawn and she looked pale. 'You look like hell.'

'Gee, thanks.'

He leaned over and took her hand. 'I'm just worried about you, Mel.' He pulled her close. 'I love you so damn much. Now will you call tomorrow and have someone check you out?'

'Okay, okay.' And the next morning he gave her a list of names, of doctors and specialists. 'You want me to see all of them?' She looked horrified and he smiled.

'One or two will do. Why don't you start with Sam Jones, and let him figure out who else you should see.'

'Why don't you just check me into the Mayo Clinic for a week?' She was teasing but he was not amused. She looked even worse than she had the night before.

'I just might.'

'The hell you will.'

She made an appointment with Sam Jones for that afternoon. It would have been a four-week wait, except that when she told the nurse who she was, miraculously, they found a spot for her that day. She stopped in at two p.m., and she had to be at work by four. Jones used every minute that he could, to take blood, do urine tests, go over her, take down a history, listen to her lungs, take her blood pressure. She felt as though he had touched and prodded every inch of her by the time he was through.

'Well, so far, you look all right to me. Tired maybe, but basically healthy. But let's see what all the lab tests say. Have you been feeling run-down for very long?' She told him all the symptoms she'd had, the queasiness, headaches, the pressure she was under at work, the move from New York, the change of jobs, Val's abortion, getting married, and adjusting to a whole new set of kids, while living with the ghost of Peter's late wife, in the house she still didn't feel at home in.

'Stop!' He fell back in his chair with a groan, clapping a hand to his head. 'I'm beginning to feel queasy too. I think you've just given your own diagnosis, my friend. I don't think you needed me at all. You need six weeks on a sandy beach.'

She smiled at him. 'I wish. But I told Peter all it was was nerves.'

'You may be right.' He offered her Valium, Librium, or sleeping pills and she declined them all. When she saw Peter that night, she told him what Sam Jones had said.

'See, there's nothing wrong with me. I'm just overworked.' They both knew that anyway, but he still wasn't convinced. He was inclined to be overly cautious about her, and Mel knew that.

'Let's see what the lab tests say.'

She rolled her eyes and went to put Matthew to bed. Pam was listening to her stereo, and the girls were doing homework in their room. Mark was out. The grapevine had told Mel a few days before that he had a new girlfriend, a freshman at UCLA, and Val didn't seem bothered at all. There was a boy in her class she said was 'really cute', and Jessica had finally found someone she liked who had taken her out on two dates. All was well with all of them for once. She returned to Peter with a happy sigh. 'All's quiet on the Western Front at least.' She reported on them all and he was pleased. Things were finally settling down after all, or so he thought. But neither of them was prepared for the news they got the next day.

Mel forgot to call Dr Jones before she left for work, and there was a message for her to call him at home when she got in. Peter saw the message first and called Sam himself, but his old colleague and friend would say nothing at all to him. 'Have your wife call me when she gets home, Pete.'

'For chrissake, Sam, what's wrong?' He was terrified but Jones would not relent, and Peter pounced on Mel the moment she walked through the door. 'Call Jones!'

'Now? Why? I just walked in, can I at least hang up my coat?'

'For chrissake, Mel ...'

'Jesus.' She looked at the worried look in his eyes, wondering what he wasn't telling her. 'What's wrong?'

'I don't know. He won't tell me a thing.'

'Did you call him?' She looked annoyed.

He confessed. 'Yes. but he wouldn't tell me anything.'

'Good.'

'For chrissake ...'

'All right, all right.' She dialled the home number he had left, and Mrs Jones went to get her husband. Peter hovered over Mel but she waved him away. She and the doctor went through the usual small talk before getting down to why he had called her.

'I didn't want to tell Peter before I told you.' He sounded serious and Mel held her breath. Maybe Peter was right. Maybe something awful was wrong with her. 'You're pregnant, Mel, but I thought you'd like to tell him that yourself.' He was beaming at his end, but Mel was not at hers. She wore a glazed expression and Peter stared at her, convinced it was bad news. He sank slowly into a chair and waited until she hung up.

'Well?'

It was difficult to fend him off. He was just sitting there, watching.

'What did he say?'

'Nothing much.'

'Bullshit!' Peter leapt to his feet in the front hall. 'I saw your face. Now are you going to tell me yourself or am I going to call him back?'

'He won't tell you a thing.'

'The hell he won't.' Peter was beginning to steam, and Mel felt as though she were in shock. She stared at him and stood up.

'Could we go in your study and talk?' He said not a word but followed her in and shut the door. She sat down again and stared at him. 'I don't understand it.'

'Tell me what he said, and I'll try and explain it to you, Mel, but for God's sake tell me what's wrong.'

And this time, she smiled. He was expecting complicated results, but there was nothing complicated about what Jones had told her. The only thing complicated about it was what it was going to do to her life. 'I'm pregnant.'

'You're what?' He stared at her in disbelief. 'You're not?'

'I am.'

And suddenly he grinned. 'Well, I'll be damned. You are?'

'I am.' She looked as though she'd just been run over by a train, and he came to her side and pulled her into his arms.

'That's the best news I've had in years.'

'It is?' She still looked shocked.

'Hell, yes.'

'For chrissake, Peter, that's all we need. We're already drowning in the responsibilities we have. And a baby? Now? I'm thirty-six years old, we have five children between the two of us ...' She was horrified at the thought, and he looked crushed.

He tried to sound matter-of-fact as he asked, 'Will you abort it?'

She stared into space remembering what Val had said about going to the abortion clinic with Mark. 'I don't know. I don't know if I could.'

'Then there's no decision to be made, is there?'

'You make it sound awfully simple.' She stared at him unhappily. 'But it isn't as simple as all that.'

'Sure it is. You have a maternity clause in your contract. You told me so.'

'Christ. I forgot.' And then she began to laugh as she remembered how amused she had been at that. And suddenly it all seemed very funny to her. She began to laugh and laugh and laugh and Peter kissed her cheek and took a bottle of champagne from the bar. He popped the cork, and poured a glass for each of them and toasted her.

'To us.' and then, 'To our baby.'

She took a sip and set it down again rapidly. It made her queasy almost at once. 'I can't.' She literally turned green before his eyes, and he set down his own glass and came to her.

'Sweetheart, are you all right?'

'I'm fine.' She smiled and leaned against him, still unable to believe the irony of it all. 'I have daughters who are almost seventeen, and I'm pregnant. Would you believe ..' She began to laugh again. 'I can't even figure out how it happened, unless you put a hole in my diaphragm.'

'Who cares? Look at it as a gift.' He looked soberly at his wife. 'Mel, I deal with death every day of the week. I fight it, I hate it, I try to outsmart it by putting plastic hearts in people's chests, pig's valves, and valves from sheep, I do transplants, I do anything I can to cheat that old boy death always watching over me. And here you are, with a precious gift of life, given to us gratuitously. It would be criminal not to appreciate that.'

She nodded quietly, touched by what he had said. What right did she have to question such a gift? 'What'll we tell the kids?'

'That we're having a baby, and we're thrilled. Hell, I thought you were sick.'

'So did I.' She smiled, feeling better again now that the champagne was far from her lips. 'I'm glad I'm not.'

'Not half as glad as I am, Mel. I couldn't live without you.'

'Well, you won't even have to try.' And with that, Matthew came and pounded on the door to announce that it was dinnertime and before they went into the dining room to eat, Peter called them all into the living room and made a little speech.

'We have something exciting to tell you all.' Peter beamed and looked at Mel.

'We're going to Disneyland next week!' Matt filled in and everyone laughed and began to offer their best guess. Mark thought they were building a tennis court, Pam thought they were buying a yacht, the twins decided on a Rolls-Royce, and a trip to Honolulu, an idea of which everyone approved, and each time Peter shook his head.

'Nope. Not quite. Although Honolulu does sound nice. Maybe at Easter time. But we have something much more important to tell you than that.'

'Come on, Dad, what is it?' Matthew was dying to know, and Peter looked straight at him.

'We're having a baby, Matt.' He looked at them all, and Mel watched their faces too, but they were no more prepared for the reactions they got from the kids than they had been for the test results from Sam Jones.

'You're what?' Pam leapt to her feet, clearly horrified, and she stared at Mel in disbelief. 'That's the most disgusting thing I've ever heard.' And with that she burst into tears and fled to her room, as Matthew looked at them with trembling lip.

'We don't need another kid around here. We've already got five.'

'But it might make a nice friend for you, Matt.' Peter looked at him as tears filled the child's eyes. 'The others are so much older than you are.'

'I like it like that.' He followed his sister to his room, and Mel turned to her own children, to see Val dissolve in tears.

'Don't expect me to be pleased for you, Mom.' She stood up and her copious bosom heaved. 'I just killed my baby two months ago, and now I suppose you expect me to be pleased about yours?' She ran from the room in tears, and Mark shrugged, but he didn't seem to think it was much of an idea either. Jessica simply stared at them, stricken. It was as though she knew how much they already had on their backs, and couldn't understand how they could even consider taking on more. And the worst of it was that Mel thought she was right. She went upstairs with the excuse of checking on her twin and Mark disappeared too. They sat alone in the living room, as Mel wiped tears from her own eyes.

'Well, so much for that.'

'They'll come round.' He put an arm around his wife, and looked up to see Hilda Hahn staring at them.

'The dinner is getting cold.' She looked fierce, and Mel stood up, obviously depressed. The children were all in an uproar at the prospect of another child, and she was still having problems at work. Somehow it all seemed like more than she could cope with right now, and they went in to dinner, as Mel felt her heart drag. And she looked up to see Mrs Hahn staring at her.

'I couldn't help overhearing the news.' Her heavy German accent always grated on Mel's nerves, there was nothing warm or kindly about the way she spoke, unlike the other German women Mel had known. And she stared at Mel again now. 'Isn't it dangerous to have a baby at your age?'

'Not at all' – Mel smiled sweetly – 'I'm only fifty-two.' Knowing full well that Mrs Hahn was fifty-one. Peter smiled at her. Anything that Mel did now was okay with him. And he didn't give a damn how their kids behaved, he was thrilled and he wanted Mel to know it. But she couldn't eat dinner, all she could think of was the children and their reactions. She went up to see them, but all doors were closed and nowhere did she get a warm reception. When she came downstairs to their bedroom, Peter insisted that she lie down, and she laughed at him. 'I'm only about four or five weeks pregnant, for chrissake.'

'Never mind. You might as well start out right.'

'I think we did that in the living room about two hours ago.' She sighed as she lay on their bed. 'That was some reception we got, wasn't it?' Their reactions had cut her to the quick, and left her feeling unprotected and unwanted and alone.

'Give them a chance. The only ones who really have grounds to be upset are Val and Matt, and I'm sure they'll both survive the shock.'

'Poor Matt.' Mel smiled thinking of him. 'He wants to be our baby, and I don't blame him a bit.'

'Maybe it'll be a girl.' Peter looked thrilled and Mel groaned.

'Not another one. We already have three.' She was already adjusting to the idea and the miracle of it seemed remarkable to her. They talked about it that night for hours, and he kissed her tenderly the next morning before he left. But when she went down to breakfast and saw Matt and Pam and the twins, she felt as though she had ventured into the enemy camp. She looked around at them and felt despair wash over her. They would never adjust.

'I'm sorry you all feel this way.' Val wouldn't look her in the face, and Jess looked intensely depressed, Matthew wouldn't touch anything on his plate, and when Mel looked into Pam's eyes she was terrified by what she saw there – hatred and fury mixed with terror. It was as though she had run away to a distant place in her head where Mel could no longer reach her.

Of all of them, Pam was by far the most upset. Mel tried to talk to her about it that day when she came home from school, but when Mel went up to her room, she slammed the door in her face, and locked the door. Even when Mel pounded on it, she wouldn't open it again.

Theirs became a house filled with grief, and hurt and anger. It was as though they each wanted to punish her, each in their own way, Mark by never being home, to his father's despair, the twins by keeping away from her and shutting her out, Matt by whining all the time and having trouble at school, and Pam by turning off and skipping school. They called Mel four times in as many weeks that Pam had disappeared before her second class, and when she questioned the child about it, she shrugged and went upstairs and locked her door. Her final

act of viciousness was to hang her mother's portrait boldly over the bed in
Mel and Peter's room. When Mel came home one day and saw it there, she
gasped and stared.

'Did you see her do this?' she asked Mrs Hahn, as she held the portrait of
Anne in trembling hands.

'I see nothing, Mrs Hallam.' But Mel knew that she had. When they called
Mel from Pam's school again to tell her that she had cut class again, she
decided to stay home that day and wait for her to turn up. But by four
o'clock she still had not. And this time Mel began to wonder if there was a
boy involved. At five o'clock, she sauntered in with a grin on her face,
amused that Mel had waited for her all day long, and when Mel took a good
look at her, she could see that the girl was stoned. She sent her to her room
after confronting her, then left for the newsroom. Later, she told Peter what
she thought.

'I really doubt that, Mel. She's never done that before.'

'Take my word for it.' But he shook his head. He didn't believe his wife,
and when he questioned Pam, she denied everything Mel said. Pam was
beginning to cause a serious rift between them, and Mel felt she was losing
her only ally now. Peter always took Pam's side against her. Her home was
filled with enemies, and it wasn't even her home, and now Peter was on his
daughter's side. 'Peter, I know that she was stoned.'

'I just don't think she was.'

'I think you should talk to her school.' When Mel attempted to discuss it
with Val and Jess, they were distant but polite. They didn't want to get
involved, nor did Mark. Mel was a pariah now, to all of them, because of the
unborn child she was carrying. She had betrayed them.

And two weeks later when the L.A.P.D. called, it was an empty victory.
She had been right. Pam had been caught buying a lid of grass from some kids
downtown when she should have been in school. Peter went right through
the roof and threatened to send her to boarding school, but again the child
turned on Mel. 'You turned him against me. You want me sent away.'

'I want no such thing. But I want you to behave, and I think it's about time
you did, time you stopped cutting school every other day, and smoking
grass, and behaving like a little beast around this house. This is your home
and we love you, but you can't behave any way you want. In every society,
in every community, in every home, there are rules.'

But as usual, Peter let Pam off the hook, put her on restriction for a week
and let it go at that. He didn't back the position Mel took, and two weeks
later, Pam was picked up again. This time she got even more attention than
before, and Peter called up her old psychiatrist. A series of appointments
were set up and he asked Mel if she could get Pam there. And the result of
that was that Mel had to almost drag her there four times a week, break her
neck to get to work, and run home again at night, trying to pay some
attention to Matt and the twins. All she wanted to do was sleep, between
throwing up the heavy meals persistently prepared by Mrs Hahn.

'This is what the doctor likes,' she'd say as she put another plate of sauer-
kraut in front of Mel, and finally after a month of it, she wound up in the

hospital one Friday night with bleeding and cramps, and her obstetrician looked at her soberly.

'If you don't slow down, you're going to lose the baby, Mel.'

Tears filled her eyes. Everything was a fight these days. 'I don't think anyone would give a damn.'

'Would you?'

She nodded her head, tired, sad. 'Yeah, I'm beginning to think I would.'

'Then you better tell everyone around you to shape up.'

Peter came to see her the next day, and looked mournfully at her. 'You don't really want the baby, do you, Mel?'

'Do you think I'm trying to get rid of it?'

'That's what Pam says. She says you went horseback riding last week.'

'*What*? Are you crazy? Do you think I'd do that?'

'I don't know. I know this interferes with your work, or you think it will.' She stared at him in disbelief, got out of bed, and packed her bag. 'Where are you going?'

She turned to look at him. 'Home. To kick your daughter.'

'Mel, come on ... please ...' But she checked out of the hospital, and went home, climbed into bed, despite all of Peter's apologies, and that afternoon she went downstairs and ordered Mrs Hahn to make chicken and rice that night, something *she* could eat for a change, and she literally lay in wait until all of the children came home. By six o'clock they were all there, surprised to see her again. And when they came downstairs to eat, she was waiting at the table, with eyes of fire.

'Good evening, Pam.' She started with her. 'How was your day?'

'Fine.' She attempted to look confident, but she kept glancing nervously at Mel. 'I understand that you told your father I went horseback riding last week. Is that true?' There was dead silence in the room. 'I repeat. Is that true?'

Her voice was low. 'No.'

'I can't hear you, Pam.'

'No!' She shouted at Mel, and Peter reached for his wife's arm.

'Mel, please, don't upset yourself ...'

Mel looked him right in the eye. 'We need to clear the air. Did you hear what she said?'

'I did.'

Mel turned back to Pam. 'Why did you tell your father a lie? Did you want to make trouble for us?' Pam shrugged. 'Why, Pam?' She reached out and touched the girl's hand. 'Because I'm having a baby? Is that so awful that you have to punish me? Well, I'll tell you something, no matter how many babies we have, we'll still love you.' She saw Pam's eyes fill with tears while Peter kept his grip on her arm. 'But if you don't knock off the trouble you've been pulling ever since I moved in, I'm going to kick your behind from here to the other side of town.' Pam smiled through her tears and looked at Mel.

'Would you really do that?' She sounded almost pleased. It told her they cared about her, still.

'I would.'

Mel looked around the rest of the table then. 'And that goes for the rest of you too.' She softened her voice as she looked at Matt. 'You're always going to be our baby, Matt. This one will never take your place.' But he didn't look as though he believed her. Then she turned to the twins. 'And you two.' She looked specifically at Val. 'I didn't plan the timing of this to hurt you, Val. I couldn't know what was going to happen any more than you planned what happened to you, and the two of you have been totally insensitive about how I feel, and I think it's lousy of you.' She turned to Mark then, 'And frankly, Mark, I'm surprised to see you here tonight. We don't seem to see much of you any more. Did you run out of funds so you had to eat here for a change?'

'Yeah.' He grinned.

'Well, I think you ought to keep in mind that as long as you're living at home, you have a responsibility to this family to be here more than once a month. We expect to see a little more of you than we have lately.'

He looked startled by what she said, and subdued as Peter watched. 'Yes, ma'am.'

'And Pam' – Peter's only girl looked at her cautiously 'from now on you take yourself to the psychiatrist. You can take the bus just like everyone else. I'm not going to drive you all over town. If you want to see him, you can get there by yourself, but I'm not going to drag you there by the hair. You're almost fifteen years old. It's time you took some responsibility for yourself.'

'Do I have to take the bus home from school?' Matt piped up hopefully. He loved the bus, but Mel smiled and shook her head.

'No, you don't.' She looked around the table then. 'I hope I've made myself clear to all of you. For your own reasons, you've all behaved like little beasts since your father and I told you that I was pregnant, and personally I think it stinks. I can't change what you feel, but I can change how you act, and I'm not willing to accept the way you've been treating me, all of you' – her eyes even took in Mrs Hahn – 'there's room for everyone here, for you, for me, for your father, this baby, but we have to be nice to each other. And I'm not going to let you go on punishing me' – tears suddenly sprang to her eyes and overflowed – 'for this unborn child.' And with that she threw down her napkin and went upstairs, not having touched a morsel of food, but at least she had proved a point with that too, and Mrs Hahn had actually produced salad, and roasted chicken, and rice. Peter looked around at all of them. They looked embarrassed and, subdued, as well they should have, and they knew it.

'She's right, you know. You've all been rotten to her.' Pam tried to stare him down, but it didn't work, and Mark squirmed uncomfortably in his seat, as Val hung her head. 'I didn't mean to ...'

Jess spoke up too. 'Yes, you did. We all did. We were mad at her.'

'It isn't fair to take it out on her like that.'

'It's okay, Dad. We'll be good now.' Matt patted his father's arm and they all smiled, and a few minutes later Peter took a plate up to their room where she lay crying on the bed.

'Come on, sweetheart, don't get so upset. I brought you something to eat.'

'I don't want to eat. I feel sick.'

'You shouldn't get excited like that, it's bad for you.' She turned around to look at him in disbelief.

'Bad for me? Do you ever think how bad for me it is to have everyone in this house treat me like dirt?'

'They'll shape up now.' She didn't answer him. 'And you shouldn't be so hard on them, Mel. They're just kids.'

She narrowed her eyes and looked at him. 'I don't count Matt because he's six years old and he has a right to be mad about this, but the others are practically adults, and they've stomped all over me for the past month. Pam even told you a blatant lie so that you'd think I was trying to lose our child, and you believed her!' Suddenly she was raging at him, and he hung his head, and then finally he looked at her.

'Well, I know this baby will interfere with your work, and you didn't want it at first.'

'I'm not even sure I want it now. But it's there for chrissake, and that's another thing. Just where do you think we're going to put it in this house?'

'I hadn't thought of that.'

'I didn't think you had.' She looked depressed. She didn't want to fight with him, but in his own way he was hurting her too. She spoke more quietly to him. 'Can we finally sell this place?'

He looked horrified. 'Are you out of your mind? This is my children's home.'

'And you built it with Anne.'

'That's beside the point.'

'It's not to me. And there's no room for our baby here.'

'We'll add on a wing.'

'Where? Above the swimming pool?' It was an absurd idea and he knew that.

'I'll call my architect and see what he suggests.'

'You're not married to him.'

'And I'm not married to you. You're married to that job you bitch about so much.'

'That's not fair.'

His rage continued. 'And you wouldn't give it up for a day, would you? Even if it cost you our child ...' You could hear their voices across the house.

'It won't.' She leapt off the bed and confronted him. 'But you and the children will if you don't all get off my back and start doing something for me for a change. They want to take it out on me for daring to get pregnant, and you want to squash me into your old life, while your daughter puts her mother's portrait over my bed.'

'Once. Big deal.' He looked unimpressed.

'That thing shouldn't even be in this house.' And then she stared at him. It had gone too far. 'And neither should I. In fact' – she stalked to the closet, pulled out a case and threw it on the bed, then marched to her chest of drawers and began throwing things into the open suitcase – 'I'm getting out until you all think this out. Those kids, all of them, damn well better behave, and you'd better stop treating Pam like a little wilting flower with a head of glass or she's going to wind up a junkie or some other crazy thing by the time she's sixteen. There's nothing wrong with that kid that a whole lot of discipline won't cure.'

'May I remind you that my daughter is not the one who got pregnant earlier this year.' It was a low blow and he knew it as soon as the words were out. But it was too late to turn back now.

Mel stared at him with hatred in her eyes. 'Touché. And we can thank your son for that.'

'Look, Mel ... why don't we calm down and talk ...' He was suddenly frightened by the look in her eyes, and he knew she wasn't supposed to get upset, but she had made him so angry.

'You're half right at least. I'm going to calm down, but we are not going to talk. Not now anyway. I'm walking out of here tonight, and you can manage the kids on your own. In fact, you can sit here and figure out what you want to do about them, this house, and me.'

'Is that an ultimatum, Mel?' His voice was strangely still.

'Yes, it is.'

'And what do you do in the meantime?'

'I'm going away to make up my mind about a few things myself. What I want to do about living in this house, whether or not I want to quit my job, and if I want to get rid of this kid.'

'Are you serious?' He looked shocked, but she suddenly looked frighteningly calm.

'I am.'

'You'd get rid of our child?'

'I might. You all seem to assume that I have to do as I'm told, what's expected of me. I have to be here day after day, I have to put up with Mrs Hahn, I have to take anything the kids dish out, I have to live with Anne's pictures staring me in the face, I have to drive Pam to the psychiatrist day after day, I have to have this baby no matter what ... Well, guess what? I don't. I have choices to make too.'

'And I have nothing to say about any of it?' He looked furious again.

'You've said enough. You defend Pam every time I open my mouth. You tell me how marvellous Mrs Hahn is and I tell you I hate her guts, and you tell me this is your house, and you assume that I have to have our child. Well, I don't. I'm thirty-six years old and frankly I think I'm too old for this. And I'm much too old to be taking this kind of dirt from anyone, you, or the kids.'

'I wasn't aware I'd been giving you dirt, Mel.'

She looked sadly at him. 'I've changed my whole life for you in the past six months, given up my job, my home, my town, my independence. I have a job out here which may or may not work out, but is something of a step down for me, and working with a real sonofabitch. You don't seem to appreciate any of that. And for you, everything is status quo. Your kids still have their own rooms, own house, pictures of their mom everywhere, their housekeeper, their dad. The only inconvenience is that now they have to put up with me. Well, if any of you expect me to stick around, maybe you'd all better start thinking about what changes you're going to make. Or I may make a few big changes and go home.'

He looked terrified but his voice was firm. 'Mel, are you leaving me?'

'Will you have the abortion while you're gone?'

She shook her head and fought back tears. 'I wouldn't do that to you. If that's what I decide, I'll tell you first.'

'It's getting awfully late for that. There would be a risk involved.'

'Then I'll have to take that into consideration too. But right now, I'm going to think about what I want, not what you want, or you expect, or what makes you comfortable or the kids need. I have needs too, and no one has given two dots about them in a long time, not even me.' He nodded slowly; devastated that she would leave, even for a week.

'Will you let me know where you are?'

'I don't know.'

'Do you know where you're going?'

'No, I don't. I'm going to get in the car and drive, and I'll see you in a week.' She was leaving him with a lot to think about. She wasn't going to be the only one thinking things out that week.

'What about your work?'

'I'll tell them I'm sick again. I'm sure Paul Stevens will be thrilled.'

And he knew that he had to say something to her then, before she left, before she threw it all away in her head. 'I won't be, Mel. I'll miss you terribly.'

She looked sad as she walked away with her case. 'So will I. But maybe that's the whole point of this. Maybe it's time we both figured out how much this all means to us, how much it's worth, how much we're willing to pay for what we want. I don't know any more, I thought I did, but suddenly I wonder about it all, and I need to think it out.' He nodded, and watched as she walked out the door, and a moment later he heard the front door close behind her. He had wanted to take her in his arms, to tell her he loved her more than life itself, that he wanted their child, but he had been too proud, he had only stood there. And now she was gone. For a week. For longer? Forever?

'Where's Mom?' Val looked in, in surprise, as she passed their room.

'Out.' He stared at her. 'Gone.' He decided to tell her the truth. He would tell them all. They deserved to know. They had played a part in it too. They were all responsible for how she felt. He wouldn't take the blame alone, although he realised now that a good part of it was his. He had been so damn stubborn about the house, about everything. She had made all the changes required for their new life, and he had made none. She was right, it wasn't fair. He looked sadly at Val now, who didn't seem to understand.

'Gone? Gone where?'

'I don't know. She'll be back in a week.' And then Val simply stood and stared at him. She understood. They'd all gone too far. But they had all been so damn mad at her, and she had been too. It didn't seem worth it now.

'Will she be okay?'

'I hope so, Val.' He walked into the hall and put an arm around her as Jess came up the stairs and looked at them.

'Did Mom go out?'

'Yeah.' Val answered for him. 'She left for a week.' And as the rest of them came up the stairs, they heard what Val said, and they simply stood where they were and stared at him.

Chapter 30

When Mel left the house that night, she simply got in the car and drove, with no set plan of where to go, no one she wanted to see. All she wanted to do was get away, from her house, her job, their kids, and him. And for the first fifty miles, all she thought of was where she was leaving from, not where she was going to.

But after that, she began to relax, and suddenly after almost two hours, she stopped for petrol, and grinned to herself. She had never done anything quite as outrageous in her life. But she couldn't take any more. Everyone was pushing her, and it was time she thought of herself instead of all of them. Even as far as this baby was concerned. She didn't have to do a damn thing she didn't want to. Hell, she made a million bucks a year, she could buy her own goddamn house, she told herself. She didn't have to live with Anne's ghost, if she didn't want to, and she already knew that she did not. And as she began driving again, with a full tank of petrol, she began thinking of all the changes she had made in her life in the last six months, and how few changes had been required of Peter. He still worked in the same place, with the same people who respected his work, slept in the same bed he had slept in for a number of years. His children hadn't been moved out of their home. He even had the same housekeeper. The only thing that had changed for him was the face he kissed before he left the house for work, and maybe he didn't even notice that. And as Mel pulled into Santa Barbara, she began to steam again, and was glad she'd left. She was only sorry she hadn't done it before, but who had time, between driving Pam to her psychiatrist, trying to pacify the twins, keep a remote eye on Mark, and play Mommy to Matthew, hold Peter's hand when his transplant patients died, not to mention doing interviews, specials, and the six-o'clock news every night? It was a wonder she had time to dress and comb her hair. To hell with all of them. Peter, the kids, and Paul Stevens. Let him anchor alone for a while, they could always say that she was sick. To hell with them. She didn't care.

She pulled into a motel and paid for a room, which looked like it could have been anywhere in the world, from Beirut to New Orleans, when she glanced at the rust-coloured shag rug on the floor, the orange vinyl chairs, the spotless white tile bathroom, the rust-coloured bedspread. It was definitely not the Bel-Air, or even the Santa Barbara Biltmore where she had stayed years before, and she didn't give a damn. She took a hot bath, turned on the TV, watched the news when it came on at eleven o'clock, by habit more than desire, and turned out the light without calling home. Screw them all, she thought to herself, and for the first time in months she felt free, to do what she wanted to do, to be herself, to make up her own mind without considering a living, breathing soul.

As she lay in bed, she thought of what was inside her, and realised that even here she wasn't totally alone. The baby had come with her ... the baby ... as though it were already a person separate from herself ... She laid a hand on her stomach, which had been so flat a month before, and now there was a small but distinct bulge where the hollow between her hip bones had been. It was odd to think what would happen if she went on with the pregnancy. The baby would become real to her, she would feel it move in about six weeks ... for a tiny moment, there was a tender feeling deep inside her, and then she let it go. She didn't want to think of that right now. She didn't want to think of anything. She closed her eyes and went to sleep, without dreaming of Peter, or the children or their unborn child, or anything. She just lay in bed in the motel room and slept, and when she woke up the next day, the sun was streaming into her room, and she couldn't remember where she was at first. When she looked around and realised where she was, she laughed to herself. She felt good, and strong, and free.

When Peter woke up that morning in Bel-Air, he reached over to the other side of the bed, instinctively feeling for her, and when his hand and leg met smooth, empty sheets, he opened one eye, and remembered with a sinking heart that she was gone. He turned over and lay staring up at the ceiling for a long time, wondering where she was, and remembering why she had gone. It was really all his fault, he told himself, you couldn't blame the kids, or Paul Stevens at her job, or Mrs Hahn. It was that he had done everything wrong from the first. He had expected too much of her, expected her to change her entire life ... for him. And he knew she regretted everything she'd done. He lay there re-proaching himself, thinking of how much she loved her life in New York, and wondering how he had even dared to think she could give that up. A job that any man in the country would have drooled to have, a house she loved, her friends, her life, her town ...

And as Melanie began driving slowly north, she thought of Peter's face the first time they had met, those endless first days during the interview, the exhausting hours they shared when the President had been shot ... his first trip to New York. She began to think not so much of what she'd had there, but what she'd got in exchange ... the first time Matt had climbed into her lap ... a look in Pam's eyes once or twice ... the moments when Mark had clung to her and cried when Val almost died on their skiing trip. Suddenly it was difficult to exorcise them all from her life. Her anger now was directed more at the twins, at Jess for expecting too much of her, for expecting her to be there for everyone and especially for her, at Val for resenting this baby in her mother's life because she hadn't been able to have her own.

She owed them more than that. But how much more did she have to give? No more than she had already given them, that was the tragedy of it, and it wasn't enough, she knew. And now there was one more pair of eyes to look into hers one day and tell her that she didn't have enough to give to him, or her ... and there was nothing at all left of herself. It exhausted her to think of it, and she was relieved when she saw Carmel at last. All she wanted to do was check into another motel and go back to sleep again ... to get away ... to dream ... to escape ...

'When's Mommy coming back?' Matthew stared glumly at his plate, and then at the rest of them. No one had said a word since they had sat down to dinner that night. It didn't feel like Sunday night without her. It was Mrs Hahn's day off, and usually Mel made them all something they liked to eat. She talked and laughed and listened to them, kept an eye on everyone, and spoke about what she had lined up in the week ahead, knowing full well that everything would change before the week was halfway out. But she would tease and joke, and manage to include everyone, or try to. Matthew looked up at Peter then, his eyes filled with reproach. 'Why did you make her go away?'

'She'll be back.' Jessica was the first to speak, as tears filled her eyes. 'She just went away for a little rest.'

'Why can't she rest here?' He looked accusingly at her. She was the only one who would speak to him. The rest of them seemed to have been struck dumb, but Mark addressed him now.

'Because we all wear her out, Matt. We expect too goddamn much of her.' Mark looked pointedly at Pam, and then let his glance take in everyone, and after dinner Peter heard him shouting at Val. 'You blamed her for goddamn everything ... that you had to leave New York ... your friends ... your school ... you even blamed her for what happened to us. It wasn't her fault, Val.' But the pretty little blonde sat down and cried so hard that he didn't have the heart to go on. Peter walked slowly up the stairs to Val's room, and found them all sitting there except for Pam who was lying on her bed, staring at the ceiling with the radio on. She had wanted her to go. She admitted it to herself, even if she wouldn't have told her psychiatrist. She wanted her own mother back. But she understood now that that was never going to be. It was either Mel or this incredible emptiness, the same way it had been when her mom was first gone, with only Mrs Hahn there for them, and suddenly Pam knew that wasn't what she wanted, for them, or for herself. She got up and walked into the twins' room and found the others there, even Matt, sitting sadly on the floor.

'Boy, this room is small.' She looked around. Her room was twice that size. Val and Jess didn't say anything, but they turned as they saw Peter in the doorway.

'Yes, it is.' But it only reminded him of what Mel had said, that the twins had never shared a room in their life. And here, they were squashed in like orphans, while Pam had a room twice the size. Had everything she said been true? Most of it, he told himself. Not all of it. But too much for him to be able to discard all that she had said.

'A double room?' The man at the motel in Carmel asked.

'No.' She smiled tiredly. 'A single will be fine.' He looked at her sorrowfully. They always said that, and then a guy and two kids would make a mad dash into the room, thinking he wouldn't know that they were there. And they probably had a large slobbering dog. But this time he was wrong. She took her small overnight bag out of the car, walked inside and closed the door, and lay down on the bed without looking around. It was almost identical to the room she'd had the night before. There was a sameness to everything new as she lay down in another orange vinyl room with a rust-coloured shag rug, and went to sleep from sheer exhaustion.

'Dr Hallam?'

'Hmmm?' A nurse had spoken to him, and he sat in a cubicle with a stack of charts, grateful that they had only had two bypasses to do that morning.

'Is something wrong?' She was terrified of him. He was a great man and if she made a mistake, her neck would be on the line, but he only looked at her and shook his head with a tired smile.

'Everything is fine. What about Iris Lee? Is there any reaction to the drugs yet?'

'Not yet.' She had had the transplant two weeks before, and everything seemed to be going well, but Peter didn't have a lot of hope for her. They hadn't got a heart in time, and had had to put a child's heart piggyback with her own. Sometimes the technique had worked well for him, but Iris had been so frail, in her case it had been a desperate move, and he had been expecting the worst for days. This time, Mel wouldn't be there for him. It was like in the days after Anne's death. He was alone now. And even lonelier than he had been when Anne died.

'Jess?'

'Yeah?'

Val lay on her bed after school, while Jessie sat at the desk in their room. 'Do you ever wish we'd go back to New York?'

'Sure.' She turned to look at her twin. 'Lots of times. There's nothing wrong with that. We lived there for a long time.'

'Do you suppose that's where Mom went?' She had been thinking about it all day.

'I don't know. I don't know where she'd go. She might even be in LA.'

'And not call us?' Val looked horrified and Jessie smiled.

'Would you call us if you felt like that?'

Val shook her head. 'I guess not.'

'Neither would I.' She stared out the window then with a small sigh. 'I blamed everything on her, Val. Everything. It was so unfair, but all the decisions were hers. She always used to ask us what we thought about things, and this time she just went ahead, and pulled us out of school, moved out here ...' She thought about it for a long time. 'I guess I was annoyed at her for taking the decisions out of our hands.'

'She must have thought she was doing the right thing.' Val looked sad and Jess nodded her head and looked at her.

'The bitch of it is that she did. I like Peter, don't you?'

Val nodded her head again. 'All I could think of when I heard we were moving out here was Mark.'

Jess smiled. 'I know that. It sure didn't help me much while we were leaving New York. Mom had Peter, you had Mark. And I had nothing.' She grinned. It didn't seem so awful now. She liked their school, and she had met a nice boy a month or so before. For the first time in her life, she had met someone she really cared about. He was twenty-one, and she had a feeling that her mom was going to have a fit, especially after what had happened with Val and Mark. But she knew that this was going to be someone special to her, and she sat staring into space with a distant smile.

'What are you grinning about?' Val had been watching her. 'And you sit there with a happy smile. What's up?'

'Nothing much.'

But instantly Val knew. Jess might have got better grades, but Val knew men. She zeroed in on her sister with narrowed eyes. 'Are you in love?'

Jess looked at her with a smile. She hadn't wanted to tell her yet. 'Not yet. But I met someone nice.'

'You?' Val looked stunned, and Jessie nodded, unwilling to say more. But Val didn't look impressed. 'Just watch out.' They both knew what she meant, and Val had been right. She'd learned one of the toughest lessons of life, and she wouldn't forget.

Mrs Hahn served them dinner silently that night, and Peter didn't get home till nine o'clock. Matthew was already in bed, tucked in by Jess, Pam, and Val and Peter went upstairs to check on them. 'Everyone all right?' They were a quiet group, but everyone nodded as he went from room to room. He had had a rough day but there was no one to tell, he stopped in the twins' room and stared at Jess. 'Any word from your mom?' She only shook her head and he went back downstairs, just as Mel drove up San Francisco's California Street on Nob Hill, and checked into the Stanford Court Hotel. It was a refreshing change from the motels she'd been staying at, and the room was all done in grey velvets and silks and moiré, and she collapsed on the bed with a tired groan. She felt as though she had been driving for days and days and days, and she reminded herself to slow down a bit. She hadn't made her mind up yet, and she didn't want to lose the baby before she did. She had a responsibility to it, if it was going to live. She lay awake thinking about it that night, about how angry Val had been, Jess's fury over just how many changes she expected them to make ... Pam's hostility and ploys for attention for herself, even poor little Matt's hurt, and Peter's expectation that she would have the baby in spite of it all, as an antidote to his constant bouts with death in the operating room. It all seemed terribly unfair. She had to have it, or not have it, for all of them. Once again, the issue was them and not herself.

She walked through Chinatown the next day, and then drove to Golden Gate Park, and wandered through the flowers. It was almost May ... May ... she had met Peter almost a year before, and now here she was, and when she got back to the hotel, she took her little phone book out of her bag, dialled 8 for long distance, and called Raquel. It was eight o'clock in New York and they hadn't heard from her in months, Mel didn't even know if she had a job. Or she could have been out, but she picked the phone up on the first ring.

'Hello?' She sounded as suspicious as she always did and on her end Mel grinned.

'Hi, Raquel, it's me.' It was like calling home from far away in the old days, and she had to remind herself not to ask how the twins were. 'How are you?'

'Mrs Mel?'

'Of course.'

'Is something wrong?'

'No, I just thought I'd call and see how you were.'

'I'm fine.' She sounded pleased. 'How are the girls?'

'They're wonderful.' She wouldn't tell her about Val. She was all right now. 'They like their school, everything seems to be working out.' But as she said it, her voice trembled and tears filled her eyes.

'Something's wrong!' It was an accusation this time, and Mel felt tears rise in her throat.

'Absolutely not. I was in San Francisco for a few days and I got lonely for you.'

'What you doing there? You still working too hard?'

'No, it's not as bad. I only have to do the six o'clock.' She didn't tell her what an agony the job had been. 'And I'm just here to take it easy for a few days.'

'Why? You sick?' She had always been to the point and Mel smiled. What was the point of fooling her?

'To tell you the truth, you old witch, I ran away.'

'From who?' She sounded shocked.

'Everyone. Peter, the kids, my job, myself.'

'What's happening to you?' It was obvious that she disapproved.

'I don't know. I guess I just needed some time to think.'

'About what?' She sounded angry at Mel now. 'You always think too much. You don't need to think.' And then, 'Is your husband there?'

'No, I'm here alone.' She could just see Raquel's face, and she wondered why she had called, but she had wanted to hear a familiar voice and she didn't want to call home.

'You go home right now!'

'I will in a few days.'

'I mean now. What's wrong with you? You going crazy out there?'

'A little bit.' She didn't want to tell her about the baby yet. She still needed time to make a decision about that. And there was no point telling anyone if she was going to get rid of it. In LA, she could always say that she lost it because she worked too hard, and no one knew at work yet. 'I just wanted to know if you were all right.'

'I'm fine. Now you go home.'

'I will. Don't worry about me, Raquel. I send you a big kiss.'

'Don't kiss me, go home and kiss him. Tell him you're sorry you ran away.'

'I will. And write to me sometime.'

'Okay, okay. And give my love to the twins.'

'I will.' They hung up then and Mel lay on the bed for a long time. Raquel didn't understand any better than they did. In her mind, Mel belonged at home, no matter what they said or did. It was her place. And the truth was that she thought so too.

She ordered room service that night, had a hot bath, and watched a couple of hours of TV. She didn't feel like going out. There was nowhere she wanted to go, and at eleven o'clock, before the news came on, she dialled, got a long-distance line, and held the phone in her hand for a long time. Maybe Raquel was right . . . but she didn't want to call unless she wanted to . . . She dialled the number, not sure yet if she'd hang up or speak to him, but when she heard his voice, her heart leapt as it had almost a year before.

'Hello?' She could tell that he hadn't been asleep yet. And she hesitated for one beat.

'Hi.' It was a cautious sound.

'Mel?'

'No. Chicken Delight. Yeah, it's me.'

'For God's sake, are you all right? I've been worried sick.'

'I'm okay.'

He didn't dare to ask, but he had to know. 'The baby? Did you . . . did you get rid of it?'

She sounded hurt. 'I told you I wouldn't do that until I told you what I'd decided to do.'

'And did you decide?'

'Not yet. I haven't really given it a lot of thought.'

'Then what the hell have you been thinking about?'

'Us.'

There was a long pause. 'Oh.' And then, 'So have I. I've been a real sonofabitch, Mel. The kids think so too.'

'No, they don't.' She smiled. He had been breast-beating while she was gone, and that really wasn't the point. 'That's silly, Peter. We both had a lot of adjustments to make.'

'Yeah, and I let you make them all.'

'That's not entirely true.' But it was in part, and he knew it now. She didn't totally want to take the truth from him. 'One of us had to move, ourselves, our kids, had to give up our old lives. And it was impossible for you. It was my choice.'

'And I let it go at that. I let everything fall on you. I even expected you to step into Anne's shoes. It makes me sick when I think about it now.'

She sighed. He wasn't entirely wrong, but there was more to it than that, and she knew that now. 'And in a way, I think I expected to continue my old independent life, to make all my decisions for myself without consulting you, bring up my kids the way I want, and coincidentally yours too. I expected you and your children to throw out all your old ways at once because I told you to. And that wasn't right.'

'It wasn't wrong.' He sounded desperately contrite and she was touched.

'Maybe we were both half right and half wrong.' She smiled.

He wasn't smiling yet. She wasn't home. And he still didn't know where she was. 'Where does that leave us now?'

'A little wiser than we were.'

He wasn't sure what she meant. 'And you, Mel? Are you going back to New York?' He heard her gasp.

'Are you crazy?' And then, 'Are you throwing me out?'

This time he laughed. 'I don't know if you remember this, but last time I looked you ran away. In fact, I don't even know where you are.'

She smiled at that. She had forgotten to tell him when she first called. 'I'm in San Francisco.'

'How did you get there?' He seemed surprised.

'I drove.'

'That's too far, Mel.' He was thinking of the pregnancy, but he didn't want to tell her that.

'I stopped in Santa Barbara and Carmel on the way up.'

'Do you feel all right?'

'I'm fine.' And then she smiled as she lay on her bed at the Stanford Court. 'I miss you a lot.'

'Well, that's nice to hear.' And then he finally dared to ask. 'When are you coming home?'

'Why?' She sounded suspicious again and he groaned.

'Because I want you to clean the place and mow the lawn, you idiot. Why do you think? Because I miss you too.' And then he had an idea. 'Why don't you stay there for a few more days, and I'll meet you there.'

Melanie's face suddenly burst into a smile. 'That's a nice idea, love.' It was the first time she had called him that in a long while and he beamed.

'I love you so much, Mel. And I've been such a fool.'

'No, you haven't. We've both been. So much happened in so little time and our work puts so much pressure on us both.' He couldn't disagree with that.

'What do you want to do about the house? Do you still want to move? I will if you want us to.' He had thought about it a lot in the past few days, and he didn't want to give up the house he loved, but if it meant that much to her, and there really wasn't enough room for the twins, unless maybe they exchanged rooms with Pam, and he knew she'd have a fit. 'What do you think?'

'I think we should stay where we are for a while, and let everyone settle down before we make any more changes at all, and that goes for Mrs Hahn too.' He was relieved at what she said and he thought she was right. They all needed time to settle down now. So everything was resolved, except her miseries at her job, and what to do about their unborn child. 'Do you really want to come up here?'

'Yes, I do. I feel like we haven't been alone for years. We even took the kids to Mexico on our honeymoon.'

She laughed at that. 'Whose idea was that?'

'All right ... mea culpa ... but anyway, a romantic weekend sounds fabulous to me right now.'

'I'll do my best. Keep your fingers crossed.'

She did and he called her back the next day. He had got two surgeons on the team to split the weekend and cover for him. It had taken a little negotiation, but he had been so intense about it that they had both agreed.

'I'll be there in two days.'

'Good.' And she needed that much time to herself to think about whether she wanted an abortion or not. She really wasn't sure. 'How are the kids, by the way?'

'Fine. And really beginning to appreciate you.' And so was he. He could hardly wait to see her on Friday night. It was like the days when she was living in New York, only worse, because he knew what he was missing now. And he told her so. 'I miss you too, Mel, more than you know.' It had been a ghastly week for him. And Iris Lee had died that day, but he had expected it. He didn't tell Mel. They had their own problems now, without adding another thing. He was more worried about her than his patients now. 'Are you feeling all right?'

'I'm fine.'

He didn't ask her if she'd made up her mind yet. The next day she took a long walk in Muir Woods, and tried to think about what she wanted to do. Again and again she came back to what she had told Val ... 'I don't know if I could have done what you did ...' It was not a condemnation, whatever Val might have thought at the time. There was something about aborting a child at her age, married to a man she loved, with plenty of money between them both. There was no reason for it, no way she could explain it to herself, and perhaps there would be no way she could live with it. 'But do you want the child?' she asked herself, and that was where she got hung up. She wasn't sure. But what an ugly luxury to dispose of a life because she wasn't in the mood, it didn't fit in with her job, it annoyed her other kids ... and there they were again ... the all-powerful others in her life, husband, children ... what she owed *them*. What did she owe *herself*? And suddenly she heard her own voice in the woods. 'I want this child.' She was so startled that she looked around, as though to see who had spoken these words, but she knew she had. She felt a thousand-pound weight lift off her heart and she smiled. She looked at her watch. It was time for lunch. She had to take care of the baby if she were having it ... *I want this child* ... the words had been so strong and sure, and so was she as she made her way back to her car, walking through the woods.

Chapter 31

As she stood at the gate waiting for him, Mel felt dampness in her palms, and the same nervousness she had felt a year before. It was like starting all over again, except that it would be better this time. He was the third one off the plane and she flew into his arms. It had been an endless week.

'Oh, Mel ...' Tears filled his eyes and he was beyond words as he clung to her. He didn't even care what she did about the baby now. He wanted her and only her ... and no more so than she wanted him.

'God, I missed you so much.' But as she pulled away from him, smiling and with tears in her eyes, he saw that she looked better than she had in months. She looked rested and relaxed and the frown between her brows was gone.

'You look wonderful, Mel.'

'So do you.' And then she looked down at the zipper in her slacks that had barely closed and was straining now. 'I've gained a little weight here and there.' He wasn't sure what to say and she smiled at him. 'I've decided that ...' She felt strange saying the words. Who was she to decide about a life. It was what she had said to him a long time ago. God decided that, he didn't, and neither did she. 'The baby's going to be fine.'

'Is it?' He wanted to be sure he understood what she meant.

'Yes.' She beamed.

'Are you sure?'

'I am.'

'For me?' He didn't want her to do that. She had to want it too, and it was a lot to ask, given the fact that they had five others at home, and the ultra-demanding job she had.

'For myself, for you, for us ... for all of us ...' She blushed and he took her hand. 'But mostly for me.' She told him what had happened when she was walking in the woods and tears filled his eyes as he pulled her close to him again.

'Oh, Mel.'

'I love you.' It was all she could say, and arm in arm they walked outside, and shared a weekend like no other they had ever shared.

They started the drive home slowly Sunday afternoon, and took Route 5 so it wouldn't be quite as long. By ten o'clock they were home, and as she looked at the house, Mel felt as though she had been gone for years. She stood outside for a moment or two and just smiled, but Peter took her hand and walked her inside. 'Come on, kiddo, let's get you to bed. That's a long drive for you.' He was treating her like Venetian glass and she smiled at him.

'I think I'll live.' But as soon as she stepped inside the house, there was an explosion of sound. The kids had heard them drive up, and Pam had looked outside and given a horrendous squeal.

'They're home!' She was first down the stairs, and threw her arms around Mel. 'Welcome back!' It wasn't welcome home, but it was close. The twins hugged her, and Mark, and Matthew woke up from all the noise and wanted to sleep in her bed that night. When they had all finally returned to their rooms again after almost an hour of clatter and noise and talk, Mel lay on their bed and looked at Peter with a happy smile.

'They're all good kids, aren't they?'

'They have a good mother.' He sat down on the edge of the bed and took her hand in his. 'I promise, Mel. I'll do everything I can to make things easier for you.' But there was only so much he could do, and that night he got a call at two a.m. He was back on call, and one of his bypasses needed him at once. The next time Mel saw him was when he came home at noon to change his clothes. She had the house back in control, had told Mrs Hahn what she wanted served for dinner that night, and Peter noticed with a grin that Mrs Hahn did not look pleased, but she made no complaint to him. Peter changed his clothes and hurried off to work, just as Mel left. She smiled and waved as they pulled out of the driveway in their separate cars. Pam was getting herself to the psychiatrist alone that day, as she had done the week before when Mel was absent. Mark had said he'd be home after dinner but not too late, since he had exams the next day, the twins were playing tennis with friends, but would be in by five o'clock. Mrs Hahn was picking Matthew up at school, as she had a year before, and Mel was off to work for the first time in a week, and when she got in, even Paul Stevens's viciousness couldn't dampen her spirits today. Everything felt too good.

But at six forty-five, after she had done the news, the producer sought her out and found her in her office, jotting down some notes before she went home. He walked in and closed the door, and Mel looked up.

'Hi, Tom. Is something wrong?'

He hesitated and Mel felt a chill. Were they firing her? Could they? Had Stevens finally won? 'Mel, I have to talk to you.' Oh dear.

'Sure. Sit down.' She waved him to a chair. The office didn't feel like home yet but it was all she had there.

'I don't know how to tell you this, Mel ...' Her heart stopped. My God, she was being canned. She had been the biggest newsroom star at the network in New York, she had won four prizes for the documentary interviews she'd done and that little horror had got her canned.

'Yes?' She might as well make it easy for him, she just hoped she didn't cry, and all she wanted was to go home to Peter now. To hell with their job and their lousy show. She'd go home and have the baby and take care of their kids.

'I don't want to frighten you.' That didn't make sense. 'But we've had several threats ...' She looked blank. 'They started coming in during the week you were gone. And they began again today.'

'What kind of threats?' She didn't understand. Was that little sonofabitch threatening to quit? Let him then. The ratings would soar. But she didn't want to tell Tom that yet.

'Threats on your life, Mel.' She stared at him.

'On me?' It had happened once in New York, years ago, some kook didn't like a piece she'd done and called the network for months, threatening to strangle her, but eventually he'd got bored or given up. Mel looked amused. 'At least someone's watching out there.'

'I'm serious, Mel. We've had problems like this before. This is California, not New York. We've had several assassination attempts on presidents out here.'

She couldn't help but smile. 'I'm flattered, Tom, but I'm hardly in those leagues.'

'You're important to us.'

She was touched. 'Thank you, Tom.'

'And we've hired a bodyguard for you.'

'You've what? Oh that's ridiculous ... you don't really think ...'

'You have children, Mel. Do you want to take that chance?' His question stopped her dead.

'No, I don't, but ...'

'We didn't want to frighten your husband while you were gone, but we think it's serious.'

'Why?' She still looked amused. It happened in their business all the time.

'Because we got a call last week, and the man said there was a bomb in your desk. There was, Mel. It would have gone off in exactly one hour, when you opened your desk, and blown us all to kingdom come, if you'd been here.' Suddenly she felt sick.

'They think they might know who it is. But in the meantime, while they figure it out, we want you safe. We were very glad that you were gone last week.'

'So am I.' She felt an unconscious twitch in her left eye as she spoke, and she looked up to see a tall stern-looking man walk into the room. Tom introduced him at once. He was her bodyguard, and two others had been hired as well. They wanted her escorted whenever she came and went, and they left it up to her, but they thought she should have them at home as well. It was no secret who she was married to, and anyone could look them up. The bodyguard's name was Timothy Frank and as he left the building at her side, she felt as though she had a wall with her. He was the biggest, broadest, toughest man she'd ever seen. And she thanked him when he got her home. She had been asked to leave her car at the station that night, and go home with Tim in the limousine. As she rolled up, she saw that Peter was home.

'Hi.' He looked up from some papers he was going through and smiled. It was good to have her home again, but the frown was back, and she looked extremely strained.

'Trouble at work?'

'You might say that.' She looked dazed. Tim had left again with the limousine.

'What's wrong?' She told him then about the bomb and he stared at her. 'My God, Mel. You can't live like that, and neither can we.'

'What do you expect me to do?'

He hated to say the words, but she was pregnant now, and it was just too much strain for her. Even if they caught the guy in a week or two, just knowing that it could happen again would put too much pressure on her, and on him. He didn't want her going through that. And if they didn't catch the guy ... He shuddered at the thought, and stood up to close his study door. He stood there, looking down at her. 'I think you should quit.'

'I can't.' Her face turned to rock. 'It happened once in New York and I didn't quit then. I won't do it for a reason like that.'

'What reason do you need?' He was shouting at her. Life never seemed to get off their backs, patients dying, unruly kids, bomb threats, unexpected pregnancies. It was almost more than he could stand to think about as he looked at her. 'What if someone bombs this house and one of the children is killed?'

She winced at his words and turned a faint shade of green. 'We'll have bodyguards round the clock.'

'For five kids?'

'God damn it, I don't know ...' She leapt to her feet. 'I'll stay in a hotel if you want me to. But I won't quit my job, because of some lunatic. For all I know it's Paul Stevens just trying to scare me off.'

'Is that what the police think?'

She had to be honest with him. 'No, they don't. But they also think they know who the guy is.'

'Then take a leave until they pick him up.'

'I can't, Peter. I can't, dammit. I have a job to do.'

He walked over and grabbed her arm. 'You'll get killed.'

'I've taken that chance before.' Her eyes blazed. He couldn't make her quit her job, not after all these years. It was part of who she was, and he had promised to respect that, for better or worse.

'You've never taken that chance with my child's life. Think of that.'

'I can't think of anything any more.'

'Except yourself.'

'Damn you.' She walked out of the room and slammed the door, and went upstairs, and he didn't speak to her again that night. Things were off to a great start again, and the children sensed the tension in the house. She called the producer of the show that night, and accepted his offer of bodyguards, for herself, her husband, and the kids. It would take an army to keep them safe, but the station was willing to pay for it. And she told Peter about it when they went to bed. 'They start tomorrow morning, at six.'

'That's ridiculous. What am I supposed to do? Do rounds with a bodyguard?'

'I don't think the problem is you. Maybe he could just go with you when you go outdoors. The real problem is me.'

'I'm aware of that.' He felt sick at the thought. And the next morning, at breakfast, she explained it to the kids. Their eyes were wide as she explained, and she assured them that they'd all be safe and in a few days the man would be caught. It was just something they had to live with for a little while. Matt thought it was fabulous, Mark was embarrassed to have to take a bodyguard to college with him, and the girls looked terrified. But as they each left for school with the policeman assigned to the task, Mrs Hahn sought Mel out upstairs.

'Mrs Hallum?' She always pronounced it that way, and Mel turned to speak to her.

'Yes, Mrs Hahn?' Peter called her Hilda now and then, but Mel never did. And there was no 'Mrs Mel' as there had been in New York with Raquel.

'I wanted to tell you that due to the circumstances, I quit.'

Mel stared at her. 'You do?' Peter would be shocked, and possibly even angry at her. She was wreaking havoc on their house and it was not her fault.

'I really don't think that you're in any danger here, and as I explained to the children this morning, there will be full protection here at all times.'

'I've never worked in a house where there had to be police before.'

'I'm sure you haven't, Mrs Hahn. But if you'll be patient for a little while ...' She owed it to Peter at least to try.

'No.' She shook her head decidedly. 'I won't. I'm leaving now.'

'With no notice at all?'

She shook her head, looking at Mel accusingly. 'Nothing like this ever happened before when the doctor's wife was here.' The doctor's wife being Anne of course, the *real* Mrs Hallam as opposed to Mel. And now Mel couldn't help pushing her a little, with a barely concealed grin. She was hardly heart-broken to see the woman go. She had hated her from the first.

'Things must have been pretty dull here then.' She looked nonchalant and Hilda Hahn was clearly horrified. She didn't even offer to shake Mel's hand.

'Goodbye. I left the doctor a letter in my room.'

'I'll see that he gets it then. You don't want to stay long enough to say goodbye to the children yourself?' That seemed mean to Mel, but she knew that they'd survive.

'I don't want to be in this house for another hour.'

'Fine.' Mel looked unperturbed and watched her go, and she almost shouted hallelujah as the front door closed. But that night, Peter was a little less than thrilled.

'Who's going to run this place Mel? You don't have time.' She searched his eyes for accusation, but it was more concern.

'We'll find someone else.' She called Raquel, but she still refused to come out, and she urged Mel to be careful with the girls. 'In the meantime, I can do it myself with the kids.'

'That's great. Someone is out there planting bombs with your name on them and you have to worry about doing laundry and making beds.'

'You can help too.' She smiled.

'I have other things to do.' And a bodyguard to endure. The entire situation wore on his nerves as the days went on and the bomber wasn't caught. There had been four more threats, and a defective bomb was found in Mel's desk. At long last even Paul Stevens felt sorry for her. He knew she was pregnant now, and there were dark circles under her eyes from lying awake at night, wondering if the man would be caught. He would in time, they always were, but how long would that be?

'I'm sorry this is happening to you, Mel.' He finally called a truce one day and held out a hand.

'So am I.' She smiled tiredly after they went off the air. The bodyguard had stood close by during the entire time. She was constantly aware of him, and in the morning when the kids left for school, the house seemed to be full of cops. It was driving Peter nuts and they were fighting all the time. He had almost got used to his own man, but the others seemed 'de trop' for him. 'It goes with the turf, I guess,' she told Paul.

He looked sadly at her. 'You know, I used to envy you.'

'I know.' She smiled. And she knew why. 'But at least you don't have to contend with this.'

'I don't know how the hell you stand the strain.'

'Mostly, I worry about the kids ... my own ... his ... if something happens to one of them, I'll never forgive myself.' It had been going on for a month by now, and she was seriously beginning to think she ought to give in and leave. She hadn't said anything to Peter yet, because she didn't want to get him started, or let him think that it was sure. But she had promised herself that if the bomber wasn't caught in the next two weeks, she would quit.

Paul Stevens looked horrified as he contemplated it all. 'If there's anything that I can do ...' She shook her head and said goodnight, and went home to her family, but it wasn't the casual group it used to be. There were unmarked police cars outside, and inside the house everyone was aware of the danger that lurked near them every day.

'Do you think they'll catch him, Mom?' Matthew asked her that night.

'I hope so, Matt.' She held him on her lap, praying that the danger would not touch him ... or any of them ... she looked from him to Pam to the twins. Mark was out. And that night Peter talked to her about it again.

'Why don't you resign?'

She didn't want to tell him that she was thinking the same thing. 'I'm not a quitter, that's why.' But she had thought of something else. 'What if we go away?'

'Where?'

It was June by then, and she thought of it with a sigh, as she looked at Peter hopefully. 'What about taking everyone to Martha's Vineyard for a while?' She hadn't rented the house this year, but maybe she could still get it for a few weeks, or rent another one. But he shook his head.

'That's too far away for you.' She was four months pregnant by then, and just beginning to show. 'And I'll never see you if you go there. Why not something nearby?'

'That defeats the whole purpose of the trip.' She was exhausted by the whole idea, and she was staggered by what the station was spending on bodyguards, but nobody begrudged them to her. It certainly wasn't their fault they got on her nerves. That morning as she poured a glass of milk for Matt, one of the men had asked her to 'Step back from the window, please.' It certainly reminded one day and night of what was going on, and the threat to their lives. 'What about Aspen again?' She looked hopelessly at Peter then.

'I don't think the altitude is good for you.'

'Neither is the tension here.'

'I don't know. I'll think about it today.' And so did she. Suddenly all she wanted to do was run away again. She had lived with the nightmare for a month, and she couldn't stand it any more. She went to work that afternoon, and sat at her desk, her bodyguard just outside the room and suddenly she looked up and saw the producer staring down at her with a smile.

'Mel, we've got good news for you.'

'You're sending me to Europe for a year?' She smiled, and for the first time, she thought she felt the baby move. They hadn't mentioned her pregnancy on the show because they were afraid that the madman who was hunting her would do something even worse to her if he found out. So the secret she was carrying remained invisible and unknown beneath the desk.

'Better news than that.' The smile grew wider and she saw Paul Stevens in the hall looking at her benevolently.

'You're giving Paul my job.' Paul grinned and nodded yes as Mel laughed. They were almost friends now, as a result of the agonies of the past month.

'They caught the lunatic who's been threatening you.'

'They did?' Her eyes grew wide and filled with tears. 'It's all over then?' He nodded and she began to shake.

'Oh my God.' She put her head down on her desk and began to sob.

Chapter 32

'Well, my love,' Peter looked happily across at her, as they sat beside their pool; all the kids were out, and they had peace again. 'What'll we do for fun this week?' He smiled at her. 'No one can accuse us of having a dull life at least.'

'God forbid.' She lay back and closed her eyes. She knew what she wanted to do. She wanted to go to Martha's Vineyard and lie in the hot sand, but all the kids had other plans by then, Peter was tied up with his work, and she had agreed to forfeit her holiday that year, and take maternity leave instead. The baby was due around Thanksgiving, and she was leaving on October first.

'I have an idea, Mel.'

'If it involves anything more than falling into the pool, don't tell me now.' Her eyes were closed as he smiled at her, and walked slowly over to where she sat.

'Why don't we look at some houses today?' She opened one eye.

'You're kidding of course.'

'I'm serious.'

She looked absolutely amazed. 'You are?'

'Well, much as I hate to admit it, there's nowhere to put the new baby, except maybe in the garage, and I think a whole lot of construction would drive us nuts. The twins need their own rooms ...' Mel knew how hard it was for him to admit mistakes, and she held out her arms. He knew how badly she had wanted to move out of Anne's house, and she had long since given up.

'Wouldn't you rather stay here? I really wouldn't mind. We can figure something out for a couple of years, and Mark will be gone soon.' He had decided to go east to college for his junior and senior two years, which meant he had only one more year at home, and Jess already knew she wanted to go to Yale if she could get in ... 'The kids are practically grown-up.'

'That's nice for them. I wish I could say the same for me.'

'You're the nicest man I know.' She kissed him gently on the lips and he let his fingers drift up her leg. 'Hmm ... Do you suppose anyone can see us here?'

'Only a neighbour or two, and what's a little passion between friends?'

He took her inside then, and their lovemaking renewed the bond between them. Afterwards he brought her lunch on a tray, and she lay in bed looking comfortable and happy and relaxed. 'Why are you so good to me?'

'I don't know. I must love you a lot.'

'Me too.' She smiled happily. 'Did you really mean that about a new house?' The idea delighted her, but she didn't want to push. She knew how much the old one meant to him and how much effort he had put into it, standing behind Anne. But in Mel's mind, it would always be Anne's house, not even his, but Anne's. Even now.

'Yes, I did.' She beamed and finished lunch, and then they got up and went for a drive, and here and there they saw a house they liked, but none of them was for sale.

'You know, it could take us years to find the right place.'

'We have the time.'

She nodded, feeling relaxed, and enjoying the Sunday afternoon. The next weekend was the Fourth of July. And it was then that they saw the perfect house for them. 'My God' – Mel looked at Peter as they walked around for a second time – 'it's huge.'

'This may come as a shock to you, Mrs Hallam, but we have six kids.'

'Five and a half.' She smiled, but there were rooms for each of them, with studies for both Peter and Mel to us whenever they worked at home, there was a handsome garden, an enormous pool, and a little pool house for the kids to use with their friends. It had absolutely everything they wanted and it was still in Bel-Air, which Peter preferred.

'Well, Mrs Hallam?'

'I don't know, Doctor. What do you think? Can we afford it?'

'Probably not. But once we sell my house we can.' It was the first time he had admitted it was his, not theirs, and Mel grinned. She loved the new house. 'Why don't we make a down payment on it?' But it was a project in which they would both have to invest, otherwise they couldn't manage it, and that suited Mel just fine. She wanted something that was equally theirs, hers as well as his, and she still had her money from the house in New York to invest. They put their house on the market the following week, and it didn't sell until Labor Day, but the other one was still available.

'Let's see.' Peter glanced at the calendar as they closed on the new house. 'The baby's due November twenty-eight ... today is September third ... you go on leave from the network in four weeks. That gives you exactly two months to get this place in shape for us, and with any luck at all we'll be in by Thanksgiving.' He looked totally matter-of-fact and Mel laughed at him.

'Are you kidding? It'll take months.' Even though the place was in perfect shape, they wanted to paint and change the wallpapers, alter the garden here and there, they had to pick out fabrics and order drapes ... new carpeting ... 'Dream on.'

Peter looked surprised. 'Don't you want your baby born in the new house?' In truth, she did, the nesting instinct was strong, but she still had three major interviews to do before she left on her four-month leave.

'It's your baby too, by the way.'

'Our baby.' And with that, his beeper went off, and the estate agent stared at them.

'Don't you two ever stop?'

'Not much.' Mel smiled. They were almost used to it after being married for eight months, during which time he had done nineteen heart transplants, countless bypasses, and she had done twenty-one major interviews and the news five nights a week. And predictably, the show's ratings had gone up. Peter had gone to call his office in another room just then, and he came rushing back and kissed Mel goodbye.

'I've got to go. We have a heart.' It was a donor they had desperately been waiting for, and he had almost given up hope. 'Will you finish here?' She nodded and he vanished, and they heard his car speed away, as the estate agent shook his head again and Mel only smiled.

Chapter 33

'... and thank you, God, for my Grandma' – he looked around sheepishly and grinned as he lowered his voice – and my new bike. Amen.' The entire Thanksgiving table laughed. Matthew had turned seven that week, and his grandmother had given him a brand-new bike. Suddenly he clasped his hands again and squeezed his eyes shut. 'And thank you for Mel too.' He looked apologetically at Val and Jess after that, but it was too late to start again. Everyone was dying to attack their food. Peter had already carved the turkey, and Pam had cooked her favourite recipe for candied yams. The twins had helped with the rest, and everyone was in a festive mood, including Mel, who claimed she had no room for anything. The baby felt huge now. Peter had teased her for the past two months that it was twins again, but the doctor swore that it was not. He could only hear one heart this time, and despite her age, she had opted not to have the amniotic-fluid test, so they had no idea what the baby was. But whatever it was, it was large. It was due in another two days, and most of all, Mel was grateful to have Thanksgiving with them. She had been worried that she would be in the hospital by then. And although they had a new housekeeper, she had wanted the day off, so Mel had cooked the dinner herself.

'Seconds anyone?' Peter looked around with a contented smile. His latest transplant patient was doing well. They had moved into the new house three weeks before and could still smell fresh paint all around them, but they didn't seem to mind. Everything looked beautiful and fresh, and each of them had their own rooms, even the new baby whose room was already filled with toys they all had bought. Matthew had contributed a teddy bear and an old set of cowboy guns, and without saying a word to Mel, Pam had knitted a little dress for the baby to wear home from the hospital. She had been desperately nervous about doing it right, and the entire family knew about the project except Mel, who cried when she opened the gift on her last day at work, when she came home, feeling the letdown of her last Friday-night news for a while.

It had taken them all almost a year to settle down, and in some ways they never would. She would always be dashing off to cover the news, and Peter would be gone at two a.m. to try to repair another damaged heart. But there was something different between them all now. It was a stronger bond than had been there before. They had survived a lot in a year, the threats on Mel, the disastrous romance between Val and Mark ... the new baby ... the threat the new marriage presented to them all ... even the ghost of Anne. Mel had brought the portrait with them; it hung in Pam's room now and it looked well there, and her furniture from New York was unpacked and out of storage at long last.

'Happy, love?' Peter smiled down at her as they sat by the fire in their room. The children were all downstairs in the huge playroom near the pool, playing games and having fun. And Mel looked up at Peter and took his hand.

'Yes, except I ate too much.'

'It doesn't even show.' They both laughed at the enormous bulge which seemed to shift slightly from side to side as Mel watched the baby kick. It seemed to do that constantly these days, and she was ready to be rid of it. Especially after tonight. With Thanksgiving done, she felt free to have the child, she told Peter as they went to bed that night. 'Don't say that tonight, or he'll hear you and come out.' They both laughed and went to bed, and two hours later, Mel got up and felt a familiar pain in her lower back. She got up and sat down in a chair, but all she wanted to do was walk around. She wandered downstairs and looked out into the garden that would be pretty the following spring, but already looked nice now, and sat down in their living room, feeling it was their home, and not just his or hers, but something they had built together and started fresh, like a whole new life.

She went back to their bedroom then, and tried to lie down again, but the baby was kicking too hard and suddenly she felt a short searing pain in her lower abdomen and she gave a small gasp. She sat up and waited to see what would come next, and suddenly there was another pain, and with a feeling of exultation, she touched Peter's hand.

'Hmm?' He barely stirred, and it was only four o'clock.

'Peter.' She whispered his name after the third pain came. She knew it would be hours, but she didn't want to be alone. She wanted to share the excitement of it all with him. This was the moment they had waited for, Peter most of all.

'What?' He suddenly lifted up his head and looked at her more seriously. 'Maybe it's just a false alarm.' She looked down at her enormous stomach and laughed, but the laughter was brief as another pain came, this time joined with a searing arc that shot across her back. She gasped and grabbed his hand, and he supported her as she breathed. And when the pain was over he looked at the clock. 'How often are you getting them?'

She laughed again and looked at him with love in her eyes. 'I don't know. I forgot to look.'

'Oh my God.' He sat up in bed. Hearts he knew, but babies were something else to him, and he had been secretly nervous about her for nine months. 'How long have you been up then?'

'I don't know. Most of the night.' It was five o'clock by then.

'How long were you in labour with the twins?'

'Hell, I don't know. That was seventeen and a half years ago. A while, I guess.'

'You're a big help.' He sat up, still keeping an eye on her. 'I'll call the doctor. You get dressed.' She had another pain this time, and it seemed longer than the ones before. He was panicking but he didn't want to show it. He did not want to deliver his own child at home. He wanted her at the hospital in case anything went wrong. 'Go on.' He helped her up, and she came back a minute later with a vague look.

'What'll I wear?'

'For chrissake, Mel! Anything ... jeans ... a dress ...' She was smiling to herself as she padded off again, and then the waters broke, and she called out to him from the bathroom where she stood wrapped in towels. The obstetrician told Peter to bring her in right away, and they left a note for the kids on the kitchen table where they'd all see it when they got up. 'Gone to pick baby up at hospital, Love, Mom' she wrote with a smile, as Peter urged her out the door. 'Will you hurry up?'

'Why?' She looked supremely calm and Peter envied her.

'Because I don't want to deliver our child in our new car.' He had finally sold Anne's Mercedes and bought a new one for Mel.

'Why not?'

'Never mind, love, never mind.' But he had never felt closer to her as he drove the familiar route he drove so often late at night and as he walked her into the hospital and wheeled her into the maternity ward, he was unbearably proud.

'I can walk, you know.'

'Why walk if you can ride?' But the banter barely covered up all that he felt for her. A thousand thoughts were rushing through his head and he was praying that everything was all right. The baby looked awfully large to him, and he had been wondering about a Caesarean. He asked the obstetrician about it again just outside the labour room, and his old friend patted his arm.

'She's fine, you know. She's doing just fine.' By then it was almost eight o'clock, and she had been in labour for five or six hours.

'How much longer do you think it'll take?' He spoke sotto voce so Mel wouldn't hear and the doctor smiled.

'A while.'

'You sound like Mel.' Peter glared at him and they went back inside. Mel said she wanted to push and the obstetrician said it was too soon, but when he looked again, he saw that things had progressed by leaps and bounds in the last half hour, and he had her wheeled into the delivery room, where she turned red-faced and pushed ferociously as Peter and the nurses urged her on.

'I can see the baby's head, Mel.' The doctor crowed and she beamed.

'You can?' Her face was dripping wet and her hair looked more than ever like flame against the white drapes, and Peter had never loved her more, as she pushed again, and suddenly they heard a cry. Peter took one long step to see the baby born, and the tears poured down his face as he smiled.

'Oh, Mel ... it's so beautiful ...'

'What is it?' But she had to push again.

'We don't know yet.' Everybody laughed and then suddenly the shoulders came out, the body, hips, and legs ... 'A girl!'

'Oh, Mel.' Peter returned to her head and kissed her full on the mouth and she laughed and cried with him, and they handed the baby to her. He knew how much she had wanted a boy, but she no longer seemed to remember that as she held her daughter in her arms, and then suddenly she made an awful face and grabbed Peter's arm, as someone gently took the baby from her.

'Oh ... God ... that hurts ...'

'It's just the placenta now.' The doctor looked unconcerned, and then Peter saw him frown, and a ripple of panic ran down his limbs. Something was happening to her, and she was in hideous pain again, even more so than before.

'Oh ... Peter ... I can't ...'

'Yes, you can.' The doctor spoke softly to her as Peter held her hand, and he wondered why the hell they didn't put her out and see what was wrong, and suddenly as she pushed with all her might there was another wail and Peter's eyes grew wide, and Mel stared at him, already knowing what had happened.

'Not again ...' Peter still didn't understand and the doctor was laughing now, and he began to laugh too. She had had twins again, and no one knew, just as they hadn't with Jess and Val. She looked up at him half rueful, half amused. 'Doubles again.'

'Yes, ma'am.' The doctor handed the baby to Peter this time who held him with a look of awe and then presented him to Mel to hold. 'Madam' – the love spilled from his eyes as they met hers – 'your son.'

FULL CIRCLE

To Alex Haley,
my brother,
my friend,
with much, much love.
And with special love
and thanks
to Lou Blau.

D.S.

PART I
THE EARLY YEARS

Chapter 1

On the afternoon of Thursday, December 11th, 1941, the country was still in a daze. The casualty list was complete, the names of those killed had already been released, and slowly, slowly, in the past few days, the monster of vengeance was raising its head. In almost every American breast pounded a pulse that had been unknown before. It had finally hit us at home, and it wasn't simply a matter of Congress declaring war. There was much more to it than that, much, much more. There was a nation of people filled with dread, with rage, and the sudden fear that it could happen here. Japanese fighter planes could appear overhead at any time of day or night and suddenly wreak destruction in cities like Chicago and Los Angeles, Omaha ... Boston ... New York ... it was a terrifying thought. The war was no longer happening to a distant, remote 'them', it was happening to *us*.

And as Andrew Roberts hurried east in the chill wind, his coat collar up, he wondered what Jean would say. He had already known for two days. When he had signed his name, there hadn't been any doubt in his mind, yet when he'd come home, he had looked into her face and the words had caught in his throat. But there was no choice now. He had to tell her tonight. Had to. He was leaving for San Diego in another three days.

The Third Avenue E1 roared overhead, as his feet pounded on the front steps of the narrow brownstone in which they lived. They had lived there for less than a year, and they hardly even noticed the train anymore. It had been awful at first, at night they had held each other tight and laughed as they lay in bed. Even the light fixtures shook as the elevated train careered by, but they were used to it now. And Andy had come to love the tiny flat. Jean kept it spotlessly clean, getting up sometimes at five o'clock to make him homemade blueberry muffins and leave everything immaculate before she left for work. She had turned out to be even more wonderful than he'd thought ... and he smiled to himself as he turned the key in the lock. There was a chill wind whistling through the hall and two of the lights were burned out, but the moment he set foot inside, everything was cheery and bright. There were starched white organdy curtains, which Jean had made, a pretty little blue rug, slipcovers she had gone to a night class to learn how to make. And the furniture they'd bought secondhand shone like new beneath her hardworking hands. He looked around now, and suddenly felt the first shaft of grief he had felt since he signed up. It was an almost visceral ache as he thought of telling her that he was leaving New York in three days, and suddenly there were tears in his eyes as he realized that he didn't know when he'd be back ... when ... or even if ... but hell, that wasn't the point, he told himself. If he didn't go to fight the Japs, then who the hell would? And if they didn't, then one of these days the bastards would be flying overhead and bombing the hell out of New York ... and this house ... and Jean.

He sat down in the armchair she had upholstered herself in a deep, cozy green, and was lost in his own thoughts ... San Diego ... Japan ... Christmas ... Jean ... he didn't know how long he'd been sitting there when suddenly, startled, he looked up. He had just heard the key in the lock. She flung the door wide, her arms filled with brown bags from the A&P. She didn't see him at first, and then jumped as she turned on the light, and saw him smiling at her, his blond hair falling over one eye as it always did, the green eyes looking straight at her. He was still as handsome as he had been when they first met. He had been seventeen then, and she had been fifteen ... six years ... he was only twenty-three.

'Hi, sweetheart, what are you doing here?'

'I came home to see you.' He walked toward her and easily grabbed the bags in his powerful arms, and she turned her big, dark brown eyes up to him with the same look of awe she always wore when she looked up at him. She was so impressed with him, always had been, he'd had two years of college, going at nights, had been on the track team in school, the football team for a few months till he hurt his knee, and had been a basket ball star when they met during his senior year. And he seemed no less heroic to her now. In fact, he seemed more so to her, and she was so proud of him. He had landed a good job. He sold Buicks in the biggest dealership in New York, and she knew that he'd be the manager eventually ... one day ... or maybe he'd go back to school. They had talked about that. But he brought home a nice paycheck for now, and combined with her own, they did all right. She knew how to stretch a dollar more than a mile. She'd been doing it for a long time. Both her parents had died in a car accident when she was just eighteen, and she'd been supporting herself since then. Fortunately, she had just finished secretarial school when they died, and she was a bright girl. She'd had a job in the same law firm now for almost three years. And Andy was proud of her too. She looked so cute when she went off to work in the well tailored suits that she made herself, and hats and gloves she always bought so carefully, checking the styles in the magazines, and then consulting with Andy to make sure they looked just right. He smiled at her again now, as she peeled off her gloves, and tossed her black felt fedora onto the big green chair. 'How was your day, cutie pie?' He loved to tease her, pinch her, whisk her into his arms, nuzzle into her neck and threaten to ravish her as she walked in from work. It was certainly a far cry from her constantly proper demeanour at work. He dropped in to see her there once in a great while, and she looked so serious and sedate that she almost frightened him. But she had always been that kind of girl. And actually, she'd been a lot more fun since she'd been married to him. She was finally beginning to relax. He kissed her on the back of the neck now and she felt a shiver run up her spine.

'Wait till I put the groceries away. ...' She smiled mysteriously and tried to wrest one of the bags from his hand, but he pulled it away from her and kissed her on the lips.

'Why wait?'

'Andy ... come on. ...' His hands were beginning to rove passionately over her, pulling off the heavy coat, unbuttoning the jet buttons on the suit jacket she wore underneath. The grocery bags had long since been cast aside, as they suddenly stood, their lips and bodies pressed tight against each other, until Jean finally pulled away for air. She was giggling when they stopped, but it didn't discourage his hands. 'Andy ... what's gotten into you ...?'

He grinned mischievously at her, afraid to make a remark that would shock her too much. 'Don't ask.' He silenced her with another kiss, and relieved her of coat, jacket, and blouse, all with one hand, and a moment later, her skirt dropped to the floor as well, revealing the white lace garter belt with matching pants, silk stockings with seams, and a pair of absolutely sensational legs. He ran his hands across her behind, and pressed hard against her again, and she didn't object as he pulled her down on the couch. Instead she pulled his clothes off as suddenly the elevated train roared by and they both started to laugh. 'Damn that thing ...' he muttered under his breath as he unhooked her bra with one hand and she smiled.

'You know, I kind of like the sound of it by now....' This time it was Jean who kissed him, and a moment later their bodies were enmeshed just as their mouths had been, and it seemed hours before either of them spoke in the silent room. The kitchen light was still on, near the front door, but there was no light in the living room where they lay, or the tiny bedroom beyond. But even in the darkness of the room, he could sense that Jean was looking at him. 'Something funny's going on, isn't it?' There had been a small hard rock in the pit of her stomach all week. She knew her husband too well. 'Andy ...?' He still didn't know what to say. It was no easier now than it would have been two days before. And it was going to be even worse by the end of the week. But he had to tell her sometime. He just wished it didn't have to be now. For the first time in three days, he suddenly wondered if he'd done the right thing.

'I don't quite know what to say.'

But instinctively she knew. She felt her heart lurch as she looked up at him in the dark, her eyes wide, her face already sad, as it always was. She was very different from him. There was always laughter in his eyes, always a quick line on his tongue, a joke, a funny thought. He had happy eyes, an easy smile. Life had always been gentle with him. But it was not so with Jean. She had the tense nervousness of those who have had hard times from birth. Born to two alcoholic parents, with an epileptic sister who died in the bed next to Jean when she was thirteen and Jean nine, orphaned at eighteen, struggling almost since the day she was born, and yet in spite of it all, she had a certain kind of innate style, a joie de vivre which had never been allowed to bloom and which Andy knew would blossom in time, if nurtured enough. And he did nurture her, in every way he could. But he couldn't make it easier for her now, and the old sorrow he had seen when they first met suddenly stood out in her eyes again. 'You're going, aren't you?'

He nodded his head, as tears filled the deep, dark eyes and she laid her head back on the couch where they'd just made love. 'Don't look like that, baby, please....' She made him feel like such a son-of-a-bitch, and suddenly unable to face her pain, he left her side and strode across the room to fish a pack of Camels out of his coat. He nervously tapped one out, lit it, and sat down in the green chair across from the couch. She was crying openly now, but when she looked at him, she didn't seem surprised.

'I knew you'd go.'

'I have to, babe.'

She nodded her head. She seemed to understand, but it didn't ease the pain. It seemed to take hours to get up the courage to ask the only thing she wanted to know, but at last she did. 'When?'

Andy Roberts gulped hard. It was the hardest thing he'd ever said. 'Three days.'

She visibly winced and closed her eyes again, nodding her head as the tears slid down her cheeks.

And for the next three days, nothing was ever normal again. She stayed home from work, and seemed to go into a frenzy, doing everything she possibly could for him, washing underwear, rolling socks, baking him cookies for the train. Her hands seemed to fly all day long, as though by keeping them as busy as she could, she would be able to keep a grip on herself, or perhaps even on him. But it was no use, by Saturday night, he forced her to put it all down, to stop packing the clothes he didn't need, the cookies he'd never eat, the socks he could have done without, he took her in his arms and she finally broke down again.

'O God, Andy ... I can't ... how will I live without you...?' He felt as though he had a hole in his guts the size of a fist when he looked into her eyes and saw what he had done to her. But he had no choice ... no choice ... he was a man ... he had to fight ... his country was at war ... and the worst of it was that when he didn't feel sick over what he'd done to her, he felt a strange, unfamiliar thrill of excitement about going to war, as though this was an opportunity he might never have again, something he had to do almost like a mystic rite, in order to become a man. And he felt guilty about that too. And by late Saturday night, it had gotten to him too. He was so torn between Jean's clinging little hands and what he knew he had to do that he wished it was already over with and he was on the train, heading west, but he would be soon enough. He had to report to Grand Central Station at five a.m. And when he finally got up in the tiny bedroom to get dressed, he turned and looked at her, she was quieter now, her tears were spent, her eyes swollen and red, but she looked a little bit more resigned than she had before. For Jean, in some terrible, desperate, frightening way, it was like losing her sister, or her parents, again. Andy was all she had left. And she would rather have died herself than lose him. And suddenly he was leaving her too.

'You'll be all right, won't you, babe?' He sat on the edge of the bed, looking at her, desperate for some reassurance from her now, and she smiled sadly and reached a hand out for his.

'I'll have to be, I guess, won't I?' And then she smiled again, almost mysteriously. 'You know what I wish?' They both knew that, that he weren't going to war. She read his thoughts, and kissed his fingertips. 'Aside from that ... I hope you got me pregnant this week. ...' In the emotions of the past few days, they had thrown caution to the winds. He had been aware of it, but there had been so much else going on. He had just hoped that it wasn't her dangerous time. But he wondered now, as he looked at her. They had been so careful about that for the past year, they had agreed from the first that they didn't want babies for a while, at least not for the first few years until they both got better jobs, or maybe Andy went back to college for another two years. They were in no hurry, they were both young, but now ... in the past week, their whole life had turned upside down.

'I kind of wondered what was happening this week. ... Do you think you could have ...?' He looked worried. That hadn't been what he wanted at all. He didn't want her to be pregnant alone, with him God knows where, at war.

She shrugged. 'I might. ...' And then she smiled again and sat up. 'I'll let you know.'

'Great. That's all we need.' He looked suddenly upset, and then glanced nervously at the bedside clock. It was ten after four. He had to go.

'Maybe it is.' And then suddenly, as though she had to tell him before he left, 'I meant what I said just now, Andy. I'd like that a lot.'

'Now?' He looked shocked as she nodded her head, her voice a whisper in the tiny room.

'Yes.'

Chapter 2

The elevated train roared past the windows of Jean Roberts' apartment, providing the only breeze she had felt in days as she sat motionless in front of the open windows. It felt as though the entire building had turned into an inferno, as the blazing August heat rose off the sidewalks, and seemed to bake right into the walls of the brownstone building. And sometimes at night, she had to leave her bed and sit on the stoop, just to get some air as the train hurtled by. Or she would sit in her bathroom, wrapped in a wet sheet. There seemed to be no way to cool down, and the baby made it worse. She felt as though her whole body were about to explode, and the hotter it got, the more the baby would kick her, as if it knew, as if it were stifling too. Jean smiled to herself at the thought. She could hardly wait to see the baby now ... there were only four weeks left ... four weeks until she held their baby ... she hoped that it would look just like Andy. He was in the Pacific now, doing just what he had wanted to do, 'fighting the Japs', as he said in his letters, although somehow the words always pained her. One of the girls in the law firm she had worked in was Japanese and she had been so nice to Jean when she found out she was pregnant. She even covered for her when Jean was almost too sick to move in the beginning. She would drag herself in to work, and stare into her type-writer, praying that she wouldn't throw up before she reached the bathroom. They had kept her for six months, which was decent of them, it was longer than most firms would have kept her, she knew, but they felt it was the patriotic thing to do, because of Andy, as she told him in one of her letters. She wrote to him almost every day, although she rarely heard from him more than once a month. Most of the time, he was too tired to write, and the letters took forever to reach her. It was a long way from selling Buicks in New York, as he said in one letter, making her laugh about the bad food, and his buddies. Somehow he always seemed to make her laugh with his letters. He made everything sound better than it was, and she was never as frightened after she heard from him. She had been terrified at first, particularly when she felt so ill. She had gone through agonies of conflict after she first found out she was pregnant. It had seemed like such a good idea at first, during those last few days before he left, but when she found out, she had panicked. It meant she had to give up her job, she'd be alone, and how would she support herself, and the baby? She had been desperately afraid of his reaction too, only when he finally wrote to her, he sounded so thrilled that it all seemed fine to her again, and by then, she was almost five months pregnant, and she wasn't as nervous.

And in the last few months she'd had plenty of time to turn their bedroom into a nursery for the baby. She had sewn everything herself in white eyelet with yellow ribbons, sewing and knitting, and making little hats and booties and sweaters. She had even painted pretty little murals on the baby's walls and clouds on the ceiling, although one of her neighbors had given her hell when he found out that she was doing the painting herself and standing on the ladder. But she had nothing else to do now that she wasn't working. She had saved every penny she could, and she wouldn't even go to a movie now, for fear of eating into those savings, and she was receiving part of Andy's paycheck from the army. She was going to need everything she had for the baby, and she was going to stay home for the first few months if she could, and after that she'd have to find a sitter and go back to work. She was hoping that elderly Mrs Weissman on the fourth floor would baby-sit for her. She was a warm, grand-motherly woman who had lived in the building for years, and had been excited to hear about Jean's baby. She checked on her every day, and sometimes she would even come down late at night, unable to sleep herself in the heat, and tap on Jean's door, if she saw a light beneath it.

But tonight, Jean never turned on the lights. She just sat in the dark, feeling breathless and stifled in the killing heat, listening to train after train come by until they stopped and then started again just before the dawn. Jean even watched the sun come up. She wondered if she would ever be able to breathe normally again, or lie down without feeling as though she was being smoth-ered. There were days when it was really very tiring and the heat and the train didn't help. It was almost eight o'clock in the morning when she heard the knock on her door, and assumed it was Mrs Weissman. She put her pink bathrobe on, and with a tired sigh padded toward the front door in bare feet. Thank God she only had four weeks to go. She was beginning to think she couldn't take it for much longer.

'Hi. . . .' She pulled the door open with a weary smile, expecting to see her friend, and blushed to find herself looking into the face of a stranger, a stranger in a brown uniform with a cap and mustard colored braid, holding a yellow envelope toward her. She looked at him, uncomprehending, not wanting to understand because she knew only too well what that meant, and the man seemed to be leering at her. It was as though his face was distorted as she reeled from the shock and the heat, clutching the envelope and tearing it open without saying a word to him. And it was there, just as she had feared, and she looked at the messenger of death again, focusing on the words on his uniform as her mouth formed a scream, and she sank to his feet in a quiet heap on the floor, as he gaped at her in silent horror, and then suddenly called out for help. He was sixteen years old and he had never been that close to a pregnant woman before. Two doors opened across the hall, and a moment later, there was the sound of running feet on the stairs above, and Mrs Weissman was putting damp cloths on Jean's head, as the boy backed slowly away and then hurried down the stairs. All he wanted to do was get out of the stifling little building. Jean was moaning by then, and Mrs Weissman and two other ladies were leading her to the couch where she slept now. It was the same couch where the baby had been conceived, where she had lain and made love with Andy ... Andy ... Andy. ... 'We regret to inform you ... your husband died in the service of his country ... killed in action at Guadalcanal ... in action ... in action ...' Her head was reeling and she couldn't see the faces.

'Jean . . .? Jean. . . .' They kept calling her name, and there was something cold on her face, as they looked at her and at each other. Helen Weissman had read the telegram, and had quickly shown it to the others. 'Jean. . . .' She came around slowly, barely able to breathe, and they helped her to sit and forced her to drink a little water. She looked blankly at Mrs Weissman, and then suddenly she remembered, and the sobs strangled her more than the heat, and she couldn't catch her breath anymore, all she could do was cry and cling to the old woman who held her . . . he was dead . . . just like the others . . . like Mommy and Daddy and Ruthie ... gone ... he was gone ... she would never see him again ... she whimpered almost like a small child, feeling a weight in her heart that she had never felt before, even for the others. 'It's all right, dear, it's all right. ...' But they all knew that it wasn't, and never would be again, not for poor Andy.

The others went back to their apartments a little while later, but Helen Weissman stayed. She didn't like the glazed look in the girl's eyes, the way she sat and stared and then suddenly began to sob, or the terribly endless crying she heard that night when she finally left Jean for a little while, and then returned to open the unlocked door and check on her again as she had all day. She had even called Jean's doctor before he left his office, and he had told Helen to tell Jean how sorry he was to hear the news, and warned Helen that Jean could go into labor from the shock, which was exactly what she was afraid of, and it was exactly what she suspected when she saw Jean press her fists into her back several times later that evening, and walk restlessly around the tiny apartment, as though it had grown too small for her in the past few hours. Her entire world had shattered around her, and there was nowhere left to go. There wasn't even a body to send home ... just the memory of a tall, handsome blond boy ... and the baby in her belly.

'Are you all right?' Helen Weissman's accent made Jean smile. She had been in the country for forty years, but she still spoke with a heavy German accent. She was a wise, warm woman, and she was fond of Jean. She had lost her own husband thirty years before, and she had never remarried. She had three children in New York, who visited her from time to time, mostly to drop their respective children off so she could baby-sit, and a son who had a good job in Chicago. 'You have pains?' Her eyes searched Jean's, and Jean started to shake her head. Her whole body ached after the day of crying, and yet inside she felt numb. She didn't know what she felt, just achy and hot and restless. She arched her back as though to stretch it.

'I'm all right. Why don't you get some sleep, Mrs Weissman?' Her voice was hoarse after the long day. She glanced at the kitchen clock and registered the fact that it had been fifteen hours since she had gotten the telegram telling her about Andy ... fifteen hours, it felt like fifteen years ... a thousand years ... she walked around the room again as Helen Weissman watched her.

'You want to go for a walk outside?' The train whizzed past nearby and Jean shook her head. It was too hot to go for a walk, even at eleven o'clock at night. And suddenly Jean was even hotter than she'd been all day.

'I think I'll have something cold to drink.' She fixed herself a glass of the lemonade she kept in a pitcher in the ice box, and it tasted good going down, but it came back up almost as quickly. She rushed to the bathroom, where she threw up and retched repeatedly and then emerged wanly a little while later.

'You should lie down.' Meekly, she agreed. She was more uncomfortable when she did. It was easier to sit up than lie down, so she tried the comfortable old green chair again, but after a few minutes she found that she couldn't do that either. She had gnawing pains in her lower back and an unsettled feeling in her stomach, and Helen Weissman left her alone again at midnight, but only after insisting that Jean come and get her during the night if she had a problem. But Jean was sure she wouldn't have to. She turned off the lights, and sat alone in the silent apartment, thinking of her husband ... Andy ... of the big green eyes and straight blond hair ... track star ... football hero ... her first and only love ... the boy she had fallen head over heels in love with the first time she saw him, and as she thought of him, she felt a shaft of pain slice through her from her belly to her back, and then again, and again, and yet again, so that she couldn't catch her breath at all now. She stood up unsteadily, nausea overwhelming her, but determined to get to the bathroom, where she clung miserably to the toilet for almost an hour, the pains pounding her body, the retching tearing at her soul, until weakly at last, barely conscious, she began calling for Andy. It was there that Helen Weissman found her at one thirty in the morning. She had decided to check on her once more before going to bed. It was too hot for anyone to sleep that night, so she was awake unusually late. And she thanked God that she was, when she found her. She went back to her own apartment just long enough to call Jean's doctor and the police, who promised to send an ambulance at once. She climbed into a cotton housedress, grabbed her purse, kept the same sandals on her feet, and hurried back to Jean, to drape a bathrobe around her shoulders, and ten minutes later, they heard the sirens. Helen did, but Jean seemed to hear nothing at all as she retched and cried, and Helen Weissman tried to soothe. She was writhing with pain and calling Andy's name by the time they reached New York Hospital, and the baby didn't take long to come after that. The nurses whisked Jean away on a gurney, and they didn't have time to give her anything at all, before the wiry five pound four ounce little girl emerged with jet black hair, and tightly clenched fists, wailing loudly. Helen Weissman saw them both barely an hour later. Jean mercifully drugged at last, the baby dozing comfortably.

And she went back to the apartment house that night, thinking of the lonely years Jean Roberts had ahead, bringing up her baby girl alone, a widow at twenty-two. Helen brushed the tears from her cheek as the elevated train roared by at four thirty that morning. The older woman knew what kind of devotion it would take to bring the child up alone, a kind of religious zeal, a solitary passion to do all for this baby that would never know her father.

Jean gazed at her baby the next morning when they brought her to nurse for the first time; she looked down at the tiny face, the dark silky hair that the nurses said would fall out eventually, and she knew instinctively what she would have to do for her. It didn't frighten Jean at all. This was what she had wanted. Andy's baby. This was his last gift to her, and she would guard her with her life, do all she could, give her only the best. She would live and breathe and work and do, and give her very soul to this baby.

The tiny rosebud mouth worked as she nursed and Jean smiled at the unfamiliar feeling. She couldn't believe that it was twenty-four hours since she had learned of Andy's death, as a nurse came into the room to check on them both. They seemed to be doing fine, and the baby was a good size, considering that she'd been almost four weeks early.

'Looks like she has a good appetite.' The woman in the starched white uniform and cap glanced at mother and child. 'Has her daddy seen her yet?' They couldn't know ... no one did ... except Jean, and Helen Weissman. Her eyes filled with tears and she shook her head as the nurse patted her arm, not understanding. No, her daddy hadn't seen her yet, and he never would. 'What are you going to name her?'

They had written back and forth to each other about that, and had finally agreed on a name for a girl, although they both thought they wanted a boy. Funny, how after the first moment of surprise and near disappointment a girl seemed so much better now, as though that had been their choice all along. Nature somehow managed things well. Had she been a boy, she would have been named after her father. But Jean had found a girl's name that she loved, and she tried it out on the nurse now as her eyes glowed with pride as she held her baby. 'Her name is Tana Andrea Roberts. Tana ...' She loved the sound of it, and it seemed to suit her to perfection.

The nurse smiled as she lifted the tiny bundle from Jean's arms when she was finished nursing. She smoothed the covers expertly with one hand and looked at Jean. 'Get some rest now, Mrs Roberts. I'll bring Tana back to you when she's ready.' The door closed, and Jean laid her head back against the pillow, with her eyes closed, trying not to think of Andy, but only of their baby ... she didn't want to think of how he had died, what they had done to him ... if he had screamed her name ... a tiny sob broke from her as she turned in her bed, and lay on her stomach for the first time in months, her face buried in the pillows ... and she lay there and sobbed for what seemed like hours, until at last she fell asleep ... and dreamt of the blond boy she had loved ... and the baby he had left her ... Tana ... Tana....

Chapter 3

The phone rang on Jean Roberts' desk only once before she answered it. She had a brisk, efficient way about her, which came from long years of managing a mammoth job. It had fallen into her lap twelve years before. She had been twenty-eight, Tana six, and Jean thought she would scream if she had to work one more day in another law firm. There had been three jobs in six years, in law firms that were one more boring than the other. But the pay was good, and she had Tana to think of now. Tana always came first, Tana upon whom the sun rose and set, in Jean's eyes.

'For God's sake, let the kid breathe ...', one of her co-workers had told her once, and Jean had been cool to her after that. She knew exactly what she was doing, taking her to the theater and the ballet, museums, libraries, art galleries and concerts when she could afford to, helping her inhale every drop of culture. Almost every dime she made went to the education and support and entertainment of Tana. And she had saved every penny of the pension from Andy. And it wasn't that the child was spoiled, she wasn't. But Jean wanted her to have the good things in life, the things she herself had seldom had, and which she thought were so important. It was hard to remember objectively now if they would have had that kind of life with Andy. More likely he would have rented a boat and taken them sailing on Long Island Sound, taught Tana to swim at an early age, gone clam digging, or running in the park, riding a bike ... he would have worshipped the pretty little blonde child who looked so exactly like him. Tall, lanky, blonde, green eyed, with the same dazzling smile as her father. And the nurses in the hospital had been right when she was born, the silky black hair had fallen out and had been replaced by pale golden peach fuzz, which as she got older, grew into straight wheat-like shafts of golden hair. She was a lovely looking little girl, and Jean had always been proud of her. She had even managed to get her out of public schools when she was nine and send her to Miss Lawson's. It meant a lot to Jean, and was a wonderful opportunity for Tana. Arthur Durning had helped her in, which he insisted was a small favor. He knew himself how important good schools were for children. He had two children of his own, although they went to the exclusive Cathedral and Williams Schools in Greenwich, and were respectively two and four years older than Tana.

The job came to Jean almost by accident when Arthur came to the law firm where she worked for a series of lengthy conferences with Martin Pope, the senior partner. She had worked for Pope, Madison and Watson for two years by then, and was bored to death, but the salary was more than she dared to hope for. She couldn't afford to run around looking for a 'fun job', she always had Tana to think of. She thought of her night and day. Her whole life revolved around her daughter, as she explained to Arthur when he invited her to drinks after seeing her for almost two months during his meetings with Martin Pope.

Arthur and Marie were separated then, in fact, she had been in New England, at a 'private institution'. He seemed loath to discuss it and she didn't press him. She had her own problems and responsibilities. She didn't go around crying on other people's shoulders about the husband she had lost, the child she supported on her own, the responsibilities, the burdens, the fears. She knew what she wanted for Tana, the kind of life, the education, the friends. She was going to give her security, no matter what, the kind of life she herself had never had. And without Jean having to say too much, Arthur Durning had seemed to understand that. He was the head of one of the largest conglomerates in the country, in plastics, in glass, in food packaging, they even had enormous holdings in oil in the Middle East. He was an enormously wealthy man. But he had a quiet, unassuming way about him that she liked.

In fact, there had been a lot about Arthur Durning that appealed to her, enough so that when he asked her out to dinner shortly after that first drink, she went. And then she went again, and somehow, within a month they were having an affair. He was the most exciting man Jean Roberts had ever met. There was a quiet aura of power about the man that one could almost touch, he was so strong, and yet he was vulnerable too, and she knew that he had suffered with his wife. Eventually he told her about that. Marie had become an alcoholic almost immediately after their second child was born, and Jean knew the pain of that only too well, having watched her parents attempt to drink themselves to death, and in the end, they killed themselves in their car, drunk on an icy road on New Year's Eve. Marie had also cracked up the car, driving a car pool full of little girls one night. Ann and her friends were ten years old, and one of the children had almost been killed. Marie Durning had agreed to put herself away after that, but Arthur didn't have much hope. She was thirty-five and she'd been a hopeless drunk for ten years, and Arthur was desperately tired of it. Enough so to be swept off his feet by Jean. At twenty-eight, there was something unusually dignified about her that he liked, and at the same time, there was something kind and gentle in her eyes. She looked as though she cared a great deal, about everything and in particular her daughter. Her basic warmth came through, and it was precisely what he had needed just then. He hadn't known what to do with her at first, or what to make of what he felt for her. He and Marie had been married for sixteen years, and he was forty-two years old. He didn't know what to do about the children, about his house ... his life ... about Marie. Everything seemed to be hanging so precariously that year, and it was an unusual way of life for him, and one that he didn't like. He didn't take Jean home at first, for fear of upsetting the children, but eventually he saw Jean almost every night, and she began to take care of things for him. She hired two new maids, a gardener he didn't have time to see, she orchestrated some of the small business dinners he liked to give, a party for the children at Christmas, helped him pick out a new car. She even took a few days off to take a couple of brief trips with him. Suddenly it seemed as though she were running his whole life and he couldn't function without her, and she began to ask herself more and more what it meant, except that deep in her heart she knew. She was in love with him, and he was in love with her, and as soon as Marie was well enough to be told, they'd get divorced, and he would marry Jean ....

Except that instead, after six months, he offered her a job. She wasn't sure what to do about that. She didn't really want to work for him. She was in love with him, and he was so wonderful to her, but the way he described it was like throwing open a window onto a vista she had longed for, for years. She could do exactly what she'd done for him in the past six months, just as a friend. Organize parties, hire help, make sure that the children had the right clothes, the right friends, the right nurses. He thought she had fabulous taste, and he had no idea that she made everything she and Tana wore herself. She had even upholstered the furniture in their tiny apartment. They still lived in the narrow brownstone, near where the Third Avenue E1 had been, and Helen Weissman still baby-sat for Tana, when Jean was at work. But with the job Arthur described, she could send Tana to a decent school, he'd even help her get in. She could move to a bigger place, there was even a building Arthur owned on the Upper East Side, it wasn't Park Avenue, he said with his slow smile, but it was far nicer than where they were. When he told her the salary he had in mind, she almost died. And the job would be so easy for her.

If she hadn't had Tana, she might have held out. It would have been easier not to be indebted to him, and yet it was such a wonderful chance to be side by side all the time ... and when Marie was well .... He already had an executive secretary at Durning International, but there was a small secluded office just beyond the conference room which adjoined the handsome wood-panelled office he used. She would see him every day, be right nearby, she would be virtually essential to him, as she was rapidly becoming now. 'It would just be more of the same', he explained, begging her to take the job, offering her even more benefits, an even higher salary. He was already dependent on her now, he needed her, and indirectly his children did too, although they hadn't met her yet. But she was the first person he had relied on in years. For almost two decades everyone else had relied on him, and suddenly here was someone he could turn to, who never seemed to let him down. He had given the matter a great deal of thought and he wanted her near him always, he said, in bed that night as he begged her again to take the job.

In the end, although she seemed to fight so hard, it was an easy choice to make, and her whole life seemed like a dream now as she went to work every day, sometimes after he had spent the night with her. His children were used to his spending a few nights in town. And the house in Greenwich was efficiently staffed now, Arthur was no longer as worried about them, although Ann and Billy had had a hard time at first when Marie left, but they seemed less anxious about it now. And once they met Jean, it was as though they had always been old friends. She took them to movies with Tana constantly, bought them toys, shopped for their clothes, drove their car pools, went to their schools, and their school plays when Arthur was out of town, and she took even better care of him. He was like a well-fed cat, polishing his paws by the fire as he smiled at her one night in the apartment he'd gotten her. It wasn't sumptuous but for Tana and Jean, it was more than enough, two bedrooms, a living room, dining room, handsome kitchen. The building was modern and well built and clean, and they had a view of the East River from the living-room windows. It was a far cry from the elevated train in Jean's old apartment.

'Do you know,' she looked at him with a smile, 'I've never been happier in my life.'

'Neither have I.'

But that was only days before Marie Durning tried to take her own life. Someone told her that Arthur was having an affair, although they didn't say with whom, and things were touch and go with her after that. Six months later, the doctors began talking of letting her go home, and by then Jean had worked for Arthur Durning for over a year. Tana was happy in her new school, new home, new life, as was Jean. And suddenly it was as though everything stopped. Arthur went to see Marie and came home looking grim.

'What did she say?' Jean looked at him with wide, terrified eyes. She was thirty years old now. She wanted security, stability, not a clandestine affair for the rest of her life. But she had never objected to their life because she knew how desperately ill Marie Durning was, and how it worried him. But only the week before he had been talking about marriage to Jean. He looked at her now with a bleak expression she had never seen before, as though he had no hope left, no dreams.

'She said that if she can't come home to us, she'll try to commit suicide again.'

'But she can't do that to you. She can't keep threatening you for the rest of your life.' Jean wanted to scream, and the bitch of it was that Marie could threaten, and did. She came home three months after that, with only a tenuous grip on her own sanity. She was back at the hospital by Christmas that year, home by spring, and this time she held out until fall, and began drinking heavily over bridge lunches with her friends. All in all it went on for more than seven years.

When she came out of the hospital the first time, Arthur was so upset that he actually asked Jean to help her out. 'She's so helpless, you don't understand ... she's nothing like you, sweetheart. She can't cope ... she can barely think.' And for love of Arthur, Jean found herself in the unenviable position of being the mistress caring for the wife. She spent two or three days a week, during the day, in Greenwich with her, trying to help her run the house. Marie was desperately afraid of the help; they all knew that she drank. And so did her kids. At first they seemed to view her with despair, and eventually with scorn. It was Ann who hated her most, Billy who cried when she got drunk. It was a nightmarish scene, and just like Arthur, within a few months, Jean was trapped. She couldn't let her down, let her go ... it would have been like deserting her parents. It was as though this time she could make things happen right. Even though, in the end, Marie came to an almost identical end as Jean's parents. She was going to meet Arthur in town for a night at the ballet, and Jean swore that she was sober when she left, at least she thought she was, but she must have had a bottle with her. She spun out on an icy patch on the Merritt Parkway halfway to New York, and died instantly.

They were both still grateful that Marie never knew of their affair, and the agony of it all was that Jean had been fond of her. She had cried at the funeral more than the children had, and it had taken her weeks to be willing to spend a night with Arthur again. Their affair had gone on for eight years, and now he was afraid of what his children would say. 'In any case, I've got to wait a year.' She didn't disagree with that, and anyway he spent a great deal of time with her. He was thoughtful and attentive. She had never had any complaints. But it was important to her that Tana not suspect their long standing affair ... but finally a year after Marie died, she turned and accused Jean.

'I'm not stupid, you know, Mom. I know what's going on.' She was as long and lanky and beautiful as Andy had been, and she had the same mischievous light in her eyes, as though she were always about to laugh, but not this time. She had hurt for too long, and her eyes almost steamed as she glared at Jean. 'He treats you like dirt and he has for years. Why doesn't he marry you instead of sneaking in and out of here in the middle of the night?' Jean had slapped her for that, but Tana didn't care. There had been too many Thanksgivings they spent alone, too many Christmases with expensive boxes from fabulous stores, but no one but the two of them there, while he went to the country club with his friends. Even the year that Ann and Billy were gone with their grandparents. 'He's never here when it counts! Don't you see that, Mom?' Huge tears had rolled down her cheeks as she sobbed and Jean had had to turn away. Her voice was hoarse as she tried to answer for him.

'That's not true.'

'Yes, it is. He always leaves you alone. And he treats you like the maid. You run his house, drive his kids around, and he gives you diamond watches and gold bracelets and briefcases and purses and perfume, and so what? Where is *he*? That's what counts, isn't it?' What could she say? Deny the truth to her own child? It broke her heart to realize how much Tana had seen.

'He's doing what he has to do.'

'No, he's not. He's doing what he wants to do.' She was very perceptive for a girl of fifteen. 'He wants to be in Greenwich with all his friends, go to Bar Harbor in the summer, and Palm Beach in the winter, and when he goes to Dallas on business, he takes you. But does he ever take you to Palm Beach? Does he ever invite us? Does he ever let Ann and Billy see how much you mean to him? No. He just sneaks out of here so I won't know what's going on, well I do ... dammit ... I do. ...' Her whole body shook with rage. She had seen the pain in Jean's eyes too often over the years, and she was frighteningly close to the truth, as Jean knew. The truth was that their arrangement was comfortable for him, and he wasn't strong enough to swim upstream against his children. He was terrified of what his own children would think of the affair with Jean. He was a dynamo in business, but he couldn't fight the same wars at home. He had never had the courage to call Marie's bluff and simply walk out, he had catered to her alcoholic whims right till the end. And now he was doing the same with his kids. But Jean had her own worries too. She didn't like what Tana had said to her, and she tried to talk to Arthur about it that night, but he brushed her off with a tired smile. He had had a hard day, and Ann was giving him some trouble.

'They all have their own ideas at that age. Hell, look at mine.' Billy was seventeen, and had been picked up on drunk driving charges twice that year, and Ann had just gotten kicked out of her sophomore year at Wellesley, at nineteen. She wanted to go to Europe with her friends, while Arthur wanted her to spend some time at home. Jean had even tried to take her to lunch to reason with her, but she had brushed Jean off, and told her that she'd get what she wanted out of Daddy by the end of the year.

And true to her word, she did. She spent the following summer in the South of France, and picked up a thirty-seven-year old French playboy, whom she married in Rome. She got pregnant, lost the child, and returned to New York with dark circles under her eyes and an enormous diamond ring. Not bad for a twenty-year-old girl. It had made the international press, of course, and Arthur had been sick about it when he met the 'young man'. It had cost him a fortune to buy him off, but he had, and he left Ann in Palm Peach to 'recuperate' as he said to her, but she seemed to get into plenty of trouble there, carousing all night with boys her own age, or their fathers if she had the chance. She was a racy one, in ways of which Jean did not approve, but she was twenty-one now, and there was little Arthur could do. She had gotten an enormous trust from her mother's estate, and she had the funds she needed now to run wild. She was back in Europe, raising hell, before she was twenty-two. And the only thing that cheered Arthur a little bit was that Billy had managed to stay in Princeton that year in spite of several near fatal scrapes he'd been in.

'I must say, they don't give one much peace of mind, do they, love?' They had quiet evenings together in Greenwich now, but most nights she insisted on driving home, no matter how late she got in. His children were no longer there, but she still had Tana at home, and Jean wouldn't dream of staying out for the night unless Tana was at a friend's, or skiing for the weekend somewhere. There were certain standards she expected to maintain and it touched him about her. 'You know, in the end they do what they want anyway, Jean. No matter how good an example you set.' It was true in a way, but he didn't fight her very hard. He was used to spending his nights alone now, and it made it more of a treat when they awoke side by side. There was very little passion left in what they shared. But it was comfortable for them both, particularly for him. She didn't ask him for more than he was willing to give, and he knew how grateful she was for all that he had done for her over the years. He had given her a security she might never have had without him, a wonderful job, a good school for her child, and little extras whenever he could, trips, jewels, furs. They were minor extravagances to him, and though Jean Roberts was still a wizard with a needle and thread, she no longer had to upholster her own furniture or make their own clothes, thanks to him. There was a cleaning woman who came twice a week, a comfortable roof over their heads, and Arthur knew that she loved him. He loved her too, but he was set in his ways, and neither of them had mentioned marriage in years. There was no reason to now. Their children were almost grown, he was fifty-four years old, his empire was doing well, and Jean was still attractive and fairly young, although there had been a matronly look to her now for the past several years. He liked her that way, though, and it seemed hard to believe that it had been twelve years. She had just turned forty that spring. And he had taken her to Paris for the week. It was almost like a dream. She brought back dozens of tiny treasures for Tana, and enchanted her with endless tales, including that of her birthday dinner at Maxim's. It was always sad coming home after trips like that, waking up in bed alone again, reaching out to him in the night and finding no one there, but she had lived that way for so long that it no longer bothered her, or at least she pretended that to herself, and after her outbreak three years before, Tana had never accused her again. She had been ashamed of herself afterwards. Her mother had always been so good to her. 'I just want the best for you ... that's all ... I want you to be happy ... not to be alone all the time....'

'I'm not, sweetheart,' tears had filled Jean's eyes, 'I have you.'

'That's not the same.' She had clung to her mother then, and the forbidden subject had not come up again. But there was no warmth lost between Arthur and Tana when they met, which always upset Jean. Actually, it would have been harder on her if he'd insisted on marrying her after all, because of the way Tana felt about him. She felt that he had used her mother for the past dozen years, and given nothing in exchange.

'How can you say that? We owe him so much!' She remembered the apartment beneath the elevated train, which Tana did not, the meager checks, the nights she couldn't even afford to feed the child meat, or when she bought lamb chops or a little steak for her and ate macaroni herself for three or four days.

'What do we owe him? A deal on this apartment? So what? You work, you could get us an apartment like this, Mom. You could do a whole lot of things for us without him.' But Jean was never as sure. She would have been frightened to leave him now, frightened not to work for Durning International, not to be at his right hand, not to have the apartment, the job, the security that she always knew was there ... the car he replaced every two years so that she could go back and forth to Greenwich with ease. Originally, it had been a station wagon so that she could carpool his kids. The last two had been smaller though, pretty little Mercedes sedans he bought and replaced for her. And it wasn't as though she cared about the expensive gifts, there was more to it than that, much, much more. There was something about knowing that Arthur was there for her, if she needed him. It would have terrified her not to have that, and they had been together for so long now. No matter what Tana thought, she couldn't have given that up.

'And what happens when he dies?' Tana had been blunt with her once. 'You're all alone with no job, nothing. If he loves you, why doesn't he marry you, Mom?'

'I suppose we're comfortable like this.'

Tana's eyes were big and green and hard, as Andy's had been when he disagreed with her. 'That's not good enough. He owes you more than that, Mom. It's so damn easy for him.'

'It's easy for me too, Tan.' She hadn't been able to argue with her that night. 'I don't have to get used to anyone's quirks. I live the way I please. I make my own rules. And when I want, he takes me to Paris or London or LA. It's not such a bad life.' They both knew it wasn't entirely true, but there was no changing it now. They were set in their ways, both of them. And as she tidied the papers on her desk, she suddenly sensed him in the room. Somehow, she always knew when he was there, as though years ago, someone had planted a radar in her heart, designed to locate him. He had walked silently into her office, not far from his own, and was looking at her, as she glanced up and saw him standing there.

'Hello,' she smiled the smile that only they had been sharing for more than twelve years, and it felt like sunshine in his heart as he looked at her. 'How was your day?'

'Better now.' He hadn't seen her since noon, which was unusual for them. They seemed to touch base half a dozen times during the afternoons, met for coffee each morning, and often he took her to lunch with him. There had been gossip on and off over the years, particularly right after Marie Durning died, but eventually it had died down, and people just assumed they were friends, or if they were lovers, it was both discreet and dead-end, so no one bothered to talk about them anymore. He sat in his favorite comfortable chair across from her desk and lit his pipe. It was a smell she had come to love as part of him for more than a decade, and it pervaded all the rooms in which he lived, including her own bedroom with the East River view. 'How about spending the day in Greenwich with me tomorrow, Jean? Why don't we both play hookey for a change?' It was rare for him to do that, but he'd been pushing very hard on a merger for the past seven weeks, and she thought the day off would do him good, and wished he would do things like that more frequently. But now she smiled at him regretfully.

'I wish I could. Tomorrow's our big day.' He often forgot things like that. But she didn't really expect him to remember Tana's graduation day. He looked blankly at her and she smiled as she said the single word. 'Tana.'

'Oh, of course,' he waved the pipe and frowned as he laughed at her, 'how stupid of me. It's a good thing you haven't depended on me the way I have on you, or you'd be in trouble most of the time.'

'I doubt that.' She smiled lovingly at him, and something very comfortable passed between them again. It was almost as though they no longer needed words. And in spite of the things Tana had said over the years, Jean Roberts needed nothing more than she had. As she sat there with the man she had loved for so long, she felt totally fulfilled.

'Is she all excited about graduation day?' He smiled at Jean. She was a very attractive woman in her own way. Her hair was peppered with gray, and she had big, beautiful dark eyes, and there was something delicate and graceful about her. Tana was longer, taller, almost coltlike, with a beauty that would surely stop men in the street in the next few years. She was going to Green Hill College in the heart of the South, and had gotten in under her own steam. Arthur had thought it a damn odd choice for a girl from the North, since it was filled mostly with Southern belles, but they had one of the finest language programs in the States, excellent laboratories, and a strong fine arts program. Arthur had long since told Jean what he thought about that, 'Ridiculous stuff for a girl to take', but Tana had made up her own mind, the full scholarship had come through, based on her grades, and she was all set to go. She had a job in New England at a summer camp, and she would be going to Green Hill in the fall. And tomorrow was going to be her big day – graduation.

'If the volume of her record player is any indication of how she feels,' Jean smiled, 'then she's been hysterical for the last month.'

'Oh God, don't remind me of that ... please ... Billy and four of his friends are coming home next week. I forgot to tell you about that. They want to stay in the pool house, and they'll probably burn the damn thing down. He called last night. Thank God they'll only be here for two weeks before moving on.' Billy Durning was twenty now, and wilder than ever, from the correspondence Jean saw from school. But she knew that he was probably still reacting to his mother's death. It had been hard on all of them. Billy most of all, he had been only sixteen when she died, a difficult age at best, and things were a little smoother now. 'He's giving a party next week, by the way. Saturday night, apparently. I was 'informed', and he asked me to tell you.'

She smiled. 'I shall make due note. Any special requests?'

Arthur grinned. She knew them all well. 'A band, and he said to be ready for two or three hundred guests. And by the way, tell Tana about that. She might enjoy it. He can have one of his friends pick her up here in town.'

'I'll tell her. I'm sure she'll be pleased.' But only Jean knew how big a lie that was. Tana had hated Billy Durning all her life, but Jean had forced her to be courteous whenever they met, and she would make the point to her again now. She owed it to Billy to be polite, and to go to his party if he invited her, after all his father had done for them. Jean never let her forget that.

'... I will not.' Tana looked stubbornly at Jean, as the stereo blared deafeningly from her room. Paul Anka was crooning 'Put Your Head On My Shoulder' and she had already played it at least seven times.

'If he's nice enough to invite you, you could at least go for a while.' It was an argument they had had before, but Jean was determined to win this time. She didn't want Tana to be rude.

'How can I go for a while? It takes at least an hour to drive out there, and another hour back ... so what do I do, stay for ten minutes?' She tossed the long shaft of golden wheat-colored hair over her shoulder with a look of despair. She knew how insistent her mother always was about anything that emanated from the Durnings. 'Come on, Mom, we're not little kids anymore.

Why do I have to go if I don't want to? Why is it rude just to say no? Couldn't I have other plans? I'm leaving in two weeks anyway, and I want to see my friends. We'll never see each other again anyway....' She looked forlorn and her mother smiled at her.

'We'll talk about it another time, Tana.' But Tana knew just how those discussions went. She almost groaned. She knew how stubborn her mother was going to be about Billy Durning's party, and he was a creep, as far as she was concerned. There were no two ways about it, and Ann was even worse in Tana's eyes. She was snobby, stuck up, and she looked easy, no matter how polite she pretended to be to Jean. Tana knew she was probably a whore, she had seen her drink too much at some of Billy's other parties, and she treated Jean in a condescending manner that made Tana want to slap her face. But Tana also knew that any hint of her feelings to her mother would lead them into a major battle again. It had happened too often before, and she wasn't in the mood tonight.

'I just want you to understand how I feel now, Mother. I'm not going.'

'It's still a week away. Why do you have to decide tonight?'

'I'm just telling you....' The green eyes looked stormy and ominous and Jean knew better than to cross her when she looked like that.

'What did you defrost for dinner tonight?'

Tana knew the tactic of avoidance, her mother was good at that, but she decided to play the game for now, and followed her mother into the kitchen. 'I took out a steak for you. I'm having dinner with some of my friends.' She looked sheepish then. As much as she wanted her own life, she hated leaving Jean alone. She knew just how much her mother had given her, how much she had sacrificed. It was that which Tana understood all too well. She owed everything to her mother, not to Arthur Durning, or his selfish, spoiled, over-indulged children. 'Do you mind, Mom? I don't have to go out.' Her voice was gentle, and she looked older than her eighteen years as Jean turned to look at her. There was something very special between the two of them. They had been alone together for a very long time, and had shared bad times and good; her mother had never let her down, and Tana was a gentle, thoughtful child.

Jean smiled at her. 'I want you to go out with your friends, sweetheart. Tomorrow is a very special day for you.' They were going to dinner at '21' the following night. Jean never went there except with Arthur, but Tana's graduation day was occasion enough to warrant the extravagance, and Jean didn't need to be as careful now. She made an enormous salary from Durning International, at least compared to what she had made as a legal secretary twelve years before, but she was cautious by nature, and always a little worried. She had worried a lot over the past eighteen years since Andy had died, and sometimes she told Tana that was why things had turned out so well. She had worried all her life, in sharp contrast to Andy Roberts' easy ways, and Tana seemed to be a great deal like him. There was more joy in her than in her mother, more mischief, more laughter, more ease with life, but then again life had been easier for her with Jean to love and protect her, and Tana smiled now as Jean took out a pan to cook the steak.

'I'm looking forward to tomorrow night.' She had been touched to learn that Jean was taking her to '21'.

'So am I. Where are you all going tonight?'

'To the Village, for a pizza.'

'Be careful.' Jean frowned. She always worried about her, anywhere she went.

'I always am.'

'Will there be boys along to protect you?' She smiled. Sometimes it was hard to know if they were protection or a threat, and sometimes they were both. Reading her mind, Tana laughed and nodded.

'Yes. Now will you worry more?'

'Yes. Of course.'

'You're silly, but I love you anyway.' She threw her arms around her neck, gave her a kiss, and disappeared into her room to turn the music up even louder, as Jean winced, and then found that she was singing along. She had certainly heard it all often enough, but by the time Tana finally turned it off and reappeared, wearing a white dress with big black polka dots and a wide black patent leather belt, with black and white spectator shoes, Jean was suddenly struck by how pleasant the silence sounded. And at the same moment she realized how quiet the apartment would be once Tana was gone, too much so. It would be tomblike when Tana was away.

'Have a good time.'

'I will. I'll be home early.'

'I won't count on it.' Her mother smiled. At eighteen, she no longer had a curfew. Jean knew better than that, and Tana was reasonable most of the time. Jean heard her come in that night, around eleven thirty. She knocked softly on Jean's door, whispered 'I'm home', and went off to her own room, and Jean turned over and went to sleep.

The next day was one that Jean Roberts would long remember, with the long line of innocent looking young girls strung together with garlands of daisies, the boys coming in solemnly behind them, all of them singing in unison, their voices raised, so young, so strong, so powerful, and all of them so new and fresh, as though they were about to be born into the world, a world full of politics and ruses and lies and heartbreaks, and all of it out there, waiting to hurt them. Jean knew that life would never be as simple for them again, as the tears rolled slowly down her cheeks, and they filed slowly out of the auditorium, their voices raised together for the last time. She was embarrassed that a single sob escaped her, but she was not alone, and the fathers cried as hard as their wives, and suddenly all was pandemonium, and the graduates were shouting and cheering in the hallway, kissing and hugging, and making promises that couldn't possibly be fulfilled, to come back, to travel together, to never forget...to always...forever...next year... someday.... Quietly, Jean watched them, and most especially Tana, her face alight, her eyes almost an emerald green, and all of them so excited, so happy.

Tana was still bubbling over with excitement that night when they went to '21', where they ate a delicious dinner, and Jean surprised her by ordering champagne. Generally, she wasn't much in favor of Tana drinking. Her own experience with her parents, and Marie Durning, still frightened her, especially for someone as young as Tana, but graduation day was an exception. And after the champagne, she handed Tana the little box from Arthur. He had had Jean pick it out for him, like all the presents he gave, even those to his own children. Inside was a beautiful gold bangle which Tana slipped on her wrist with cautious pleasure.

'That was nice of him, Mom.' But she didn't look overly excited. They both knew the reasons why, and Tana did not discuss it now. She didn't want to upset her mother. And by week's end, Tana had lost a major battle to her mother. She couldn't stand hearing about it anymore, and she had finally agreed to go to Billy Durning's party. 'But this is the last time I'm going to one of their parties. Is that a deal?'

'Why do you have to be so rigid, Tana? It's nice of them to invite you.'

'Why?' Tana's eyes flashed, and her tongue was too quick to control. 'Because I'm an employee's daughter? Does that make it a special favor from the almighty Durnings? Like inviting the maid?' Tears quickly filled Jean's eyes, and Tana stalked into her room, furious with herself for losing her temper. But she couldn't stand the way her mother felt about the Durnings, not just Arthur, but Ann and Billy too. It was nauseating, as though every little word or gesture were some giant favor to be grateful for. And Tana knew all too well what Billy's parties were like. She had suffered through them before, with too much drinking, too much necking, everybody getting fresh, getting drunk. She hated going to his parties, and tonight was no different.

A friend of his who lived nearby picked her up in a red Corvette he had gotten from his father, and he drove to Greenwich driving eighty miles an hour to impress her, which it didn't, and she arrived feeling as annoyed as she had when she left her apartment. She was wearing a white silk dress, with flat white shoes, and her long slim legs looked particularly graceful as she climbed out of the low slung car, tossing her hair over her shoulder, glancing around, knowing that she would know no one at all. She had particularly hated coming to their parties when she was younger, and the children had pointedly ignored her, but it was easier now. Three boys in madras jackets made a beeline for her, and offered to get her a gin and tonic, or whatever else might be her pleasure. She was noticeably vague and managed to get lost in the crowd, anxious to ditch the boy who had driven her out there. She wandered in the garden for half an hour, wishing she hadn't come, and watching clumps of giggling girls, drinking beer or gin and tonics, the boys watching them. A little while later the music started, and couples began forming, and within half an hour the lights were dim, bodies were chafing happily, and Tana even noticed several couples strolling outside. It was only then that she finally saw Billy Durning. He had been nowhere when they arrived. He walked over to her, and seemed to be giving her a cool appraisal. They had met often enough before, but he always looked her over again, as though he might buy her. It made her angry at him every time she saw him, and tonight was no exception.

'Hello, Billy.'

'Hi. Shit, you're tall.' As a greeting it didn't excite her, and anyway he was

considerably taller than she was, what was the point? But she noticed then that
he was staring at the fullness of her breasts and for a minute she wanted to kick
him, and then gritting her teeth, she decided to make one stab at good manners,
for her mother's sake, if nothing else.

'Thank you for inviting me tonight.' But her eyes said she didn't mean it.

'We can always use more girls.' Like cattle. So many head ... so many tits
... legs ... or better....

'Thanks.'

He laughed at her and shrugged. 'Want to go outside?' She was about to turn
him down, and then figured, why not? He was two years older than Tana, but
he usually acted as though he were ten. Except ten years old with drinking. He
grabbed her arm, and led her through the unfamiliar bodies until they reached
the Durnings' elaborate garden which led, eventually, to the pool house in the
distance, and Tana felt annoyance sweep over her, knowing that it would be
her mother's job to replace everything they damaged, to set it to rights again,
and also to calm Arthur down when he saw the mess.

'Why don't you just try not to behave like animals?' She looked sweetly at
him, and for a moment he was shocked, and then suddenly, something evil and
angry glinted in his eyes as he glared back at her.

'That's a dumb thing to say, but I guess you were always dumb, weren't you?
If my old man hadn't paid to keep you at that fancy school in New York, you'd
probably have wound up in some public school whorehouse on the West Side,
giving your teacher a blow job.' She was so shocked that for a moment she was
breathless as she stared at him, and then wordlessly, she turned and walked
away, as behind her, she could hear him laugh. What an evil little bastard he
was, she thought to herself, as she fought her way back into the house, noticing
that the crowd had thickened considerably in the past half hour, and that most
of the guests were several years older than she was, especially the girls.

She saw the boy who had driven her out from town, a little while later, his fly
open, his eyes red, his shirttail out, and there was a girl frantically sliding her
hands over his body as they shared a half full bottle of scotch. Tana looked at
them in despair, and knew that she had just lost her ride to the city. There was
no way she would have driven anywhere with anyone that drunk. Which left
the option of the train, or finding someone sober, which did not, for the
moment at least, appear likely.

'Wanna dance?' She turned, surprised to see Billy again, his eyes redder, his
mouth leering at her, still gazing at her breasts, barely able to tear his eyes
away, which he did at last, in time to see her shake her head.

'No, thanks.'

'They're banging their asses off in the pool house. Wanna go watch?' Her
stomach turned over at the prospect, and if he hadn't been so revolting she
would have laughed. It was incredible how blind her mother could be to the
Sacred Durnings.

'No, thanks.'

'Whatsa matter? Still a virgin?' The look on his face made her sick, but she
didn't want to let on that he was right. She'd rather he thought simply that he
repulsed her, which was also correct. He did.

'I'm not into watching.'

'Shit, why not? Best sport there is.' She turned and tried to lose him in the crowd, but for some reason he was following her around tonight, and he was beginning to make her uncomfortable. She glanced around the room again, saw that he had disappeared, probably to the pool house to join his friends, and she figured that she had been there for long enough. All she had to do was call a cab, get to the train station, and go home. Not pleasant, but at least not difficult, and glancing over her shoulder to make sure that no one had followed her, she tiptoed up a small back staircase that she knew about, to a private phone. It was very simple, she called information, got the number, and called the cab. They promised to be out there within the next fifteen minutes, and she knew that she was in plenty of time for the last train. And for the first time all night, she felt relief, having gotten away from the drunks and creeps downstairs, and she wandered slowly down the thickly carpeted hall, glancing at the photographs of Arthur and Marie, Ann and Billy as children, and somehow it seemed as though the photographs should have included Jean. She had been so much a part of them, so much of their well being had been because of her, it didn't feel fair to leave her out, and then suddenly without thinking, Tana opened a door. She knew it was the family room her mother often used as a kind of office when she was there. The walls were covered with photographs too, but she didn't see them tonight. As the door opened slowly, she heard a nervous squeal, a 'Shit! ... Hey ... !' She saw two white moons leap into the air, and heard a scuffle of embarrassment as she quickly closed the door again, and then jumped in horror as someone right behind her laughed.

'Ah!' She turned, and found Billy leering at her. 'For heaven's sake....' She had thought he was downstairs.

'I thought you weren't into watching, Miss Lily Pure.'

'I was just wandering around, and I stumbled across. ...' Her face flushed to the roots of her hair as he grinned at her.

'I'll bet ... what'd you come up here for, Tan?' He had heard her mother call her that over the years, but it annoyed her hearing it from him. It was a private name and he had never been her friend.

'My mom usually works in that room.'

'Nah.' He shook his head, as though surprised at her mistake. 'Not in there.'

'Yes, she does.' Tana was sure of it, as she glanced at her watch. She didn't want to miss her cab. But she hadn't heard him honk yet, anyway.

'I'll show you where she does work, if you want.' He began to walk down the hall the other way, and Tana wasn't sure whether or not to follow. She didn't want to argue with him, but she knew that her mother used the family room where they stood. But it was his house after all, and she felt awkward standing there, particularly as groans began reaching her from the couple inside. She had five minutes until her cab and for lack of something better to do, she followed Billy down the hall. It was no big deal, and he swung open a door into another room. 'That's it.' Tana walked to the doorway and stepped in and looked around, realizing instantly that this wasn't where her mother worked. The most dominant thing in the entire room was an enormous bed, covered with gray velvet, trimmed in silk, there was both a gray opossum blanket and a chinchilla one draped across a matching chaise longue. The carpeting was gray too, and there were beautiful prints everywhere. Tana turned to him, looking annoyed.

'Very funny. That's your father's room, isn't it?'

'Yeah. And that's where your old lady works. Hell of a lot of work she does in here, old Jean.' Suddenly Tana wanted to grab him by the hair and slap his face, but forcing herself not to say anything she started to walk out of the room, and instead he grabbed her arm, and yanked her back into it, kicking the door closed with his foot.

'Let go of me, you little shit!' Tana tried to pull her arm away, but was amazed to discover the strength he had. He grabbed her brutally by both arms and shoved her against the wall, knocking the air out of her.

'Want to show me what kind of work your mama does, you little bitch?' She gasped, he was hurting her arms, and tears suddenly came into her eyes, more out of anger than fear of him.

'I'm getting out of here, right now.' She attempted to pull herself away from him, but he slammed her hard against the wall, banging her head against it, and she looked into his eyes, and suddenly she was genuinely afraid of him. There was the look of a madman on his face, and he was laughing at her. 'Don't be a jerk.'

His eyes glinted evilly then, as he crushed her wrists in one powerful hand . . . she had never realized what strength he had . . . and with the other hand, he unzipped his fly and undid his pants, exposing himself, and then grabbing one of her hands in his own, pulling it down towards him. 'Grab onto that, you little cunt.' She was terrified of him now, her face deathly white, pulling away from him, as he pushed up against her, against the wall, and she pushed him away as hard as she could, getting nowhere, as he laughed at her. And suddenly, in horror, she realized what was happening, as she struggled against him . . . the limp penis he had exposed was getting hard and grinding against her . . . it felt like an evil ugly stump, as he smashed her back against the wall again and again, pulling at her dress suddenly, tearing it along the side, to expose the flesh he wanted to see, and suddenly his hands were all over her, her abdomen, her breasts, her thighs . . . he was pressing hard against her, crushing her, smearing her face with his tongue, breathing alcohol fumes in her face, touching her, holding her, grabbing her . . . he felt as though he were tearing at her, and suddenly his fingers plunged into her, between her legs, as she screamed, and bit him hard on the neck, but he didn't even move back. He just grabbed a hunk of her hair and twisted it around his hand . . . until she felt it would come out by the roots . . . and he bit her face viciously. She flailed at him . . . she attempted to fight him with her legs. She was breathless now, fighting for her life more than her virginity, and suddenly crying, sobbing, gasping for air, she felt him throw her down onto the thick gray carpeting . . . and tear her dress from collar to hem, revealing the last of her, tearing the white lace underpants off too, leaving her brown and bare and beautiful, and suddenly begging him, crying, gnashing her teeth, almost hysterical, as he pushed his pants down, and then kicked them off somewhere onto the carpeting, pressing his full weight on her, pinning her down, and only letting up to tear her flesh again, almost limb from limb, his fingers digging into her, ripping her flesh apart, tearing her, and then sucking at her flesh with his mouth as she cried and howled … and each time she attempted to move away from him he would smash her down again until at last she was barely conscious when he entered her, mounting her with all the force he had, plunging into her, as rivers of blood cascaded out onto the thick carpeting, until at last in final orgiastic glory, he exploded atop the barely whining, raggedly breathing girl, her eyes glazed, a trickle of blood coming from her mouth, another from her nose, as Billy Durning stood up and laughed at her, grabbing his own pants off the floor as she didn't move. She looked almost dead as she lay there and he looked down at her.

'Thanks.'

And with that, the door opened, and one of Billy's friends walked in. 'Christ, what did you do to her?' Tana still hadn't moved, although she could hear voices somewhere far, far away.

'No big deal.' Billy shrugged. 'Her old lady is my father's hired cunt.'

The other boy laughed. 'Looks like one of you had a good time at least.' It was impossible not to see the sea of blood beneath her on the gray carpeting. 'She got her period?'

'I guess.' Billy seemed unconcerned as he zipped his pants and she still lay there with her legs spread like a rag doll's, while his friend looked down at her. Billy bent over and slapped her face. 'Come on, Tan, get up.' She didn't move, and he went into the bathroom, wet a towel and dropped it on her, as though she would know what to do with it, but it was another ten minutes before she slowly rolled over in her own mire and threw up. And he grabbed her by the hair again as the other boy watched, and yelled at her. 'Shit, don't do that here, you little pig.' He pulled her roughly to her feet and dragged her into the bathroom where she hung over the bowl, and then finally, reached over and slammed the door. It seemed hours before she could revive herself and there were jagged sobs in her throat. Her cab was long since gone and she had missed the last train, but more than that something hideous had happened to her that she knew she would never recover from. She had been raped. She was shaking from head to foot, trembling violently, her teeth were chattering, her mouth was dry, her head ached, and she couldn't begin to figure out how she was ever going to leave the house. Her dress was torn, her shoes were smeared with blood, and as she sat in the bathroom crouching on the floor, the door opened and Billy strode into the room and threw some things at her. She saw a moment later that it was a dress and a pair of shoes that were some of Ann's things. He looked at Tana tentatively now, and she could see how drunk he was. 'Get dressed. I'll take you home.'

'And then what?' She suddenly screamed at him. 'How do you explain to your father about this?' She was hysterical and he glanced behind him into the room.

'About the rug?' He looked nervous now and she got totally hysterical.

'About *me!*'

'That's not my fault, you little tease.' The horror of what he was saying to her made her even sicker than she was before, but suddenly all she wanted to do was get out of there, and she didn't care if she had to walk back to New York. She pushed past him, clutching the clothes to her, and dashed into the room where the rape had taken place. Her eyes were wild, her hair matted and tangled, her face streaked with tears, and she bolted naked from the room and smack into his friend, who laughed at her nervously.

'You and Billy had a good time, huh?' He laughed at her and wild eyed, she ran past him, and into a bathroom she knew was there. She pulled on the clothes he had given her, and she ran downstairs. It was too late to catch a train, no point to call a cab. She saw that the musicians were gone, and she ran down the driveway, leaving her torn dress and her handbag behind, but she didn't give a damn. She just wanted to get away from there. She could hitchhike if she had to, stop a police car ... anything ... the tears were caked on her face, and she was breathing hard as she began to run, and then suddenly bright head-lights shone on her and she ran harder knowing instinctively that he was coming after her. She could hear his tires on the gravel road, and she began to dart in and out of the trees, crying softly, as the tears rolled into her hair, as he honked the horn and shouted at her.

'Come on, I'll take you home.'

She didn't answer him. She just kept running as fast as she could, but he wouldn't go away. He just kept driving after her, zigzagging, following her course on the deserted road until finally she turned and screamed hysterically at him. 'Leave me alone!' She stood bent over in the road, crying, sobbing, hugging her knees, and slowly he got out of the car and walked towards her. The night air was beginning to sober him, and he looked different than he had before, no longer crazed, but gray and grim, and he had brought his friend along, who was silently watching them from the passenger seat of Billy's long, sleek, dark green XKE.

'I'll drive you home.' He stood in the road, legs spread, the car headlights behind him glaring eerily at them. 'Come on, Tan.'

'Don't call me that.' She looked like a frightened little girl. He had never even been her friend, and now ... and now ... she wanted to scream each time she thought of it, but now she couldn't even scream anymore, and she no longer had the strength to run away from him. Her whole body ached, her head pounded, there was dried blood over her face and on her thighs, and now she stared blankly at him, stumbling along the road, as he reached out and tried to grab her arm, and she screamed at him and darted away again. He stood and stared at her for a moment, and then got back in the car and drove off. He had offered to take her home, if she didn't want to go, to hell with her, and she stumbled along the road, aching from head to foot. Not twenty minutes later he was back again. He screeched to a halt beside her, got out and grabbed her by the arm. She saw that the other boy was no longer in the car, and suddenly she wondered if he was going to rape her again. A wave of terror ran through her as he pulled her toward the car, and she pulled away, but this time he jerked her hard and shouted at her, and she could smell whiskey on his breath again.

'Goddammit, I told you I'd take you home. Now get in the fuckin' car!' He almost threw her onto the seat, and she realized that there was no arguing with him. She was alone with him, and he would do whatever he wanted with her.

She had already learned that. She sat bleakly beside him in the XKE, and he roared off into the night, as she waited for him to take her somewhere else to torture her again, but he got on the highway, sank his foot to the floor, and the breeze whipping through the car seemed to sober both of them. He glanced over at her several times, and waved at the box of tissues on the floor. 'You'd better clean yourself up before you go home.'

'Why?' She looked straight ahead at the empty road. It was after two o'clock, and even her eyes felt numb. Only a few trucks went whizzing by, driving straight through the night.

'You can't go home like that.' She didn't answer him, and she didn't turn to look at his face. She still half expected him to stop and try to rape her again, and this time she was expecting it. She would run as fast as she could, across the highway if she dared, and maybe one of the trucks would stop. She still couldn't believe what he had done to her, and she was wondering now if it had somehow been her fault, had she not fought him hard enough, had she done something to encourage him...? They were hideous thoughts as she noticed the powerful sports car beginning to weave. She turned and glanced at him, and noticed that he was falling asleep at the wheel. She jerked on his sleeve, and he started and looked at her. 'Why the hell'd you do that? You could've caused an accident.' She would have liked nothing better for him. She would have liked to see him lying dead by the side of the road.

'You were falling asleep. You're drunk.'

'Yeah? So what?' He sounded more tired than surly now, and he seemed all right for a while, until she saw the car weave again, but this time before she had a chance to grab his arm or shake him awake, an enormous trailer truck sped by, and the sports car veered. There was a hideous, grinding shriek of brakes, as the truck jack-knifed and overturned, and miraculously the XKE whizzed just past the cab and came to rest with its nose crushed by a tree. Tana hit her head hard as they stopped, and she sat staring ahead for a long time, and then suddenly she was aware of a soft moaning beside her. His face was covered with blood and she didn't move. She just sat and stared, and then suddenly the door opened and there was a strong pair of hands on her arm, and then she began to scream. Suddenly the events of the endless night had caught up with her and she totally lost control, sobbing and hysterically trying to run from the car, as two passing trucks stopped, and the drivers tried to subdue her until the cops came, but her eyes were uncomprehending and wild. They had cold compresses on Billy's head, and he had a terrible gash over one eye. The police arrived a short time later, followed by an ambulance, and all three victims were taken to the New Rochelle Hospital Medical Center nearby. The truck driver was almost instantly released. His vehicle had suffered more damage than he had, miraculously. Billy was being stitched up. It was also noted that he had been driving under the influence of alcohol, and as his third offence, it would cost him his driver's license, which seemed to worry him more than the wounded eye. Tana's entire body seemed to be covered with blood, but oddly enough the staff noticed that most of it was dried. They couldn't seem to get her to explain what had happened to her, and she hyperventilated each time she tried. A pleasant young nurse gently wiped her off, while Tana just lay on the examining table and cried. They administered a sedative, and by the time her mother arrived at four o'clock she was half asleep.

'What happened...? my God!' She was looking at the bandage on Billy's eye. 'Billy, will you be all right?'

'I guess.' He smiled sheepishly, and she noticed again what a handsome boy he was, although he had always looked less like his father and more like Marie. And suddenly the smile faded and he looked terrified. 'Did you call Dad?'

Jean Roberts shook her head. 'I didn't want to frighten him. They told me you were all right when they called, and I thought I'd take a good look at you both first myself.'

'Thanks.' He glanced over at Tana's dozing form and then shrugged almost nervously. 'I'm sorry about ... that I ... we wrecked the car....'

'The important thing is that neither of you were badly hurt.' She frowned as she looked at Tana's matted blonde hair, but there was no longer any evidence of blood anywhere, and the nurse tried to explain how hysterical Tana had been.

'We gave her a sedative. She should sleep for a while.'

Jean Roberts frowned. 'Was she drunk?' She already knew that Billy was, but there would be hell to pay if Tana was too, but the young nurse shook her head.

'I don't think she was. Mostly frightened, I think. She got a nasty little bump on her head, but nothing more than that. We don't see any evidence of concussion or whiplash, but I'd keep an eye on her.' And as she said the words, hearing them talking around her, Tana woke up, and she looked at her mother as though she had never seen her before, and then silently began to cry, as Jean took her in her arms and made gentle cooing sounds.

'It's all right, baby ... it's all right....'

She shook her head violently, taking great gulps of air, 'No, it's not ... it's not ... he ...' But Billy stood there staring at her, with an evil look in his eye, and she couldn't say the words. He looked as though he would hit her again, and she turned away, choking on her sobs, still feeling his eyes on her. She couldn't look at him again ... couldn't see him ... never wanted to see him again....

She lay on the back seat of the Mercedes her mother had driven out, and they took Billy home. And Jean was inside with him for a long time. They threw the last people out, made half a dozen others get out of the pool, tossed two couples out of Ann's bed, and told the group in the pool house to settle down, and as Jean walked back to the car where Tana still was, she knew she had her week's work cut out for her. They had destroyed half the furniture, set fire to some of the plants, spoiled the upholstery, left spots on the rugs, and there was everything from plastic glasses to whole pineapples in the pool. She didn't want Arthur to even see the place until she had had it set to rights again. She got in to the car with a long tired sigh, and glanced at Tana's still form. Her daughter seemed strangely calm now. The sedative had taken effect.

'Thank God they didn't go into Arthur's room.' She started the car, and Tana shook her head with a silent no, but she couldn't say the words. 'Are you all right?' That was really all that mattered. They could have been killed. It was a miracle they hadn't been. It was all she could think of when the phone rang at three o'clock. She had already been worried sick for several hours, and instinctively, when she had heard the phone, she had known. And she had answered it on the first ring.

'How do you feel?' All she could do was stare at her mother and shake her head. 'I want to go home.' The tears slid down her cheeks again, and Jean wondered again if she was drunk. It had obviously been a wild night, and Tana had been part of it. She also noticed that she wasn't wearing the same dress she'd been wearing when she left.

'Did you go for a swim?' She sat up, her head reeling, and shook her head, as her mother glanced at her in the mirror and saw the strange look in Tana's eyes. 'What happened to your dress?'

She spoke in a cold hard voice that didn't even sound like her to Jean's ears. 'Billy tore it off.'

'He did what?' She looked surprised, and then smiled. 'Did he throw you in the pool?' It was the only image she had of him, and even if he had been a little drunk, he was harmless enough. It was just damn lucky he hadn't hit the truck. It was a good lesson for them both. 'I hope you learned a lesson tonight, Tan.' She began to sob again at the sound of the nickname Billy had used until finally Jean pulled off the road and stared at her. 'What's happening to you? Are you drunk? Did you take drugs?' There was accusation in her voice, in her eyes, and none of that had been there when she drove Billy home. How unfair life was, Tana thought to herself. But her mother just didn't understand what Precious Little Billy Durning had done. She looked straight into her mother's eyes.

'Billy raped me in his father's room.'

'*Tana!*' Jean Roberts looked horrified. 'How can you say a thing like that? He would never do such a thing!' Her anger was at her own child, not at her lover's son. She couldn't believe a thing like that about Billy, and it was written all over her face as she glared at her only child. 'That's a terrible thing to say.' It was a terrible thing to do. But Jean only stared at her.

Two lonely tears rolled relentlessly down Tana's cheeks. 'He did.' Her face crumbled at the memory. 'I ... swear....' She was getting hysterical again as Jean turned and started the car, and this time she did not glance into the back seat again.

'I don't ever want to hear you say a thing like that again, about anyone.' Surely not someone they knew ... a harmless boy they had known for half his life ... she didn't even care to think about what would make Tana say a thing like that, jealousy perhaps of Billy himself, or Ann, or Arthur.... 'I never want to hear you say that again. Is that clear?' But there was no answer from the back seat. Tana just sat there, looking glazed. She would never say it again. About anyone. Something inside her had just died.

Chapter 4

The summer sped past Tana easily after that. She spent two weeks in New York, recuperating, while her mother went to work every day. And Jean was concerned about her, but in an odd, uncomfortable way. There seemed to be nothing wrong with her, but she would sit and stare into space, listening to nothing, not seeing her friends. She wouldn't answer the phone when Jean, or anyone else, called. Jean even mentioned it to Arthur at the end of the first week. She almost had the house in Greenwich put to rights again, and Billy and his friends had moved on to Malibu. They had all but destroyed the house at the pool, but the worst damage of all was a section of the rug in Arthur's room which looked as though it had been cut out with a knife. And Arthur had had plenty to say to his son about that.

'What kind of savages are all of you? I ought to be sending you to West Point instead of Princeton for chrissake so they can teach you a thing or two about how to behave. My God, in my day, no one I'd ever known would behave like that. Did you see that carpeting? They tore the whole damn thing up.' Billy had looked both subdued and chagrined.

'I'm sorry, Dad. Things got a little out of hand.'

'A little? And it's a wonder you and the Roberts girl weren't killed.' But on the whole he'd been all right. His eye was still bothering him a little when he left, but the stitches on the eyebrow had already been removed. And he still seemed to be out every night right up until they left for Malibu. 'Damn wild kids ...' Arthur had growled at her. 'How's Tana now?' She had mentioned to Arthur several times how oddly Tana had behaved, and she really wondered if she hadn't had a worse blow on the head than they had first thought.

'You know she was almost delirious that first night ... in fact she was....' She still remembered the ridiculous tale about Billy that Tana had tried to tell. The girl really wasn't all there ... and Arthur looked worried too.

'Have her looked at again.' But when Jean tried to insist, Tana refused. Jean almost wondered if she was well enough to go to New England for her summer job, but on the night before she was due to leave, she quietly packed her bag, and the next morning she came to the breakfast table with a pale, wan, tired face, but for the first time in two weeks, when Jean handed her a glass of orange juice, she smiled, and Jean almost sat down and cried. The house had been like a tomb since the accident. There were no sounds, no music, no laughter, no giggles on the phone, no voices, only dead silence everywhere. And Tana's deadened eyes.

'I've missed you, Tan.' At the sound of the familiar name, Tana's eyes filled with tears. She nodded her head, unable to say anything. There was nothing left for her to say. To anyone. She felt as if her life were over. She never again wanted to be touched by a man, and she knew she never would again. No one would ever do to her what Billy Durning had done, and the tragedy was that Jean couldn't face hearing it, or thinking of it. In her mind, it was impossible, so it didn't exist, it hadn't happened. But the worst of it was that it had. 'Do you really think you're up to going to camp?'

Tana had wondered about that herself; she knew that the choice was an important one. She could spend the rest of her life hiding there, like a cripple, a victim, someone shrivelled and broken and gone, or she could begin to move out again, and she had decided to do that. 'I'll be all right.'

'Are you sure?' She seemed so quiet, so subdued, so suddenly grown up. It was as though the bump on her head in the car accident had stolen her youth from her. Perhaps the fear itself had done that. Jean had never seen such a dramatic change in such a short time. And Arthur kept insisting that Billy had been fine, remorseful, but almost his old self by the time he left for his summer holiday, which was certainly not the case here. 'Look, sweetheart, if you don't feel up to it, just come home. You want to start college in the fall feeling strong.'

'I'll be all right.' It was almost all she said before she left, clinging to her single bag. She took the bus to Vermont as she had twice before. It was a summer job she had loved, but it was different this year, and the others noticed it too. She was quieter, kept to herself, and never seemed to laugh anymore. The only time she talked to anyone at all was with the campers themselves. It saddened the others who had known her before, 'Something must be wrong at home....' 'Is she sick...?', 'Wow, she's like a different girl....' Everyone noticed, and no one knew. And at the end of the summer, she got on the bus and went home again. She had made no friends this year, except among the kids, but even with them, she wasn't as popular as she'd been before. She was even prettier than she'd been in previous years but all of the kids agreed this time, 'Tana Roberts is weird.' And she knew herself that she was.

She spent two days at home with Jean, avoided all her old friends, packed her bags for school, and boarded the train with a feeling of relief. Suddenly, she wanted to get far, far from home ... from Arthur ... from Jean ... from Billy ... from all of them ... even the friends she'd had at school. She wasn't the same carefree girl who had graduated three months before. She was someone different now, someone haunted and hurt, with scars on her soul. And as she sat on the train and rolled through the south, she slowly began to feel human again. It was as though she had to get far, far from them, from their deceptions, their lies, the things they couldn't see, or refused to believe, the games they played ... it was as though ever since Billy Durning had forced his way into her, no one could see her anymore. She didn't exist, because they couldn't acknowledge Billy's sin ... but that was only Jean, she told herself. But who else was there? If her own mother didn't believe her ... she didn't want to think about it anymore. Didn't want to think about any of it. She was going as far away as she could, and maybe she'd never go home, although she knew that too was a lie. Her mother's last words to her had been, 'You'll come home for Thanksgiving, won't you, Tan?' It was as though her mother was afraid of her now, as though she had seen something in her daughter's eyes that she just couldn't face, a kind of bleeding, open, raw pain that she couldn't help and didn't want to be there. She didn't want to go home for Thanksgiving, didn't want to go home ever again. She had escaped their tiny, petty lives ... the hypocrisy ... Billy and his barbaric friends ... Arthur and the years and years he had used Jean ... the wife he had cheated on ... and the lies Jean told herself ... suddenly Tana couldn't stand it anymore, and she couldn't go far enough to get away from them. Maybe she'd never go back ... never.

... She loved the sound of the train, and she was sorry when it stopped in Yolan. Green Hill College was two miles away and they had sent a lumbering old station wagon for her, with an old black driver with white hair. He greeted her with a warm smile, but she looked at him suspiciously as he helped her load her bags.

'You been on the train long, miss?'

'Thirteen hours.' She barely spoke to him on the brief drive to the school, and had he ever seemed about to stop the car, she would have leapt out and begun to scream. But he sensed that about her, and he didn't push her by trying to get too friendly with her. He whistled part of the way, and when he got tired of that he sang, songs of the Deep South that Tana had never heard before, and in spite of herself, when they arrived, she smiled at him.

'Thanks for the ride.'

'Anytime, miss. Just come on down to the office and ask for Sam, I'll give you a ride anywhere you want to go.' And then he laughed the warm black laugh, smiling at her. 'There ain't too many places to go around here.' He had the accent of the Deep South, and ever since she had gotten off the train she had noticed how beautiful everything was. The tall majestic looking trees, the bright flowers everywhere, the lush grass, and the air still, heavy and warm. One had a sudden urge to just stroll off somewhere quietly, and when she saw the college itself for the first time, she just stood there and smiled. It was all she had wanted it to be. She had wanted to come here to visit the winter before, but she just hadn't had time. Instead, she had interviewed with their travelling representative up North, and gone on what she'd seen in the brochures. She knew that academically they were one of the best schools, but she had actually wanted something more – their reputation, and the legends she had heard about what a fine old school it was. It was old-fashioned, she knew, but in a way that appealed to her. And now as she looked at the handsome white buildings, perfectly kept, with tall columns, and beautiful French windows looking out on a small lake, she almost felt as though she had come home.

She checked in at the reception room, filled in some cards, wrote down her name on a long list, found out what building she'd be living in, and a little while later, Sam was helping her again, loading all of her luggage on an old country cart. It was almost like a trip back in time just being there, and for the first time in months, she felt peaceful again. She wouldn't have to face her mother here, wouldn't have to explain how she felt or didn't feel, wouldn't have to hear the hated Durning name, or see the unknowing pain Arthur inflicted on her mother's face ... or hear about Billy again ... just being in the same town with them had stifled her, and for the first month or two after the rape, all she had wanted to do was run away. It had taken all the courage she had to go on to camp that summer anyway, and each day there had been a battle too. She wanted to flinch each time someone came too close, especially the men, but even the boys frightened her now too. At least she didn't have to worry about that here. It was an all-women's school, and she didn't have to attend the dances or proms, or nearby football games. The social life had appealed to her when she had first applied, but she didn't care about that now. She didn't care about anything ... or at least she hadn't in three months ... but suddenly ... suddenly ... even the air here smelt good, and as Sam rolled the luggage cart along, she looked at him with a slow smile and he grinned at her.

'It's a long way from New York.' His eyes seemed to dance, and the nubby white hair looked soft.

'It sure is. It really is beautiful here.' She glanced out at the lake and then back at the buildings behind her, fanned out, with still smaller buildings ahead of them. It looked almost like a palatial estate, which was what it had once been, everything was so perfectly manicured, immaculately kept. She was almost sorry her mother couldn't see it now, but perhaps she would eventually.

'It used to be a plantation, you know.' He told hundreds of girls that every year. He loved to tell the story to the girls. His grand daddy had been a slave right here, he always bragged, as they looked at him with wide eyes. They were so young and so fine, almost like his own daughter had been, except she was a grown woman now, with children of her own. And these girls would be married and have children soon too. He knew that every year, in the spring, girls came back from everywhere to get married in the beautiful church right there on the grounds, and after graduation ceremonies, there were always at least a dozen who got married in the ensuing days. He glanced at Tana as she loped along at his side, wondering how long this one would last. She was one of the prettiest girls he had ever seen, with long shapely legs, and that face, the shaft of golden hair, and those enormous green eyes. If he'd known her for a while he would have teased her and told her she looked like a movie star, but this one was more reserved than most. He had noticed all along that she was unusually shy. 'You been here before?' She shook her head, looking up at the building where he had just stopped the cart. 'This is one of the nicest houses we got. Jasmine House. I've already brought five girls here today. There should be about twenty-five or so here in all, and a housemother to keep an eye on all of you,' he beamed, 'though I'm sure none of you will be needing that.' He laughed his deep, rich burst of laughter again, which sounded almost musical, and Tana smiled, helping him with some of the bags. She followed him inside, and found herself in a pleasantly decorated living room. The furniture was almost entirely antique, English and Early American, the fabrics were flowery and bright, and there were big bouquets of flowers in large handsome crystal vases on several tables and a desk. There was a homely atmosphere as Tana stepped in and looked around, and one of the first things that struck her about the place was that it was ladylike. Everything looked proper and neat, and as though one ought to be wearing a hat and white gloves, and suddenly Tana looked down at her plaid skirt, her loafers and knee socks, and smiled at the woman coming across the room to her in a neat gray suit. She had white hair and blue eyes. She was their housemother, Tana soon learned. She had been housemother of Jasmine House for more than twenty years, she had a gentle Southern drawl, and when her jacket opened, Tana noticed a single strand of pearls. She looked like someone's aunt, and there were deep smile lines around her eyes.

'Welcome to Jasmine House, my dear.' There were eleven other houses on campus much like this, 'But we like to think that Jasmine is the very best.' She beamed at Tana, and offered her a cup of tea as Sam took her bags upstairs. Tana accepted the flowered cup with the silver spoon, declined a plate of bland looking little cakes, and sat looking at the view of the lake, thinking of how strange life was. She felt as though she had landed in a different universe. Things were so different from New York ... suddenly here she was, far from everyone she knew, drinking tea, eating cakes, talking to this woman with blue eyes and pearls ... when only three months before she had been lying on Arthur Durning's bedroom floor being raped and beaten by his son.... '... don't you think, dear?' Tana stared blankly at the housemother, not sure of what she had just said, and demurely nodded her head, feeling suddenly tired. It was so much to take in all at once.

'Yes ... yes ... I do....' She wasn't even sure what she was agreeing with, and suddenly all she wanted to do was escape to her room. At last, they finished their tea, set down their cups, and Tana had a sudden urge to laugh, wondering just how much tea the poor woman had had to drink that day, and then as though sensing Tana's impatience to settle in, she led the way to her room. It was up two handsomely curved flights of stairs, on a long hall, with flower prints and photographs of alumnae interspersed. Her room was at the very end of the hall. The walls were a pale pink, the curtains and bedspreads chintz. There were two narrow beds, two very old chests, two chairs, and a tiny corner sink. It was a funny old-fashioned room and the ceiling sloped directly over their beds. The housemother was watching her and seemed satisfied as Tana turned to her with a smile.

'This is very nice.'

'Every room in Jasmine House is.' She left the room shortly after that, and Tana sat staring at her trunks, not quite sure what to do, and then she lay down on her bed, looking out at the trees. She wondered if she should wait for her roommate to arrive before simply taking over one of the chests or half of the hanging space, and she didn't feel like unpacking anyway. She was thinking of taking a walk around the lake when she heard a knock on the door and suddenly Old Sam appeared. She sat up quickly on the edge of the bed, and he walked into the room carrying two bags with a strange look on his face. He glanced over at where Tana sat, seemed to shrug, and just looked at her.

'I guess this is a first for us.' What is? Tana looked confused as he shrugged again and disappeared, and Tana glanced over at the bags. But there seemed nothing remarkable there, two large navy blue and green plaid bags with railroad tags, a make-up case, and a round hat box, just like the ones filled with

Tana's junk. She wandered slowly around the room, wondering when their owner would appear. She expected an endless wait as she imagined the tea ritual, but in the end she was surprised at how quickly the girl appeared. The housemother knocked first, stared into Tana's eyes portentously as she opened the door, and then stood aside, as Sharon Blake seemed to float into the room. She was one of the most striking girls Tana thought she had ever seen, with jet black hair pulled tightly back, brilliant onyx eyes, teeth whiter than ivory in a pale cocoa face that was so finely etched it barely seemed real. Her beauty was so unique, her movements so graceful, her style so marked that she literally took Tana's breath away. She was wearing a bright red coat, and a small hat, and she tossed both swiftly into one of the room's two chairs, to reveal a narrow tube of gray wool dress, the exact same color as her well-made gray shoes. She looked more like a fashion plate than a college girl, and Tana inwardly groaned at the things she had brought. They were all kilts and slacks, old wool skirts that she didn't really care about, a lot of plain shirts, V neck sweaters, and two dresses her mother had bought her at Saks just before she left.

'Tana,' the housemother's voice said that she took the introduction *very* seriously, 'this is Sharon Blake. She's from the North too. Although not as far north as you. She's from Washington, DC.'

'Hello.' Tana glanced shyly at her, as Sharon shot her a dazzling smile and extended a hand.

'How do you do.'

'I'll leave you two girls alone.' She seemed to look at Sharon almost with a look of pain, and Tana with immeasurable sympathy. It cut her to the core to do this to her, but someone had to sleep with the girl, and Tana was a scholarship student after all. It was only fair. She had to be grateful for whatever she got. And the others wouldn't have put up with it. She softly closed the door, and walked downstairs with a determined step. It was the first time this had ever happened at Jasmine House, at Green Hill for that matter, and Julia Jones was wishing that she could have had something a little stronger than tea that afternoon. She needed it. It was a terrible strain after all.

But upstairs Sharon only laughed as she threw herself into one of the room's uncomfortable chairs and looked at Tana's shining blonde hair. They were an interestingly contrasted pair. The one so fair, the other dark. They eyed each other curiously as Tana smiled, wondering what she was doing there. It would have been easier for her to go to a college in the North, than to come here. But she didn't know Sharon Blake yet. The girl was beautiful, there was no doubt about that, and she was expensively dressed. Tana noticed that again, too, as Sharon kicked off her shoes.

'Well,' the delicate, dark face broke into a smile again, 'what do you think of Jasmine House?'

'It's pretty, don't you think?' Tana still felt shy with her, but there was something appealing about the lovely girl. There was something raw and courageous and bold that stood out on the exquisite face.

'They gave us the worst room, you know.' Tana was shocked at that.

'How do you know?'

'I looked as we walked down the hall.' She sighed then and carefully took off her hat. 'I expected that.' And then she looked Tana over appraisingly. 'And what sin did you commit to wind up rooming with me?' She smiled gently at Tana. She knew why she was there, she was the only token Negro to be accepted at Green Hill, and she was unusual, of course. Her father was an author of distinguished prose, winner of the National Book Award and the Pulitzer Prize, her mother was an attorney, currently in government, she would be different from most Negro girls. At least they expected her to be ... although one could never be sure, of course ... and Miriam Blake had given her oldest child a choice before sending her to Green Hill. She could have gone somewhere in the North, to Columbia in New York, her grades were good enough, or Georgetown closer to home ... there was UCLA if she was serious about an acting career ... or there was something important she could do, her mother said ... 'something that will mean something to other girls one day, Sharon.' Sharon had stared at her, not sure what she meant. 'You could go to Green Hill.'

'In the South?' Sharon had been shocked. 'They wouldn't even let me in.'

Miriam had glared at her. 'You don't understand yet, do you, babe? Your father is Freeman Blake. He's written books that people have read all around the world. Do you really think they'd dare to keep you out today?'

Sharon had grinned nervously. 'Hell, yes. Mama, they'd tar and feather me before I even unpacked.' The thought terrified her. She knew what had happened in Little Rock three years before. She read the news. It had taken tanks and the National Guard to keep black children in a white school. And this wasn't just any little old school they were talking about. This was Green Hill. The most exclusive woman's junior college in the South, where daughters of Congressmen and Senators, and the governors of Texas and South Carolina and Georgia sent their little girls, to get two years of smarts before settling down with boys of their own kind. 'Mama, that's nuts!'

'If every black girl in this country thinks like that, Sharon Blake, then a hundred years from now we'll still be sleeping in black hotels, sitting at the back of the bus, and drinking out of water fountains that reek of white boys' piss.' Her mother's eyes had blazed at her as Sharon winced. Miriam Blake thought that way, she always had. She had gone to Radcliffe on a scholarship, law school at UC, and ever since, she had fought hard for what she believed, for the underdog, the common man, and she was fighting for her people now. Even her husband admired her. She had more guts than anyone he'd ever known and she wasn't going to stop now. But it frightened Sharon sometimes. It frightened her a lot. As it had when she applied to Green Hill.

'What if I get in?' That scared her most of all and she told her father that. 'I'm not like her, Daddy ... I don't want to prove a point ... to just get in ... I want to have friends, to have a good time ... what she wants me to do is too hard....' Tears had filled her eyes and he understood. But he couldn't change either of them, Miriam and what she expected of them all, or the gentle, lovely girl, who was less fiery, and much more like him. She wanted to be an actress on the Broadway stage one day. And she wanted to go to UCLA.

'You can go there for your last two years, Shar,' her mother said, 'after you pay your dues.'

'Why do I have to pay any dues at all?' she screamed. 'Why do I owe anyone two years of my life?'

'Because you live here in your father's house, in a comfortable suburb of Washington, and you sleep in your nice, warm bed, thanks to us, and you've never known a life of pain.'

'So beat me, then. Treat me like a slave, but let me do what I want to do!'

'Fine.' Her mother's eyes had blazed black fire. 'Do what you want. But you'll never walk proud, girl, not if all you think of is yourself. You think that's what they did in Little Rock? They walked every step of the way, with guns pointed at their heads, and the Klan itching for their necks every day. And you know who they did it for, girl? They did it for you. And who're you going to do it for, Sharon Blake?'

'Myself!' She had screamed before running up the stairs to her room and slamming the door. But the words had haunted her. Her mother's words always did. She wasn't an easy person to live with, or to know, or to love. She never made things comfortable for anyone. But in the long run, she made things good. For everyone.

Freeman Blake had tried to talk to his wife that night. He knew how Sharon felt, how badly she wanted to go to the western school. 'Why don't you let her do what she wants for a change?'

'Because she has a responsibility. And so do I, and so do you.'

'Don't you ever think of anything else? She's young. Give her a chance. Maybe she doesn't want to burn for a cause. Maybe you do enough of that for all of us.' But they both knew that that wasn't entirely true. Sharon's brother Dick was only fifteen, but he was Miriam to the core, and he shared most of her ideas, except that his were angrier, more radical. No one was ever going to shove him down, and Freeman was proud of that, but he also recognized that Sharon was a different child. 'Just let her be.'

They had, and in the end, the guilt had won, as she told Tana later that night. 'So here I am.' They had been to dinner in the main dining hall, and were back in their room. Sharon in a pink nightgown that had been a going away present from her best friend at home, and Tana in a blue flannel nightgown, her hair in a long silky ponytail as she watched her new friend. 'I guess I'll go to UCLA after I finish here.' She sighed and looked at the pink polish she had just applied to her toes, and then looked up at Tana again. 'She expects so damn much of me.'

Tana smiled. 'So does mine. She's devoted her whole damn life to doing the right thing for me, and all she wants me to do is come here for a year or two, and then marry some 'nice young man.'' She made a face which suggested she found it an unappealing idea, and Sharon laughed.

'Secretly that's what all mothers think, even mine, as long as I promise to crusade even after I marry him. What does your father say? Thank God for mine, he gets me off the hook whenever he can. He thinks all that stuff is a pain in the ass too.'

'Mine died before I was born. That's why she gets so excited about everything. She's always scared to death that everything's going to go wrong, so she

clutches whatever security we have, and she expects me to do the same.' She
looked strangely at Sharon then, 'You know, actually your mother sounds
more like my cup of tea.' The two girls laughed and it was another two hours
before they turned off the lights, and by the end of the first week at Green Hill,
the two girls were fast friends. They shared much of the same schedule, met for
lunch, went to the library, went for long walks around the lake, talking about
life, about boys, about parents and friends. Tana told Sharon about her
mother's relationship with Arthur Durning, even when he was married to
Marie, and how she felt about him. The hypocrisy, the narrow views, the
stereotyped life in Greenwich with children and friends and associates all of
whom drank too much, in a house that was all for show, while her mother
slaved for him night and day, lived for his calls, and had nothing to show for it
after twelve years. 'I mean, Christ, Shar, it really burns me up. And you know
the worst thing about it?' Her eyes smouldered like fiery green rocks as she
looked at her friend. 'The worst thing is that she accepts all that shit from him.
It's all right with her. She'd never walk out on him, and she'd never ask for
more. She'll just sit there for the rest of her life, grateful for all the menial
things she does for him, totally unaware that he does nothing for her, while she
insists that she owes everything to him. What everything? She's worked like a
dog all her life for whatever she has, and he treats her like a piece of furniture....' ... *a paid cunt* ... Billy's words still rang in her ears and she forced
them from her head for the ten thousandth time. 'I don't know ... she just sees
things differently, but it makes me mad as hell. I can't go around kissing his ass
for the rest of my life. I owe mother a lot, but I don't owe Arthur Durning a
damn thing, and neither does she, but she just doesn't see it that way. She's so
damn scared all the time ... I wonder if she was like that before my father
died....' Her mother often told her that she was a lot like him, and her face
kind of lit up.
   'I like my dad better than my mom.' Sharon was always honest about what
she felt, especially with Tana. They had told each other countless secrets by the
end of the first month, although the one thing Tana had said nothing about was
the rape. Somehow she could never quite bring the words to her mouth, and
she told herself that it didn't matter anyway, but a few days before the first
dance was scheduled on Halloween with a neighboring boys' school, Sharon
rolled her eyes and lay back on her bed. 'So much for that. What do I do? Go as
a black cat, or in a white sheet as a member of the Klan?' The girls had all been
careful not to get too close to her. They were polite to her, and none of them
stared anymore, and all of the teachers treated her courteously, but it was
almost as though they wanted to pretend that she wasn't there, as though by
ignoring her, she would disappear. And the only friend she had was Tana, who
went everywhere with her, and as a result, Sharon was Tana's only friend.
Everyone stayed away from her. If she wanted to play with niggers, she was
going to find herself playing alone. Sharon had shouted at her about it more
than once. 'Why the hell don't you go play with your own kind!' She had tried
to sound harsh but Tana had always seen through the ruse.
   'Go to hell.'
   'You're a damn fool.'

'Good. That makes two of us. That's why we get along so well.'

'Nah,' Sharon would grin at her, 'we get along because you dress like shit and if you didn't have my wardrobe and my expert advice at hand you'd go out looking like a total jerk.'

'Yeah,' Tana grinned delightedly, 'you're right. But can you teach me to dance?' The girls would collapse on their beds, and you could hear their laughter out in the hall almost every night. Sharon had an energy and a spunk and a fire about her that brought Tana back to life again, and sometimes they just sat around and told jokes and laughed until the tears ran down their cheeks and they cried. Sharon also had a sense of style which Tana had never seen before, and the most beautiful clothes she had ever seen. They were both about the same size and after a while, they just began to shove everything into the same drawers, and wear whatever came to hand.

'So ... what are you going to be for Halloween, Tan?' Sharon was doing her nails a bright orange this time, and it looked spectacular against her brown skin. She glanced at the wet polish and then over at her friend, but Tana looked noncommittal as she looked away.

'I don't know ... I'll see. ...'

'What does that mean?' She was quick to sense something different in Tana's voice, something she had never heard there before, except maybe once or twice when Sharon suspected that she had hit a nerve, but she wasn't yet sure what that nerve was, or precisely where it lay. 'You're going, aren't you?'

Tana stood up and stretched, and then looked straight into Sharon's eyes. 'No. I'm not.'

'For heaven's sake, why not?' She looked stunned. Tana liked having a good time. She had a great sense of humor, she was a pretty girl, she was fun to be around, she was bright. 'Don't you like Halloween?'

'It's all right ... for kids. ...' It was the first time Sharon had seen her behave like that and she was surprised.

'Don't be a party pooper, Tan. Come on, I'll put your costume together for you.' She began digging into the closet they shared, pulling things out and throwing them on the bed, but Tana did not look amused, and that night when the lights were out, Sharon questioned her about it again. 'How come you don't want to go to the Halloween Dance, Tan?' She knew that she hadn't had any dates yet, but so far none of them had. For Sharon it was a particularly lonely road, as the only black girl at the school, but she had resigned herself to that when she had agreed to come to Green Hill, and none of them really knew anyone yet. Only a few lucky girls had already won dates, but they were sure to meet a flock of young men at the dance, and Sharon was suddenly dying to get out. 'Do you have a steady at home?' She hadn't mentioned it yet, but Sharon knew that it was possible she had held back. There were some things they still hadn't shared. They had avoided the subject of their virginity, or lack of it, which Sharon knew was unusual at Jasmine House. It seemed as though everyone else was anxious to discuss their status as far as that went, but Sharon had correctly sensed Tana's reticence, and she wasn't anxious to discuss the subject herself. But she propped herself up on one elbow now and looked at Tana in the moonlit room. 'Tan ...?'

'No, nothing like that.... I just don't like going out.'

'Any particular reason why not? You're allergic to men?... get dizzy in heels?... turn into a vampire after twelve o'clock? ... although actually,' she grinned mischievously, 'that might be kind of a neat trick on Halloween.'

In the other bed, Tana laughed. 'Don't be a jerk. I just don't want to go out, that's all. It's no big deal. You go. Go fall in love with some white guy and drive your parents nuts.' They both laughed at the prospect of that.

'Christ, they'd probably kick me out of school. If old Mrs Jones had her choice, they'd be fixing me up with Old Sam.' The housemother had several times looked patronizingly at Sharon, and then glanced at Sam, as though there were some kind of kinship between them.

'Does she know who your father is?' Freeman Blake had just won another Pulitzer, and everyone in the country knew his name, whether they had read his books or not.

'I don't think she can read.'

'Give her an autographed book when you come back from the holidays.' Tana grinned and Sharon roared.

'She'd die....' But it still didn't solve the problem of the Halloween Dance. In the end, Sharon went as an excruciatingly sexy black cat, in a black leotard, her warm cocoa face peeking out, her eyes huge, her legs seeming to stretch forever, and after an initial tense moment or two, someone asked her to dance, and she was on the floor all night long. She had a terrific time, although none of the girls talked to her, and Tana was tucked into bed and sound asleep when she got home just after one o'clock. 'Tan?... Tana?...Tan...?' She stirred faintly, lifted her head, and opened one eye with a groan.

'D'ya have a good time?'

'It was great! I danced all night!' She was dying to tell her all about it but Tana had already turned over in bed.

'I'm glad ... g'night. ...' Sharon watched the other girl's back and wondered again why she hadn't gone, but nothing more was said, and when Sharon tried to bring it up again the next day, it was obvious that Tana didn't want to talk about it. The other girls began going out after that. The phone in the downstairs hall seemed to ring all the time, but only one boy called Sharon Blake. He asked her to a movie and she went, but when they arrived, the ticket taker wouldn't let them in. 'This ain't Chicago, friends,' he glared at them and the boy blushed a deep, anguished red, 'you're in the South now.' He addressed the young man, 'Go home and find yourself a decent girl, son.' Sharon was reassuring when they left.

'I didn't want to see it anyway. Honest, Tom, it's all right.' But the silence was agonizing as he drove her back, and finally when they reached Jasmine House, she turned to him. Her voice was sultry and soft, her eyes kind, her hand like velvet as she touched his. 'It really is all right, Tom. I understand. I'm used to this.' She took a deep breath. 'That's why I came to Green Hill.' It seemed an odd thing to say and he looked questioningly at her. She was the first black girl he had ever asked out, and he thought her the most exotic creature he had ever seen.

'You came here to be insulted by some turd in a movie house in a one horse town?' He was still burning inside, he was angry for her even if she was not.

'No,' she spoke softly, thinking of her mother's words, 'I came here to change things, I guess. It starts like this, and it goes on for a long time, and eventually no one gives a damn, black girls and white guys go to movies, ride in cars, walk down streets, eat hamburgers anywhere they want. It happens in New York. Why shouldn't it happen here? People may look, but at least there they don't throw you out. And the only way to get to that point is to start small like tonight.' The boy looked at her, suddenly wondering if he'd been used but somehow he didn't think he had. Sharon Blake wasn't like that, and he had already heard who her father was. You had to be impressed by someone like that. And he admired her more after what she had just said. It confused him a little bit, but he knew that there was truth in it.

'I'm sorry we didn't get in. Why don't we try again next week?'

She laughed at that. 'I didn't mean that we had to change it all at once.' But she liked his spunk. He was getting the idea, and maybe her mother hadn't been so wrong.

'Why not? Sooner or later that guy'll get tired of kicking us out. Hell, we can go to the coffee shop ... the restaurant across town....' The possibilities were limitless and Sharon was laughing at him, as he helped her out of the car and walked her into Jasmine House. She offered him a cup of tea, and they were going to sit in the living room for a while, but the looks they got from the other couples sitting there were so ominous that eventually Sharon got up. She walked him slowly to the door, and for a moment she looked sad. It would have been so much easier at UCLA ... anywhere in the North ... anywhere but here.... Tom was quick to sense her mood, and he whispered as he stood in the open door, 'Remember ... it doesn't happen overnight.' He touched her cheek then and was gone, as she watched him drive away ... he was right of course ... it didn't happen overnight.

And as she walked upstairs, she decided that it hadn't been a totally wasted night. She liked Tom, and wondered if he would call her again. He was a good sport.

'Well? Did he propose?' Tana was grinning at her from the bed as Sharon walked in, and groaned.

'Yeah. Twice.'

'That's nice. How was the movie?'

Sharon smiled. 'Ask someone else.'

'You didn't go?' She was surprised.

'They didn't let us in ... you know ... white boy ... brown girl ... 'Find yourself a *decent* girl, son....' 'She pretended to laugh but Tana could see the pain in her eyes, and she frowned.

'The shits. What did Tom say?'

'He was nice. We sat downstairs for a while when we got back, but that was even worse. There must be seven Snow Whites sitting downstairs with their Prince Charmings, and all of them had their eyes glued on us.' She sighed and sat down, looking at her friend. 'Shit ... my mother and her bright ideas ... for about a minute outside the movie house I felt very noble and brave and pure, and by the time we got back, I decided it was really a huge pain in the ass. Hell, we can't even go out for a hamburger. I could starve to death in this town.'

'Not if you went out with me, I'll bet.' They hadn't gone out to eat yet, they were too comfortable where they were, and the food was surprisingly good at school. They had both already gained three or four pounds, much to Sharon's chagrin.

'Don't be so sure, Tan. I'll bet they'd raise hell if I tried to go somewhere with you too. Black is black and white is white, no matter how you look at it.'

'Why don't we try?' Tana looked intrigued, and the next night they did. They walked slowly into town, and stopped for a hamburger and the waitress gave them a long, slow, ugly look and then walked away without serving them, as Tana looked at her in shock. She signalled for her again, and the woman appeared not to see, until finally Tana walked over to her, and asked if they could order their dinner now, and the waitress looked at her with chagrin.

She spoke in a low voice so that Sharon wouldn't hear. 'I'm sorry, honey. I can't serve your friend. I was hoping you two'd get the idea.'

'Why not? She's from Washington,' as though that would make a difference, '... her mother is an attorney and her father has won the Pulitzer twice....'

'That don't make no difference here. This ain't Washington. It's Yolan.' Yolan, South Carolina, home of Green Hill.

'Is there anywhere in town we can eat?'

The waitress looked nervously at the tall, green eyed blonde, there was a hardness in her voice that suddenly frightened her. 'There's a place for her just down the street ... and you could eat here.'

'I mean together,' Tana's eyes were as hard as green steel, and for the first time in her life she felt something tighten in her spine. She almost wanted to hit someone. It was a feeling she hadn't known before, an unreasoning, helpless rage. 'Is there anyplace in this town where we can eat together, without taking the train to New York?' Tana glared at her, and slowly the waitress shook her head. But Tana wasn't moving an inch. 'Okay, then I'll have two cheeseburgers, and two Cokes.'

'No, you won't.' A man appeared form the kitchen behind where they stood. 'You'll go back to that damn fancy school you two come from.' They were easily spotted in Yolan. Sharon's clothes alone were enough to draw attention anywhere. She was wearing a skirt and sweater her mother had bought her at Bonwit Tellers in New York. 'And you can eat anything you damn well please there. I don't know what's gotten into them over there, but if they choose to let niggers into the school, then let them feed 'em over at Green Hill, we don't gotta feed 'em here.' He looked pointedly at Tana, then at Sharon where she sat, and it was as though an enormous force had entered the room, and for a minute Tana thought he might physically throw them out. She hadn't been as frightened or as angry since she'd been raped.

And then, ever so quietly, and in her graceful, long-legged, ladylike way, Sharon stood up. 'Come on, Tan.' Her voice was a sexy purr, and for an instant, Tana saw the man's eyes almost paw at her and she wanted to slap his face. It reminded her of something she never wanted to think of again, and a moment later she followed Sharon out.

'Son-of-a-bitch....' Tan was fuming as they walked slowly back to school, but Sharon was amazingly calm. It was the same feeling she had had the night before, with Tom, when they hadn't let them in to the movie house. For an instant, there had been a quiet surge of power, an understanding of why she was there, and then depression had set in. But tonight, the depression hadn't hit her yet.

'Life is strange, isn't it? If this were in New York or LA, or almost anywhere else, no one would give a damn. But down here, it's all important that I'm black, you're white. Maybe my mother is right. Maybe it is time for a crusade. I don't know, I always thought that as long as I was comfortable, it didn't matter if things like that were happening to someone else. But all of a sudden that someone else is me.' Suddenly she knew why her mother had insisted on her coming here, and for the first time since she'd arrived, she wondered if she'd been right. Maybe she did belong here after all. Maybe she owed it to someone else for all the time that she had been comfortable. 'I don't know what to think, Tan....'

'Neither do I....' They were walking along side by side. 'I don't think I've ever felt so helpless or been so mad....' And then suddenly Billy Durning's face came to mind, and she visibly winced, 'Well ... maybe once....'

They suddenly felt closer than they ever had before. Tana almost wanted to put an arm around her to protect her from more hurt, as Sharon glanced over at her with a gentle smile. 'When was that, Tan?'

'Oh a long time ago....' She tried to smile, '... like five months....'

'Oh yeah ... a *real* long time ago....' The two girls exchanged a smile and walked on as a car sped by, but no one bothered them, and Tana wasn't afraid. No one would ever do to her again what Billy Durning did. She would kill them first. And there was a strange ugly look in her eyes as Sharon glanced at her. 'Must've been pretty bad.'

'It was.'

'Wanna talk about it?' Her voice was as soft as the charcoal gray night, and they walked along in silence for a time as Tana thought. She had never wanted to tell anyone about it before, not since she'd tried to tell her mom.

'I don't know.'

Sharon nodded, as though she understood. Everyone had one of those. She had one herself. 'It's okay, Tan.' But as she said the words, Tana looked at her, and suddenly the words burst from her, almost of their own accord.

'Yeah, I do....' And then, 'I don't know ... how do you talk about something like that?' She began to walk faster as though to run away, and Sharon followed her easily on her long, graceful legs; unconsciously Tana ran a hand through her hair nervously, looked away, and began to breathe harder than she had before. 'There's nothing much to say. ... I went to a party after I graduated in June ... my mother's boss's house ... he has this real little shit of a son ... and I told my mother I didn't want to go....' Her breath was coming in little short gasps and Sharon knew she wasn't aware of it as they hurried along. She knew that whatever it was, it was torturing the girl, and it would be better if she got it out. 'Anyway, she said I had to go anyway ... she always says that ... that's the way she is, about Arthur Durning anyway, and his kids ... she's blind to what they are, and ...' the words stopped, and they walked on hurrying, hurrying, as though she could still run away, and Sharon kept pace, watching her as she struggled with the memories and then began to speak again, '... anyway, this dumb boy picked me up and we got there ... to the party, I mean ... and everyone got drunk ... and the dumb guy who brought me got drunk and disappeared and I was wandering around the house ... and Billy ... Arthur's son ... asked me if I wanted to see the room where my mother worked, and I knew where it was. ...' There were tears running down her cheeks now, but she didn't feel them in the wind, and Sharon didn't say anything to her, 'and he took me to Arthur's bedroom instead and every-thing was gray ... gray velvet, gray satin ... gray fur ... even the rug on the floor was gray,' it was all she could remember, the endless field of gray and her blood on the floor afterwards and Billy's face, and then the accident, she could barely breathe thinking of it, and she pulled at the neck of her shirt as she began to run, sobbing now, as Sharon followed her, keeping close, staying near. She wasn't alone anymore, there was a friend running through the nightmare with her and it was as though she sensed that as she went on, '... and Billy started to slap me and he pushed me down ... and everything I did ...,' she remembered the helplessness again now, the desperation she felt, and then in the night air she screamed and then she stopped, burying her face in her hands, '... and I couldn't do anything to make him stop ... I couldn't....' Her whole body was shaking now as Sharon took her quietly in her arms and held her tight, '... and he raped me ... and he left me there with blood all over me ... my legs and my face ... and then I threw up ... and later he followed me all down the road and he made me get in his car and he almost hit this truck,' the words just wouldn't stop now as she cried and Sharon began to cry with her, 'and we hit a tree instead and he cut his head and there was blood all over him too and they took us to the hospital and then my mother came ...' And suddenly she stopped again, and with her face ravaged by the memory she had tried to flee for five months, she looked up into Sharon's eyes, 'and when I tried to tell her, she wouldn't believe anything I said ... she said Billy Durning wouldn't do a thing like that.' The sobs were deep and wracking now, but she looked better than she had before and Sharon dried her eyes.

'I believe you, Tan.'

Tana nodded, looking like a bereft little girl. 'I never want anyone to touch me again.'

She knew exactly how Tana felt, but not for the same reasons as her friend. She hadn't been raped. She had gladly given it, to the boy she loved. 'My mother never believed a single word I said. And she never will. The Durnings are gods to her.'

'All that matters is that you're okay, Tan.' They sat down on a tree stump, and Sharon offered her a cigarette, and for once Tana took a puff. 'And you are okay, you know. A lot more so than you think.' She smiled gently at her friend, deeply moved by her confidence, and she wiped the tears from her cheeks as Tana smiled at her.

'You don't think I'm awful because of that?'

'That's a dumb thing to ask. It's no reflection on you, Tan.'

'I don't know ... sometimes I think it is ... as though I could have stopped him if I tried hard enough.' It felt good just to say the words, just to get them out. They had haunted her for months.

'Do you really believe that, Tan? Do you really think you could have stopped him? Tell the truth.'

She shook her head. 'No.'

'Then don't torture yourself. It happened. It was horrible. Worse than that. It was probably the worst thing that'll ever happen to you in your whole life, but no one will ever do that to you again. And it wasn't really you he touched. He couldn't touch the real you, no matter what, Tan. Just cut it off. Sump the memory. And move on.'

'That's easy to say,' Tana smiled tiredly, 'but not so easily done. How do you forget something like that?'

'You make yourself. You don't let it destroy you, Tan. That's the only time a guy like that wins. He's sick. You're not. Don't make yourself sick over what he did. As awful as it was, put it out of your mind, and move on.'

'Oh Sharon. . . .' She sighed and stood up, looking down at her friend. It was a beautiful night. 'What makes you so smart, for a kid?'

Sharon smiled, but her eyes were serious tonight, almost sad, as Tana looked down at her. 'I have my secrets too.'

'Like what?' Tana felt calmer now than she ever had in her life, it was as though a raging animal had been released from her, as though Sharon had let it out of its cage and set it free, and Tana was finally at peace again. Her mother hadn't been able to do that for her five months before, but this girl had, and she knew that whatever else happened after that, they would always be friends. 'What happened to you?' Tana searched her eyes, knowing now that there was something there. And she was sure of it when Sharon looked up at her. She didn't mince any words. She had never told anyone, but she had thought about it a lot, and she and her father had talked about it one night before she left for Green Hill. He had told her the same thing she had just told Tana, that she couldn't let it destroy her life. It had happened. And now it was done. And she had to let it stay that way, and move on, but she wondered if she ever would.

'I had a baby this year.'

For an instant Tana's breath caught and she looked at Sharon in shock. 'You did?'

'Yeah. I've been going with the same boy at home since I was fifteen and when I was sixteen he gave me his senior ring ... I don't know, Tan ... it kind of seemed so cute ... he looks like an African god, and he's smart as hell, and he dances ...' she looked pretty and young as she thought of him. . . . 'He's at Harvard now,' her eyes grew sad, 'but I haven't talked to him in almost a year. I got pregnant, I told him, and he panicked, I guess. He wanted me to have an abortion at this doctor's his cousin knew, and I refused ... hell, I'd heard about girls who died. . . .' Her eyes filled with tears at the memory, and she forgot that Tana was standing there, looking down at her. 'I was going to tell my mom, but ... I just couldn't ... I told my father instead ... and then he told her ... and everybody went nuts ... and they called his parents, and everyone cried and screamed, my mother called him a nigger ... and his father called me a slut ... it was the worst night in my life, and when it was all over, my parents gave me a choice. I could have an abortion at a doctor's my mother had found out about, or I could have the baby and give it up. They said,' she took a deep gulp of air as though this were the worst part, 'that I couldn't keep it ... that it would ruin my life ...,' her whole body shook, 'to have a baby at seventeen ... and I don't know why but I decided to have the baby, I think because I thought that Danny would change his mind ... or my parents would ... or a miracle would happen ... but nothing did. I lived in a home for five months and I kept up with all the work for my senior year, and the baby was born on April nineteenth ... a little boy....' She was trembling and Tana wordlessly reached out and took her hand, 'I wasn't supposed to see him at all ... but I did once ... he was so little.... I was in labor for nineteen hours and it was horrible and he only weighed six pounds....' Her eyes were a thousand miles away thinking of the little boy she would never see again, and she looked up at Tana now, 'He's gone, Tan,' she whimpered almost like a child and in many ways she still was a child. They both were. 'I signed the final papers three weeks ago. My mother drew them up ... some people adopted him in New York....' She couldn't stop the sobs as she bent her head, 'Oh God, Tan, I hope they're good to him ... I never should have let him go ... and all for what?' She looked angrily up at her friend, 'For this? To come to this dumb school to prove a point, so that other colored girls can come here one day. So what?'

'That had nothing to do with this. They wanted you to have a fresh start, with a husband and a family at the right time.'

'They were wrong, and so was I. You'll never know what it felt like ... that emptiness when I went home ... with nothing ... with no one ... nothing will ever replace that.' She took a deep breath. 'I haven't seen Danny since I went into the home in Maryland ... and I'll never know where the baby is.... I graduated with my class ...,' with a lead weight in her heart, '... and no one knew what I felt....' Tana shook her head, watching her. They were both women now. It had been hard earned, hard won, and it was too soon to know if things would get better in time, but one thing they both knew as they walked slowly home, and that was that they each had a friend. Tana pulled Sharon off the stump, and they hugged each other tight, their tears fell on each other's cheeks, each feeling the other's pain, as much as they could.

'I love you, Shar.' Tana looked at her with her gentle smile, and Sharon dried her eyes.

'Yeah ... me too....'

And they walked home arm in arm, in the silent night, went back to Jasmine House, got undressed and into their beds, each with her own thoughts.

'Tan?' It was Sharon's voice in the dark room.

'Yeah?'

'Thanks.'

'For what? Listening. That's what friends are for ... I need you too.'

'My father was right, you know. You've got to move on in life.'

'I guess.' But how? 'Did he have any suggestions about how to pull that off?'

Sharon laughed at that. 'I'll have to ask him that.' And then suddenly, she had an idea. 'Why don't you ask him yourself? Why don't you come home for Thanksgiving with me?'

Tana mulled it over from her bed, with the beginnings of a smile. She liked the idea. 'I don't know what my mother will say.' But all of a sudden she wasn't sure she cared, and if she did, it wasn't as much as she would have cared six months before. Maybe it was time to try her wings and do what she wanted to do this time. 'I'll call her tomorrow night.'

'Good.' Sharon smiled sleepily and turned over in her bed, with her back to her friend. 'G'night, Tan....' And a moment later, they were both asleep, more at ease than either of them had been in months, Tana's hands cast childlike above the blonde hair, and Sharon cuddled up into a little black purring ball. Even the long legs seemed to disappear and she looked like a kitten as she slept peacefully.

Chapter 5

Jean Roberts was disappointed when her daughter called to say that she had decided not to come home for Thanksgiving.

'Are you sure?' She didn't want to insist, but she would have preferred it if Tana were coming back. 'You don't know this girl very well....'

'Mother, I live with her. We share the same room. I know her better than I've known anyone in my life.'

'Are you sure her parents won't mind?'

'Positive. She called them this afternoon. They have a room for me, and she said they were delighted that she was bringing someone home.' Of course they were. From what Sharon had said, it proved Miriam's point that Sharon could be happy at Green Hill, even if she was the only black girl there, and now she was bringing one of 'them' home, the ultimate proof of how well they had accepted her. They didn't know that Tana was her only friend, that there wasn't a single place in Yolan where she could be served, that she hadn't been able to go to a movie since she'd arrived, and even in the cafeteria at school, the girls avoided her. But, according to Sharon, even if they had known, Miriam would have felt it proved even more that Sharon was needed there. 'They' had to accept Negroes one day, and the time was now. It was a good challenge for Sharon, particularly after last year, this would keep her from dwelling on herself, Miriam Blake thought, it would give her something else to think about, or so she had said. 'Really, they said it was fine.'

'All right, then be sure you invite her up sometime during the Christmas holidays.' Jean smiled into the phone, 'In fact, I have a little surprise for you. Arthur and I were going to tell you over Thanksgiving....' Tana's heart stopped. Was he finally marrying her? She was robbed of speech as her mother went on. 'Arthur made it possible for you to have a little coming out party of your own. There's a small cotillion here in town ... well, not a cotillion really, but a deb party of sorts, and Arthur put up your name, I mean you did go to Miss Lawson's after all, dear, and ... you're going to be a debutante, sweetheart. Isn't that wonderful?' For a moment, no words came to Tana's mind. It didn't seem particularly wonderful at all, and once again her mother would be kissing Arthur Durning's feet ... marry her ... what a joke. How could she have thought a thing like that ... a 'cotillion of sorts' ... shit.... 'Why don't you invite your new friend to come up then?' Tana almost choked. *Because my new friend is black, Mom.*

'I'll ask, but I think she's going away over the holidays.' Shit. A debutante. And who would her escort be? Billy Durning? The son-of-a-bitch.

'You don't sound very excited, sweetheart.' There was disappointment in Jean Roberts' voice, both because Tana wouldn't be coming home, and because she didn't sound very excited about the party Arthur had arranged. He knew how much it meant to Jean. Ann had come out at the International Ball four years before, of course, not at a small deb party like this, but nonetheless it would be a wonderful experience for Tana to have, or at least Jean thought it would.

'I'm sorry, Mom. I guess I'm just surprised.'

'It is a beautiful surprise, isn't it?' No. She didn't really care. Things like that didn't matter to her. They never had. All the social nonsense of the Durnings' world seemed irrelevant to her, but it meant so much to Jean. It always had, ever since she had fallen in love with him. 'You'll have to think of an escort for the dance. I was hoping Billy could,' Tana felt her heart pound and her chest get tight, 'but he's going skiing in Europe with friends. In Saint Moritz, the lucky boy,' ... lucky boy ... *he raped me, Mom....* 'You'll just have to think of someone else. Someone suitable, of course.' Of course. *How many other rapists do we know?*

'It's too bad I can't go alone.' Tana's voice sounded dead at her end of the phone.

'That's a ridiculous thing to say.' Jean sounded annoyed. 'Well, anyway, don't forget to invite your friend ... the one you're going home for Thanksgiving with.'

'Sure.' Tana smiled. If she only knew. Jean Roberts would have died if Tana had invited a black friend to the little 'coming out' party Arthur had arranged. It almost amused Tana to think of it, but she would never have taken advantage of Sharon like that. They were all a bunch of rude pricks. She knew that even her mother wasn't ready for that. 'What'll you do for Thanksgiving, Mom? Will you be all right?'

'I'll be fine. Arthur had already invited us to Greenwich for the day.'

'Maybe now that I won't be there, you can spend the night.' There was a dead silence on the phone, and Tana regretted the words. 'I didn't mean it like that.'

'Yes, you did.'

'Well, what difference does it make? I'm eighteen years old now. It's not a secret....' Tana felt sick as she thought of the endless gray room where ... 'I'm sorry, Mom.'

'Take care of yourself.' She drew herself up. She would miss seeing her, but she had a lot to do now, and Tan would be home in a month anyway. 'And don't forget to thank your friend for having you there.' Tana smiled to herself, it was like being seven years old again. Maybe it always would be.

'I will. Have a good Thanksgiving, Mom.'

'I shall. And I'll thank Arthur for you.' Jean said the words pointedly and Tana looked blank at her end.

'What for?'

'The ball, Tana, the ball ... I don't know if you realize it yet, but something like that is very important for a young girl, and it's not something that I could provide for you myself.' Important ...? Important to whom ... ? 'You have no idea what something like this means.' Tears stung Jean Roberts' eyes. In some ways, it was a dream come true. Andy and Jean Roberts' little girl, the baby Andy had never seen, would be coming out in New York society, and even if it was on the fringe, it was an important event for both of them ... for Tana ... and especially for Jean ... it would be the most important moment in her life. She remembered Ann's coming out ball. She had planned every exquisite detail and had never thought that one day Tana would be coming out too.

'I'm sorry, Mom.'

'You'd better be. And I think you ought to write Arthur a nice note. Tell him what it means to you.' She wanted to scream into the phone. What the hell does it mean? That she'd find a rich husband some day, that they could mark it on her pedigree? Who cared? What accomplishment was that, to curtsy at a dumb ball, being gaped at by a lot of drunks? She didn't even know who she was going to take with her, and she shuddered at the thought. She had gone out with half a dozen different boys during her last two years at school, but there had never been anyone serious, and after what had happened in Greenwich in June, there was no one she wanted to go out with at all.

'I have to go, Mom.' She was suddenly desperate to get off the phone, and when she returned to her room, she looked depressed and Sharon looked up. She was doing her nails again. It was an eternal process with both of them. Recently they had both tried beige, 'Show Hat' by Fabergé.

'She said no?'

'She said yes.'

'So? You look like someone just burst your balloon.'

'I think she did.' Tana sat down on her bed with a thump. 'Shit. She got her damn friend to sign me up for some dumb coming out ball. Jesus Christ, Shar, I feel like a complete fool.'

Sharon looked up at her and started to laugh. 'You mean you're going to be a debutante, Tan?'

'More or less.' Tana looked embarrassed and groaned at her friend. 'How could she do that to me?'

'It might be fun.'

'For who? And what the hell's the point? It's like a big cattle drive. They shove you around in a white dress and show you off to a lot of drunks, and you're supposed to find a husband somewhere in the bunch. Pretty cute, huh?' She looked sick, and Sharon put her nail polish away.

'Who're you going to take?'

'Don't ask. She wanted Billy Durning to be my escort, of course, but thank God he'll be out of town.'

'Be grateful for that.' Sharon looked pointedly at her.

'I am. But the whole thing sounds like a farce.'

'So are a lot of things in life.'

'Don't be so cynical, Shar.'

'Don't be so chicken, Tan. It'll do you good.'

'Says who?'

'Says I.' Sharon advanced towards her and tried to stare her down. 'You live like a nun around here.'

'So do you. So what?'

'I don't have any choice.' Tom had never called her again, it was more than he could cope with, Sharon knew, and in truth she understood. She hadn't expected more of him. But it didn't make her life very interesting at Green Hill. 'You do.'

'Never mind.'

'You've got to start going out.'

'No, I don't.' Tana looked her right in the eye. 'I don't have to do a goddamn thing I don't want to do. I'm eighteen years old, and I'm free as a bird.'

'A lame duck.' Sharon stared her down. 'Get out there again, Tan.' But Tana said nothing at all. She walked into the bathroom they shared with the next room, locked the door, ran a bath, and didn't come out for an hour. 'I meant what I said.' Sharon's voice was husky in the darkened room, once they were both in their beds.

'About what?'

'You should start going out again.'

'So should you.'

'I will one of these days.' Sharon sighed. 'Maybe over the holidays when I'm home. There's no one for me to go out with here.' And then she laughed. 'Hell, Tan, I don't know what I'm complaining about. At least I've got you.'

Tana smiled at her and they chatted for a few minutes and then drifted off to sleep.

The following week Tana went home to Washington with her. They were met at the train by Sharon's father, Freeman Blake, and Tana was instantly struck by how tall and handsome he was. He was a regal looking man, with a proud, beautifully carved, almost mahogany face, broad shoulders, and Sharon's same endlessly long legs. He had a warm smile, brilliantly white teeth, and he was quick to pull his daughter into his arms and hold her tight. He knew just how much she'd been through in the last year, and she'd come through it like a champ, just as he'd known she would, and he was desperately proud of her.

'Hi, baby, how's school?' She rolled her eyes, and turned quickly towards her friend.

'Tana, this is my dad, Freeman Blake. Daddy, this is Tana Roberts, my roommate at Green Hill.' He gave Tana's hand a powerful shake and she was magnetized by his eyes and the sound of his voice on the way home. He was filling Sharon in on all the local news, her mother's appointment to an even more important post, her brother Dick's big new romance, the remodelling of the house, the neighbor's new child, his new book. It was a warm friendly patter that touched Tana's heart, and she felt envious of the life that Sharon obviously had. And she felt it even more at dinner that night in the handsome colonial dining room. They had a beautiful house with a huge lawn and back yard, three cars in the garage, one of which was a Cadillac Freeman drove, despite the rude things his friends said. But he admitted that he had always wanted a Cadillac convertible and he had one now after all these years. They were obviously all four closely knit, and Tana found Miriam more than a little formidable. She was so intelligent and so direct that it took one's breath away, and she seemed to constantly expect the ultimate of everyone. One was never safe from her questions, her demands, and her ever searching gaze.

'See what I mean?' Sharon said when they were alone upstairs. 'It's like being on the witness stand, just having dinner with her.' She had wanted to know everything Sharon had done in the last two months, and she was interested in both the incident with Tom at the movie house, and the one at the coffee shop with Tana after that.

'It's just that she cares so much, Shar ... about everything!'

'I know that. And it drives me nuts. Daddy is just as smart as she is for chrissake, and he's so much gentler about everything.' He was that, he told exquisite tales, made everyone laugh, and he had a way of making everyone comfortable, of bringing them closer together and forming an irresistible bond. Tana had noticed it all night long and she thought him the most remarkable man she had ever met.

'He's the most incredible man, Shar.'

'I know.'

'I read one of his books last year. I'm going to go home now and read them all.'

'I'll give them to you.'

'Only if I can have an autographed set.' They both laughed, and a moment later, Miriam knocked at the door, anxious to know that they were all right.

'Do you have everything you need?' Tana smiled almost shyly at her.

'I do. Thank you very much, Mrs Blake.'

'Not at all. We're so glad you could come.' The smile was even more dazzling that Shar's, and the eyes were driving, omniscient, almost frightening they plunged so deep and so hard. 'How do you like Green Hill?'

'I do. Very much. The professors are pretty interesting.' But there was a lack of enthusiasm in her voice which Miriam picked up at once.

'But?'

Tana smiled. She was sharp. Very sharp. 'The atmosphere isn't as warm as I thought it would be.'

'Why is that?'

'I don't know. The girls seem to stay in cliques.'

'And the two of you?'

'We're together most of the time.' Sharon looked at Tana and smiled, and Miriam didn't seem displeased. She thought that Tana was a bright girl, and there was a lot of potential there. Far more than Tana herself knew. She was quick, she was bright, she was funny at times, but cautious, laced up. She would have to open up one day, and when she did, God only knew what would be there.

'Maybe that's your problem then, girls. Tana, how many other friends do you have at Green Hill?'

'Just Shar. We're in class together most of the time. We share the same room.'

'And you're probably being punished for that. I'm sure you realize that. If your closest friend is the only Negro girl there they're going to penalize you, you know.'

'What for?'

'Don't be naive.'

'Don't be so cynical, Mom.' Sharon sounded suddenly annoyed.

'Maybe it's time you both grew up.'

'What the hell's that supposed to mean?' Sharon lashed out at her. 'Hell, I've been home for nine hours and you're already on my back with your speeches and your crusades.'

'I'm not making any speeches. I'm just telling you to face facts.' She looked at them both then. 'You can't hide from the truth, girls. It isn't easy being black today ... or a black girl's friend ... you're both going to have to realize that and be willing to pay the price if you expect the friendship to last.'

'Can't you do anything without turning it into a political crusade, Mom?'

Miriam looked at her and then at her friend. 'I want you to do something for me, both of you, before you go back to school on Sunday night. There's a man I know speaking this Sunday in Washington. He's one of the most extraordinary men I've ever known, Martin Luther King, and I want you to come listen to him with me.'

'Why?' Sharon was still glaring at her.

'Because it's something neither of you will ever forget.'

And as they rode back toward South Carolina late that night, Tana was still thinking of it. Miriam Blake had been right. He was the most visionary man Tana had ever listened to. He made everyone else seem stupid and blind, and it was hours before she could even talk about what she had heard. Simple words about being black and being a black man's friend, about civil rights and the equality of everyone, and afterwards they had sung a song, swaying together, arms crossed, holding hands. She looked at Sharon an hour after they left Washington.

'He was amazing, wasn't he?'

Sharon nodded, thinking of his words again. 'You know, it feels dumb just going back to school. I feel as though I should be doing something.' She leaned her head back against the seat and closed her eyes, and Tana stared out into the dark night as they rode into the South. It seemed to make his words even more important than they had been. This was where it was happening, where people were being hurt, and ignored, and abused. And as the thoughts wandered through her head, she thought of the debutante party her mother had set up, and it was as though the two thoughts were so diametrically opposed that they just wouldn't fit into her head at the same time. When Sharon opened her eyes again, Tana was looking at her.

'What are you going to do?' One had to do something after hearing him. There was no choice at all. Even Freeman Blake had agreed.

'I don't know yet.' Sharon looked tired, but she had been thinking of it since they'd left Washington, of what she could do to help ... in Yolan ... in Green Hill ... 'What about you?'

'I don't know.' Tana sighed. 'Anything I can, I guess. But I'll tell you, after hearing Dr King speak, I know one thing ... that party my mother is forcing me into in New York is the dumbest thing I've ever done.'

Sharon smiled. She couldn't really disagree now, but there was another side to it as well. A more small-scale, human one. 'It'll do you good.'

'I doubt that.' The two girls exchanged a smile, and rode on into the South until they reached Yolan, and took one of the town's two cabs to Green Hill.

Chapter 6

The train roared into Pennsylvania Station on December 21st just after two o'clock in the afternoon and there was a light snow falling as Tana watched. It made everything look Christmasy and almost like a fairy tale, and yet as she gathered her things, fought her way through the station and went outside to hail a cab, she realized again how depressed she was about coming home. It made her feel instantly guilty toward Jean, and she knew that she wasn't being fair, but she would rather have been anywhere, than on her way home to her own coming out dance. And she knew how excited her mother was. For the past two weeks, she had called Tana almost every night, about the guests, the flowers, the table decor, her date, her dress. She had picked the dress out for Tana herself, an exquisite white silk with white satin trim and tiny little white beads embroidered in floral patterns around the hem. It had cost a fortune, and Arthur had told her to charge it to his account at Saks.

'He's so good to us, sweetheart....' As she rode home to the apartment in the cab, Tana closed her eyes and imagined her mother's face as she said the words ... why, why was she so everlastingly grateful to him? What on earth did he do for her, except let her work her fingers to the bone, and wait for him all those times he never came when Marie was still alive ... and even now, everything else always seemed to come first with him. And if he loved Jean so much, why the hell didn't he marry her? It depressed Tana to think about that too. Everything was such a goddamn farce ... her mother and Arthur, how 'good' the Durnings were to them, yeah, like the way Billy had been good to her ... and the party she would have to go to the following night. She had invited a boy she had known for years and never liked, but he was the right type for an event like that, Chandler George III. She had gone to a couple of dances with him before, and he bored her to tears, but she knew her mother would be pleased. And she also knew that she'd have a miserable time but that couldn't be helped.

The apartment was dark when she got in, Jean was still at work as Tana looked around. Everything looked the same except smaller somehow, and drearier than she had remembered it. She knew how hard her mother tried to keep a nice home for them both, and she always had. But Tana felt as though things were different now, as though imperceptibly she had changed and no longer fit in this comfortable scene. She found herself thinking of the comfortable Blake house in Washington, and how much she had enjoyed being there. It wasn't pretentious, like the Durnings' house, but it was warm and beautiful and real. And she missed the Blakes as well, especially Sharon. Tana had watched her get off the train, feeling as though she were losing her best friend, and Sharon had turned back once to give her a big smile and a wave, and then she was gone and the train moved north, and now she was here, feeling as though she wanted to cry as she set her bags down in her room.

'Is that my little girl?' The front door slammed and Jean's voice rang out as Tana turned with a frightened look. What if her mother could read her thoughts, could see how uncomfortable she was just being there? But Jean saw nothing of the sort, all she saw was the daughter she loved, and she held her tight for an instant before stepping back again. 'Boy, you look good!' And so did Jean. Her cheeks were pink from the cold, there were kisses of frost on the tips of her hair, and her eyes looked big and dark. She was so excited that she didn't even wait to take off her coat before running into her own room and emerging again with Tana's dress. It was exquisite as it hung from the padded satin hanger they had delivered it with. It looked almost like a wedding dress, and Tana smiled.

'Where's the veil?'

Her mother smiled back, 'You never know. That'll come next.'

Tana laughed and shook her head at the thought. 'Now let's not rush into that. I'm only eighteen.'

'That doesn't mean anything, sweetheart. You might meet the man of your dreams tomorrow night, you know. And who knows after that?' Tana stared at her in disbelief. Something in Jean's eyes said she was serious.

'Do you mean that, Mom?'

Jean Roberts smiled again. It was wonderful to see Tana again, and now that she saw the dress next to her, she knew just how fabulous it was going to look. A victory all around. 'You're a beautiful girl, Tana. And some man is going to be very lucky to have you as his wife.'

'But wouldn't you be upset if I met him now?'

'Why?' She didn't seem to understand and Tana looked stunned.

'But I'm eighteen years old. Don't you want me to go on with college and make something of myself?'

'You're doing that now.'

'But this is just the beginning, Mom. When I finish my two years at Green Hill, I want to go on and do something else.'

Jean frowned. 'There's nothing wrong with getting married and having kids.'

'Is that what this is all about?' Suddenly Tana felt sick. 'This coming out bullshit ... it's kind of like a slave auction, isn't it?'

Jean Roberts looked shocked. 'Tana, that's a terrible thing to say.'

'Well, it's true, isn't it? All these young girls lined up, curtsying like fools, and a bunch of men checking them out.' She squinted her eyes as though the girls were lined up in front of her, '... let's see, I'll take ... that one over there.' Her eyes opened wide again, and she looked upset. 'Hell, there has to be more to life than that.'

'You make it sound sick somehow, and it's not. It's a beautiful tradition that means a lot to everyone.' No, it doesn't, Mom, at least not to me ... just to you ... but she couldn't bring herself to say those words. Jean looked at her unhappily. 'Why are you being so difficult about this? Ann Durning came out four years ago, and she had a wonderful time.'

'Good for her. But I'm not Ann.' She also hadn't run off with some twit in Italy who had to be bought off.

Jean sighed and sat down, looking up at Tana from the chair. She hadn't seen Tana in three months and she could already feel the tension mounting between them. 'Why don't you just relax and enjoy yourself, Tana? You never know, you might meet someone you like.'

'I don't want to meet someone I 'like'. I don't even want to go, Mom.'

Tears filled Jean's eyes as she looked at her, and Tana couldn't stand the look on her face. 'I just wanted you to ... I wanted you to have....' Tana knelt and hugged her close.

'I'm sorry, Mom. I'm sorry ... I know it'll be beautiful.'

Jean smiled through her tears and kissed Tana's cheek. 'One thing's for sure, you will be beautiful, sweetheart.'

'I'd have to be in that dress. You must have spent a fortune on it.' She was touched but it seemed such a useless expense. She would rather have had clothes to wear at school. She was borrowing Sharon's all the time.

But Jean was smiling at her. 'It's a gift from Arthur, sweetheart.' Tana felt her stomach tie in a knot. Another reason to be 'grateful' to him. She was so tired of Arthur and his gifts.

'He shouldn't have done that.' Tana was visibly less than thrilled, and Jean couldn't understand why except that Tana had always been jealous of him.

'He wanted you to have a pretty dress.' And indeed it was. As she stood in front of the mirror the following night, her hair teased and swept up, the way her mother had seen Jackie Kennedy's hair done in *Vogue*, with the beautiful silk dress, she looked like a fairy princess with her spun gold hair and big green eyes. It filled Jean's eyes with tears just to look at her. She looked exquisite. Moments later, Chandler George arrived to pick her up, and Jean left with them. Arthur had said that he would try to come by, but he wasn't sure. There was a dinner he had to attend that night, and he'd do his 'best'. Tana didn't say anything about it to Jean in the cab, but she had heard that line before, and knew that it meant nothing at all. It had applied to Christmas, Thanksgiving, Jean's birthdays over the years. And usually doing his 'best' meant that he wouldn't arrive, but a bunch of flowers, or a telegram, or a note would instead. She always remembered her mother's crestfallen face at those times, but not tonight. Jean was too excited about her to worry about Arthur very much. She hovered like a mother hen, joining a group of the other mothers at one side of a long bar. The fathers had found each other, too, and there were clumps of well wishers and old family friends, but most of the room was filled with young people about Tana's own age, girls in pink dresses, or red satin, or bright green, and only a dozen in the white dresses their parents had bought them to come out in that night. For the most part, they were a motley adolescent herd, with faces that would take years to thin out, with waistlines to match. There was something singularly undistinguished about girls that age, and because of that, Tana especially stood out. She was tall and slim, and she held her head high.

Jean watched her proudly from across the room. When the big moment came, and the drum roll came halfway into the night, and each girl was led out on her father's arm to curtsy to the guests, there were unrestrained tears of pride on Jean's cheeks. She had hoped that Arthur Durning would be there by then, and had even dared to hope that he might lead her out. But he couldn't make it, of course. He had done enough for them, she couldn't expect him to do more. Tana came out looking nervous and flushed on the arm of Chandler George. She curtsied prettily, lowered her eyes, and disappeared into the rest of the group, and the music began again shortly after that. It had happened, it was done. Tana had officially come out. She looked around the room afterwards, feeling like a complete fool. There was no exhilaration, no thrill, no romantic tingle up and down her spine. She had done it because her mother wanted her to and it was over now. She was grateful for the hubbub that happened afterwards, which allowed her to get lost for a while. Chandler looked as though he had fallen madly in love with a chubby redheaded girl with a sweet smile and an elaborate white velvet dress, and Tana had discreetly disappeared, allowing him to go in pursuit of his prize, as Tana wandered into an alcove and collapsed in a chair. She laid her head back, closed her eyes, and sighed, grateful to be away from it all, from the music, the people, Chandler, whom she couldn't stand, and the desperately lonely look of pride in her mother's eyes. Tana sighed again just thinking of it, and then jumped halfway off her seat as she heard a voice.

'It can't be as bad as all that.' She opened her eyes to see a powerfully built, dark-haired young man with eyes as green as hers. There was something rakish about him, even in black tie, a casual air about the way he stood, looking down at her, holding a glass, and smiling cynically at her, as a piece of dark hair fell over one emerald eye. 'Bored, lovely one?' He managed to look both sarcastic and amused and Tana nodded her head tentatively in embarrassment and began to laugh.

'You caught me.' She looked into his eyes and smiled. She had the feeling that she'd seen him somewhere, but couldn't imagine where. 'What can I say? It's a drag.'

'It certainly is. The cattle show. I make the rounds every year.' But he didn't look as though he'd been doing them for long. Despite the air of sophistication, he didn't look very old.

'How long have you been doing this?'

He grinned boyishly. 'This is my second year. Actually, this should be my first, but they invited me to the cotillion by mistake last year. And all the rest of the coming out balls, so I went.' He rolled his eyes with a grin, 'What a pain in the ass.' And then he looked appraisingly at her, and took a sip of his scotch. 'And how did you find your way here?'

'By cab.' She smiled sweetly at him and he grinned.

'Lovely date you had.' The sarcasm dripped from his words again and she laughed. 'Engaged to him yet?'

'No thanks.'

'That shows at least minimal good judgment on your part.' He spoke in a lazy laconic way, with the accent of the upper crust, and yet he seemed to be laughing at it all, and Tana was amused by him. There was something outrageous about the boy, as proper as he was, as well dressed. But at the same time there was a shocking irreverence which showed through and suited her mood perfectly. 'Do you know Chandler, then?'

The young man smiled again. 'We went to the same boarding school for two years. He plays a great game of squash, stinks at bridge, handles himself pretty well on the tennis court, flunked math, history, and biology, and has absolutely nothing between his ears.'

Tana laughed in spite of herself. She didn't like him anyway, but it seemed an almost surgically accurate, albeit unkind, portrait of him. 'That sounds about right. Not nice, but right.'

'They don't pay me to be nice.' He looked mischievous as he sipped his drink again, and made an obvious appraisal of her cleavage and small waist.

'Do they pay you to do anything?'

'Not yet actually.' He smiled benevolently at her. 'And with luck they never will.'

'Where do you go to school?'

He frowned, as though he had just forgotten something somewhere, and then gazed blankly at her. 'Do you know ... I can't seem to remember.' He smiled again as she wondered what that meant. Maybe he wasn't going to college at all, although he didn't look that type either. 'What about you?'

'Green Hill.'

The impish smile appeared again, with one eyebrow raised. 'How ladylike. Majoring in what? Southern plantations, or pouring tea?'

'Both.' She grinned and stood up. 'At least I go to school.'

'For two years anyway. Then what, princess? Or is that what tonight is all about? The Great Hunt for Husband Number One.' He pretended to speak into a megaphone. 'Will all candidates line up against the far wall. All healthy young white males with pedigrees ... have your fathers' D&B's in hand, we will also want to know your schools, blood type, whether or not you drive, how large your personal trust is and how soon you come into it ...' He went on as she laughed at him, and he lowered his voice. 'Seen any likely ones so far, or are you too madly in love with Chandler George?'

'Much.' She began to walk slowly toward the main ballroom and he followed her, just in time to see her escort kissing the chubby redhead on the other side of the room.

The tall dark handsome young man turned to Tana somberly. 'I've got bad news for you. I think you're about to be jilted, princess.'

She shrugged and met the green eyes so like her own. 'Them's the breaks, I guess.' There was laughter in her eyes. She didn't give a damn about Chandler George.

'Would you like to dance?'

'Sure.'

He whirled her around the floor expertly. There was something very dashing and worldly about this boy, which seemed to belie his youth. One had the feeling that he had been around, although Tana didn't know where, or even who he was, a circumstance he remedied at the end of the first dance.

'By the way, what's your name, princess?'

'Tana Roberts.'

'My name's Harry.' He looked at her with the boyish grin and she smiled, and then unexpectedly he swept her a low bow. 'Harrison Winslow the fourth, actually. But Harry will do.'

'Should I be impressed?' She was, but she wouldn't give him the satisfaction of letting him know.

'Only if you read the social columns regularly. Harrison Winslow the third usually makes an ass of himself, in cities that circle the globe ... Paris and London most of the time, Rome when he has time ... Gstaad, Saint Moritz ... Munich, Berlin. And New York when he has absolutely no choice, and needs to fight with the trustees my grandmother left in charge of her estate. But he isn't very fond of the States, or of me, come to think of it.' He spoke in a flat monotone as Tana watched, wondering what was going on inside of him, but there was no clue as yet. 'My mother died when I was four. I don't remember her at all, except once in a while, something comes back in a wave ... like a perfume ... or a sound, her laughter on the stairs when they went out ... a dress that reminds me of her, but that's probably impossible. She committed suicide. 'Highly unstable', as my grandmother used to say, 'but a pretty piece.' And poor Dad's been licking his wounds ever since ... I forgot to mention Monaco and St. Jean Cap Ferrat. He licks his wounds there too. With help-mates, of course. There's a regular one he parks in London for most of the year, a very pretty one in Paris ... one with whom he likes to ski ... a Chinese girl in Hong Kong. He used to take me along when I wasn't in school, but eventually I got too disagreeable, so he stopped. That, and ...' the eyes grew vague, '... other things. Anyway,' his eyes came back into focus and he smiled cynically at Tana again, 'that's who Harrison Winslow is, or at least one of them.'

'And you?' Her voice was soft and his eyes were sad. He had told her more than he had intended to. But it was also his fourth scotch, and although it hadn't hurt his feet when they danced, it had loosened his tongue, not that he cared. Everyone in New York knew who Harry Winslow was, both father and son. 'Are you like him?' She doubted it. For one thing, he hadn't had time to develop all those skills. He couldn't have been much older than she, after all.

He shrugged carelessly. 'I'm working on it.' And then he smiled again. 'Beware, lovely one! Beware!' And with that, he swept her into his arms and onto the dance floor again, and she saw her mother watching them. She watched them for a long time, and then inquired of someone who he was, and she didn't look displeased.

'Do you see your father very much?' She was still thinking of what he had said as he whirled her around the floor. It sounded like a lonely life ... boarding schools ... his mother dead by suicide when he was four ... the father halfway around the world most of the time, and obviously a libertine.

'Actually, no. He doesn't have time.' For just a minute, he sounded like a very young boy, and she was sorry for him, but he was quick to turn the tables on her. 'What about you? What's your story, Tana Roberts, other than the fact that you have deplorable taste in men?' He glanced in the direction of Chandler George, crushing the little redhead to him, and they both laughed.

'I'm single, eighteen years old, and I go to Green Hill.'

'Jesus. How dull. What else. Any major loves?'

Her face slammed shut, and he noticed it. 'No.'

'Relax. I meant other than Chandler, of course.' She relaxed a little again. 'Although admittedly, he's hard to beat.' Poor guy, they were both being rotten to him, but he was the dullest boy she had ever known, and he was an easy target for the scorn of his peers. 'Let's see, what else? Parents? Illegitimate children? Dogs? Friends? Hobbies? Wait,' he patted his pockets, as though he had misplaced something. 'I should have a form here somewhere....' They both laughed. 'All of the above ...? none of the above ...?'

'One mother, no dogs, no illegitimate kids.'

He looked sad. 'I'm disappointed in you. I thought you would have done better than that.' The music was winding down and Harry looked around. 'What a bunch of bores. Want to go somewhere for a hamburger or a drink?'

She smiled. 'I'd like that, but do we take Chandler along?' She laughed and Harry bowed.

'Leave that to me.' He vanished and returned again with an outrageous grin.

'Oh God, what did you do?'

'I told him you were upset about the way he's behaved all night with that redheaded tart, and I'm dropping you off at your psychiatrist's....'

'You didn't!'

'I did.' She feigned innocence and then laughed. 'Actually, I just told him that you'd seen the light and preferred me. He congratulated you on your good taste, and ran off with his chubby little friend.' But whatever Harry had said, Chandler was waving happily at them and leaving with the redhead, so there was obviously no harm done.

'I have to say something to my mother before we go. Do you mind?'

'Not at all. Well, actually, I do, but I guess I don't have much choice.' But he behaved himself when Tana introduced him to Jean, and he looked very proper, much to her delight, as they left the ball, and Jean went home alone, wishing Arthur had been there to see it all. It had been a beautiful evening, and it was obvious that Tana had had a wonderful time. And she was leaving now with Harry Winslow IV. Jean knew who he was, or at least she knew the name.

'What about your old man?' He stretched his legs out in the cab, after giving the driver the address of '21'. It was the hangout of his choice when he was in town, and Tana had been impressed. It was certainly a lot more fun than going out with Chandler George. And it was so long since she'd been out on a date, she'd forgotten how it felt, and her dates had never been like this. Usually, they all went out for a pizza in a group on Second Avenue.

'My father died before I was born, in the war.'

'That was considerate of him. It's less of a wrench that way, than if they stick around for a few years.' It made Tana wonder why his mother had committed suicide, but she would never have dared to ask. 'Did your mother remarry?'

'No,' Tana shook her head hesitantly, and then, 'She has a friend.'

He raised the mischievous eyebrow again. 'Married?'

She blushed beet red but he couldn't see. 'What made you say that?'

'Just smart, I guess.' He was so impossible, one would have wanted to slap his face if he weren't so boyish and so appealing all at once. And he was so openly impudent that it somehow made it all right. 'Was I right?'

Normally, she wouldn't have admitted it to anyone, but she did now. 'Yes, or at least he was for a long time. He's been a widower now for four years, and he still hasn't married her. He's a real selfish son-of-a-bitch.' It was the strongest thing she had ever said about him publicly, even to Sharon at school.

But Harry didn't look perturbed. 'Most men are. You should meet my old man. He leaves them bleeding by the side of the road at least four times a week, just to keep his hand in.'

'Sounds nice.'

'He's not.' Harry's eyes were hard. 'He's only interested in one thing. Himself. It's no wonder she killed herself.' He had never forgiven his father for that, and Tana's heart suddenly ached for him, as the cab pulled up in front of '21', and Harry paid and they stepped out. And a moment later, they were swept up in the excitement of the exclusive restaurant. Tana had only been there once or twice, like on graduation night, and she loved the toys hanging over the bar, the well-dressed people crowded in, there were even two movie stars she recognized at once, and the head waiter pounced on Harry with glee, obviously ecstatic to see him again. It was clearly his favorite haunt and he went there all the time. They stayed at the bar for a while, and then went to their table, where Harry ordered steak tartare for himself, and Tana ordered eggs benedict; but as they sipped the Louis Roederer champagne he had ordered for them, Harry saw her face go taut. She was looking across the room at a table of people who seemed to be having a good time and there was an older man with his arm around a fairly young girl. Harry watched her face, and then her eyes and a moment later he patted her hand. 'Let me guess . . . an old love?' He was surprised to see that she went for older men. She didn't look the type.

'Not mine, anyway.' And then he instantly knew.

'Your mother's friend?'

'He told her he had a business dinner tonight.'

'Maybe it is.'

'It doesn't look like it to me.' Her eyes were hard as she turned to Harry again. 'What irritates me more than anything is that he can do no wrong in her eyes. She always makes excuses for him. She sits and she waits and she's so goddamn grateful to him.'

'How long have they been together?'

'Twelve years.'

He winced. 'Jesus, that's a long time.'

'Yeah.' Tana glanced malevolently in Arthur's direction again. 'And it doesn't seem to be cramping his style.' Seeing him made her think of Billy again, and she turned her head as though to avoid the thought, but Harry saw the sudden look of pain in her eyes.

'Don't take it so hard, princess.' His voice was gentle in her ears and she turned to look at him.

'It's her life, not mine.'

'That's right. Don't forget that. You can make your own choices with your life.' He smiled, 'And that reminds me, you never answered all my rude questions before. What are you going to do after Green Hill?'

'God knows. Maybe Columbia. I'm not sure. I want to go on.'

'Not get married and have four little kids?' They both laughed.

'Not for a while, thanks, although it's my mother's fondest dream.' And then she turned to him with a curious look. 'And what about you, where did you go to school?'

He sighed as he put down his champagne. 'Harvard actually. Sounds obnoxious, doesn't it?' It was why he hadn't told her at first.

'Is it true?'

'Unfortunately, yes.' He grinned. 'But there's hope. I may flunk out before the end of the year. I'm working on it.'

'You can't be that bad or you wouldn't have gotten in.'

'A Winslow not get in? Don't be absurd, my dear. We *always* get in. We practically built the place.'

'Oh . . .' She looked impressed. 'I see. And you didn't want to go?'

'Not especially. I wanted to go out West somewhere. I thought Stanford or UC, but Dad had a fit, and it wasn't worth arguing about it . . . so there I am, being a pain in the ass, and making them sorry they let me in.'

'You must be a real treat for them.' Tana laughed, and she noticed that Arthur Durning and his group had just left. He hadn't noticed her.

'I try to be, princess. You'll have to come up and see me sometime, maybe during spring break.'

She laughed at that and shook her head. 'I doubt that.'

'Don't you trust me?' He looked amused and very debonair for a boy of eighteen.

'As a matter of fact, no.' She took another sip of champagne and they both laughed. She was feeling giggly now and she was having a good time with him. He was the first boy she had liked in a long time, and she liked him as a friend. He was fun to laugh with and she could say things to him that she hadn't been able to say to anyone else recently, except Shar. And then she had an idea. 'I might come up if I could bring a friend.'

'What kind of friend?' he asked suspiciously.

'My roommate at Green Hill.' She told him about Sharon Blake then and he looked intrigued.

'The daughter of Freeman Blake? That's something else. Is she as wonderful as you say?'

'Wonderfuler.' She told him then about their being unable to get served at the coffee shop in Yolan, and the lecture given by Martin Luther King and he seemed interested in all of it.

'I'd like to meet her sometime. Do you really think you'd come up to Cambridge at spring break?'

'Maybe, I'll have to ask her.'

'What are you two, joined at the hip?' He looked Tana over appraisingly. She was one of the prettiest girls he had ever seen, and it would be worth putting up with someone else, just to see her.

'More or less. I visited them at Thanksgiving, and I want to go back.'

'Why don't you have her here?'

There was a long pause and then Tana looked at him. 'My mother would have a fit if she knew Sharon was black. I've told her everything except that.'

'Great.' Harry smiled. 'I did tell you that my maternal grandmother was black, didn't I?' For an instant he looked so honest that she almost believed what he said and then he started to laugh and she made a face.

'Pain in the ass ... why don't I just tell my mother about you?'

'Be my guest.'

And she did the next day when he called to take her to lunch in two days. They had Christmas to endure in between.

'Isn't that the boy you met last night?' It was Saturday morning and Jean was relaxing with a book. She hadn't heard from Arthur since the day before and she was dying to tell him about the ball, but she didn't want to bother him. She usually waited for him to call. It was a habit she had picked up when he was still married to Marie. And it was Christmas after all. He'd be busy with Billy and Ann.

'Yes, it is.' Tana explained to her mother about Harry's call.

'He seems nice.'

'He is.' But not in any way Jean would approve of, as Tana knew only too well. He was irreverent and outrageous and he drank too much, and he was obviously spoiled, but he had behaved decently when he had brought her home. He had said goodnight and there was no wrestling match. She had been nervous about that, but she hadn't needed to be. And when he came to pick her up for lunch two days later he wore a blazer and a tie and gray slacks, but as soon as they got downstairs, he put on roller skates and a crazy hat, and proceeded to behave like a complete madman as they walked downtown and Tana laughed at him. 'Harry Winslow, you are completely nuts, do you know that?!'

'Yes, ma'am.' He smiled and crossed his eyes, and insisted on wearing his roller skates into the Oak Room for lunch. The maitre d' didn't look pleased but he knew who he was and he didn't dare throw him out. He ordered a bottle of Roederer champagne, and guzzled a glass as soon as it was uncorked, and then set down the empty glass and smiled at Tana. 'I think I'm addicted to that stuff.'

'You mean you're a drunk.'

'Yup.' He said it with pride, ordered lunch for them both, and after lunch they walked through Central Park and stopped at Wollman Rink where they watched the ice skaters for more than an hour and talked about life, and he sensed that there was a strange reticence about her. She didn't offer herself, in a romantic sense, she was careful and closed, and yet at the same time she was intelligent and warm. She cared about people and causes and things. But there was no hand held out. He knew that he had made a new friend, and no more, and she saw to it that he understood, in so many words, and it aroused his curiosity. 'Are you involved with someone near Green Hill?'

She shook her head, and her eyes met his. 'No, nothing like that. I don't want to get involved with anyone right now.' He was surprised at her honesty. And it was a challenge too, of course, one he couldn't completely resist.

'Why not? Afraid to get hurt the way your mother has been?' She had never thought of it that way. It was why he didn't want kids. He didn't want to hurt anyone as badly as he himself had been hurt. And she had just told him how Arthur had stood her mother up for Christmas again that year.

'I don't know. Maybe. That, and other things.'

'What kind of 'other things'?'

'Nothing I want to talk about.' She looked away, and he tried to imagine what had marked her that way. She kept a safe distance between them, and even when they laughed and played, she sent out messages that said 'don't get too close to me.' He hoped that there was nothing strange about the girl, about her sexual propensities, but he didn't think it was that. It was more that she seemed to be hiding in a protective shell, and he wasn't sure why. Someone had driven her into it and he wondered who it was.

'Was there someone important in your life before?'

'No.' She looked him square in the eye. 'I don't want to talk about that.' The look on her face made him back off at once. It was anger and hurt and something he couldn't even define, but it was so powerful it took his breath away, and he didn't scare easily. But this time he got the point. A blind man would have.

'I'm sorry.' They changed the subject then and went back to talking about easier things. He liked her a lot, and he saw her several times during that Christmas holiday. They went to dinner and lunch, went ice skating in the park, to a movie one night, and she even invited him to dinner one night with

Jean. But that was a mistake, she recognized at once. Jean was grilling him as though he were a hot marriage candidate, asking about his future plans, his parents, his career goals, his grades. She could hardly wait for him to leave, and when he did, she screamed at Jean.

'Why did you do that to him? He just came here to eat, not to ask me to marry him.'

'You're eighteen years old, you have to start thinking about things like that now.'

'Why?' Tana was enraged. 'All he is is a friend, for chrissake. Don't act like I have to get married by next week.'

'Well, when do you want to get married, Tana?'

'Never, dammit! Why the hell do I have to get married at all?'

'What are you going to do for the rest of your life?' Her mother's eyes were hunting her, shoving her into corners and pushing her hard and she hated it.

'I don't know what I'm going to do. Do I have to figure that out now? Right now? Tonight? This week? Shit!'

'Don't talk to me like that!' Now her mother was angry too.

'Why not? What are you trying to do to me?'

'I want to see you have some security, Tana. Not to be in the same boat I'm in when you're forty years old. You deserve more than that!'

'So do you. Did you ever think of that? I hate seeing you like this, waiting around for Arthur all the time, like his slave. That's all you've been for all these years, Mother. Arthur Durning's concubine.' She was tempted to tell her about seeing him with another girl at '21', but she couldn't do that to her mother. She didn't want to cause her that much pain and it would have for sure. Tana restrained herself but Jean was irate anyway.

'That's not fair and it's not true.'

'Then why don't you want me to be like you?' Jean turned her back on her, so that she wouldn't see her tears, and then suddenly she turned on Tana, and twelve years of sorrow showed in her eyes, and a lifetime before that.

'I want you to have all the things I didn't have. Is that too much to ask?'

Tana's heart suddenly went out to her and she backed down. Her voice was gentler as she spoke again. 'But maybe I don't want the same things you did.'

'What is there not to want? A husband, security, a home, children – what's wrong with all that?' She looked shocked.

'Nothing. But I'm too young to think about all that. What if I want a career?'

Jean Roberts looked shocked. 'What kind of career?'

'I don't know. I just mean theoretically.'

'That's a lonely life, Tana.' She looked worried about her. 'You'd be better off if you just settled down.' But to Tana that felt like giving up, and she thought about it as she rode south on the train and she and Sharon talked about it their first night back in Jasmine House, once the lights were off.

'Jesus, Tan, she sounds just like mine ... in a different way, of course. But they all want for us what they wanted for themselves, no matter who we are, or how different we are from them, or what we think and feel and want. My dad understands, but my mom ... all I hear about is law school, and sit-ins, and being 'responsible' about being black. I'm so goddamn tired of being 'responsible', I could scream. That's why I came here in the first place, to Green Hill. I wanted to go somewhere where there would be other blacks. Hell, here I can't even date, and she tells me that there's plenty of time for that. When? I want to go out now, I want to have a good time, I want to go to restaurants and movies and football games.' She reminded Tana then, and the pretty blonde smiled in the dark.

'Want to go to Harvard with me at spring break?'

'How come?' Sharon propped herself up on one elbow in the dark with an excited look. And Tana told her about Harry Winslow then. 'He sounds neat. Did you fall for him?'

'No.'

'Why not?'

There was a silence which they both understood. 'You know why.'

'You can't let that screw you up for the rest of your life, Tan.'

'You sound like my mother now. She wants me engaged to anyone by next week, as long as he's willing to marry me, buy me a house, and give me kids.'

'It beats the hell out of going to sit-ins and getting raw eggs in your hair. Doesn't that sound like fun?'

Tana smiled. 'Not much.'

'Your Harvard friend sounds nice.'

'He is.' Tana smiled to herself. 'I like him a lot, as a friend. He's the most honest, straightforward person I've ever met.' The call he made to her later that week underlined why she so enjoyed him. He called pretending to be the owner of a laboratory in Yolan, and they needed young ladies to perform experiments on, he explained.

'We're trying to find out if young ladies are as intelligent as young men,' he said, disguising his voice. 'We realize of course that they are not, however ...', and just before she flew into a rage, she recognized his voice.

'You shit!'

'Hi, kiddo. How's life in the Deep South?'

'Not bad.' She let him speak to Sharon eventually, and the two girls stood beside the phone, passing it back and forth, and eventually Sharon went upstairs and Tana talked to him for hours. There were no romantic overtones at all, he was more like a brother to her, and after two months of phone calls, aside from Sharon he was her closest friend. He was planning to see her at spring break, and she tried to get Sharon to come along, but to no avail. She decided to brave her mother, and invite Sharon to stay with them, but Miriam Blake had been on the phone to Sharon almost every night. There was an enormous black rally scheduled in Washington with a candlelight vigil for Civil Rights over Easter weekend and she wanted Sharon to be there. She felt that it was an important part of their life, and this was no time for a vacation trip. Sharon was depressed about it when they both left Green Hill.

'All you had to do was say no, Shar.' Tana looked at her and shook her head and for a moment something angry flashed in the pretty black girl's eyes.

'Just like you did about the coming out party, huh, Tan?'

There was a silence, and then slowly Tana nodded her head. Her friend wasn't far wrong. It was difficult to fight with them all the time. She shrugged, with a sheepish grin. 'Okay, you win. I'm sorry. We'll miss you.'

'I'll miss you too.' She flashed her the dazzling smile, and they chatted and played cards on the train. Sharon got off in Washington, and Tana went on to New York. It was balmy and warm when she walked out of the station and hailed a cab, and the apartment looked the same as it always had, and somehow, for no reason she could explain, it was depressing to be back. There was a sameness to it all. Nothing grew, nothing changed. There were never fresh drapes, new plants, wonderful flowers, something exciting going on. There was the same thing, the same life, the same worn-out couch, the same dreary looking plants year after year. It hadn't seemed quite so bad when she was living there every day, but now that she came and went, it looked different to her. Everything was shabbier, and the whole apartment seemed to have shrunk. Her mother was at work, and she threw her bags down into her room, just as the phone rang. She went back to the living room to pick it up, glancing around again.

'Hello?'

'Winslow here. How's it going, kid?'

She grinned. It was like a burst of fresh air in the stale, musty room. 'Hello.'

'When'd you get in?'

'About four seconds ago. How about you?'

'I drove down last night with a couple of guys. And,' he looked lazily around the apartment his father owned at the Pierre, 'here I am. Same old dump, same old town.' But he looked boyish when he smiled, Tana recalled, and she was excited at the prospect of seeing him again. They had learned so much about each other in the last four months on the phone, it was as though they were old friends now. 'Want to come up for a drink?'

'Sure. Where are you?'

'At the Pierre.' He sounded unimpressed by his own whereabouts and Tana grinned.

'That's nice.'

'Not very. My father had the apartment redone by some decorator last year. It looks like a fag hangout now, but at least it's free when I'm in New York.'

'Is your father there?' She was intrigued and Harry laughed derisively.

'Don't be ridiculous. I think he's in Munich this week. He likes spending Easter there. The Germans are so emotional about Christian events. That and the Oktoberfest.' He was slightly over her head. 'Never mind. Come on over, and we'll drive room service nuts. What do you want? I'll order something now, and it'll take two hours to show up.'

She was impressed. 'I don't know … a club sandwich and a Coke? Does that sound all right?' There was something very impressive about all this, but Harry was nonchalant about it all and when she arrived, he was lying on the couch in jeans and bare feet watching a soccer match on TV. He swept her off her feet, and gave her a huge bear hug, and it was obvious that he was genuinely pleased to see her, much more than she realized. His whole body tingled as he gave her a friendly peck on the cheek. And there was a moment of awkwardness, translating the intimacy they had developed on the phone into real life, but by the end of the afternoon, they were like old friends, and Tana hated to leave to go home.

'Then stay. I'll put some shoes on and we'll go to '21'.'

'Like this?' She looked down at her plaid skirt and loafers and wool socks, but she shook her head. 'I have to go home anyway. I haven't seen my mother in four months.'

'I keep forgetting rituals like that.' His voice was flat, and he looked even handsomer than he had before, but nothing stirred in Tana's heart for him, only the friendship that had continued to grow since they first met, nothing more than that, and she was sure that he had nothing other than platonic feelings for her as well.

She turned to look at him now, as she picked her raincoat up off the chair. 'Don't you ever see your father at all, Harry?' Her voice was soft and her eyes were sad for him. She knew how alone he was. He had spent the holidays alone, he said he always did, or with friends, or in empty houses or hotels, and he only mentioned his father in the context of bad jokes about his women and his friends and his gallivanting here and there.

'I see him once in a while. We run into each other about once or twice a year. Usually here, or in the South of France.' It sounded very grand, but Tana easily sensed how lonely Harry was. It was why he had opened up so much to her. There was something inside him which was dying to reach out and be loved. And there was something like that in her too. A part of her which had only had Jean and had wanted more, a father, sisters and brothers, a family ... something more than just a lonely woman who spent her life waiting for a man who didn't appreciate her. And Harry didn't even have that. Tana hated his father, just thinking about him.

'What's he like?'

Harry shrugged again. 'Good looking, I guess. At least that's what the women say ... smart ... cold....' He looked Tana square in the eye. 'He killed my mother, what do you think he's like?' Something shrivelled up in her as she watched her friend's eyes, and she didn't know what to say. She was sorry that shehe had asked, but Harry put an arm around her shoulders as he walked her to the door. 'Don't let it upset you, Tan. It happened a long time ago.' But she was sad for him. There was something so lonely about him, and he was so funny and decent and nice, it wasn't fair ... and he was also spoiled and self-indulgent and mischievous. He had put on a British accent for the first room service waiter who'd come up, and pretended to the second one that he was French, and afterwards he and Tana were convulsed. She wondered if he always behaved like that and suspected that he did. And as she took the bus back uptown, she suddenly didn't mind the depressing little apartment she shared with Jean. Better that than the lavish, chilly decor of the Winslow suite at the Hotel Pierre. The rooms were large, and everything was chrome and glass and white, predictably expensive, there were two huge fabulous white fur rugs on the floor and there were priceless paintings and objects everywhere, but that's all there was. There was no one there when he arrived from school, and there wouldn't be that night or the next. There was only Harry, with an ice box filled with booze and Cokes, a wardrobe filled with expensive clothes, and a TV.

'Hi ... I'm home ... !' She called out as she got in and Jean came running to her, and held her tight with a look of delight.

'Oh baby, you look so good!' It made her think of Harry again, and all that he didn't have, in spite of his trusts, and his houses, and his fancy name ... he didn't have this. And somehow Tana wanted to make it up to him. Jean was looking at her now and there was such obvious pleasure in her eyes that it actually felt good to be home. 'I saw your bags. Where did you go?'

'I went to see a friend downtown. I didn't think you'd be home for a while.'

'I left early, in case you'd come in.'

'I'm sorry, Mom.'

'Who did you go to see?' Jean always liked to know what she did, who she saw. But Tana wasn't as used to the questions anymore, and she hesitated for just a moment before she smiled.

'I went to see Harry Winslow at the Pierre. I don't know if you remember him.'

'Of course I do.' Jean's eyes lit up. 'Is he in town?'

'He has an apartment here.' Tana's voice was quiet, and there were mixed reviews in Jean's eyes. It was good that he was mature enough, and solvent enough, to have his own place, but also dangerous at the same time.

'Were you alone with him?' Jean looked concerned.

This time Tana laughed. 'Sure. We shared a club sandwich and watched TV. All perfectly harmless, Mom.'

'Still ... I don't think you should.' She watched Tana's eyes, as the pretty blonde's face began to tense.

'He's my friend, Mom.'

'He's still a young man, and you never know what could happen in a situation like that.'

'Yes, I do.' Her eyes were instantly hard. She knew only too well. Only it had happened at precious Billy Durning's house, in his own father's bedroom, with a hundred kids right downstairs. 'I know who I can trust.'

'You're too young to be able to judge things like that, Tan.'

'No, I'm not.' Tan's face was like a rock. Billy Durning's raping her had changed her whole life. She knew everything about things like that, and if she sensed any threat from Harry at all, she would never have gone to his hotel, or stayed. But she knew instinctively that he was her friend and she would come to no harm at his hands, unlike her mother's lover's son. 'Harry and I are just friends.'

'You're being naive. There's no such thing between boys and girls, Tan. Men and women can't be friends.'

Tana's eyes opened wide. She couldn't believe her mother was saying those words. 'How can you say a thing like that, Mom?'

'Because it's true. And if he's inviting you to his hotel, he has something else in mind, whether you recognize it or not. Maybe he's just biding his time.' And then she smiled. 'Do you think he could be serious about you, Tan?'

'Serious?' Tana looked as though she were about to explode. '*Serious?* I just told you, all we are is friends.'

'And I told you I didn't believe that.' There was something almost insinuating about her smile. 'You know, Tan, he would be quite a catch.'

But it was too much for Tana to stand. She jumped to her feet, and looked down at her mother with scorn. 'You make him sound like a fish, for chrissake. I don't want a 'catch.' I don't want to get married. I don't want to get laid. All I want is to have some friends and go to school. Can you understand that?' There were tears in her eyes, mirrored by those in Jean's.

'Why do you have to get so violent about everything? You never used to be like that, Tan.' Jean's voice sounded so sad that it tore at Tana's heart, but she couldn't help how she felt or what she said anymore.

'You never used to push me all the time.'

'When do I push?' She looked shocked. 'I don't even see you anymore. I've seen you twice in six months. That's pushing?'

'That coming out party was pushing, and what you just said about Harry is pushing, and talking about catches, and settling down, and getting married is pushing. For chrissake, Mom, I'm eighteen years old!'

'And you're almost nineteen. And then what? When *are* you going to think about it, Tan?'

'I don't know, Mom. Maybe never, how's that? Maybe I'll never get married. So what? If I'm happy, who cares?'

'I care. I want to see you married to a nice man with nice children in a nice house....' Jean was crying openly now, it was what she had always wanted for herself ... yet, she was alone ... with a couple of nights a week with a man she loved, and a daughter who was almost gone.... She bent her head and sobbed, as Tana came to her and hugged her close.

'Come on, Mom, stop ... I know you want the best for me ... but just let me work things out for myself.'

Her mother looked at her with big, sad, dark eyes. 'Do you realize who Harry Winslow is?'

Tana's voice was soft. 'Yes. He's my friend.'

'His father is one of the richest men in the United States. He even makes Arthur Durning look poor.' Arthur Durning. The measuring stick for everything in Jean's life.

'So what?'

'Do you realize what kind of life you could have with him?'

Tana looked sad for her, and she suddenly felt sad for herself. Her mother was missing the point, and probably had all her life. But by the same token, Jean had given her so much. And Tana felt as though she owed her a lot now. But in spite of that, she hardly saw Jean during the entire two weeks she was in New York. She ran around with Harry almost every day, although she didn't admit it to Jean. She was still furious at what her mother had said. *Do you realize who he is?* As though that made a difference to her. She wondered how many people felt that way about him. It seemed a hideous thought, to be evaluated because of his last name.

Cautiously, she even asked Harry about it one day, when they were having a picnic in Central Park. 'Doesn't that bug you, Harry? I mean people wanting to get to know you because of who you are?' The thought still horrified her, but he only shrugged and munched his apple as he lay on the grass.

'That's just the way people are, I guess. It gives them some kind of a thrill. I used to see people do that to my father all the time.'

'Doesn't it get to him?'

'I don't really think he cares.' Harry smiled at her. 'He's so insensitive, I don't think he actually feels anything at all.' Tana watched Harry's eyes.

'Is he really that bad?'

'Worse.'

'Then how come you're so nice?'

He laughed. 'Just lucky, I guess. Or maybe it's my mother's genes.'

'Do you still remember her?' It was the first time she had asked him that, and he looked away from her.

'Sometimes ... a little bit ... I don't know, Tan.' He looked back at her again. 'Sometimes, when I was a kid, I'd pretend to my friends that she was alive, that she was out shopping or whatever when they came over to play. I didn't want to be different from the rest of them. But they always found out. Their mothers would tell them or something when they went home, and then they'd think I was weird, but I didn't give a damn. It felt nice to be normal just for a few hours. I'd just talk about her like she was out ... or upstairs ...' Tan saw tears stand out in his eyes, and then he looked at her almost viciously. 'Pretty dumb, huh, to be hung up on a mother you never even knew?'

Tana reached out to him with her heart and her words, and the gentleness of her voice. 'What else do you have? I'd do the same thing in your shoes.'

He shrugged and looked away, and a while later they went for a walk and talked about other things, Freeman Blake, Sharon, Tana's classes at Green Hill, and then suddenly out of the blue, Harry took her hand. 'Thanks for what you said before.' She knew instantly what he meant. They had that kind of rapport, had from the moment they first met.

'It's okay.' She squeezed his hand, and they walked on, and she was amazed at how comfortable she was with him. He didn't push her at all, didn't ask her anymore why she didn't go out with anyone. He seemed to accept her as she was, and she was grateful to him for that. She was grateful to him for a lot of things, for the way he saw life, for the fun they had, the sense of humor that always made her laugh. It felt wonderful to have someone to share her thoughts with.

He was almost like a sounding board for everything she had in her head, and she was particularly grateful for that when she went back to Green Hill. When she saw Sharon again, it was as though her family had sent someone else instead, and all of her moderate political ideas had disappeared. She had attended a series of rallies and sit-ins with her mother and her friends, and suddenly she was as rabid as Miriam Blake was. Tana couldn't believe the change that had taken place, and finally, after listening to her for two days, Tana turned to her and screamed.

'For chrissake, Shar, what's happened to you? This room has been like a political rally ever since we got back. Get off your soap box, girl. What the hell has happened to you?' Sharon just sat there and stared and suddenly the tears flooded her eyes and she bowed her head, the sobs choked her and her shoulders shook and it was almost half an hour before she could speak, as Tana watched her in astonishment. Something terrible had happened to the girl, but it was impossible to say what it was. She held her and rocked her, and at last Sharon spoke, as Tana's heart went out to her.

'They killed Dick on Easter Eve, Tan ... they killed him ... he was fifteen years old ... and he was hanged ...' Tana felt instantly sick. That couldn't be. That didn't happen to people one knew ... to blacks ... to anyone ... but she could see on Sharon's face that it was true, and when she called Harry that night, she cried when she told him the news.

'Oh, my God ... I heard something about it in school, that the son of an important black had been killed, but it didn't click ... shit....'

'Yeah.' Tana's heart felt like lead. And when her mother called her later that week, she still sounded depressed.

'What's the matter, sweetheart? Did you and Harry have a fight?' She was trying a new tack, she was going to pretend to herself and Tana that it was a romance and maybe the idea would take, but Tana didn't have any patience with her and she was instantly blunt.

'My roommate's brother died.'

'Oh, how terrible ...' Jean sounded horrified. 'In an accident?'

There was a long pause as Tana weighed her words ... No, Mom, he was hanged, you see he's black ... 'Sort of.' Wasn't death always an accident? Who expected it?

'Tell her how sorry I am. Those are the people you spent Thanksgiving with, aren't they?'

'Yes.' Tana's voice sounded flat and dead.

'That's just terrible.'

Tana couldn't stand talking to her anymore. 'I've got to go, Mom.'

'Call me in a few days.'

'I'll try.' She cut her off and hung up. She didn't want to talk to anyone, but she and Sharon were talking again late into the night. Suddenly everything in Sharon's life had changed. She had even contacted the local black church, and she was helping to organize sit-ins on weekends for the remainder of the spring. 'Do you think you should, Shar?'

Sharon looked angrily at her. 'Is there a choice anymore? I don't think there is.' There was anger in her soul now, an anger that nothing would help, a fire that no love could quench. They had killed the little boy she had grown up with. '... and he was always such a pain in the ass ...' She laughed through her tears one night as they talked in the dark, '... he was so much like Mom, and now ... and now ...' She gulped her sobs down, and Tana went to sit on her bed. It went on like that every night, either talking about marches elsewhere in the South, or sit-ins in town, or Dr Martin Luther King, it was as though she wasn't really there anymore, and by mid terms she was panicking. She hadn't done any studying at all. She was a bright girl, but she was desperately afraid now that she was going to flunk. Tana helped her as much as she could, sharing notes, underlining her books for her, but she didn't have much hope, and Sharon's mind was on the sit-in she had organized in Yolan for the following week. The townspeople had already complained about her twice to the Dean of Green Hill, but because of who her father was, they had only called her in and talked to her. They understood what a strain she was under, after her brother's, er ... unfortunate accident, but she had to behave herself nonetheless, and they didn't want her causing trouble in town anymore.

'You better lay off, Shar. They're going to kick you out of school if you don't stop.' Tana had warned her more than once, but it was something she couldn't change now. She had no choice. It was something she had to do, and the night before the big sit-in in Yolan she turned to Tana just before they turned off the lights and there was something so intense in her eyes that it almost frightened Tana as she looked at her. 'Is something wrong?'

'I want to ask you a favor, and I won't be mad if you say no. I promise, so do whatever you want. Is that a deal?'

'Okay. What's up?' Tana just prayed that she didn't want her to cheat on a test.

'Reverend Clarke and I were talking today, at the church, and I think it would make a big difference if there were whites involved in the sit-in tomorrow in town. We're going to walk into the white church.'

'Holy shit.' Tana looked shocked, and Sharon grinned.

'That's about right.' The two girls exchanged a smile. 'Dr Clarke is going to see who he can get, and I ... I don't know ... maybe it's wrong, but I wanted to ask you. But if you don't want to, Tan, don't.'

'Why would they get upset if I walk into their church? I'm white.'

'Not if you walk in with us, you're not. That makes you white trash, or worse. If you walk in holding my hand, standing between me and Reverend Clarke or another black ... that's different, Tan.'

'Yeah,' she felt a twinge of fear in her gut, but she also wanted to help her friend, 'I guess I can see that.'

'What do you think?' Sharon looked her square in the eye and Tana did the same.

'Honestly? I'm scared.'

'So am I. I always am.' And then very gently, 'So was Dick. But he went. And I'm going too. I'm going to go every time I can for the rest of my life now, until things change. But it's my fight, Tana, not yours. If you come, you come as my friend. And if you don't come, I love you anyway.'

'Thanks. Can I think about it tonight?' She knew that it could have repercussions if it got back to the school, and she didn't want to jeopardize her scholarship for the following year. She called Harry late that night, but he was out, and she woke up the next morning at dawn, thinking about going to church when she was a little girl, and things her mother had said about all people being the same in God's eyes, the rich, the poor, the white, the black, everyone, and then she thought about Sharon's brother Dick, a fifteen-year-old child, hanged until he died, and when Sharon turned over in bed as the sun came up, Tana was waiting for her.

'Sleep okay?'

'More or less.' She sat up on the edge of the bed and stretched.

'You getting up?' There was a question in Sharon's eyes, and Tana smiled.

'Yeah. We're going to church today, aren't we?' And with that Sharon grinned broadly at her friend. She hopped out of bed, and gave her a hug and a kiss and a victorious smile.

'I'm so glad, Tan.'

'I don't know if I am, but I think it's the right thing to do.'

'I know it is.' It was going to be a long bloody fight, but Sharon would be there, and Tana, just this once. She put on a simple blue cotton shirtdress, the color of the sky, brushed her long blonde hair into a sleek ponytail, put her loafers on, and they walked into town side by side.

'Going to church, girls?' The housemother had smilingly asked and both had answered yes. They both knew that she had meant different ones, but Tana went to the black church with Sharon where they met Dr Clarke and a small crowd of ninety-five blacks and eleven whites. They were told to stay calm, to smile if it seemed appropriate, but not if it would provoke anyone, and to remain silent no matter what anyone said to them. They were to hold hands and to enter the church solemnly and respectfully, in groups of five. Sharon and Tana were to remain together. There was another white girl with them, and two black men, both burly and tall, and they told Tana on the way to the other church that they worked at the mill. They were about Tana's own age, both were married, one had three children, the other four, and they didn't seem to question her being there. They called her Sister, and just before they walked into the church, the five companions exchanged a nervous smile. And then quietly, they stepped inside. It was a small Presbyterian church on the residential side of town, heavily attended every Sunday, with a Sunday School that was well filled, and as the black faces began to file in, every man and woman in the church turned around. There was a look of complete shock on everyone, the organ stopped, one woman fainted, another began to scream, and within a matter of moments all hell broke loose, the minister began to shout, someone ran to call the police, and only Dr Clarke's volunteers remained calm, standing solidly along the back wall, causing no trouble at all, as people turned and jeered, hurled insults at them, even though they were in church. Within moments the town's tiny squad of riot police had arrived. They had been recently trained for the sit-ins that had begun to occur and were mostly composed of highway patrolmen, but they began to push and shove and drag the uncooperating black bodies out, as they made themselves limp, and allowed themselves to be dragged away ... and suddenly Tana realized what was happening to them. She was next ... this was not happening to a remote 'them', it was happening to 'us' ... and suddenly two enormous policemen hovered over her and grabbed her roughly by both arms, waving their sticks in her face.

'You should be ashamed of yourself ... white trash!' Her eyes were huge as they dragged her off, and with every ounce of her being she wanted to hit and bite and kick, thinking of Richard Blake and how he had been killed, but she didn't dare. They threw her into the back of the truck, with much of Dr Clarke's group, and half an hour later she was being fingerprinted and she was in jail. She sat in a jail cell for the rest of the day, with fifteen other girls, all of them black, and she could see Sharon across the way. They had each been allowed one phone call, the whites at least, the blacks were still being 'processed' according to the cops, and Sharon shouted to her to call her mom, which Tana did. She arrived in Yolan at midnight, and released Sharon and

Tana simultaneously, congratulating them both. Tana could see that she looked harder and more drawn than she had six months before, but she seemed pleased with what the girls had done. She wasn't even upset when Sharon told her the news the next day. She was being kicked out of Green Hill, effective immediately. Her things had already been packed by the housemother of Jasmine House, and she was being asked to leave the campus before noon. Tana was in shock when she heard, and she knew what she could expect for herself when she was ushered into the Dean's office. It was just as she had thought. She was being asked to leave. There would be no scholarship the following year. In fact, there would be no following year at all. Like Sharon, it was all over for her. The only difference was that if she was willing to stay on in a probationary state, she could do so until the end of the year, which would at least mean that she could take her final exams and apply to another school. But where? She sat in her room in shock after Sharon had left. Sharon was going back to Washington with her mother, and there had already been talk of her spending a little time as a volunteer for Dr King.

'I know Daddy'll be mad because he wants me to go to school, but you know, truthfully, Tan, I've had it up to here with school.' She looked sorrowfully at Tana then. 'But what about you?' She was devastated about the price of the sit-in for her friend. She had never gotten arrested before, although they had been warned before the church sit-in that it was a real possibility, yet she really hadn't expected it.

'Maybe it's all for the best.' Tana tried to cheer her up, and she was still in shock when Sharon left, and she sat alone in her room until dark. Her probation meant that she had to eat alone at Jasmine House, keep to her room at night, and avoid all social activities including the freshman prom. She was a pariah of sorts, but she also knew that school would be over in three weeks.

The worst of it was that, as they had warned Tana they would, they informed Jean. She called, hysterical, that night, sobbing into the phone. 'Why didn't you tell me that little bitch was black?'

'What difference does it make what color she is? She's my best friend.' But tears filled Tana's eyes and the emotions of the past few days overwhelmed her suddenly. Everyone at school was looking at her as though she had killed someone, and Sharon was gone. She didn't know where she would go to school next year, and her mother was screaming at her ... it was like being five years old and being told you had been very, very bad, but not being sure why.

'You call that a friend?' Her mother laughed through her tears. 'She cost you your scholarship, and got you kicked out of school. And do you think you'll get accepted anywhere else after this?'

'Of course you will, you jerk.' Harry reassured her through her sobs the next day. 'Shit, there are zillions of radicals at Boston University.'

'I'm not a radical.' She cried some more.

'I know that. All you did was go to a sit-in, for chrissake. It's your own goddamn fault for going to that prissy redneck school. I mean shit, you aren't even in the civilized world down there. Why the hell don't you come up here to school?'

'You really think I might be able to get in?'

'With your grades, are you kidding? They'd let you run the place.'

'You're just trying to make me feel better.' She started to cry again.

'You're giving me a mamoth pain in the ass, Tan. Why don't you just let me get you an application and see what happens?' And what happened was that she got in, much to her own astonishment and her mother's chagrin.

'Boston University? What kind of school is that?'

'One of the best in the country, and they even gave me a scholarship.' Harry had taken the application over himself, put in a good word for her, which seemed like a crazy thing to do and touched her to the core, and by July 1st, it was settled. She was going to Boston University in the fall.

She was still numb from the events of two months before, and her mother still wanted to wrestle about it with her.

'I think you should get a job for a while, Tan. You can't hang around in school for the rest of your life.'

Tana looked horrified. 'How about for another three years, like until I get a degree?'

'And then what? What are you going to do then, Tana, that you couldn't do now?'

'Get a decent job.'

'You could go to work for Durning International right now. I spoke to Arthur last week....'

Tana seemed to be screaming at her all the time now, but she never understood. 'For chrissake, don't condemn me to that for the rest of my life.'

'Condemn you! *Condemn* you! How dare you say such a thing? You get arrested, kicked out of school, and you think you have a right to the world. You're lucky a man like Arthur Durning would even consider hiring you.'

'He's lucky I didn't bring charges against his son last year!' The words flew out of Tana's mouth before she could stop them and Jean Roberts stared at her.

'How dare you say a thing like that?'

Her voice was quiet and sad, 'It's true, Mom.'

She turned her back to Tana, as though shielding herself from the look on Tana's face, not wanting to hear. 'I don't want to hear you tell lies like that.' Tana walked quietly out of the room, and a few days later she was gone.

She went to stay with Harry at his father's place in Cape Cod, and they played tennis and sailed, swam, and visited his friends, and she never felt threatened by him at all. The relationship was entirely platonic as far as she was concerned and therefore comfortable for her. Harry's feelings were something else but he kept them carefully veiled. She wrote to Sharon several times, but the answers she got back were brief, scrambled, and obviously in haste. She'd never been so busy, or so happy, in her life. Her mother had been right, and she had a wonderful job working as a volunteer for Dr Martin Luther King. It was amazing how their lives had changed in one short year.

And when Tana started school at Boston University, she was astonished at how different it was from Green Hill, how open, how interesting, how avant garde. She liked being in class with boys as well. Interesting issues were constantly raised and she did well in every class she took.

And secretly Jean was proud of her, although her rapport with Tana was no longer as good as it had once been. She told herself it was a passing phase. She had other things on her mind anyway. By the end of Tana's first year at Boston University, Ann Durning was getting married again. There was going to be an enormous wedding at Christ Episcopal Church in Greenwich, Connecticut, and a reception, organized by Jean, at the house. At the office, her desk was littered with lists, photographs, caterers' lists and Ann called her at least fourteen times a day. It was almost as though her own daughter was getting married, and after fourteen years as Arthur Durning's mistress and right arm, she felt possessive about the children anyway. And she was especially pleased at how well Ann had chosen this time. He was a lovely man of thirty-two, also previously married, and he was a partner at Sherman and Sterling, the law firm in New York, and from everything that Jean Roberts had heard, he was a very promising attorney, and he had plenty of money of his own. Arthur was also pleased about the match, and he gave Jean a beautiful gold bracelet from Cartier to thank her for all the work she did to make Ann's wedding a success.

'You're really a wonderful woman, you know.' He sat in her living room, drinking a scotch, looking at her, wondering why he had never married her. Once in a while he felt like that, although most of the time he was comfortable now by himself. He was used to it.

'Thank you, Arthur.' She handed him a small plate of the hors d'oeuvres he liked best, Nova Scotia salmon on little thin slices of Norwegian pumpernickel, little balls of steak tartare on white toast, the macadamia nuts she always kept in the house, in case he came by, along with his favorite scotch, favorite cookies ... soap ... eau de cologne ... everything he liked. It was easier to be always ready for him now, with Tana gone. In some ways, that had helped their relationship, and in others, it had not. She was freer now, more available, always ready for him to come by at the drop of a hat, but at the same time, she was much lonelier with Tana gone, more anxious for his company. It made her hungrier, and lonelier, and less understanding when two weeks slid by without his spending a night in her bed. She realized that she should be grateful to him that he came to her at all, and he made so many things in her life easier, but she wanted so much more of him, she always had, ever since they first met.

'Tana's coming to the wedding, isn't she?' He ate another mouthful of steak tartare, and she tried to look vague. She had called Tana about it only a few days before. She hadn't responded to the invitation Ann had sent, and she had chided her for it, telling her it wasn't polite, and her Boston University manners didn't apply here, which of course had done nothing to warm Tana's heart.

'I'll answer as soon as I get around to it, Mom. I have exams right now. It only came last week.'

'It only takes a minute to respond.'

Her tone annoyed Tana as it always did now, and she was curt when she replied. 'Fine. Then tell her no.'

'I'll do nothing of the sort. You answer that invitation yourself. And I think you should go.'

'Well, that comes as no surprise. Another command performance from the Durning clan. When do we get to say no to them?' She still cringed every time she imagined Billy's face. 'I think I'm busy anyway.'

'You could make the effort for my sake at least.'

'Tell them that you have no control over me. That I'm impossible, that I'm climbing Mount Everest. Tell them whatever the hell you want!'

'You're really not going then?' Jean sounded shocked, as though that weren't possible.

'I hadn't thought about it till now, but now that you mention it, I guess I'm not.'

'You knew it all along.'

'Oh, for chrissake ... look, I don't like Ann or Billy. Scratch that. I don't like Ann, and I hate Billy's guts. Arthur is your affair, if you'll pardon the pun. Why do you have to drag me into this? I'm grown up now, so are they, we've never been friends.'

'It's her wedding, and she wants you there.'

'Bullshit. She's probably inviting everyone she knows, and she's inviting me as a favor to you.'

'That's not true.' But they both knew it was. And Tana was getting stronger and stronger as time went on. In some ways, it was Harry's influence over her. He had definite ideas about almost everything, and it brought something similar out in her in order to respond to him. He made her think about how she felt and what she thought about everything, and they were as close as they had ever been. And he'd been right about BU too. Moving to Boston had been good for her, much more so than going to Green Hill. And in an odd way, she had grown up more in the last year than ever before. She was almost twenty years old.

'Tana, I just can't understand why you behave this way.' It was back to the wedding again, and her mother was driving her nuts.

'Mom, can we talk about something else? How are *you*?'

'I'm fine, but I'd like to think that you'll at least think about this....'

'All right!' She screamed into the phone at her end. 'I'll think about it. Can I bring a date?' Maybe it would be more bearable if Harry came along.

'I was expecting that. Why don't you and the Winslow boy take a lesson from Ann and John and get engaged?'

'Because we're not in love. That's the best reason why not.'

'I find that hard to believe after all this time.'

'Fact is stranger than fiction, Mom.' Talking to her mother always drove her nuts, and she tried to explain it to Harry the next day. 'It's as though she spends the whole day planning what to say to me so that it will irritate me the most possible, and she never fails. She hits the nail right on the head every time.'

'My father has the same knack. It's a pre-requisite.'

'For what?'

'For parenthood. You have to pass a test. If you're not irritating enough, they make you try again until you get it right. Then after the kid is born, they have to renew it every few years, so that after fifteen or twenty years, you've really got it down.' Tana laughed at the idea as she looked at him. He was even more handsome than he had been when they first met, and the girls went crazy for him. There were always about half a dozen he was juggling at once, but he always made time for her. She came first, she was his friend, in fact she was much more than that to him, but Tana had never understood that. 'You're going to be around for a long time, Tan. They'll be gone by next week.' He never took any of them seriously, no matter how desperately they wanted him. He didn't fool anyone, he was careful that no one got hurt, he was sensible about birth control. 'No casualties, thanks to me, Tan. Life is too short for that, and there's enough hurt out there without making more for your friends.' But there was no pretense offered either. Harry Winslow wanted to have fun, and nothing more than that. No I love you's, no wedding rings, no starry eyes, just some laughs, a lot of beer, and a good time, if possible in bed. His heart was otherwise engaged, albeit secretly, but other interesting parts of him were not.

'Don't they want more than that?'

'Sure they do. They've got mothers just like you. Only most of them listen to their mothers more than you do. They all want to get married and drop out of school as soon as possible. But I tell them not to count on me to help them out. And if they don't believe me, they figure it out soon enough.' He grinned boyishly and Tana laughed at him. She knew that the girls dropped like flies every time he looked at them. She and Harry had been inseparable for the past year and she was the envy of all her friends. They found it impossible to believe that nothing was going on between them, they were as puzzled as her own mother was, but the relationship stayed chaste. Harry had come to understand her by now, and he wouldn't have dared to scale the walls she had put up around her sexuality. Once or twice he tried to fix her up with one of his friends, just as a friendly double date, but she wanted nothing to do with it. His roommate had even asked him if she was a lesbian, but he was sure that it wasn't that. He had a strong feeling that something had traumatized her, but she never wanted to talk about it, even with him, and he let it be. She went out with Harry, or her friends from BU, or by herself, but there were no men in her life, not in a romantic sense.

'It's a hell of a waste, you know, kid.' He tried to talk to her about it teasingly, but she brushed him off as she always did.

'You do enough of that for both of us.'

'That doesn't do you much good.'

She laughed. 'I'm saving it for my wedding night.'

'A noble cause.' He swept her a low bow and they both laughed. People at Harvard and BU were used to seeing them, raising hell, cavorting, playing pranks on each other and their friends. Harry bought a bicycle for two at a garage sale one weekend, and they rode around Cambridge on it, with Harry in a huge raccoon hat in the winter months, and a straw boater when the weather got warm.

'Want to go to Ann Durning's wedding with me?' They were wandering across the Harvard Quad, the day after her mother had harassed her about it on the phone.

'Not particularly. Is it liable to be fun?'

'Not a chance.' Tana smiled angelically. 'My mother thinks I should go.'
'I'm sure you expected that.'
'She also thinks we should get engaged.'
'I'll second that.'
'Good. Then let's make it a double ceremony. Seriously, do you want to go?'
'Why?' There was something nervous in her eyes and he was trying to figure out what it was. He knew her well, but every now and then she hid from him, albeit not too successfully.
'I don't want to go alone. I don't like any of them. Ann's a real spoiled brat, and she's already been married once, but her daddy seems to be making a big fuss about this. I guess she did it right this time.'
'What does that mean?'
'What do you think? It means the guy she's marrying has bucks.'
'How sensitive.' Harry smiled angelically and Tana laughed.
'It's nice to know where people's values are, isn't it? Anyway, the wedding's right after we get out of school, in Connecticut.'
'I was going to the South of France that week, Tan, but I could put it off for a few days, if it'll help you out.'
'That wouldn't be too big a pain in the ass for you?'
'It would.' He smiled at her honestly. 'But for you, anything.' He bowed low, and she laughed, and he slapped her behind and they got back on the bicycle built for two, and he dropped her off at her dorm at BU. He had a big date that night. He had already invested four dinners in the girl, and he expected her to come through for him tonight.
'How can you talk like that!' Tana laughed and scolded him as they stood outside her dorm.
'I can't feed her forever, for chrissake, without getting something for it. Besides, she eats those huge steaks with the lobster tails. My income is suffering from this broad, but ...' he smiled, thinking of her mammaries, '... I'll let you know how it works out.'
'I don't think I want to know.'
'That's right ... virgin ears ... oh well....' He waved as he rode off on their bicycle.
That night, she wrote a letter to Sharon, washed her hair, and had brunch with Harry the next day. He had gotten nowhere with the girl, 'The Eater' as he called her now. She had devoured not only her own steak, but most of his as well, her lobster as well as his once more, and then told him that she didn't feel well and had to go home and study for exams. He got nothing whatsoever for his pains except a large check at the restaurant and a night of good, restful sleep, alone in his bed. 'That's the end of her. Christ, the trouble you have to go to, to get laid these days.' But she knew from all she heard that he did fine most of the time, and she teased him about it all the way to New York in June. He dropped her off at her apartment and went on to the Pierre. When he picked her up the next day to go to the wedding, she had to admit that he looked spectacular. He was wearing white flannel slacks, a blue cashmere blazer, a creamy silk shirt his father had made for him in London the year before, and a navy and red Hermes tie.

'Shit, Harry, if the bride had any sense, she'd ditch this guy and run off with you.'

'That headache I don't need. And you don't look bad yourself, Tan.' She was wearing a green silk dress almost the exact same color as her eyes, her hair hung long and straight down her back, and she had brushed it until it shone, just like her eyes, which sparkled as she looked at him.

'Thanks for coming with me. I know it's going to be a bore, but I appreciate it.'

'Don't be silly. I didn't have anything else to do anyway. I'm not leaving for Nice until tomorrow night.' And from there he was driving to Monaco, where his father was picking him up on a friend's yacht. Harry was going to spend two weeks with him, and then his father was dropping him off and going on with friends, leaving Harry alone in the house on Cap Ferrat. 'I can think of worse fates, Tan.' He was hinting at the hell he would raise, chasing girls in the South of France, and living in the house alone, but it sounded lonely to her. He would have no one to talk to most of the time, no one who really cared about him. On the other hand, she was going to spend the summer being smothered by Jean. In a moment of weakness, feeling guilty for the independence that had been so hard won, she had agreed to take a summer job, working for Durning International. And her mother was thrilled.

'I could kill myself every time I think about it.' She groaned to Harry every time the subject came up. 'I was nuts. But I feel so sorry for her sometimes. She's so alone now that I'm gone. And I thought it would be a nice thing to do for her, but Christ, Harry ... what have I done?'

'It won't be that bad, Tan.'

'Want to make a bet?' Her scholarship had come through for the following year, and she wanted to make some pocket money to spend. At least this would help. But it depressed her beyond words to think of spending the whole summer in New York, living with Jean, and watching her kiss Arthur's feet at work every day. The very thought made her sick.

'We'll go to the Cape for a week when I come back.'

'Thank God for that.' They exchanged a smile as he drove her to Connecticut, and a little while later, they were standing in Christ Episcopal Church with the rest of the guests, painfully hot in the stifling June air, and then mercifully they were released and they drove to the Durning house, passing through the enormous gates, as Harry watched her face. It was the first time she had been back since the nightmare two years before. Exactly two years in fact.

'You really don't like it here, do you, Tan?'

'Not much.' She glanced out the window and looked vague as he watched the back of her head. But he could sense something inside her go tense, and it was worse once they parked the car and got out. They wandered down the receiving line saying the appropriate things. Tana introduced Harry to Arthur and the bride and groom, and then as she ordered a drink, she saw Billy staring at her. He was watching her intently, and Harry was watching him, as he wandered away, and Tana seemed to be in a stupor after that. She danced with Harry several times, with several people she didn't know, chatted with her mother once or twice, and then suddenly in a lull, she found herself face to face with Billy.

'Hello there. I wondered if you'd come.' She had an overwhelming urge to slap his face, but instead she turned away. She couldn't breathe just looking at him. She hadn't seen him since that night, and he looked as malevolent as he had then, as weak and evil and spoiled. She could remember his hitting her, and then....

'Get away from me.' She spoke in a barely audible voice.

'Don't be so uptight. Hell, this is my sister's wedding day. It's a romantic event.' She could see that he was more than slightly drunk. She knew that he had graduated from Princeton a few days before and he had probably been drinking non-stop since then. He was going into the family firm, so he could screw around and chase secretaries. She wanted to ask him who he'd raped recently, but instead she just started to walk away and he grabbed her arm. 'That was a pretty rude thing to do.'

She turned back to him, her teeth clenched, her eyes wild. 'Get your hand off me or I'm going to throw this drink in your face.' She hissed like a snake, and suddenly Harry materialized at her side, watching her, seeing something he had never seen before, and also noting the look in Billy Durning's eyes.

Billy Durning whispered one word, 'Whore,' with a vicious look in his eyes, and with a single gesture Harry grabbed his arm and twisted it back painfully until Billy groaned and tried to fight back, but he didn't want to make a scene and Harry whispered in his ear.

'Got the picture, pal? Good, then why don't you just take yourself off right now?' Billy wrenched his arm free, and without saying a word, he walked away as Harry looked at Tana. She was shaking from head to foot. 'You all right?' She nodded, but he wasn't convinced. She was deathly pale, and her teeth were chattering despite the heat. 'What was that all about? An old friend?'

'Mr Durning's adorable son.'

'I take it you two have met before.'

She nodded. 'Not very pleasantly.' They stayed for a little while after that, but it was obvious that Tana was anxious to leave so Harry suggested it first. He didn't say anything for a while as they drove back to town, and he could see her visibly unwind as they put some distance between them and the Durning house. He had to ask her then. Something so powerful had been in the air, it frightened him for her.

'What was that all about, Tan?'

'Nothing much. An old hatred, that's all.'

'Based on what?'

'He's a complete prick, that's what.' They were strong words for her and Harry was surprised, and there was no humor in her voice. 'A rotten little son-of-a-bitch.'

'I figured you two weren't the best of friends.' Harry smiled but she didn't respond. 'What did he do to you, to make you hate him so much, Tan?'

'It's not important now.'

'Yes, it is.'

'No, it's not!' She was shouting at him, and there were suddenly tears rolling down her cheeks. None of it had healed in the past two years, because she hadn't allowed the air to get to it. She hadn't told anyone except Sharon, hadn't fallen in love, hadn't gone on any dates. 'It doesn't matter anymore.'

He waited for her words to die down. 'Are you trying to convince me or yourself?' He handed her his pocket handkerchief and she blew her nose.

'I'm sorry, Harry.'

'Don't be. Remember me? I'm your friend.' She smiled through her tears and patted his cheek.

'You're the best friend I've got.'

'I want you to tell me what happened with him.'

'Why?'

He smiled. 'So I can go back and kill him if you want.'

'Okay. Go ahead.' She laughed for the first time in hours.

'Seriously, I think you need to get it off your chest.'

'No, I don't.' That frightened her more than living with it. She didn't even want to talk about it now.

'He made a pass at you, didn't he?'

'More or less.' She was looking out the window again.

'Tana ... talk to me ...'

She turned to him with a wintry smile. 'Why?'

'Because I give a damn.' He pulled the car off the road, turned off the ignition and looked at her. He knew suddenly that he was about to open a door that had been sealed tight, but he knew that for her sake he had to open it. 'Tell me what he did to you.'

She stared into Harry's eyes and spoke expressionlessly. 'He raped me two years ago. Two years ago tomorrow night, in fact. Happy Anniversary.' Harry felt sick.

'What do you mean he raped you? Did you go out with him?'

She shook her head. 'No. My mother insisted that I go to a party here in Greenwich, at the house. His party. I went with one of his friends, who got drunk and disappeared, and Billy found me wandering around the house. He asked me if I wanted to see the room where my mother worked. And like a complete fool, I said yes, and the next thing I knew he dragged me into his father's bedroom, threw me down on the floor and beat me up. He raped me and beat me for a few hours, and then he took me home and cracked up the car.' She slowly began to sob, choking on her own words, feeling them rush out, almost physically. 'I had hysterics at the hospital ... after the police came ... my mother came out ... and she wouldn't believe me, she thought I was drunk ... and little Billy could do no wrong in her eyes ... I tried to tell her another time ...' She buried her face in her hands, and Harry pulled her into his arms, and cooed to her the way no one had ever done to him, but listening to her almost broke his heart. It was why she had never gone out with anyone since they'd met, nor with him.

'Poor baby ... poor Tan....' He drove her back to the city then, took her to dinner at a quiet place, and then they went back and talked for hours at the Pierre. She knew her mother would be staying in Greenwich again that night.

She had been staying there all week, to make sure that everything went all right. And after Harry dropped her off, he wondered if things would change for Tana now, or even if possibly things might change between them. She was the most remarkable girl he had ever met, and if he had let himself, he would have fallen head over heels in love with her. But he had known better for the past two years, and he reminded himself of that now. He didn't want to spoil what they had, for what? A piece of ass? He had plenty of that, and she meant more than that to him. It was still going to take her a long time to heal, if she ever did, and he could help her more as a friend, than trying to meet his own needs by jumping into bed and playing therapist with her.

He called her the next day before he left for the South of France, and he had flowers sent to her the day after that, with a note that read, 'Screw the past. You're okay now. Love, H.' And he called her from Europe whenever he thought of it and had the time. His summer was a lot more interesting than hers, and they compared notes when he came back a week before Labor Day, and she finished her job and drove to Cape Cod with him. She was relieved to be out of Durning International at last. It had been a mistake, but she had lived up to her end.

'Any big romances while I was gone?'

'Nope. Remember me? I'm saving it for my wedding night.' But they both knew why now. She was still traumatized by the rape, and they both also knew that she had to get over that. And after talking to him before he left, it seemed a little less painful now. It was finally beginning to heal.

'There won't be a wedding night if you never go out, you jerk.'

'You sound like my mother again.' She smiled. It was so good to see him again.

'How is your mother, by the way?'

'The same. Arthur Durning's devoted slave. It makes me sick. I never want to be like that with anyone.'

He snapped his fingers with a look of despair. 'Shit ... and I was hoping that....' They both laughed, and the week sped by as it always did when they had a good time, and there was something magical about being together on Cape Cod. But in spite of Harry's hidden feelings for her, they kept the relationship as it had been. And they both went back to their respective schools for their junior year, which seemed to fly by. The following summer Tana stayed in Boston to work, and Harry went to Europe again, and when he came back they went back to Cape Cod, and the easy days were almost over with. They had only one year left before real life set in. And each in their own way, they were trying to keep reality at bay.

'What are you going to do?' she asked him somberly one night. She had finally agreed to date one of his friends, but things were going very slowly and Tana wasn't really interested in him. Secretly, Harry was glad. But he thought that a few superficial dates would do her good.

'He's just not my type.'

'How the hell do you know? You haven't gone out with anyone in three years.'

'From what I can see, that's no loss.'

'Bitch.' He grinned.

'I'm serious. What the hell are we going to do next year? Have you thought about graduate school?'

'God, no! That's all I need. I've had enough of this place to last me the rest of my life. I'm getting the hell out.'

'And doing what?' She had been tormenting herself for the past two months.

'I don't know. I guess I'll stay in the house in London for a while. My father seems to be in South Africa all the time these days so it wouldn't bother him. Maybe Paris . . . Rome, then I'll come back here. I just want to play, Tan.' And he was running away from something he wanted and knew he couldn't have. Not yet.

'Don't you want to work?' She looked shocked and he roared.

'Why?'

'That's disgusting!'

'What's disgusting about it? The men in my family haven't worked in years.'

'How can you admit that?'

'Because it's true. They're a bunch of rich, lazy bums. Just like my old man.' But there was more to them than that, especially him. Much, much more.

'Is that what you want your children to say about you?' She looked horrified.

'Sure, if I'm dumb enough to have any, which I doubt.'

'You sound like me now.'

'God forbid.' They both smiled.

'Seriously, aren't you at least going to pretend to work?'

'Why?'

'Stop saying that.'

'Who cares if I work, Tan? You? Me? My old man? The columnists?'

'Then why did you go to school?'

'I had nothing else to do with myself, and Harvard was fun.'

'Bullshit. You studied your ass off for exams.' She tossed the gold mane over her shoulder with an earnest look. 'You were a good student. What for?'

'Myself. What about you? What were you doing it for?'

'Same thing. But now I don't know what the hell to do.'

But two weeks before Christmas, the choice was made for her. Sharon Blake called, and asked her if she would be willing to go on a march with Dr King. Tana thought about it for a night, and called Sharon back the next day, with a tired smile. 'You got me again, kid.'

'Hurray! I knew you would!' She filled Tana in on the details. It was to take place three days before Christmas in Alabama and it was relatively low risk. It all sounded fine to her, and the two girls chatted like old times. Sharon had never gone back to school, much to her father's chagrin, and she was in love with a young black attorney now. They were talking about getting married in the spring. Tana was excited for her when she hung up, and she told Harry about the march the following afternoon.

'Your mother's going to have a fit.'

'I don't have to tell her about it, for chrissake. She doesn't have to know everything I do.'

'She will when you get arrested again.'

'I'll call you and you can come bail me out.' She was serious and he shook his head.

'I can't. I'll be in Gstaad.'

'Shit.'

'I don't think you should go.'

'I didn't ask you.'

But when the time came, she was in bed with a fever of 102 degrees and a virulent flu. She tried to get up and pack the night before, but she was just too sick, and she called Sharon at the Blakes' home in Washington, and Freeman Blake answered the phone.

'You've heard the news then ... ?' His voice sounded as though it came from the bottom of a well, and it was filled with gloom.

'What news?'

He couldn't even say the words. He just sat there and cried, and without knowing why, Tana began to cry too.

'She's dead ... they killed her last night ... they shot her ... my baby ... my little girl....' He was totally unglued and Tana was sobbing along with him, feeling frightened and hysterical, until Miriam Blake came to the phone. She sounded distraught but she was calmer than her husband had been. She told Tana when the funeral was. And Tana flew to Washington, fever and all, on the morning of Christmas Eve. It had taken that long to get the body home, and Martin Luther King had made arrangements to come and speak about her.

There was national news coverage, press pushing their way into the church, flashbulbs going off in everyone's face, and Freeman Blake was completely undone. He had lost both of his children now, to the same cause, and afterwards Tana spent a little quiet time with them, with close friends, at their home.

'Do something useful with your life, child.' Freeman Blake looked bleakly at her. 'Get married, have kids. Don't do what Sharon did.' He began to cry again, and eventually Dr King and another friend led him upstairs and it was Miriam who came to sit beside Tana then. Everyone had been crying all day, and for days before, and Tana felt wrung out both from the emotions and the flu.

'I'm so sorry, Mrs Blake.'

'So am I....' Her eyes looked like rivers of pain. She had seen it all, but she was still on her feet and always would be. She was that kind of woman, and in some ways Tana admired her. 'What are you going to do now, Tana?'

She wasn't sure what Miriam meant. 'Go home, I guess.' She was going to catch a late flight that night to spend Christmas with Jean. As usual, Arthur had gone away with friends, and Jean was going to be alone.

'I mean when you finish school.'

'I don't know.'

'Have you ever thought about going into government? That's what this country needs.' Tana smiled, she could almost hear Sharon speaking to her. Here, her daughter had just died, and she was already back at her crusades. It was frightening in some ways, and yet admirable too. 'You could go into law. You could change things, Tana. You're that kind of girl.'

'I'm not sure I am.'

'You are. You've got guts. Sharon did too, but she didn't have your kind of mind. In some ways, you're like me.' It was a frightening thought because Tana had always found her cold, and she didn't want to be like that.

'I am?' She looked a little stunned.

'You know what you want, and you go for it.'

Tana smiled. 'Sometimes.'

'You didn't even skip a beat when you got kicked out of Green Hill.'

'That was just luck, a friend, and Harry Winslow suggested BU.'

'If he hadn't, you'd have landed on your feet anyway.' She stood up with a small sigh. 'Anyway, think about it. There aren't enough lawyers like you, Tan. You're what this country needs.' It was a heady thing to say to a twenty-one-year-old girl, and on the plane home the words echoed in her head, but more than that, she kept seeing Freeman's face, hearing him cry ... hearing things Sharon had said to her at Green Hill ... the times they had walked into Yolan ... the memories flooded her, and she dried her eyes again and again to no avail, and she found herself thinking constantly of the baby Sharon had given up four years before, wondering where he was, what had happened to him. And she wondered if Freeman had been thinking of him too. They had no one left now.

And at the same time, she kept thinking of Miriam's words. This country needs you ... she tried the thought on her mother before she went back to school, and Jean Roberts looked horrified.

'Law School? Haven't you been in school for long enough? Are you going to stay there for the rest of your life?'

'Only if it does me some good.'

'Why don't you get a job? You might meet someone that way.'

'Oh, for chrissake, never mind ...' It was all she thought about ... meet someone ... settle down ... get married ... have kids.... But Harry wasn't much warmer to the idea when she tried it out on him the following week.

'Jesus Christ, why?'

'Why not? It might be interesting, and I might be good at it.' She was getting more excited about it every day, and suddenly it seemed like the right thing to do. It made some sense, gave some purpose to her life. 'I'm going to apply to Boalt, at UC Berkeley.' She had already made up her mind. There were two other schools she was going to apply to also, but Boalt was her first choice.

Harry stared at her. 'You're serious?'

'Yes.'

'I think you're nuts.'

'Want to come?'

'Hell, no!' He grinned. 'I told you. I'm going to play ... just kick up my heels.'

'That's a waste of time.'

'I can hardly wait.'

And neither could she. In May she got the word. She'd been accepted at

Boalt. They would give her a partial scholarship, and she had already saved the rest.

'I'm on my way.' She grinned at Harry as they sat on the lawn outside her dorm.

'Tan, are you sure?'

'Never more so in my whole life.' The two exchanged a long smile. The road would part for them soon. She went to his graduation at Harvard in June, and cried copiously for him, for herself, for Sharon Blake who was no more, for John F. Kennedy who had been killed seven months before, for the people they had met, and never would. An era had come to an end, for them both. And she cried at her own graduation, too. As Jean Roberts did, and Arthur Durning came along. And Harry sat in the back row, pretending to make conquests among the freshman girls.

But it was Tana his eyes were rivetted to, his heart leapt with pride for her and then sank as he thought of their going separate ways. He knew that inevitably their paths would cross again. He would see to that. But for her, it was still too soon. And with all his heart, he wished her godspeed, that she would be safe and well in California. It made him nervous to think of her so far from him. But he had to let her go for now ... for now ... tears filled his eyes as he watched her come down the steps with her diploma in hand. She looked so fresh and young, the big green eyes, the bright shining hair ... and the lips he so desperately longed to kiss and had for almost four years ... the same lips brushed his cheeks as he congratulated her again, and for an instant, just an instant, he felt her hold him close, and it almost took his breath away.

'Thanks, Harry.' There were tears in her eyes.

'What for?' He had to fight back tears in his own.

'For everything.' And then the others pressed in on them and the moment was gone. Their separate lives had begun.

PART II
LIFE BEGINS

Chapter 7

The ride to the airport seemed endless this time. Tana took a cab, and Jean insisted on coming with her. There were endless silences, pauses, staccato bursts of words, like machine-gun fire at the enemy as it disappeared into the brush, and then finally they were there. Jean insisted on paying for the cab, as though it were her last chance to do something for her little girl, the only chance she'd ever have, and it was easy to see she was fighting back the tears as they checked Tana's bags in.

'That's all you had, dear?' She turned to Tana nervously, as Tana nodded and smiled. It had been a difficult morning for her, too. There was no pretending anymore. She wouldn't be coming home again, not for a long, long time. For a few days, a week, a brief trip. But if she managed to hang in at Boalt, she would probably never live at home again. She hadn't had to face that before when she went to Green Hill, or BU, and she was ready to go now. But it was easy to see the panic on Jean's face. It was the same expression she had worn twenty-three years before when Andy Roberts had gone to war. That look that comes of knowing that nothing will ever be the same again. 'You won't forget to call me tonight, will you, dear?'

'No, Mother. I won't. But I can't promise after this.' Tana smiled. 'If everything I hear is true, I won't come up for air for the next six months.' And she had already warned her that she wouldn't be coming home for Christmas that year. The trip was too expensive anyway. And Jean had resigned herself to that. She was hoping that Arthur might give her a ticket out, but then there would be no hope of spending Christmas with him. Life wasn't easy sometimes. For some, it never was.

They both had a cup of tea, and watched the planes take off as Tana waited for her plane to be called, and she saw her mother staring at her more than once. Twenty-two years of caring for her was officially coming to an end, and it was difficult for both of them. And then suddenly Jean took her hand and looked into her eyes. 'Is this what you really want, Tan?'

Tana answered her quietly. 'Yes, Mom, it is.'

'You're sure?'

Tana smiled. 'I am. I know it seems strange to you, but it really is what I want. I've never been so sure of anything, no matter how hard it is.'

Jean frowned and slowly shook her head before looking at Tana again. It was a strange time to be talking about it, just before she took off, and a strange place, with thousands of people all around, but this was where they were and what was in Jean's heart as she looked into her daughter's eyes again. 'It seems more like a career for a man. I just never thought ...'

'I know.' Tana looked sad. 'You wanted me to be like Ann.' She was living in Greenwich, near her dad, and had just had her first child. Her husband was a full partner of Sherman and Sterling now. He drove a Porsche, and she a Mercedes sedan. It was every mother's dream. 'That just isn't me. It never was, Mom.'

'But why not?' She didn't understand. Maybe she had gone wrong.

'Maybe I need more than that. Maybe I need it to be my accomplishment, instead of my husband's. I don't know, but I don't think I could be happy like that.'

'I think Harry Winslow is in love with you, Tan.' Her voice was gentle, but Tana didn't want to hear the words.

'You're wrong, Mom.' It was back to that again. 'We love each other dearly, as friends, but he's not in love with me, and I'm not in love with him.' That wasn't what she wanted. She wanted him as her brother, her friend. Jean nodded and said nothing as they called Tana's plane. It was as though she were making a last attempt to change Tana's mind, but there was nothing to change it with, no lifestyle, no man, no overwhelming gift, and nothing would have changed it anyway. She looked into her mother's eyes, and then held her close in a long hug as she whispered in her ear. 'Mom, this is what I want. I'm sure. I swear it to you.' It was like leaving for Africa, as she said goodbye. As though she were leaving for a different world, a different life, and in a way she was. Her mother looked so grief-stricken that it broke her heart, and Jean's tears flowed unchecked down her cheeks as she waved goodbye and Tana boarded the plane, shouting back, 'I'll call you tonight!'

'But it'll never be the same again,' Jean whispered to herself, as she watched the doors close, the gangway pull back, and the giant bird head down the runway at last, and finally take off. And then at long, long last, it was only a speck in the sky, and feeling very small and very alone, she went outside, hailed a cab, and went back to the office where Arthur Durning needed her. At least someone still did, but she dreaded going home that night.

Chapter 8

Tana had taken a plane which landed at Oakland airport, and it seemed a small and friendly place when she arrived. Smaller than both Boston and New York, and much, much larger than Yolan, which didn't have an airport at all. She took a cab to the Berkeley campus with her conglomeration of things, checked into the room that had been rented for her as part of her scholarship, unpacked her bags, and looked around. Everything felt different and strange and new. It was a beautiful, warm, sunny day, and people looked relaxed in everything from blue jeans to cords to flowing robes. There was more than one caftan in sight, lots of shorts and T shirts, sandals, sneakers, loafers, bare feet. Unlike Boston University, the Jewish princesses from New York were not in evidence here, wearing expensive wools and cashmeres from Bendel's. This was strictly 'come as you are', and it was anything but neat. But there was an excitment about it, too, and she felt exhilarated as she looked around. It was an exhilaration which stayed with her once classes began, and into the next month, as she ran from one class to the other everyday, and then dashed home to study all afternoon and all night. The only other place she ever saw was the library, and whenever possible she ate in her room or on the run. She had lost six pounds which she didn't need to lose by the end of the first month. And the only good thing about the schedule she kept was that she didn't miss Harry quite as much as she feared she would. For three years, they had been almost joined at the hip, even though they attended different schools, and now suddenly he wasn't there, although he would call at off-hours. And on October 5th, she was in her room, when someone knocked on her door and told her that there was a call on the pay phone for her. She figured it was her mother again, and she really didn't want to go downstairs. She had a quiz the next day on contract law, and she had a paper due in another course.

'Find out who it is. Can I call back?'

'Okay, just a sec.' And then she came back again. 'It's from New York.'

'Shit.' Her mother again. 'I'll call back.'

'He says you can't.' He? Harry? Tana smiled. For him, she would even interrupt her work.

'I'll be right out.' She grabbed a pair of rumpled jeans off the back of a chair, and pulled them on as she ran to the phone. 'Hello?'

'What the hell are you doing? Making it with some guy on the fourteenth floor? I've been sitting here for an hour, Tan.' He sounded annoyed and he also sounded drunk, to her practised ear. She knew him well.

'I'm sorry. I was in my room, studying, and I thought it was my mom.'

'No such luck.' He sounded strangely serious.

'Are you in New York?' She was smiling, happy to hear him again. 'Yeah.'

'I thought you weren't coming back till next month.'

'I wasn't. I came back to see my uncle. Apparently, he thinks he needs my help.'

'What uncle?' Tana looked confused. Harry never mentioned an uncle before.

'My uncle Sam. Remember him, the guy on the posters in the ridiculous red and blue suit with the long white beard.' He was definitely drunk and she started to laugh, but the laughter faded on her lips. He was serious. Oh my God ...

'What the hell do you mean?'

'I got drafted, Tan.'

'Oh shit.' She closed her eyes. That was all they heard about Vietnam ...
Vietnam ... Vietnam ... everyone had something to say about it ... kick the
shit out of them ... stay out of it ... remember what happened to the French
... go to it ... stay home ... police action ... war ... it was impossible to
know what was going on, but whatever it was, it wasn't good. 'Why the hell
did you come back? Why didn't you stay over there?'

'I didn't want to do that. My father even offered to buy me out if he could,
which I doubt. There are some things which even his Winslow money won't
buy. But that's not my style, Tan. I don't know, maybe secretly I've wanted to
go over there and make myself useful for a while.'

'You're nuts. My God ... You're worse than that. You could be killed.
Don't you realize that? Harry go back to France.' She was shouting at him
now, standing in an open corridor, shouting at Harry in New York. 'Why the
hell don't you go to Canada, or shoot yourself in the foot ... do something,
resist the draft. This is 1964, not 1941. Don't be so noble, there's nothing to be
noble about, asshole. Go back.' There were suddenly tears in her eyes and she
was afraid to ask what she wanted to know. But she had to. She had to know.
'Where are they sending you?'

'San Francisco.' Her heart soared. 'First. For about five hours. Want to meet
me at the airport, Tan? We could have lunch or something. I have to get to
some place called Fort Ord by ten o'clock that night, and I arrive at three. And
somebody told me it was about a two hour drive from San Francisco ...' His
voice trailed off, they were both thinking the same thing.

'And then what?' Her voice was suddenly hoarse.

'Vietnam, I guess. Cute, huh?'

She suddenly sounded pissed. 'No, not cute, you dumb son-of-a-bitch. You
should have come to law school with me. Instead, you wanted to play and get
yourself laid in every whorehouse in France, and now look at you, you're
going to Vietnam to get your balls shot off ...' There were tears rolling down
her face, and no one dared walk past her in the hall.

'You make it sound intriguing anyway.'

'You're a jerk.'

'So what else is new? You fallen in love yet?'

'Who has time, all I do is read. What time does your place come in?'

'Three o'clock tomorrow.'

'I'll be there.'

'Thanks.' He sounded so young again, on the last word, and when she saw
him the next day, she thought he looked pale and tired. He didn't look as well
as when she had seen him in June, and their brief visit was nervous and
strained. She didn't know what to do with him. Five hours wasn't very long.
She took him to her Berkeley room, and then they drove into town for lunch
in Chinatown, wandered around, and Harry kept looking at his watch. He had
a bus to catch. He had decided not to rent a car to get to Fort Ord after all, but
that shortened the time he had with her. They didn't laugh as much as usual,
and they were both upset all afternoon.

'Harry, why are you doing this? You could have bought your way out.'

'That's not my style, Tan. You must know that by now. And maybe, secretly, I think I'm doing the right thing. There's a patriotic part of me I didn't know I had.'

Tana felt her heart sink. 'That's not patriotism, for chrissake. It isn't our war.' It horrified her that he had an out he wouldn't use. It was a side of him she had never seen. Easygoing Harry had grown up, and she saw a man in him she had never known before. He was stubborn and strong, and although what he was doing frightened him, it was clearly what he wanted to do.

'I think it will be soon, Tan.'

'But why you?' They sat silently for a long time and the day went too fast. She held him tight when they said goodbye, and she made him promise to call whenever he could. But that wasn't for another six weeks, and by then basic training would be over. He had been planning to come back to San Francisco to see her, but instead of going north, he was being sent south. 'I leave for San Diego tonight.' It was Saturday. 'And Honolulu, the beginning of the week.' And she had mid-term exams, so she couldn't just run down to San Diego for a day or two.

'Shit. Will you stay in Honolulu for a while?'

'Apparently not.' She sensed instantly that he wasn't telling her what she wanted to know.

'What does that mean?'

'It means I'm being sent to Saigon by the end of next week.' His voice sounded cold and hard, almost like steel, and it didn't sound like Harry at all. She wondered how this had happened to him, and it was something he had wondered himself every day for six weeks. 'Just lucky, I guess,' he had said jokingly to his friends, but there was nothing to joke about, and you could have cut the air with a knife when they handed the assignments out. No one dared say anthing to anyone, least of all those who had fared well, for fear that others had not. And Harry was one of the unlucky ones. 'It's a bitch, Tan, but there it is.'

'Does your father know?'

'I called last night. No one knows where he is. In Paris, they think he's in Rome. In Rome, they think he's in New York. I tried South Africa, and then I figured fuck the son-of-a-bitch. He'll find out sooner or later where I am.' Why the hell didn't he have a father one could reach? Tana would even have called for him, but he had always sounded like the kind of man she didn't want to know anyway. 'I wrote to him at the London address, and I left a message at the Pierre in New York. That's the best I can do.'

'It's probably more than he deserves anyway. Harry, is there anything I can do?'

'Say a prayer.' He sounded as though he were serious, and she was shocked. This wasn't possible. Harry was her best friend, her brother, practically her twin, and they were sending him to Vietnam. She had a sense of panic she had never known before and there was absolutely nothing she could do.

'Will you call me again before you leave ... ? and from Honolulu ... ?' There were tears in her eyes ... what if something happened to him? But nothing would, she gritted her teeth, she wouldn't even let herself think like that. Harry Winslow was invincible, and he belonged to her. He owned a piece of her heart. But she felt lost for the next few days, waiting constantly for his calls. There were two from San Diego before he left, 'Sorry I took so long, I was busy getting laid, probably got the clap, but what the hell.' He was drunk most of the time, and even more so in Hawaii, and he called her twice from there, too, and after that he was gone, into the silence, the jungles and the abyss of Vietnam. She constantly imagined him in danger, and then began to get outrageous letters describing life in Saigon, the hookers, the drugs, the once lovely hotels, the exquisite girls, the constant use he had for his French, and she began to relax. Good old Harry, nothing ever changed, from Cambridge to Saigon, he was the same. She managed to get through her exams, Thanksgiving, and the first two days of the Christmas holiday, which she was spending in her room with a two-foot tall stack of books, when someone came and pounded on her door at seven o'clock one night.

'Call for you.' Her mother had been calling her a lot, but Tana knew why, although neither of them ever admitted it. The holidays were difficult for Jean. Arthur never spent much time with her, and somehow she always hoped that he would. There were excuses and reasons and parties where he just couldn't take her along, and Tana suspected that there were probably other women too, and now there was Ann and her husband and her baby, and maybe Billy was there too, and Jean just wasn't family, no matter how many years she'd been around.

'I'll be right there,' Tana called out, pulled on her bathrobe, and went to the phone. The hall was cold, and she knew it was foggy outside. It was rare for the fog to come this far east, but sometimes it did on particularly bad nights. 'Hello?' She expected her mother's voice and was shocked when she heard Harry's instead. He sounded hoarse and very tired, as though he'd been up all night, which was understandable, if he was in town. His voice sounded exquisitely close. 'Harry ... ?' Tears instantly filled her eyes, 'Harry! Is that you?'

'Hell, yes, Tan.' He almost growled at her, and she could almost feel the beard stubble on his face.

'Where are you?'

There was only a fraction of a pause. 'Here. San Francisco.'

'When did you arrive? Christ, I'd have picked you up if I'd known.'

'I just got in.' It was a lie, but it was easier to tell her that than to explain why it had taken so long to call.

'You sure didn't stay long, thank God.' She was so grateful to hear his voice that she couldn't stop the tears. She was smiling and crying all at once, and at his end, so was he. He had never thought he would hear her voice again, and he loved her more than he ever had before. He wasn't sure that he could hide it now. But he would have to, for her sake, and his own. 'Why'd they let you come back so soon?'

'I guess I gave them a bad time. The food stank, the girls had lice. Shit, I caught crabs twice, and the worst case of clap I ever had ...' He tried to laugh but it hurt too much.

'You creep. Don't you ever behave yourself?'

'Not if I have a choice.'

'So where are you now?'

There was that pause again. 'They're cleaning me up at Letterman.'

'Hospital?'

'Yeah.'

'For the clap?' She said it so loud that two girls turned halfway down the hall and she started to laugh. 'You know, you're impossible. You're the worst person I know, Harry Winslow the fourth, or whoever the hell you are. Can I come and visit you or will I get it too?' She was still laughing, and he still sounded tired and hoarse.

'Just don't use my toilet seat.'

'Don't worry, I won't. I may not shake your hand either unless I see it boiled. God only knows where it's been.' He smiled. It was so goddamn good to hear her voice. She looked at her watch. 'Can I come over now?'

'Don't you have anything better to do on a Saturday night?'

'I was planning to make love to a stack of law books.'

'You're about as amusing as you used to be, I see.'

'Yeah, but I'm a lot smarter than you are, asshole, and nobody sent me to Vietnam.' There was a strange silent pause, and Harry wasn't smiling when he answered her.

'Thank God, Tan.' She felt strange as she heard his voice, and an odd feeling crept over her, that sent chills up her spine. 'Do you really want to come over tonight?'

'Hell, yes, do you think I wouldn't come? I just don't want to catch the clap, that's all.'

He smiled. 'I'll behave myself.' But he had to say something to her ... before she came ... it wasn't fair. 'Tan ...' His voice caught on the words. He hadn't said anything to anyone yet. He hadn't even talked to his father yet. They hadn't been able to locate him anywhere although Harry knew he'd be in Gstaad by the end of the week. He always spent Christmas there, whether Harry was there or not. Switzerland meant Christmas to him. 'Tan ... I've got a little more than the clap ...' An odd chill raced up her spine and she closed her eyes.

'Yeah, asshole? Like what?' She wanted to fight back the words, to make him laugh, to make him all right in case he was not, but it was too late ... to stop either the truth or the words ...

'I got a little bit shot up ...' She heard his voice crack, and felt a sudden pain in her chest as she fought back a sob.

'Oh, yeah? Why'd you go do a thing like that?' She was fighting back tears and so was he.

'Nothing better to do, I guess. The girls were really all dogs ...' His voice grew sad and soft, '... compared to you, Tan.'

'Jesus, they must have shot you in the brain.' They both laughed a little bit, and she stood in her bare feet feeling as though her whole body had turned to ice. 'Letterman. Right?'

'Yeah.'

'I'll be there in half an hour.'

'Take your time. I'm not going anywhere.' And he wouldn't be for quite a while. But Tana didn't know any of that as she pulled on her jeans, shoved her feet into shoes, she didn't even know which ones, pulled a black turtleneck over her head, dragged a comb through her hair, and yanked her pea jacket off the foot of her bed. She had to get to him now, had to see what had happened to him ... *I got a little bit shot up* ... It was all she could hear again and again in her head as she took the bus into town, and then found a cab to take her to Letterman Hospital in the Presidio. It took twice as long as she had said it would be, but she had run like hell, and fifty-five minutes after she hung up, she walked into the hospital and asked for Harry's room. The woman at the reception desk asked Tana what department he was in, and she had a strong urge to say 'The department for the clap', but she wasn't feeling funny now, and she felt even less so as she ran down the halls labelled Neurosurgery, praying that he was all right. Her face was so pale it was almost gray, but so was his when she walked into the room. There was a respirator standing by, and he was lying flat on a bed with a mirror overhead. There were racks and tubes, and a nurse watching over him. She thought he was paralyzed at first. Absolutely nothing moved, and then she saw him move a hand and tears filled her eyes, but she had been half right anyway. He was paralyzed from the waist down. He had been shot in the spine as he explained to her that night, as tears filled his eyes. He could finally talk to her, cry with her, tell her how he felt. He felt like shit. He wanted to die. He had wanted to die ever since they brought him back.

'So this is it ... 'He could hardly speak, and the tears ran down the sides of his face, down his neck, onto the sheets. 'I'll be in a wheelchair from now on ...' He was sobbing openly. He had thought he would never see her again, and suddenly there she was, so beautiful and so good and so blonde ... just as she had always been. Everything was the same as it always had been. No one knew about Vietnam here. About Saigon or Da Nang or the Viet Cong, whom you never even saw. They just shot you in the ass from their hiding place in a tree, and maybe they were only nine years old, or just looked that way. But no one gave a damn about that here.

Tana was watching him, trying not to cry. She was grateful he was alive. From the story he had told, of lying face down in the mud, in the driving rains, in the jungle for five days, it was obviously a miracle that he was alive at all. So what if he could never walk again? He was alive, wasn't he? And the thing Miriam Blake had seen in her so long before began to surface now. 'That's what you get for screwing cheap whores, ya jerk. Now, you can lie there if you want to, for a while, but I want you to know right now that I'm not going to put up with much of this. Got that?' She stood up, and they were both unable to stop their tears, but she took his hand and she held it fast. 'You're going to get off your ass and do something with yourself. Is that clear?' He stared at her in disbelief, and the crazy thing was that she was serious. 'Is that clear?'

'You know you're a crazy girl. Do you know that, Tan?'

'And you're a lazy son-of-a-bitch, so don't get too excited about this lie-on-your-ass life of yours, because it's not going to last long. Got that, asshole?'

'Yes, ma'am.' He saluted her, and a few minutes later, a nurse came in and gave him a shot for the pain, and Tana watched him drift off to sleep, holding his hand, as the tears rolled down her face and she cried, silently whispering her prayers and her thanks. She watched him for hours, just holding his hand, and at last she kissed his cheek, and his eyes, and she left the hospital. It was after midnight by then, and all she could think of as she took a bus back to Berkeley that night was 'Thank God'. Thank God he was alive. Thank God he hadn't died in that godforsaken jungle, wherever the hell it was. Vietnam had a new meaning to her now. It was a place where people went to be killed. It wasn't just someplace one read about, something to talk about between classes, with professors or friends. It was real to her now. She knew exactly what it meant. It meant Harry Winslow would never walk again. And as she stepped off the bus in Berkeley that night, the tears still running down her cheeks, she jammed her hands in her pockets, and walked back to her rented room, knowing that neither of them would ever be the same again.

Chapter 9

Tana sat at his side for the next two days, and never moved, except to go home and get a few hours' sleep, bathe, change her clothes and come back again, to hold his hand, talk to him when he was awake, about the years when he was at Harvard and she was at BU, the tandem bicycle they had, the vacations on Cape Cod. They kept him pretty doped up most of the time, but there were times when he was so lucid it hurt to look at him, and to realize the thoughts going through his mind. He didn't want to spend the rest of his life paralyzed. He wanted to die, he told Tana again and again. And she screamed at him and called him a son-of-a-bitch. But she also afraid to leave him at night, for fear he would do something about it himself. She warned the nurses about how he felt, but they were used to it and it didn't impress them much. They kept a close eye on him, and there were others who were worse off, like the boy down the hall who had lost both arms and his entire face.

On the morning of Christmas Eve, her mother called just before she left for the hospital. It was ten o'clock in New York, and she had gone into the office for a few hours, and she thought she'd call Tana to see how she was. She had hoped right up until the last minute that Tana would change her mind and come home to spend Christmas with her, but Tana had insisted for months that there was no chance of that. She had stacks and stacks of work to do. And she said there wasn't even any point in Jean coming out. But it seemed a depressing way to spend the Christmas holidays, almost as depressing as the way she was spending them herself. Arthur was having a family Christmas in Palm Beach with Ann and Billy and his son-in-law, and the baby Ann had just had, and he hadn't included Jean. She understood, of course, that it would have been awkward for him.

'So what are you up to, sweetheart?' Jean hadn't called her in two weeks. She was too depressed to call, and she didn't want Tana to hear it on the phone. At least when Arthur was in New York over the holidays, there was some hope that he might stop by for a few hours, but this year she didn't even have that held out to her, and Tana was gone ... 'Studying as hard as you thought?'

'Yes ... I ... no ...' She was still half asleep. She had stayed with Harry until four o'clock. His fever had suddenly shot up the night before and she was afraid to leave him again, but at four in the morning, the nurses had insisted she go home and get some sleep. It was going to be a long, hard climb for him, and if she burned herself out now, she wouldn't do him any good later on, when he needed her most. 'I haven't been. At least not for the past three days.' She almost groaned with fatigue, as she sat down in the straight-backed chair they left near the phone. 'Harry got back from Vietnam.' Her eyes glazed as she thought of it. This would be the first time she had told anyone, and the thought of what there was to say made her sick.

'You've been seeing him?' Jean sounded instantly annoyed. 'I thought you had studying to do. If I'd thought you could take time off to play, Tana, I wouldn't be sitting here spending the Christmas holidays by myself ... if you have time to play around with him, the least you could have ... '

'Stop it!' Tana suddenly shrieked in the empty hall. '*Stop it*! He's in Letterman. No one's playing around, for God's sake.' There was silence at Jean's end. She had never heard Tana sound like that. There was a kind of hysterical desperation in her voice, and a frightening despair.

'What's Letterman?' She imagined it was a hotel, but something instantly told her she was wrong.

'The military hospital here. He was shot in the spine ...' She began to take in great gulps of air so she wouldn't cry, but it didn't work. Nothing happened. She cried all the time when she wasn't with him. She couldn't believe what had happened to him. And she nearly collapsed now in the chair, like a little child. 'He's a paraplegic now, Mom ... he may not even live ... he got this terrible fever last night ...' She just sat there, crying, shaking from head to foot and unable to stop, but she had to let it out, as Jean stared at her office wall in shock, thinking about the boy she had seen so many times. He was so confident, almost debonair, if one could say that about a boy his age, he laughed all the time, he was funny and bright and irreverent and he had annoyed her most of the time, and now she thanked God Tana hadn't married him ... imagine the life that would have been for her.

'Oh sweetheart ... I'm so sorry ... '

'So am I.' She sounded exactly as she had as a child when her puppy died, and it broke Jean's heart to listen to her. 'And there's nothing I can do, except sit there and watch.'

'You shouldn't be there. It puts too much strain on you.'

'I *have* to be there. Don't you understand?' Her voice was harsh. 'I'm all he has.'

'What about his family?'

'His father hasn't shown up yet, and he probably never will, the son-of-a-bitch, and Harry's just lying there, barely hanging on.'

'Well, there's nothing you can do. And I don't think you should see something like that, Tan.'

'Oh, no?' She was belligerent now. 'What should I see, Mom? Dinner parties on the East Side, evenings in Greenwich with the Durning clan? That's the worst crock of shit I've ever heard. My best friend had just had his ass shot off in Vietnam and you don't think I should do something like that. Just what do you think should happen to him, Mom? Should I cross him off my list because he can't dance anymore?'

'Don't be so cynical, Tana.' Jean Roberts sounded firm.

'Why the hell not? What kind of world do we live in anyway? What's wrong with everyone? Why don't they see what we're getting into in Vietnam?'

'That's not in your hands or mine.'

'Why doesn't anyone care what we think ... ? what I think ... what Harry thinks ... Why didn't anybody ask him before he went?' She was sobbing again and she couldn't go on.

'Get hold of yourself.' Jean waited for a moment, and then, 'I think you should come home for the holidays, Tan, especially if you're going to spend them around the hospital with that boy.'

'I can't come home now.' Her voice was sharp and suddenly there were tears in Jean's eyes.

'Why not?' Now she sounded like the child.

'I don't want to leave Harry now.'

'How can he mean that much to you ... ? more than I do ... ?'

'He just does. Aren't you spending Christmas with Arthur anyway, or at least part of it?' Tana blew her nose and wiped her eyes, but Jean shook her head at her end.

'Not this year, Tan. He's going to Palm Beach with the kids.'

'And he didn't invite you?' Tana sounded shocked. He was really the consummate selfish son-of-a-bitch, second only to Harry's dad, perhaps.

'It would be awkward for him.'

'Why? His wife's been dead for eight years, and you're no secret anymore. Why couldn't he invite you?'

'It doesn't matter. I have to work to do here anyway.'

'Yeah,' it drove her nuts thinking about her mother's subservience and devotion to him, 'work for him. Why don't you just tell him to jump in the lake one of these days, Mom? You're forty-five years old, you could still find someone else, and no one could treat you worse than Arthur does.'

'Tana, that's not true!' She was instantly outraged.

'No? Then how come you're spending Christmas alone?'

Jean's tongue was quick and sharp. 'Because my daughter won't come home.'

Tana wanted to hang up in her face. 'Don't lay that shit on me, Mom.'

'Don't talk to me like that. And it's true, isn't it? You want him around so there isn't any responsibility on you. Well, it doesn't work like that. You may not choose to come home, but you can't pretend it's the right thing to do.'

'I'm in law school, Mom. I'm twenty-two years old. I'm grown up. I can't be there for you all the time anymore.'

'Well, neither can he. And his responsibilities are far more important than yours.' She was crying softly now and Tana shook her head. Her voice was calm when she spoke again.

'He's the one you should be mad at, Mom, not me. I'm sorry I can't be there for you, but I just can't.'

'I understand.'

'No, you don't. And I'm sorry about that, too.'

Jean sighed into the phone. 'I guess there's nothing we can do about it now. And I suppose you are doing the right thing.' She sniffed, 'But please, sweetheart, don't spend all your time at the hospital. It's too depressing, and you can't do the boy any good. He'll pull out of it on his own.' Her attitude made Tana sick, but she didn't say anything to her.

'Sure, Mom.' They each had their own ideas, and neither of them was going to change anymore. It was hopeless now. They had gone their own ways, and Jean knew it too. She thought of how lucky Arthur was to still have his children around so much of the time. Ann always wanted his help, financially and otherwise, and her husband practically kissed Arthur's feet, and even Billy was living at home. It was wonderful for him, she thought as she hung up. It meant he never really had enough time for her. Between his business obligations, his old friends who had been too close to Marie to accept Jean, according to him anyway, and Billy and Ann, there was scarcely ever time for her. And yet, there was still something so special between them, and she knew there always would be.

It was worth all the hours she spent alone, waiting for him. At least that was what she told herself, as she straightened her desk and went home to her apartment to stare into Tana's empty room. It looked painfully neat, so empty and deserted now. So unlike the room she was living in, in Berkeley, where her things were spread all over the floors, as she rapidly gathered her things, desperate to get back to Harry again. She had called the hospital after she and her mother hung up, and they said his fever was up again. He was asleep, and he had just had a shot, but she wanted to get back to him before he woke up again. And as she pulled a comb through her hair, and climbed into her jeans, she thought of the things her mother had said. It was unfair of Jean to blame her loneliness on her. What right did she have to expect Tana to always be there for her? It was her mother's way of absolving Arthur of his responsibilities. For sixteen years she had made excuses for him, to Tana, to herself, to her friends, to the girls at work. How many excuses could one make for the man?

Tana grabbed her jacket off a hook and ran downstairs. It took her half an hour to cross the Bay Bridge on the bus, and another twenty minutes to get to Letterman, peacefully nestled in the Presidio. The traffic was worse than it had been in the past few days, but it was the morning of Christmas Eve, and she had expected it. She tried not to think of her mother as she got off the bus. She could take care of herself at least, better than Harry could right now. That was all she could think about as she went up to his room on the third floor and walked softly inside. He was still asleep, and the curtains were drawn. It was a brilliantly sunny winter day outside, but none of the bright light and cheer entered here. Everything was darkness and silence and gloom. She slipped quietly into a chair next to the bed, and watched his face. He was deep in a heavy, drugged sleep, and he didn't stir for the next two hours, and finally just to move around a little bit, she walked out into the hall, and wandered up and down, trying not to look into rooms, or see the hideous machines everywhere, the stricken faces of parents coming to see their sons, or what was left of them, the bandages, the half faces, severed limbs. It was almost more than she could stand, and she reached the end of the hall, and took a deep breath, as suddenly she saw a man who literally took her breath away. He was the tallest, most handsome man she had ever seen. Tall, dark haired, with brilliant blue eyes, a deep tan, broad shoulders, long, almost endless legs, an impeccably cut dark blue suit, and a camel's hair coat tossed over his arm. His shirt was so perfect and creamy white that it looked like something in an ad. Everything about him was beautiful and immaculate and magnificently groomed. He wore a crest ring on his left hand, and a troubled look in his eyes, and he stood watching her for a fraction of an instant, just as she stood watching him.

'Do you know where the neurosurgical area is?' She nodded, feeling childlike and stupid at first, and then shyly smiled at him.

'Yes, it's down this hall.' She pointed in the direction she had come, and he smiled, but only with his mouth, and not with his eyes. There was something desperately sad about the man, as though he had just lost the one thing he cared about, and he had, or almost.

But Tana found herself wondering why he was there. He looked about fifty years old, although he seemed youthful for his age and he was certainly the most striking man she had ever seen. The dark hair peppered with gray made him look even more handsome as he walked swiftly past her and down the hall, and she followed slowly back the way she had come, and saw him turn left in the direction of the nurses' station that they were all so dependent on. Her thoughts turned back to Harry then, and she realized that she had better get back. She hadn't been gone long, but he might have woken up, and there were a lot of things she wanted to say to him, things she had thought about all night, ideas that she had about what they could do now. She had meant what she'd said, she wasn't going to just let him lie on his ass. He had his whole life ahead of him. Two of the nurses smiled at her as she walked past where they stood, and she walked on tiptoe into Harry's room. The room was still dim, and the sun was going down outside anyway, and instantly she saw that Harry was awake. He looked groggy but he recognized her, and he didn't smile. Their eyes met and held, and she felt suddenly strange as she entered the room, as though something was wrong, something more than had been wrong before, as though that could even be. Her eyes swept the room as though searching for a clue, and she found him standing there, in a corner, looking grim, the handsome man with the gray hair, in the dark blue suit, and she almost jumped. It had never occurred to her ... and now suddenly she knew ... Harrison Winslow III ... Harry's father ... he had finally come.

'Hi, Tan.' Harry looked unhappy and uncomfortable. It was easier before his father had come. Now he had to deal with him, and his grief too. Tana was so much easier to have around, she always understood how he felt. His father never had.

'How do you feel?' For an instant, they both ignored the older man, as though deriving strength from each other first. Tana didn't even know what to say to him.

'I'm okay.' But he looked a lot less than that, and then he looked from her to the well-dressed man. 'Father, this is Tana Roberts, my friend.' The elder Winslow said very little, but he held out his hand. He almost looked at her as though she was an intrusion. He wanted the details of how Harry had gotten there. He had reached London from South Africa the day before, had gotten the telegrams that were waiting for him and had flown to San Francisco at once, but he hadn't realized until he arrived what the full implications were. He was still reeling from the shock. Harry had just told him that he would be confined to a wheelchair for life, before Tana had walked into the room. He hadn't wasted much time in telling him, and he hadn't been gentle or kind. But he didn't have to be, as far as he was concerned. They were his legs, and if they weren't going to work anymore, that was his problem, no one else's, and he could talk about it any way he wanted to. And he wasn't mincing words just then. 'Tan, this is my father, Harrison Winslow,' a sarcastic tone came into his voice, 'the third.' Nothing between them had changed. Not even now. And his father looked chagrined.

'Would you like to be alone?' Tana's eyes went back and forth between the two men and it was easy to read that Harry would not, and his father would prefer that they were. 'I'll go get a cup of tea.' She glanced at his father with a cautious glance. 'Would you like some, too?'

He hesitated, and then nodded his head. 'Yes, thanks. Very much.' He smiled, and it was impossible not to notice how devastatingly handsome he was, even here, in a hospital, in his son's room, listening to bad news. There was an incredible depth to the blue eyes, a strength about the chiselled jaw line, something both gentle and decisive about his hands. It was difficult to see him as the villain Harry had described, but she had to take Harry's word for it. Yet sudden doubts began to come to mind, as she took her time going to the cafeteria to get their tea. She returned in slightly less than half an hour, wondering if she should leave and come back the following day, or later that night. She had all that studying to do anyway, but there was a dogged look in Harry's eyes when she returned, as though he wanted to be rescued from his father, and the nurse saw it too when she came in, and not knowing what was causing Harry's distress, or who, and in a little while she asked them both to leave. Tana bent to kiss Harry goodbye and he whispered in her ear.

'Come back tonight ... if you can ... '

'Okay.' She kissed his cheek, and made a mental note to call the nurses first. But it was Christmas Eve, after all, and she thought maybe he didn't want to be alone. She wondered, too, if he and his father had just had an argument. His father glanced back over his shoulder at him, sighed unhappily as they left the room, and walked down the hall. His head was bowed, as he stared at his highly polished shoes, and Tana was afraid to say anything. And she felt like a total slob in her scuffed loafers and jeans, but she hadn't expected to meet anyone there, least of all the legendary Harrison Winslow III. She was even more startled when he suddenly turned to her.

'How does he seem to you?'

Tana took a sharp breath. 'I don't know yet ... it's too soon ... I think he's still in shock.' Harrison Winslow nodded. So was he. He had spoken to the doctor before coming upstairs and there was absolutely nothing they could do. Harry's spinal cord had been so badly damaged, the neurosurgeon had explained, that he would never walk again. They had made some repairs, and there would be more surgery in the next six months, but there were some things about which he was very pleased. They had told Harry as much, but it was too soon for it all to have set in. The best news of all was that he would be able to make love, with some instruction, as that part of his nervous system still functioned, to a degree, and although he wouldn't have complete feeling or total control, he still had a considerable amount of sensation there. 'He could even have a family,' the doctor told his father as he stared, but there were other things that he would never do, like walk or dance, or run or ski ... tears filled the father's eyes as he thought of it, and then he remembered the girl walking along at his side. She was pretty, he had noticed her when he first saw her walking down the hall, and had been struck by the lovely face, the big green eyes, the graceful way she moved, and had been surprised to see her walk into Harry's room.

'I take it you and Harry are close friends?' It was odd, Harry had never mentioned the girl to him, but Harry never mentioned anything to him anyway.

'We are. We've been friends for four years.'

He decided not to beat around the bush as they stood in the lobby of Letterman Hospital. But he wanted to know what he was up against, and maybe this was the time to find out. Just how involved was Harry with this girl, another casual affair, a hidden love, maybe a hidden wife? He had Harry's financial affairs to think of, too, even if the boy wasn't sophisticated enough yet to protect himself. 'Are you in love with him?' His eyes bore into hers and she was momentarily stunned.

'I ... no ... I ... that is,' she wasn't sure why he had asked, 'I love him very much ... but we ... I'm not 'involved with him' physically, if that's what you mean.' She flushed to the roots of her hair to be explaining that to him and he smiled apologetically.

'I'm sorry to even ask you a thing like that, but if you know Harry well, you know how he is. I never know what the hell is going on and I assume that one of these days I'll arrive and find our that he has a wife and three kids.' Tana laughed. It was unlikely but not impossible. More likely three mistresses. And she suddenly realized that she was finding it difficult to dislike him as much as Harry would want her to, in fact, she wasn't sure she disliked him at all.

He was obviously powerful, and not afraid to ask what he wanted to know. He looked her over now, glanced at his watch, and at the limousine waiting at the curb outside for him. 'Would you come to have a cup of coffee with me somewhere? At my hotel perhaps? I'm staying at the Stanford Court, but I could have the driver take you back to wherever you like afterwards. Does that sound all right?' Actually, it sounded faintly traitorous to her, but she didn't know what to say to him. The poor man had been through a lot, too, and he had come an awfully long way.

'I ... I really should get back ... I have an awful lot of studying to do ...' She blushed and he looked hurt, and suddenly she was sorry for him. As elegant and dashing as he was, there was at the same time something vulnerable about him. 'I'm sorry, I didn't mean to sound rude. It's just ...'

'I know.' He looked at her with a rueful smile that melted her heart. 'He's told you what a bastard I am. But it's Christmas Eve, you know. It might do us both good to go and talk for a while. I've had a hell of a shock, and you must have too.' She nodded sadly and followed him to the car. The driver opened the door and she got in, and Harrison Winslow sat next to her on the gray velvet seat. He looked pensive as the city slid by and it seemed moments when they reached Nob Hill, and drove down the east face of it, turning sharply into the courtyard of the Stanford Court. 'Harry and I have had a rough time of it over the years. Somehow we never managed to hit it off ...' He almost seemed to be talking to himself as she watched his face. He didn't look as ruthless as Harry had described. In fact, he didn't look ruthless at all. He looked lonely and sad, and he seemed very much alone. Harrison looked pointedly at Tana then. 'You're a beautiful girl ... inside as well, I suspect. Harry is lucky to have you as a friend.'

And the oddest thing about her was something Harry couldn't really have known. She looked so much like his mother at the same age. It was uncanny as Harrison watched her step lightly out of the car, and he followed her into the hotel. They went to the Potpourri restaurant and slid into a booth. He seemed to be constantly watching her, as though trying to understand who she was, and what she meant to his son. He found it difficult to believe that she was only his 'friend' as she claimed, and yet she was insistent about that as they talked and she had no reason to lie to him.

Tana smiled as she watched his eyes. 'My mothers feels that same way about it that you do, Mr Winslow. She keeps telling me that "boys and girls can't be friends," and I tell her she's wrong. That's exactly what Harry and I are ... he's my best friend in the whole world ... he's like a brother to me ...' Her eyes filled with tears and she looked away thinking of what had happened to him. '... I'll do anything I can to help make him all right again.' She looked at Harrison Winslow defiantly, not angry with him, but at the fate which had crippled his son. 'I will, you'll see ... I won't just let him lie there on his ass,' she blushed at the word, but went on, 'I'm going to get him up and moving and giving a damn again.' She looked at him strangely then. 'I have an idea, but I have to talk to Harry about it first.' He was intrigued. Maybe she had designs on the boy after all, but he didn't think that would be so bad now. Aside from being pretty, she was obviously bright and the girl had a hell of a lot of spunk. When she spoke, her eyes lit up like green fire, and he knew that she meant everything she said.

'What kind of idea?' He was intrigued by her, and if he hadn't been so worried about his son, he would have been amused.

She hesitated. He'd probably think she was nuts, particularly if he was as unambitious as Harry said. 'I don't know ... it probably sounds crazy to you, but I thought ... I don't know ...' It was embarrassing, admitting it to him. 'I thought that maybe I could get him to go to law school with me. Even if he never uses it, it would be good for him, especially now.'

'Are you serious?' There were laugh lines coming to light beside Harrison Winslow's eyes. 'Law school? My son?' He patted her hand with a grin, she was an amazing child, a little ball of fire, but he wouldn't put anything past this girl, including that. 'If you can talk him into that, especially now,' his face sobered rapidly, 'you really would be even more remarkable than I think you are.'

'I'm going to give it a try when he's well enough to listen to me.'

'That'll be a while, I'm afraid.' They both nodded silently, and in the silence heard someone singing carols outside, and then suddenly Tana looked at him.

'Why do you see so little of him?' She had to ask, she had nothing to lose, and if he got angry with her, she could always leave. He couldn't do anything to her, but he didn't actually look upset as he gazed into her eyes.

'Honestly? Because Harry and I have been a lost cause until now. I tried for a long, long time, but I never got anywhere. He's hated me ever since he was a small boy, and it's only gotten worse over the years. There was no point inflicting new wounds after a while. It's a big world, I have a lot to do, he has his own life to lead,' tears flooded his eyes and he looked away, '... or at least he did, until now ... '

She reached across the table and touched his hand. 'He will again. I promise you ... if he lives ... oh God ... if he lives ... please God, don't let him die.' Tears flooded her eyes, too, and she brushed them from her cheeks. 'He's so wonderful, Mr Winslow, he's the best friend I've ever had.'

'I wish I could say the same.' He looked sad. 'We're almost strangers by now. I felt like an intruder in his room today.'

'Maybe that's because I was there. I should have left you two alone.'

'It wouldn't make any difference anymore. It's gone too far, for too long. We're strangers now.'

'You don't have to be.' She was talking to him as though she knew the man, and somehow he didn't seem so impressive anymore, no matter how worldly or debonair or handsome or sophisticated he was. He was only another human being, with a devastating problem on his hands, a very sick son. 'You could make friends with him now.'

Harrison Winslow shook his head, and after a moment he smiled at her. He thought Tana a remarkably beautiful girl, and he suddenly wondered again exactly what the story was between Harry and this girl. His son was too much of a libertine, in his own way, to let an opportunity like this pass him by, except if he cared about her even more than she knew ... maybe that was it ... maybe Harry was in love with her ... he had to be. It couldn't be what she said it was between them. It seemed impossible to him.

'It's too late, my friend. Much, much too late. And in his eyes, my sins are unforgivable.' He sighed. 'I suppose I'd feel the same way in his shoes.' He looked unwaveringly at her now. 'He thinks I killed his mother, you know. She committed suicide when he was four.'

She almost choked on her words. 'I know.' And the look in his eyes was devastating, raw pain that still lived in his soul. His love for her had never died, nor had his love for their son. 'She was dying of cancer and she didn't want anyone to know. In the end, it would have disfigured her and she couldn't have tolerated that. She'd already had two operations before she died ... and ...' he almost stopped, but went on, '... it was terrible for her ... for all of us ... Harry knew she was sick then, but he doesn't remember it now. It doesn't matter anyway. She couldn't live with the operations, the pain, and I couldn't bear to watch her suffer. What she did was a terrible thing, but I always understood. She was so young, so beautiful. She was very much like you, in fact, and almost a child herself ...' He wasn't ashamed of the tears in his eyes, and Tana looked at him horrified.

'Why doesn't Harry know?'

'She made me promise I'd never tell.' He sat back against the banquette as though he'd been punched. The feeling of despair over her death never really went away. He had tried to run away from it for years, with Harry at first, with women, with girls, with anyone, and finally by himself. He was fifty-two years old and he had discovered that there was only so far he could run, and he couldn't run that far anymore. The memories were there, the sorrow, the loss ... and now Harry might go too ... he couldn't bear the thought as he looked at this lovely young girl, so full of life, so filled with hope. It was almost impossible to explain it all to her, it was all so long ago. 'People felt differently about cancer then ... it was almost as though one had to be ashamed of it. I didn't agree with her at the time, but she was adamant that Harry not know. She left me a very long letter at the time. She took an overdose of pills when I went to Boston overnight to see my great aunt. She wanted Harry to think her flighty and beautiful, and romantic, but not riddled with disease, and so she went ... she's a heroine to him.' He smiled at Tana, 'And she was to me. It was a sad way to die, but the other way would have been so much worse. I never blamed her for what she did.'

'And you let him think it was your fault.' She was horrified, and her green eyes were huge in her face.

'I never realised he would, and by the time I understood, it was already too late. I ran around a great deal when he was a child, as though I could flee from the pain of losing her. But it doesn't really work that way. It follows you, like a mangy dog, always waiting outside your room when you wake up, pawing at your door, whining at your feet, no matter how dressed up and charming and busy you are, how many friends you surround yourself with, its always there, nipping at your heels, gnawing at your cuffs ... and so it was ... by the time Harry was eight or nine, he had come to his own conclusions about me, and he got so hateful for a while that I put him into boarding school, and he decided to stay, and then I had nothing at all, so I ran even harder than before ... and,' he shrugged philosophically, 'she died almost twenty years ago, and here we are ... she died in January ...' His eyes looked vague for a moment and then focused on Tana again, but that didn't help. She looked too much like her anyway, it was like looking into the past, just seeing her. 'And now Harry is in this awful mess ... life is so rotten and so strange, isn't it?' She nodded, there wasn't much she could say. He had given her a great deal to think about.

'I think you should say something to him.'

'About what?'

'About how his mother died.'

'I couldn't do that. I made a promise to her ... to myself ... it would be self-serving to tell him now ... '

'Then why tell me?' She was shocked at herself, at the anger in her voice, at what she felt, at the waste people allowed in their lives, lost moments in which they could have loved each other, like this man and his son. They had wasted so many years they could have shared. And Harry needed him now. He needed everyone.

Harrison looked apologetically at her. 'I suppose I shouldn't have told you all that. But I needed to talk to someone ... and you're ... so close to him.' He looked at her point blank. 'I wanted you to know that I love my son.' There was a lump in her throat the size of a fist and she wasn't sure if she wanted to slap him or kiss him, or perhaps both. She had never felt that way about any man before.

'Why the hell don't you tell him yourself?'

'It wouldn't do any good'

'It might. Maybe this is the time.'

He looked at her pensively, and then down at his hands, and then finally into her green eyes again. 'Perhaps it is. I don't know him, though ... I wouldn't know where to begin ... '

'Just like that, Mr Winslow. Just the way you said it to me.'

He smiled at her, and he suddenly looked very tired. 'What makes you so wise, little girl?'

She smiled at him, and she felt an incredible warmth emanating from him. He was a lot like Harry in some ways, and yet he was more, and she realized with a pang of embarrassment that she was attracted to him. It was as though all the senses that had been deadened for years, ever since the rape, had suddenly come alive again.

'What were you thinking then?'

She flushed pink and shook her head. 'Something that had nothing to do with all this ... I'm sorry ... I'm tired ... I haven't slept for a few days ... '

'I'll get you home, so you can get some rest.' He signalled for the check, and when it came he looked at her with a gentle smile, and she felt a longing for the father she had never had, or even known. This was the kind of man she would have wanted Andy Roberts to have been, not Arthur Durning who breezed in and out of her mother's life when it suited him. This man was a great deal less selfish than Harry had wanted her to believe, or insisted on believing himself. He had put a lot of energy into hating this man over the years and Tana knew instinctively now that he had been wrong, very wrong, and she wondered if Harrison was right, if it was too late. 'Thank you for talking to me, Tana. Harry is lucky to have you as his friend.'

'I've been lucky to have him.'

He put a twenty dollar bill under the check and looked at her again. 'Are you an only child?' He suspected that about her, and she nodded with a smile.

'Yes. And I never knew my father, he died before I was born, in the war.' It was something she had said ten thousand times in her life, but it seemed to have new meaning now. Everything did, and she didn't understand what they meant or why. Something strange was happening to her as she sat with this man, and she wondered if it was just because she was so tired. She let him walk her back to his car, and he surprised her by getting in with her, rather than letting the driver take her home.

'I'll ride with you.'

'You really don't need to do that.'

'I have nothing else to do. I'm here to see Harry, and I think he's better off resting for the next few hours.' She agreed with him and they chatted on the drive across the bridge. He mentioned that he had never been to San Francisco before. He found it an attractive place, but he seemed distracted as they drove along. She assumed he was thinking about his son, but he was actually thinking about her, and he shook her hand when they arrived. 'I'll see you at the hospital again. If you need a ride, just call the hotel and I'll send the car for you.' She had mentioned that she'd been taking the bus back and forth and that worried him. She was young after all and pretty and anything could have happened to her.

'Thank you for everything, Mr Winslow.'

'Harrison.' He smiled at her, and he looked exactly like Harry when he smiled, not quite as mischievous, but there was a sparkle there too. 'I'll see you soon. Get some rest now!' He waved, and the limousine drove off, as she slowly climbed the stairs, thinking of all he had said. How unfair life was at times. She feel asleep thinking of Harrison ... and Harry ... and Vietnam ... and the woman who had killed herself, and in Tana's dream she had no face, and when she woke it was dark, and she sat up with a start and couldn't catch her breath in the tiny room. She glanced at the clock and it was nine o'clock, and she wondered how Harry was. She went to the pay phone and called and discovered that the fever was down, he had been awake for a while, and was now dozing again, but he hadn't gone to bed for the night. They hadn't given him his sleeping medicine yet, and they probably wouldn't for a while, and suddenly, as Tana heard caroling outside, she realized that it was Christmas Eve, and Harry needed her. She showered quickly and decided to dress for him. She wore a pretty white knit dress, high heeled shoes, and put on a red coat and a scarf that she hadn't worn since the winter before in New York, and thought she would never wear here. But somehow it all looked and felt Christmassy, and she thought that might be important to him. She put on some perfume, brushed her hair, and rode back into town on the bus, thinking of his father again. It was ten thirty at night when she arived at Letterman, and there was a sleepy holiday air about it all. Little trees with blinking lights, plastic Santa Clauses here and there. But no one seemed to be in a particularly holiday mood, there were too many desperate things going on, and when she reached his room, she knocked softly and tiptoed in, expecting him to be asleep, and instead, he was lying there, staring at the wall, with tears in his eyes. He started when he saw her, and he didn't even smile.

'I'm dying, aren't I?' She was shocked at his words, at his tone, at the lifeless look in his eyes, and she suddenly frowned and approached the bed.

'Not unless you want to die.' She knew she had to be blunt with him. 'It's pretty much up to you.' She stood very close to him, looking into his eyes, and he did not reach for her hand.

'That's a dumb thing to say. It wasn't my idea to get shot in the ass.'

'Sure it was.' She sounded nonchalant and for a moment he looked pissed. 'What the hell is that supposed to mean?'

'That you could have gone to school. And you decided to play instead. So you got the short end of the stick. You gambled and you lost.'

'Yeah. Only I didn't lose ten bucks, I lost my legs. Not exactly small stakes.'

'Looks like they're still there to me.' She glanced down at the useless limbs and he almost snarled at her.

'Don't be an ass. What good are they now?'

'You've got them, and you're alive, and there's plenty you can still do. And according to the nurses, you can still get it up,' she had never been so blunt with him and it was a hell of a speech for Christmas Eve, but she knew that it was time to start pushing him, especially if he thought he was going to die. 'Hell, look at the bright side, you might even get the clap again.'

'You make me sick.' He turned away, and without thinking she grabbed his arm, and he turned to look at her again.

'Look, dammit, you make *me* sick. Half the boys in your platoon were killed, and you're alive, so don't lie there whining at what you don't have. Think of what you do. Your life isn't over, unless you want it to be, and I don't want it to be,' tears stung her eyes, 'I want you to get off that dead ass of yours, if I have to drag you by the hair for the next ten years to make you get up and live again. Is that clear? The tears were pouring down her cheek. 'I'm not going to let go of you. Ever! Do you understand that?' And slowly, slowly ... she saw a smile dawn in his eyes.

'You're a crazy broad, do you know that, Tan?'

'Yeah, well maybe I am, but you'll find out just how crazy I am until you start making life easier for both of us by doing something with yourself.' She wiped the tears from her cheeks and he grinned at her, and for the first time in days, he looked like the Harry she knew.

'You know what it is?'

'What?' She looked confused. It was the most emotional few days of her life and she had never felt so overwrought as she did now.

'It's all the sexual energy you've got pent up, that's what gives you all this oomph to put into everything else. It makes you a real pain in the ass sometimes.'

'Thanks.'

'Anytime.' He grinned, and closed his eyes for a minutes and then he opened them again. 'What are you all dressed up for? Going someplace?'

'Yes. Here. To see you. It's Christmas Eve.' Her eyes softened and she smiled at him. 'Welcome back to the human race.'

'I liked what you said before.' He was still smiling and Tana could see that the tides had turned. If he hung on to the will to live, he'd be all right, relatively. That was what the neurosurgeon had said.

'What did I say ... ? you mean about booting you in the ass making something of yourself ... it's about time.' She looked pleased.

'No, about getting it up, and getting the clap again.'

'Shit.' She looked at him with total contempt and one of the nurses walked in and they started to laugh, and suddenly, for just a minute it was just like old times, and then Harry's father walked into the room, and they both looked like nervous kids, and the laughter stopped, and Harrison Winslow smiled. He wanted so desperately to make friends with his son, and he already knew how much he liked the girl.

'Don't let me spoil your fun. What was that all about?'

Tana blushed. It was difficult talking to someone as cosmopolitan as he was, but she had talked to him all afternoon after all.

'Your son was being as rude as he usually is.'

'That's nothing new.' Harrison sat down in one of the room's two chairs, and glanced at them both. 'Although you'd think on Christmas Eve, he could make an effort to be a little more polite.'

'Actually, he was talking about the nurses and ...' Harry blushed and began to object, Tana laughed, and suddenly Harry's father was laughing too. There was something very tenuous in the room, and none of them looked totally at ease, but they chatted for half an hour and then Harry began to look tired, and Tana stood up. 'I just came to give you a Christmas kiss, I didn't even think you'd be awake.'

'Neither did I.' Harrison Winslow stood up too. 'We'll come back tomorrow, son.' He was watching Harry look at her, and he thought he understood. She was innocent of what Harry felt for her, and for some reason he was keeping it a secret from her, and Harrison couldn't understand why. There was a mystery here which made no sense to him. He looked at his son again. 'Do you need anything before we leave?'

Harry looked sad for a long moment and then shook his head. He needed something, but it was nothing they had to give. The gift of his legs. And his father understood and gently touched his arm.

'See you tomorrow, son.'

'Goodnight.' Harry's greeting to his father wasn't warm, but his eyes lit up when he looked at the beautiful blonde. 'Behave yourself, Tan.'

'Why should I? You don't.' She grinned and blew him a kiss, as she whispered, 'Merry Christmas, asshole.' He laughed and she followed his father out into the hall.

'I thought he looked better, didn't you?' They were becoming friends over the disaster that had befallen his son.

'I did. I think he's over the worst. Now its just going to be a long, slow climb back uphill.' Harrison nodded, and they took the elevator downstairs again. There was a familiarity to it now, as if they had done this dozens of times before, when actually it had only been once. But their talk that afternoon had brought them much closer, and Harrison held the door open for her now, as she saw that the same silver limousine was there.

'Would you like something to eat?'

She started to say no and then realized that she hadn't had dinner yet. She had been thinking about going to midnight mass, but she didn't really want to go alone. She looked at him, wondering if it would mean something to him, too, particularly now.

'I might. Could I interest you in midnight mass afterwards?'

He looked very serious as he nodded his head, and Tana was struck once again by how handsome he was. They went out for a quick hamburger, and chatted about Harry, and their Cambridge days. She told Harrison some of the more outrageous things they'd done and he laughed with her, still puzzled by the odd relationship they shared. Like Jean, he couldn't quite figure them out. And then they went off to midnight mass, and tears streamed down Tana's cheeks as they sang Silent Night. She was thinking of Sharon, her beloved friend, and Harry and how lucky he was to be alive, and when she glanced over at his father, standing tall and proud at her side, she saw that he was crying too. He discreetly blew his nose when they sat down, and as he took her back to Berkeley afterwards, she noticed how comfortable it was just being with him. She was almost dozing as he drove her home. She was desperately tired.

'What are you doing tomorrow?'

'Seeing Harry, I guess. And one of these days I've got a lot of studying to do.' She had all but forgotten it in the past few days.

'Could I take you to lunch before you go to the hospital?' She was touched that he would ask, and she accepted, worrying instantly what she would wear as soon as she stepped out of the car, but she didn't even have time to think of it when she got back to her room. She was so exhausted that she peeled off her clothes, dropped them on the floor, climbed into bed, and was instantly dead to the world. Unlike her mother in New York, who had been awake, sitting lonely in a chair and crying all night. Tana had not called, nor had Arthur in Palm Beach, and she had spent the entire night wrestling with the darker side of her soul, contemplating something she would never have thought she would do.

She had gone to midnight mass, as she and Tana used to do, and at one thirty she came home, watched a little late night TV.

By two o'clock the most desparate loneliness she had ever felt in her life had set in. She was riveted to her seat, unable to move, almost unable to breathe. And for the first time in her life, she began to think of committing suicide, and by three o'clock it was an almost impossible urge to resist. Half an hour later, she went to her bathroom and got out a bottle of sleeping pills she never used, and trembling, she forced herself to put them down. She wanted to take them more than she had ever wanted to do anything in her life, and at the same time she did not. She wanted someone to stop her, to tell her that everything would be all right. But who could tell her that now? Tana was gone, and would probably never live at home again, and Arthur had his own life, he only included her when it suited him, and never when she needed him. Tana was right about that, but it hurt her too much to admit it to her. Instead she defended everything he did, and his miserable selfish kids, that bitch Ann, who was always so rude to her, and Billy, he had been so sweet as a boy, but now ... he seemed to be drunk all the time, and Jean wondered if Tana was right, if he wasn't the kind of young man she had always thought he was, but if that was true ... the memory of what Tana had said four years before came crashing down on her now. What if it were true ... if he had ... if she hadn't believed ... it was almost more than she could bear ... it was as if her whole life were crashing in on her tonight and she couldn't bear it, as she sat staring longingly at the pills she held in her hand. It seemed the only thing left to do, and she wondered what Tana would think when they called her in California to tell her the news. She wondered who would find her body ... the superintendent maybe ... one of her co-workers ... if they waited for Arthur to find her it could take two weeks. It was even more depressing to realize that there wasn't even anyone left who would discover her soon. She thought of writing Tana a note, but that seemed so melodramatic and there was nothing left to say, except how much she had loved her child, how hard she had tried. She cried as she thought of Tana growing up, the tiny apartment they had shared, meeting Arthur, hoping that he would marry her ... her whole life seemed to be flashing before her eyes as she clutched the vial of sleeping pills, and the night ground agonizingly. She didn't even know what time it was when the phone finally rang. It was five a.m., and Jean was shocked when she saw the clock. She wondered if it was Tana, maybe her friend had died ... with a shaking hand, she lifted the phone, and at first she didn't recognize the voice that identified itself as John.

'John?'

'John York, Ann's husband. We're in Palm Beach.'

'Oh. Of course.' But she was still stunned, and the emotions of the night had left her drained. She quietly set down the bottle of pills, she could tend to them afterwards. She couldn't understand why they would be calling her, but John York was quick to explain.

'It's Arthur. Ann thought I should call. He's had a heart attack.'

'Oh, my God.' She could feel her heart pound in her breast, and she was suddenly crying into the phone. 'Is he all right? Is he ... did ... '

'He's all right now. But it was pretty bad for a while. It happened a few hours ago, and it's still touch and go, which is why Ann thought I should call.'

'Oh, my God ... oh, my God ...' Here she had been thinking of taking her own life, and Arthur had almost died. What if she had ... she almost shuddered at the thought. 'Where is he now?'

'At Mercy Israel Hospital. Ann thought you might want to come down.'

'Of course.' She jumped to her feet, still holding the phone, grabbed a pencil, a pad, knocking over the vial of pills, and as they fell to the floor, she stood looking at them. She was herself again. It was incredible to think what she might have done, and he needed her now. Thank God she hadn't done it after all. 'Give me the details, John. I'll catch the next plane.' She scribbled down the name and address of the hospital, jotted his room number down, asked if there was anything they would need, and a moment later set down the phone, closed her eyes, thinking of him, and when she opened them there were tears on her cheeks thinking of Arthur, and what might have been.

Chapter 10

Harrison Winslow sent the car to Berkeley to pick Tana up at noon the next day, and they went to Trader Vic's for lunch. The atmosphere was festive and the food was good; he had been told at the hotel that it would be an appropriate place to go. And he enjoyed her company almost too much as they chatted again, about Harry, but other things as well. He was impressed by how bright she was, and she told him about Freeman Blake, and her friend who had died, and Miriam who had influenced her into going to law school. 'I just hope I survive. It's even harder that I thought it would be.' She smiled.

'And you really think Harry could do something like that?'

'He can do anything he wants to do. The trouble is he'd rather screw around,' she blushed and he laughed. 'I'm sorry ... I've been out here talking to students for too long.'

'I agree with you. He does like to screw around. He thinks it's congential. But actually, I was a lot more serious than he in my youth, and my father was a very scholarly man. He even wrote two books on philosophy.' They chatted on for a while, and it was the most pleasant interlude Tana had spent in a long, long time. She looked guiltily at her watch eventually, and they hurried off to the hospital, bringing Harry a bag of fortune cookies. Tana had insisted on bringing him a drink. They brought him a huge Scorpion with a gardenia floating in it, and he took a long sip and grinned.

'Merry Christmas to you too.' But she could see that he didn't look pleased that she and his father had made friends, and finally when his father left the room and went downstairs to make a call, he glared at her.

'What are you looking so pleased about?' It was good for him to be mad, she didn't mind. It would help bring him back to life.

'You know how I feel about him, Tan. Don't let him do a snow job on you.'

'He's not. He wouldn't be here if he didn't care about you. Don't be so goddamn stubborn and give him a chance.'

'Oh, for chrissake.' He'd have walked out of the room and slammed the door if he could. 'What a crock of shit that is. Is that what he's been telling you?' She couldn't tell him all that Harrison had been telling her because she knew he wouldn't want her to, but she also knew by now how he felt about his son, and she was convinced of his sincerity. She was growing fonder of him by the hour, and she wished Harry would try to be more open to him.

'He's a decent man. Give him a chance.'

'He's a son-of-a-bitch and I hate his guts.' And with that, Harrison Winslow walked into the room, just in time to hear Harry's words. And Tana went pale. The three looked at each other, and Harrison was quick to reassure her.

'That's not the first time I've heard that. And I'm sure it won't be the last.'

Harry turned in his bed to snarl at him. 'Why the hell didn't you knock?'

'Does it bother you that I heard? So what? You've said it to me before, usually to my face. Are you getting more discreet now? Or less courageous?' There was an edge to the older man's voice and a fire in Harry's eyes.

'You know what I think of you. You were never there when I needed you. You were always somewhere goddamn else, with some girl, in some spa, or on some mountaintop, with your friends ...' He turned away. 'I don't want to talk about it.'

'Yes, you do.' He pulled up a chair and sat down. 'And so do I. You're right, I wasn't there, and neither were you. You were in the boarding schools you chose to be in, and you were a goddamn impossible little snot every time I laid eyes on you.'

'Why shouldn't I have been?'

'That was a decision you made. And you never gave me a chance from the time your mother died. I knew by the time you were six that you hated me. I could accept it at the time. But you know, at your age, Harry, I would have thought that you would have gotten a little smarter by now, or at least more compassionate. I'm not really as bad as you like to think, you know.' Tana tried to fade into the wall, it was embarrassing being there, but neither of them seemed to mind. And as she listened, she realized that she had forgotten to call her mother again. She made a mental note to do it as soon as she left the hospital, maybe even from one of the phones downstairs, but she couldn't leave the room now, with World War III going on.

Harry stared angrily at his father now. 'Why the hell did you come here anyway?'

'Because you're my son. The only one I've got. Do you want me to leave?' Harrison Winslow III quietly stood up and his voice was low when he spoke. 'I'll leave anytime you like. I will not inflict myself on you, but I will also not allow you to continue to delude yourself that I don't give a damn about you. That's a very nice fairy tale, poor little rich boy and all that, but in the words of your friend here, it's a crock. I happen to love you very much,' his voice cracked but he went on anyway, struggling with the emotions and the words and Tana's heart went out to him. 'I love you very, very much, Harry. I always have and I always will.' He walked over to him then, bent and kissed him gently on the top of his head, and then strode out of the room, as Harry looked away and closed his eyes, and when he opened them, he saw Tana standing there with tears running down her cheeks at what she had just heard.

'Get the hell out of here.' She nodded, and quietly left, and as she closed the door softly behind here, she heard the sobs from the direction of Harry's bed.

Harrison was waiting outside for her, he looked more composed now, and relieved as he smiled at her. 'Is he all right?'

'He will be now. He needed to hear the things you said to him.'

'I needed to say them to him. I feel better now too.' And with that, he took her arm, and they walked downstairs arm in arm. It felt as though they had always been friends. And he looked at her with a broad smile. 'Where are you going now, young lady?'

'Home, I guess. I still have all that work to do.'

'That's a crock.' He imitated her, and they both laughed. 'How about playing hookey and going to the movies with an old man? My son has just thrown me out of his room, and I don't know a soul in this town, and it's Christmas for God's sake. How about it, Tan?' He had picked the name up from his son and she smiled, wanting to tell him that she had to go home, but she couldn't do it somehow; she wanted to be with him.

'I really should go home.' But she didn't convince either of them, and he was in a festive mood as they climbed into the limousine.

'Good. Now that you've gotten that out of the way, where shall we really go?' She giggled like a little girl, and he told the limousine driver to drive them around. Eventually, they bought a newspaper, picked out a movie they both liked, ate as much popcorn as they could stand, and went to L'Etoile afterwards, for a small supper and drinks at the bar. She was getting spoiled just being with him. And she was trying to remind herself of what a cad Harry said he was, but she didn't believe that anymore, and she had never been as happy in her life, as when he drove her home to Berkeley again, and took her in his arms, and kissed her as naturally as if they had both been waiting for that all their lives. He looked at her afterwards, touching her lips with his fingertips, wondering if he should regret what he'd done, but he felt younger and happier than he had in years. 'Tana, I've never met anyone like you before, my love.' He held her tight and she felt a warmth and safety she had never even dreamed of before, and then he kissed her again. He wanted to make her his for the rest of time, but he also wondered if he was half mad. This was Harry's friend . . . his girl . . . but they both insisted that they were just friends, and yet he sensed something different than that, on Harry's part anyway. He looked deep into her eyes. 'Tell me the truth about something, Tan. Are you in love with my son?'

Slowly, she shook her head. The driver of the limousine seemed to have disappeared. Actually, he had gone outside for a discreet walk. They were parked outside Tana's house. 'No. I've never been in love with anyone . . . until now . . .' They were brave words for her, and she decided to tell him the truth all at once. He had been honest with her since they'd met. 'I was raped four and a half years ago. It kind of stopped everything for me. As though my emotional clock no longer ran, and it hasn't since. I didn't go out at all for the first couple of years I was in college, and then finally Harry forced me into double dating with him a few times. But it was no big deal, and I don't go out with anyone here. All I do is work.' She smiled tenderly at him. She was falling head over heels in love with the father of her best friend.

'Does Harry know?'

'That I was raped?' He nodded. 'Yes. I told him eventually. He thought I was weird, and eventually I told him why. Actually, we saw the guy at a party we went to, and he guessed.'

'Was it someone you knew?' Harrison looked shocked.

'The son of my mother's boss. Lover and boss, actually. It was awful . . . no,' she shook her head, 'it was much, much worse than that.' He pulled her into his arms again, and he understood things better now. He wondered if that was why Harry had never allowed himself to be more than friends with her. He instinctively sensed that the desire was there, even if she was innocent of what was in his mind. And he also knew what he felt for the girl. He hadn't been so taken with anyone since he met his wife twenty-six years before, and then he began to think of the age difference between them, wondering if it would bother her. He was exactly thirty years older than Tana, and there were those who would be shocked. But more importantly, would she? 'So what?' She answered him. 'Who cares about them?' She kissed him this time and she felt something come alive in herself that she had never felt before, a passion and desire which only he could fulfill, and she tossed and turned all night thinking about him, just as he did about her. She called him at seven o'clock the next day, and he was already awake, and surprised by her call. But he would have been even more surprised had he known what she felt for him.

'What are you doing up at this hour, little one?'

'Thinking about you.' He was flattered and touched and enchanted and infatuated and a thousand other things. But there was much more to it than that. Tana trusted this man as she had trusted no other man before, not even his son, and he represented a great many things to her, even the father she had never known. He was all men in one, and had Harrison known, he might have been frightened that she expected too much of him. They visited Harry, they met for lunch, they had dinner together that night, and he had an over-whelming urge to take her to bed, but something told him that he could not, that it was dangerous, that he would form a lasting bond and that was wrong. For the next two weeks, they met and they walked and they kissed and they touched and the feelings and needs they had for each other grew. They visited Harry separately, for fear that he would find out, and finally Harrison sat down beside his son one day. The matter had to be broached, it was getting serious for both of them, and he didn't want to hurt the girl. But more than that, he wanted to offer her something he hadn't offered anyone in years, his heart and his life. He wanted to marry her, and he had to know how Harry felt, now, before it was too late, before anyone got hurt, especially the one person he cared about most, his son. He would have sacrificed anything for Harry, especially now, even the girl he loved, and he had to know now.

'I want to ask you something. Honestly. And I want you to answer me.' There had been a tenuous peace between the two men in the past two weeks, thanks to efforts on Tana's part, and Harrison had been enjoying the fruits of it.

'What's this all about?' Harry looked suspiciously at him.

'What's between you and that enchanting child?' He fought hard to keep his face blank, his eyes calm, and prayed that his son wouldn't see anything there, particularly not how much he loved the girl, although he couldn't imagine how Harry could not see. He felt as though he was wearing a neon sign.

'Tana?' Harry shrugged.

'I told you, I want you to answer me.' His whole life depended on it now, as did hers.

'Why? What's it to you?' Harry was restless and his neck had hurt all day. 'I told you, she's my friend.'

'I know you better than that, whether you like it or not.'

'So what? That's all it is. I've never slept with her.' But he already knew that, though he didn't tell Harry that.

'That doesn't mean a damn thing. That could have to do with her and not you.' There was no joking in his eyes or words. This was no joking matter to him, but Harry laughed and conceded the point.

'That's true, it could.' And then suddenly he lay back against his pillows and looked up at the ceiling, feeling an odd closeness to his father he had never felt before. 'I don't know, Dad . . . I was crazy about her when we first met, but she was so locked up as a stone . . . she still is.' He told him about the rape then, and Harrison pretended to hear it for the first time. 'I've never known anyone like her before. I guess I've always known that I'm in love with her, but I've been afraid to fuck it up by telling her that. This way, she won't run away. The other way, she might.' His eyes filled with sudden tears. 'I couldn't stand losing her. I need her too much.' Harrison felt his heart sink like a rock, but he had to think for his son now. That was all he really cared about, all he would let himself care about now. He had finally found him and he wasn't willing to lose him again. Not even for Tana, whom he loved so desperately. But Harry's words burned through him like fire. 'I need her so much . . .' The funny thing was the elder Winslow needed her too, but not as Harry did, and he couldn't take her from him, not now . . .

'One of these days, maybe you should be brave enough to tell her some of this. Maybe she needs you too.' Harrison knew now how lonely and isolated Tana had been, but even Harry hadn't fully realized those depths.

'And what if I lose?'

'You can't live like that, son. Afraid to lose, afraid to live, afraid to die. You'll never win like that. She knows that better than anyone. It's the one lesson you can learn from her.' And there were so many others he had learned from her too. Lessons he would have to abandon now.

'She's got more guts than anyone I know . . . except about men.' Harry shook his head. 'She scares me to death as far as that goes.'

'Give her time. Lots of time.' He fought to keep his voice strong. He couldn't let Harry know. 'And lots of love.'

Harry was silent for a long time, searching his father's eyes. In the past two and a half weeks they had begun to discover each other as they never had before. 'Do you think she could ever be in love with me?'

'Possibly.' Harrison felt his heart tear again. 'You have plenty of other things to think about right now. But once you're up again,' he avoided saying 'on your feet', 'and out of here, you can think about things like that.' They both knew that he wasn't totally impaired sexually, and the doctor had told them both that with a little 'creativity' Harry would have a near-normal sex life again one day, he could even impregnate his wife, if he chose, which didn't turn Harry on much, at least not for now, but Harrison knew it would mean a great deal to him one day. He would have loved to have Tana's child. The very thought brought him near to tears.

They chatted on for a little while, and eventually Harrison left. He was supposed to have dinner with Tana that night, but instead he called it off. He explained over the phone that he had a stack of cables that had arrived, and he had to compose answers to all of them. They met for lunch the next day instead, and Harrison was honest with her. It was the worst day in his life, since his wife had died. His eyes looked sad and his face was grim, and she knew the moment she met him at the restaurant that he didn't have good news, and she felt her heart stop for an instant as he began to speak once they sat down. She knew instantly that he was going to say something she didn't want to hear.

'I spoke to Harry yesterday.' He fought the emotions that were rising up in him. 'I had to, for both our sakes.'

'About us?' She looked stunned. It was so soon. Nothing had even happened yet. It was an innocent romance ... but Harrison shook his head.

'About him, and what he feels for you. I had to know before we went any further with this.' He took her hand and looked into her eyes, and she felt her heart melt again. 'Tana, I want you to know right now, that I'm in love with you. I've only loved one woman in my life as I think I love you, and that was my wife. But I also love my son, and I wouldn't hurt him for anything in this world, no matter what kind of son-of-a-bitch he thinks I am, and I've been one at times. I would have married you ... but not until I knew where Harry stood.' He didn't pull any punches with her. 'He's in love with you, Tan.'

'What?' She was shocked. 'He is not!'

'He is. He's just scared to death to scare you off. He told me about the rape, about how you felt about going out with men. He's been biding his time for years, but I don't have any doubt. He has been in love with you for years. He admitted it himself.' Harrison's eyes looked sad.

'Oh, my God.' She looked shocked. 'But I'm not ... I don't ... I don't think I ever could ... '

'I suspected that too. But that's between you and him. If he ever does get up the guts to declare himself, you'll have to deal with that yourself. What I wanted to know was how he felt. I know how you feel now. I knew it before I talked to him.' There were tears spilling in her eyes, and suddenly in his, too, as he reached for her hand. 'Darling, I love you more than life itself, but if I walked off with you now, if you'd even be willing to do that with me, it would kill my son. It would break his heart, and maybe destroy something he needs very much right now. I can't do that to him. Nor can you. I really don't think you could.' She was crying openly, and he pulled her into his arms as tears rolled down his cheeks. They had nothing to hide here, or anywhere, only in front of his son. But it was the cruelest trick life had played on her so far, the first man she had loved couldn't love her because of his son ... who was her best friend, whom she loved, but not like that. She didn't want to do anything that would hurt Harry either, but she was so much in love with Harrison ... it was a ghastly day filled with tears and regrets. She wanted to sleep with him anyway, but he wouldn't let her do that to herself. 'The first time that happens to you, after that awful experience you had, should be with the right man.' He was gentle, and loving, and he held her while she cried, and once he almost cried himself. And the next week was the most painful in her life, as at last he left for London again, and Tana felt as though she had been left on the beach. She was alone, with her studies, with Harry again. She went to the hospital every day, took her books with her, and she looked tired and pale and grim.

'Boy, you're a pleasure to see. What the hell's wrong with you? Are you sick?' She almost was, over Harrison, but she knew he had been right, no matter how painful it was. They had both done the right thing for someone they loved. And now she was merciless with him, forcing Harry to do what the nurses asked, urging him on, insulting him, cajoling him, encouraging him when he needed it. She was tireless, and devoted beyond anything imaginable, and when Harrison called from halfway round the world, sometimes she would talk to him and she would feel her heart leap again, but he hadn't gone back on his resolve. It was a sacrifice he had made for his son, and Tana had to go along with it. He had given her no choice. Or himself, although he knew that he would never recover from what he felt for her. He only hoped she would.

Chapter 11

The sun streamed into the room as Harry lay on his bed, trying to read a book. He had already had an hour in the pool and two hours of therapy, and he was sick to death of his schedule. There was a sameness about it all, a tediousness he couldn't stand anymore. He glanced at his watch, knowing Tana would be there soon. He had been at Letterman for more than four months, and she came to see him every day, bringing her stacks of papers and notes, and mountains of books. And almost as soon as he thought of her, the door opened and she walked in. She had lost weight in the past few months. She was working too hard at school, and running herself ragged going back and forth between Berkeley and the hospital. His father had offered to buy her a car, but she had absolutely refused to even consider it.

'Hi kid, what's up, or is that rude?' She grinned at him and he laughed.

'You're disgusting, Tan.' But at least he wasn't as sensitive about that anymore. Five weeks before, he had actually made love to a student nurse, a little 'creativity' as he had said to his therapist, but with a little imagination here and there, things had gone fairly well for both of them, and he didn't give a damn that she was engaged. True love hadn't been on his mind, and he had no intention of trying beginner's luck on Tan. She meant much, much too much to him, as he had told his dad, and she had enough problems of her own. 'What'd you do today?'

She sighed and sat down with a rueful smile. 'What do I ever do? Study all night, turn in papers, take exams, Christ, I may not live through another two years of this.'

'Sure you will.' He smiled. She was the light of his life, and he would have been lost without her visits every day.

'What makes you so sure?' Sometimes she doubted it herself, but somehow she always went on. Always. She wouldn't let herself stop. She couldn't let Harry down and she couldn't flunk out of school.

'You've got more guts that anyone I know. You'll make it, Tan.' It was something they gave each other now – courage, faith. When he'd get depressed, she'd stand there and shout at him until he wanted to cry, but she made him try all the things he was supposed to do, and when she thought she couldn't make it through another day of Boalt, he quizzed her for exams, woke her up after she got a little sleep, underlined some of the textbooks for her. And now suddenly, he grinned at her. 'Besides, law school's not that hard. I've been reading some of that stuff you left here.'

She smiled. That was what she had in mind. But she looked nonchalant as she turned to him. 'Oh yeah, then why don't you give it a try?'

'Why should I bust my hump?'

'What else have you got to do? Except sit on your can, and pinch nurses' aides. And how long will that last? They're going to kick you out of here in June.'

'That's not sure yet.' He looked nervous at the thought. He wasn't sure he was ready to go home. And home where? His father moved around so much, and he couldn't keep up with him no, even if he wanted to. He could go to a hotel, of course, there was the apartment at the Pierre in New York, but that sounded terribly lonely to him.

'You sure don't look excited about going home.' Tana was watching him. She had talked to Harrison in Geneva several days before, and they had discussed the same thing. He called her at least once a week to see how Harry was, and she knew that he still felt the same about her as he had before, and she did for him as well, but they had taken their resolve and there was no turning back anymore. Harrison Winslow would not betray his son. And Tana understood.

'I don't have a home to go to, Tan.' She had thought of it before, but not with any great seriousness, yet she had an idea. Maybe it was time to broach it to him.

'What about moving in with me?'

'In that dismal room of yours?' He laughed and looked horrified at the same time. 'Being confined to a wheelchair is bad enough. I might kill myself. Besides, where would I sleep? On the floor?'

'No, you ass.' She was laughing at him as he made a hideous face. 'We could get a place of our own, as long as it's reasonable so I could pay my share too.'

'Like where?' The idea hadn't quite sunk in yet, but it had a certain appeal.

'I don't know ... the Haight Ashbury maybe?' The hippie boom was just taking hold, and she had driven through the Haight only recently. But she was teasing him. Unless one wore flowing robes and were permanently stoned on LSD, it would have been impossible to tolerate living there. 'Seriously, we could find something if we looked.'

'It would have to be on the ground floor.' He looked pensively at the wheel-chair parked at the end of the bed.

'I know that. And I have another idea too.' She decided to hit him with it all at once.

'Now what?' He lay back against his pillows and looked happily at her. As difficult as these months had been, it had given them something very special to share, and they were closer than either of them had ever thought two human beings could be. 'You know, you never give me a moment's peace. You've always got some plot or plan. You exhaust me, Tan.' But it wasn't a complaint and they both knew it.

'Horseshit. It's good for you.'

'So, what's your thought?'

'How about applying to Boalt?' She held her breath and he looked shocked. 'Me? Are you *nuts*? What the hell would I do there?'

'Probably cheat, but failing that, you could study your ass off like I do every night. It would give you something to do other than pick your nose.'

'What a charming image you have of me, my dear.' He swept her a bow from the bed and she laughed. 'Why in God's name would I torture myself with law school? I don't have to do a dumb thing like that.'

'You'd be good at it.' She looked at him earnestly and he wanted to argue with her, but the worst of it was that he liked the idea.

'You're trying to ruin my life.'

'Yes.' She grinned. 'Will you apply?'

'I probably won't get in. My grades were never as good as yours.'

'I already asked, you can apply as a veteran. They might even make an exception for you ...' She was cautious about the way she said it, but he looked annoyed anyway.

'Never mind that shit. If you got in, so can I.' And the damnedest thing was that suddenly he wanted to. He almost wondered if he had wanted to for a long time. Maybe he felt left out with all that studying she did, while he had nothing at all to do except lie around and watch the nursing shifts change.

She brought him the application forms that afternoon, and they mulled them over endlessly, and finally sent them in, and by then Tana was looking at flats for them. It had to be exactly right, and something that would work for him.

She had just seen two she liked when her mother called on an afternoon in late May. It was unusual for her to be home, but she had some things to take care of at home, and she knew Harry was all right. One of the girls from down the hall came and knocked at her door. She assumed it was Harry, wanting to know how the apartments were. One of them was in Piedmont, and snob that he was, she knew he would like that one best, but she wanted to be sure she could afford it too. She didn't have the income he had, even though she had lined up a good job for herself that summer. Maybe after that ...

'Hello?' There was a long-distance whir and her heart stopped, wondering if it was Harrison calling her again. Harry had never realised what had passed between them, or, more important, what could have and what sacrifice they had made. 'Hello?'

'Tana?' It was Jean.

'Oh. Hi, Mom.'

'Is something wrong?' She had sounded strange at first.

'No. I thought it was someone else. Is something wrong?' It was an unusual hour for her to call. Maybe Arthur had had another heart attack. He had stayed in Palm Beach for three months, and Jean had stayed there with him. Ann and John and Billy had gone back to New York, and Jean had stayed to nurse him back to health even after he left the hospital. They had only been back in New York for two months, and she must have had her hands full, because Tana almost never heard from her now.

'I wasn't sure you'd be home at this hour.' She sounded nervous, as though she wasn't sure what to say.

'Usually I'm at the hospital, but I had something to do here.'

'How's your friend?'

'Better. He's getting out in about a month. I was just looking at some apartments for him.' She hadn't told her yet that they were thinking of living together. It made perfect sense to her, but she knew that it wouldn't to Jean.

'Can he live alone?' She sounded surprised.

'Probably if he had to, but I don't think he will.'

'That's wise.' She had no idea what that meant, but she had other things on her mind. 'I wanted to tell you something, sweetheart.'

'What's that?'

She wasn't at all sure how Tana would react, but there was no way to beat around the bush any longer. 'Arthur and I are getting married.' She held her breath and at her end, Tana stared.

'You're *what*?'

'Getting married ... I ... he feels that we've gotten older ... we've been foolish for long enough ...' She stumbled over some of the words he had said to her only days before, blushing furiously and at the same time terrified of what Tana would say. She knew that she hadn't liked Arthur for years, but maybe now ...

'You weren't the fool in all that, Mom. He was. He should have married you fifteen years ago, at least.' She frowned for a moment, mulling over what Jean had said. 'Is this what you really want to do, Mom? He's not young anymore, and he's sick ... he's kind of saved the worst for you.' It was blunt, but true, but until his heart attack he hadn't even wanted to marry her. He hadn't thought of it in years, not since his wife had come home from the hospital sixteen years before in fact. But suddenly, everything had changed, and he realized his own mortality. 'Are you sure?'

'Yes, Tana, I am.' Her mother sounded strangely calm suddenly. It was what she had waited almost twenty years for, and she wouldn't have given it up for anything, not even for her only child. Tana had her own life now, and she had nothing at all, without Arthur. She was grateful to him for finally marrying her. They would have a comfortable, easy life, and she could finally relax. All those years of loneliness and worrying; would he show up, would he come by, should she wash her hair, and then just in case ... and he didn't come for two weeks, until the night when Tana had flu, or she herself had a bad cold ... and it was all over now, and real life was about to begin. At last. She had earned every minute of it, and she was going to enjoy every minute of it now. 'I'm very sure.'

'All right then.' But Tana did not sound thrilled. 'I guess I should say congratulations or something like that.' But somehow she didn't feel like it. It seemed like such a boring bourgeois life, and after all Jean's years of sitting there waiting for him, she would have liked to see her tell him to go to hell. But that was youth thinking, and not Jean. 'When are you getting married?'

'In July. You'll come, won't you sweetheart?' She sounded nervous again, and Tana nodded to herself. She had planned to go home for a month anyway. She had worked it out with her summer job. She was working at a law firm in town, and they understood, or so they said.

'I'll sure try.' And then she had an idea. 'Can Harry come?'

'In a wheelchair?' Her mother sounded horrified, and something hardened instantly in Tana's eyes.

'Obviously. It's not exactly as though he has a choice.'

'Well, I don't know ... I should think it would be embarrassing for him ... I mean, all those people, and ... I'll have to ask Arthur what he thinks ... '

'Don't bother.' Tana's nostrils flared and she wanted to strangle someone, primarily Jean. 'I can't make it anyway.'

Tears instantly sprang to Jean's eyes. She knew what she'd done, but why was Tana always so difficult? She was so stubborn about everything. 'Tana, don't do that, please ... it's just ... why do you have to drag him along?'

'Because he's been lying in a hospital for six months and he hasn't seen anyone except me, and maybe it would be nice for him. Did that occur to you? Not to mention the fact that this did not happen in a car accident, it happened defending a stinking country we have no right to be in anyway, and the least people can do for him now is show him some gratitude and courtesy ...' She was in a blind rage and Jean was terrified.

'Of course ... I understand ... there's no reason why he can't come ...' And then suddenly, out of nowhere, 'John and Ann are having another baby, you know.'

'What the hell does that have to do with anything?' Tana looked blank. It was hopeless talking to her. They never saw eye to eye about anything.

'Well, you could be thinking of that one of these days. You're not getting any younger, dear. You're almost twenty-three.'

'I'm in law school, Mom. Do you have any idea what that's like? How hard I work night and day? Do you have any idea how ridiculous it would be for me to be thinking of marriage and babies right now?'

'It always will be if you spend your time with him, you know.' She was picking on Harry again and Tana saw red at the words.

'Not at all.' Her eyes were fierce, but her mother couldn't see that. 'He can still get it up, you know.'

'Tana!' Jean was appalled by Tana's vulgarity. 'That's a disgusting thing to say.'

'But it's what you wanted to know, isn't it? Well, you can relax, it works. I hear he screwed a nurse a few days ago, and she said it was great.' She was like a big dog refusing to release its prey, and her mother was hanging there, by the neck, unable to escape. 'Feel better now?'

'Tana Roberts, something has happened to you out there.' In the flash of a moment, Tana thought of the gruelling hours of studying she had put in, the love she had felt for Harrison, to no avail, the heartbreak of seeing Harry return crippled from Vietnam ...

'Yeah ... I think I've grown up. That's not always real pretty, is it, Mom?'

'It doesn't have to be ugly or rude, except in California, I suppose. They must be savages out there at that school.'

Tana laughed. They were worlds apart. 'I guess we are. Anyway, congratulations, Mom.' It suddenly dawned on her that she and Billy were going to be stepbrother and sister now, and the thought almost made her sick. He would be at the wedding, and it was almost more than she could stand. 'I'll try and be home in time.'

'All right.' Jean sighed, it was exhausting talking to her. And bring Harry, if you must.'

'I'll see if he's up to it. I want to get him out of the hospital first, and we've got to move ...' She cringed at the slip, and there was a deafening silence at the other end. That really was too much.

'You're moving in with him?'

Tana took a breath. 'I am. He can't live alone.'

'Let his father hire a nurse. Or are they going to pay you a salary?' She could be as cutting as Tana when she tried, but Tana was undaunted by her.

'Not at all. I'm going to split the rent with him.'

'You're out of your mind. The least he could do is marry you, but I'd put a stop to that.'

'No, you wouldn't.' Tana sounded strangely calm. 'Not if I wanted to marry him, but I don't. So relax. Mom ... I know this is hard for you, but I just have to live my life my own way. Do you think you can just try and accept that?' There was a long pause and Tana smiled. 'I know, it's not easy.' And then suddenly she heard Jean crying at the other end.

'Don't you see that you're ruining your life?'

'How? By helping a friend out? What harm is there in that?'

'Beacuse you'll wake up next week and you'll be forty years old and it'll be over, Tan. You'll have wasted your youth, just like I did, and at least mine wasn't a total waste, I had you.'

'And maybe one day I'll have children of my own. But right now I'm not thinking of that. I'm going to law school so I can have a career and do something useful with my life. And after that, I'll think about all that other stuff. Like Ann.' It as a dig, but a friendly one, and it went right over Jean's head.

'You can't have a husband and a career.'

'Why not? Who said that?'

'It's just true, that's all.'

'That's bullshit.'

'No, it's not, and if you hang around with that Winslow boy long enough, you'll marry him. And he's a cripple now, you don't need a heartbreak like that. Find someone else, a normal boy.'

'Why?' Tana's heart ached for him. 'He's human, too. More so than most, in fact.'

'You hardly know any boys. You never go out.' Thanks to your darling stepson, Mom. But actually, lately it was thanks to law school. Ever since Harrison, she had begun to feel differently about men, in some ways more trusting and open, and yet so far no one measured up to him. He had been so good to her. It would have been wonderful to find someone like him. But she never had time to go out with anyone now. Between going to the hospital every day and preparing for exams ... everyone complained of it. Law school was enough to destroy an existing relationship, and starting a new one was almost impossible.

'Just wait a couple of years, Mom. And then I'll be a lawyer, and you'll be proud of me. At least I hope you will.'

'I just want a normal life for you.'

'What's normal? Was your life so normal, Mom?'

'It started out to be. It wasn't my fault that your father was killed and things changed after that.'

'Maybe not, but it was your fault you waited almost twenty years for Arthur Durning to marry you.' And the truth was that if he hadn't had his heart attack, he might never have married her. 'You made that choice. I have a right to my choices, too.' ·

'Maybe so, Tan.' But she didn't really understand the girl, she didn't even pretend to anymore. Ann Durning seemed so much more normal to her. She wanted what every other girl wanted, a husband, a house, two kids, pretty clothes, and if she'd made a mistake early on, she'd been smart enough to do better the second time. He had just bought her the most beautiful sapphire ring at Cartier's, and that was what Jean wanted for her child, but Tana didn't give a good goddamn.

'I'll call you soon, Mom. And tell Arthur I said congratulations to him too. He's the lucky one in this deal, but I hope you'll be happy too.'

'Of course I will.' But she didn't sound it when she hung up. Tana had upset her terribly, and she told Arthur about it, as much as she could, but he just told her to relax. Life was too short to let one's children get the best of one. He never did. And they had other things to think about. Jean was going to redecorate the Greenwich house, and he wanted to buy a condo in Palm Beach, as well as a little apartment in town. They were giving up the apartment she had had for years. And Tana was shocked when she discovered that.

'Hell, I don't have a home anymore either.' She was shocked when she told Harry that, but he looked unimpressed.

'I haven't had one in years.'

'She said there'll always be a room for me wherever they live. Can you imagine my spending the night in the Greenwich house, after what happened there? I get nightmares thinking of it. So much for that.' It depressed her more than she wanted to admit to him, and she knew that marrying Arthur was what Jean wanted, but somehow it seemed so depressing to her. It was so ultimately middle class, so boring and bourgeois, she told herself, but what really bothered her was that Jean was still at Arthur's feet after all the shit she had taken from him over the years. But when she told Harry that, he got annoyed with her.

'You know you've been turning into a radical, and it bores the shit out of me, Tan.'

'Have you ever considered the fact that you're more than a little right wing?' She started to look uptight.

'Maybe I am, but there's nothing wrong with that. There are certain things I believe in, Tan, and they aren't radical, and they aren't leftist, and they aren't revolutionary, but I think they're good.'

'I think you're full of shit.' There was an unusual vehemence about what she said, but they had already disagreed about Vietnam several times. 'How the hell can you defend what those assholes are doing over there?' She leapt to her feet and he stared at her, there was an odd silence in the room.

'Because I was one of them. That's why.'

'You were not. You were a pawn. Don't you see that, you fucking jerk? They used you to fight a war we shouldn't be fighting in a place we shouldn't be in.'

His voice was deathly quiet as he looked at her. 'Maybe I think we should.'

'How can you say a dumb thing like that? Look what happened to you over there!'

'That's the whole point.' He leaned forward in his bed, and he looked as though he wanted to strangle her. 'If I don't defend that ... if I don't believe in why I was there, then what the hell good was it anyway?' Tears suddenly sprang to his eyes and he went on, 'What does it all mean, goddamn it, Tana ... what did I give them my legs for if I don't believe in them? Tell me that!' You could hear him shouting all the way down the hall. 'I have to believe in them, don't I? Because if I don't, if I believe what you do, then it was all a farce. I might as well have gotten run over by a train in Des Moines ...' He turned his face away from her and started to cry openly and she felt terrible. And then he turned to her, still in a rage. 'Now get the hell out of my room you insensitive radical bitch!'

She left, and she cried all the way back to school. She knew that he was right for him. He couldn't afford to feel about it as she did, and yet, since he had come back from Vietnam, something had begun to rage in her that had never been there before, a kind of anger that nothing could quench, and possibly never would. She had talked to Harrison about it on the phone one night and he had put it down to youth, but she knew it wasn't just that, it was something more. She was angry at everyone because Harry had been maimed, and if people were willing to take more chances politically, to stick their necks out ... Hell, the President of the United States had been killed a year and a half before, how could people not see what was happening, what they had to do ... but Tana didn't want to hurt Harry with all of it. She called him to apologize but he wouldn't talk to her. And for the first time in six and a half months since he'd gotten to Letterman, she didn't go and see him for three days. And when she finally did, she stuck an olive branch through the door of his room, and followed it in sheepishly.

'What do you want?' He glared at her, and she smiled tentatively.

'The rent, actually.'

He tried to suppress a grin. He wasn't angry at her anymore. So she was turning into a crazy radical. So what? That's what Berkeley was all about. She'd grow out of it. And he was more intrigued by what she had just said. 'You found a place?'

'I sure did.' She grinned at him. 'It's on Channing Way, a teeny two-bedroomed house with a living room and a kitchenette. It's all on one floor, so you'd have to behave yourself somewhat or at least tell your lady friends not to scream too loud,' they both grinned and Harry looked ecstatic at the news, 'you're going to love it!' She clapped her hands and described it in detail to him, and that weekend the doctor let her drive him over there. The last of the surgeries had been completed six weeks before; his therapy was going well. They had done all for him they were going to do. It was time to go home. Harry and Tana signed the lease as soon as he saw it. The landlord didn't seem to object to the fact that they had different last names, and neither of them offered to explain. Tana and Harry shook hands with a look of glee, and she drove him back to Letterman. Two weeks later, they moved in. He had to arrange for transportation for his therapy, but Tana promised to take him. And the week after her exams, he got the letter congratulating him on his acceptance to Boalt. He sat in his wheelchair waiting for her when she got home, with tears streaming down his cheeks.

'They took me, Tan ... and it's all your fault ...' They hugged and kissed, and he had never loved her more. And Tana knew only that he was her very dearest friend as she cooked him dinner that night and he uncorked a bottle of Dom Perignon champagne.

'Where did you get that?' She looked impressed.

'I've been saving it.'

'For what?' He had been saving it for something else, but he decided that enough good things had happened in one day to warrant drinking it.

'For you, you jerk.' She was wonderfully obtuse about the way he felt. But he loved that about her too. She was so engrossed with her studies and her exams and her summer job and her political ideas that she had no idea what was going on right beneath her nose, at least, not with regard to him, but he wasn't ready yet anyway. He was still biding his time, afraid to lose.

'It's good stuff.' She took a big gulp of champagne and grinned at him, slightly drunk, happy and relaxed. They both loved their little house and it was working out perfectly, and then she remembered that she had to ask him something. She had meant to ask him before, but with the rush to move, and buy furniture, she had forgotten to ask. 'Listen, by the way, I hate to ask you this ... I know it's going to be a drag ... but ... '

'Oh Jesus, now what? First she forces me to go to law school, and now God knows what other torture she has in mind ...' He pretended to look terrified, but Tana looked sincerely grim.

'Worse than that. My mother's getting married in two weeks.' She had long since told him that, but she hadn't asked him to go to the wedding with her. 'Will you come with me?'

'To your mother's wedding?' He looked surprised as he set down his glass. 'Is that appropriate?'

'I don't see why not.' She hesitated, and then went on, her eyes huge in her face. 'I need you there.'

'I take it her charming stepson will be on hand.'

'Presumably. And the whole thing is a little much for me. The happily married daughter with one child and another on the way, Arthur pretending that he and my mother fell in love only last week.'

'Is that what he's saying?' Harry looked amused and Tana shrugged.

'Probably. I don't know. The whole thing is just hard for me. It's not my scene.'

Harry thought it over, looking into his lap. He hadn't been out like that yet, and he had been thinking of going to Europe to meet his dad. He could stop on the way ... he looked up at her. There was nothing he would have denied her, after all she had done for him. 'Sure, Tan, no sweat.'

'You don't mind too much?' She looked doggedly grateful to him and he laughed.

'Sure I do, but so do you. At least we can laugh together.'

'I'm happy for her ... I just ... I just can't play those hypocritical games anymore.'

'Just behave yourelf while we're there. We can fly in and I'll go to Europe the day afterwards, I thought I'd meet Dad in the South of France, for a while.' It was so good to hear him talking about things like that again. It was amazing to realize that only a year before he had been talking about playing for the rest of his life, and now, thank God, he was playing again, at least for a month or two, before he started law school in the fall. 'I don't know how I let you talk me into that.' But they were both glad she had. Everything was working out perfectly. They had divided the chores in the house. She did the things he was unable to do, but it was amazing how much he did. Everything from dishes to beds, although he had practically strangled himself vacuuming one week, and now that was her task to do. They were both comfortable. She was about to start her summer job. Both of them thought life pretty damn grand in the summer of '65, and Harry picked up two of the stewardesses on their flight to New York in July. And Tana sat back in her seat, laughing at him.

Chapter 12

The wedding was simple and well done. Jean wore a very pretty gray chiffon dress, and she had bought a pale blue one for Tana to wear, in case she herself didn't have time to shop. It certainly wasn't the kind of thing she would have bought herself, and she was horrified when she saw the price tag on it. Her mother had bought it at Bergdorf's, and it was a gift from Arthur, of course, so Tana couldn't say anything.

Only the family were present at the ceremony, but Tana had insisted on bringing Harry along, much to his chagrin, since they arrived from the city in the same limousine. Tana was staying with him at the Pierre. She insisted to her mother that she couldn't leave him alone. And she was relieved that her mother and Arthur were leaving the next day on a honeymoon so she didn't have to stay in New York for an extended period after all. She would have refused to stay in the Greenwich house, and she was going to fly out of New York when Harry did. He was going to Nice to meet Harrison in St. Jean Cap Ferrat, and she was flying back to San Francisco to her summer job. And Jean and Arthur were threatening to come out and see her in the fall. Her mother looked pointedly at Harry each time she spoke of it, as though she expected him to disappear by then and eventually Tana had to laugh at it.

'It's really awful, isn't it?' But worst of all was Billy, who managed to sidle up to her halfway through the afternoon, drunk as usual, and make some sly comment about her boyfriend not being able to get it up, and he'd be glad to help her out anytime, as he recalled she had been a fairly worthwhile piece of ass, but just as she contemplated putting her fist through his mouth, she saw a larger one come whizzing by, meet Billy's chin, and Billy reeled backwards before collapsing neatly on the lawn. Tana turned to see Harry smiling in his wheelchair just behind where she stood. He had reached up and put Billy out cold with one blow and he was immensely pleased with himself.

'You know, I wanted to do that a year ago.' he smiled at her, but her mother was horrified at how they had behaved. And as early as possible Tana and Harry got back into the limousine and went back to New York. There was a tearful goodbye between Tana and Jean before that. Or, at least, Jean cried and Tana was tense. Arthur had kissed her on the cheek and announced that she was his daughter now, too, and there wouldn't have to be any more scholarships. But she insisted that she couldn't accept a gift like that, and she couldn't wait to get away from all of them, especially cloying, pregnant Ann, with her whiny voice, her showy gems, and her boring husband, making eyes at someone else's wife halfway through the afternoon.

'Jesus, how can they live like that?' She had fumed to Harry on the way home and he patted her knee.

'Now, now, one day the same thing will happen to you, little one.'

'Oh, go fuck yourself.' He laughed at her and they went back to the Pierre. They were both leaving the next day, and he took her to '21' that night. Everyone was happy to see him there, although chagrined to see that he was in a wheelchair now. And for old times' sake, they drank too much champagne, and were drunk when they got back to the hotel. Just drunk enough for Harry to do something he had promised himself he wouldn't do for another year or two. They were into their second bottle of Roederer, and actually they had been drinking all day, when he turned to her with a gentle look and touched her chin, and unexpectedly kissed her lips.

'Do you know that I've always been in love with you?' At first Tana looked shocked, and then suddenly she looked as though she might cry.

'You're kidding me.'

'I'm not.' Was her mother right? Was Harrison?

'But that's ridiculous. You're not in love with me. You never were.' She focused on him tipsily.

'Oh yes I am. I always was.' She stared at him, and he took her hand in his. 'Will you marry me, Tan?'

'You're crazy.' She pulled her hand away and stood up and suddenly there were tears in her eyes. She didn't want him to be in love with her. She wanted them to be friends forever, just friends, no more than that. And he was spoiling everything. 'Why are you saying that?'

'Couldn't you love me, Tan?' Now he looked as though he was going to cry and she felt more sober than she had all night.

'I don't want to spoil what we have ... it's too precious to me. I need you too much.'

'I need you too. That's the whole point. If we get married then we'll always be there.' But she couldn't marry him ... she was still in love with Harrison ... it was insane, the whole thing ... all of it ... she lay on her bed and sobbed that night, and Harry never went to bed at all. He was waiting for her when she came out of her room the next morning, looking pale and tired, with circles under her eyes. He wanted to retrieve what they'd had before, and it wasn't too late yet. That meant everything to him. He could live without being married to her, but he couldn't stand losing her. 'I'm sorry about what happened last night, Tan.'

'So am I.' She sat down next to him in the room's spacious sitting room. 'What happens now?'

'We put it down to one drunken night. It was a rough day for both of us ... your mother getting married ... my first time out socially in the chair ... no big deal. We can put it behind us. I'm sure of it.' He was praying that she would agree with him and slowly she shook her head, as his heart sank.

'What happened to us? Have you really been ... in love with me for all that time?'

He looked at her honestly. 'Some of it. Sometimes, I hate your guts.' They both laughed and she felt some of what they had shared before, and she put her arms around his neck then.

'I'll always love you, Harry. Always.'

'That's all I wanted to know.' He could have cried if he'd let himself, but instead they ordered room service, laughed, raised hell, teased, trying desperately to regain the ease of what they'd had before, and as she watched his plane take off that afternoon, there were tears in her eyes. It might never be quite the same again, but it would be close. They'd see to that. They both had too much invested in each other by now to let anything spoil it for them.

When Harry finally arrived at Cap Ferrat, brought there by the car and driver Harrison had sent for him, his father came running across the lawn to help his son from the car and into his chair, gripping his arm powerfully and looking at him.

'You all right, son?' There was something in Harry's eyes that worried him.

'More or less.' He looked tired. It had been along flight, a long couple of days, and this time he hadn't played games with the stewardesses. He had been thinking of Tana as he flew to France. She would always be his first great love, the woman who had brought him back to life again. Feelings like that couldn't be lost, and if she didn't want to marry him ... he had no choice. He had to accept it. He could see in her eyes that it simply wasn't there for her. And as much as it hurt, he knew that he had to force himself to accept that now. But it wasn't going to be easy for him, He had waited for so long to tell her what he felt. And it was all over now. It was never going to happen between them. The thought of that reality brought tears to his eyes again and Harrison took his son's shoulders in his powerful hands.

'How's Tana?' Harrison was quick to ask, and for just an instant he saw Harry hesitate, and then instinctively he understood. Harry had tried and lost. His father's heart went out to him.

'Tana's fine ...' He tried to smile '... but difficult.' He smiled cryptically, and Harrison instantly understood. He knew that one day it would come to that.

'Ah yes ...' he smiled, as a pretty girl walked across the lawn to him and caught Harry's eye, '... but difficult.'

Chapter 13

When Harry returned from Europe in the fall he was deeply tanned and happy and rested. He had followed his father everywhere, to Monaco, to Italy, to Madrid for a few days, Paris, New York. It had been the whirlwind life again, the life he had felt so left out of as a boy, but suddenly there was a place reserved in it for him. Pretty women, lovely girls, galas, endless concerts and parties and social events. He was actually tired of it when he finally got on the plane in New York and flew west. Tana met him at the Oakland airport, and she looked reassuringly as she had before. She looked healthy and brown, her blonde mane flying in the wind, she had loved her summer job, gone to Malibu for a few days with some friends she'd made at work, and she was talking about going to Mexico over the holidays, and when law school began, they were constantly together, yet apart. She would drop him off at the library, but her classes were different than his. She seemed to be making new friends now. With Harry out of the hospital, she had more free time, and the survivors of the first year grind seemed to stick together now. It was a healthier arrangement than they'd had before, and by Christmas there always seemed to be three of them, including a pretty, petite blonde girl from Australia, named Averil. She seemed to be Harry's shadow. She was studying for a master's degree in art, but she seemed far more interested in following Harry around everywhere, and he didn't seem to object. Tana tried to be nonchalant the first time Averil emerged from his room on a Saturday morning and suddenly all three of them laughed nervously.

'Does this mean you guys are kicking me out?' Tana laughed nervously.

'Hell no, you jerk. There's room for all of us.' And by the end of Harry's first year, she was living with them. She was actually adorable, shared the chores, was cheerful, pleasant, helpful, she was so sweet she made Tana nervous sometimes, particularly when she had exams, but on the whole the arrangement worked out perfectly. She flew to Europe with Harry that summer to meet Harrison, and Tana worked in the same law firm again. She had promised her mother that she would come East, but she was looking for every possible excuse not to go, and was spared a lie when Arthur had another heart attack, a mild one this time, but her mother took him to Lake George to rest, and promised to come out and see Tana in the fall. But Tana knew what that meant by now. She and Arthur had flown out once the year before, and it was nightmarish. She was 'revolted' by the house they shared, 'shocked' that she and Harry were still living under one roof, and she would be even more so now when she discovered that they had added another girl. Tana laughed at the thought. She was obviously beyond hope, and the only consolation was that Ann had gotten divorced again, through no fault of hers, of course. John had actually had the nerve to walk out on her, and was having a flagrant affair with her best friend. So all was not entirely wholesome anywhere these days ... poor Ann ... Tana smiled at the thought.

Tana actually enjoyed her summer alone that year. She loved Harry and Averil, too, but there was so much pressure on her with law school, that it was nice to be alone now and then. And she and Harry seemed to fight about politics all the time these days. He continued to support the war in Vietnam, and she became crazed when the subject came up at all, as Averil would try desperately to keep the peace. But Harry and Tana had known each other for too long. After six years, they no longer felt they had to be polite and the language they threw at each other made Averil cringe, although he would never have spoken in that way to her, nor she to him. Averil was a far gentler soul than Tana was. Tana had been on her own for a long time. And at twenty-four, she was powerful and unafraid, and sure of her own ideas. She had a long, strong stride, and eyes that did not shy from anything or anyone. She was curious about everything around her, definite about what she thought, and courageous enough to say it to anyone. It got her into trouble sometimes, but she didn't mind. She liked the discussions that arose like that. And when she registered for school that year, hallelujah her last, she thought to herself with a grin, she found herself in the midst of a lengthy conversation in the cafeteria. There were at least eight or nine people talking heatedly about Vietnam, as usual, and she was quick to leap into it, as she always did. It was the subject she felt strongest about, because of Harry of course, no matter how he chose to feel, she had her own ideas, and Harry wasn't there anyway. He was off somewhere with Averil, probably, copping a quick feel before class, as Tana teased him often enough. The two of them seemed to spend most of their life in bed, challenging his creativity, which seemed to pose no problem at all. But Tana was deep in the ideologies of Vietnam and not thinking of Harry specifically as she spoke that day, and was surprised to find herself sitting next to someone even more radical than she. He had a wild mane of tightly curled black hair that sprang from his head almost angrily, sandals, blue jeans, a turquoise T shirt, strangely electric blue eyes, and a smile that tore at something deep inside of her. When he stood up, every muscle seemed to ripple through his flesh, and everything about him seemed oddly sensual, and she had an almost irresistible urge to reach out and touch his arm, hanging so near to her.

'Do you live nearby?' She shook her head. 'I didn't think I'd seen you here before.'

'I usually hang out in the library. Third year law.'

'Shit.' He looked impressed. 'That's tough.'

'You?'

'The master's program in political science, what else?' They both laughed. He had chosen well anyway, and he followed her to the library where she left him regretfully. She liked his ideas and he was strikingly beautiful, and she knew instantly that Harry wouldn't approve of him. He had very square ideas these days, especially with Averil around. It was something Tana knew about them both and it didn't bother her. Harry could have grown ferns on his head and sprouted horns, and she would have loved him anyway. He was her brother by then, and Averil was part of him, so she accepted that. Most of the time, she tried not to discuss politics with them. It made things easier.

And she was intrigued to see her new friend making a speech on campus a few days later, about the same issues they had discussed. It was an impassioned, brilliant confrontation of the mind and she told him as much when she saw him afterwards. She knew by then that his name was Yael McBee. It was a funny name, but he was not a funny man. He was brilliant and intense and his anger reached out almost like a lash to touch those he wished to reach. She admired his skill in addressing crowds, and she went to see him several more times that fall, before he finally asked her out to dinner one night. They each paid their share, and went back to his apartment to talk afterwards. There were at least a dozen people living there, some of them on mattresses, and it didn't have the neat, well-polished air of the cottage which Harry and Tana and Averil shared. She would, in fact, have been embarrassed to bring Yael there. It was too bourgeois, too sweet, almost too foreign to him. And she liked visiting him where he lived. She felt uncomfortable at home anyway these days. Averil and Harry were always making love or hiding out, going in his room and closing the door. She wondered how he got any studying done at all, and yet she knew he did from the look of his grades, which were surprisingly good. But it was more fun being with Yael and his friends, and when Harry flew to Switzerland at Christmastime, and Averil flew home, Tana finally invited Yael to come and see her. And it was odd to see him in the tidy little house, without his strident friends around. He had worn a deep green turtleneck and his well worn jeans. He had military combat boots, although he had served a year in jail for refusing to be drafted and to to Vietnam. They sent him to a prison in the south west, and paroled him after a year.

'That's incredible.' She was awed by him, by his remarkable, almost Rasputin-like eyes, his courage in going against every current imaginable, there was something outstanding about the man, and she wasn't surprised that he had been fascinated by communism as a child. Everything about him was intriguing and unusual, and when he gently took her in his arms and made love to her on Christmas Eve, that seemed intriguing too. Only once did she have to force Harrison Winslow from her mind. And in a peculiar way he had readied her for this. Not that he had anything in common with Yael McBee. Yael managed to unleash her flesh in a way she had never dreamed could happen to her, reaching deep into her, into all she had wanted and denied herself for so long. He reached into her very soul, and pulled out a passion and desire she had never suspected in herself, and gave her something she had never dreamed a man could give, until she felt addicted to everything he gave to her. She was almost his slave by the time Harry and Averil came home, and more often than not, she slept at Yael's apartment now, on a mattress with him, curled up, cold, until he laid a hand on her, and then suddenly life was exotic and tropical, there wre brilliant hues everywhere. She couldn't live without him now, and after dinner, they would sit around the living room with the others, talking politics and smoking dope, and Tana suddenly felt like a woman now, a woman in full bloom, living daringly at the feet of her man.

'Where the hell are you all the time, Tan? We never see you anymore.' Harry questioned her.

'I have a lot of work to do at the library for exams.' She had five months of law school left before finals came up, and then the bar to face, and in some ways it panicked her, but actually most of the time she was with Yael, and she had still said nothing about him to Harry or Averil. She didn't know what to say. They lived in such different worlds that it was impossible to conceive of them in the same place, same house, same school.

'You have a romance going on or something, Tan?' He was suspicious of her now, in addition to her absences. She was looking strange to him, numb almost, glazed, as though she had joined a Hindu cult, or smoked dope all the time, which he suspected too. But it wasn't until Easter that he saw her with Yael, and when he did he was horrified. He waited for her after class, and like an irate parent, he berated her. 'What the hell are you doing with that creep? Do you know who he is?'

'Of course I do ... I've known him all year ...' She had known he wouldn't understand and she told him as much.

'Do you know what kind of reputation he has? He is a violent radical, a Communist, a trouble maker of the worst sort. I watched him get arrested last year, and someone told me he's served time in prison before this ... for chrissake, Tan, wake up!'

'You fucking jerk!' They were screaming at each other outside the main library, and now and then someone turned around but neither of them cared. 'He served time for evading the draft, which I'm sure you think is worse than Murder One, but as it so happens, I don't.'

'I'm well aware of that. But you better watch your goddamn fucking ass, or you won't have to worry about taking the bar in June. He'll get you arrested and kicked out of school so fast your head will spin.'

'You don't know what you're talking about!' But the next week, over Easter holiday, he arranged a major demonstration outside the administration building, and two dozen students were carted off to jail.

'See what I mean?' Harry had been quick to rub it in and she had slammed out of the house again. Harry didn't understand anything. Mostly, he didn't understand what Yael meant to her. Fortunately, he had managed not to get arrested himself, and she stayed with him for the following week. Everything about him excited her. Every sense was aroused when he walked into the room, and things were pretty interesting at his place these days. Everyone seemed to be getting more wound up for demonstrations set up for the end of the school year, but she was so panicked about exams that she had to stay at her own house more than once just to get some studying done. And it was there that Harry tried to reason with her, gently this time, he was terrified that something would happen to her, and he'd do anything to stop it if he could, before it was too late. 'Please, Tan, please ... listen to me ... you're going to get into trouble with him ... are you in love with him?' He looked heartbroken at the thought, not because he was still in love with her himself, but because he considered it a hideous fate for her. He hated the guy, he was a rude, boorish, uncivilized, selfish creep, and Harry had heard plenty about him around the school in the last six months. The guy was violent and sooner or later there was going to be serious trouble involving him. Harry just didn't want him to pull Tana down with him when he went. And he thought there was a good chance he might. If she let him. And she looked as though she would. She had a blind passion for the man. Even his politics excited her, and the thought of that made Harry sick. She insisted that she wasn't in love with him, but he knew that it wasn't that simple for her, that this was the first man she had willingly given herself to, and she had been so chaste for so long that in some ways her judgment was impaired. He knew that if the right man, or the wrong one as it were, came along and aroused her in a way she'd never known before, she might fall prey to him, and in this instance she had. She was mesmerized by Yael, and his unorthodox life and friends. She was fascinated by something she had never seen before, and at the same time he played her body like a violin. It was a difficult combination to defeat. And then, just before her final exams, six months into their relationship, Yael took matters into his own hands, and put her to the test.

'I need you next week, Tan.'

'What for?' She looked over her shoulder distractedly. She had two hundred pages more to read that night.

'Just a meeting, sort of ...' He was vague, smoking his fifth joint of the night. Usually, it didn't affect him visibly, but lately he was tired.

'What kind of meeting?'

'We want to make a point with the people who count.'

She smiled at him. 'Who's that?'

'I think it's time we took things directly into government. We're going to the mayor's house.'

'Christ, you'll get busted for sure.' But it didn't seem to faze her much. She was used to that by now, not that she'd gotten arrested with him yet, although all the others had.

'So what?' He was unconcerned.

'If I'm with you, and I go, and no one bails me out, I'll miss my exams.'

'Oh, for chrissake, Tan, so what? What are you going to be after all? Some two-bit lawyer to defend society as it exists? It sucks, get rid of it first, then go to work. You can wait a year to take your exams, Tan. This is more important.' She looked at him, horrified at what she had just heard him say to her. He didn't understand her at all if he could say something like that. Who was this man?

'Do you know how hard I've worked for this, Yael?'

'Don't you realize how meaningless it it?'

It was the first fight they had ever had, and he pressured her for days but in the end she did not go. She went back to her own house to study for exams, and when she watched the news that night, her eyes almost fell out of her head. The mayor's house had been bombed, and two of his children had almost been killed. As it turned out, they were going to be all right, but an entire side of the house had been destroyed, his wife was badly burned by a bomb that had exploded nearby. 'And a radical student group of UC Berkeley had taken credit for it.' Seven students had been arrested on charges of attempted murder, assault, assorted weaponry charges, and sundry other things, and among them Yael McBee ... and if she had listened to him, she realized with trembling knees, her whole life would have been over ... not just law school, but her freedom for many, many years. She was deathly pale as she sat watching them being loaded into police wagons on TV and Harry watched her face and said nothing at all. She stood up after a long moment and looked down at him, grateful that he hadn't said anything. In one second, everything she had felt for Yael exploded into nothingness, like one of his bombs.

'He wanted me to be there tonight, Harry ...' She started to cry. 'You were right.' She felt sick. He had almost destroyed her life, and she had been completely under his spell. And for what? A piece of ass? How sick was she? She felt sick thinking of it. She had never realized how deeply commited they were to their ideals, and it terrified her now to have known them at all. She was afraid that she might be taken in for questioning. And eventually she was, but nothing ever came of it. She was a student who had slept with Yael McBee. She wasn't the only one. She took her exams. She passed the bar. She was offered a job in the district attorney's office, as a prosecutor, and grown-up life began there and then. The radical days were past, along with student life, and living with Harry and Averil in their little house. She rented an apartment in San Francisco, and slowly packed up her things. Everything was suddenly painful to her, everything was over, finished, done.

'You look a picture of cheer.' Harry wheeled slowly into her room, as she threw another stack of law books into a box. 'I guess I should call you Madam Prosecutor now.' She smiled and looked at him. She was still shocked at what had happened to Yael McBee, and almost to her through him. And she was still depressed at the thought of what she had felt for him. Now it had all begun to seem unreal. They hadn't come to trial yet, but she knew that he and his friends would be sent away for a long, long time.

'I feel like I'm running away from home.'

'You can always come back, you know, we'll still be here.' And he suddenly looked sheepishly at her. Tana laughed as she looked at him. They had known each other for too long to be able to get away with anything.

'Now what does that look like? What mischief are you up to now?'

'Me? Nothing.'

'Harry ...' she advanced on him menacingly and he wheeled away as he laughed.

'Honest, Tan ... oh shit!' He ran smack into her desk and she carefully put her hands around his handsome throat. He looked more like his father every day, and she still missed him sometimes. It would have been a lot healthier having an affair with him than Yael McBee. 'All right ... all right ... Ave and I are getting married.' For a moment, Tana looked shocked. Ann Durning had just gotten married for the third time, to a big movie producer in LA. He had given her a Rolls-Royce as a wedding present and a twenty carat diamond ring, which Tana had heard a lot about from Jean, But that was something people like Ann Durning did. Somehow she never thought about Harry getting married.

'You are?'

He smiled. 'I thought after all this time ... she's a terrific girl, Tan ... '

'I know that, you dummy,' Tana grinned. 'I've been living with her too. That just seems like such a grown-up thing to do.' They were all twenty-five years old, but she didn't feel old enough to get married yet, she wondered why they did. Maybe they had had more sex, she laughed to herself, and then she smiled at him and bent to kiss his cheek. 'Congratulations. When?'

'Pretty soon.' And then suddenly Tana saw something funny in his eye. It was, at the same time, both embarrassment and pride.

'Harry Winslow ... do you mean to tell me that ... you didn't ...' She was laughing now, and Harry was actually blushing for one of the few times in his life.

'I did. She's knocked up.'

'Oh, for chrissake.' And then her face sobered suddenly. 'You don't have to get married, you know. Is she forcing you to?'

He laughed and Tana thought she'd never seen him look so happy in his life. 'No. I forced her. I told her I'd kill her if she got rid of it. It's our kid, and I want it, and so does she.'

'My God,' Tana sat down hard on the bed, 'marriage *and* a family. Jesus, you guys don't mess around.'

'Nope.' He looked about to burst with pride and his intended walked into the room with a shy smile.

'Is Harry telling you what I think he is?' Tana nodded, watching their eyes. There was something so peaceful and satisfied there. She wondered what it felt like to feel like that, and for a moment she almost envied them. 'He has a big mouth.' But she bent and kissed his lips and he patted her behind, and a little while later he wheeled out of the room. They were getting married in Australia, where Averil was from, and Tana was invited to the wedding, of course, and after that they would come back to the same little house, but Harry was starting to look for a nice place in Piedmont for them to live until he finished school, it was time for the Winslow funds to come into play a little bit. He wanted Averil living decently now. And he turned to Tana later that night.

'You know, if it weren't for you, Tan, I wouldn't be here at all.' He had told that to Averil ten thousand times at least in the past year, and he believed it with all his heart.

'That's not true, Harry, you know that. You did it yourself.'

But he grabbed her arm. 'I couldn't have made it without you. Give yourself credit for that, Tan. The hospital, law school, all of it ... I wouldn't even know Ave, if it weren't for you ...'

She was smiling gently at him and she was touched. 'What about the baby, is that my doing too?'

'Oh, you jerk ...' He tugged at the long blonde hair and went back to his future wife, sound asleep in the bed where their baby had been conceived. His 'creativity' had paid off, and Tana smiled to herself wistfully that night as she fell asleep. She was happy for him, for them both. But she suddenly felt so alone. She had lived with him for two years, with Averil for half of that, it would be strange living alone without them, and they would have their own life ... it all seemed so strange ... why did everyone want to get married ... Harry ... her mother ... Ann ... what was the magic about? All Tana had wanted was to get through law school, and when she had finally had an affair with someone, he had turned out to be some wild nut, and had wound up in jail for the rest of his life ... it was mystifying as she fell asleep ... she didn't have any of the answers, not then or when she moved out.

She moved into a pleasant little flat in Pacific Heights, with a view of the bay, and it took her fifteen minutes to get to City Hall in the secondhand car she bought. She was trying to save everything she could to go to Harry and Averil's wedding, but Harry insisted on giving her the ticket as a gift. She went just before she started her new job, and she could only stay in Sydney with them for four days. Averil looked like a little doll in a white organza dress, and nothing showed yet at all. Her parents had no idea that there was a baby on the way, and Tana even forgot about it. She forgot everything when she saw Harrison Winslow walk toward her again.

'Hello, Tan.' He kissed her gently on the cheek and she thought she would melt. And he was as he had always been, charming, and debonaire, sophisticated in every possible way, but the romance that had been stopped so long ago was not destined to be revived again. They talked for hours, and went for a long walk late one night. He found her different and more grown up, but in his mind, she would always be Harry's friend, and he knew that no matter what, in Harry's mind, Tana would always belong to him, and he still respected that.

He took her to the airport when she left. Harry and Averil had already left on their honeymoon, and he kissed her as he had so long ago, and every ounce of her soul reached out to him. There were tears rolling down her cheeks as she boarded the plane, and the stewardesses left her alone, wondering who the handsome man had been. They wondered if she was his girlfriend or his wife, and they watched her curiously. She was a tall, pretty blonde, in a simple beige linen suit, with an assurance about the way she moved, a proud way she held her head, and what they didn't know was that inside she felt frightened and alone. Everything she was going back to was going to be new all over again. New job, new home, and no one to share it with. She suddenly understood why people like Ann Durning and her mother got married. It was safer than being out there on your own, and yet, it was the only way Tana knew by now.

PART III
REAL LIFE

Chapter 14

The apartment Tana had rented had a pretty view of the bay and a little garden in the back. There was a tiny bedroom, a living room, a kitchen with a brick wall and a little French window that looked out into the garden, where she sat sometimes, soaking up the sun. Unconsciously, she had looked for something on the ground floor, so that when Harry came to see her, he wouldn't have a problem with the chair. And she felt comfortable living there. She was surprised at how quickly she adapted to living alone, Harry and Averil came to see her frequently at first, they missed her, too, and Tana was surprised at how rapidly Averil lost her shape. She blew up into a pretty little balloon, and the whole thing seemed foreign to her. Her own life was involved in such a different world. The world of prosecution of the DA, of murders and robberies and rapes. It was all she thought of all day, and the idea of having babies seemed light years away, although her mother had reported that Ann Durning was pregnant again, not that Tana gave a damn. All of that was too far behind her now. Hearing about the Durnings had no effect at all, even her mother knew that, she had all but given up. And it was the final blow when she heard that Harry had married that other girl. Poor Tana, all those years taking care of him, and he'd gone off with someone else.

'What a rotten thing to do.' Tana had been stunned by her words at first and then she had begun to laugh. It seemed so funny to her. Her mother really never had believed that they were just friends.

'Of course it's not. They're perfect for each other.'

'But don't you mind?' What was wrong with all of them? How did they think these days? And she was twenty-five years old, when was she ever going to settle down?'

'Of course I don't mind. I told you years ago, Mom, Harry and I are just friends. The best of friends. And I'm thrilled for them.' She waited a respectable interval to tell her about the child, when she called again.

'And what about you, Tan? When are you going to thing about settling down?'

Tana sighed. What a thought. 'Don't you ever give up, Mom?'

'Have you, at your age?' What a depressing thought.

'Of course not. I haven't even started to think about that.' She was just out of her affair with Yael McBee, who was the last person one would have though of settling down with, and she didn't even have time to think of romance at her new job. She was too busy learning to be an assistant DA. It was almost six months into the job before she even had time for her first date. A senior investigator asked her out, and she went because he was an interesting guy, but she had no real interest in him. She went out with two or three lawyers after that, but her mind was always on her work, and in February she had her first important case, covered by national press. She felt as though all eyes were on her, and she was anxious to do well. It was a fiercely ugly rape. The rape of a fifteen-year-old-girl, who had been lured into an abandoned house by her mother's lover. She had been raped nine or ten times, according to the testimony, badly disfigured and eventually killed, and Tana wanted to get the gas chamber for him. It was a case that struck a chord near her heart, although no one knew that, and she worked her ass off, preparing the case, and reviewing the testimony and the evidence every night. The defendant was an attractive man of about thirty-five, well educated, decently dressed, and the defense was trying to pull every trick in the book. She was up until two o'clock every night. It was almost like trying to pass the bar again.

'How's it going, Tan?' Harry called her late one night. She glanced at the clock, surprised that he was still up. It was almost three.

'Okay. Something wrong? Averil all right?'

'Sure she is.' She could almost see him beam. 'We just had a baby boy, Tan. Eight pounds one ounce, and she's the bravest girl in the whole world ... I was there, and oh Tan, it was so beautiful ... his little head just popped out, and there he was, looking at me. They handed him to me first ...' He was breathless and excited and he sounded as though he were laughing and crying at the same time. 'Ave just went to sleep so I thought I'd give you a call. Were you up?'

'Of course I was. Oh Harry, I'm so happy for both of you!' There were tears in her eyes too, and she invited him up for a drink. He was there five minutes later, and he looked tired, but the happiest she'd ever seen. And it was the strangest feeling, watching him, listening to him tell it all, as though it had been the first baby that had ever been born, and Averil were miraculous. She almost envied them, and yet at the same time, she felt a terrible void deep in her soul, as though that part of her just wasn't there, almost as though it had been left out. It was like listening to someone speak a foreign tongue and admiring them tremendously, but having no understanding of the language at all. She felt completely in the dark, and yet she thought it was wonderful for them.

It was five o'clock in the morning before he left, and she slept for a little less than two hours before getting up to get ready for court, and she went back to her big case. It dragged on for more than three weeks, and the jury stayed out for nine days, after Tana argued before them heroically. And when they finally came in, she had won. The defendant was convicted of every charge and although the judge refused to impose capital punishment on him, he was sentenced to prison for life, and deep within her, Tana was glad. She wanted him to pay for what he had done, although his going to prison would never bring the girl back to life.

The newspapers said that she had argued the case brilliantly, and Harry teased her about it when she came to see the baby in Piedmont after that, calling her Madam Hotshot, and giving her a bad time.

'All right, all right, enough. Let me see this prodigy you've produced, instead of giving me a bad time.' She was fully prepared to be acutely bored and was surprised to discover how sweet the baby was. Everything was tiny and perfect and she hesitated when Averil tried to hand him to her. 'Oh God ... I'm afraid to break him in two ...'

'Don't be silly.' Harry grabbed the baby easily from his wife and plopped him into Tana's arms, and she sat staring down at him, utterly amazed at how lovely he was, and when she handed him back, she felt as though she had lost something and she looked at them both almost enviously, so much so that when she left, he told Averil victoriously, 'I think we got to her, Ave', and indeed she thought about them a great deal that night, but by the following week, she had another big rape case on her hands, and two big murder cases after that. And the next thing she knew, Harry called her victoriously. He had not only passed the bar, but he'd been offered a job, and he could hardly wait to start.

'Who hired you?' She was happy for him. He had worked hard for it. And now he laughed.

'You won't believe this, Tan. I'm going to work for the PD.'

'The public defender's office?' She laughed too. 'You mean I have to try my cases against you?' They went out to lunch to celebrate and all they talked about was work. Marriage and babies were the last thing on her mind. And the next thing she knew, the rest of the year had flown by, and another one on its heels, trying murders and rapes and assaults and assorted other crimes. Only once or twice did she actually find herself working on the same case Harry was on, but they had lunch whenever they could, and he had been in the public defender's office for two years when he told her that Averil was pregnant again. 'So soon.' Tana looked surprised. It seemed as though Harrison Winslow V had been born just moments before, but Harry smiled.

'He'll be two next month, Tan.'

'Oh my God. Is that possible?' She didn't see him often enough, but even at that it seemed impossible. He was going to be two. It was incredible. And she herself was twenty-eight years old, which didn't seem so remarkable actually, except that everything had gone so fast. It seemed like only yesterday when she was going to Green Hill with Sharon Blake, and taking long walks with her into Yolan. Only yesterday when Sharon was alive, and Harry could dance....

Averil had a baby girl this time, with a tiny pink face, a perfect little mouth, and enormous almond shaped eyes. She looked incredibly like her grandfather, and Tana felt an odd tug at her heart when she looked at her, but again, it didn't feel like anything she could ever do herself. She said as much to Harry when they had lunch the following week.

'Why not for chrissake? You're only twenty-nine years old, or you will be in three months.' He looked at her seriously then. 'Don't miss out on it, Tan. It's the only thing I've ever done that really matters to me, the only thing I really give a damn about ... my children and my wife.' She was shocked to hear him say that. She thought his career was more important to him than that, and then she was even more startled to hear that he was thinking of giving up his job with the PD, and going into practice for himself.

'Are you serious? Why?'

'Because I don't like working for someone else, and I'm tired of defending those bums. They all did whatever it is they claim they didn't do, or at least most of them anyway, and I'm just sick of it. It's time for a change. I was thinking of going into partnership with another lawyer I know.'

'Wouldn't it be dull for you? Ordinary civil law?' She made it sound like a disease and he laughed as he shook his head.

'No. I don't need as much excitement as you do, Tan. I couldn't run the crusades you do every day. I couldn't survive that day in, day out. I admire you for doing it, but I'll be perfectly happy with a small comfortable prac- tice, and Averil and the kids.' He had never set his sights high, and he was happy with things just as they were. She almost envied him that. There was something deeper and hungrier that burned within her. It was the thing that Miriam Blake had seen in her ten years before, and it was still there. It wanted tougher cases, across the board convictions, it wanted harder and more, and greater challenges all the time. She was particularly flattered when, the fol- lowing year, she was assigned to a panel of attorneys that met with the governor over a series of issues that affected the criminal processes all over the state. There were half a dozen lawyers involved, all of them male except for Tana, two of them from Los Angeles, two from San Francisco, one from Sacramento, and one from San Jose, and it was the most interesting week she thought she had ever spent. She was exhilarated day after day. The attorneys and the judges and politicians conferred long into the night, and by the time she got into bed every night, she was so excited about what they'd been talking about that she couldn't sleep for the next two hours. She lay awake running it all through her mind.

'Interesting, isn't it?' The attorney she sat next to on the second day leaned over and spoke to her in an undervoice as they listened to the governor discuss an issue she had been arguing about with someone the night before. He was taking exactly the position she had herself and she wanted to stand up and cheer.

'Yes, it is.' She whispered back. He was one of the attorneys from Los Angeles. He was tall and attractive and had gray hair. They were seated next to each other at lunch the next day, and she was surprised to discover how liberal he was. He was an interesting man, from New York originally, he had gone to Harvard Law School, and had then moved to Los Angeles. 'And actually, I've been living in Washington for the last few years, working with the government, but I just came back out West again, and I'm glad I did.' He smiled. He had an easy way, a warm smile, and she liked his ideas when they talked again that night, and by the end of the week, all of them felt as though they had become friends. It had been a fascinating exchange of ideas for the past week.

He was staying at the Huntington. And he offered her a drink at L'Etoile before he left. Of all the people there, they had had the most thoughts in common, and Tana had found him a pleasant companion on the various panels they'd been on. He was hard-working and professional, and pleasant almost all the time.

'How do you like working in the DA's office?' He had been intrigued by that. Generally, the women he knew didn't like it there. They went into family practices, or other aspects of the law, but female prosecutors were rare everywhere, for obvious reasons. It was a damn tough job, and no one made things easy for them.

'I love it.' She smiled. 'It doesn't leave me much time for myself, but that's all right.' She smiled at him, and smoothed back her hair. She still wore it long, but she wore it in a knot when she worked. She was given to wearing suits and blouses when she went to court, but she still lived in jeans at home. And she was wearing a gray flannel suit now, with a pale gray silk shirt.

'Married?' He raised an eyebrow and glanced at her hand, and she smiled.

'No time for that either, I'm afraid.' There had been a handful of men in her life in recent years, but they never lasted long. She ignored them for weeks on end, preparing trials, and just never had enough time for them. It wasn't a loss that had bothered her very much, although Harry kept insisting she'd be sorry one day. 'I'll do something about it then.' 'When? When you're ninety-five?'

'What were you doing in government, Drew?' His name was Drew Lands and he had the bluest eyes she'd ever seen. She liked the way he smiled at her, and she found herself wondering how old he was, and correctly guessed that he was around forty-five.

'I had an appointment to the Department of Commerce for a while. Someone died, and I was filling in until they made a permanent change.' He smiled at her, and she realized again that she liked the way he looked, more than she had anyone in a long time. 'It was an interesting job for a time. There's something incredibly exhilarating about Washington. Everything centers arounds the government, the people involved with it. If you're not in government, you're absolutely no one there. And the sense of power is overwhelming. It's all that matters there, to anyone.' He smiled at her, and it was easy to see that he had been part of that.

'That must be hard to give up.' She was intrigued by that, and she herself had wondered more than once if she would be interested in politics, but she didn't really think it would suit her as well as the law.

'It was time. I was happy to get back to Los Angeles.' He smiled easily and put down his scotch again, looking at her. 'It almost feels like home again. And you, Tana? What's home to you? Are you a San Francisco girl?'

She shook her head. 'New York originally. But I've been here since I went to Boalt.' It had been eight years since she arrived, and that in itself was incredible, since 1964. 'I can't imagine living anywhere else now ... or doing anything else....' She loved the district attorney's office more than anything. There was always excitement for her there, and she had grown up a lot in her five years on the job. And that was another thing ... five years as an Assistant DA. That was as hard to believe as the rest ... where did the time run to, while one worked? Suddenly one woke up and ten years had drifted past ...

ten years ... or five ... or one ... it all seemed the same after a while. Ten years felt like one felt like an eternity.

'You looked awfully serious just them.' He was watching her, and they exchanged a smile.

She shrugged philosophically. 'I was just thinking how quickly time rushes by. It's hard to believe I've been out here this long ... and in the DA's office for five years.'

'That was how I felt about Washington. The three years felt more like three weeks, and suddenly it was time to go home.'

'Think you'll go back one day?'

He smiled, and there was something there she couldn't quite read. 'For a while anyway. My kids are still there. I didn't want to pull them out of school halfway through the year, and my wife and I haven't resolved yet where they're going to live. Probably half and half eventually. It's the only thing that's fair to us, although it might be difficult for them at first. But kids adjust.' He smiled at her. He had obviously just gotten divorced.

'How old are they?'

'Thirteen and nine. Both girls. They're terrific kids, and they're very close to Eileen, but they've stayed close to me too, and they're really happier in LA than they are in Washington. That's not really much of a life for kids back there, and she's awfully busy,' he volunteered.

'What does she do?'

'She's assistant to the ambassador to the OAS, and actually she has her sights on an ambassadorial post herself. That'll make it pretty impossible to take the kids with her, so I'd have them then. Everything is still pretty much up in the air.' He smiled again, but a little more hesitantly this time.

'How long have you two been divorced?'

'Actually, we're working it out right now. We took our time deciding while we were in Washington, and now it's definite. I'm going to file as soon as things settle down. I'm hardly unpacked yet.'

She smiled at him, thinking of how difficult it had to be, children, a wife, traveling three thousand miles, Washington, Los Angeles. But it didn't seem to shake up his style. He had made incredible sense at the conference. Of the six attorneys involved, she had been most impressed with him. She had also been impressed with how reasonable he was about being liberal. Ever since her experiences with Yael McBee five years before, her liberalism had been curbed considerably. And five years in the DA's office was making her less liberal by the hour. She was suddenly for tougher laws, tighter controls, and all the liberal ideas she had believed in for so long no longer made as much sense to her, but somehow Drew Lands made them palatable again, and even if the actual positions no longer appealed to her, he didn't alienate anyone expressing his views. 'I thought you handled it beautifully.' He was touched and pleased, and they had another drink, before he dropped her off at her place with his cab, and went on to the airport to go back to Los Angeles.

'Could I call you sometime?' He asked hesitantly, as though he were afraid there might be someone important to her, but at the moment there was no one at all. There had been a creative director in an ad agency for a few months the year before, and actually no one at all since then. He had been too busy and too harassed and so had she, and the affair had ended as quietly as it had begun. She had taken to telling people that she was married to her work, and she was the DA's 'other wife', which made her colleagues laugh. But it was almost true by now. Drew looked at her hopefully, and she nodded with a smile.

'Sure. I'd like that.' God only knew when he'd be back in town again anyway. And she was trying a big Murder One case anyway for the next two months.

But he astounded her and called her the next day, as she sat in her office, drinking coffee and making notes, as she outlined her approach for the case. There was going to be a lot of press involved and she didn't want to make a fool of herself. She wasn't thinking of anything but the case when she grabbed the phone and barked into it. 'Yes?'

'Miss Roberts, please.' He was never surprised by the rudeness of people who worked for the DA.

'That's me.' She sounded playful suddenly. She was so damn tired, she was slap happy. It was almost five o'clock, and she hadn't left her desk all day. Not even for lunch. She hadn't eaten anything since dining the night before, except for the gallons of coffee she'd consumed.

'It didn't sound like you.' His voice was almost a caress, and she was startled at first, wondering if it was a crank call.

'Who's this?'

'Drew Lands.'

'Christ ... I'm sorry ... I was so totally submerged in my work, I didn't recognize your voice at first. How are you?'

'Fine. I thought I'd give you a call and see how *you* were, more importantly.'

'Preparing a big murder case I'm starting next week.'

'That sounds like fun.' He said it sarcastically and they both laughed. 'And what do you do in your spare time?'

'Work.'

'I figured as much. Don't you know that's bad for your health?'

'I'll have to worry about that when I take my retirement. Meanwhile, I don't have time.'

'What about this weekend? Can you take a break?'

'I don't know ... I ...' She usually worked weekends, especially right now. And the panel had cost her a whole week she should have spent preparing her case. 'I really should ... .'

'Come on, you can afford a few hours off. I thought I'd borrow a friend's yacht in Belvedere. You can even bring your work along, although it's a sacrilege.' But it was late October then, and the weather would have been perfect for an afternoon on the bay, warm and sunny with bright blue skies. It was the best time of the year, and San Francisco was lyrical. She was almost tempted to accept, but she just didn't want to leave her work undone.

'I really should prepare ... .'

'Dinner instead ... ? lunch ... ?' And then suddenly they both laughed. No one had been that persistent in a long time and it was flattering.

'I'd really like to, Drew.'

'Then, do. And I promise, I won't take more time than I should. What's easiest for you?'

'That sail on the bay sounded awfully good. I might even play hookey for a day.' The image of trying to juggle important papers in the breeze did not appeal to her, but an outing on the bay with Drew Lands did.

'I'll be there then. How does Sunday sound?'

'Ideal to me.'

'I'll pick you up at nine. Dress warmly in case the wind comes up.'

'Yes, sir.' She smiled to herself, hung up and went back to work, and promptly at nine o'clock Sunday morning, Drew Lands arrived, in white jeans, sneakers, a bright red shirt, and a yellow parka under his arm. His face already looked tan, his hair shone like silver in the sun, and the blue eyes danced as she followed him out to the car. He was driving a silver Porsche he had driven up from LA on Friday night, he said, but true to his word, he hadn't bothered her. He drove her down to the Saint Francis Yacht Club where the boat was moored, and half an hour later they were out on the bay. He was an excellent sailor, and there was a skipper aboard, and she lay happily on the deck, soaking up the sun, trying not to think of her murder case, and suddenly glad she'd let him talk her into taking the day off.

'The sun feels good, doesn't it?' His voice was deep, and he was sitting on the deck next to her when she opened her eyes.

'It does. Somehow everything else seems so unimportant all of a sudden. All the things one scurries around about, all the details that seem so monumental, and then suddenly poof ... they're gone.' She smiled at him, wondering if he missed his kids a lot, and it was as though he read her mind.

'One of these days, I'd like you to meet my girls, Tana. They'd be crazy about you.'

'I don't know about that.' She sounded hesitant, and her smile was shy. 'I don't know much about little girls, I'm afraid.'

He look at her appraisingly, but not accusingly. 'Have you ever wanted children of your own?'

He was the kind of man one could be honest with and she shook her head. 'No, I haven't. I've never had the desire, or the time,' she smiled openly then, 'or the right man in my life, not to mention the right circumstances.'

He laughed. 'That certainly takes care of pretty much everything, doesn't it?'

'Yup. What about you?' She was feeling breezy and carefree with him. 'Do you want more?'

He shook his head, and she knew that that was the kind of man she would want one day. She was thirty years old and it was too late for children for her. She had nothing in common with them anyway. 'I can't anyway, or not at least without going to an awful lot of trouble. Eileen and I decided when Julie was born that that was it for us. I had a vasectomy.' He spoke of it so openly that it shocked her a little bit. But what was wrong with not wanting more kids? She didn't want any, and she didn't have any at all.

'That solves the problem anyway, doesn't it?'

'Yes,' he smiled mischievously, 'in more ways than one.' She told him about

Harry then, his two children, Averil … and when Harry came back from Vietnam, the incredible year of watching him fight for his life and go through surgery, and the courage he had had.

'It changed my life in a lot of ways. I don't think I was ever the same after that. …' She looked out over the water pensively, and he watched the sunlight dancing on her golden hair. '… it was as though things mattered so much after that. Everything did. You couldn't afford to take anything for granted after that.' She sighed and looked at him. 'I felt that way once before too.'

'When was that?' His eyes were gentle as he looked at her and she wondered what it would be like to be kissed by him.

'When my college roommate died. We went to Green Hill together, in the South,' she explained seriously and he smiled.

'I know where it is.'

'Oh.' She smiled back. 'She was Sharon Blake … Freeman Blake's daughter, and she died on a march with Martin Luther King nine years ago … She and Harry changed my life more than anyone else I know.'

'You're a serious girl, aren't you?'

'Very, I guess. Maybe "intense" is the right word. I work too hard, I think too hard. I find it hard to turn all that off a lot of the time.' He had noticed that, but he didn't mind that. His wife had been like that too, and it hadn't bothered him. He hadn't been the one who wanted out. She was. She was having an affair with her boss in Washington, and she wanted some 'time off', she said, so he gave it to her and came home, but he didn't want to go into details about that.

'Have you ever lived with anyone? I mean, romantically, not your friend, the Vietnam vet.' It was funny to hear Harry referred to that way, it was so impersonal.

'No. I've never had that kind of relationship.'

'It would probably suit you very well. Closeness without being tied down.'

'That sounds about right.'

'It does to me too.' He looked pensive again, and then he smiled at her almost boyishly. 'Too bad we don't live in the same town.' It was a funny thing to say so soon, but everything happened quickly with him. In the end, it turned out that he was just as intense as she said she was. He came back to see her for dinner twice that week, flying up from Los Angeles, and then flying back afterwards, and the following weekend he took her sailing again, even though she was totally immersed in her murder case and she was anxious for it to go well. But if anything he soothed her, and made things easier for her, and she was amazed at that. And after their second day on the bay in his friend's boat, he brought her home, and they made love in front of the fire in her living room. It was tender and romantic and sweet, and he made her dinner afterwards. He spent the night, and remarkably, he didn't crowd her at all. He got up at six o'clock, showered, dressed, brought her breakfast in bed, and left in a taxi for the airport at seven fifteen. He caught the eight o'clock plane to Los Angeles, and was in his office by nine twenty-five, looking neat as a pin. And within weeks, he had established a regular commuting schedule, almost without asking her, but it all hapenned so easily, and made her life so much happier that she suddenly felt as though her whole life had improved. He came to see her in court twice, and she won her case. He was there when the verdict came in and took her out to celebrate. He gave her a beautiful gold bracelet that day that he had bought her at Tiffany in Los Angeles, and that weekend she went down to Los Angeles to visit him. They had dinner at Morton's and Ma Maison, and spent the days shopping on Rodeo Drive or lounging around his swimming pool, and on Sunday night, after a quiet dinner he cooked her himself on his barbecue, she flew back to San Francisco alone. She found herself thinking about him all the way home, about how quickly she had gotten involved with him, and it was a little frightening to think about, but he seemed so definite, so anxious to establish a relationship with her. She was also aware of how lonely he was. The house he lived in was spectacular, modern, open, filled with expensive modern art, and with two empty rooms for his two girls. But there was no one else there, and he seemed to want to be with her all the time. By Thanksgiving she had grown used to his spending half the week in San Francisco with her, and after almost two months, it didn't even seem strange to her anymore. It was the week before the holiday when he suddenly turned to her.

'What are you doing next week, sweetheart?'

'For Thanksgiving?' She looked surprised. She really hadn't thought of it. She had three small cases in her files that she wanted to close out, if the defendants would agree to making a deal. It would certainly make life simpler for her, and none of them were really worth taking to trial. 'I don't know. I haven't given it much thought.' She hadn't gone home in years. Thanksgivings with Arthur and Jean were absolutely unbearable. Ann had gotten divorced again several years before, and she lived in Greenwich now, so she was on hand with her unruly kids. Billy came and went if he had nothing better to do. He hadn't gotten married. Arthur got more tiresome with age, her mother more nervous, and she seemed to whine a lot now, mostly about the fact that Tana had never married and probably wouldn't now. 'A wasted life', was usually the headline of time spent with her, to which Tana could only answer, 'Thanks, Mom.' The alternative was Thanksgiving with Averil and Harry, but as much as she loved them, their friends in Piedmont were so painfully dull, with their little children and large station wagons. Tana always felt totally out of place with them, and infinitely glad she was. She marvelled at how Harry could tolerate it. She and his father had laughed about it together one year. He couldn't stand it any better than Tana could, and he rarely appeared. He knew that Harry was happy, well cared for, and didn't need him, so he kept to the life he enjoyed.

'Want to go to New York with me?' Drew looked at her hopefully.

'Are you serious? Why?' She looked surprised. What was in New York for him? Both of his parents were dead, he had said, and his daughters were in Washington.

'Well,' he had already thought it all out ahead of time, 'you could see your family, I could stop off in Washington first to see the girls, and then meet you in New York and we could play a little bit. Maybe I could even bring them up with me. How does that sound?'

She thought about it and slowly nodded her head, her hair falling around her like a fan. 'Possible.' She smiled up at him. 'Maybe even very possible, if you leave out the part about my family. Holidays with them are what drive people to suicide.'

He laughed. 'Don't be so cynical, you witch.' He gently tugged a lock of hair and kissed her lips. He was so deliciously affectionate, she had never known a man like him before, and parts of her were opening up to him that had never opened up to anyone. She was surprised at how much she trusted him. 'Seriously, could you get away?'

'Actually, right now I could.' And that was unusual for her too.

'Well?' Stars danced in his eyes and she threw herself into his arms.

'You win. I'll even offer a visit to my mother up as a sacrifice.'

'You'll go to heaven for that for sure. I'll take care of everything. We can both fly East next Wednesday night. You spend Thursday in Connecticut, and I'll meet you in New York on Thursday night with the girls at ... let's see ....' He looked pensive and she grinned. 'The Hotel Pierre?' She fully intended offering to pay her share, but he shook his head.

'The Carlyle. I always try to stay there if I can, especially with the girls, it's nice for them up there.' It was also where he had gone with Eileen for the last nineteen years, but he didn't tell Tana that. He arranged everything, and Wednesday night found them on separate planes, heading East, she wondering for a moment at how easily she had let him make her plans for her. It was sort of a novelty for her, no one had ever done that before, and he seemed to do it so well and so easily. He was used to it. And when she arrived in New York, she suddenly realized that she was actually there. It was bitter cold, and traces of the first snow were already on the ground as she rode in the cab to Connecticut from John F. Kennedy Airport. She was thinking of Harry as they rode along, and the time he had punched Billy in the face. She was sorry he wasn't there now. She was really not looking forward to Thanksgiving with them. She would have preferred to go to Washington with Drew, but she didn't want to intrude on his private Thanksgiving with his girls after not seeing them for two months. Harry had invited her to join them in Piedmont, as he did every year, but she explained that she was going to New York this year.

'My God, you must be sick,' he laughed.

'Not yet. But I will be by the time I leave. I can already hear my mother now ... "a wasted life ... ."'

'Speaking of which, I wanted to introduce you to my associate, finally.' He had started his own law firm after all, and Tana had never gotten around to meeting the other half. She just never had time, and they were actually surprisingly busy. Things were going well for them on a small but pleasant scale. It was exactly what they had both wanted, and Harry was ecstatic about it whenever he talked to her.

'Maybe when I get back.'

'That's what you always say. Shit, you're never going to meet him, Tan, and he's such a nice guy.'

'Oh oh, I smell a blind date. Am I right? A hungry one even ... oh no!' She was laughing now, the way they used to in the old days and Harry laughed too.

'You suspicious bitch. What do you think, everyone wants to get into your pants?'

'Not at all. I just know you. If he's under ninety-five and has no objection to getting married, you want to fix him up with me. Don't you know I'm a hardened case, Winslow? Give up, for chrissake. Never mind, I'll have my mother call you from New York.'

'Don't bother, you jerk. But you don't know what you're missing this time. He's *wonderful*, Averil thinks so too.'

'I'm sure he is. Fix him up with someone else.'

'Why? Are you getting married?'

'Maybe.' She was teasing him, but his ears instantly perked up and she regretted saying it.

'Yeah? To who?'

'Frankenstein. For chrissake, get off my back.'

'The hell I will. You're seeing someone, aren't you?'

'No ... yes! ... I mean no. Shit. Yes, but not seriously. Okay? Will that suffice?'

'Shit, no. Who is he, Tan? Is is serious?'

'No. He's just a guy I'm seeing like all of the others. That's all. Nice guy. Nice date. No big deal.'

'Where's he from?'

'LA.'

'What's he do?'

'He's a rapist. I met him in court.'

'Not cute. Try again.' It was like being a hunted animal and she was getting annoyed at him.

'He's an attorney, now lay off, dammit. It's no big deal.'

'Something tells me that it is.' He knew her well. Drew was different from the others, but she didn't want to admit that yet, least of all to herself.

'Then you have your head up your ass, as usual. Now, give Averil my love, and I'll see you both when I get back from New York.'

'What are you doing for Christmas this year?' He was half inviting and half prying, and she felt like hanging up on him.

'I'm going to Sugar Bowl, is that all right with you?'

'Alone?'

'Harry!' Of course not. She was going with Drew. They had already decided that. Eileen was taking the girls to Vermont with her, so he would be alone, and the holidays were going to be difficult for him. They both expected it. But Tana wasn't going to tell Harry any of it. 'Goodbye. See you soon.'

'Wait ... I wanted to tell you more about ...'.

'No!' She had finally hung up on him, and as she approached Greenwich in the cab, she smiled to herself, wondering what he'd think of Drew. She suspected that they'd like each other, even though Harry would give him the third degree, which was why she wanted to wait a while. It was rare that she introduced any of her men to him. Only after she decided she didn't give a damn about them. But this time was different ....

Her mother and Arthur were waiting for her when she arrived, and it shocked her to see how much he had aged. Her mother was only fifty-three years old, which was still young, but Arthur was sixty-seven now and he wasn't aging gracefully. The years of stress with his alcoholic wife had taken their toll, running Durning International, and it all showed now. He had had several heart attacks and a small stroke, and he looked terribly old and frail, and Jean was very nervous, watching him. She seemed to cling to Tana like a raft in a troubled sea, and when Arthur went to bed that night, her mother came to her room and sat at the foot of the bed. It was the first time Tana had actually stayed at the house, and she had the newly decorated bedroom her mother had promised her. It was just too much trouble to stay in town, or at a hotel, and Tana knew her mother would have been terribly hurt. They saw too little of her as it was. Arthur only went to Palm Beach, to their condominium there, and her mother didn't like to leave him to fly out to San Francisco, so they only saw Tana when she came East, which was more and more infrequently.

'Is everything all right, sweetheart?'

'Fine.' It was better than that, but she didn't want to say anything about it to Jean.

'I'm glad.' She usually waited a day to start complaining about Tana's 'wasted life', but this time she didn't have much time so she would have to move fast, Tana knew. 'Your job's all right?'

'It's wonderful.' She smiled and Jean looked sad. It always depressed her that Tana liked her job as much as she did. It meant she wouldn't be giving it up soon. She still secretly thought that one day Tana would drop everything for the right man, it was hard for Jean to imagine that she wouldn't do that. But she didn't know her daughter very well. She never really had, and she knew her even less now.

'Any new men?' It was the same conversation they always had, and Tana usually said no, but this time she decided to throw her mother a small bone.

'One.'

Jean's eyebrows shot up. 'Anything serious?'

'Not yet.' Tana laughed. It was almost cruel to tease her that way. 'And don't get excited, I don't think it ever will be. He's a nice man, and it's very comfortable, but I don't think it's more than that.' But the sparkle in her eyes said that she lied and Jean saw that too.

'How long have you been seeing him?'

'Two months.'

'Why didn't you bring him East?'

Tana took a deep breath and hugged her knees on the single guest bed, her eyes fixed on Jean's. 'As a matter of fact, he's visiting his little girls in Washington.' She didn't tell her that she was meeting him in New York the following night. She had let Jean think she was flying back out West. It gave her brownie points for coming home just for a day, and gave her the freedom to float around New York at will with Drew. She didn't want to drag him out to meet her family, especially not with Arthur and his offspring around.

'How long has he been divorced, Tana?' Her mother sounded somewhat vague as she glanced away.

'A while.' She lied, and suddenly her mother's eyes dug into her.

'How long?'

'Relax, Mom. He's actually working on it right now. They just filed.'

'How long ago?'

'A few months. For heaven's sake ... relax!'

'That's exactly what you shouldn't do.' She got off the foot of Tana's bed and suddenly paced the room nervously, and then stood glaring at Tana again. 'And the other thing you shouldn't do is go out with him.'

'What a ridiculous thing to say. You don't even know the man.'

'I don't have to, Tana.' She spoke almost bitterly. 'I know the syndrome. The man doesn't even matter sometimes. Unless he's already divorced, with his papers in his hand, steer clear of him.'

'That's the dumbest thing I ever heard. You don't trust anyone, do you, Mom?'

'I'm just a whole lot older than you are, Tan. And as sophisticated as you think you are, I know better than you. Even if he thinks he's going to get divorced, even if he's absolutely sure of it, he may not. He may be so totally wound up in his kids, for all you know, that he just can't divorce his wife. Six months from now, he could go back to her, and you'll be left standing there, in love with him by then with no way out, and you'll talk yourself into sticking around for two years ... five years ... ten ... and the next thing you know, you'll be forty-five years old, and if you're lucky,' her eyes were damp, 'he'll have his first heart attack and need you by then ... but his wife may still be alive, and then you'll never have a chance at him. There are some things you can't fight. And most of the time, that's one of them. It's a bond that no one else can break for him. If he breaks it himself, or already has, then more power to you both, but before you get badly hurt, sweetheart, I'd like to see you stay out of it.' Her voice was so compassionate and so sad that Tana felt sorry for her. Her life hadn't been much fun since she and Arthur had gotten married, but she had won him at last, after long, hard, desperately lonely years. 'I don't want that for you, sweetheart. You deserve better than that. Why don't you stay out of it for a while, and see what happens to him?'

'Life is too short for that, Mom. I don't have much time to play games with anyone. I have too much else to do. And what difference does it make? I don't want to get married anyway.'

Jean sighed and sat down again. 'I don't understand why. What do you have against marriage, Tan?'

'Nothing. It makes sense if you want kids, I guess, or have no career of your own. But I do, I have too much else in my life to be dependent on anyone, and I'm too old for children, now. I'm thirty years old, and I'm set in my ways. I could never turn my life upside down for anyone.' She thought of Harry and Averil's house which looked as though a demolition squad stopped to visit them every day. 'It's just not for me.' Jean couldn't held wondering if it was something she had done, but it was a combination of everything, knowing that Arthur had cheated on Marie, seeing how badly her mother had been hurt for so long, and not wanting that for herself, she wanted her career, her independence, her own life. She didn't want a husband and kids, she was sure of it. She had been for years.

'You're missing out on so much.' Jean looked sad. What hadn't she given this child to make her feel like that?

'I just can't see that, Mom.' She searched her mother's eyes for something she saw but didn't understand.

'You're the only thing that matters to me, Tan.' She found that hard to believe and yet for years her mother had sacrificed everything for her, even putting up with Arthur's gifts of charity, just so she would have something more for her child. It tore at Tana's heart to remember that, and it reminded her of how grateful she should be. She hugged her mother tight, remembering the past.

'I love you, Mom. I'm grateful for everything you did for me.'

'I don't want gratitude. I want to see you happy, sweetheart. And if this man is good for you, then wonderful, but if he's lying to you or himself, he'll break your heart. I don't want that for you ... ever ....'

'It's not like what happened to you.' Tana was sure of it, but Jean was not.

'How can you know? How can you be sure of that?'

'I just can. I know him by now.'

'After two months? Don't be a fool. You don't know anything, anymore than I did twenty-four years ago. Arthur wasn't lying to me then, he was lying to himself. Is that what you want, seventeen years of lonely nights, Tan? Don't do that to yourself.'

'I won't. I've got my work.'

'It's no substitute.' But in her case it was, she substituted it for everything. 'Promise me you'll think about what I said.'

'I promise.' She smiled and the two women hugged each other goodnight again. Tana was touched by her mother's concern, but she knew for certain that she was wrong about Drew. She went to sleep with a smile on her face, thinking of him and his little girls. She wondered what he was doing with them. She had the name of his hotel in Washington, but she didn't want to intrude on them.

The Thanksgiving dinner at the Durning home the next day was predictably dull for everyone, but Jean was grateful that Tana was there. Arthur was somewhat vague, and fell asleep twice in his chair, the maid gave him a gentle nudge, and eventually Jean helped him upstairs. Ann arrived with her three brats, who were even worse than they had been several years before. She was talking about marrying a Greek shipping magnate and Tana tried not to listen to her, but it was impossible. The only blessing of the day was that Billy had gone to Florida with friends instead of being there.

And by five o'clock Tana was checking her watch regularly. She had promised Drew she would be at the Carlyle by nine, and they hadn't called each other all day. She was suddenly dying to see him again, to look into his eyes, touch his face, feel his hands, peel away his clothes as she dropped her own. She had an almost veiled smile as she went upstairs to pack her bags, and her mother came into the room as she did. Their eyes met in the large mirror over the chest of drawers, and Jean spoke to her first.

'You're going to meet him, aren't you?'

She could have lied to her, but she was thirty years old, what was the point? 'Yes.' She turned to face her mother across the room. 'I am.'

'You frighten me.'

'You worry about things too much. This isn't a replay of your life, mother, it's mine. There is a difference.'

'Not always as much as we'd like to think, I'm afraid.'

'You're wrong this time.'

'I hope for your sake that I am.' But she looked grief-stricken when Tana finally called a cab, and rode into New York at eight o'clock. She couldn't get her mother's words out of her mind, and by the time she arrived at the hotel, she was angry with her. Why did she burden her with her own bad experiences, her disappointments, her pain? What right did she have to do that? It was like a blanket of cement one had to wear everywhere to prove that one had been loved, well, she didn't want to be loved that much. She didn't need it anymore. She wanted to be left alone to lead her own life now.

The Carlyle was a beautiful, exquisite hotel, the thickly carpeted steps down to the lobby's marble floor, the Persian rugs, the antique clocks, the gentlemen at the desk in morning coats. It was all from another world, and Tana smiled to herself. This was not her mother's life, it was her own. She was sure of that now. She gave Drew's name, and went upstairs to the room. He had not yet arrived, but they obviously knew him well. The room was as sumptuous as the lobby had promised it would be, a sweeping view of Central Park, the skyline shimmering like jewels, more antiques, this time upholstered in a deep rose silk, heavy satin drapes, and a magnum of champagne waiting in a bucket of ice, a gift from the management. 'Enjoy your stay' were the bellboy's final words, and Tana sat down on the handsome couch, wondering if she should run a bath for herself, or wait. She still wasn't sure if he was bringing the girls, but she thought he was. She didn't want to shock them by being undressed when they came. But an hour later, they had not yet arrived, and it was after ten o'clock when he finally called.

'Tana?'

'No, Sophia Loren.'

He laughed. 'I'm disappointed. I like Tana Roberts better than her.'

'Now I know you're nuts.'

'I am. About you.'

'Where are you?'

There was the briefest pause. 'In Washington. Julie has an awful cold, and we thought that Elizabeth might be coming down with the flu. I thought maybe I ought to wait here, and I might not bring them up at all. I'll come up tomorrow, Tan. Is that all right?'

'Sure.' She understood, but she had also noticed the 'we' that had snuck in. 'We thought that Elizabeth ... .' And she wasn't too crazy about that. 'The room is fabulous.'

'Aren't they wonderful? Were they nice to you?'

'They sure were.' She looked around the room, 'But it's no fun without you, Mr Lands. Keep that in mind.'

'I'll be there tomorrow. I swear.'

'What time?'

He thought for a minute. 'I'll have breakfast with the girls ... see how they feel ... that should make it ten o'clock. I could catch a noon plane ... I'll be at the hotel by two without fail.' That meant half the day was shot, and she wanted to say something about that, but thought wiser of it.

'All right.' But she didn't sound pleased, and when she hung up the phone she had to push her mother's words out of her head again. She took a hot bath, watched television, ordered a cup of hot chocolate from room service, and wondered what he was doing in Washington, and then suddenly she felt guilty for what she hadn't said to him. It wasn't his fault the kids were sick. It was certainly a pain in the ass for them, but it was no one's fault. She picked up the phone and asked for the hotel where he was staying in Washington, but he wasn't there. She left a message that she had called, watched the late show, and fell asleep with the television still on. She woke at nine o'clock the next day, and went out to discover that it was an absolutely gorgeous day. She went for a long walk down Fifth Avenue, and over to Bloomingdale's where she puttered for a while and bought a few things for herself, a handsome blue cashmere sweater for him, and gifts for the girls, a doll for Julie and a pretty blouse for Elizabeth, and then she went back to the Carlyle to wait for him, but there was a message this time. Both the girls were deathly ill, 'will arrive Friday night', another night at the Carlyle alone. On Saturday she went to the Metropolitan, and on Saturday afternoon at five o'clock, he arrived finally, in time to make love to her, order room service, apologize to her all night, and take the plane back to San Francisco with her the next day. It had been a great weekend for them in New York.

'Remind me to do that again with you sometime,' she said half sarcastically as they finished dinner on the plane.

'Are you furious with me, Tan?' He had looked miserable ever since he'd arrived in New York, consumed with guilt toward her, worried about the girls, he talked too much, too fast, and he wasn't himself for days.

'No, disappointed more than furious. How was your ex-wife by the way?'

'Fine.' He didn't seem anxious to talk about her and was surprised Tana had asked. It didn't seem an appropriate subject for them, but she was haunted by her mother's words. 'What made you ask that?'

'Just curious.' She took a mouthful of the dessert on the tray, looking strangely cool as she glanced at him. 'Are you still in love with her?'

'Of course not. That's ridiculous. I haven't been in love with her for years.' He looked downright annoyed and Tana was pleased. Her mother was wrong. As usual. 'You may not be aware of it, Tan,' he hesitated, looking pale, 'but I happen to be in love with you.' He looked at her for a long time, and she watched his face searchingly. And then at last she smiled, but she said nothing at all. She kissed his lips, put down her fork, and eventually closed her eyes for a nap. There was nothing she wanted to say to him, and he was oddly uncomfortable. It had been a difficult weekend for both of them.

Chapter 15

December flew by, with a series of small cases on Tana's desk, and a number of parties she went to with Drew. He seemed to think nothing of flying up for the night, and sometimes he came just to have dinner with her. They shared delicious tender moments, quiet nights at home, and a kind of intimacy that Tana had never known before. She realized now how lonely she had been for so long. There had been her mad affair with Yael years before, and since then only casual relationships that came and went, without meaning much to her. But everything about Drew Lands was different. He was so sensitive, so intense, so thoughtful in small ways that meant a great deal to her. She felt surrounded and protected and alive, and they laughed most of the time. By the time the holidays came, he was excited about seeing his two little girls again. They were coming out from Washington to spend Christmas with him. He had cancelled his skiing trip to Sugar Bowl with her.

'Will you come down and spend some time with us, Tan?'

She smiled at him; she knew how crazy he was about his kids. 'I'll try.' She had a big case coming up, but she was pretty sure it wouldn't actually go to trial for a while. 'I think I can.'

'Do your best. You could come down on the twenty-sixth, and we could spend a few days in Malibu.' He was renting a little weekend place there, but she was not surprised by that so much as by the date he had said ... the twenty-sixth ... she realized then he wanted to be alone with the girls for the holidays. 'Will you, Tan?' He sounded like a little kid and she hugged him tight and laughed at him.

'Okay, okay, I'll come down. What do you think the girls would like?'

'You.' They exchanged a smile and he kissed her again.

He spent the week before getting everything ready for them in LA. Tana was trying to clean up the work on her desk so she could take a few days off from the district attorney's office, and she had lots of shopping to do. She bought Drew a suede shirt, and a very expensive briefcase that he'd seen and loved, and eau de cologne that he wore, and a wild tie she knew he'd love. And she bought each of the girls a beautiful doll at F.A.O. Schwarz, some stationery, some barettes, an adorable sweat suit for Elizabeth that looked just like one Tana had, and a rabbit made of real fur for the little one. She wrapped all the gifts, and put them in a suitcase to take to LA with her. She hadn't bothered with a tree this year; she didn't really have time and there was no one to see it anyway. She spent Christmas Eve with Harry and Averil and their kids, and it was relaxing just being with them. Harry had never looked better, and Averil looked contented as little Harrison ran around waiting for Santa Claus. They sliced carrots for the reindeer, put chocolate chip cookies out, a big glass of milk, and finally got him into bed. His sister was already asleep, and when he finally fell asleep too, Averil tiptoed into their rooms to look at them with a quiet smile, as Harry watched her go, and Tana watched him. It made her feel good just to see him like that, contented and alive. His life had turned out well, although it certainly wasn't what he had expected to do with his life. He glanced at Tana with a smile, and it was as though they both understood.

'Funny, isn't it, Tan, how life works out ....'

'Yeah, it is.' She smiled at him. They had known each other for twelve years, almost half their lives. It was incredible.

'I figured you'd be married in two years when I met you that first time.'

'And I thought you'd die a hopeless degenerate ... no ...', she looked pensive and amused, '... a playboy drunk ....'

He laughed at the idea. 'You've got me mixed up with my old man.'

'Hardly.' She still had a soft spot for Harrison, but Harry had never been quite sure of that. He had suspected it once, but he had never been sure, and his father had never let on to anything. Nor had Tan.

Harry looked at her oddly then. He hadn't expected to be spending Christmas with her this year, not after the hints she had dropped about Drew once or twice. He had the strangest feeling that it was serious for her, more so even than she would let on to him. 'Where's your friend, Tan? I thought you were going to Sugar Bowl.' She looked blank at first, but she knew instantly who he meant and he grinned. 'Come on, don't pull that "who do you mean" shit on me. I know you better than that.'

She laughed at him. 'All right, all right. He's in LA with his kids. We cancelled Sugar Bowl because his kids were coming out. I'm going down on the twenty-sixth.' Harry thought that strange but he didn't say anything to her.

'He means a lot to you, doesn't he?'

She nodded cautiously, but she didn't meet his eyes. 'He does ... for whatever that's worth.'

'What's it worth, Tan?'

She sighed and leaned back in her chair. 'God only knows.'

Harry kept wondering something and he finally had to ask. 'How come you're not down there today?'

'I didn't want to intrude.' But that wasn't true. He hadn't invited her.

'I'm sure you're not an intrusion to him. Have you met his kids yet?' She shook her head.

'Day after tomorrow will be the first time.'

Harry smiled at her. 'Scared?'

She laughed nervously. 'Hell, yes. Wouldn't you be? They're the most important thing in his life.'

'I hope you are too.'

'I think I am.'

And then Harry frowned. 'He's not married, is he, Tan?'

'I told you before, he's in the process of getting a divorce.'

'Then why didn't he spend Christmas with you?'

'How the hell do I know?' She was annoyed at the persistent questions and she was beginning to wonder where Averil was.

'Didn't you ask?'

'No. I was perfectly comfortable like this,' she glowered at him, 'until now.'

'That's the trouble with you, Tan, you're so used to being alone that it doesn't even occur to you to do things differently. You should be spending Christmas with him. Unless ... .'

'Unless what?' She was angry at him now. It was none of his business whether or not she spent Christmas with Drew, and she respected his need to be alone with his kids.

But Harry wasn't content to leave it alone. 'Unless he's spending Christmas with his wife.'

'Oh, for chrissake ... what an assinine thing to say. You are the most cynical, suspicious son-of-a-bitch, I know ... and I thought I was bad ... .' She looked furious, but there was something else lurking in her eyes, as though he had hit a nerve. But that was ridiculous.

'Maybe you're not bad enough.'

'Shit.' She stood up and looked for her bag, and when Averil finally came back, she found them both tense, but she didn't think anything of it. They were like that sometimes. She was used to them by now, they had their own special relationship and sometimes they fought like cats and dogs but they didn't mean any harm.

'What have you two been up to out here? Beating each other up again?' she smiled.

'I'm considering it.' Tana glared irritatedly at her.

'It might do him good.' All three of them laughed then.

'Harry's been making an ass of himself, as usual.'

He suddenly grinned at her. 'You make it sound as though I've been exposing myself.'

Averil laughed. 'Did you do that again, sweetheart?' And then finally Tana warmed up again.

'You know, you're the biggest pain in the ass in the world. World cup goes to you.'

He bowed politely from his chair, and Tana went to get her coat. 'You don't have to leave, Tan.' He was always sorry to see her go, even when they disagreed. They still had a special bond between them. It was almost like being twins.

'I should go home and get organised. I brought home a ton of work.'

'To do on Christmas Day?' He looked horrified, and she smiled.

'I have to do it sometime.'

'Why don't you come here instead?' They were having friends over, his partner and another dozen or so, but she shook her head. She didn't mind being home alone, or at least so she said.

'You're weird, Tan.' But he kissed her cheek and his eyes were filled with the love he felt for her.

'Have a good time in LA.' He wheeled beside her to the door and looked at her pensively. 'And Tan ... take care of yourself ... Maybe I was wrong ... but it doesn't hurt to be careful about things ....'

'I know.' Her voice was soft again, and she kissed them both as she left. But driving home in the car, she found herself thinking about what he had said. She knew he couldn't be right. Drew was not spending Christmas with his wife ... but nonetheless she should have been spending it with him. She had tried to tell herself that it didn't matter, but it did. And suddenly it reminded her of all the lonely years she had felt so sorry for Jean ... waiting for Arthur, sitting by the phone, hoping he would call ... they were never able to spend their major holidays together when Marie was alive, and even afterwards there was always an excuse ... his in-laws, his children, his club, his friends ... and there was poor Jean, with tears in her eyes, holding her breath ... waiting for him ... Tana fought back the thoughts. It was *not* like that with Drew. It was *not*. She wouldn't let it be. But the next afternoon, as she worked, the questions kept coming to her. Drew called her once, but it had been a very brief call, and he sounded rushed. 'I have to go back to the girls,' he had said hastily and then hung up on her.

And when she landed in Los Angeles the next day, he was waiting for her at the airport, and he swept her into his arms, and held her so tight she could barely breathe.

'My God ... wait ...! stop ...!' But he crushed her to him, and they were laughing and kissing all the way to the parking lot as he juggled her bags and packages, and she was ecstatic to see him. It had been a lonely holiday without him after all. And she had secretly wanted it to be different and exciting this year. She hadn't even admitted that to herself, but suddenly she knew it was true. And it was, it was wonderful driving into town with him. He had left the girls at the house with a baby-sitter he knew, just so he could pick her up alone, and spend a few quiet minutes with her.

'... before they drive us both nuts.' He looked at her and beamed.

'How are the girls?'

'Wonderful. I swear they've doubled in size in the last four weeks. Wait till you meet them, Tan.' And she was enchanted with them when she did. Elizabeth was lovely and grown up and looked strikingly like Drew, and Julie was a cuddly little ball who almost instantly climbed onto Tana's lap. They loved the presents she had brought, and they seemed to have no resistance to her, although Tana saw Elizabeth looking her over more than once. But Drew handled it remarkably well. He cut out all the necking and the cuddly stuff. It was as though they were just friends, spending a cozy afternoon. It was obvious that he knew Tana well, but it would have been impossible to guess the relationship they shared from the way he behaved to her. And Tana wondered if he always acted that way around the girls.

'What do you do?' Elizabeth was looking her over again, and Julie was watching them both, as Tana smiled, shaking back her mane of pale blonde hair. Elizabeth had envied that since they first met.

'I'm an attorney like your dad. In fact, that's how we met.'

'So's my mom.' Elizabeth was quick to add. 'She's assistant to the ambassador of the OAS in Washington, and they might give her her own ambassadorship next year.'

'Ambasssadorial post.' Drew corrected her and glanced at the three 'girls'.

'I don't want her to do that.' Julie pouted. 'I want her to come back here to live. With Daddy.' She stuck her lower lip out defiantly, and Elizabeth was quick to add, 'He could come with us wherever Mom's sent. It depends on where it is.' Tana felt an odd feeling in her gut, and she looked at him, but he was doing something else, and Elizabeth went on. 'Mom may even want to come back here herself, if they don't offer her the right job. That's what she said, anyway.'

'That's very interesting.' Tana noticed that her mouth felt dry, and she wished that Drew would regain control of the conversation again, but he didn't say anything. 'Do you like living in Washington?'

'Very much.' Elizabeth was painfully polite and Julie hopped into Tana's lap again, and smiled up into Tana's eyes.

'You're pretty. Almost as pretty as our mom.'

'Thank you!' It was definitely not easy talking to them, and other than with Harry's children, it was rare for Tana to be in a spot like this, but she had to make the effort for Drew. 'What will we do this afternoon?' Tana felt almost breathless as she asked, desperate to divert them from the topic of his almost ex-wife.

'Mommy's going shopping on Rodeo Drive.' Julie smiled up at her, and Tana almost gasped.

'Oh?' Her eyes turned toward Drew in astonishment and then back to them. 'That's nice. Let's see, how about a movie? Have you seen *Sounder*?' She felt as though she were running up a mountain as fast as she could and she wasn't getting anywhere ... Rodeo Drive ... that meant she had come to Los Angeles with the girls ... and why hadn't he wanted Tana to come down yesterday? Had he spent Christmas with her after all? The next hour seemed to trickle by as Tana chatted with the girls, and finally they ran outside to play, and Tana finally turned to him. Her eyes spoke volumes before her mouth said a word. 'I take it your wife is in Los Angeles.' She looked rigid and inside something had gone numb.

'Don't look at me like that.' His voice was soft while his eyes avoided her.

'Why not?' She stood up and walked toward him. 'Did you spend the holiday with her, Drew?' He couldn't avoid her now, she was standing directly in front of him. And she already assumed he had. And when he lifted his eyes to face her, she knew instantly that she was right and the girls had given him away. 'Why did you lie to me?'

'I didn't lie to you. I didn't think ... oh, for chrissake ... .' He looked at her almost viciously. She had cornered him. 'I didn't plan it that way, but the girls have never had a Christmas with us separated before, Tan ... it's just too damn hard on them ... .'

'Is it now?' Her eyes and voice were hard, concealing the pain she felt inside ... the pain he had inflicted on her by lying to her ... . 'And just exactly when do you plan to let them get used to it?'

'*Goddammit*, do you think I like seeing my children hurt by this?'

'They look fine to me.'

'Of course they do. That's because Eileen and I are civilized. That's the least we can give them now. It's not their fault things didn't work out for us.' He looked at Tana sorrowfully and she had to fight the urge to sit down and cry, not for him or the girls, but for herself.

'Are you sure it's not too late to salvage it with Eileen?'

'Don't be ridiculous.'

'Where did she sleep?' He looked as though he had received an electric shock.

'That's an inappropriate thing to ask, and you know it damn well.'

'Oh, my God ....' She sat down again, unable to believe how transparent he was. 'You slept with her.'

'I did *not* sleep with her.'

'You did, didn't you?' She was shouting now and he strode around the room like a nervous cat as he turned to face her again.

'I slept on the couch.'

'You're lying to me. Aren't you?'

'Goddammit, Tana! Don't accuse me of that! It isn't as easy as you think. We've been married for almost twenty years, Goddammit ... I can't just walk out on everything from one day to the next, and not when the girls are involved,' he looked at her mournfully and then walked slowly to where she sat. 'Please ....' There were tears in his eyes. 'I love you, Tan ... I just need a little time to work this out ....' She turned away from him and walked across the room, keeping her back to him.

'I've heard that before.' She wheeled to face him then, and there were tears in her eyes, too. 'My mother spent seventeen years listening to bullshit like that, Drew.'

'I'm not giving you bullshit, Tan. I just need time. This is very difficult for all of us.'

'Fine.' She picked up her bag and coat from a chair. 'Then call me when you've recovered from it. I think I'd enjoy you more then.' But before she reached the door, he grabbed her arm.

'Don't do this to me. Please ....'

'Why not? Eileen in in town. Just give her a call. She'll keep you company tonight.' Tana smiled at him sardonically to hide the hurt. 'You can sleep on the couch ... together, if you like.' She yanked open the door and he looked as though he were going to cry.

'I love you, Tan.' But as she heard the words, she wanted to sit down and cry. And suddenly she turned to him and her energy seemed to drain as she looked at him.

'Don't do this to me, Drew. It's not fair. You're not free ... you have no right to ....' But she had opened the door to her heart just wide enough for him to slip into it again. Wordlessly, he pulled her into his arms, and kissed her hard, and she felt everything inside her melt. And when he pulled away from her, she looked at him. 'That doesn't solve anything.'

'No.' He sounded calmer now. 'But time will. Just give me a chance. I swear to you, you won't regret it.' And then he said the words that frightened her the most. 'I want to marry you one day, Tan.' She wanted to tell him to stop, to move the film back to before he had said those words, but it didn't matter anyway, the girls came running in, laughing and shouting and ready to play with him and he looked over their heads at her and whispered two words to her, 'please stay.' She hesitated. She knew she should go back, and she wanted to. She didn't belong here with them. He had just spent the night with the woman he was married to, and they had had Christmas with their two girls. Where did Tana belong in all this? And yet when she looked at him, she didn't want to leave. She wanted to be part of it, to be his, to belong to him and the girls, even if he never married her. She didn't really want that anyway. She just wanted to be with him, the way they had been since they first met, and slowly she put down her bag and coat and looked at him, and he smiled at her, and her insides turned to mush, and Julie hugged her around the waist while Elizabeth grinned at her.

'Where were you going, Tan?' Elizabeth was curious, she seemed fascinated by everything that Tana did and said.

'Nowhere.' She smiled at the pretty adolescent child. 'Now, what would you girls like to do?' The two girls laughed and teased and Drew chased them around the room. She had never seen him as happy as this, and later that afternoon they went to the movies, and ate buckets of popcorn, then he took them to the La Brea Tar Pits, and to Perino's for dinner that night, and when they finally came home all four of them were ready to fall into bed. Julie fell asleep in Drew's arms, and Elizabeth made it into bed before falling asleep too, and Tana and Drew sat in front of a fire in the living room, whispering, as he gently touched the golden hair he loved.

'I'm so glad you stayed, sweetheart ... I didn't want you to go ... .'

'I'm glad I stayed too.' She smiled at him, feeling vulnerable and young, which didn't make sense for a woman her age, at least not to her. She imagined that she should be more mature than that by now, less sensitive. But she was more sensitive to him than she had ever been to any man. 'Promise it won't happen again ... .' Her voice drifted off and he looked at her with a tender smile.

'Baby, I promise you.'

Chapter 16

The spring Tana and Drew shared was so idyllic it was almost like a fairy tale. Drew flew up roughly three times a week, she went to LA every weekend. They went to parties, sailed on the bay, met each other's friends. She even introduced him to Harry and Ave, and the two men had gotten along splendidly. And Harry gave her the okay when he took her out to celebrate the following week.

'You know, kid, I think you finally did good for yourself.' She made a face and he laughed. 'I mean it. I mean, look at the guys you used to drag around. Remember Yael McBee?'

'Harry!' She threw her napkin at him in the restaurant and they both laughed. 'How can you compare Drew to him? Besides, I was twenty-five years old. I'm almost thirty-one now.'

'That's no excuse. You're no smarter than you used to be.'

'The hell I'm not. You just said yourself ....'

'Never mind what I said, you jerk. Now, are you going to give me some peace of mind and marry the guy?'

'No.' She laughed, and she said it too fast, and Harry, looking at her, saw something he had never seen before. He had been looking for it for years, and suddenly there it was. He saw it as clearly as he saw the big green eyes, a kind of vulnerable, sheepish look she had never worn before for anyone.

'Holy shit, it's serious, isn't it, Tan? You're going to marry him, aren't you?'

'He hasn't asked.' She sounded so demure that he roared.

'My God, you will! Wait till I tell Ave!'

'Harry, calm down.' She patted his arm. 'He isn't even divorced yet.' But it didn't worry her. She knew how hard he was working on it. He told her every week about his meetings with his lawyer, his conversations with Eileen to speed things up, and he was going East to see the girls for Easter week, and hopefully she'd sign the settlement papers then, if they were drawn up in time.

'He's working on it, isn't he?' Harry looked momentarily concerned, but he had to admit, he liked the guy. It was almost impossible not to like Drew Lands. He was easy going, intelligent, and it was easy to see he was crazy about Tan.

'Of course he is.'

'Then relax, you'll be married six months from now, and nine months after that, you'll have a baby in your arms. Count on it.' He looked thrilled and Tana sat back and laughed at him.

'Boy, do you have a wild imagination, Winslow. In the first place, he hasn't asked me to marry him yet, at least not seriously. And in the second, he's had a vasectomy.'

'So he'll have it reversed. Big deal. I know plenty of guys who've done that.' But it made him a little nervous thinking about it.

'Is that all you think about? Getting people pregnant?'

'No,' he smiled innocently, 'just my wife.'

She laughed and they finished the meal, and they both went back to their offices. She had an enormous case coming up, probably the biggest of her career. There were three murder defendants involved in the most gruesome series of murders committed in the state in recent years, and there were three defense attorneys and two prosecutors and she was in charge of the case for the DA. There was going to be a lot of press involved and she had to really know her stuff, which was why she wasn't going East with Drew when he went to see the girls over the Easter holiday. It was probably just as well she didn't anyway. Drew would be a nervous wreck getting the papers signed, and she had the case on her mind. It made more sense to stay home and do her work than to sit around in hotel rooms waiting for him.

He came up to San Francisco to spend the weekend with her before he left, and they lay on the rug in front of the fire for hours on his last night, talking, thinking aloud, saying almost anything that came to mind, and she realized again how deeply she was falling in love with him.

'Would you ever consider marriage, Tan?' He looked pensively at her and she smiled in the firelight. She looked exquisite in the soft glow, her delicate features seeming to be carved in a pale peach marble, her eyes dancing like emeralds.

'I never have before.' She touched his lips with her fingertips and he kissed her hands and then her mouth.

'Do you think you could be happy with me, Tan?'

'Is that a proposal, sir?' He seemed to be beating around the bush and she smiled at him. 'You don't have to marry me, you know, I'm happy like this.'

'You are, aren't you?' He looked at her strangely and she nodded her head. 'Aren't you?'

'Not entirely.' His hair looked even more silvery, his eyes a bright topaz blue, and she never again wanted to love any man but him. 'I want more than this, Tan ... I want you all the time ... .'

'So do I ... .' She whispered the words to him, and he took her in his arms and made love to her ever so gently in front of the fire, and afterwards he lay for a long, long time and looked at her, and then finally he spoke, his mouth nestled in her hair, his hands still stroking the body he loved so much.

'Will you marry me when I'm free?'

'Yes.' She said the word almost breathlessly. She had never said it to anyone, but she meant it now, and suddenly she understood what people felt when they promised ... for better or worse ... until death do us part. She never wanted to be without him again, and when she took him to the airport the next day, she was still a little overwhelmed by what she felt, and she looked at him searchingly. 'Did you mean what you said last night, Drew?'

'How can you ask me something like that?' He looked horrified, and instantly crushed her against his chest as they stood in the terminal. 'Of course I did.'

She grinned at him, looking more like his thirteen-year-old child than the Assistant DA. 'I guess that means we're engaged then, huh?' And suddenly he laughed, and he felt as happy as a boy as he looked at her.

'It sure does. I'll have to see what kind of ring I can find in Washington.'

'Never mind that. Just come back safe and sound.' It was going to be an endless ten days of waiting for him. And the only thing that would help was her enormous case.

He called her two and three times a day for the first few days, and told her everything he did from morning till night, but when things began to get rough with Eileen, he called once a day and she could hear how uptight he was, but they had started jury selection by then and she was totally engrossed in that, and by the time he got back to Los Angeles, she realized that they hadn't spoken to each other in more than two days. He had stayed longer than he had expected to, but it was for a 'worthy cause' he said, and she agreed with him, and she could barely think straight anymore by then. She was too worried about the jury that was being picked, and the tack they were going to take, the evidence that had just turned up, the judge to whom they had been assigned. She had plenty on her mind, and one of Drew's rare litigation situations had occurred. Almost everything he did settled before it went to court, and this was a rare exception for him, and it kept him away from her for almost another week, and when they both finally met, they almost felt like strangers again. He teased her about it, asked if she had fallen in love with anyone else, and made passionate love to her all night long.

'I want you to be so bleary eyed all day in court that everyone wonders what the hell went on last night.' And he got his wish. She was half asleep and she couldn't get him out of her mind she was so hungry for him. She never seemed to get enough of him anymore, and all through her trial, she was lonely for him, but it was too important to screw up and she kept her nose to the grindstone constantly. It went on till late May, and finally, in the first week in June, the verdict came in. It went just the way she had wanted it to, and the press gave her high praise as usual. Over the years, she had earned a reputation for being rigid, tough, conservative, merciless in court, and brilliant at the cases she tried. They were nice reviews to have, and it often made Harry smile when he read about her.

'I'd never recognize the liberal I knew and loved in this, Tan.' He grinned broadly at her.

'We all have to grow up sometime, don't we? I'm thirty-one this year.'

'That's no excuse to be as tough as you are.'

'I'm not tough, Harry, I'm good.' And she was right, but he knew it too. 'Those people killed nine women and a child. You can't let people get away with shit like that. Our whole society will fall apart. Someone has to do what I do.'

'I'm glad it's you and not me, Tan.' He patted her hand. I'd lie awake at night, worrying that they'd get me eventually.' He hated even saying it, and he worried about it sometimes for her, but it didn't seem to bother her at all. 'By the way, how's Drew?'

'Fine. He's going to New York on business next week, and he's bringing the girls back with him.'

'When are you getting married.'

'Relax.' She smiled. 'We haven't even talked about it since I started this case. In fact, I've hardly talked to him.' And when she told him about her success before it hit the press, he sounded strange.

'That's nice.'

'Well, don't get too excited. It might be bad for your heart.'

He laughed at her. 'All right, all right, I'm sorry. I had something else on my mind.'

'What?'

'Nothing important.' But he was that way until he left, and he sounded worse from the East, and when he got back to Los Angeles, he didn't call her at all. She almost wondered if something was wrong, or if she should fly down to surprise him and get everything on the right track again. All they needed was a little time alone to sort things out, they'd both been working too hard, and she knew all the signs. She looked at her watch late one night, trying to decide if she should catch the last plane down, and decided to call him instead. She could always go down the next day, and they had a lot of catching up to do after her two months of grueling work. She dialed the phone number she knew by heart, heard it ring three times and smiled when it was picked up, but not for long. A woman's voice answered it.

'Hello?' Tana felt her heart stop, and she sat there endlessly staring into the night, and then hurriedly she put the down the phone.

Her heart was pounding hideously, she felt dizzy, awkward, disoriented, strange. She couldn't believe what she had heard. She had to have dialled the wrong number, she told herself, but before she could compose herself to try again, the phone rang, and she heard Drew's voice, and suddenly she knew. He must have known she'd called and now he was panicking. She felt as though her whole life had just come to an end.

'Who was that?' She sounded half hysterical, and he sounded nervous too.
'What?'

'The woman who answered your phone.' She fought for composure but her voice was totally out of control.

'I don't know what you mean.'

'Drew ... ! answer me ... ! please ...' She was half crying, half shouting at him.

'We have to talk.'

'Oh my God ... Goddammit, what have you done to me?'

'Don't be so melodramatic, for chrissake ... .' She cut him off with a shriek.

'Melodramatic? I call you at eleven o'clock at night and a woman answers your phone, and you tell me I'm being melodramatic? How would you like to have a man answer you when you call me here?'

'Stop it, Tan. It was Eileen.'

'Obviously.' Instinctively, she had known.

'And where are the girls?' She didn't even know why she had asked.

'In Malibu.'

'In Malibu? You mean you're alone with her?'

'We had to talk.' His voice sounded dead suddenly.

'Alone? At this hour? What the hell does that mean? Did she sign?'

'Yes, no ... look, I have to talk to you ...'

'Oh, now you have to talk to me ... .' She was being cruel to him and now they were both beginning to sound hysterical. 'What the fuck is going on down there?' There was an endless silence which he couldn't fill. Tana hung up and cried all night, and he arrived in San Francisco the next day. It was Saturday and he found her at home, as he knew he would. He used his key and let himself in, and he found her sitting mournfully on her deck looking out over the bay. She didn't even turn when she heard him come in, but spoke to him with her back turned. 'Why did you bother to come up?'

He knelt beside her and touched her neck with his fingertips. 'Because I love you, Tan.'

'No, you don't.' She shook her head. 'You love her. You always did.'

'That's not true ... .' But they both knew it was, in fact, all three of them did.

'The truth is that I love both of you. That's an awful thing to say, but it's the truth. I don't know how to stop loving her, and at the same time I'm in love with you.'

'That's sick.' She continued to stare out at the bay, passing judgment on him, and he yanked her hair to make her look at him, and when she did, he saw tears on her face and it broke his heart.

'I can't help what I feel. And I don't know what to do about what's happening. Elizabeth almost flunked out of school, she's so upset about us, Eileen and me. Julie is having nightmares. Eileen quit her job at OAS, she turned down the ambassadorial post they tried to tempt her with, and she came home, with the girls . . . .'

They're living with you?' Tana looked as though he had just driven a stake into her heart, and he nodded. He didn't want to lie to her anymore. 'When did this happen?'

'We talked about it a lot in Washington on Easter week . . . but I didn't want to upset you when you were working so hard, Tan . . . .' She wanted to kick him for what he'd said. How could he not tell her something like that? 'And nothing was sure. She did it all without consulting me, and just showed up last week. And now what do you expect me to do? Throw them out?'

'Yes. You should never have let them in again.'

'She's my wife, and they're my kids.' He looked as though he were on the verge of tears but Tana stood up then.

'I guess that solves it then, doesn't it?' She walked slowly to the door and looked at him. 'Goodbye, Drew.'

'I'm not leaving here like this. I'm in love with you.'

'Then get rid of your wife. It's as simple as that.'

'No it's *not*, goddammit!' He was shouting now. She refused to understand what he was going through. 'You don't know what it's like . . . what I feel . . . the guilt . . . the agony . . . .' He started to cry and she felt sick as she looked at him. She turned away and had to fight to speak above the tears in her own voice.

'Please go . . . .'

'I won't.' He pulled her into his arms, and she tried to push him away, but he wouldn't let her do that, and suddenly, without wanting to, she succumbed, and they made love again, crying, begging, shouting, railing at each other and the Fates, and when it was all over, they lay spent in each other's arms and she looked at him.

'What are we going to do?'

'I don't know. Just give me time.'

She sighed painfully. 'I swore I'd never do something like this . . . .' But she couldn't bear the thought of losing him, nor he the pain of giving her up. They cried and lay in each other's arms for the next two days, and when he flew back to Los Angeles, nothing was solved, except that they both knew it wasn't over yet. She had agreed to give him more time, and he had promised her he'd work it out, and for the next six months they drove each other mad with promises and threats, ultimatums and hysteria. Tana called and hung up on Eileen a thousand times. Drew begged her not to do anything rash. The children were even aware of what terrible shape he was in. And Tana began avoiding everyone, especially Harry and Averil. She couldn't bear the questions she saw in his eyes, the sweetness of his wife, the children which only reminded her of Drew's. It was an intolerable situation for all of them, and Eileen was even aware of it, but she said that she wasn't moving out again. She could wait for him to work it out, she wasn't going anywhere, and Tana felt as though she were going mad. She spent her birthday and the Fourth of July and Labor Day and Thanksgiving alone, predictably .....

'What do you expect of me, Tana? You want me to just walk out on them?'

'Maybe I do. Maybe that's exactly what I expect of you. Why should I be the one who's always alone? It matters to me too .....'

'But I've got the kids .....'

'Go fuck yourself.' But she didn't say that for real, until she had spent Christmas alone. He had promised to come up, both then and on New Year's Eve, and she sat and waited for him all night and he never came. She sat in an evening dress until nine a.m. on New Year's Day, and then slowly, irrevocably, she took it off and threw it in the trash. She had bought the dress just for him. She had the locks changed the next day, and packed up all the things he'd left with her over the past year and a half and had them sent to him in an unmarked box. And after that she sent him a telegram which said it all. 'Goodbye. Don't come back again.' And she lay drowning in her tears. For all the bravery, the final straw had almost broken her back, and he came flying up as soon as he began to get the messages, the telegram, the package, he was terrified that she might mean it this time, and when he tried his key in her lock, he knew she did. He drove frantically to her office and insisted on seeing her, and when he did her eyes were cold and the greenest he had ever seen.

'I have nothing left to say to you, Drew.' A part of her had died. He had killed it with the hopes that had never been fulfilled, the lies he'd told to both of them, and most of all himself. She wondered now how her mother had stood it for all those years without killing herself. It was the worst torture Tana had ever been through and she never wanted to go through it again, for anyone. And least of all for him.

'Tana, please .....'

'Goodbye.' She walked out of her office and down the hall, disappearing into a conference room, and she left the building shortly after that, but she didn't go home for hours. And when she did, he was still waiting there, outside, in the driving rain. She slowed her car, as she saw him and drove off again. She spent the night in a motel on Lombard Street, and the next morning when she went back, he was sleeping in his car. When, instinctively, he heard her step, he woke and leapt out to talk to her. 'If you don't leave me alone, I'll call the police.' She sounded tough and threatening, looked furious to his eyes, but what he didn't see was how broken she felt inside, how long she sobbed once he was gone, how desperate she felt at the thought of never seeing him again. She actually thought of jumping off the Bridge, but something stopped her when she thought of it and she didn't even know what. And then, as though by miracle, Harry sensed something wrong when he called her repeatedly and no one answered the phone. She thought it was Drew, and she lay on the living room floor and sobbed, thinking of the time when they had made love there and he had proposed to her. And then suddenly there was a pounding on the door and she heard Harry's voice. She looked like a derelict when she opened it, standing there in her tear-stained face and bare feet, her skirt covered with lint from the rug, her sweater all askew.

'My God, what happened to you?' She looked as though she'd been drinking for a week, or had been beaten up, or as though something terrible had happened to her. Only the last was true. 'Tana?' She dissolved in tears as he looked at her, and he held her close to him as she hovered awkwardly over his chair, and then he sat her down on the couch and she told him her tale.

'It's all over now ... I'll never see him again ... .'

'You're better off.' Harry looked grim. 'You can't live like this. You've looked like shit for the past six months. It's just not fair to you.'

'I know ... but maybe if I'd waited ... I think eventually ... .' She felt weak and hysterical, and suddenly she had lost her resolve and Harry shouted at her.

'No! Stop that! He's never going to leave his wife if he hasn't by now. She came back to him seven months ago, damn it, Tan, and she's still there. If he wanted out, he'd have found the door by now. Don't kid yourself.'

'I have been for a year and a half.'

'That's how things go sometimes.' He tried to sound philosophical, but he wanted to kill the son-of-a-bitch who had done this to her. 'You just have to pick yourself up and go on.'

'Oh yeah, sure ... .' She started to cry again, forgetting who she was talking to, 'That's easy for you to say.'

He looked long and hard at her. 'Do you remember when you dragged me back to life by the teeth, and then into law school the same way? Remember me? Well, don't give me that shit, Tan. If I made it, so can you. You'll live through it.'

'I've never loved anyone like I loved him.' She whimpered horribly and it broke his heart as she looked at him, with those huge green eyes. She didn't look more than twelve years old and he wanted to make everything all right for her, but he couldn't make Drew's wife disappear, although he would have liked to do that for her. Anything for Tan, his best and dearest friend.

'Someone else will come along. Better than him.'

'I don't want someone else. I don't want anyone.' And Harry feared that more than anything.

And in the next year she set out to prove just that. She refused to see anyone except her colleagues at work. She went nowhere, saw no one, and when Christmas came, she even refused to see Averil and Harry. She had turned thirty-two alone, had spent her nights alone, would have eaten Thanksgiving turkey alone, if she'd bothered to eat any at all, which she didn't. She worked overtime and double time and golden time and all the time, sitting at her desk until ten and eleven o'clock at night, taking on more cases than she ever had before, and for literally a year, she had no fun at all. She rarely laughed, called no one, had no dates with anyone, and took weeks to answer Harry's calls.

'Congratulations.' He finally reached her in February. She had mourned Drew Lands for more than a year, and she had inadvertently learned through mutual friends that he and Eileen were still together and had just bought a beautiful new home in Beverley Hills. 'Okay, asshole.' Harry was tired of chasing her. 'How come you don't return my calls anymore?'

'I've been busy for the last few weeks. Don't you read the papers? I'm waiting for a verdict to come in.'

'I don't give a fuck about that, in case you're interested, and that doesn't account for the last thirteen months. You *never* call me anymore. I always call you. Is it my breath, my feet, or my IQ?' She laughed. Harry never changed.

'All of the above.'

'Asshole. Are you going to go on feeling sorry for yourself for the rest of your life? The guy wasn't worth it, Tan. And a whole year is ridiculous.'

'It had nothing to do with that.' But they both knew that wasn't true. It had everything to do with Drew Lands, and his not leaving his wife.

'That's new too. You never used to lie to me.'

'All right, all right. It's been easier not to see anybody.'

'Why? You ought to celebrate! You could have done what your mother did and sat there for fifteen years. Instead, you were smart enough to get the hell out. So what did you lose, Tan? Your virginity? Eighteen months? So what? Other women lose ten years over married men ... they lose their hearts, their sanity, their time, their lives. You got off lucky if you ask me.'

'Yeah.' Somewhere in her heart, she knew he was right, but it still didn't feel good yet. Maybe it never would. She still alternated between missing him and being angry at him. It wasn't the difference she would have like to feel, and she finally admitted that to Harry when she let him take her to lunch.

'That takes time, Tan. And a little water over the dam. You have to go out with some other people. Fill your head with other stuff, not just him. You can't just work all the time.' He smiled gently at her, he loved her so much, and he knew he always would. It wasn't like what he felt for his wife. She was more like a sister to him now. He remembered the tremendous crush he had had on her for years and he reminded her of that now. 'And I survived.'

'That wasn't the same thing. Shit, Drew had proposed marriage to me. He was the only man I'd ever even wanted to marry. Do you know that?'

'Yes, I do.' He knew her better than anyone. 'So, he's a jerk. We already know that. And you're a little slow. But you'll want to get married again. Someone else will come along.'

'That's all I need.' She looked revolted at the thought. 'I'm going to be thirty-three years old this year. Teen romance is not my style anymore, thanks.'

'Fine, then find some old fart who thinks you're cute, but don't sit around like this and waste your life.'

'It isn't exactly wasted, Harry.' She looked somberly at him. 'I have my work.'

'That's not enough. Christ, you're a pain in the ass.' He looked at her and shook his head, and invited her to a party they were giving the following week, but she never showed up in the end. And he had to go on a campaign to drag her out of her shell. It was as though she had been raped again. And then, to make matters worse, she lost a major case and got depressed about that. 'Okay,

okay, so you're not infallible., Give yourself a break, for chrissake. Get off the cross. I know it's Easter week, but one's enough. Can't you find something else to do except torment yourself? Why don't you come spend a weekend in Tahoe with us?' They had just rented a house, and Harry loved going up there with the kids. 'We can't go up for much longer anyway.'

'Why not?' She glanced at him as he paid the check, and he smiled at her. She had given him a hard time for the past few months, but she was starting to come out of it.

'I can't take Averil up much longer. She's pregnant again, you know.' For a minute, Tana actually looked shocked and he laughed at her, and then blushed. 'It's happened before after all ... I mean, it's not that remarkable ... .' But they both knew it was. And suddenly Tana grinned at him. It was as if life had come back into focus again, and suddenly Drew Lands was gone and she wanted to shout and sing. It was like having had a toothache for over a year, and discovering miraculously that the tooth was gone.

'Well, I'll be damned. Don't you two ever stop?'

'Nope. And after this, we'll go for four. I want another girl this time, but Ave wants a boy.' Tana was beaming at him, and she gave him a big hug as they left the restaurant.

'I'm going to be an aunt again.'

'That's the easy way, if you ask me. Not fair, Tan.'

'It suits me just fine.' One thing she knew she didn't want was children, no matter what man wandered into her life. She didn't have time for that, and she was too old now anyway. She had made that decision long ago; her baby was the law. And she had Harry's children to spoil when she wanted someone little to sit on her lap. They were both adorable, and she was happy for them that a third one was coming along. Averil always had a pretty easy time, and Harry was always so proud of himself, and he could certainly afford as many as they chose to have. Only her mother disapproved when she talked to her.

'That seems awfully unreasonable to me.' She was always opposed to every-thing these days; babies, trips, new jobs, new homes. It was as though she wanted to play out the rest of her life cautiously and thought everyone else should too. It was a sign of age which Tana recognized but her mother seemed too young for that. She had aged rapidly since she and Arthur had gotten married. Nothing had turned out quite right for her, and when she had gotten what she'd wanted for so long, it was not the same as it had once been. Arthur was sick and getting old.

But Tana was happy for Harry and Ave, and when the baby came on November 25th, Averil got her wish. It was a bouncing, squalling boy. They named him after his great grandfather, Andrew Harrison, and Tana smiled down at him in his mother's arms and felt tears come to her eyes. She hadn't had that reaction to the others before, but there was something so sweet and touching about the baby's innocence, his perfect pink flesh, the big round eyes, the tiny fingers so gently curled. Tana had never seen such perfection, and all of it so small. She and Harry looked at each other and exchanged a smile, thinking of how far they had come, and he looked so proud, one hand tightly holding his wife's, and the other gently touching his son.

Averil went home the day after Andrew was born, and made the Thanksgiving dinner herself, as she always did, practically refusing any help at all, as Tana stared at her, amazed at all she did, and did so well.

'It kind of makes you feel dumb, doesn't it?' She was nursing in the window seat looking out at the bay, and Tana looked at her as Harry grinned.

'Shit, Tan, you could do it too, if you wanted to.'

'Don't count on it. I can barely boil myself an egg, let alone give birth, and cook a turkey two days later for my family, making it seem as though I had nothing to do all week. You'd better hang on to her, Harry, and don't get her knocked up again.' She grinned at him, and she knew that they had never been happier. Averil just radiated happiness and so did he.

'I'll do my best. Will you come to the christening, by the way. Ave wants to do it on Christmas Day, if you're going to be here.'

'Where else would I be?' She laughed at him.

'What do I know? You might go home to New York. I was thinking of taking the kids to see Gstaad to see Dad, but now he says he's going to Tangiers with some friends, so that blows that.'

'You're breaking my heart.' She laughed at him. She hadn't seen Harrison in years, but Harry had said he was all right. He seemed the kind of man who would be handsome and healthy for all his life. It was a little startling to realize that he was in his early sixties now, sixty-three, to be exact, Harry reminded her, though he didn't look more than half of it, Harry had told her. It was odd to remember how much Harry had once hated him, but he didn't anymore. It was Tana who had changed all that, and Harry never forgot any of it. He wanted her to be godmother again, and she was touched by it.

'Don't you have any other friends? You're kids are going to be sick to death of me by the time they grow up.'

'Too bad for them. Jack Hawthorne is Andrew's godfather. At least you two will finally meet. He thinks you've been avoiding him.' In all the years of Harry's partnership with him, the two had never met. But Tana had no reason to meet him, although she was curious to now. And when they met at St. Mary the Virgin Church on Union Street on Christmas Day, he was almost as she had expected him to be. Tall, blond, handsome, he looked like an All-American football player in a college game, and yet he looked intelligent as well. He was tall and broad and had enormous hands, and he held the baby with a gentleness that startled her. He was talking to Harry outside afterwards and she smiled at him.

'You do that awfully well, Jack.'

'Thanks. I'm a little rusty, but I can still manage in a pinch.'

'Do you have children?' It was casual conversation outside the church. The only thing they could have talked about was law, or their mutual friend, but it was easier and more pleasant to talk about the new godchild that they shared.

'I have one. She's ten.'

'That seems incredible.' Ten seemed so old somehow ... of course Elizabeth had been thirteen, but Drew had been a lot older than this man. Or at least he looked that way. Tana knew Jack was about thirty-seven or eight, but he had a boyish air. And at the party at Averil and Harry's house later that day, he told funny stories and jokes, and had everyone laughing, including Tana, for most of the day. She smiled at Harry when she found him in the kitchen pouring someone another drink. 'No wonder you like him so much. He's a nice guy.'

'Jack?' Harry didn't look surprised. Other than Tana and Averil, Jack Hawthorne was his best friend, and they had worked well together for the past few years. They had established a comfortable practice, and they worked in the same way, not with Tana's burning drive, but with something a little more reasonable. And the two men were well matched. 'He's smart as hell, but he's very relaxed about it.'

'I noticed that.' At first he seemed very casual, almost indifferent to what was going on, but Tana had noticed rapidly that he was a lot sharper than he looked.

Eventually, at the end of the day, he offered her a ride home, and she accepted gratefully. She had left her own car outside the church in town. 'Well, I finally met the famous Assistant DA. They certainly like to write about you, don't they?' She was embarrassed by what he said but he seemed unconcerned.

'Only when they have nothing else to do.'

He smiled at her. He liked her modesty. He also liked the long shapely legs peeking out beneath the black velvet skirt she wore. It was a suit she had bought at I. Magnin just for her godchild's christening day. 'Harry is very proud of you, you know. I feel as though I know you myself. He talks about you all the time.'

'I'm just as bad. I don't have kids, so everyone has to listen to stories about Harry and when we went to school.'

'You two must have been hell on wheels back then.' He grinned at her and she laughed.

'More or less. We had a hell of a good time, at times. And some nasty run-ins now and then.' She smiled at the memories and then smiled at Jack. 'I must be getting old, all this nostalgia ... .'

'It's that time of year.'

'It is, isn't it? Christmas always does that to me.'

'Me too.' She wondered where his daughter was, if that was part of the nostalgia for him. 'You're from New York, aren't you?' She nodded her head. That seemed light years away too.

'And you?'

'I'm from the Midwest. Detroit, to be exact. A lovely place.' He smiled and they both laughed again. He was easy to be with, and it seemed harmless to her when he offered to take her out for drinks. But everything seemed so empty when they looked around and it was depressing to go to a bar on Christmas night, she wound up inviting him back to her place instead, and he was perfectly agreeable to her. So much so he was almost innocuous, and she didn't even recognize him at first when she ran into him at City Hall the next week. He was one of those tall, blond, handsome men who could have been almost anyone, from a college pal, to someone's husband or brother or boyfriend and then suddenly she realized who he was and blushed with embarrassment.

'I'm sorry, Jack ... I was distracted ... .'

'You have a right to be.' He smiled at her, and she was amused at how impressed he was by her job. Harry must have been lying to him again. She knew he exaggerated a lot about her, about the rapists she had fought off in holding cells, the judo holds she knew, the cases she cracked herself without investigators' help.

'. . . Why do you lie like that?' She had challenged him more than once but he felt no remorse.

'Some of it's true anyway.'

'The hell it is. I ran into one of your friends last week who thought I had been knifed by a coke dealer in the holding cell. For chrissake, Harry, knock it off.'

She thought of it now and assumed he had been at it again as she smiled at Jack. 'Actually, things are pretty quiet right now. How 'bout you?'

'Not bad. We have a few good cases. Harry and Ave went up to Tahoe for a few weeks, so I'm holding the fort on my own.'

'He's such a hardworking type.' They both laughed and he looked at her hestitantly. He had been dying to call her for a week and he hadn't dared.

'You wouldn't have time for lunch, would you?' Oddly enough, for once she did. He was ecstatic when she said yes, and they went to the Bijou, a small French restaurant on Polk, which was more pretentious than good, but it was pleasant chatting with Harry's friend for an hour or so. She had heard about him for so many years, and between her heavy caseload and her turmoil over Drew Lands they'd never met.

'It's ridiculous, you know. Harry should have gotten us together years ago.'

Jack smiled. 'I think he tried.' He didn't say anything that indicated that he knew about Drew, but Tana could talk about it now.

'I was being difficult for a while.' She smiled.

'And now?' He looked at her with the same gentle look he had used on their godchild.

'I'm back to my old rotten self again.'

'That's good.'

'Actually, Harry saved my life this time.'

'I know he was worried about you for a while.'

She sighed. 'I made an ass of myself . . . I guess we all have to sometime.'

'I sure did.' He smiled at her. 'I got my kid sister's best friend pregnant in Detroit ten years ago when I went home over the holidays. I don't know what happened to me, except I must have gone nuts or something. She was this pretty little redhead . . . twenty-one years old . . . and bang, the next thing I knew I was getting married. She hated it out here, she cried all the time. Poor little Barb had colic for the first six months of her life, and a year later, Kate went back again and it was all over. I now have an ex-wife and a daughter in Detroit, and I don't know anything more about them than I did then. It was the craziest thing I ever did, and I'm not about to do it again!' He looked extremely determined as he said the words, and it was easy to see that he meant every bit of it. 'I've never drunk straight rum either since then.' He grinned ruefully and Tana laughed.

'At least you have something to show for it.' It was more than she could say, not that she would have wanted Drew's child, even if he hadn't had the vasectomy. 'Do you see your daughter sometimes?'

'She comes out once a year for a month,' he sighed with a careful smile. 'It's a little difficult to build a relationship based on that!' He had always thought it was unfair to her, but what else could he do? He couldn't ignore her now. 'We're really strangers to each other. I'm the oddball who sends her birthdays cards every year and takes her to baseball games when she's here. I don't know what else to do with her. Ave was pretty good about keeping an eye on her in the daytime last year. And they lent me the house in Tahoe for a week. She loved that,' he smiled at Tana, 'and so did I. It's awkward making friends with a ten-year-old child.'

'I'll bet it is. The relationship ... the man I was involved with had two of them, and it was odd for me. I don't have children of my own, and it wasn't like Harry's kids, suddenly here were these two big people staring at me. It felt awfully strange.'

'Did you get attached to them?' He seemed intrigued by her and she was surprised at how easy it was to talk to him.

'Not really. There wasn't time. They lived in the East,' she remembered the rest of it, 'for a while.'

He nodded, smiling at her. 'You've certainly managed to keep your life simpler than the rest of us.' He laughed softly then. 'I guess you don't drink rum.'

She laughed too. 'Usually not, but I've managed to do a fair amount of damage to myself in other ways. I just don't have any kids to show for it.'

'Are you sorry about that?'

'Nope.' It had taken thirty-three and a half years to say it honestly. 'There are some things in this life that aren't for me, and children are one of them. Godmother is more my style.'

'I probably should have stuck to that myself, for Barb's sake, if no one else's. At least her mother is remarried now, so she has a real father figure to relate to for the eleven months I'm not around.'

'Doesn't that bother you?' She wondered if he felt possessive about the child. Drew had been very much so about his, especially Elizabeth.

But Jack shook his head. 'I hardly know the kid. That's an awful thing to say, but it's true. Every year I get to know her again, and she leaves and when she comes back she's grown up by a year and changed all over again. It's kind of a fruitless venture, but maybe it does something for her. I don't know. I owe her that much. And I suspect that in a few years she'll tell me to go to hell, she has a boyfriend in Detroit and she's not coming out this year.'

'Maybe she'll bring him.' They both laughed.

'God help me. That's all I need. I feel the way you do, there are some things in this life I never want inflicted on me ... malaria ... typhoid ... marriage ... kids ....' She laughed at his honesty, it was certainly not a popular view or one that one could admit to most of the time, but he felt he could with her, and she with him.

'I agree with you. I really think it's impossible to do what you do well and give enough to relationships like that.'

'That sounds noble, my friend, but we both know that that has nothing to do with it. Honestly? I'm scared stiff, all I need is another Kate out from Detroit and crying all night because she has no friends out here ... or some totally dependent woman with nothing to do all day except nag me at night, or decide after two years of marriage that half of the business Harry and I built is hers. He and I see too much of that as it is, and I just don't want any part of it.' He smiled at her. 'And what are you scared of, my dear? Chillblains, childbirth? Giving up your career? Competition from a man?' He was surprisingly astute and she smiled appreciatively at him.

'Touché. All the above. Maybe I'm afraid of jeopardizing what I've build, of getting hurt ... I don't know. I think I had doubts about marriage years ago, although I didn't know it then. It's all my mother ever wanted for me, and I always wanted to say 'but wait ... not yet ... I've got all these other things to do first.' It's like volunteering to have your head cut off, there's never really a good time.' He laughed, and she remembered Drew proposing to her in front of the fire one night, and then she forced it from her with a flash of pain. Most of the time the memories of him didn't hurt much now, but a few still did. And that one most of all, maybe because she felt he had made a fool of her. She had been willing to make an exception for him, she had accepted the proposal and then he had gone back to Eileen ... Jack was watching her as she frowned.

'No one is worth looking that sad for, Tana.'

She smiled at him. 'Old, old memories.'

'Forget them, then. They won't hurt you anymore.'

There was something wonderfully easy and wise about the man, and she began going out with him almost without thinking of it. A movie, an early dinner, a walk on Union Street, a football game. He came and went, and became her friend, and it wasn't even remarkable when they finally went to bed with each other late that spring. They had known each other for five months by then, and it wasn't earth shattering, but it was comfortable. He was easy to be around, intelligent, and he had a wonderful understanding of what she did, a powerful respect for her job, they even shared a common best friend, and by summertime when his daughter came out, even that was comfortable. She was a sweet eleven-year-old child with big eyes and hands and feet and bright red hair, like an Irish Setter puppy. They took her to Stinson Beach a few times, went on picnics with her. Tana didn't have much time – she was trying a big case just then – but it was all very pleasant, and they went up to Harry's place where Harry eyed them carefully, curious as to whether it was serious with them. But Averil didn't think it was and she was usually right. There was no fire, no passion, no intensity, but also no pain. It was comfortable, intelligent, amusing at times, and extremely satisfying in bed. And at the end of a year of going out with him, Tana could well imagine herself going out with Jack for the rest of her life. It was one of these relationships one saw between two people who had never married, and never wanted to, much to the chagrin of all their friends who had been in and out of divorce courts for years; one saw people like that eating in restaurants on Saturday nights, going on holidays attending Christmas parties and gala events, and enjoying each other's company and sooner or later they'd wind up in bed, and the next day the other one would go home to his or her own place, to find the towels exactly the way they wanted them, the bed undisturbed, the coffee pot in perfect readiness for their needs. It was so perfect for both of them that way, but they drove Harry nuts and that amused them too.

'I mean, look at you both, you're so goddamn complacent I could cry.' The three of them were having lunch, and neither Tana nor Jack looked concerned.

She looked up at Jack with a smile. 'Hand him a handkerchief, sweetheart.'

'Nah, let him use his sleeve. He always does.'

'Don't you have any decency? What's wrong with you?'

They exchanged a bovine glance. 'Just decadent, I guess.'

'Don't you want kids?'

'Haven't you ever heard of birth control?' Jack looked at him and Harry looked as though he wanted to scream as Tana laughed.

'Give it up, kid. You aren't gonna win this one with us. We're happy like this.'

'You've been dating for a year. What the hell does that mean to you both?'

'That we have a lot of stamina. I now know that he gets homicidal if anyone touches the sports section on Sundays and he hates classical music.'

'And that's it? How can you be so insensitive?'

'It comes naturally.' She smiled sweetly at her friend and Jack grinned at her.

'Face it, Harry, you're outnumbered, outclassed, outdone.' But when Tana turned thirty-five six months later, they surprised Harry after all.

'You're getting *married*?' Harry barely dared to breathe the words to Jack when he told him they were looking for a house, but Jack laughed at him.

'Hell no, you don't know your friend Tan if you think there's even a chance of that. We're thinking about living together.'

Harry spun his wheelchair around, glaring at Jack. 'That's the most disgusting thing I've ever heard. I won't let you do that to her.'

Jack roared. 'It was her idea, and besides – you and Ave did it.' His daughter had just gone home, and it had gotten very complicated going back and forth from his house to hers for a month. 'Her place is too small for both of us, and so is mine. And I'd really like to live in Marin. Tana says she would too.'

Harry looked miserable. He wanted a happy ending, rice, rose petals, babies, and neither of them was cooperating with him. 'Do you realize how complicated it is to invest in real estate if you're not married?'

'Of course I do, and so does she. That's why we'll probably rent.' And it was exactly what they did. They found the house they wanted with an overwhelming view, in Tiburon. It had four bedrooms, and was dirt cheap compared to what it might have cost, and it gave them each an office, a bedroom for them, and a bedroom for Barb when she came to town from Detroit, or if they had guests. It had a lovely sun deck, a porch, a hot tub, which looked out at the view, and neither of them had ever been happier. Harry and Averil came to check it out with the kids, and they had to admit that the setting was beautiful but it still wasn't what Harry had hoped for her, but she only laughed at him. And, worst of all, Jack shared all of her views. He had no intention of getting hooked into marriage again, by anyone. He was thirty-eight years old, and his little escapade in Detroit twelve years before had cost him dearly.

Jack and Tana did Christmas dinner that year, and it was beautiful, with the bay below, and the city shimmering in the distance. 'It's like a dream, isn't it, sweetheart?' Jack whispered to her after everyone went home. They had exactly the life that suited them, and she had even finally given her own apartment up in town. She had hung onto it for a while to play it safe, but in the end, she had let it go. She was safe with him, and he took good care of her. When she had appendicitis that year, he took two weeks off from work to take care of her. When she turned thirty-six, he gave her a party in the Trafalgar Room at Trader Vic's for eighty-seven of her closest friends and the following year, he surprised her with a cruise in Greece. She came home rested and brown, and happier than ever with their life. There was never any talk of marriage between the two, although once in a while they talked about buying the house in which they lived, but Tana wasn't even sure about that, and secretly Jack was wary of it too. Neither of them wanted to rock the boat that had sailed along so comfortably for so long. They had lived together for almost two years and it was perfect for them both. Until October after the cruise to Greece. Tana had a big case coming up, and she had stayed up almost all night going over her notes and the files, and she'd fallen asleep at her desk, looking out over the bay in Tiburon. The phone woke her before Jack did with a cup of tea, and she stared at him as she picked it up.

'Huh?' She looked blank and Jack grinned at her. She was a mess when she stayed up all night like that, and as though hearing his thoughts, she turned her eyes toward him, and then suddenly he saw them open wide and stare at him. 'What? Are you crazy? I'm *not* ... oh God. I'll be there in an hour.' She put down the phone and stared at him as he set down the cup of tea with a worried frown.

'Something wrong?' It couldn't be anything back home if she'd promised to be there in an hour, it had to be work ... and it wasn't for him. 'What happened, Tan?' She was still staring at him.

'I don't know ... I have to talk to Frye.'

'The district attorney?'

'No. God. Who the hell do you think?'

'Well, what are you getting so excited about?' He still didn't understand. But neither did she. She had done a fantastic job. It just didn't make sense. She'd been there for years ... there were tears iner her eyes when she looked at Jack and stood up at her desk, spilling the tea across her files, but she didn't even care now.

'He said I'm being fired.' She started to cry and sat down again as he stared at her.

'That can't be, Tan.'

'That's what I said ... the DA's office is my whole life .....' And the saddest thing of all was that they both knew it was true.

Chapter 17

Tana showered, dressed and drove into the city within the hour, her face set, eyes grim. It was obvious that it was an emergency. She looked as though someone had died. Jack offered to go with her, but she knew he had his own problems that day, and Harry had been out of the office a lot recently, so everything rested on him

'Are you sure you don't want me to drive you in, Tan? I don't want you to have an accident.' She kissed him vaguely on the lips and shook her head. It was so odd. They had lived together for so long, but they were almost more friends than anything else. He was someone to talk to at night, as she worked on her strategy. He understood her life, her quirks, he was content with the life they shared and he wanted relatively little from her, it seemed. Harry claimed it was unnatural, and it was certainly different from what he and Averil shared. But she felt Jack's concern now as she started her car and he watched her leave. He still couldn't understand what had happened to her, and neither could she. She walked into her office, feeling numb, half an hour later, and without even knocking walked into the office of the DA. She couldn't hold the tears back anymore, and they rolled down her face as she looked at him.

'What the hell did I do to deserve this?' She looked stricken and he felt instant remorse at what he'd done. He had just thought it would be fun to give her the news in a roundabout way, but he never realized she'd be so heart-broken. It made him all the sorrier to lose her now. But he had been sorry anyway.

'You're too good at your job, Tan. Stop crying and sit down.' He smiled at her and she felt even more confused.

'So you're firing me?' She was still on her feet, staring at him.

'I didn't say that. I said you were out of a job.' She sat down with a thump.

'Well, what the hell does that mean?' She reached into her handbag and pulled out a handkerchief and blew her nose. She was unashamed of how she felt. She loved her job, and she had from the first day. She'd been in the DA's office for twelve years. That was a lifetime to give up now, and she would have preferred to give up anything but that. Anything. The district attorney felt sorry for her then, and he came around his desk to put an arm around her.

'Come on, Tan, don't take it so hard. We're going to miss you, too, you know.' A fresh burst of tears escaped from her and he smiled. It brought tears to his eyes too. She would be leaving soon, if she accepted it. And she had suffered long enough. He forced her to sit down, looked her square in the eye. 'You're being offered a seat on the bench, sweetheart. Judge Roberts. How does that sound to you?'

'I am?' She stared at him, unable to absorb it all. 'I am? I'm not being fired?' She started to cry all over again, and she blew her nose again, suddenly laughing at the same time. I'm not ... you're kidding me ....'

'I wish I were.' But he looked delighted for her and she suddenly gave a small scream, realizing what he'd done to her.

'Oh, you son-of-a-bitch ... I thought you were firing me!' He laughed.

'I apologize. I just thought I'd create a little excitement in your life.'

'Shit.' She looked at him in disbelief and blew her nose again but she was too stunned at what he was telling her to even be angry at him. 'My God ... how did that happen?'

'I've seen it coming for a long time, Tan. I knew it would happen eventually. I just didn't know when. And I'll lay you odds you're in the Superior Court by this time next year. You're perfect for it after your track record here.'

'Oh, Larry ... my God ... an appointment to the bench ....' The words were almost beyond her ken. 'I just can't believe it.' She looked up at him. 'I'm thirty-seven years old, and I never even thought of that.'

'Well, thank God someone did.' He held out a hand and shook hers as she beamed. 'Congratulations, Tan, you deserve every bit of it. They want to induct you in three weeks.'

'So soon? What about my work ... Christ, I have a case that goes to trial on the twenty-third ....' She knit her brows and he laughed at her and waved a hand magnanimously.

'Forget it, Tan. Why don't you take some time off, and get ready for the new job? Just dump it all on someone else's desk for a change. Use this week to wrap and then get yourself sorted out at home.'

'What do I have to do?' She still looked stunned and he smiled at her. 'Shop for robes?'

'No.' He laughed. 'But I think you may have some house hunting to do. Do you still live in Marin?' He knew she'd lived with someone for the past couple of years, but he wasn't sure if she'd kept her own place in town or not. She nodded at him. 'You've got to have a place in town, Tan.'

'How come?'

'It's a condition of being a San Francisco judge. You can keep the other place, but your main residence has to be here.'

'Do I really have to stick to that?' She looked upset.

'Pretty much. During the week anyway.'

'Christ.' She stared into space for a minute, thinking of Jack. Suddenly her whole life had turned upside down. 'I'll have to do something about that.'

'You've got plenty to do in the next few weeks, and first of all you have to respond.' He put on an official voice. 'Tana Roberts, do you accept the seat on the bench that has been offered you, to serve as a municipal court judge in the city and county of San Francisco?'

She looked at him in awe. 'I do.'

He stood up and smiled at her, happy at the good fortune that had befallen

her so deservedly. 'Good luck, Tan. We'll miss you here.' Tears sprang to her
eyes again and she was still in shock when she went back to her own desk and
sat down. There were a thousand things she had to do. Empty her desk, look
over her caseload, brief someone else about the cases she was passing on, call
Harry, tell Jack ... Jack ... ! She suddenly looked at her watch and grabbed
the phone. The secretary said he was in a meeting but Tana told her to get him
anyway.

'Hi babe, you okay?'

'Yes.' She sounded breathless on the phone. She didn't know where to start.
'You won't believe what happened, Jack.'

'I wondered what the hell was going on when they called you at home. What
is it, Tan?'

She took a deep breath. 'They just offered me a seat on the bench.' There was
total silence at the other end.

'At your age?'

'Isn't that incredible?' She was beaming now. 'I mean, would you believe ...
I never thought ....'

'I'm happy for you, Tan.' He sounded quiet, but pleased, and then she
remembered what the DA had said. She had to find a place in town, but she
didn't want to tell him that on the phone.

'Thank you, sweetheart. I'm still in shock. Is Harry there?'

'No, he's not in today.'

'He's sure out a lot lately, isn't he? What's up?'

'I think he's in Tahoe with Ave and the kids for a long weekend. You can call
him there.'

'I'll wait till he gets back. I want to see his face.' But the face she didn't want
to see was Jack's when she told him she had to move out of Marin.

'I wondered about that after you called.' He looked sad when she told him
that night. He was obviously upset and so was she, but she was terribly excited
too. She had even called her mother, and Jean had been stunned. 'My daughter, a judge?' She had been thrilled for Tana. Maybe things did work out in the
end, and she had met Jack once and he seemed nice to her. She hoped they
would get married eventually, even if Tana was too old for children now. But
as a judge, maybe that didn't matter as much. Even Arthur had been thrilled
for her. Jean had explained it to him several times.

Tana looked at Jack now. 'How do you feel about living in town during the
week?'

'Not great.' He was honest with her. 'It's so damn comfortable for us here.'

'I thought I'd look for something small that we don't have to worry about.
An apartment, a condo, a studio, even ....' As though she could pretend it
wasn't happening but he shook his head.

'We'd go nuts after all the room we're used to here.' For two years they had
lived like kings, with a huge master bedroom, offices for each of them, a living
room, dining room, quest room for Barb, sweeping view of the bay. A studio
would feel like a jail cell after that.

'Well, I've got to do something, Jack, and I only have three weeks.' She
looked faintly annoyed at him, he wasn't making it easier for her, and she

wondered if the appointment bothered him. It would be natural that it would, at least at first, but she hardly had time to think of that in the next few weeks. She divided her caseload up, emptied her desk, and ran around looking at every condo available until the real estate agent called halfway into the second week. She had something 'very special' she wanted Tana to see, in Pacific Heights.

'It's not exactly what you had in mind, but it's worth a look.' And when she went, it was more than that. It was a dollhouse that took her breath away, a tiny ginger-bread jewel, painted beige with dollops of cinnamon and cream. It was absolutely impeccable, with inlaid floors, marble fireplaces in just about every room, huge closets, perfect lighting, double French doors, and a view of the bay. Tana would never have thought of looking for something like it, but now that she was here, there was no way she could resist.

'How much is the rent?' She knew it would be ferocious. The place looked like something out of a magazine.

'It's not for rent.' The agent smiled at her. 'It's for sale.' She told her the price, and Tana was amazed at how reasonable it was. It wasn't cheap, but it wouldn't have destroyed her savings at one blow, and at the price that was being asked, it was actually a good investment for her. It was irresistible in every possible way, and it was perfect for her. One large bedroom on the second floor, a dressing room with mirrored walls, a tiny den with a brick fireplace, and downstairs, one large, beautiful living room, and a tiny country kitchen that gave out onto a patio framed with trees. She signed away her life, put the deposit down, and turned up in Jack's office, looking nervous about what she'd done. She knew it wasn't a mistake, but still ... it was such an independent thing to do, so solitary, so grown up ... and she hadn't asked him.

'Good lord, who died?' He stepped into the anteroom and saw her face, as she laughed nervously. 'That's better.' He kissed her neck. 'You practicing to be a judge? You're going to scare people half to death running around with a face like that.'

'I just did a crazy thing.' The words tumbled out and he smiled. He had had a rough day, and it wasn't even two o'clock yet.

'So what else is new? Come on in and tell me about it.' Tana saw that Harry's door was closed, and she didn't knock. She passed right into Jack's large, pleasant room in the Victorian they'd bought five years before. That had been a good investment for them, maybe it would help make him understand what she'd done. He smiled at her from across his desk. 'So what'd you do?'

'I think I just bought a house.' She looked like a frightened kid and he laughed at her.

'You think you did. I see. And what makes you think that?' He sounded as he always did, but his eyes were different now and she wondered why.

'Actually, I signed the papers ... oh Jack ... I hope I did the right thing!' Do you like it?'

'I'm in love with it.' He looked surprised, neither of them had wanted to own a house before. They had talked about it several times. They had no need of permanance, and he hadn't changed his mind. But apparently she had and he wondered why. A lot seemed to have changed in the last ten days, mostly for her. Nothing had changed for him.

'Won't that be a lot of trouble for you, Tan? Keeping it up, worrying about a leaky roof, and all that stuff we talked about before and didn't want.'

'I don't know ... I guess ....' She looked nervously at him. It was time to ask. 'You'll be there too, won't you?' Her voice was frightened and soft and he smiled at her. She was at once so vulnerable and soft, and yet so incredibly powerful as well. He loved that about her and knew he always would. It was what Harry loved in her too, that and her loyalty, her fierce heart, bright mind. She was such a lovely girl, judge or not. She looked like a teenager sitting there, watching him.

'Is there room in it for me?' His voice sounded tentative and she nodded vehemently, and her hair swung wild. She had cut it straight to her shoulders only weeks before she got the news, and it looked very elegant and sleek, hanging in a smooth blonde sheet from crown to nape.

'Of course there is.' But he wasn't sure he agreed when he saw the place that night. He agreed that the place was beautiful, but it was awfully feminine to his eyes. 'How can you say a thing like that? There's nothing here but walls and floors.'

'I don't know. It just feels that way, maybe because I know it's your house.' He turned to her and he looked sad all at once. 'I'm sorry, Tan, its beautiful ... I don't mean to rain on your parade.'

'It's all right. I'll make it comfortable for both of us. I promise you.' He took her to dinner that night and they talked for hours, about her new job, the 'judges' school' she would have to attend in Oakland for three weeks, holed up in a hotel with other recent appointees. Everything seemed suddenly exciting and new, and she hadn't felt that way in years.

'It's like starting life all over again, isn't it?' Her eyes danced as she looked at him and he smiled at her.

'I guess.' They went home after that and made love, and nothing seemed to have changed in important ways. She spent the next week shopping for furniture for her new house, closing the deal, and buying a new dress for her induction ceremony. She had even asked her mother to come out, but Arthur wasn't well enough and Jean didn't want to leave him alone. But Harry would be there, and Averil, and Jack, and all the friends and acquaintances she had collected over the years. In the end, there were two hundred people at the ceremony, and Harry gave her a reception afterwards at Trader Vic's. It was the most festive occasion she had ever been to, and she laughed as she kissed Jack halfway through the afternoon.

'It's kind of like getting married, isn't it?' He laughed back at her and they exchanged a look which said they both understood.

'Better than that, thank God.' They laughed again and he danced with her, and they were both a little drunk when they went home that night, and the following week, she started 'judges' school'.

She stayed at the hotel, in the room they had given her, and she had planned to spend weekends in Tiburon with Jack, but there was always something to do at her new house, a painting she wanted to hang up, lights she had to fix, a couch that had arrived, a gardener she wanted to interview, and for the first two weeks she slept in town when she wasn't at 'judges' school'.

'Why don't you come sleep here with me?' There was a plaintive note in her voice and she sounded irritable. He hadn't seen her in days but that was par for the course these days. She had too much else to do.

'I've got too much work to do.' He sounded curt.

'You can bring it here, sweetheart. I'll make some soup and a salad, you can use my den.' He noticed the possessive term, and like everything else these days, it rankled him, but he had a lot on his mind just then.

'Do you know what it's like to drag all your work over to someone else's house?'

'I'm not someone else. I'm me. And you live here too.'

'Since when?' She was hurt by his tone and she backed off, and even Thanksgiving was strained, spent with Harry and Averil and the kids.

'How's the new house, Tan?' Harry was happy about everything that had happened to her, but she noticed that he looked tired and drawn, and Averil looked strained too. It was a difficult day for everyone and even the children whined more than usual, and Jack and Tana's godchild cried most of the day. She sighed as they drove back to town at last, and Jack visibly unwound in the silence in the car.

'Doesn't it make you glad you don't have kids?' He looked at her as he spoke and she smiled at him.

'Days like this do, but when they're all dressed up and cute, or sound asleep, and you watch Harry look at Ave ... sometimes I think it would be sweet to be like that ....' She sighed then and glanced at him. 'I don't think I could stand it though.'

'You'd look cute on the bench, with a string of kids.' He said it sarcastically and she laughed. He had been sharp with her a lot recently and she noticed that he was driving her into town and not to Tiburon, and she looked at him, surprised.

'Aren't we going home, sweetheart?'

'Sure ... I thought you wanted to go back to your place ....'

'I don't mind ... I ....' She took a deep breath. It had to be said eventually. 'You're mad at me for buying the house, aren't you?'

He shrugged and drove on, keeping his eyes on the other cars. 'I guess it was something you had to do. I just didn't think you'd do something like that.'

'All I did was buy a little house because I had to have a place in town.'

'I just didn't think you wanted to *own* something, Tan.'

'What difference does it make if I own or rent? It's a good investment this way. We've talked about doing something like that.'

'Yeah, and we decided not to. Why do you have to get yourself locked into something permanent?' The thought of that almost gave him hives. He was happy renting where they were in Tiburon. 'You never thought like that before.'

'Things change sometimes. This just made sense at the time, and I fell in love with it.'

'I know you did. Maybe that's what bothers me. It's so 'yours', not ours.'

'Would you rather have bought something with me?' But she knew him better than that and he shook his head.

'That would just complicate our lives. You know that.'

'You can't keep things simple all the time. And as those things go, I think we've done damn well. We're the most unencumbered people I know.' And they had done it purposely. Nothing was permanent, written in stone. Their whole life could be unwound in a matter of hours, or so they thought, at least it was what they had told themselves for two years.

Tana went on, 'Hell, I used to have an apartment in town. What's the big deal?' But it wasn't the house, it was her job, she had begun to suspect it weeks before. It bothered him, the fuss, the press, he had tolerated it before because she was only an assistant DA, but suddenly she was a judge ... Your Honor ... Judge Roberts, she had noticed the look on his face every time someone said the words to her. 'You know, it really isn't fair of you to take it out on me, Jack. I can't help it. Something wonderful happened and now we have to learn to live with it. It could have happened to you too. The shoe could be on the other foot, you know.'

'I think I'd have handled it differently.'

'How?' She was instantly hurt by his words.

'Actually,' he looked at her accusingly, the anger between them finally had words put to it, like a symphony with a chorale, but it was a relief to get it out. 'I think I'd have turned it down. It's a goddamn pompous thing to do.'

'Pompous? What an awful thing to say. Do you think I'm pompous for accepting the seat they offered me?'

'Depends on how you handle it.' He answered cryptically.

'Well?'

They stopped at a light and he turned to look at her, and then suddenly looked away. 'Look ... never mind ... I just don't like the changes it's made for us. I don't like you living in town, I don't like your goddamn house, I don't like any of it.'

'So you're going to punish me, is that it? Christ, I'm doing my best to handle it gracefully, give me a chance. Let me figure it out. It's a big change for me too, you know.'

'You'd never know it to look at you. You look happy as can be.'

'Well, I am happy.' She was honest with him. 'It's wonderful and flattering and interesting, and I'm having fun with my career. It's very exciting for me, but it's also scary and new, and I don't quite know how to handle it and I don't want it to hurt you ....'

'Never mind that ....

'What do you mean, never mind? I love you, Jack. I don't want this to destroy us.'

'Then it won't.' He shrugged and drove on, but neither of them was convinced, and he remained impossible for the next few weeks. She made a point of spending the night in Tiburon whenever she could, and she cajoled him constantly, but he was angry at her, and the Christmas they spent at her house was grim. He made it clear that he hated everything about her house, and he left at eight o'clock the next day, claiming he had things to do. He made life difficult for her for the next few months, and in spite of it, she enjoyed her job. The only thing she didn't like were the long hours she kept. She stayed in her chambers until midnight sometimes, but she had so much to learn, so many points of law to read and refer to for each case. So much depended on her that she became blind to almost all else, so much so that she didn't see how unwell Harry looked, never realized how seldom he went to work anymore, and it was late April before Jack turned to her and screamed.

'What are you, blind? He's dying, for God's sake. He has been for the last six months, Tan. Don't you give a shit about anyone else anymore?' His words cut her to the quick and she gaped at him in horror.

'That's not true ... he can't be ....' But suddenly the pale face, the ghostly eyes, all of it suddenly made sense. But why hadn't he told her? Why? She looked up at Jack accusingly. 'Why didn't you say something?'

'You wouldn't have heard. You're so fucking wrapped up in how important you are these days, you don't see anything that goes on.' They were bitter accusations, angry words, and without saying a word she left Tiburon that night and drove home to her own house, called Harry on the phone, and before she could say anything, she began to cry.

'What's the matter, Tan?' He sounded tired, and she felt as though her heart were going to break.

'I can't ... I ... oh God, Harry ....' All the pressures of the past months suddenly began to pile up on her, Jack's anger, and what he had told her that night about Harry being ill. She couldn't believe he was dying, but when she saw him the next day for lunch, he looked at her quietly and told her it was true. She felt her breath catch as though on a sharp nail and she stared at him. 'But that can't be true ... that's not fair ....' She sat there and sobbed like a little child, unable to comfort him, desolate, in too much pain herself to help anyone, and he wheeled to where she sat and put his arms around her. There were tears in his eyes too, but he was strangely calm. He had known for almost a year, and they had told him that a long time ago. His wounds could cut his life short and they were. He was suffering from hydronephrosis, which was devouring him by degrees as he headed towards kidney failure. They had tried everything they could, but his body was just quietly giving up. She looked at him with terror in her eyes. 'I can't live without you.'

'Yes, you can.' He was more worried about Averil and the kids. He knew Tana would survive. She had saved him. She would never give up. 'I want you to do something for me. I want you to make sure Ave is all right. The kids are all set, and she has everything she'll need, but she's not like you, Tan ... she's always been so dependent on me.'

She stared at him. 'Does your father know?'

He shook his head. 'No one does, except Jack and Ave, and now you.' He was angry that Jack had said something to her and especially in anger, but he wanted a promise from her now. 'You promise you'll keep an eye on her?'

'Of course I will.' It was hideous, he was talking as though he were planning to leave on a trip. She looked at him and twenty years of love raced before her eyes ... the dance where they had met ... the years at Harvard and BU ... coming West ... Vietnam ... the hospital ... law school ... the apartment they had shared ... the night his first child was born ... it was incredible, impossible. His life wasn't over yet, it couldn't be. She needed him too much.

But then she remembered the spate of bladder infections and she knew suddenly where all this would lead – he was dying. She began to cry again and he held on to her, and then she looked at him and sobbed. 'Why . . . ? It's not fair.'

'Damn little in life is.' He smiled at her, a small, gray, wintry smile. He didn't care so much for himself as he did for his wife and kids. He had been worried sick about them for months, and he was trying to teach Averil to handle everything herself, to no avail. She was totally hysterical, and she refused to learn anything, as though that way she could keep it from happening, but nothing would. He was getting weaker by the day, and he knew it himself. He only came in to the office now once or twice a week; it was why he was never there when she went in to see Jack from time to time, and she talked to him about that now.

'He's beginning to hate me now.' She looked so bleak that it frightened him. He had never seen her like that. These were difficult times for all of them. He still couldn't believe he was going to die, but he knew he would. It was like stuffing running out of a rag doll, he felt as though he were slowly disappearing until he would be no more one day. Only that. They would wake up and he would be gone. Quietly. Not with the squall and pushes and the screams with which one comes into the world, but with a tear and a sigh and a breath of air as one passes on into the next life, if there even was such a thing. He didn't even know that anymore, and he wasn't sure he cared. He was too worried about the people he was leaving behind, his partner, his wife, his children, his friends. They all seemed to be resting on him and it was exhausting for him. But in some ways it also kept him alive, like right now with Tana. He felt he had something to share with her, before he went. Something important for her. He wanted her to change her life before it was too late. And he had said the same thing to Jack, but he didn't want to hear.

'He doesn't hate you, Tan. Look, the job is threatening to him. Besides, he's been upset about me for the past few months.'

'He could have said something at least.'

'I made him swear he wouldn't, you can't blame that on him. And as for the rest, you're an important woman now, Tan. Your job is more important than his. That's just the way things are. It's difficult for both of you, and he'll have to adjust to it.'

'Tell him that.'

'I have.'

'He punishes me for what's happened. He hates my house, he's not the same man.'

'Yes he is.' Too much so for Harry's taste. He was still devoted to the same ridiculous things; staying unattached, a total lack of commitment or permanence. It was an empty life, and Harry had told him he was full of shit, but Jack only shrugged. He liked the way he lived, or at least he had until Tana's new job came along. That was giving him a major pain in the ass, and he made no bones about it to Harry. 'Maybe he's jealous of you. That's not attractive, but it's possible, and he's human after all.'

'So when will he grow up? Or do I have to resign?' It was a relief talking about normal things, as though the nightmare weren't happening, as though she could make it stop by talking about something else with him. Like the old days ... they had been so sweet ... tears filled her eyes as she thought of them ...

'Of course you don't have to resign. Just give him time.' And then he looked at Tana, with something else on his mind. 'I want to say something to you, Tan. Two things.' He looked at her so intensely it was as though his whole body turned to flame, she could feel the strength of his words boring into her soul. 'I don't know from one day to the next what tomorrow will bring, if I'll be there ... if ... I have two things to say to you, and it's all I have to leave you, my friend. Listen well. The first is thank you for what you did for me. The last sixteen years of my life have been a gift from you, not from my doctor, or anyone else, but from you. You forced me to live again, to go on ... if it weren't for you I'd never have met Averil, or have had the kids ....' There were tears in his eyes now, too, and they rolled slowly down his cheeks. Tana was grateful that they had met in her chambers for lunch. They had needed to be alone. 'And that brings me to the second thing. You're cheating yourself, Tan. You don't know what you're missing, and you won't know till you're there. You're depriving yourself of marriage, commitment, real love ... not borrowed, or rented, or temporary, or kind of. I know that fool's in love with you and you love him but he's devoted to 'hanging loose', to not making a mistake again and that's the biggest mistake of all. Get married, Tan ... have kids ... it's the only thing that makes sense in life ... the only thing I care about ... the only important thing I'm leaving behind ... no matter who you are or what you do, until you have that and are that and give that, you are nothing and no one ... you're only half alive ... Tana, don't cheat yourself ... please ....' He was crying openly now. He had loved her so much for so long and he didn't want her to miss what he and Averil had shared. And as he spoke to her, her mind went instantly to the countless looks she had watched them share, the quiet joy, the laughter that never seemed to end ... and would end so soon now, and deep in her heart she had always known that what he said was true, in some ways she had wanted it for herself, and in other ways she was scared ... and the men in her life had always been wrong for that ... Yael McBee ... Drew Lands ... and now Jack ... and the people who didn't matter in between. There had never been anyone who might have come close. Maybe Harry's father would, but that was so long ago now .... 'If the opportunity ever comes, grab it, Tan. Give up everything, if you have to. But if it's the right thing, you won't.'

'What do you propose I do? Go out on the street and wear a sign? Marry me. Let's have kids.' They laughed together, for a moment, just like old times.

'Yeah, asshole, why not?'

'I love you, Harry.' The words sprung from her and she was crying again and he held her tight.

'I'll never really be gone, Tan. You know that. You and I had too much to ever lose that ... just like Ave and I do in a different way. I'll be here, keeping an eye on things.' They were crying openly and she didn't think she could live without him. And she could only imagine how Averil felt. It was the most painful time of their lives, and for the next three months, they watched him roll slowly downhill, and on a warm summer day, with the sun high in the sky, she got a call. It was from Jack. There were tears in his voice, and she felt her heart stop. She had seen Harry only the night before. She went to see him every day now, no matter what, at lunchtime or at night, or sometimes before her day began. She never knew how hectic things would get, but she wouldn't give that up. And he had held her hand and smiled just the night before. He could barely talk, but she had kissed his cheek, and suddenly thought of the hospital so long ago. She wanted to shake him back to life, to make him fight for what he had been, but he couldn't anymore, and it was easier to go.

'He just died.' Jack's voice broke, and Tana began to cry. She wanted to see him just once more ... to hear him laugh ... see those eyes .... She couldn't speak for a minute, and then she nodded her head and took a breath to fight back the sobs.

'How's Ave?'

'She seems all right.' Harrison had arrived the week before and he was staying with them. Tana looked at her watch.

'I'll go over there right now. I just called a recess for the afternoon anyway.' She could feel him tense at her words, as though he felt she were showing off for him. But that was what she did. She was a municipal court judge, and she had called a recess. 'Where are you?'

'I'm at work. His father just called.'

'I'm glad he was there. Are you going over now?'

'I can't for a little while.' She nodded, realizing that if she had said that, he would have said something unpleasant to her about how important she thought she was. There was no winning with him now and Harry hadn't been able to soften him before he died, no matter how hard he tried. There had been so much he wanted to say, so much to share with those he loved. And it was over so soon. Tana drove over the Bay Bridge with tears streaming down her face, and then suddenly, it was as though she felt him next to her and she smiled. He was gone, but he was everywhere now. With her, with Ave, with his father, his kids ....

'Hi, kid.' She smiled into the air as she drove, and the tears continued to flow and when she arrived at the house, he was already gone. They had taken him to prepare him for the services, and Harrison was sitting in the living room, looking stunned. He looked suddenly very old, and Tana realized he was almost seventy now. And with grief etched on his still handsome face, he looked even older than that. She said nothing at all, she just went to him, and they held each other tight, and Averil came out of the bedroom after that, wearing a simple black dress, her blonde hair pulled back and her wedding ring on her left hand. Harry had given her some beautiful things from time to time, but she wore nothing now – only her grief and her pride and their love, as she stood surrounded by the life and the home and the children they had shared. She looked oddly beautiful as she stood there, and in a strange way Tana envied her. She and Harry had shared something that few people ever had, for how-ever long, and it had been worth everything to them. And suddenly, for the first time in her life, she felt a void. She was sorry that she hadn't married him a long time before, or someone else ... gotten married ... had kids ... it left an aching hole in her that refused to be filled. All through the services, at the cemetery as they left him there, and afterwards, when she was alone again, she felt something she couldn't have explained to anyone, and when she tried to tell Jack, he shook his head and stared at her.

'Don't go crazy now, Tan, just because Harry died.' She had told him that she suddenly felt her life was a waste because she had never married and had kids. 'I've done both, and believe me it doesn't change a damn thing. Don't kid yourself, not everyone has what they did. In fact, I've never known anyone who did, except them. And if you got married looking for that, you'd be disappointed, because it wouldn't be there.'

'How do you know that? It might.' She was disappointed by what he said.

'Take my word for it.'

'You can't make a judgment on that. You knocked up some twenty-one-year-old girl and got married lickety split because you had to. That's different from making an intelligent choice at our age.'

'Are you trying to put pressure on me, Tan?' He suddenly looked angrily at her, and all the handsome blond good looks seemed suddenly drawn and tired. Losing Harry had been rough on him too. 'Don't do that to me now. This isn't the time.'

'I'm just telling you what I feel.'

'You feel like shit because your best friend just died. But don't go getting all romantic about it, and the secret of life being marriage and kids. Believe me, it's not.'

'How the hell do you know that? You can't decide for anyone but yourself. Don't try to evaluate things for me, goddammit, Jack.' All her feelings suddenly came rushing out, 'You're so fucking scared to give a damn about anyone, you squeak anytime someone comes too close. And you know what? I'm fucking sick of you punishing me all the time because I got made a judge last year!'

'Is that what you think I do?' It was a relief for both of them to scream a little bit, but there was truth in her words, and they hit home so hard he slammed out of her house, and she didn't see him for three weeks. It was the longest they'd been apart voluntarily since they'd met, but he didn't call her and she didn't call him. She heard nothing at all from him until his daughter arrived in town for her annual visit, and Tana invited her to stay with her in town. Barb was excited at the idea, and when she arrived at the little house on her own the following afternoon, Tana was stunned by how much she had changed. She had just turned fifteen, and she suddenly looked like a woman now, with long lean lines, and pretty little hips and big blue eyes with her flash of red hair.

'You look great, Barb.'

'Thanks, so do you.' Tana kept her for five days, and even took her to court with her, and it was only toward the end of the week that they finally talked about Jack, and how things had changed with them.

'He yells at me all the time now.' Barbara had noticed it too, and she wasn't having a very good time with him. 'My mom says he was always like that, but he never was when you were around, Tan.'

'I think he's probably pretty nervous these days.' She was making excuses for him for Barb's sake, so she didn't think it was her fault, but in truth it was a conglomerate of things. Tana, Harry, pressures in his work. Nothing seemed to be going right for him, and when Tana attempted to have dinner with him after Barbara when back to Detroit, it ended in more bickering again. They were arguing about what Averil should do with the house. He thought she should sell and move into town, and Tana disagreed. 'That house means a lot to her; they've been there for years.'

'She needs a change, Tan. You can't hang on to the past.'

'Why the hell are you so desperately afraid to hang on to anything? It's almost as if you're afraid to give a damn.' She had noticed that a lot about him of late. He always wanted to be free and unattached, never tied down. It was a wonder the relationship had lasted as long as it had, but it certainly wasn't in good shape now, and at the end of the summer, fate dealt them another blow. Just as she had been told, when she was offered her seat on the municipal court bench a year before, an opening had come up, and she was being kicked up into superior court. She almost didn't have the heart to tell Jack, but she didn't want him to hear it from someone else first. Gritting her teeth, she dialed him at home one night. She was in her cozy little house, reading some law books she had brought home, to check some remote statutes of the penal code, and she held her breath as he answered the phone.

'Hi, Tan, what's up?' He sounded more relaxed than he had in months, and she hated to spoil his good mood, which she knew her news would. And she was right. He sounded as though someone had punched him in the gut when she told him she was being made a superior court judge.

'That's nice. When?' He sounded as though she had just planted a cobra at his feet.

'In two weeks. Would you come to my induction, or would you rather not be there?'

'That's a hell of a thing to say. I gather you'd just as soon I not come.' He was so sensitive, there was no talking to him.

'I didn't say that. But I know how uptight you get about my work.'

'What makes you think that?'

'Oh please, Jack ... let's not get into that now ....' She was tired after a long day, and everything seemed harder and sadder and more difficult now that Harry was gone. And with the relationship with Jack on the rocks, it wasn't the happiest time of her life, to say the least. 'I hope you'll come.'

'Does that mean I won't see you till then?'

'Of course not. You can see me when ever you want.'

'How about tomorrow night?' It was almost as if he were testing her.

'Great. Your place or mine?' She laughed but he did not.

'Yours gives me claustrophobia. I'll pick you up outside City Hall at six.'

'Yes, sir.' She put a mock salute in her voice, but he didn't laugh, and when they met the next day, their mood was gray. They both missed Harry terribly and the only difference was that Tana talked about it, and Jack would not. He had taken another attorney into the partnership, and he seemed to like the man. He talked about that a lot, and about how successful the man had been, how much money they were going to make. It was obvious that he still had a chip on his shoulder over Tana's work, and by the next morning, it was a relief when he dropped her off at City Hall again. He was going to Pebble Beach that week end to play golf with a bunch of guys and he hadn't invited her, and she was relieved as she walked up the steps of City Hall with a sigh. He certainly didn't make her life easy these days, and now and then she thought of what Harry had said to her before he died. But it was hopeless thinking of anything permanent with Jack. He just wasn't that kind of man. And Tana didn't kid herself anymore. She wasn't that kind of girl anyway. It was probably why they had gotten along for as long as they had. Not that that seemed to apply anymore. The friction between them was almost more than she could bear, and she was actually grateful when she discovered that he was going to be in Chicago on a business trip when she was inducted into superior court.

It was a small, simple ceremony this time, presided over by the presiding judge of the superior court. There were half a dozen other judges there, her old friend the DA, who happily said, 'I told you so' over her swift move up, and a handful of other people she cared about, and Averil was in Europe with Harrison and the kids. She had decided to winter in London that year, just to get away for a while, and she had put the children in school there. Harrison had talked her into it, and he looked happy when he left with his grandchildren in tow. There had been a heart-breaking moment alone with Tana just before that, when he actually put his face in his hands and cried, wondering if Harry had known how much he had loved him, and she insisted that he had. It helped assuage his sorrow and his guilt over the early years to take care of his daughter-in-law and his grandchildren now. But it wasn't the same without them at Tana's swearing-in and it was odd to look around and not see Jack.

The actual swearing-in was done by a judge of the court of appeals, a man Tana had met once or twice over the years. He had thick black hair, ferocious dark eyes, and a look which would have frightened anyone, as he towered over them all in his dark robes, but he also had quick laughter, a keen mind, and a surprising gentleness. He was particularly well known for some very controversial decisions he had made, which had been played up in the national press, and in particular the *New York Times*, and the *Washington Post*, as well as the *Chronicle*. Tana had read about him a lot, and wondered just how ferocious he was, but she was intrigued to see now that he was less lion and more lamb, or at least he was at her swearing-in. They chatted for while about his superior court days, and she knew that he had also run the biggest law firm in town, before being made a judge. He had an interesting career behind him, though she suspected that he wasn't more than forty-eight or forty-nine. For a long time, he had been kind of '*Wunderkind*,' and she liked him very much as he shook her hand, and congratulated her warmly again, before he left.

'I'm impressed.' Her old friend, the DA, smiled at her. 'That's the first time I've ever seen Russell Carver at a swearing-in. You're getting to be awfully important, my friend.'

'He probably had to pay his parking tickets downstairs, and someone re-cruited him.' They both laughed. Actually, he was a close friend of the presiding judge, and had volunteered his services for the swearing-in. He looked the part anyway, with his dark hair and serious face.

'You should have seen him when he was the presiding judge here, Tan. Shit, he threw one of our DA's into the can on contempt of court for three weeks and I couldn't get the poor bastard out.'

Tana laughed, just imagining it. 'I'm lucky that never happened to me, I guess.'

'Didn't you ever have him as a judge?'

'Only twice. He's been on the court of appeals for a hell of a long time.'

'I guess he has. He's not very old though, as I recall. Forty-nine, fifty, fifty-one ... something like that ....'

'Who's that?' The presiding judge wandered over to them and shook Tana's hand again. It was a nice day for her, and she was suddenly glad that Jack wasn't there. It was so much easier like this, and not having to hold her breath or apologize to him.

'We were talking about Justice Carver.'

'Russ? He's forty-nine. He went to Stanford with me.' The presiding judge smiled, 'although I'll admit he was a few years behind.' In fact, he had been a freshman when the presiding judge graduated from law school, but their families had been friends. 'He's a hell of a nice guy, smart as hell.'

'He has to be.' Tana spoke admiringly. There was another leap to contemplate. The court of appeals. What a thought. Maybe in another decade or two. And in the meantime, she was going to enjoy this. Superior Court was going to be just her cup of tea. They were going to have her trying criminal cases in no time at all, since that was her area of expertise. 'It was nice of him to do my swearing-in today.' She smiled at everyone.

'He's a nice guy.' Everyone said that about the man, and she sent him a little note, thanking him for taking the time to make her induction an even more special event, and the next day, he called and there was laughter in his voice.

'You're awfully polite. I haven't had a bread and butter letter like that in twenty years at least.'

She laughed in embarrassment and thanked him for the call. 'It was just a very nice thing to do. Like having the Pope around when you take religious vows.'

'Oh my God ... what a thought. Is that what you were doing last week? I take it all back ....' They both laughed and they chatted for a while. She invited him to stop into her court whenever he was around, and she felt a comfortable warmth at the confrerie she was a part of now, judges and justices, all working together. It was like having arrived at Mount Olympus at last, and it was a hell of a lot easier in some ways than prosecuting cases against rapists and murderers, building a case and arguing, although she had enjoyed that too. Here, she had to keep a clearer head, and objective outlook, and she had never studied so much law in her life. She was buried in a stack of books in her chambers two weeks later, when Justice Carver took her at her word and came by. 'Is this what I condemned you to?' He stood in her doorway and smiled. Her clerk had long since gone home, and she was frowning in concentration as she pored over six open books at once, comparing statutes and precedents as he wandered in and she looked up with a smile.

'What a nice surprise.' She stood up quickly and waved him toward a large, comfortable leather chair. 'Please sit down.' He did and she looked at him. He was good looking, in a quiet, virile, rather intellectual way. They weren't the same football team good looks as Jack's. They were much quieter, and much more powerful, just as he was in myriad ways. 'Would you like a drink?' She kept a small bar well hidden for occasions such as this.

'No, thanks. I have too much homework to do tonight.'

'You too? How do you ever get through it all?'

'I don't. Sometimes it makes you want to just sit there and cry, but you get through it eventually. What are you working on?' She described the case to him as briefly as she could and he nodded thoughtfully. 'That should be an interesting one. It may even wind up in my lap eventually.'

She laughed. 'That's not much of a vote of confidence if you think they'll appeal my decision.'

'No, no,' he was quick to explain, 'it's just that you're on new turf there and whatever you decide, if they don't like it, they may try to overturn it. Be careful you don't give them grounds.' It was good advice and they chatted on for quite a while. He had dark, thoughtful eyes that gave him an almost sensual air, which didn't seem in keeping with his seriousness. There were a lot of contrasts about the man, and she was intrigued by him. He walked out eventually, and helped her carry a stack of books to her car, and then he seemed to hesitate. 'I couldn't talk you into a hamburger somewhere, could I?'

She smiled at him. She liked this man. She had never known anyone quite like him before. 'You might, if you promise to get me home early enough to do some work.' They chose Bill's Place on Clement. It was a simple, wholesome environment amidst the hamburgers and french fries and milkshakes and kids, and no one would have suspected who they were, how important their jobs, as they chatted on about cases they had suffered with years before, and the comparison of Stanford to Boalt, and eventually Tana laughed at him.

'All right, all right I concede. Your school is better than mine.'

'I didn't say that.' He laughed. 'I said we had a better football team.'

'Well, that's not my fault at least. I had nothing to do with that.'

'I somehow didn't think you did.' It was very relaxing being with him. They had common interests, common friends, and the time flew by. He took her home, and was about to drop her off when she invited him inside for a drink, and he was surprised by how pretty the little bijou house was, how well she'd decorated it. It was a real haven, that made one want to stretch out in front of the fire and stay for a while.

'I'm happy here.' And she was, whenever she was alone. It was only when Jack was there, that it got so uncomfortable. But especially now, with him there, it suited her perfectly. Russ lit the fire for her, and she poured him a glass of red wine, and they chatted for a while, about their families, their lives. She discovered that he had lost his wife ten years before, and he had two daughters who were both married now.

'At least I'm not a grandfather yet.' Russell Carver smiled at her. 'Beth is going to architectual school at Yale, while her husband studies law, and Lee is a fashion designer in New York. She's actually pretty good, and I'm proud of them ... but grandchildren,' he almost groaned, and she smiled at him, 'I'm not ready for that yet?'

'Did you ever want to marry again?' She was curious about him. He was an interesting man.

'No. No one that important has come along, I guess.' He looked around her house and then back at her. 'You know how it is, you get comfortable with your own way of life. It's difficult to change all that for someone else.'

She smiled. 'I suppose. I've never really tried. Not very courageous of me, I suppose.' Sometimes she regretted it now, and if Jack had twisted her arm before things began to fall apart ... She looked up at Russ and smiled. 'Marriage used to scare the hell out of me.'

'As well it should. It's a mightly delicate operation at best. But when it works, it's wonderful.' His eyes glowed and it was easy to guess that he'd been happy with his wife. 'I have nothing but good memories about that.' And they both knew that that made it harder to marry again too. 'And my girls are great. You'll have to meet them sometime.'

'I'd like that very much.' They chatted on for a few minutes, he finished his wine, and then he left. She went up to her den with the books he'd helped her bring home, and she worked late into the night and the next day she laughed when a court messenger appeared with an envelope in his decisive hand. He had written her a bread and butter letter much like the one she'd written him for her swearing-in and she called to laugh with him. It was a far easier conversation than the one she shared with Jack later that day. He was on the warpath again, and they were fighting about their weekend plans, so much so that eventually she got out of them, and sat peacefully in her house alone on Saturday, going through some old photographs when the doorbell rang. Russell Carver was standing there, looking at her apologetically, with a bunch of roses in his hands.

'This is a terribly rude thing to do, and I apologize in advance.' He looked handsome in a tweed jacket and a turtleneck and she smiled at him delightedly.

'I never heard that bringing someone roses was rude before.'

'That's to compensate for dropping by unannounced, which is rude, but I was thinking of you and I didn't have your number at home. I gather it's unlisted, so I took a chance ...' He smiled sheepishly and she waved him in.

'I had absolutely nothing to do, and I'm delighted you came by.'

'I'm surprised I found you here. I was sure you'd be out.' She poured him a glass of wine, and they sat down on the couch.

'Actually, I had plans but I cancelled them.' Things were impossible with Jack, and she wondered how to handle it. Sooner or later, they'd either have to work things out or give up, but she didn't want to face that now, and he was away anyway.

'I'm glad you did.' Russ Carver smiled at her. 'Would you like to go to Butterfield's with me?'

'The auction house?' She looked intrigued, and half an hour later they were wandering amidst antiques and Oriental works of art, chatting about sundry things. He had an easy way about him that was relaxing to her, and they shared similar views about almost everything. She even tried to explain her mother to him. 'I think that's a big part of the reason why I never wanted to get married. I kept thinking of her sitting there waiting for him to call ....' She hated the memory, even now.

'Then all the more reason to marry him and have security.'

'But I knew he was cheating on his wife by then. I never wanted to be either one of those women ... my mother ... or the wife he cheated on.'

'That must have been difficult for you, Tana.' He was sympathetic about so many things. And she told him about Harry that afternoon when they walked on Union Street. She told him about the friendship they had shared, the years at school, the time at the hospital, and how lonely it was without him now. Tears came to her eyes as she talked about him, but there was something gentle on her face too as she looked up at him. 'He must have been a fine man.' His voice touched her like a caress and she smiled at him.

'He was more than that. He was the best friend I'll ever have. He was remarkable ... even as he died, he gave something to everyone, a piece of himself ... some part of himself ....' She looked up at Russ again. 'I wish you'd known him.'

'So do I.' He looked at her gently then. 'Were you in love with him?'

She shook her head, and then she smiled, remembering. 'He had a crush on me when we were kids. But Averil was perfect for him.'

'And you, Tana?' Russell Carver looked searchingly at her. 'Who was perfect for you? Who has there been? Who was the love of your life?' It was an odd question to ask, but he had the feeling that there had been someone. It was impossible that a girl like this should be unattached. There was a mystery there, and he couldn't find the answer to it.

'No one.' She smiled at him. 'Some hits, some misses ... the wrong people mostly. I haven't had much time.'

He nodded. He understood that too. 'You pay a price for getting where you are today. It can be a very lonely place sometimes.' He wondered if it was for her, but she looked content to him. He wondered who there was in her life now, and he asked her as much, in so many words.

'I've been seeing someone for the last few years, more than that actually, I 'Sguess. We lived together for a while. And we still see each other,' she smiled wistfully and looked into Russ' dark eyes, 'but things aren't what they used to be. 'The price you pay', as you put it. Things haven't been the same since I got appointed to the bench last year ... and then Harry died ... it's made a lot of dents in us.'

'Is it a serious affair?' He looked both concerned and intrigued.

'It was for a long time, but it's limping badly now. I think we're still together out of loyalty.'

'You're still together, then?' He watched her face carefully, and she nodded. She and Jack had never really called it quits. At least not yet, although neither of them knew what the future would bring.

'We are for now. It suited us both for a long time. We had the same philosophy. No marriage and no kids. And as long as we both agreed on that, it worked pretty well ...'

'And now?' The big dark eyes were probing hers and she looked at him, suddenly hungry for his touch, his hands, his lips. He was the most attractive man she'd ever seen, but she had to reproach herself. She still belonged to Jack ... didn't she? She was no longer quite so sure.

'I don't know. Things have changed for me since Harry died. Some of what he said makes me wonder about my own life.' She looked hard at Russ. 'I mean is this it? Is this all there is? I go on from here, with my work ... with or without Jack,' Russ gathered who she meant, 'and that's all? Maybe I want more of a future than that. I've never felt that way before, and suddenly I do. Or at least I wonder about it sometimes.'

'I think you're on the right track.' He sounded worldly and wise, and in some ways he reminded her of Harrison.

She smiled at him. 'That's what Harry would say.' And then she sighed. 'Who knows, maybe it doesn't matter anyway. Suddenly it's all over, and then so what, who cares, you're gone ....'

'It matters all the more then, Tana. But I felt that way too after my wife died ten years ago. It's difficult to adjust to something like that, it forces the realization on us that we hve to face our own mortality one day. It all counts, every year, every day, every relationship, if you're wasting it, or unhappy where you are, one day you wake up, and it's time to pay the check. So, in the meantime, you might as well be happy where you are.' He waited a moment and then looked at her. 'Are you?'

'Happy?' She hesitated for a long time and then looked at him. 'In my work, I am.'

'And the rest?'

'Not very, right now. It's a difficult time for us.'

'Am I intruding, then?' He wanted to know everything, and sometimes it was difficult to answer him.

She shook her head and looked into the brown eyes she was coming to know so well. 'No, you're not.'

'You're still seeing your friend ... the one you lived with for a while?' He smiled at her and he looked terribly sophisticated and grown up. She felt almost like a child with him.

'Yes, I still see him off and on.'

'I wanted to know how things stand with you.' She wanted to ask him why, but she didn't dare. Instead, he took her to his house, and showed her around. It took her breath away, from the moment they walked into the front hall. Nothing about him bespoke that kind of wealth. He was simple, easy, quietly well dressed, but when you saw where he lived, you understood who he was. It was a house on Broadway, in the last block before the Presidio, with small, carefully kept grounds, a marble entrance hall in inky green and sparkling white, tall marble columns, a Louis XV chest with a white marble top and a silver tray for calling cards, gilt mirrors, parquet floors, satin curtains sweeping the floor. The main floor was a series of exquisite reception rooms. The second floor was more comfortable, with a large master suite, a pretty wood panelled library, a cozy little den with a marble fireplace, and upstairs were the children's rooms he no longer used.

'It doesn't make much sense for me anymore, but I've been here for so long, I'd hate to move ....'

There was nothing she could do but laugh as she sat down and looked at him. 'I think I'll burn my house down after this.' But she was happy there too. This was just another life, another world. He had need of this and she did not. She remembered hearing now that he had considerable personal wealth, knew he had owned a profitable law firm a number of years ago. The man had done well in his life, and he had nothing to fear from her. She wanted nothing from him materially. He showed her proudly from room to room, the billiard room and the gym downstairs, the racks of guns he kept for duck hunting. He was a whole man, of many interests and pursuits. And as they went back upstairs, he turned to her and took her hand with a small, careful smile.

'I'm very taken with you, Tana .... I'd like to see more of you, but I don't want to complicate your life just now. Will you tell me when you're free?' She nodded, totally amazed by all that she had seen and heard. A little while later, he took her home, and she sat staring into the fire in her living room. He was like the kind of man one read about in books, or saw in magazines. And suddenly there he was, on the threshold of her life, telling her that he was 'taken with her', bringing her roses, walking her through Butterfield's. She didn't know what to make of him, but one thing she knew, and that was that she was 'very taken' with him too.

It made things difficult with Jack for the next few weeks. She attempted to spend several nights in Tiburon, almost out of guilt, and all she could think about was Russ, especially when they made love. It was beginning to make her as testy as Jack was with her, and by Thanksgiving she was a nervous wreck. Russ had gone East to see his daughter Lee, and he had invited her to go with him, but that would have been dishonest of her. She had to resolve the situation with Jack, but by the time the holidays came, she felt hysterical every time she thought of him. All she wanted to do was be with Russ, for their quiet talks, their long walks in the Presidio, their ventures into antique shops, art galleries, their long hours over lunch in tiny coffee shops and restaurants. He brought something into her life that had never been there before and which she longed for now, and whenever a problem arose, it was Russ she called, not Jack. Jack would only bark at her. He still had a need to punish her, and it was tiresome now. She wasn't feeling guilty enough to put up with it anymore.

'Why are you hanging on to him?' Russ asked her one day.

'I don't know.' Tana stared miserably at Russ over lunch before court was recessed for the holidays.

'Maybe because in your mind he's attached to your friend.' It was a new idea to her, but she thought it might be a possibility. 'Do you love him, Tan?'

'It isn't that ... it's that we've been together for so long.'

'That's no excuse. From what you say, you're not happy with him.'

'I know. That's the crazy part. Maybe it's just that it's been so safe.'

'Why?' He pushed her hard sometimes, but it was good for her.

'Jack and I have always wanted the same things ... no commitment, no marriage, no kids ....'

'Is that what you're afraid of now?'

She took a breath and stared at him. 'Yes ... I think I am ....'

'Tana,' he reached out and took her hand. 'Are you afraid of me?' Slowly, she shook her head, and then he said what she had both feared and wanted most. She had wanted it since they'd met, since she'd first looked into his eyes. 'I want to marry you. Do you know that?' She shook her head, and then stopped and nodded it, and they both laughed, she with tears in her eyes.

'I don't know what to say.'

'You don't have to say anything. I just wanted to make things clear for you. And now you have to clear up the other situation, for your own peace of mind, whatever you decide about us.'

'Wouldn't your daughters object?'

'It's my life, not theirs, isn't it? Besides, they're lovely girls, there's no reason for them to object to my happiness.' Tana nodded her head. She felt as though she were living a dream.

'Are you serious?'

'Never more so in my life.' His eyes met hers and held. 'I love you very much.' He hadn't even kissed her yet, and she felt herself melting toward him where they sat. And as they left the restaurant, he gently pulled her toward him and kissed her lips, and she felt as though her heart would melt as he held her in his arms.

'I love you, Russ.' The words were suddenly so easy for her. 'I love you so much.' She looked up at him and there were tears in her eyes and he smiled down at her.

'I love you too. Now go straighten out your life, like a good girl.'

'It may take a little time.' They walked slowly back toward City Hall. She had to go back to work.

That's all right. How about two days?' They both laughed. 'We could go to Mexico over the holidays.'

She cringed. She had already promised Jack she would go skiing with him. But she had to do something now. 'Give me till the first of the year and I promise I'll straighten everything out.'

'Then maybe I'll go to Mexico alone.' He frowned pensively and she glanced worriedly at him. 'What are you worried about, little one?'

'That you'll fall in love with someone else.'

'Then hurry up.' He laughed at her, and kissed her again before she went back to court. And all afternoon she sat on the bench with a strange expression in her eyes, a small smile on her lips. She couldn't concentrate on anything, and when she saw Jack that night, she felt breathless every time she looked at him. He wanted to know if she had all her skiing gear. The condo was rented and they were going with friends, and then suddenly halfway through the evening, she stood up and looked at him.

'What's wrong, Tan?'

'Nothing ... everything ....' She closed her eyes. 'I have to go.'

'Now?' He looked furious. 'Back to town?'

'No.' She sat down and started to cry. Where could she begin? What could she say? He had finally driven her away, with his resentment of her work and her success, his bitterness, his unwillingness to commit. She wanted something now that he didn't have to give, and she knew she was doing the right thing, but it was so difficult. She stared unhappily up at him, sure of what she was doing now. She could almost feel Russ sitting next to her, and Harry on the other side, cheering her on. 'I can't.' She looked at Jack and he stared at her.

'Can't what?' He was mystified. She wasn't making any sense and that was unusual for her.

'Can't go on like this.'

'Why not?'

'Because it's no good for either of us. You've been pissed at me for the past year, and I've been miserable ...' She stood up and walked across the room, glancing at familiar things. This house had been part hers for two years, and now it looked like a stranger's house to her. 'I want more than this, Jack.'

'Oh, Christ.' He sat down, looking furious. 'Like what?'

'Like something permanent, like what Harry and Averil had.'

'I told you, you'll never find something like that. That was them. And you're not like Averil, Tan.'

'That's no excuse to give up. I still want someone for the rest of my life who's *mine*, who's willing to stand up in front of God and man and take me on for the rest of my life ....'

He looked at her horrified. 'You want me to marry you? I thought we agreed ...' He looked terrified but she shook her head and sat down again.

'Relax, we did, and that isn't what I want from you. I want out, Jack, I think it's time.' He was silent for a long, long time, he knew it too, but it hurt anyway. And it spoiled all his plans for the holidays.

He looked at her. 'This is why I believe what I do. Because sooner or later it comes to an end. And it's easier like this. I pack my bag, you pack yours, we say goodbye, and we hurt for a while, but at least we never lied to each other, and we're not dragging along a flock of kids.'

'I'm not even sure that would be so terrible. At least we'd know how much we'd cared.' She looked sad, as though she had lost someone dear to her, and she had. She had cared about him for a long time.

'We cared a lot, Tan. And it was good.' There were tears in his eyes and he came to her and sat down. 'If I thought it was right, I'd marry you.'

'It wouldn't be right for you.' She looked at him.

'You'd never be happy married anyway, Tan.'

'Why not?' She didn't want him to say that. Not now. Not with Russ standing in the wings, wanting to marry her. It was like putting a curse on her. 'Why would you say a thing like that?'

'Because you're not the type. You're too strong.' She was stronger than he was, she knew. But she had only come to understand that recently, mostly since she had known Russ. He was so different from Jack. So much stronger than anyone she had known before. 'You don't need marriage anyway,' he smiled bitterly, 'you're married to the law. That's a full time love affair for you.'

'Can't one have both?'

'Some can. You can't.'

'Did I hurt you that much, Jack?' She looked woefully at him and he smiled and stood up, opened a bottle of wine and handed her a glass, and somehow she felt as though she had never known this man. Everything was so bitter, so shallow. Nothing in him ran deep, and she wondered how she could have stayed with him for so long, but it had suited her. She hadn't wanted a depth during those years. She had wanted to be as free as he did. Only now she had grown up, and as much as the challenge Russ offered terrified her, she wanted it, wanted it more than anything she'd ever done before. She looked into Jack's eyes and smiled at him as he toasted her.

'To you, Tan. Good luck.' She drank, and a moment later she set down her glass and looked at him.

'I'm going now.'

'Yeah. Call me sometime.' He turned his back to her, and she felt a knife of pain slice through her. She wanted to reach out to him, but it was too late. For both of them. She touched his back and whispered one word.

'Goodbye.'

And then she drove home as fast as she could, took a bath and washed her hair, as though she were washing away the disappointments and the tears. She was thirty-eight years old and she was starting all over again, but in a way she never had before, with a man like no man she had ever known. She thought of calling him that night but her mind was still filled with Jack, and she was suddenly afraid to tell Russ that she was free. She didn't say anything to him until their lunch the day he left for Mexico, and then suddenly she looked at him and smiled mysteriously.

'What are you grinning at, Funny Face?'

'Just life, I guess.'

'And that amuses you?'

'Sometimes. I ... uh ... er ...' He was laughing at her and she was blushing furiously.

'Oh shit. Don't make things so hard for me.'

He took her hand in his and smiled at her. 'What are you trying to say?' He had never seen her so tongue-tied before.

She took a deep breath. 'I straightened things out this week.'

'With Jack?' He looked amazed as she nodded her head with a shy smile. 'So soon?'

'I couldn't go on like that.'

'Was he very upset?' Russ looked concerned.

She nodded, looking sad for a moment. 'Yes, but he wouldn't admit it. He likes to keep everything easy and free'. She sighed jaggedly, then, 'He says I'd never be happy married to anyone.'

'That's nice.' Russ smiled and showed absolutely no concern. 'When you move out, be sure to burn the house down. It's an old custom with some men. Believe me, it doesn't mean a thing. I'll take my own chances, thanks.' Russ smiled ecstatically at her.

'Do you still want to marry me?' She couldn't believe what was happening to her, and for just a minute ... just a minute ... there was the temptation to run back to her old life, but that wasn't what she wanted anymore. She wanted this ... and him ... she wanted both marriage and a career, no matter how frightening it was to her. It was a chance she had to take. She was ready now. It had taken her a long, long time, but she had gotten there and she was proud of herself.

'What do you think? Of course I do.' He reassured her at once and his eyes smiled at her.

'Are you sure?'

'Are you?' That's more to the point.'

'Maybe we should talk about this for a while?' She was suddenly very nervous at the thought and he laughed at her.

'How long? Six months? A year? Ten years?'

'Maybe more like five ...' She was laughing too, and then suddenly she looked at him. 'You don't want children, do you?' She hadn't gone that far. She was too old for that, but he only shook his head and grinned at her.

'You worry about everything, don't you? No, I don't want children. I'll be fifty years old next month and I already have two. And no, I will not have a vasectomy, thanks, but I'll do anything else you want to guarantee that I won't knock you up. Okay? Want me to sign it in blood?'

'Yes.' They were both laughing and he paid the check and they walked outside and he held her as no man had ever held her before, pulling her heart right through her soul, and she had never been happier. And then suddenly he looked at his watch, and hurried her to his car. 'What are you doing?'

'We have a plane to catch.'

'We do? But I can't ... I'm not ...'

'Is your court recessed over the holidays?'

'Yes, but ....'

'Is your passport in order?'

'I ... yes ... I think it is ...'

'We'll check when I get you home ... you're coming with me ... we can plan the wedding there ... I'll call the girls ... what do you think about February ... say in about six weeks? ... Valentine's Day? ... corny enough for you, Tan?' He was crazy and she was crazy about him. They caught the plane to Mexico that night, and spent a blissful week soaking up the sun, and making love at last. He had waited until she had broken things off with Jack for good. And when they returned he bought her an engagement ring, and they told all their friends. Jack called her when he read it in the papers, and what he said cut her to the quick.

'So that was what that was all about? Why didn't you tell me you were shacked up with somebody else? A justice, too. That must be a step up for you.'

'That's a rotten thing to say ... and I wasn't shacked up with him.'

'Tell that to someone else. Come to think of it,' he laughed bitterly, 'tell it to the judge.'

'You know, you've been so damn busy trying not to get involved with anyone all your life that you don't know your ass from a hole in the ground anymore.'

'At least I know when I'm cheating on someone, Tan.'

'I wasn't cheating on you.'

'What were you doing then, fucking him at lunchtime, it doesn't count before six o'clock?' She had hung up on him, sorry that it had to end that way. And she had written to Barbara, too, explaining that her marriage to Russ was precipitous, but he was a lovely man, and when she came out to see her father the following year, the door to Tana's home would be open to her as it had been before. She didn't want the girl to feel that she was pushing her away. And there were so many other things to do too. She wrote to Averil in London, and her mother almost had a heart attack when she called her.

'Are you sitting down?'

'Oh Tana, something's happened to you.' Her mother sounded on the verge of tears. She was only sixty-one years old, but mentally she was twice that, and Arthur was getting senile now at seventy-four, which was hard on her.

'It's something nice, Mother. Something you've waited for, for a long, long time.'

Jean stared blankly at the far wall, holding the phone. 'I can't imagine what it is.'

'I'm getting married in three weeks.'

'You're *what*? To whom? That man you've been living with all these years?' She had never thought much of him, but it was about time they took a decent position in the world, especially with Tana being a judge. But she was in for a shock.

'No. To someone else. A justice on the court of appeals. His name is Russell Carver, Mom.' She went on to tell her the rest and Jean cried, and smiled and laughed and cried some more.

'Oh sweetheart ... I've waited so long for this.'

'So have I.' Tana was laughing and crying too. 'And it was worth waiting for, Mom. Wait till you see him. Will you come out for the wedding? We're getting married on February 14th.'

'Valentine's Day? ... oh, how sweet ...' It still embarrassed Tan but it seemed funny to both her and Russ. 'I wouldn't miss it for the world. I don't think Arthur will be well enough to come, so I can't stay long.' She had a thousand arrangements to make before she left, and she could hardly wait to get off the phone. Ann had just gotten married for the fifth time, and who gave a damn anymore? Tana was getting married! And to a justice on the court of appeals! And she said he was handsome too. Jean dithered around the house for the rest of the afternoon, in a total state, and she had to go into the city to Saks the following day. She needed a dress ... no ... maybe a suit ... she couldn't believe it had happened finally. And that night she whispered silent prayers.

Chapter 18

The wedding was absolutely beautiful. They had it at Russ' house, with a piano and two violins playing something delicate from Brahms as Tana came slowly down the stairs in a simple dress of off-white crêpe de chine. She wore her blonde hair long, covered by a wide-brimmed picture hat, with a faint hint of veil, and ivory satin shoes. There were roughly a hundred people there, and Jean stood in a corner and cried ecstatically for most of the day. She had bought a beautiful beige Givenchy suit, and she looked so proud it made Tana cry every time she looked at her.

'Happy, my love?' Russ looked at Tana in a way that made her heart fly. It seemed impossible that she could be lucky enough to find a man like him, and she had never dreamed of anything like what she shared with him. It was as though she had been born to be his, and she found herself thinking of Harry as she walked down the aisle. 'Okay, asshole? Did I do good?' She smiled through her tears.

'You did *great*!' She knew that Harry would have been crazy about Russ, and it would have been mutual. And she felt Harry very much there with her. Harrison and Averil sent a telegram. Russ' daughters were there too. They were both slender, attractive, pleasant girls, with husbands that Tana liked. They were an easy group to love, and they did everything to welcome her. Lee was particularly warm in her reception of her new stepmother, and they were only twelve years apart in age.

'Thank God he had the sense to wait until we grew up before marrying again.' Lee laughed. 'For one thing, the house is a hell of a lot quieter now, and for another thing, you don't have to put up with us, behaving like turds. He's been single for so long, Beth and I are grateful as hell that you married him. I hate to think of him alone in this house.' She was a little bit zany, and wonderfully dressed in her own designs. She was clearly crazy about Russ, nuts about her own husband, and Beth doted on her entire family. It was the ideal group, and as Jean looked at them, she was suddenly grateful that Tana hadn't been foolish enough to fall for Billy, in the years when she was pushing that. How sensible Tana had been to wait for this extraordinary man to come along. And what a life. The house was the most beautiful place she'd ever seen. And Tana felt totally at ease with the butler and the maid he'd had for years. She floated from room to room, entertaining his friends, as people said 'Your Honor' to her, and somebody else cited a funny poem about a justice and a judge.

It was a wonderful afternoon, and they went back to Mexico for their honeymoon, returning via La Jolla and Los Angeles. Tana had taken a month's leave from work, and when she returned she smiled to herself whenever she said her new name. Judge Carver ... Tana Carver ... Tana Roberts Carver ... She had added his name to everything, none of this women's lib crap for her. She had waited thirty-eight years for him, almost thirty-nine, and resisted marriage for almost four decades, and if she had taken the plunge now, she was going to enjoy all the benefits. She came home every night, relaxed and happy to see him. So much so that he teased her about it one night.

'When are you going to start behaving like a real wife and nagging me a little bit?'

'I forgot, I guess.' He smiled at her, and they talked about her house again. She had been thinking about renting it. It was so pretty that she didn't want to sell it, yet she knew she would never live there again. 'Maybe I should just sell it after all.'

'What if I rent it from you for Beth and John when they come home?'

'That would be wonderful.' She smiled at him. 'Let's see ... you can have it for two kisses and ... a trip to Mexico ...' He laughed at her, and eventually they decided to keep the house and rent it out and Tana had never been happier in her life. It was one of those rare times when everything feels in total control, going just the way you want, when she ran full tilt into someone one day. She was hurrying from her courtroom to meet Russ for lunch, and suddenly found herself staring into Drew Lands' face. He looked as though someone had just struck oil on his front lawn when he saw who she was, and they stood chatting amiably for a minute or two. It was incredible to realize how much pain he had caused her once. It was even more amazing to realize that Julie and Elizabeth were eighteen and twenty-two. 'Good lord, is it as long ago as that?'

'It must be, Tan.' His voice was smooth, and suddenly she was annoyed by him. She could see from his eyes that he was making assumptions that were no longer appropriate, and hadn't been for a long, long time. 'Eileen and I have been divorced for six years now.' How dare he tell her that ... how dare he have gotten divorced after hurting Tan so much for her ...

'That's too bad.' Her voice was cool, and she was losing interest in what he said. She didn't want to be late for Russ. She knew he was working on an important case.

'Gee ... I wonder if ... maybe we could see each other sometime. I'm living in San Francisco now ...'

She smiled at him. 'We'd love to see you sometime. But my husband is just buried in a big case right now.' She smiled almost evilly at him, waved her hand with a few garbled words, and was gone. And Russ could still see the victory in her eyes when he met her for lunch at the Hayes Street Grill. It was one of their favorite haunts, and she often met him there, kissing at a corner table, and necking happily over lunch, while people smiled at them.

'What are you looking so pleased about?' He knew her very well.

'Nothing ...' And then, she kept no secrets from him, she couldn't have anyway. 'I just ran into Drew Lands for the first time in almost seven years. What a bastard he is. I guess he always was, the weak little shit.'

'My, my, what did he do to deserve so many epithets?'

'He was the married man I told you about ...'

'Ah!' Russ looked amused at the fire in her eyes. He knew he was in no danger of losing her to anyone, not because he was so sure of himself, but because he knew the kind of love they shared. It was one of those rare, rare things in life, and he was deeply grateful for it. He had never had a love like this before with anyone.

'And you know what? He finally divorced his wife.'

'Predictably.' Russ smiled. 'And now he wanted to take you out again. Right?'

She laughed at him. 'I told him we'd love to see him sometime, and then I skibbled off.'

'You're a little witch. But I love you anyway. How was court today?'

'Not bad. I have an interesting case coming up, an industrial injury. It's going to be messy but it brings up some very intriguing points and technicalities. How's your monster case coming along?'

He smiled at her. 'I'm finally getting it back into its cage. And,' he looked at her strangely for a minute, 'I had a call from Lee.'

'How is she?'

'Fine.' He looked at his wife, and she looked at him. There was something odd in the air.

'Russ, what's wrong?' She was worried about him. He looked strange.

'It's happened. They've finally done it to me. I'm going to be a grandfather.' He looked at once delighted and distressed and Tana laughed at him.

'Oh no! How can she do a thing like that to you?'

'That's exactly what I said to her!' And then he smiled at Tana again. 'Can you imagine that?'

'With difficulty. We'll have to buy you a white wig so you look the part. When is she having it?'

'January. For my birthday, apparently. Or New Year's Eve, something like that.'

As it turned out, the baby was born on New Year's Day, and Russ and Tana decided it would be a lark to fly to New York and visit her. He wanted to see this first grandchild of his, another girl, like his own two. And he reserved a suite for them at the Sherry Netherland, and off they went. Lee was happily ensconced at New York Hospital's Lying-in, in the best room they had, and the baby was sweet and pink, and Russell made all the appropriate noises and when they went back to the hotel, he made passionate love to his wife. 'At least I'm not totally over the hill yet. How does it feel; to make love to a grandfather, my love?'

'Even better than it was before.' But there was something odd in her eyes when she looked at him, and he saw it instantly. He grew very quiet and pulled her into his arms next to him, their naked flesh touching, and he loved to feel how velvety she was, but he was worried about her. Sometimes, when something mattered to her a lot, she burrowed deep inside herself and he could see her do it now.

'What's wrong, sweetheart?' He spoke in a whisper near her ear, and she turned toward him with a look of surprise.

'What makes you think something's wrong?'

'I know you better than that. You can't fool an old man like me. At least not one who loves you as much as I love you.' She tried to deny it for a long time, and then much to his astonishment, she broke down and cried in his arms. There was something about seeing Lee and her baby that had filled her with the most awful pain ... an emptiness ... a void more terrible than any she had ever known. He sat looking at her, amazed at the emotions pouring out of her, and she was even more startled than he. She had never realized she felt that way before.

'Do you want a baby, Tan?'

'I don't know ... I've never felt this way before ... and I'm almost forty years old ... I'm too old for that ...' But suddenly she wanted that more than anything, and she was suddenly haunted by Harry's words again.

'Why don't you think about it, and we'll talk again.' And for the next month, the sight of Lee and her baby haunted her. And suddenly, after they went home, she began seeing pregnant women everywhere, and babies in strollers on every street corner; it was as though everyone had a baby except her ... and there was an envy and a loneliness she couldn't even begin to describe. Russell saw it on her face, but he didn't mention it again until their anniversary, and then she was sharp with him, which was rare for her. It was almost as though it hurt too much to talk about.

'You said you were too old for that. And so am I.'

'Not if it matters to you. It might seem a little foolish to me at first, but I could live with it. Other men have second families at my age, older in fact ... a lot older,' he smiled. And he himself had been surprised by how touched he was by Lee's baby in her arms, and then his own. He wouldn't have minded that at all. And Tana's child would have meant the world to him. But she got more and more sensitive about it, until finally he no longer mentioned it to her. In March, they went to Mexico again, and had a fabulous holiday. Tana barely got *tourista* that time, although she didn't feel well when she got back.

'I think you've been working too hard.' She had had the flu on and off for almost three weeks and he was insisting on her going to see the doctor finally.

'I don't have time for that.' But she was so tired and draggy and so frequently sick to her stomach that she finally went, and she got the shock of her life. It was what she had wanted so desperately, but now, suddenly it was there. And it terrified her. She didn't have time for that. She had an important job. She would look ridiculous ... she had never wanted that ... Russ would be upset with her ... she stewed so terribly that she didn't even go home until seven o'clock that night and Russ knew there was something terribly wrong the minute he laid eyes on her. But he let her unwind for a while, fixed her a drink, opened a bottle of Chateau Latour with their dinner, but she didn't drink a drop of it, and she was still tense when they went upstairs that night and there was an odd look in her eyes. He was actually getting very worried about her, and as soon as she sat down, he pulled a chair up next to her.

'All right, now tell me what happened to you today. You either lost your job or your best friend died.'

She smiled sheepishly and visibly relaxed as he took her hand. 'You know me too well.'

'Then do me the favor of taking me into your confidence.'

'I can't.' She had already made up her mind. She wasn't keeping it. But Russ was not going to fool around. His voice rose ominously, the famous frown appeared, and her knees would have shaken if she didn't know him as well as she did. Instead she laughed at him. 'You know, you're very scary when you look like that.'

He laughed exasperatedly at her. 'That's the whole point. Now talk to me, dammit. What the hell is going on with you?'

She stared at him for a long, long time, lowered her eyes, and then raised them to his again. 'You're not going to believe this, sweetheart.'

'You want a divorce.'

'No, of course not.' She smiled at him. Somehow he always made things less terrible. She had been hysterical all day, and now he had her laughing again.

'You're having an affair?'

'Wrong again.'

'You were kicked off the bench.'

'Worse than that ...' She was beginning to look serious again, because in her mind what had happened meant the same thing. How could she keep her job with that? And then suddenly there were tears in her eyes and she was looking at him. 'I'm pregnant, Russ ...' For a moment everything around them stopped and then suddenly he swept her into his arms and he was laughing and smiling, and acting as though it were cause for celebration and not suicide.

'Oh, sweetheart ... I'm so glad.' He absolutely beamed at her and she stared at him.

'You are? I thought you didn't want any children.' She was stunned. 'We agreed ...'

'Never mind. Our baby is going to be so beautiful ... a little girl that looks just like you ...' He had never looked happier and he held her close as she frowned unhappily. She had wanted this, but now that it had happened, she couldn't imagine it, except in the worst light.

'But it'll ruin everything ...' She was on the verge of tears again, and he was anxious to comfort her.

'Like what?'

'Like my job. How can I be a judge with a baby at my breast?'

He laughed at the image she had in mind. 'Be practical. You work right up till the last day before it's born, and then you take six months off. We get a good nurse, and you go back to work.'

'As easy as that?' She looked shocked.

'It can be as easy as you want, my love. But there's no reason why you can't have a career and a family. It may take a little juggling sometimes, but it can be done with a little resourcefulness.' He smiled at her, and a long slow smile began to dawn in her eyes. There was the possibility that he was right about that, and if he was ... if he was ... it was what she had wanted more than anything, and she wanted both. For years she had thought she could only have one ... But she wanted more than just her work ... she wanted Russ ... she wanted his child ... she wanted everything ... and suddenly the void she had been feeling for months, that ache, the terrible emptiness, was gone again ... 'I'm so proud of you, sweetheart.' She looked at him, and the tears slowly overflowed as she smiled at him. 'Everything is going to be just fine, you know ... and you're going to look just wonderful.'

'Ha!' She laughed at him. 'I've already gained six pounds ...'

'Where?' Tickling and teasing her, he began to look for them, and Tana lay in his arms and laughed.

Chapter 19

The judge walked ponderously to the bench and sat down carefully, rapped the gavel smartly twice, and went on with the morning's calendar. Her bailiff brought her a cup of tea, at ten o'clock, and when she stood up at the noon recess, she could barely walk back to her chambers again. The baby was, by then, exactly nine days late. She had planned to stop working two weeks before, but she had everything so well organized at home that she had decided to work until the bitter end. Her husband picked her up right outside City Hall that night, opening the door smiling at her.

'How'd it go today?' The pride he felt showed easily in his eyes and she smiled back at him. It had been a beautiful time for them, even these extra days. She enjoyed the opportunity to spend these last days alone with him, although she had to admit that she was getting terribly uncomfortable. Her ankles looked like lamp posts by four o'clock in the afternoon, and she had trouble sitting for that long, but she didn't have anything else to do.

She sighed. 'Well, the verdict is in. I think I might give it up at the end of this week, whether the baby shows up or not. What do you think?'

He smiled at her as he drove her home in the new Jaguar he had just bought. 'I think that's a pretty good idea, Tan. You could sit around for a couple of days, you know.'

'Fancy that.'

But she never got time for that. Her water broke at eight o'clock that night, and she suddenly turned to Russ, terrified. She knew it was going to happen eventually, but suddenly it was *now*, and she had the overwhelming urge to run away, and there was no place to run. Her body would follow her everywhere. But Russ saw easily what she felt, and tried to comfort her.

'Everything's going to be just fine.'

'How do you know that?' She snapped at him. 'What if I need a Caesarean? Christ, I'm a hundred years old, for chrissake.' Actually, she was forty years old plus four months. She suddenly looked at Russell and began to cry. She was terrified, and the contractions started almost as soon as her water broke.

'Do you want to lie down here for a while, Tan, or do you want to go to the hospital?'

'I want to stay here.' He called the doctor for her, brought her a glass of ginger ale, flipped on the television across from their bed, and smiled to himself. It was going to be a big night for them, and he also hoped that everything would go well. He was confident that it would, and he was particularly excited. She had insisted on their doing Lamaze training together, and although he hadn't been present at the birth of his girls so many years before, he was going to be with Tana for the birth of their child. He had promised her, and he could hardly wait. She had had the amniocentesis five months before, but they had opted not to know the sex of the child. And Russ could feel a mounting feeling of excitement now for both of them. By midnight, Tana had had a short nap, and she was in control again. She smiled up at him, and he timed her pains, and at two o'clock he called the doctor again, and this time they were told to come in. He picked her bag up from the hall closet where it had sat for the last three weeks, helped her into the car, and out again at the hospital, and helped her to walk inside. She could hardly walk now, and the contractions took all her concentration and his help, just to get her through them, but they were nothing like the pains she felt once she went into transition three hours after that. She was writhing in pain on the bed in the labor room, and she was clutching at his arm, as he felt his own panic begin to rise. He hadn't expected it to be quite like this, she was in such agony, and by eight o'clock the baby still hadn't come. The sun was up, and she lay panting horribly, her hair damp, eyes wild, looking at him as though he could do something for her. And all he could do was breathe with her and hold her hand and tell her how proud he was of her, and then suddenly at nine o'clock everyone began to run around. They wheeled her into the delivery room, strapped her legs up, and she cried as the pains came now. It was the worst pain she had ever known in her entire life, and she felt as though she were drowning as she clutched at him, and the doctor urged her on, and Russell cried, and Tana knew she couldn't stand it anymore. She wanted to die ... to die ... to. ...

'I can see the head ... oh God ... sweetheart ... it's here. ...' And suddenly a tiny red face popped out, as Russell cried, and Tana looked at him and gave another ferocious push which forced the baby from her womb, and the doctor held him in his hands as the baby began to wail. They cut the cord, tied it, and cleaned him rapidly, suctioned his nose, wrapped him in a warm blanket and handed him to Russ.

'Your son, Russ. ...' The doctor smiled at them both. They had worked so hard and so long, and Tana looked at him victoriously now.

'You were wonderful, sweetheart.' Her voice was hoarse and her face was gray, as he kissed her tenderly.

'*I* was wonderful?' He was deeply impressed by what he had just seen her do. It was the greatest miracle he had ever seen. And at forty years of age, she had it all now. She looked at him. Everything she had ever wanted ...

everything ... her eyes filled with tears as she reached out to him, and Russ gently put the baby in her arms, as he had once put it in her womb.

'Oh, he's so beautiful. ...'

'No.' Russell smiled at her through his tears. 'You are, Tan. You're the most beautiful woman in the world.' And then he looked at his son. 'But he's pretty cute too.' Harrison Winslow Carver. They had long since agreed on that. He came into the world blessed in name, and life, and love.

They wheeled her back to her room that night, and she knew she would never want to do it again, but she was glad she had this once. Russell stayed with her until she drifted off to sleep, the baby asleep in the little bed they had left there for him, and Tana, all clean again, and so much in love with him. She opened her eyes once, drifting from the shot they'd given her for the pain afterwards. 'I love you so much, Russ. ...'

He nodded, smiling again, his heart forever hers after tonight. 'Sshh ... sleep now ... I love you too. ...'

Chapter 20

When baby Harry was six months old, Tana looked at her calendar with despair. She had to go back to work the following week. She had promised she would, and she knew it was almost time, but he was so sweet, and she loved spending the afternoons with him. They went on long walks, and she laughed when he smiled. They even dropped in on Russ at his office once in a while. It was a leisurely way of life she had never known, and she hated to give it up, but she was not yet ready to give up her career.

And once she was back on the bench, she was glad she hadn't given it up for good. It felt good to be back again. The cases, the verdicts, the juries, the decisions, the routine. It was incredible how fast the days flew by, and how anxious she was to come home at night, to Harry and Russ. Sometimes she would find Russ already at home with him, crawling around on the rug, and playing games with him. He delighted them both, and he was like the first child born on earth to them. Lee teased them about it when she came out to visit with Francesca, her little girl, and she was already expecting another one.

'And what about you, Tan?'

'Listen, at my age, Harry is enough of a miracle. Let's not push my luck, thanks.' And even though the pregnancy had been a breeze, the delivery had been more painful than she thought. Though, with time, even that didn't seem quite as awful as it once had. And they were both so happy with the baby. 'If I were your age, I might, Lee, and even then ... you can't have everything, a career and ten kids.' Not that it frightened Lee, though. She still had her job, and even now with the second one on the way, she was planning to work right till the end, and come back afterwards. She had just won the Coty Award and she wasn't giving that up. She didn't see why she should. She could do both, so why not?

'How was your day, sweetheart?' She threw her briefcase on a chair and bent to kiss him as he scooped the baby into his arms, as she glanced at her watch. She was still nursing him three times a day. Morning, evening, and late at night, and she wondered when his last feeding was. She loved the closeness it gave her to the child, the silent moments in the nursery at three a.m. when only she and Harry were up. She had a sense of providing for his well-being which satisfied her too, and then there were other benefits as well. She'd been told that she was unlikely to get pregnant again as long as she was still nursing him. 'Do you think it would matter if I did it till he's twelve?' she had asked Russ one day and he had laughed at her. They had such a good life, the two of them. It had been worth waiting for, no matter how long it took. At least she said that now. She had just turned forty-one, and he was fifty-two.

'You know, you look tired, Tan.' Russell was looking carefully at her. 'Maybe the nursing is too much for you, now that you're back at work.' She fought the idea, but her body voted with him, as slowly, in the next few weeks, her milk dried up. It was as though her body didn't want to be nursing Harry anymore. And when she went to the doctor for a check-up, he weighed her, felt her, checked her breasts, and then said he wanted to do a blood test on her.

'Something wrong?' She glanced at her watch. She had to be back in court at two.

'I just want to check something out. I'll call you this afternoon.' On the whole, he had found her all right, and she didn't have time to worry about it. She rushed back to City Hall, and when her clerk signalled her at five o'clock, she had forgotten that she was expecting the doctor's call.

'He said he had to speak to you.'

'Thanks.' She took the phone, scratching some notes as she listened to him, and suddenly she stopped. That couldn't be. He had to be wrong. She had been nursing until the week before ... hadn't she ... she sat down hard in a chair, thanked him, and hung up. Shit. She was pregnant again. And Harry was wonderful, but she didn't want another one. She was too old for that ... she had her career ... this time, she had to get rid of it ... it was impossible ... she didn't know what to do. She had a choice of course, but what would she say to Russ? Tell him she had aborted his child? She couldn't do that. She spent a sleepless night that night, resisting him when he asked her what was bothering her. She couldn't tell him this time. It was all wrong ... she was too old ... her career meant too much to her ... but Lee was going to continue her career after her second child ... or was it meaningless? Should she resign from the bench? Would the children mean more to her in the end? She felt torn ten thousand ways and she looked like a nightmare when she woke up. Russ looked at her over breakfast and didn't say anything to her at first. And then, just before he left, he turned to her.

'You busy for lunch today, Tan?'

'No ... not that I know of ...' But she didn't want to have lunch with him. She had to think. 'There's some stuff I really should get off my desk.' She avoided his eyes.

'You have to eat. I'll bring sandwiches.'

'Fine.' She felt like a traitor not telling him, and her heart felt like lead as she went to work. She had dozens of small matters in and out of her court, and at eleven o'clock she looked up to see a wild-eyed man, with a mane of frizzy gray hair springing out of his head like watchsprings gone wild. He had planted a bomb in front of a foreign consulate, and the matter had to be set for trial. She began to go through all of the motions, and then suddenly stared at his name and looked up with a grin. And for no reason anyone understood in court, she had to disqualify herself. The man's name was Yael McBee, the wild-eyed radical lover she'd had in her last year of law school at Boalt. The boy who had gone to jail for bombing the mayor's house. She saw from his records that he had been in prison twice since then. How odd life was. So long ago ... it brought Harry instantly to mind ... and the funny little house they'd shared ... and Averil so young then ... and the wild hippie commune she had visited with Yael. She looked across the court at him. He had grown old. He was forty-six years old now. A man. And still fighting for his causes in his unruly ways. How far they'd come, all of them ... this man with his wild ideas. His documents said that he was a terrorist. A terrorist. And she was a judge. An endless road ... and Harry gone, and all their bright ideas a little dim, some of them forgotten, so many gone ... Sharon ... Harry ... and new lives in their places ... her son, little Harry, named after her friend, and now this new baby in her womb ... it was amazing how life went on, how far they came, all of them ... She looked up and saw her husband, standing there, looking at her, and she smiled at him, and dismissed the matter of Yael McBee from her court, called a recess for lunch, and walked into her chambers with him.

'Who was that?' Russ looked amused. Her days were certainly livelier than his, and she began to laugh as she sat down.

'His name is Yael McBee, if that means anything to you. I knew him when I went to Boalt.'

'A friend of yours?' Russ looked at her sardonically and she grinned.

'Believe it or not, he was.'

'You've come a long way since then, my love.'

'I was just thinking that.' And then she remembered something else. She looked at him, hesitantly, wondering how he would react. 'I've got something to tell you.'

He smiled gently at her. 'You're pregnant again.'

She stared at him as he laughed. 'How do you know? Did the doctor call you too?'

'No. I'm smarter than that. I figured it out last night, and I assumed you'd tell me eventually. Of course by now, you think your career is over, we'll have to give up the house, I'll lose my job, or we both will ...' She laughed and tears came to her eyes as he smiled at her. 'Am I right?'

'Perfectly.'

'And has it dawned on you that if you can be a judge with one child, you can be a judge with two? And a good judge at that.'

'That just occurred to me as you walked in.'

'My, my.' He leaned over to kiss her, and they exchanged a look that belonged only to them. 'What do you know ... ?' He kissed her and her clerk walked in and hastily backed out again, smiling to herself as Tana silently thanked her lucky stars for the road she'd come, the man she'd found ... the decisions she had made ... from a career and no man, no child, to having it all, the man, the career, and her son. She had added each one, like wild flowers to a bouquet, until she stood with full hands, full heart, having come full circle in the end.